THIS PLAN
was surveyed in
1782 and Drawn 1785.
JOHN HILLS.

River or *the* *Sound*

Carteau's Hook

REFERENCE.

a Fort George Lat: Nord 41 58
b Trinity Church
c St. Paul's Church
d St. George's Church
e Old Dutch Church
f New Dutch Church
g New Reformed Church
h Old Presbyterian Meeting
i New
k Old Lutheran Church
l New
m German Reformed Church
n French Church
o Moravian Meeting
p Anabaptist Meeting
q Methodist Meeting
r Quakers Meeting
s Seceders Meeting
t Jews Synagogue
u City Hall
v Exchange
w Prison
x House of Correction
y College
z Theatre

1 Fish.
2 Old Slip
3 Fly Market
4 Peck.
5 Oswego
6 Upper Barracks
7 Powder House.
8 Jews Burial Ground
9 Lower Barracks
10 Artillery Stores
11 New Prison
12 Hospital.

Fortifications made by the British
extended by the Americans

Corporation of New-York.

FEB 0 7 2004

Washington
and Caesar

Washington and Caesar

Christian Cameron

DELACORTE PRESS

WASHINGTON AND CAESAR
A Delacorte Book / January 2004

Published by
Bantam Dell
A Division of Random House, Inc.
New York, New York

Book design by Karin Batten

Interior map by John Gilkes
Endpaper map: Hills, John.
To his excellency George Clinton . . . this plan of the city of New-York . . . was
surveyed in 1782. New York, 1857. Used by permission of the Map Division,
The New York Public Library, Astor, Lenox and Tilden Foundation.

Library of Congress Cataloging in Publication Data
Cameron, Christian.
Washington and Caesar / Christian Cameron.
p.   cm.
Includes bibliographical references.
ISBN 0-385-33776-0
1. United States—History—Revolution, 1775–1783—Fiction.   2. United
States—History—Revolution, 1775–1783—African Americans—Fiction.
3. United States—History—Revolution, 1775–1783—Participation,
African American—Fiction.   4. Washington, George, 1732–1799—
Fiction.   5. African American loyalists—Fiction.   6. African American
soldiers—Fiction.   7. Fugitive slaves—Fiction.   8. Generals—Fiction.
I. Title.
PS3603.A448W37 2004
813'.6—dc22   2003055533

Manufactured in the United States of America
Published simultaneously in Canada

10   9   8   7   6   5   4   3   2   1
BVG

To my father

Author's Note

There can be few topics as difficult to confront for an American author as the mythology attached to George Washington. If there is a topic as difficult, it is surely those issues surrounding blacks and slavery in Colonial America. The combination of the two may provide an obstacle so far beyond my merits as an author as to be insurmountable.

Rather than seeking to excuse any failures, however, I would prefer to lull the reader with a few assurances. The events of this book are firmly rooted in history; indeed, Washington's life was so well chronicled (by his own hand, among many others) that it could not be otherwise. I have tried to portray the life of black slaves equally well, based on the handful of contemporary accounts of survivors of that pernicious system. And the events of the American Revolution occurred very much as chronicled here. The British did not inevitably fight in long straight lines, the Americans were not all "Patriots," and the results of the struggle gave birth not just to the United States but to Canada as well.

To those hard truths let me add one other. All society of the day was hierarchical; all men, black or white, had superiors and inferiors, and expected certain behavior of each, and all too many were content that it be so. They were different. I have tried to portray this throughout, but I shall leave you to judge the result.

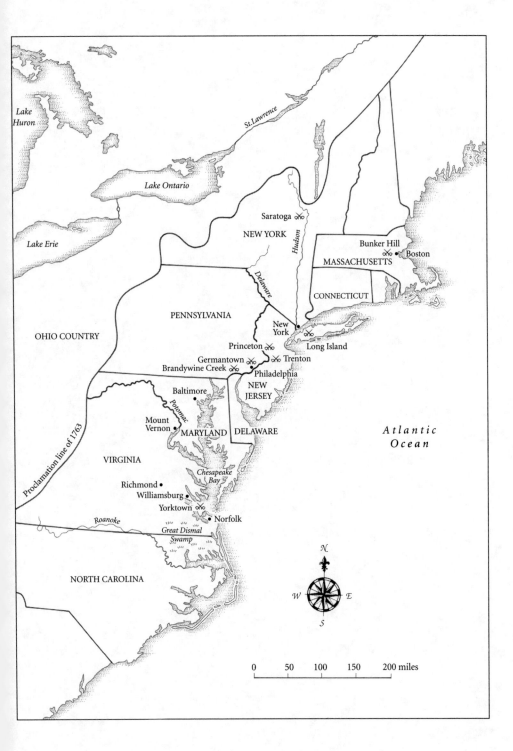

Lake Huron

Lake Ontario

St.Lawrence

Lake Erie

Saratoga ⚔

NEW YORK

Hudson

Bunker Hill
⚔ • Boston

MASSACHUSETTS

CONNECTICUT

Delaware

PENNSYLVANIA

New York ⚔

Long Island

OHIO COUNTRY

Princeton ⚔

Trenton ⚔

Germantown ⚔

Brandywine Creek ⚔

Philadelphia

NEW JERSEY

Baltimore •

DELAWARE

Potomac

Mount Vernon •

MARYLAND

Proclamation line of 1763

VIRGINIA

Chesapeake Bay

Richmond •

Williamsburg •

Roanoke

Yorktown ⚔

• Norfolk

Great Dismal Swamp

NORTH CAROLINA

Atlantic Ocean

N

W ⊕ E

S

0   50   100   150   200 miles

Washington
and Caesar

I

Wanderers in the Wilderness

Slaves, obey in all things your masters according to the flesh, not with eyeservice, as menpleasers, but in singleness of heart, fearing God. And whatsoever you do, do it heartily, as to the lord, and not unto men; knowing that of the Lord ye shall receive the reward of the inheritance, for ye serve the Lord Jesus Christ. But he that doeth wrong shall receive for the wrong which he hath done, and there is no respect of persons.

Masters, give unto your slaves that which is just and equal; knowing that you also have a Master in heaven.

—COLOSSIANS 3:22–25

Chapter One

The tall man's horse started at the distant shot, and he curbed it firmly, his attention on the woods around him. The sun, far overhead, pierced the canopy of trees with beams that played in shifting patterns on the autumn mold of the forest floor. For a moment his thoughts were in another forest, and the sound of other shots rang in his ears. His horse's uneasiness communicated itself to the rest of the horses in the party.

"Hunter?" The other white man stood in his stirrups, as if a few inches of height would improve his view of the woods.

The tall man's attention returned to the horses.

"Pompey, if you can't control that animal I'll have you walk."

The black man so addressed wheeled his horse in a tight circle, murmuring all the while. His horse stopped fidgeting. The whole party grew still.

The second shot was farther away, the low thump of a musket.

"Crogan said we'd find a hunting camp." The tall man ran his eyes over the rest of his party and touched his heels to his horse's flanks, moving off at a trot. He already seemed focused on a distant goal, but the other men, black and white, cast their eyes nervously on the woods around them as they moved off on the narrow track. He slowed his horse to a comfortable walk and flowed in next to the other white man.

"No point in hurry, Doctor. We'll need Nicholson to talk to them."

The doctor seemed oppressed by the shots, but if the tall man noticed it, he gave it no heed.

"You were speaking of the price of tobacco, Colonel."

"So I was, Doctor. Probably dwelling on it more than is healthy. But if the price continues to fall, we'll all have to find another crop or see our sons debtors."

"You've planted wheat, sir?" Dr. Craik was always a little diffident with Washington, who was not just his friend but frequently his patron.

"Indeed. I don't grow tobacco except to cover expenses, but my tenants are old-fashioned men and need to see a thing done many times before they'll consider it. I am confident that the soil will support it. And the price is better, whether I sell it in the Indies or grind it myself."

"It could make a difference, sure enough."

"I doubt it. The Virginia gentry are too used to easy money from tobacco to settle for a hard living on wheat."

"Perhaps the price will rise in time, sir."

"Oh, it may. But there are bills due now. I've had two bills refused in London, on very worthy men, at that. Gentlemen. They write bills to cover the cost of my smith and the like, you know. And those bills were refused. Very alarming."

"Ho'se behin' us, suh."

"Thank you, Pompey. Good ears, as usual. That would be Nicholson," the colonel said. "And I sold Tom. Did I tell you that?"

The two black men looked at each other, just for a moment, but neither white man remarked it.

"You said he was a problem."

"That he was. Ironical, if you can believe it. And he tried to run. I wouldn't have it, so I sold him in the Indies. I asked Captain Gibson to get me another, good with animals. We'll see what he brings." The tall man stopped his horse and turned, one hand on its rump. A white man on a small horse was trotting up the trail, a rifle across his arm and the cape of his greatcoat turned up around his face against the chill.

"Are you sober, Nicholson?"

"Aye, Colonel. Sober as a judge."

"Hear the shots?"

"Aye. That'd be the Shawnee that Crogan was on about."

"Let's go find them, then."

Nicholson glared a moment, his narrow eyes stabbing from under heavy brows. Then he shook his head, touched his mount with his heels, and passed to the front.

✯ ✯ ✯

Whatever his state of sobriety, Nicholson found the Shawnee camp so quickly that the conversation never seemed to rise again, beyond muttered comments about the beauty of the country. The party moved on at a trot until the hard-packed trail opened into a small clearing with several brush wigwams around its periphery. There was a strong smell of butchered meat and rot, overlaid with woodsmoke. Two native women were scraping a hide. An old man sat smoking. None showed any sign of alarm when the party rode in. The tall man dismounted and threw his reins to one of his blacks.

"Ask them if we can stay the night." He inclined his head civilly to the two women, who laughed and smiled.

Nicholson didn't dismount. He nudged his horse forward, raised his right hand toward the old man, and spoke a long, musical sentence. The man drew on his pipe, blew a smoke ring, and nodded. Another shot sounded, quite close. The old man batted at a fly with a horsetail whisk and waved at the tall man, then spoke for a moment.

Nicholson turned to the tall man. "Says he knows you, Colonel Washington. Says you're welcome here."

"Excellent. Dr. Craik, this is our inn for the night. Please dismount. I'll have Pompey and Jacka set up a tent."

✯ ✯ ✯

Pompey made coffee at one of the small native fires while Dr. Craik admired the skill of the women in cleaning the deer hides, a thoroughness his assistant back in Williamsburg would have done well to emulate.

"They learn as girls," said Washington in a level tone.

"Use makes master, I suppose. Handsome wenches, too."

"Oh, as to that..." Washington looked off into the middle distance and took a cup of coffee from Pompey without glancing at the man. "Beautiful country. Look at this clearing. Trees that big come out of the best soil."

"And the savages have little idea what to do with it."

"They grow corn well enough. Better than some of my tenants, if the truth were known."

"I had no idea."

"Not so savage, when it comes to farming. Of course, the women do it. Men mostly hunt and fight." He sipped his coffee appreciatively. The old man was still smoking, looking at him from time to time but otherwise off in his own thoughts. Washington couldn't place him, although he had a good memory for men he had known during the wars.

Between one thought and the next, the clearing began to fill with native men, all younger and most carrying guns. Others carried deer carcasses on poles or dragged them by the legs. Nicholson, his back against a tree and a bottle in his hand, called a greeting, and two men walked over to him. One took a drink from his bottle when it was offered, and they had a short exchange. The old man merely waved the flywhisk several times and the deer began to be sorted out.

"That fellow is a black!" Dr. Craik was pointing at a tall man in red wool leggings.

"Yes, Doctor. So he is. Probably started as a captive." Washington nodded civilly at the warrior so indicated, who inclined his head a dignified fraction in return.

"We didn't see blacks among the Shawnee during the wars."

Washington's thoughts were elsewhere, and he didn't reply.

★　★　★

The deer were being butchered. Hearts and livers were set on bark trenchers, intestines set aside, and haunches separated even as they watched. The older women moved from carcass to carcass providing advice while the younger women did all the work and got coated in the blood and ordure. The whole process seemed to take no time at all. Dr. Craik had never seen the like and watched, fascinated. The other two white men seemed oblivious to the spectacle, the tall one standing with his coffee, the small one sitting by him with his rum. Some of the native men were sitting with Nicholson; the older men had gathered in a knot around the smoker, who was now passing his pipe. None showed any curiosity about the strangers.

Pompey walked up behind his master and took the empty horn cup.

"Dat be trouble, suh." He inclined his head, the slightest gesture toward their tent.

One of the younger women had a white ruffled shirt on. It was clean and probably out of their equipment. Other women were laughing at her. They were also stealing glances at Dr. Craik. Craik remained oblivious for a moment, and then his thin face grew mottled with red.

"Doctor." The tall man put a restraining hand on his shoulder.

"That woman has my shirt on!"

"Pay her no attention, Doctor."

"I'll have my shirt back."

"You may take one of mine. We are in their country, and they are test-ing us. Think of it as the price of dinner. Resent the next theft, but not the first."

Nicholson nodded curtly and called something across the camp. One of the older women roared. The others looked uneasy.

None of the men had stirred, but their attention seemed to focus on the whites for the first time. It made Dr. Craik feel uneasy. There was menace to it, an alien scrutiny from beyond *his* world of manner and custom.

"She looks a damn sight better in that shirt than you, Doctor." Nichol-son settled himself back against his tree and set to getting a spark on to some charcloth for his pipe.

Craik took a deep breath and made himself smile. "She does, the vixen. Even with shirts at six shillings apiece and not to be bought in this country."

Nicholson was busy pulling at his pipe, clay turned black with use. He had laid his tiny scrap of lit char atop the bowl and was drawing the coal down into the tobacco. He was so fast with his flint and steel that Craik had missed the spark. When it was alight, he puffed for a moment, look-ing hard at Craik from under his unkempt eyebrows.

"Look at yon, Doctor. The men don't show what they think, and nor should you. Angry or happy, keep your thoughts to yourself. Now, when they're in drink, mind, then it's the strongest to the fore and de'il take the hindmost."

"He seems easy with them."

"Oh, aye. Well, he doesna give much away, our colonel. And he stands tall. But mostly he's a name to them. The chief there, he marked him soon as we rode in, an' that counts for something."

"It's like another country."

"It *is* another country, Doctor. This is the wilderness. He knows, and I know. Even Pompey knows. You were here in the war?"

"With the Provincials."

"Well, now you're with the savages. Best learn to please 'em." The man laughed.

Craik wanted to resent his tone, but the advice was kindly given, even from a low Scots Borderer with rum on his breath and an old plum great-coat, and the tension seeped out of his shoulders.

"That's right, Doctor. Dinna fash yersel. Dram?"

✻ ✻ ✻

Before night fell, the camp took on new life and new smells as the best of the deer went on to the fires. The men made a circle on the grass, some on blankets or robes, some already sprawled from the effects of Nicholson's rum. The women cooked and moved about, a separate community from the men, still at work while the men took their ease. Craik was handed a large mound of meat on a bark platter by the girl wearing his shirt, and he smiled at her, but she didn't meet his eyes. He wondered for a moment what he looked like to her, or to any of them. Handsome? Ugly? The shirt already had a line of black across one shoulder and a red handprint on the back.

He took out his traveling case and unfolded his fork before cutting the meat. One of Washington's blacks handed round a horn with salt and pepper. The savages just sat and ate, men with men, women off to one side.

Washington spoke into the stillness and the sound of many jaws working. "Ask him from where he knows me, Mr. Nicholson."

Nicholson spoke without slowing his meal. The old man put his pipe down on his robe and leaned forward a little, his whole attention on Washington.

"He says he nearly took you at the Monongahela."

"Tell him I was too young to know one warrior from another."

"He says you were guarded from his gun, and hopes you have a great future."

"Ask him to tell it."

The old man spoke for a moment, his right hand moving as if pointing at invisible things. Washington, too, looked at the invisible things. For the second time in a day, he thought of that bitter hour. All around them, the younger warriors stirred and settled themselves, even the drunk ones craning their heads to listen. The old man started, a singsong quality to his narration, as if the beginning had been related many times, which it had. Nicholson picked it up almost immediately, listening and speaking with conviction, mere words behind his host. It was quite a feat, only the occasional occurrence of Scots Border brogue interrupting the impression that the old man was speaking the English himself.

"I was with the French captain at the first discharge, and he fell. We fired back at the high-hats and killed many, and they broke. Then we spread to the woods on either side of the trail. I killed four men in as many shots. Then I moved again, farther off the trail. Many warriors followed me. We fired and ran, fired and ran, trying to circle to the back. For many minutes, I didn't know who was taking the worst of it."

Washington held up his hand for a moment. "Did you go to the left of the trail or the right?"

Nicholson cocked his head to listen to the old man, then nodded.

"We went up the hill, he says. He thinks that answers you." Washington nodded.

"After some time we found a little hill with thick trees and we stayed there, firing into the men below us. That was the first time I shot at you. You were on a fine horse. I shot at you and hit the horse."

"I remember that." Washington looked into the fire. The battle was not yet a disaster. The grenadiers of the Forty-fourth, the only veterans in the regiment, had formed at the base of that deadly little hill. They kept up a hot fire, and Washington's Virginians had started to gather on their flanks, staying behind trees but shooting steadily. Some of the raw battalion men of the Forty-fourth had begun to rally from their initial panic. Washington had just asked the grenadier captain to take the hill when his horse went down.

Nicholson paused in his translation to drink, but Washington was still there, kicking his feet free of the stirrups and sliding over the crupper, his boot pulls caught in the buckles of his saddlebag. By the time he was on his feet, the young captain had his jaw shot away, a third of the grenadiers were down, and they were past saving, the recruits and the Virginians with them.

It marked the bitterest moment of his life. The moment in which he knew that they were beaten, that the whole expedition, the empire, the army, the foundations of the world, were undone.

Nicholson wiped his mouth and went on.

"You disappeared when the high-hats ran. I followed you. There was nothing to stop us—most of the English had stopped shooting. The next time I saw you, you were with the big general. He was struggling with his horse. I think it was hit. I tried for you again. Perhaps I hit the general. It is possible. He fell. You caught him. You and others carried him off and I couldn't follow in the press."

Washington nodded.

"I thought I'd lost you. Then, right at the end, there you were, all alone, sitting on another tall horse."

Washington looked back into the fire. It was not a moment he liked to dwell on. He had ridden back into the rout and perhaps he had hoped to be killed. He couldn't remember that part with any clarity, but it came to him some nights, when there were bills due in England or a crop failed.

"My musket was empty, and I started loading it. You yelled at some men running by, but you didn't move. That is when it came to me that you had a spirit and it was not your day to die, and I thought, *I will take him for my own, and his spirit will join my clans.* Others fired at you. I saw you pull a long pistol and shoot it somewhere else, and I was just ramming my ball home. I pulled the rammer clear and threw it down to get a faster shot, and I began to run toward you. You just sat. You never saw me. When I was almost close enough to touch you, as close as I am now, a boy came at me out of the brush. He spooked your horse. And I hit him with my club, but you were moving away. Indeed, I took him. Since I already had my captive, I thought I would kill you. I looked down the barrel and pulled the trigger, and the pan flashed, and no shot came, and still you rode. Then I looked down at the lock, as one does . . . you know?"

Washington nodded, a brother in the fraternity of men frustrated by the vagaries of flintlocks.

"When I had the priming back in, you were gone."

The old man was done before Nicholson, and he looked at Washington and smiled. He pointed to a young man in an old French coat. "It happens often to Gray Coat here when he hunts deer, but not to me."

Most of the warriors laughed, although the one man looked sour.

"I should have ignored the boy, although he made a good slave for a while. My mother adopted him, and he was with us until the Pennsylvania men made us send him away."

Washington smiled, but he had rather the look of Gray Coat the moment before.

The old man raised his hand and smiled a feral smile. "I should have killed him and taken you. I still wonder what kind of a slave you would have made."

Mouth of the Chesapeake Bay, November 6, 1773

"You clap on to that line and haul, laddie. That's it. Handsomely now, you lot. Pull. Pull, you black bastards. Belay there, King. Right." High overhead the newly fished spar rose into the dawn light and was seated home against the mast. The black men on the deck hauled and sweated, but the sailors sweated just as hard.

The squall had hit them inside the capes, laying the vessel on her beam-ends, stripping off every scrap of sail and cracking the fore-topsail yard. The sailor called King, a free black, had cut the broken yard away from the rigging it threatened to shred, standing on the canted deck with the ropes' ends pounding him like a dozen fiendish whips.

The ship's master, Gibson, had shipped a small cargo of West Indies blacks to augment the rum and molasses in the hold. They were skilled men: two bricklayers, a carpenter, a huntsman, and a gunsmith, all likely to fetch first-rate prices among the Virginia gentry. In the meantime, they could haul ropes in an emergency.

High above them, King waved at the captain and leaned out, grabbing a stay and sliding for the deck. Something King saw at the last moment of his slide halted him, and he ran his eyes over the group standing in the waist of the ship, still holding the line that had raised the yard. One young man had scars over his eyes, hard ridges that told a story, if the watcher knew what to read. King wandered over, acknowledging the praise of his shipmates and some good-natured abuse. He turned to the man with the scars, a wave of homesickness hitting his breast and slowing his breath. "*Hello, cousin.*"

The man's eyes widened for a moment, then his white teeth flashed in an enormous smile. "*Greetings, older cousin.*"

The man looked young, young to have left home with the scars of a warrior and already have a skill worth selling in America. His face was not yet hard or closed as the slaves' too often were. "*I honor your courage in the storm, older cousin.*"

Nicely phrased. King smiled himself but turned away, headed for his hammock. It didn't do to associate too much with slaves, at least where white men could see you. It gave them ideas.

★   ★   ★

King returned topside at the changing of the watch, to see the familiar low Virginia shore clear to the southwest. The Chesapeake had become confused in his memories with Africa, where great rivers ran deep into the woods, and he thought of Virginia as home, the place where he had a wife and a family. He stood by the heads watching the shore for a moment and then moved into the waist. The sails were set and, barring a disaster, wouldn't need to be touched until the turn of the tide. Until a crisis came, sailoring was an easy life, and King liked a crisis here and there. They made good stories.

The young one with scars was watching him from the group of slaves at the base of the mainmast. It was a polite regard: The youth didn't stare, but simply glanced his way from time to time, as if inviting him to speak. King settled into the shade of the sail with the other crew on deck and accepted a draw from another man's pipe. There were sailors who wouldn't smoke with a black man, but not many around King. Gibson preferred English sailors to Americans. King had noticed that Englishmen seemed easier with blacks. It didn't stand to reason.

"You gonna jabber some more o' that black cant, King?" asked Jones, the mate.

"I might, then." King looked at Jones, who was smaller but loved to fight.

"Now then, King, boyo, don't you glare at me. I'm all for your talkin' any lingo you like. It's just funny to hear from you, that's all I'm saying." Jones was from a part of Britain called Wales, where they seemed to sing instead of talk. King was on the edge of a retort about Jones and talk, but he smiled to himself and let it pass. Instead he motioned to the scarred youngster, who rose from his squatting position against the mast in one fluid, athletic movement and walked across the deck to the sailors.

"Speak the King's English, boy?"

"Little, ya."

"*The better you speak it, the better you will be treated.* You have a name, then?"

"*Cese. Cese Mwakale. My father commands a thousand warriors—*"

"Not here, he doesn't. What were you called in Jamaica?"

"Caesar."

King nodded. He knew a dozen Caesars in Williamsburg. "*How long ago were you taken?*"

"*Four years, older cousin. You?*"

"*Twenty-five years, young one. But I was a fool, and walked to their land-ings to see the world. Who was king when you left?*"

"*King of Benin, sir? Or of my province?*"

"*Benin will do.*"

"*Callinauw was king when I last heard, sir.*"

"*And where do you hail from?*"

"*Eboe, in Esaka. My father commanded the regiment there.*"

King nodded curtly. It took him back to hear the words, to know that a man he had hated once was lording it in Benin, but it all sounded very far away. He smiled at the young man and held out the other sailor's pipe.

"Smoke, Cese?"

The lad seized the pipe greedily and sucked a great draft into his lungs. Jones watched in amazement as the inward breath went on and on. Cese held the breath for a moment and returned the pipe with more gravity than he had taken it.

Jones looked into the bottom of the pipe bowl and mimed using a glass. "Tobacco is cheap in Virginny, but not that cheap, Blackie."

"Call him Cese." King smiled at the boy. "*How were you taken?*"

"*My father's regiment was away in the north. You know of the Northern War?*"

"*I had heard. It was a small trouble in my youth.*"

"*It is a great war now. So many young men are away that kidnappers, crimi-nals, can steal children and young people from their homes; larger towns have militias of old men and women.*"

"*And the king tolerates this?*"

"*The king fears Muslims more than he cares for us. Listen, then. I was at the camp with the youngest men, those unblooded, just training. We were drilling with spears when the shots were fired, and our officers led us straight out after the raiders. The old men and women turned out with swords and shields, but the raiders shot them down with muskets.*"

"*Where were your own muskets? We had hundreds in my youth.*"

"*All our muskets were away with the regiment. Nor had we ever fought against men armed as our men were. So we charged them, like fools. In mo-ments they were all around us, in the brush on our flanks. Some of us were shot, and some stopped charging and ran. When I saw that, I knew we were done. I determined to die, and charged on. My spear bit deep into one, and then I was clubbed down. When I awoke, I was a slave.*"

"*You killed one. That's good.*"

"I paid. Perhaps I'm still paying. Some of the men who were taken were ransomed later, but I was not. I think my father took another wife. I do not know." He crossed his arms to indicate that this was not a topic he wished to discuss. *"Now I am here. Tell me about Virginny."*

"What yo' skill, Caesar?"

"Be a huntah, suh."

"Hunter. *Was your father of the Embrenake?*"

"Yes, sir."

"And weren't such men distinguished by their speech? So it is here. Say hunter."

"Hunt-ar." The other slaves had edged closer. As the foreign speech was replaced by English, they gathered courage to join in.

"You goin' to Jamaica again, then, Mista King?" asked one, a bricklayer.

"Yaas. I go twice a year, weather allowing. Mostly I sail wi' Mr. Gibson."

"You carry a message to my woman?"

"If'n you give me a good idea where to find her. I don' go too close to some plantations. I been a slave twice an' I don' mean to go that way 'gain. Won' sail again till spring."

Others asked for messages carried, or verbal messages, which King refused. He told them where to find a Quaker clerk in Williamsburg who would write out short messages for slaves, if asked nicely. Cese watched him eagerly, his head cocked a little to one side like a smart puppy awaiting instruction. King began to pass along whatever came to his mind, but they had questions of their own.

"Mista King, you know who we gon' be wo'kin' fo'?"

"I expect you be wo'kin' fo' Mr. Washington, if'n you be on his boat."

"What he like?"

"They betta, an' they worse. He be fair, and that somethin'."

"He fair? Do he let us'ns buy freedom?"

"How 'bout marriage? Do he abide black folks as marry?"

"Is it true that Christian folk can't be slaves in Virginny?"

They were clamoring now, and their different accents were hard for him to understand. He shook his head at them. West Indian slaves were the most ignorant; they were kept in pens and didn't get to hear much news.

"No. Many Christian folk is slaves."

"Is you free if you gets to England?"

"So I hear. I been there, and I ain't seen no slaves." It was common knowledge that a man was free if he could reach England. Sometimes a man could get free by enlisting in the Royal Navy, too. King had bought his freedom the first time, saving pennies from his fishing to buy his way free. The second time, he'd taken one beating too many and run, joined a navy ship hungry for men, thin on the decks from the yellow jack in the Indies and with a hard first officer not liable to ask a man questions.

He looked back at the boy. "You wan' be free, Cese?"

"I *will* be free, Mista King."

"You take care, now. Mr. Washington, he sell black boys wha' try to run."

Cese nodded. He looked out at the shore for a moment. "Maybe I go England."

"Go *to* England, Cese. Maybe so. You know who Somerset was?"

"No, suh."

"He was a black man like you. He run from his master in England. Got caught, got beat, got a white man to take him to court. He won. No slavery in England now."

Cese had heard a little of the story, but not so plain, always told elliptically so that an overseer wouldn't understand. He thought it remarkable that a black man had got into a court at all, much less that his case should be heard. In the Indies, a slave couldn't even give evidence, a fact of life that every slave knew all too well.

"Maybe I go to England," he repeated.

"You take care, boy."

King nodded to Jones and they stood, Jones carefully wrapping twine around his pipe and putting it into a fitted tin. Before the mate could call them aloft, they were standing at the base of the mainmast, ready for the last tack into the bay, the boy and the other slaves forgotten.

Cese watched the shore and thought about the raid and his last moments as a free man. He thought about it often, but now he tried to think about what England must be like, a land where men became free just by touching the ground, or so he had been told. He tried to imagine how to get to England, but he couldn't see it. What he could see in his mind's eye was the musket butt coming under his shield, into his hip and groin, the point of his spear going into the other man's innards, his hand turning the blade as he had been taught. One kill. It didn't seem like much of a tally against a life of servitude, and sometimes he wondered if he should just have died when he went down. And he thought about his father, a war captain of renown. He had probably taken another wife and forgotten Cese. Cese shook his head to send the memories away. He seldom thought of his father.

He looked at the coastline, nearer now, and decided to do the very best he could. Other slaves said Virginny was different from the Indies, the whites better, the living easier, and fewer folk died. Perhaps he could win his freedom.

"Hunt-ar." He savored the word. "Eng-land."

Williamsburg, Virginia, March 4, 1773

She meant trouble, that was plain. Martha's eyes sparkled as they always did when she had mischief on her mind, but her voice seemed serious when she asked him to explain the day's events. Of the men in the room, only Washington understood his wife's message: They had already talked politics enough. Young Henry Lee, just graduated from Princeton, did not hear the irony in her voice or catch her meaning, and he leapt to explain with a simplicity that damned him as a patronizing animal to every woman present.

"It is not a complicated matter, ma'am." Wiser heads turned to watch the man charge to his doom; his implication that she might be unequal to a more complicated matter lost him the support of the crowd.

"I'm sure you'll make it all plain to me, Mr. Lee."

"Indeed, ma'am. We have settled on choosing a committee of eleven men to obtain the most early and authentic intelligence of all such acts and resolutions of the British Parliament, or proceedings of administrations, as may relate to, or affect, the British Colonies in America..."

"So you intend to form a Committee of Correspondence, as Massachusetts has?" Martha smiled at the younger man. She was quite short, but her immense dignity and the memory of her beauty, as well as her reputation, gave her a presence that only a few of the men could match, and Lee was not one of them.

"...to keep up and maintain a correspondence and communication with our sister colonies."

"Mr. Lee, I believe you are repeating a speech that most of my guests have already heard." Martha Washington said "Mistah" with the man's name, and the drawl lengthened a bit each time she said it. "It certainly *sounds* like you have chosen a Committee of Correspondence."

Lee looked at her as if he had just perceived that she was mocking him. "I was endeavoring to explain, ma'am."

"I think you were making a speech, sir. And what I wish to understand is, why? Why must we join a league with the good wives of New England? Why have you censured our governor for bringing to justice a counterfeiter whose work threatened every person of account in this colony? Why this incessant attack on Parliament?"

"Surely, ma'am, your husband has explained..." He looked about him with the assurance of a man of twenty, expecting allies against the assault of one small middle-aged woman, but he saw only stony stares, and this stung him. His opinion of women was not very high, but his standard of rhetoric had much to recommend it, and he felt sure he could defeat her, if only he chose the right arguments.

"That the counterfeiter needed to be brought to book no one here contends, ma'am. But the governor used methods that the House of Burgesses cannot condone without it impugning our stand on a larger issue, to wit, whether Americans can be taken out of our continent to England to be tried. This counterfeiter was in Pittsylvania County. The court there was competent to execute justice on him, but our governor chose to send a special sheriff and bring him to Williamsburg to justice."

"And now he can no longer pass counterfeit five-pound notes that cause my steward to suspend business." Martha smiled at him again, a happy smile that made it difficult for him to believe that he was being led to slaughter.

"But the legality places us awkwardly, ma'am. If the governor can write a warrant to take a man from his county to Williamsburg for trial, then the Admiralty in London can write a warrant for a smuggler to be taken from Boston to London for trial."

"What of it? Are we not all English? Or is it your meaning that Americans will give their own a 'fairer' trial? Perhaps the smuggler will never be found guilty in Boston, Mr. Lee? Because if that's your meaning, I can't help but think that my steward is happier that this counterfeiter did not get a 'fairer' trial among his friends in Pittsylvania."

Lee looked like a man who had just discovered a deep pit yawning at his feet. Arguments against the tyranny of the Crown were so popular in

Virginia that he was not really ready to argue cases; he generally expected approbation in reply to any reasonable assault on the government. Martha Washington, however, was of far too much consequence to ignore, and it struck him, then, that he could forfeit his standing either by offending her, as one of the richest landowners in the colony, or by losing the debate, which would not increase his stature with the House of Burgesses, to which her husband belonged, and to which he aspired.

Lee felt doubly ambushed in that Washington himself rarely spoke in the House and was firmly a friend of liberty. It seemed astonishing that he should allow his wife to make such statements. He turned and looked at the tall colonel, who nodded gravely at him. He was actually expected to debate with her. Very well, then.

"Are you familiar, ma'am, with the *Gaspee* incident?"

"Perhaps you will help me understand it, Mr. Lee."

If he heard the warning in her voice, he ignored it.

"In June of last year, a British armed cutter of that name, engaged in the suppression of the smuggling trade, ran herself aground in Narragansett Bay. A group of men boarded the cutter and burned her. An Admiralty court of inquiry was given jurisdiction over the case and is understood to believe it has the right to send Americans to England for trial."

"And this would be harmful because..." She drawled the last word as she had drawled his name, a deliberate provocation.

"They would never receive a fair trial in England! And an attack on the rights and privileges of any one colony is an attack on them all!" His voice was powerful, and declaimed well. The words were Jefferson's, but he said them with complete conviction.

"But..." She smiled again, that happy smile that seemed to deny any possibility of open conflict. "But, Mr. Lee, those men actually *did burn that ship*, did they not?"

The laughter was pained. Lee had the sympathy of the entire audience, many of whom had also labored under delusions about Martha's native intelligence at one time or another. Washington simply looked absent, as if he refused to be a witness at another execution.

"The burning of the ship is not the issue," Lee began, but she closed her fan with a snap that distracted him, and she stepped up close for the final assault.

"No, sir, it is not the issue, and you do the friends of liberty no service to pretend it is. The issue is that we smuggle because Great Britain chokes our own trade and won't let us carry our own cargoes. That is the issue. And that they try to tax us beyond our ability to bear in prosperity, to pay her debts and ours from the Great War. That too is the issue. These are the issues, in trade, that will drive us to separate—that and the arrogance of our motherland, whose representative said at my own table that we are a race of cowards who could not stop five hundred of them from marching across our whole continent. That is the other issue. It is on these— trade, taxation, and the force of arms—that our arguments will rest. But not on the actions of law, or Dunmore's taking of a counterfeiter."

There was, quite spontaneously, a small round of applause, and Lee's training as a gentleman triumphed over his youth. He not only avoided showing resentment, but smiled and bowed deeply. "I hope you are always as passionately devoted to our cause as you are now, ma'am. You would be a devilish opponent in the House, and we're lucky your husband does not speak more often, if he has trained you to this pitch of argument."

Washington laughed aloud, a single bark that was completely different from his usual closed-mouthed laugh.

"Trained her? Trained her?" He barked again. "Perhaps, Mr. Lee, you now have a taste of why I'm so often silent."

Chapter Two

Mount Vernon, Virginia, November 1773

Queeny watched the new men come ashore from the plantation's brig; West Indians didn't hold much interest for her. They were usually so cowed by the comparative brutalities of Jamaica that Virginia seemed like paradise, and Master bought only skilled men, tradesmen who were too old for her tastes. His field hands came only from America, as they were less apt to run.

She patted the sides of her cap of crisp white linen that she had made from one of Mistress's cast-off shifts. The breeze was hard on caps, and Queeny was too vain to wear a straw bonnet like a field worker. She was tall and strong, but she had always been pretty enough to draw white eyes and clever enough to satisfy white mistresses. She had never done field work.

One of the new men was clearly young; he seemed to bounce with anticipation as the longboat came up to the plantation dock. He leapt from the thwart and helped moor the craft with a lithe agility that made her smile. The other blacks shuffled ashore, one kneeling to kiss the ground, one staring around him at the alien vegetation and neat brick buildings as if he had been delivered to another planet. The youngster looked left and right like a bird, his glance never stopping.

"You stick by me, Queeny, and we'll have this lot sorted in no time."

"As y' say, Mista Bailey."

A senior tenant farmer for the Washington and Custis farms, Bailey was in charge of the plantations while the master was away in Williamsburg on business. Bailey was not a hard man, and had never offered her the least trouble, unlike the other senior tenant, whose hands never stopped. She often translated for Mr. Bailey.

Queeny was American born, but she had grown up on a plantation where most of the slaves spoke only African tongues. Her father and mother were upcountry Ebo, and she spoke almost all the coastal languages. It was a skill that made her valuable, and like her looks and easy manner, it kept her from the fields. Queeny followed him down the gravel path to the dock, a demure three paces behind.

"Captain Gibson."

"Mr. Bailey."

"A prosperous voyage?"

"Well enough, sir, well enough. I lost a spar in the roads of the Chesapeake, and the new customs officer in Jamaica led me a merry dance on our bills of lading, but all told, why, here we are."

"I'm sure the colonel will be pleased. I see you got the slaves he asked for."

"That I did. Jones here can tell you their trades, although this one, Red Scarf, is a gunsmith. He touched up the flints on my pistols, took the locks apart and put them together neat as neat. I wanted to try him."

"An' he put right the cock o' King's barker what he bent," put in a sailor.

"So he did. And they all worked with a will to get a new spar up for me, so I've given them a penny apiece and two for the smith."

"Colonel likes his people to have a little cash. No harm in it, nor do I think. What do you have for me besides a smith? Did Colonel Washington order a smith?"

"I don't think that he did, sir, at that. But the whole lot were going off an estate sold for debt, all skilled men, an' we took the lot."

"Fair enough."

"This one's a bricklayer, answers to Jemmy." The man nodded obsequiously.

Bailey didn't like the look of the man, but the good lord knew they needed bricklayers. "Welcome to Mount Vernon, Jemmy."

Jemmy bowed his head and smiled at the tone. Queeny fixed him with a stare. He was second or third generation, she could tell, and like as not had some white in him. She couldn't see his tribe in anything obvious.

Nothing for her to do here—he understood Bailey, was already seeking his approval.

"Smith, answers to Tom."

"I hope he's an improvement over the last Tom, eh, Queeny?" She shook her head and smiled. The last Tom had been a man. He was gone, sold to the Indies, and she missed him in her bed and in her thoughts.

"Welcome to Mount Vernon, Tom."

"Yes, suh." Tom was short and swarthy, with a red flush on top of pale brown skin and curly, lank hair. He was eyeing Queeny appreciatively. She gave him no encouragement.

"Huntsman, answers to Caesar." The young one. He, too, was looking at her and he smiled, a young man's smile.

"Huntsman? We asked for a man good with animals."

"Yessir. That's your man. He got the boat's pigs and goats here in fine fettle. They say he's good with dogs."

Bailey looked at Caesar, as this was the slave the colonel had ordered himself, and the dogs boy would be close to the colonel many days in the field.

"Can you run, boy?"

He looked blank. It was an intelligent blankness; he didn't squirm or babble.

"*What is your name, boy?*" Queeny asked in the lingua franca of the Ivory Coast.

He looked at her, concentrating hard, squinting his eyes slightly, then smiled. "*Cese, madam.*"

The honorific expressed age and successful child rearing, and if it was meant to flatter her, it failed completely. Old indeed.

"*Cese, the white man wants to know if you can run.*"

"I speak Benin. Please, ma'am, I do not understand this talk you make." The last phrase rolled off his tongue smoothly, the product of frequent repetition.

"*My Benin not good.*"

"*I understand you.*"

"*White man ask you. Can run?*"

"*Like the wind in the desert. Like an antelope with the lion behind.*"

Queeny rolled her eyes at the difficult words, the poetic suggestion. "Mista Bailey, this boy say he run plenty fast. He from Africa, though. Masta don't like African boys, Mista Bailey."

"Right. Well, tell him he's welcome to Mount Vernon."

"*You from Benin, then?*"

"Yes. Obikoke. I am Yoruba!"

"*White man says you welcome here.*"

The boy looked surprised. "*Why is he talking to us at all?*"

"*They like to be polite, boy. It don't mean you aren't a slave.*"

Bailey looked interested. "What's he saying?"

"He jus' on about how he run."

"The others seem to speak well enough, Queeny. You take the boy and teach him some English, and make sure he knows the rules before the colonel comes home."

"Yes, Mista Bailey."

"You others, come with me and I'll show you your quarters. Captain Gibson, perhaps you could join me in a quarter hour for a glass."

"I'd be that pleased, Mr. Bailey. I'll just see that this lot get the unloading started."

The two white men bowed slightly, and parted.

✯ ✯ ✯

Cese followed the woman up the long gravel path from the dock toward her hut. The slave quarters were like nothing he had ever seen: a long elegant brick building on one side, with dormitories for the unmarried house slaves and a neat row of cabins on the other, larger and more open than he expected, set farther apart, the whole having more the air of a village than a prison. In Jamaica, his quarters, the "barracoon," had been fenced and locked every night. At Mount Vernon, there wasn't even a wall.

Some of the blacks smiled when they saw him and his escort. None was chained. Most of the men had shirts and trousers, most of the women had a shift and petticoats, and several, like Queeny, sported jackets or gowns. She had a jacket of India cotton, far better than anything he had seen on a Negro in the Indies, but she was probably the queen, mistress to the master. She was old to be a queen, he thought, but her shape was fine and her face good.

The woman neither looked at him nor spoke to him, but simply walked along, nodding to other slaves and once dropping a curtsy to a white woman, who smiled at her as they passed.

"Queeny, dear. Is this a new boy?"

"Yeas, Miz Bailey."

The white woman examined Cese with a careful eye. She noted the narrow rows of scars over his eyes. "He looks African, Queeny."

"I says the same to yo' husban', Miz Bailey."

"The colonel may not like it. Still, the boy's pretty enough. Run over to the well and back, boy."

Cese was aware that he had been addressed, but the words were too fast, the accent too different. He smiled to show himself willing and looked at Queeny.

"You run. Go to the well and come back."

He set his bundle down and took a deep breath before hurling himself forward. The two women watched as his long legs flashed faster, as he leaned his weight into a curve around the well and pulled himself straight with the grace of a cat. Then he dashed past them, slowed, and came back, making a small bow to Mrs. Bailey as he did so. When he took up his bundle, there was a faint line of sweat on his upper lip, but his breathing was deep and even.

Mrs. Bailey laughed aloud. "He is splendid, is he not? He runs like a god. Oh, Queeny, teach him quickly. The colonel will make a fortune on those legs."

"Yes'm."

Queeny curtsied again and moved off toward her hut. Her position allowed her half of a hut that typically housed a family of six, or up to eight men. She shared it with another woman, the house seamstress, Nelly. Nelly would be up at the big house at this hour, sewing her tiny meticulous stitches under the eyes of the colonel's wife and treating her disorders.

"You the master's queen? Is that why you are called Queeny?"

She smiled at the thought that the colonel would have a queen at all, although most plantations did. Some owners used their women as a harem; others took a preference for one woman and that made her queen, often hated by the master's wife but powerful in her own way. The colonel didn't seem to care for dark women.

"No queen here, boy. Master don't chase us. Mr. Bailey, neither."

Cese nodded thoughtfully. One of the older men was sitting on the step of his hut, smoking a black pipe. Children, naked or in shifts according to their age, dashed along the central street of the slave quarter. Queeny ducked to enter the one room of her hut, but he stayed in the doorway, looking around him. None of the slaves he could see was Yoruba, like him. Most were southerners or pagan Bakongo from the interior, or mixes from different tribes. It had been the same in the Indies.

"*Where are the gates?*"

"*No gates.*"

"*You get locked in at night, don't you?*"

"*No.*"

"*Why don't you run, sister? Are you all cowardly Bakongo, too stupid to escape?*"

She glared at him from the darkness of her hut. "*You'll learn, African boy. Shut your mouth now, and listen to me. It is my job to teach you the talk, and I will. I'll teach you more than that, if you let me. There are dogs, there's militia, there's the hunt, all out for any Negro that thinks to run. There is ways to run, hear me? But you don' know them and you better learn. Now get in here this instant. I want to teach you to speak and to stay alive.*"

He ducked his head and entered, his thoughts still outside. Most of the slaves he could see were Ebo and Luo, ignorant southern Bakongo from the interior who were prey to superstition, carried inferior weapons—pliant. Luo women were notoriously loose. This one spoke to him as no woman should speak to a man, although he had grown used to it in Jamaica. She didn't have the look of the Luo, though, and she knew more than a few words of the Benin language, which made her something. And the old sailor, King, had said to learn the language.

She was probably Ebo, it struck him. He had the urge to laugh at the irony: At home his father had kept Ebo slaves, and here the Ebo always seemed to be above him. Of course, at home, slavery was never so permanent.

The urge to laugh never lasted. The urge to violence was always there. As he did dozens of times a day, he resisted the urge to lash out. When all his training told him to fight, or resist a blow or an insult, he would think one phrase to himself.

Today I am a slave.

He sat on a stool, murmuring "*Yes, ma'am.*"

Blain's Store, Virginia, November 1773

"And Ben Carter has taken a schoolmaster from Princeton!" Henry Lee, well dressed to the point of foppery, was holding forth.

"I don't think that will cause the collapse of civilization, gentlemen." Washington was busy with accounts and tired of Lee's youth.

Dr. Thompson reached across the table to take a small basket of English gunflints. "Colonel, I think Mr. Lee means to suggest that Mr. Carter is avoiding the import of English lessons as well as English goods."

"Well put, sir. My meaning exactly."

Colonel Washington idly turned the rowel of a neat silver spur on his boot, his attention more under the table than above it. "I daresay Princeton produces some very educated men."

This was as close to a witticism as Washington ever came, as Henry Lee had just graduated from that very academy.

"I knew him there. A bit of a prig, to be sure, but he seems to know his lessons well enough. Can't dance, though." Henry Lee was suddenly contemptuous.

"Neither does Grigg, and we still pay him to carry our tobacco to England," commented Dr. Thompson, a slight man in quiet clothes.

"I can't see that it signifies much whether a man can dance a minuet, whether he's captain of a ship or a schoolteacher, Mr. Lee," Washington said quietly.

"I'd like my children to grow up to be as good as their peers in London or Jamaica. Can you imagine going out in London and not dancing?" Lee seemed unaware of the internal hypocrisy of his argument. Washington decided it was too much to correct him and let his attention wander back under the table. Alone of the seated men, he had missed education in the home country, and the slight smile that touched his mouth suggested that it was not a matter that interested him overmuch. "Are you gentlemen supporting the embargo on English goods?"

Dr. Thompson seemed rather caught out, as he had five carefully selected gunflints in one hand and a good hard English shilling in the other.

"In the main," he said, shifting in his seat.

"Tea for certain," said Lee. "Otherwise it depends on circumstances. What are we to do for cloth?"

"I've seen decent wool cloth from this country." Washington looked at them. "I'm raising a company of select militia, gentlemen, and I'll see them all uniformed in good American cloth."

"Select militia?" Lee asked with a young man's interest. He leaned forward attentively, then paused, aware that he was revealing too much enthusiasm for an aristocratic Lee.

"To train a cadre of officers and noncommissioned officers. The kind of men we lacked so badly in the last war."

"Ahh, I see," said Lee, feigning disinterest. "And while we Lees wonder about boycotting English wool, will the Washingtons still be purchasing a piano?"

Washington nodded to acknowledge the hit. "And velvet caps for my hunt boys. I suppose that the doctor's 'in the main' will have to do duty for every one of us."

Young Henry Lee had a way of pointing out men's flaws that made him difficult company at the best of times. Washington had ordered the offending pianoforte for his stepdaughter, Patsy, well before the embargo. Now she had died untimely, but he had no intention of turning it away. Nor would he turn away the parcel of velvet hunting caps, the livery jackets, or the new silver spoons. Nor discard the hallmarked English spurs on his boots.

"Mr. Blain?" Washington held out a handful of gunflints to the owner of the store.

"Colonel Washington, sir. How may I be of service?'

"Mr. Blain, Mr. Lee has just been kind enough to point out that no man of us has been perfect in our attention to the embargo on English goods, but I wonder, sir, if what I've heard of New York gunflints is true, that they are as good as English?"

"Why, truth to tell, Colonel, I'd never given it any thought. I don't think I've ever seen them offered for sale."

Washington was examining the English flints as if they carried disease. "I saw them in Albany, last war."

Lee laughed. "I've lived in New Jersey. I have a difficult time imagining anything good coming out of New York."

"I'll look into it, Colonel."

"If you manage it, Mr. Blain, I'll see my militia buy all their flints here, and other goods besides."

"Is it to be a corps of cadets, Colonel Washington?" Mr. Blain was openly curious, and thus more civil than young Lee had seemed.

"Something like, Mr. Blain."

"You don't suppose that this trouble with England will end in a struggle, sir?"

Washington rose at the sound of his wife emerging from the back of the house. He motioned to his slave, waiting against the wall, to fetch the chaise. "I know of no one who desires a struggle, sir."

"Can you honestly imagine us fighting the mother country, sir?" Henry Lee swaggered.

Washington whirled on the young man. "Seeking to provoke a quarrel by forcing the contrary opinion on every matter is uncivil, sir. First you seek to lesson me on boycotting English goods, and now you question whether we would fight England. Which way will you have it?"

"I meant no offense." But Lee was sullen.

Dr. Thompson started, worried at the sudden change in tone. He was a civil, gentlemanly man, and took his social duties as seriously as his medical. "I gather that congratulations are in order, Colonel Washington?"

The coldness around Washington's eyes suggested no such thing. He looked at the men, especially the men of quality, as if measuring them for uniforms, and was deaf to Thompson's approach. He stared at Lee and said emphatically, "If the government insists on making *slaves* of us, they will leave us little choice, sir."

With dogged social sense, Dr. Thompson pressed on. "Your son is to be married, I gather, Colonel? Allow me to present best wishes for their happiness."

Washington nodded, breathed, and nodded with a trifle more warmth. The thaw spread up from his jaw to his eyes; it did not reach them, however. "Thank you, Doctor. I will indeed tender your best wishes to the happy couple. The wedding is not for some months."

The doctor would have found that look inimical or even offensive with most men, but Washington in anger was someone to be handled gently, like a dog with a bad tooth.

Washington's slave, Jacka, reappeared at the door, and a slight nod of the head indicated that the carriage was ready. Washington gave his wife his arm, and her slave followed them in her customary silence. An ungainly man was coming up the steps of the store, and he bowed to the lady as she passed.

Henry Lee, seeking to make amends, indicated the newcomer. "Colonel Washington, this is Mr. Fithian, the Carters' schoolmaster. Mr.

Fithian is a graduate of Princeton, in far-off Jersey. Mr. Fithian, Colonel Washington, one of the heroes of the late war, and his wife."

"Your servant, sir. My condolences. I had the pleasure of your daughter's acquaintance. She danced with my pupils in Mr. Christian's class."

"Yes, I'm sure. A pleasure to meet you, Mr. Fithian."

"I have heard of your exploits my whole life, sir. Allow me to present my humble admiration." Indeed, it fairly shone from him.

Washington nodded, disconcerted by the reminder of Patsy's death and confounded by admiration as he always was. He bowed to accept the compliment, his face a little red.

"Odd accent," he noted later in the carriage. "Odd notions, in the Jerseys. Parochial. Imagine a man that age not dancing."

Martha smiled for the first time since the reminder of her daughter's death.

"And Lee can be such a pup," he added.

"Yes, dear. But hardly the first young man to behave so. Will you be coming with me up the river?" she asked.

He considered as he watched the passing countryside. "I think it would be best if I posted home to Mount Vernon and opened the house for you." Washington smiled slowly at her. He wanted her to see that things could be as they had been before, that Patsy's death was not the end of the world. She was showing signs of recovery, but he wanted more.

Martha smiled at him, the old smile that showed that the real Martha was still inside the mourner.

"You get home and make it all right," she said. "I'll just follow along, as always." They chuckled together a moment, and she began a long account of the ball.

Mount Vernon, Virginia, November 1773

Cese had worn shoes before, but never boots. He had been given trousers in Jamaica, but here received stockings and good strong breeches of hemp twill. Queeny dressed him several times, trying clothes on him until she was satisfied.

She walked around him like an artist with a sculpture, admiring her work. "I wan' cut those sca's right off you, they look so 'landish," she chastened him. The days had sharpened his English considerably, and she refused to help him in Benin or the trade language any longer, except to taunt him. He reached up and touched the scars. She pushed his hand away.

"Don' draw no 'tention to 'em."

She was a tall woman, but he stood over her, six feet or more in the boots. His legs were long for his height, and the breeches and stockings accentuated the muscles of his calf and thigh. He had a white shirt from Mr. Bailey's castoffs; the patches at the shoulders never showed under his waistcoat and the short blue jacket that Nelly had let out for him, a remnant of Mr. Jack's younger days. He held his head straight and placed his right hand on his hip like the white gentlemen, a rather striking affectation for a black man and one Queeny had never seen. Cese never considered it; he had been beaten as a child until he learned to hold his shield in just such a way, resting his spear hand, and the pose, alike in Africa and classical Rome, had been ingrained in him as it was in the men whose statues adorned the white world.

The pose made Queeny a little nervous, although she couldn't place why, but the face reassured her—an open, honest face, with a long, broad nose and large, dark, wide-set eyes still free from cynicism, his smile directed at her breasts under the boned cotton jacket she wore. It had taken her less than a day to lead him into seducing her, and she had tied him with the strings of his own notions of loyalty. Those eyes promised her some time of pleasure and comfort, as long as she could train him to his tasks and keep his arrogance at bay. He was a good man. She wanted him to stay and not go the way of Tom. But the easy confidence of his pose was troubling, and the clothes had not had the effect she expected, of cowing him, but the opposite. What he had in common with Tom was the danger—too damn smart. Queeny was old enough to know that what drew her to them was the very thing that would take them away. She smiled, a secret, bitter smile.

He smiled back, turning out his toes. "Hard to run in dese, Queeny."

"These," she said automatically. "You jes' learn, Caesa'. Colonel gon' expec' you run in those, and those clothes, too."

"Dese ones hurt the feet, Queeny."

"These, Caesa'. I don' speak like Miz Bailey, but I wants you to speak bettah, not like no field Negra. This, that, these, those. Say it."

"This . . . that . . . these . . . those," he said purposefully as he began to trot up and down the street, followed by children from all the huts. His speed was already a byword. He had beaten the plantation champion on his first evening and then downed another slave, Pompey, in a short but fair fight whose origins escaped him. Later he accepted that Pompey had seen him as a rival for Queeny before he himself had even thought of wanting her.

The boots hurt his feet, but they could be borne. His toes splayed wide from a life spent barefoot, and the short boots had been made to accommodate a more civilized foot. He changed his stride, taking longer paces to change the pressure on his feet, and leaned into the turn by the well. As he passed it, his feet went out from under him, the slick leather soles betraying him on the dry ground. He rolled over and felt the thin material around one of the patches in his shirt give way, but he bounded to his feet and increased his speed back to Queeny's distant door.

"Don' run so hard, Caesa'. Never give them all you got. They jus' wan' it every time."

He smiled at her, his big open smile full of teeth and confidence. She was angry, for some reason.

"I always got mo' of dat ting, I think. Always little mo'."

"Always *a* little mo'. *That* thing."

"Yeah, yeah. Always *a* little mo'. *That* thing."

"Now give me that shirt, you. You gon' keep me an' Nelly sewing all the time."

"Not all the time," he said neatly and clearly, and put his hands round her waist, lifting her playfully through the door of her hut. She liked to be lifted, liked when he showed his strength. She laughed, and he was caught in her again.

☆ ☆ ☆

The dogs were easy—easy in that keeping dogs had been his job in Jamaica, and easy in that these had never been mistreated and took to him from the first. They were trained, he could tell; they had good noses and fine voices, and he fed them meat—more meat than he himself got in a week, but that made no mind. The pack leader was a surprisingly small bitch with a full bell-toned voice, and he took her out and ran with her in the yard, and then with one of her mates. In Jamaica he had known all the packs and most of the ground, although the packs hunted slaves more often than animals. Cese knew the fox hunt only by repute, never having seen one, but he had learned the rules.

The master was due home in a matter of days, and the hunt season was on them. All his tests would come together. Virginia was a step up from Jamaica, and he didn't intend to go back to the beatings and the threat of worse—the barracoon and the pens. Queeny had passed to him her fears that he would be found wanting and sent back to Jamaica. He ran with the hounds and listened to anything any man could tell him about the hunts. Most of them had been beaters, one time or other; Pompey worked the hounds from time to time and seemed to bear little ill will about the fight.

Pompey resented him for Queeny and for his instant possession of the dogs, but the fight had been a matter of form. If Pompey bore him a grudge it was well hidden, and none of the hundred other blacks he had met seemed to hold his position against him. Any resentment they might have felt for his clothes and his possession of Queeny vanished in the face of the bricklayer, who already had six of the slaves working under him and was laying the front walk, formerly a broad expanse of white gravel, in brick. He was demanding and brutal as only a man who has learned his leadership on a Jamaican plantation could be. As a skilled man, he had his own hut. As an outsider, he had already earned more than his share of enemies. He was working to get the front walk paved for the master's return to keep his place, and Cese had already heard rumors from the others of things that might have been done to the walk—chalk in the mortar, holes under the bricks to make cracks appear. Cese watched and learned, keeping his thoughts to himself.

The other slaves were a mixture, their names and faces still a blur in his head, alien faces, Ebo and Efik and Teke, Luo and Seke and others from farther inland. There were no other Yoruba or Ashanti soldiers, hardly any Benin at all, and they half-castes from the coast. His mother had once said that there was good even in an Ebo, if one was patient, and he schooled himself to patience. Queeny was good company, and the work was light compared to the Indies.

He asked Queeny about the threatened attacks on the front walk.

"Oh, it do happen, Caesa'. It do."

"In the Indies they rack a slave till they know who done it."

Queeny shook her head. "This ain't the Indies, boy. You be 'spectful, you smile, but then you keep some fo' you. If'n they push hard, you break yo' tools. If'n they 'spect you to work all night, you spoil yo' work. Every one of us know to do this, Caesa'. You pay 'tention, boy. Indies slaves work too hard, too 'fraid. Make the otha's look bad."

"Queeny, I be'nt afraid. If'n you's so brave, why not run?"

"Some do. It be a hahd life, Caesa'. Hahd in woods, and hahd on the road, and the devil to pay if they catch you."

"I heah no slaves in England."

"English ship brought me heah. English mans run the farms. You know 'bout Flo-ri-da?"

"No. You tell me."

"Sometime I tell you 'bout John Canno. But you walk careful, listen to what I tell you. Be 'spectful, but keep some back."

"I heah you. I *hear* you."

" 'Cause they don' really thank you fo' it, Caesa'. If'n they nice o' if'n they nasty, you still a slave."

"You know 'bout *Somerset*, though?"

"I know I hear fools say we all be free. He one man. Good fo' him, I say. He free. I ain' free."

Cese looked at the ground a minute and kept his thoughts to himself. *Today I am a slave.*

✷   ✷   ✷

Washington rode easily, one leg cocked up over the pintle of his saddle. He had almost reached his own land and had nothing but pleasure ahead of him. He looked forward to a release from politics for a few days, because the incessant clamor against the home country could be fairly shrill. In darker moments, he wondered that they dared. In others, he suspected that they were simply grumbling like soldiers on a long march. Soon enough the debts from the Great War would be paid, and surely then the politics would return to something like normalcy.

Jacka was up on a new bay behind him, riding out in circles when the ground allowed to try to work the friskiness out of the big horse. Washington looked at him and grunted in approval. As he looked, his gaze was caught by something well to the east over Jacka's shoulder and he sat up, tacked his free foot back in the stirrup, and put his spurs to his horse. Jacka, caught off guard, was well behind him in an instant.

There was a man, a big man, taking crabs from the river in a little punt. Two black women and another man were building a fire on the bank. Washington rode up to the big man, already angry.

"What are you about, sir!" he called.

"Takin' crabs, squire," said the man. His tone was insolent. "They're God's crabs, I think."

Washington dismounted and walked along the bank until he was opposite the little boat. "What's your name, then?"

The man was as big as Washington or even bigger, with a strong, even brutal face and a squint. He was dressed in an old overshirt and filthy linen.

"I'm Hector Bludner, squire. I was in the Virginny regiment, I was." He chuckled, clearly sure that such a point would clear him of any wrongdoing. "I know you, too, Colonel."

"All right, Mr. Bludner. Bring that punt back in here and get off my land."

Bludner looked at him as if genuinely offended. Perhaps he was. "This ain't England, squire. This is Amerikay. You don' own the crabs!"

Washington stooped and lifted a rock the size of a man's fist. He cocked his arm and threw it at the boat. It went right through the flimsy timber, and in a moment Bludner was splashing and cursing in the shallow water.

"Bastard!" he yelled.

While he was floundering about, Washington turned on the little man and the two women. One was a black girl of perhaps sixteen with a fine face marred only by a collection of bruises. The other was older, perhaps her mother. She moved slowly and Washington could see she had a broken leg, badly reset.

He addressed the smaller white man. "Get off my land this instant, or I'll arrest you all as vagrants. What do you do?"

The little man scratched his head a moment. "We take slaves for folk."

Washington spat. "I have no use for your kind. My slaves don't run."

Jacka caught that remark coming up late, but if he thought anything of it, he kept it to himself.

Bludner was ashore now, soaked and raging. He struck the young woman hard, so that the impact sounded like a pistol shot. The little man just got out of his way and began to load a pony. His attack on the woman enraged Washington, who stood his ground, waiting for Bludner to approach him. Bludner spent a moment getting his blood up, cursing.

"Your kind is why we need to spill some blood in these parts, by damn. No 'nobles' in Amerikay!"

Washington watched him with calm ferocity. "You're a coward and a pimp."

Nothing spurs hatred in a man like the memory of admiration, and

Bludner had once sought Washington's approval through a whole summer as a soldier. He took his time making his move, talking a great deal,
so that when he finally shifted his weight he almost caught Washington
off guard. But Washington had wrestled Indians and Virginians all his life.
He sidestepped and sent a blow from his fist into Bludner's head that
staggered him. Then he struck him again, stepping inside his long-armed
blows and pounding a fist up under the man's arm, knocking the wind out
of him, then hammering the man's face and chest until he fell. Then he
kicked the man twice without compunction. Jacka watched with a smile,
while the little man just kept loading the group's goods on two ponies.
Washington could see the butt of an unexpectedly fine rifle standing up
from one pony.

He nodded at Bludner on the ground and at their camp. "Take any
crabs you already have ashore—I won't have them go to waste. Then get
you gone. If I see you in the country, I'll have you taken up on a charge."

The little man merely nodded.

Jacka was watching the pretty girl. She was one of the most beautiful
women he had ever seen—prettier than Queeny—with her almond eyes
and pouty lips. She met his eye boldly.

"What's you' name?" he asked.

"I'm Sally," she said, tossing her head despite a new and spreading
bruise on her cheek. Clearly mere beatings couldn't break her spirit.

Washington mounted again and rode a little apart, watching them, his
easy mood of the road broken. He handed Jacka a pistol.

"See they get clear of my land."

Jacka nodded.

★   ★   ★

Mr. Bailey wanted a great reception for Colonel Washington, and he
intended to line the drive with the servants and slaves, some old retain-
ers, and a few friends at the top, nearest the house, standing well back to
be discreet and different from the lower orders on the drive. In the meantime, fires were lit throughout the house, everything was cleaned to a
fare-thee-well, and the beds were turned down in the master bedroom.
They posted a boy well up the road to give them the signal.

When the boy came dashing back, Mr. Bailey gave the signal, ringing
his handbell, and men and women came running from the nearest farms
and outbuildings. Mr. Bailey was appalled to see his master riding up

without a coat, with one hand swollen and bleeding and his breeches all muddy. He stood at the great horse's head and welcomed the colonel, and all the servants and slaves stood silently as Washington reviewed them and nodded. He rarely praised, and in his current mood, although he was aware that a special effort had been made and that something was called for, he merely grunted to Bailey as he completed his review.

He saw new slaves, and he didn't know them. The tallest of them, a well-built lad, had tiny ridges of scars over his eyes. He'd never seen the like, and it did nothing to improve his mood, as it was a disfigurement on a noble-looking man and meant he was fresh from Africa. He didn't like Africans. He'd said so often enough.

"Let me see to your poor hand," said Mrs. Bailey, and he let himself be dragged inside.

★　★　★

Two chimes of his French watch later, he was dressed in proper clothes, the dust of the road and the dirt of the fight washed clean, and the knuckles of his hands well bandaged. He had taken a glass of rum and mint, cool from the back house, and followed Bailey out onto the lawn to inspect the front walk.

"What's the bricklayer's name?"

"Jemmy, sir."

"He's done some good work here, Bailey. But the men don't think much of him. They've spoiled the mortar in a few places."

"Yes, sir. I tried to watch them, Colonel. I made two men replace the gravel. They left holes in the work."

"I see."

"He hit them, did this Jemmy."

"I won't have it. See that he understands, Mr. Bailey, and get the walk finished. I expect to turn a nice profit on this fellow and his crew when they can pull in harness. Mrs. Carter would pay handsomely this minute to have her outbuildings touched up. I want a new kennel."

"I understand, Colonel."

"But it will be a wasted investment if he tries to come it the lord over them."

"Yes, sir."

"Good. Now, there is a smith?"

"I haven't seen much of him, sir. Perhaps I was remiss. I put him to helping at housework, as I didn't want to test him on your forge. He came with a character for being capable with firearms, but I didn't see fit to test him on yours."

"I'll see to it. I thank you for it. I fairly dread the notion of a wild man loose with my fowlers. And the dogs boy?"

"A likely lad, sir. Young and cheerful, runs like the wind. Beat Tam in a fair race and downed Pompey with his fists. And the dogs like him."

"Well, I look forward to seeing this paragon. He's African?"

"He is. Queeny says Yoruba, perhaps . . . perhaps Ashanti."

"I don't take to Africans, Bailey, but we'll see. I've always heard said Ashanti made the worst slaves."

"Perhaps this one will change your mind, sir."

"I'll expect to see him with the dogs this afternoon. Send the smith to me in a few minutes." He cast a last glance over the new brick walk and the lawn running down to the Potomac.

"You did well in my absence, Bailey. My thanks."

He was gone in a few long strides, leaving Bailey to enjoy the rare praise alone.

☆　☆　☆

The new boy was working grease into his boots in a cool corner of the shed, a small wooden tub of the stuff under one hand and the boots laid out before him, their laces stripped off to the sides. He also had several of the dog collars laid out in the straw, and a leash as well. The hounds were gathered round him, and he was speaking to them, slowly and clearly, enunciating English words: "This, these, that, those."

Washington stopped in the doorway and watched him for a moment. "He has something of the air of a soldier."

Bailey stood behind him, concerned that the floor of the kennel would spoil the boy's new breeches.

"I remember the regulars with Braddock," Washington went on. "They cleaned their gear the very same way, everything laid out neat before them."

Cese was aware of the master when the first words were spoken, and he betrayed no alarm at being caught sitting barefoot in the kennel, but put his boots off to one side and rose gracefully to his feet without his hands touching the floor. His height was just shy of Washington's, and he looked him in the eye for a moment before bowing from the waist. He saw a tall man, in a scarlet coat and buff cloth smallclothes, top boots. He had an impression of power, cloaked, a little hidden—like a chief. A more athletic man than any master he had had—more imposing. Mr. Bailey seemed a slight thing by comparison.

"What are you putting on that leather, boy?"

Cese worked it out in his head, to be sure. "Hog's fat, suh. Little linseed oil."

Washington nodded briskly. He examined the dogs; they looked clean and fit. "I hear you are fast, boy."

Cese smiled and bobbed his head.

"What do they call you?"

"Cese, suh."

Bailey actually stepped forward, as if to fight off the African name. "Caesar, Colonel."

"Ah, Caesar. He has a bit of the Roman look to him, does he not?" Washington was disconcerted for a moment—a rare feeling, quickly dismissed. Then he smiled—a quick flash, without teeth, but one that lit his face—and he turned back to Bailey.

"Am I understanding? Caesar beat Pompey?"

Bailey looked at him without understanding, and Washington shook his head and moaned inwardly; his moments of learned wit were few enough, to fall on such barren ground.

"Perhaps we'll call him Julius Caesar?"

Bailey was still trying to make out why Washington was so concerned that the new slave had beaten Pompey. "It were a fair fight, Colonel."

Washington smiled again, nodded. "I'm sure it was, Bailey. But I like the name. Julius Caesar. Tell Queeny—he's with Queeny?"

"Yes, Colonel."

"Julius Caesar. I like the look of him, Mr. Bailey. Tell him I will want him and the hounds out tomorrow morning. See to it."

"Yes, Colonel."

"He has a jacket?"

"Yes."

"I have the caps in my baggage. See that he has one. All the neighborhood will be riding tomorrow, and he must be smart." Washington leaned over the stile and looked him in the eye.

"I like to be there when the dogs are fed, Caesar. When you have their food made up, you send to the house for me, if I am by. Do you understand?"

"Yes, suh. Then dogs know you."

Washington nodded. "Exactly. Boy, what will you feed 'em tonight?"

Caesar took a moment to think over his reply. "They gun dogs, they rest tomorro'. They get meat. They hounds, they run tomorrow. They get bread soaked in broth, roll' in balls."

Washington smiled, a thin-lipped movement that hid his teeth. "And they're all well, Caesar?"

"Blue heah . . . Blue *here*, she's coat be dull, be'nt it, suh?"

"You tell me."

"An' she won' take huh food. *Her* food."

Amused at the boy's eagerness and air of confidence, Washington leaned out farther over the stile. "What do you do for a dog like that?"

"I wash her in broth and see dat . . . *that* she licks herse'f and get *her* some food."

"I take a little turbith mineral, I make it into a ball with corn syrup, and I give it her to eat."

"Neva heard that one, suh. What's turbit?"

"Mr. Bailey, would you be so good as to reach down the second tin. The very one. Look here, boy. I take as much as will cover a nail. See? I'll mix it with a dash of syrup. Damn it, there used to be corn syrup here."

"Right here, Colonel."

"Thank you, Mr. Bailey. I mix them together and then roll it in a pill, like this. Now you give it her, Caesar."

Caesar took the sticky pill and stroked the dog for a moment before running his fingers along the bottom of her jaw, where he pressed. The dog opened her mouth wide and Caesar laid the sticky pill on her tongue. It was gone in a single lick, the dog looking back and forth between the people with the weary air of one who has been practiced upon.

"Four times a day until she takes food. I do rather like the notion of bathing a dog in broth, though. Do you find that it answers?"

"They can't he'p but lick, suh."

"I learned about the turbith mineral from Lord Fairfax, and there is no man in America knows more about dogs. I long to tell him about bathing a dog in broth. Do both: I wish to see it in action."

"Yes, suh."

Washington left the boy to Bailey and headed for his house.

✳ ✳ ✳

He read in his library for a while, then looked at his latest drawing for an improved stable, made a change where he thought he could run water straight from the spring with pipes, and thought better of it. He was restless, and he walked through the house as he sometimes did when he couldn't concentrate his mind. The servants and slaves in the kitchen were surprised by his passage, but pleased at his satisfaction. Other house slaves looked worried when he passed, or were long in bed themselves, according to their tasks.

Washington stopped on the central stairs and found Martha sitting in the blue parlor. "Are you ready for bed, ma'am?"

She lifted her book to him with a smile and went back to reading, a habit he had once found rude and was now used to. The smile, at least, meant she was in good humor. He nodded, almost a bow, and went up. The stair had never satisfied him. It was too narrow, and lacked something in sweep compared to other houses. It dated from a time when Mount Vernon had been considerably smaller. He began to plan a new staircase, trying to picture where he would have the space for a broader sweep.

"Are you going to bed now, sir?" asked his personal slave, Billy.

Washington realized he was standing at the top of the stair, unmoving, and that his hands were cold. He had been there some time.

"I am, Billy. I am."

"Will you want anything while you undress?"

"I think I'll have a small brandy, Billy."

"Very well, sir. I'll be with you in an instant."

Before Washington had done more than enter his bedroom and take his watch out of his breeches, Billy was back with a trumpet-shaped glass on a silver tray. His presentation was elegant; indeed, everything about Billy was elegant, and he did it so quietly that Washington seldom heard him coming.

Washington swallowed a third of the contents in a gulp, surprising himself. He smiled. "My thanks on that, Billy. Will you see to my watch case? It's dull."

"Yes, sir." Billy took his coat and handed it to a young boy, who took it with something like reverence.

"I can get my own boots, Billy."

"I'm sure you can, sir. But you won't while I'm here."

Billy had the softest touch of the slave accent, never enough to make *sir* into *suh*, but enough to make his tone husky. He was always softly spoken. Washington sat and allowed Billy to pull off his riding boots, which were handed to the same boy for polishing. Billy left his slippers by the fire. Washington would never submit to anyone putting his slippers on. Washington turned, his aquiline profile strong against the dark outside. He sipped his brandy.

"Anything else, sir?"

"Have you met the new boy, Billy?"

"Which one, sir?"

"The African, Billy. The dogs boy."

"Cese, sir?"

"That's him, Billy. Caesar, if you please. What do you think of him?"

"He's a good boy. Queeny likes him, and that's somethin'."

Billy didn't exactly approve of Queeny, as he was a Christian man and she was easy in her affections. But at another level, they were allies.

"We'll know what he's made of when we see him on the hunting field, eh?"

Billy attended Washington even on horseback. They had been together for a long time, and Billy was probably the best black horseman in Virginia. In fact, he was better than most gentlemen, although still not the equal of Washington.

"I think he'll do fine, sir."

Washington still seemed in doubt. "I think he's too... African," he said, shaking his head. "But he has the makings of a fine young man, I'll grant you that. Get to bed, Billy."

☆ ☆ ☆

The new boy cut quite a figure in his cap and jacket. He had a stick in his hand, almost like a crop, and it seemed to Washington that the stick might be coming it a bit high for a slave, especially if that stick were meant for his dogs.

Washington edged his horse across the drive in the early morning light to the edge of the pack and watched Caesar separate one of his bitches from one of the visiting Lee hounds with the stick, never a blow, just a firm pressure with the stick and a slap of the hand.

"Where did you buy the dogs boy, sir?" young Henry Lee asked with open admiration. "He's rather fine."

Caesar recognized the look and nodded his head to Mr. Lee, leaving Washington uncomfortable again. It was an easy nod—far too easy for a slave, and yet not in any way a breach of etiquette. The nod was of a piece with the stick.

"I had him from a failed plantation in Jamaica, Henry."

"And I may wish Papa will do as well."

"He does seem singular. That's a fine mare, Henry."

"I had her from my uncle at Stratford Hall. Part Arab, they say. I hope so, for the price." The mare began to circle, and Lee was frustrated by the lack of effect his new silver spurs had on her. He pressed her with his crop and still she turned, her interest divided between worry at the dogs and interest in Washington's mount, a big bay called Nelson.

"Damn you." He hit her with his crop.

Washington shook his head. "Not her fault, sir."

Lee, unused to being checked, looked up, but Washington was already moving away, backing his horse to the open area beyond the hunt. The huntsman, a local tenant, came in and pointed off over the lane to a distant copse, motioning with a long old-fashioned whip. Lee let his horse have her head a moment and then pushed her away from the dogs, where she instantly settled down. Billy, Washington's constant attendant, trotted easily around Henry Lee and gave Caesar a smile. Then he followed his master.

The pack gave voice, answered thinly by the select pack over the hill. Someone had found a fox. The huntsman gave Caesar the signal, and he released the hounds, his eyes still following the young man his master had rebuked and the elegant black man on horseback. The hounds leapt away, and the hunt began to take shape behind them.

✽ ✽ ✽

It was the third draw that produced a fox, with the select dogs of the county behind it and the rest of the pack following from reserve. No one had expected the first draw to produce anything; the night had been very windy and the ground was cold. But the fox found in the wood hard against Dogue Run went away at a view by the schoolhouse, crossed the Alexandria road back into Mount Vernon plantation, and ran north toward Belvale, the seat of the Johnstons. Just short of the park wall he turned left and ran the whole length of the new-laid brick, but hesitation at the steep banks of the creek cost him a precious moment. He was headed at the wall and killed in the cart shed behind Belvale, the dogs in fine voice and the copper blood and ordure scent over the whole winter morning. Washington was in at the kill, his horse an extension of his will, Billy at his elbow like a standard-bearer, fine in Washington's red and buff livery. Caesar was never far from the dogs, running from scent to scent, his eyes on the country ahead. Twice he outguessed the select pack and the bitch in the lead, crossing to a new cover before the pack found a new voice, and his prowess did not pass without note.

Belvale Shrubbery was the next draw, and here there were three foxes. The field was tired, and etiquette was slipping; the pack split, with the larger part chasing an older female and the smaller a younger male. The field divided in proportion to the hounds and privately held views on the ethics of the thing. The older hunters chased the larger part of the pack; the younger members followed the younger dogs and chased over more difficult country.

Caesar stayed with his own dogs, which had the first scent, and pursued the old vixen with a will. Other dog runners paced him; an older man with the French family's hounds flashed him a smile as they ran up to the hounds at a check by Little Hunting Creek.

"You can run, boy!"

"Thanka."

"I be John. Fro' the French place."

"Why'd the pack split?"

The older man shook his head, flashing a broad smile. "Hell to pay when the leaders meet, I be thinkin'."

The pack checked at the edge of the thick cover of the wood and the rising ground toward Cameron Run. Caesar could see the other pack running well to the south, even half a mile away, straight into the wind, their noses up, tails flat out. The younger members of the field were right up on the hounds, some jumping a small hedge and some angling for the gate nearer the river. The Lee boy, the one his master had been harsh to, was riding flat out, his whip striking the horse's withers, his whole body leaning forward over the horse's neck.

The dogs were past the check and beginning to run again, and he began to lope after them. John seemed to be waiting for something.

"I'm Caesar, from Mount Vernon."

"I know, boy. I know."

Caesar wondered why he was laughing, but he lost the thought in the glory of the run.

☆　☆　☆

Washington watched him follow the hounds past the check, pleased with his purchase and angry at the day. The wind was wrecking the scent; indeed, they had been lucky to draw a fox at all, and the hounds were going to find the going harder and harder. Worse was the defection of the younger set. He thought they had ridden off willfully, and he doubted they'd make a kill. The older men and one woman had held the field on the first kill. They had done all the real work of the thing and now they were deserted for their pains. He disliked that the young people were allowed to go by the rest of the field. He liked people to follow their parts, and the defection savored of rebellion.

He turned in the saddle and rested one hand on his horse's rump, looking back into the Potomac Valley, but the lesser part of the hunt's field was gone over a hedge. He watched the last of the younger riders, their forms darkened by the winter light, balk at a stile and ride around.

"This will not do," he said aloud, as much to himself as to Billy behind him.

He trotted Nelson along the slow rise to the left, his intention to get ahead of the fox and the hunt. Washington always hunted with a military art; he read the ground and tried to outguess his opponent. The Virginian habit of hurling his horse at every obstacle that the hounds crossed had ceased to challenge him years ago.

He led Billy across country toward Rose Hill, and he noted with some surprise that his Caesar had stopped following the hounds and was running ahead of him in great leaps, like a two-legged deer, bounding over the hummocky grass. The wintry sun broke through the clouds for a moment, illuminating the three men and the winter grass around them in a brief blaze of pale gold, the slate of the sky an intimidating contrast that threatened worse weather to come.

The last of the sun's effort showed both of them the sight of the fox fully in view as she burst from the woods along the creek and turned north across the windswept open ground toward Rose Hill, her curious red-green coat gleaming with the sun's touch. Washington rose in his stirrups and yelled, then sounded a view on his horn. The cry of the hounds changed from puzzlement to pursuit within the wood and the leaders of the pack began to appear, scenting the wind and bounding along. Caesar turned to him and smiled, a personal smile that lit his face, and Washington's thin lips curled. He saluted slightly, just a wave of the whip in a gesture of acknowledgment, and he gathered the horse under him and was gone, Billy in his wake, but Billy's smile was broad, almost welcoming, and he gave Caesar a wave.

The open ground gave the field a fine burst of about ten minutes, with plenty of jumping when they came to the Rose Hill fences. But the fox was old and wise, and the wind was rising; she lay still once in a covert and doubled on her own scent when she ran, almost splitting the pack a second time.

Washington heard the other group blow a mort and knew they had killed, somewhere down in the valley on his own land. His first thought was one of sharpened competition, but he pushed that down as unworthy. Their killing did not make their actions right, and this green-red fox, this ancient vixen, had given the best of the field the kind of hunt men talked about for years—fence after fence, the sighting by the woods when the hounds were at a stand, many a twist, a true champion. He looked back at his field, eleven tired gentlemen and one gentlewoman, and then forward to where the chase had made the cover of the heavy brush at the very bank of the Dogue Run. The hounds gathered about the cover, climbing over one another but held by the tough undergrowth. Washington rode round the pack, the thong of his whip free for the first time in the afternoon. He rode over to the huntsman and William Ramsay, who were sharing a bottle.

"I say we leave her. I think she earned it."

"Huzzay, then! A well-plucked 'un."

"Leave her to have kits." They all nodded, gave a small cheer, and began to pick their way back toward Mount Vernon, except Daniel French, who was home already. He waved his whip and rode round to his stable.

"He can't be too happy, knowing you've just moved a Vernon fox into the bush behind his henhouse," said Ramsay, laughing his Scottish laugh.

" 'Twas only justice, gentlemen. She gave us good sport. She lives to do it again."

"Young Lee killed his fox."

"Young Lee broke the pack. He didn't follow the right fox."

"True enough." Ramsay looked at Washington to see if he was angry, but the man was flowing along, at one with his horse, and the look on his face was one of deep contentment.

★　★　★

The huntsman signaled the boys to call off the dogs. Again Caesar's stick stood him in good stead, as he used it deftly to separate dogs and push them back on to the greensward. He tossed tidbits from his haversack, pushing through the dogs until he had the Mount Vernon pack leader by the scruff of the neck and had carried her clear of the pack and off to the grass, where he fed her several bites of bread soaked in molasses until she had her wits about her again. The pack followed her, and Caesar kept them moving away from the covert until they began to calm down and move along with him. The older man, John, had his dogs out of the bush first and held them with his voice alone, almost crooning to them. He looked around, saw the mounted party riding away, and pushed one young pup across from his group into Caesar's.

"That 'un's yours, John," Caesar protested.

"An' you jus' take him down to Vernon. I come by latuh, pick him up, I don' miss all the pahty jus' because Missah French be tired. Right?"

"If'n you say," Caesar said with some hesitancy.

"I do say. Run 'long, now."

Caesar headed down the hill, the little stranger trying to worm his way back to his own pack for a few moments. Caesar prevented him, though not without some fellow feeling; the young dog was alone, and he felt for it. But the Rose Hill pup did not care, for soon enough he ran with the Vernon pack as if born to them.

☆　☆　☆

"It was the fastest chase, gentlemen—a young fox, and a fast one. But we kept him in view, and he never turned, just ran till the hounds had him by the heels." Lee held his horse through a little curvet, done deliberately to show his horsemanship.

"You split the pack, Mr. Lee."

"At least I caught a fox."

"Perhaps we'll leave you to hunt on your own in the future, then, Mr. Lee. Clearly the company of your elders oppresses you."

Lee had expected praise, and the dashing of his hopes and his second rebuff in a day from Colonel Washington was more than he could bear. He tried to meet Washington's eyes and fight, but failed, and his shoulders slumped. His horse felt the change and sidled a little until he curbed her with a vicious jerk at the reins, and then he turned on his dog handler.

"Didn't you see the pack was split, Hussy?"

The boy stood paralyzed. Lee's tone held the threat of violence—adolescent humiliation that couldn't be borne.

"Why did you let the dogs run off, Hussy?"

Washington thought it likely that the master had run off and the dogs boy followed, but it didn't matter now; the lad was in for a thrashing. Lee never thrashed heavy, anyway; his father had a humane reputation, and the son was thought overfriendly with his blacks.

He saw Lee let the lash fall free from the stock of his whip and then slash with it, a blow quick as the strike of a cat's claw, and his dogs boy cowered away with blood welling between his fingers where they clutched his face. The other members of the field took pulls on their flasks or headed for the house, distancing themselves from young Lee.

Old John from Rose Hill came running down the long slope from the north. Washington had missed him; he was widely known as the best and most knowledgeable of the dog handlers in the neighborhood, and Washington valued his opinion of young Caesar. But the man had his whole attention fixed on the Stratford Hall boy with a look of hatred.

"Stupid Negra!" John threw himself on the boy, pulling him to the ground and pushing his face in the dirt. The dogs ran in circles, yelping. Most of the white audience had gone, but Lee was poised above the struggling pair, his arm cocked back for another blow with his deadly whip.

Caesar was shocked by the sudden violence, and the more shocked by Old John's sudden attack on Lee's slave. Caesar didn't even know him, except as the slower of the running boys, and one without shoes. John appeared to be beating him savagely, and Lee hovered over them, his mare stepping carefully to avoid treading on the pair.

"Get clear, you bastard!" said Lee, raising the whip again.

Washington's hand seized his wrist and pulled his whip clear of his hand, disarming him so quickly and easily that it looked as if the two men had planned the whole thing. "Never strike another man's slave, young Lee."

Lee looked at him with something like loathing for a moment.

"Come into the house and have a little uncustomed brandy, Master Lee." Washington spoke in an even tone, as if nothing had happened and he didn't have Lee's whip in his hand.

"He's useless!"

"Come along." Washington thought of other men he had known whose admonitions he had heard and accepted, or resented in his own youth: Lord Fairfax, General Braddock, his brother Lawrence. All had the touch, the ability to admonish with the most result and least pain. He knew himself cold and distant—perhaps too distant for this sort of thing—but someone had to bring young Lee into line with responsibility, and today God had ordained that he be the gentleman to try.

As they rode away, Caesar could hear his master speaking softly to the violent young man, and then they reached the gravel path and turned into the outbuildings and were gone. John sat up in a moment. Caesar had the dogs under control, his own, the Lee dogs, and the remnants of several other packs and partial packs.

"They gone?"

"Yea, John. They gone." John was Ebo, through and through. Smart, though, and with a winning smile. The hint of duplicity was pure Ebo, and that he had seen a thousand times. The man winked at him and rose to his feet, dusted off his fine black cloth breeches, and helped the other boy to his feet. The whip had left a bright mark on his cheek and a deep cut, but no gash, and the blood was slowing. The boy was weeping through the mud and blood.

"Why'd you hit him, John?"

"Keep that white boy's whip off'n him, I think. Li'l whip like'n that one, it can take an eye or split you nose."

Caesar was still a little shocked by the violence of it, so different from battle because there was no resisting the hand that held the whip. "I didn' huht him none, did I, boy? Jus' roll roun' atop him."

Caesar looked the boy over. He was weeping so hard he couldn't speak. "He'll live."

"Bettah get you home wi' they dogs, boy. Get cleah 'fo' Missuh Lee get on you 'gain."

The boy nodded, still sobbing.

"Le's get they dogs settled, see what the black folks get to eat. Massa French say I can be heah to eat." He winked at Caesar again.

"You done good, boy. I see you have mah pup theyah." He whistled and the pup betrayed his new allegiance and ran to the older man's heel. "You like the hunt, boy?"

"I liked it fine, suh."

The man laughed. "No one calls a black man suh. Not heah."

Caesar opened the gate into the kennel yard and shook his head to himself, savoring the moment on the grass when he and the tall master had spotted the fox together. Then he shook his head again, as if embarrassed at his own thoughts.

★ ★ ★

The wind continued to rise, and it dished the outdoor festivities. The slaves did dance, but it was in the cart shed. Jacka played his fiddle, and played it well, and some of the house servants came. Old John danced with every girl who would have him, smiled on all, ate well, drank better, and took his leave early and with a good grace. Caesar knew the reels that he had learned in the Indies, and the Mount Vernon women took it upon themselves to show him other dances—country dances they learned from the whites, and variations on their own dances, from Africa and from the Indies. Queeny showed him steps he'd seen whites do, the complicated steps and minuets that she made into excuses to show her legs. Food came down from the house. The scraps from the hunt breakfast were scarcely a feast, but they made a change, and Mrs. Bailey passed a ration of meat and some eggs to enrich the supper. It was better than the fish and corn that they ate every day. And the estate's corn liquor flowed.

The ties that bound the house and field staff and the gulfs that kept them separate were too complex to be taken in at a single social meeting, but Caesar had begun to see them. It was plain to the simplest understanding that Nelly, the house seamstress, was attached to the white servant, Bishop; they fought and simpered in too meaningful a manner. Billy Lee, Washington's personal slave and the only slave he knew who had a surname, was seldom seen with the other blacks, but he came down for a mug of liquor and Caesar saw instantly that he wasn't so much aloof as he was a leader. He singled Caesar out.

"You were very good today," he said.

Caesar warmed to the praise. He would have kept Billy to discuss the field, but Billy was gone, first talking to Queeny and then passing through the others with a word for each.

Caesar had learned that there were other farms, other blacks on them, all satellites of Mount Vernon. The men and women who lived in the greenhouse and the cabins behind it were the elite: house slaves, trusted hands, skilled men and women. He was lucky to be included, but with his share of the estate's corn liquor in him, he didn't feel so lucky. Billy's praise had cheered him at first, but it soured.

Queeny seemed to dance without a care in the world; Old Tom from the house could jab his pipe at Billy Lee and laugh. The carpenters and the bricklayers were telling tall tales of their activities and their value.

What he resented the most was their proprietary notions. When Old Tom said Mount Vernon was the "fines' gentleman's estate on the rivah," he said it with relish, as if the estate were his own. The house girls were the same. Cook spoke of meals as if she ate them, and the sewing crew were filled with pride at their ability to alter the finest English gowns. It all sickened him because none of it was theirs or ever would be. Every pull from the jug seemed to add to his resentment.

But the hunt had been something, a challenge that he had enjoyed. The fox had never fooled him, and the run had been worth the effort. Caesar was open enough to understand that his triumph at the day's hunt might be of the same order as that of the sewing crew over an English gown. The thought that he himself was sinking into the same proprietary habit of thought made him sad, because he wasn't even sure that Washington had noticed his success, and it made him angry that he wanted the master's praise.

He didn't realize that he was pounding the doorframe of the carriage house with his hand until it hurt, and there were Queeny's hands on his arms, and her mouth on his, pulling him into the dark.

"If you jes' goin' to get drunk like a fool, I got bettah plans."

She was wearing stays and a gown that made her waist even smaller than usual; it excited him. She stayed just out of his reach, flitting in to kiss him and away.

"Sho' you ain't too drunk?" she taunted.

He swayed drunkenly to mislead her, shifted his weight against the great horse barn's wall and caught her effortlessly with both hands around her slim waist, lifted her a moment and stepped through the stable door.

"Only the horse boys 'lowed in heah," she whispered, but his hand was running up her naked leg under her petticoat and he wasn't drunk at all, though his mouth tasted of pipe smoke and corn liquor. He settled a saddlecloth under her with a consideration for her best clothes that would never have occurred to most men, and he did it without pausing in his other attentions. A fondness for him entered into her, and then she was lost in other matters.

Chapter Three

Truro Churchyard, Virginia, January 1774

The churchyard at Pohick was complete, with a breast-high brick wall surrounding a graveyard devoid of graves and the four walls of the church proper. Washington sat on his horse in the winter rain and contemplated the empty churchyard and the costs of ambition; the coveted post of warden had cost him a hefty subscription to an Anglican church to which he felt only social allegiance. All the first men of the county attended the Upper Church. Most of their business was transacted in the yard after sermon, and the vestrymen and wardens had a certain advantage, as if they were "to home" and the others visiting. In Virginia, the sacerdotal meaning of the positions was scarcely spoken of in the community.

He didn't fancy deep inquiry about the state of his soul. It sufficed him that he did good works for his peers and subordinates, that every man called him generous, and that even his slaves remembered that he had treated them by hand when the pox hit his plantations. He didn't enjoy the sort of searching often pushed by the Reverend Massey; he wasn't really sure that an afterlife existed, or that it was important that one should search. He had felt from his youngest days that such things were beyond his control and lay in God's hands, and he believed in God as he believed in the king and the empire. A preeminent spirit controlled all, as he controlled his plantation and his tenants controlled their farms, all the way down to the dogs boy controlling the dogs, all the way up to the burgesses and parliament and the king...and God.

Wolfe had been devoted to Gray's "Elegy Written in a Country Churchyard," which Washington had read without a spark of interest. It remained a title to him, but he looked at his own red-earthed country churchyard and wondered if Gray had seen the same things he saw: the value of the building, at 579 pounds Virginia currency; the bricklayer's time and the value of the land; the work to "view and examine" as the wardens were enjoined. Washington doubted that a poet saw the value of things or the work that built them.

By some freak association, his thoughts went from the churchyard to Townshend, who had loathed Wolfe and still did. If Wolfe had won Quebec by luck, where was the justice in Providence? It was the one aspect of war that had sickened him above all others—that neither courage nor hard work was necessarily rewarded or justly served by the results. Braddock's expedition could be smashed and Forbes's succeed, despite their relative merits, and while he strove with all his might to succeed, James Wolfe took Quebec by luck.

Farming did not work in such a way. Farming required planning and work, acceptance of occasional defeat...but the farmer who worked would be repaid in time. War should repay work and interest, like farming. It was a matter of reducing it to principles, but it was unlikely that he would ever be called upon to do so again. The thought left him a little sorry, but the rain was beginning to go through his greatcoat, and he turned his horse's head and trotted toward Truro Church, with time in hand to dry off when he arrived.

Pompey, behind him on a pale nag, was soaked through and cold. He was missing the Reverend Cleve, who was speaking to the slaves at Mount Vernon. He only came one week in five, and Pompey was always sorry to miss the event, as he held his soul dear.

✶   ✶   ✶

The Reverend Cleve was a wholly new experience for Caesar—a black minister, and a free man. He spoke beautifully, as Caesar himself hoped to speak. His clear diction rolled through the cart shed, and his challenges brought out the strongest responses in his congregation. His sermon was simple and direct, and on a theme calculated to appeal most strongly to his listeners: that salvation would come for the worthy, regardless of color or station; that God's house had many doors, and that all of them were open. He never went so far as to say that worldly freedom was unimportant, but his listeners were able to note that eternity would outlast life and freedom and grace defeat bondage in their own souls' lives.

Caesar was a baptized man, brought to Christ's Table when fresh from Africa and newly enslaved, but no part of the religion had moved him like the preaching he heard from the Reverend Cleve. He raised his voice in response, affirming his loyalty to Jesus. Neither his glass of rum at the dance nor his frequent tumbles with Queeny troubled him. Later in the sermon, when both acts were denounced by the minister, Caesar felt some surprise that the gentle, new-light Jesus had time for such small stuff, but he responded that he would not do such things again. He meant it, at the moment the words were spoken. And when they reached the responses in the creed, he tried to form his responses exactly as the Reverend Cleve had spoken them, syllable by syllable. He heard his own voice speaking the words so well, above the cart-shed din, and he knew he could do it always, if he practiced.

Because, though an eternity of heavenly bliss appealed to him, he still wanted freedom while on the earth.

★ ★ ★

At Truro Church, the Reverend Massey droned on toward the completion of his sermon, the attention of most of his congregation taken up in the recurrent thunder and worries about their horses or shays outside. His theme had been warm enough, and well taken at the outset, but only the parish's philosophers were still on the scent with the minister's theological pack as they finally began to pull down their ethereal fox.

Washington was elsewhere, his mind making an orderly survey of the new black children and how best to house them, the question of drainage in a new field on the upper parts of Dogue Run, the health of Old Blue and whether the African boy was all he seemed with the dogs, and most of all his stepson's coming marriage and its consequences, which were great enough, for all love.

Marriage with the Calverts of Baltimore was pleasant enough, and the girl seemed comely and proper, although a certain element of papishness clung to the family. Jack liked her out of all mind, had neglected his expensive studies at Columbia, and wouldn't be satisfied until he had her, so have her he would. Martha was insistent. In this she reminded him too much of his own mother and made him writhe, but there was nothing for it.

Providentially, the event was planned for Mount Airy; nothing he had to do but get on a horse and cross at the ferry. The effect on the estates would be negligible as long as everyone understood the precautions he had taken, and should his wife's son, Jack Custis, decide to build himself a manor house, he now had the means to support one. Washington had worked hard on the Custis estate, which was really his wife's and would now be Jack's. It pleased him that Jack was now going to enjoy the work, but Washington hoped he didn't enjoy it so much that he took either to spending his capital by selling lands or interfering with the excellent managers that Washington had installed.

He could tell by Massey's tone of voice that the end of the sermon was near, and he began to cast his mind toward his Maker in the sort of symbolic prayer the Masons taught. That was more real to him than all the talk. He thanked his Maker for the favor of the making and the Providence that made him what he was, and turned by the congruence of names and ideas to look at his friend George Mason, who was nodding like a musician at someone else's concert. George probably had a point he wanted to dispute. Then he felt Washington's attention, turned, and gave him a significant look, a long one. Washington had no idea what it meant, but it almost caused him to miss the closing words and the signal to rise.

The closing, the admonition to go with God to love and serve him, a spartan procession, not like the papist affairs in some Anglican churches, a moment of silence, and he was walking in the yard, the rain past, with George Mason, who clearly had something urgent to communicate. They walked a distance from the others.

"Boston has spoiled the East India tea."

Washington looked at him, fumbling for words and understanding simultaneously.

"A group of men thinly disguised as Indians went on board the Indiamen and threw the tea in the harbor rather than pay the tea tax."

Washington tapped the church wall with his crop. "Idle fellows? Or a decision taken by the gentlemen of the town?"

"Not known."

"I . . . I don't think it was well done."

"Would you have us submit to the tax?"

"Is the tax so illegal, Mr. Mason?"

"It is an external tax. We have resisted Parliament's attempts to impose such up till now."

"I mislike... I very much mislike the notion that men can take such an act against property into their own hands."

"So must all propertied men."

"And I fear that the government's reaction will be strong. We must await events."

But Mason's eyes burned with the evangelical zeal of the true believer. "You still avoid English goods?"

"Within bounds. I bought a pianoforte, I must confess."

"Oh, that's nothing. It is the daily stuff we must learn to do without if we are to break this legislation."

Washington looked away. His lack of response had disappointed his friend, and his friend's dejection at the reception of his news was spreading. Washington found prating about the injuries of the colonies rather like searching his soul; it didn't accomplish very much.

"This is, what, the fourth time we've embargoed goods?"

"It works well enough, if all comply."

Washington winced slightly. In the earliest embargoes, he had consistently misunderstood the complex system by which the embargo of some goods "supported" the prohibition on "taxed" goods. But the picture of property destroyed by a mob did not please him at all, and it roused him to speech.

"I still fail to see how cheaper India tea makes us slaves. I see how it harms the interests of the Boston smugglers, and this morning I resent such merchants raising a mob to destroy property—it could as easily be my tobacco or my wheat. Doubtless, my friend, you will lead me to see the error of my ways another day. Today I see the cost of Pohick Church rise before me beside the cost of Jack's wedding, and I think that our troubles with England can wait until my crops are in the ground and spring is here."

"You've other business, sir, and I will not detain you. The news is not so ominous, I allow, but the reaction of the government to this check is likely to affect us all."

Washington shook his head solemnly. Other men had gathered to hear the last of the exchange—men with greater debts in England, men with more love, or less, for the mother country—and in a moment the yard was abuzz with it. Washington left Mason retelling the dumping of the tea, motioned to Pompey for his horse, and looked at his watch. Slow.

"Care to pass me the time?" he said, bowing to the elder Mr. French, watch in hand.

"Your servant, sir. Hmm, a quarter past twelve."

Washington opened the face of his watch and put an elegant gold key to the fusee and then to the hands. French caught the engraving on the key and smiled, closed his case with a sharp snap, and bowed; Washington eased his over the catch to save wear, but his bow was just as neat.

"Thank you, sir."

"Bought that brig, did you?"

"I hadn't much choice. I took her in lieu of a debt, you know."

"Good buy, though. Will you send a cargo north, do ya think?"

"I may. First the Indies with my flour."

"If she goes north, I'd be happy to help make a cargo."

"Thankee. That's something to think on. Good day to you, sir."

"'Servant."

Washington rose from the bow and turned to find his horse to hand, mounted in one athletic movement, nodded to Pompey, and was gone before the next rain cloud opened.

Mount Vernon, Virginia, January 1774

Washington's library had a more martial character than its master admitted, these days. Charles XII of Sweden, Voltaire's beau ideal, gazed angrily down from a column that faced his ideological child, Frederick the Great of Prussia. Julius Caesar and Alexander locked gazes in the other corner, an unceasing contest between youth (Alexander and Charles) and age (Caesar and Frederick). Or sometimes the masters of war divided other ways, classical versus modern.

The other furnishings of the room were to the latest taste, if a bit much by native English standards—drapes a little too plum, carpets a little too bright. Altogether, it was the room of a man of immense wealth, and the books that lined the shelves catalogued all his interests. A 1740 Humphrey Bland on military exercise, as well as a new subscription copy of Stevenson's *Advice to Officers in Command of Detachments*, and a shelf of manuals of arms, directions on fortification with plates or without, Muller on artillery. The owner of the library had the most complete interest in war to be found in a library in Virginia.

Farming filled other shelves. The foundation of the collection had come with his wife, being her former husband's books on the subject. He added to it every year, books such as Duhamel's *Practical Treatise of Husbandry* and Young's *Annals of Agriculture*, Thomas Fairfax on sports and dogs and the preservation of game, Tull on English plowing, *The Farmer His Own Mechanic*, and dozens of other titles. The newest were newer than the military volumes, and on the whole more plentiful.

Sport for the sake of sport had its place as well: fishing, shooting, riding, and keeping horses. There weren't many of the classics: some schoolbooks, an uncut Ovid, a much-thumbed Epictetus in English and Latin—much thumbed because the owner knew that Frederick the Great had a copy and praised it. Washington liked Epictetus, because he had been a slave and spoke well of it. When Washington spoke to a slave, he tried to remember the precepts that Epictetus laid down. There was also Homer in translation by Pope—all the volumes save one, which his stepson, Jack, had lost while still in school and never replaced.

They were well kept and their leather gleamed with solid worth; their master read most of them, whether to farm or make war. He had been a soldier and now he was a farmer—head bent over a careful drawing of a drainage canal in the Great Dismal Swamp as he laboriously traced out his plans for further drainage. The Great Dismal was a watery fortress built by nature on the south coast of Virginia to keep farmers at bay. It would take more slaves, more effort, and more money to drain the swamp and till the ground, but the result would be thousands of acres of prime farmland reclaimed from the wilderness right on the coast, where cargoes would fetch the best price. The plan had started almost ten years before; it had never quite succeeded or failed, and its demands seemed to increase every year, no matter how much effort the original investors expended.

He was a farmer, and yet he planned his assault for the year on the Great Dismal like a soldier: considering each drainage ditch an approach sap on nature's fortress swamp; marshaling the forces of slaves and pressed labor available to the investors; planning against the day when the scheme would turn a profit and the siege would end.

He was a farmer, and all his thoughts were on the coming planting, on drainage and foaling, water tables and wheat prices, and the extent of the herring run, and yet none of his heroes had ever excelled as a farmer. They had all been soldiers, soldiers of the type that won their fame for the glory of their arms and not for the kingdoms that they built; indeed, Alexander, Charles, and Frederick shared a failure to build very much at

all. But they were his chosen companions in his library, as his pen gradually worked its way into the defenses built by nature to keep the European
farms at bay in the Great Dismal Swamp, where ten years of labor had yet
to yield a single crop. He looked at his new network of ditches without
confidence, laid his pen carefully in a ready holder to avoid inking the
map, scattered some sand on it, and rose.

A house slave appeared instantly, looking expectant, but Washington
waved him away. "I'm going out to the dogs, Jack."

"Yes, suh."

"Build up the fire, if you please."

"Yes, suh."

He walked out through the library hall and around the drive to the
kitchen, nodding courteously to the cook, the maid, and the little black
girl who helped with the kitchen and was clearly terrified by his appearance so late at night. He paused for a moment and looked at the stars,
missing the child streaking by him down toward the deer park, bound for
the kennel to warn the young man there that Master was headed that
way, so that he was pleasantly surprised to find Caesar up, with a small
rushlight in the kennel, sitting with Old Blue.

"She still in a bad way, Caesar?"

"She bin bettah . . . *better*, sir."

Her coat was not as dull as it had been, though, he noted, and she had
her head in the boy's lap, looking at him with some interest.

"She eating?"

"Eats a little, if'n I feed it to her slow."

"She's a good dog—used to be the best in the pack."

"Yes, sir."

"I'd like to shoot tomorrow."

"How many dogs, sir?"

"Just a pair. You work hard on your speech, don't you?"

"Yes, sir."

Washington smiled, though the subject didn't really please him very
much. He had worked hard to sound English when he joined Braddock's
staff; Lord Fairfax had helped him lose the provincial speech that might
have marked him. Slaves who spoke too well, though—that was another
matter.

"You did a very good job on the hunt. Here's a crown. That's a quarter
of an English pound. Spend it wisely."

Delighted smile, deep bow, genuine admiration. "Thank you, suh! Thank you, *sir*." The black face beamed with pleasure and willingness to please, but Washington noticed that in his flurry of spirits, Caesar's pronunciation had slipped, which was to be expected.

"But I desire you to take care, Caesar. You can be overfamiliar. Do you understand me?"

"No, sir." The light went out. Washington had never been good at admonition; he was too cold, and it always came out as criticism without leniency. It had hurt him with his regiment.

"You should not smile at me, or at Mr. Lee, as if we were your familiar friends."

The boy looked hurt and confused. He'd recover.

"Talk to Queeny, boy. Tell her what I said. Both things. You are a good hunter, and you can have a good life here. But you must know your place."

"Yes, sir."

Washington thought of clasping his shoulder, but he didn't. A slave should not need comforting when the master had spoken to him. Washington tried to regulate his slaves in the tradition of the ancients. His firmness would not have offended Epictetus, he was sure.

Chapter Four

Mount Vernon, Virginia, late January 1774

"Coward! Drunkard! That he would dare..."

Washington's voice trailed off as he realized that his angry words had been audible throughout the house and that the girl who had been tending the fire was now cowering in the corner. He colored in embarrassment, and within a moment Martha appeared from the back stairs and their own apartment just above, her pretty face a picture of concern.

"Hush there, husband. You'll wake the neighborhood."

He all but stuttered his apology; it shamed him to be so uncontrolled in front of his wife. His hand was still clenching the letter and his knuckles were white. He opened his hand as he realized how he must look, and the letter fell free to the desk.

"I think you should tell me, my dear."

"Nothing. I was a fool. Apologies."

"Nonsense, my dear. No one shouts in that manner at half past ten on a winter's night unless moved beyond the capacity of the human frame to resist."

Portraits never did her justice; she was uncommonly pretty, even now, a little thing with an elegant carriage and a firmness of purpose. He could dislike her when she was an overprotective copy of his own mother, but when she was like this, she was the woman he wanted, his partner.

"Do you recall my mentioning George Muse?"

"He admitted to cowardice at Fort Necessity, I believe. I expected to hear his name—we don't number so many cowards among our acquaintance." She smiled.

Her turn of phrase, so much wittier than he could manage, made him smile through his anger, as she had known it would, and he saw her relax as if she had expected more difficulty. It struck him that she was handling his temper, that he was being managed and that he could resent it but didn't. He knew in that moment that he had shouted the words to get her to come to him. And she had come.

"He has had the effrontery to send me a perfectly odious letter, suggesting that my interest in the veterans' grants in Ohio is all self-interest— that I have attempted to cheat him and others of my former officers. Utter rot. It sticks in my craw, madam."

She turned her head slightly, toward the pistols in the case on the desk. "Washingtons don't fight Muses, my dear."

He looked confused for a moment. Then he saw it. She thought the cleaning of the pistols went with the letter.

"I won't fight him unless he calls me. But I'll write him such a letter and make my feelings plain. To bear such an affront is beyond me. I'm speechless."

"You are not, dear. Come to bed."

"I think I will read, madam, if only for a bit."

"I'll wait for you, then."

She came and kissed him, a social kiss, and his temper cooled some, but just the sight of the letter on his desk made his pulse race again.

The room was cold, despite the fire, and the girl hadn't really done much but stir the coals and add logs that hadn't caught. He crossed the room in front of his desk and pushed the logs around until they made a blaze, smiled to think of Martha and her wit, and went to his wall of books, looking for an old friend to calm his mind. He knew that George Mason and other more learned men turned to the ancients in moments such as these. He'd never really learned his Latin and now he regretted it, because they were farmers as well as soldiers.

Another packet on his desk brushed at his attention, and with deep pleasure he withdrew careful drawings of a plow from England, with a letter from a scientific farmer there. The letter and close consultation on the plow eased him out of the worst of his temper; fifteen minutes' study required to understand the harness and he was quite ready to face her again, and bed.

✯　✯　✯

It was a troubling time. He woke with the specter of Muse's letter in his mind, and it stayed with him as he was shaved and had his hair prepared by his valet. It left him sharp all day although it couldn't contend with the cares of the estate. He was up with the dawn, and an hour later ahorse with nothing but a cup of chocolate in him, riding down the lane to see his farms with a small staff of men behind him: two slaves, Bailey, and a secretary. All the men were working. Washington noted with surly pleasure that the herring nets were out on two farms, the work of repair and restoration going along smartly. He handled the English-made linen twine himself; experiment had shown that there was no substitute for it, despite the relative expense and the trouble of keeping it stocked. Prices for herring were falling, but the fishery provided a reliable cash crop that cost him nothing but net repair and the labor of slaves. If no one bought the fish, he could feed all his farms on them for the whole year, although that might require more clay for jars. He jotted a note in his daybook.

Twice he met neighbors on the road. Both made sure to congratulate him on Jack's marriage, and both asked if he would hunt the next day, or if preparations for the wedding would keep him away. He smiled at both and gave nothing away, although most of his acquaintance knew he felt ill-used in the matter. He did the civil thing and assured both gentlemen that he would indeed hunt and that his dogs (the best dogs in the county, except perhaps the Fairfax pack) would be at their service. Both men commended him on the slave Caesar. This didn't entirely please him. Something about the boy irritated him; he did not wish to be unfair, and that annoyed him the more.

✯　✯　✯

Caesar worked with a will, washing every dog in the pack, even the gun dogs that would spend the next morning at home. He was not in his fine clothes; he was dressed in a pair of cast-off breeches and an evil cotton shirt of a weave so coarse that he could feel the sun right through it on his back.

Old Blue was better—there couldn't be much doubt of that, although whether the mineral or the broth baths or her own animal constitution saved her was open to question. He washed her and scratched her head; of all the dogs, he now knew her the best. He wondered if she'd take the pack from the temporary leader now that she was back—whether they'd fight (not likely) or if some hidden signal of speech would pass between them, like him and Pompey, where the fight was just the symbol of the thing.

When the dogs were clean, he changed their straw, mucked out the kennel until it was as clean as Queeny's cabin, swept the front of the building, and put water out for all the dogs. He was just yoking up a second pair of buckets in the yard by the stables when the master came riding down the road between the overseer's house and the new dung pit. Most of the slaves went right on with their tasks, which was odd to Caesar. In Jamaica, they would all have stood and tugged their forelocks until the master passed. But this was a freer place, so he raised his face and smiled before realizing that he had been warned against just such, by both white and black. It caused an odd spasm to cross his face, which stopped his master in his tracks.

"Bailey, find out what Julius Caesar means by that long face of his."

"Stop there, boy."

Caesar stood in confusion, knowing he was in the wrong but resentful as well. He was only seeking to please, even if that thought didn't sit well. He kept his buckets on the yoke and his head down. This generally worked in Jamaica.

"I saw that look, Caesar. What did you mean by it?" Bailey sounded more concerned than angry. He was reputed a fair man among the blacks, not like some awkward bastards they all knew.

A few seconds gave Caesar all the time he needed. "Yoke bit mah shouldah, suh." He raised his eyes for a moment, then back down. "I did'n' mean no ha'm."

Queeny had ordered him to stop speaking his "new way." It didn't please him, and he practiced in secret, both the language of his master and the language of the pulpit. But it seemed to work on Bailey, who was more relaxed with him when he spoke like the rest of the men.

Bailey rode back to Washington. "I think he had a spasm, sir."

Washington watched the boy hike his buckets again as if seeking comfort, and a little water trickled out of each and ran off into the dust. "I cannot abide rebellion, Mr. Bailey. But I'll let this pass."

Bailey could only put it down to temper. His employer never watched the blacks like some white men Bailey had known, and there was little rebellion to be found at Mount Vernon. Bailey suspected that most slaves were as smart as he—smart enough to know that they would not be as comfortable anywhere else if they were sold from Mount Vernon. The African boy was no more a rebel than the others, but the big man on the horse was in a foul temper, and he didn't seem to like the dogs boy at the best of times. Bailey wondered why. The boy was quite clearly gifted, and everyone else on the farm knew it.

★　★　★

Martha Custis, as she was then, had two children by Jack Custis before he died and she became Mrs. Washington. He loved them both, though Patsy had been frail and Jack was the very model of a wild rich boy. As Jacky got older and more spoiled by his mother, his demands on his estates grew larger, until Washington had separated them off from the other Custis and Washington holdings so that Jack could affect only his own. But this separation had been on paper only, and the final books that would allow a grown-up and married Jack Custis the full enjoyment of his own estates were a difficult and unrewarding task. Washington didn't resent the loss of revenue. It was nothing as simple as that. He had enjoyed commanding one of the largest sets of estates in Virginia, and he would miss many of the useful details from Jack's land. Among other details, Jack had the best farrier in Virginia, and now Washington would have to pay to use him.

He sought to repair his acreage in the Ohio country, where the grants to veterans of the last war would give him something like a hundred thousand acres of new land, beautiful land with big trees and fresh soil. He wanted to farm on that sort of scale, and he sometimes dreamed about what the Ohio might be like in his old age, if he got to put his schemes into production.

Selling off Martha's other child's estates was also trouble. Patsy's death had upset Martha very much—so much, indeed, that she was just recovering. Patsy had always been a sickly child and no one who knew her well had expected a long life for her, but as she reached her teens and continued to dance and read, the Washingtons had begun to imagine that she might live a normal life, marry, and have children of her own.

Selling her shares of stock in London would clear the very last of his debts, but the details seemed to drag, and he sat with his pen scratching carefully away on the business of his farms and his livelihood while he could hear the real life of his estate going on behind him—horses being led out and walked, sheep being fed, chickens, and then the distant music of his hounds. The boy was feeding them.

He got up and walked out, his anger rising from a small curiosity to a rage before he reached the kennel. The boy was rolling balls of bread and soaking them in broth, then throwing them to each hound by name. It was a curious ritual, and not the way he did the feedings himself. It neither slowed his anger nor increased it. It was a subject for another day.

"Caesar! I told you to call me every day before the dogs were fed."

Caesar fairly leapt in the air at the sound of his name, and his sudden tension threw the dogs into confusion. They sensed their master's anger and the boy's worry, and some barked. Others milled, biting each other. Caesar recovered and moved slowly, trying for calm. Washington had to look at the scars over his eyes.

"Sorry, suh."

"Is that all, boy? You are sorry?"

Bailey was hurrying out from the overseer's house, his coat off, clearly torn from his supper. Someone had seen the master headed for the kennel and called him out. Washington resented this as an intrusion.

"Caesar, did you forget, or were you deliberately sullen? Answer me, boy."

The slave looked up to him slowly, and his eyes were a little hard—not reproachful or hurt, as might be expected from an innocent slave, nor wary or deceitful, either. Washington was a good judge of men, and this one was hard to read. The eyes held his for one flash, then were cast down.

"I'm sorry, *sir*. I *didn't* do it on purpose." The sentences were delivered like a verdict; the enunciation was strong and crisp.

Bailey wiped some crumbs from his chin but stayed mute, waiting for the explosion, worried that the enunciation might be read as rebellion.

Washington waited with the rest of them, balanced on the sword's point of his own conflicting feelings of anger and fairness, until fairness won out. The boy had done nothing. If called, he would not have come to the feeding. His business held him, and he was still angry at Muse's letter, at his stepson's stubbornness in marrying a Maryland papist without reflection, at the loss of prestige involved in Jack's estates. It was a witch's brew of discontent and no mistake; he was fair enough a man to know that the black boy had little to do with it.

The boy's way of speaking was another matter entirely, but like his careful feeding of the dogs, it needed to be dealt with another time. The boy was arrogant; arrogance had no place in a slave, a point he had made to Bailey countless times.

"Look at me, Julius Caesar." His voice was calm, and as he hoped, the eyes that met his were not hard or rebellious but concerned now.

"Always call me before the dogs are fed."

"I won't forget again, suh."

Washington shook his head, smiled very slightly, made a small bow to Bailey, and went inside.

Bailey stopped a moment longer. "For God's sake, call him next time. Or you'll be the worse for it, young Caesar. I can't be plainer than that." He tried to project a number of pieces of information through those sentences, because he worried about fairness at times. But his dinner was waiting, and his wife. His wife often chided him about slaves. "Catch more flies with honey than you do with vinegar," she said, meaning that a little conversation was often better than punishment. But he lacked the knack of it. She always carried herself above the blacks but spoke to them all the time; he couldn't do it.

He wanted to warn the boy, but he couldn't find any words that wouldn't betray his own notions of loyalty to the colonel. So he stood for a moment, a short man in his smallclothes with a napkin tied under his chin, leaning on the rail of the kennel. And when nothing came, he simply nodded to the boy and went back to his dinner, his spirits lowered.

★ ★ ★

The next morning dawned with more bad news. His party of indentures and Palatine Germans going to open the farms in his new land in the Ohio was held up by the incompetence of his agent in the matter, and, as was all too often the case, only his own intervention could solve the matter. He rode to Alexandria through a light rain and back through a heavier, and the chance to hunt was long washed away by the time he had his riding horse back at the beautiful brick barn at Mount Vernon.

The next day Washington took a party of his family and two grooms and set out on horseback to reach Mount Airy, the Calvert main estate in Maryland. An encounter with a discourteous ferryman showed him that his temper hadn't improved, but by the time he arrived he was calm, and the ceremony was simple, moving, and unmistakably Anglican. Moreover, young Nelly showed every sign of utter devotion to Jack, which commended her in Washington's eyes. He smiled at them both, reconsidered his position a little, and stayed on for the wedding breakfast the next morning, although he'd only packed the one shirt. Lund laughed at him, as well he might. Everyone at Mount Vernon had heard him mutter about the wedding for weeks, and now he had enjoyed it, rather as Martha had predicted.

☆ ☆ ☆

The wedding of Master Jack, even at some distance over in Maryland, was a cause for celebration on the estate. Master Jack, although given to high spirits, was popular with the slaves and known to be free with praise and money. On the day of his wedding, Martha gave Mr. Bailey permission to serve out ham and some good rum to the estate's slaves and servants, and they cleared the drying floor in a tobacco barn for a dance floor.

Caesar hadn't recovered from Washington's admonition about being "too familiar." He thought about it, over and over, trying to see the right of it. He couldn't bring himself to cringe, but he noticed that Queeny didn't cringe, either. She was just careful. Always careful. He would try to model himself more on her behavior.

Despite his misgivings, he enjoyed the dance with something like content. He was growing stronger and faster, because the food was better than anything in Jamaica and the life was so easy by comparison. His hands were clean, his clothes were good, and now he had several new shirts and different waistcoats and jackets for different days. He even enjoyed the respect of most of the other men at Mount Vernon. The white servants were polite to him, even respectful. None of them seemed to think he was overfamiliar.

He watched Nelly dance with one of the white servants. Was she overfamiliar?

"There you ah', thinkin' them dahk thoughts again. Come dance wi' me an' show a little smile." Queeny reached out and pulled him to his feet. He walked with her out to the floor and she took him boldly to the top of the set, so that they would be head couple.

"Hole in the wall," said one of the fiddlers. Queeny nodded in time to the first bars of the music, and Caesar took a moment to see how beautiful she was, and how happy, living in the moment. Then they turned away from each other and headed down the set, the two of them in perfect time. When they met again he turned her, not by one hand like a proper gentleman, but with an arm locked around her waist so that his lips were at her ear.

"I think I should marry you, Queeny."

Her smile lit her face, and then the dance took them apart.

☆　☆　☆

The mountain of business that awaited Washington when he returned to Mount Vernon might have prompted a rebellion of spirit in a lesser man. Jack Custis's wedding required a final pile of paper to be cleared, although it seemed obvious that he would reside at Mount Vernon with his new wife for a while. Gibson's accounts had to be cleared, and the problems of shipping goods and grain dealt with. He looked over his accounts, wondering why he had bought the brig and where it might make a profit.

He heard the gentle rustle of Martha's gown as she paused in the door to his study and he looked up. She shook her head and frowned, very slightly.

"I wish you found my son's wedding as interesting as you find his accounts," she said.

"The best gift I can give Jack is a clean bill and unencumbered estates." Washington waved his pen at the ledger next to him, as if the book held all Jack's fields and houses within leather covers. They locked eyes for a moment.

"We have guests, George. Come be hospitable and leave the books for a bit."

It was something he enjoyed, the process of management. He liked building the tools that allowed him to do the jobs that ran the estates, watching the careful plans of years come slowly to fruition. He considered a protest. There was more to be done. In fact, there was always more to be done. Between them, he and Martha and Jack owned a great deal and were likely to own more. But as always, Martha was more in the right, and he bowed in his chair, wiped his pen, and rose to join her.

Several of their guests talked about George Muse and his notions of fairness, and while George Mason speculated for the thirtieth time that winter on the Crown's reaction to the dumping of tea, Washington writhed at their comments. As soon as he could free himself, he settled himself to write the strong letter he had promised.

As he wrote the draft, his pen flew along, the strokes as powerful as sword thrusts.

> *As I am not accustomed to receive such from any man, nor would have taken the same language from you personally, without letting you feel some marks of my resentment; I would advise you to be cautious of writing me a second of the same tenor, for though I understand you were drunk when you did it, yet give me leave to tell you that drunkenness is not an excuse for rudeness . . .*

He paused, licked the tip of his pen and failed even to note the taste, but dipped and wrote on, fueled by anger.

> *. . . all my concern is that I ever engaged in behalf of so ungrateful and dirty a fellow as you are.*

Hugh Mercer, late in the library because he couldn't sleep, committed the unpardonable offense of reading it over his host's shoulder, because his strong eyes had caught the phrase "dirty a fellow" from the shelves.

"No, please feel free," Washington said with a hint of stiffness, when he realized that the doctor was reading the letter on the table.

"Damn, sir. My apologies. I should never—"

"Nonsense, sir. I welcome your opinion. You must know to whom it is addressed."

"I assume it is to that whelp Muse."

"It is."

Thus invited, Mercer read what was offered him. The lengthy justification of the process by which officers' land claims were settled was worded awkwardly, but it made sense and it utterly dished the arguments Muse was making in public. But the personal attack at the end was a shock, the more so from such an old stoic as Washington.

"But it is the most deliberate provocation, George." Mercer had known Washington for a long time. He was in his lodge, though he didn't use his first name without a little hesitation. This was serious—pistols-in-the-morning-and-Martha-a-widow serious.

"He's a coward. He won't fight."

Mercer looked at Washington, amazed that so mature and noble a man could see the world in such a schoolyard manner, could base his expectations of men's actions on such simple stuff.

"He'll fight if you drive him to it, coward or not. Would you fight his like, sir? He's a rascal, I'll own, but the entire world knows it. You'll lose nothing—"

"That is not the matter to hand, sir. He has said things, monstrous things, of me and my intentions on these land grants. I won't stand it; I'll not be called names by this coward."

Washington's voice was calm but his hand almost trembled with indignation. Mercer couldn't remember when he had himself last been so indignant, although he thought he might have approached it when the Townshend Acts were announced. To be so enraged by some fool's tattle— but Washington had ever been a proud, *noli me tangere* sort of fellow, and allowances had to be made.

"I don't want to pull a bullet out of you. You are too important to us for that, George."

The comment went right to him, the sort of flattery Washington liked, but the anger was still present. He folded the letter. "Just a draft. Perhaps I'll cool off by tomorrow."

And with that, Mercer had to be content.

Mount Vernon, Virginia, early May 1774

It was really too late in the season for a hunt, with the wheat and the tobacco in the ground, but Washington wanted the pack out one more time and his neighbors joined in happily enough despite the business of the time. Even George Mason, the most bookish of the men in the parish, was to be seen approaching, though, to be sure, his clothes suggested more of the scholar than the huntsman, and he had gaiters on, not boots. Washington watched him ride and smiled at the way his head rose and fell with the horse's stride like a cock crossing the yard. Not exactly a natural horseman.

They had fewer dogs than usual: just Washington's pack and French's, because the chance of a decent fox was low, and because Cedar Grove was not represented in the field today and none of the Cedar Grove people seemed disposed to offer hounds. Washington knew why, but his neighbor's relative financial troubles didn't matter to him, except that he would eventually be asked to help them and he would. It was certainly nothing he would think to discuss. And young Lee had insisted on joining the small hunt, despite the fact that he would be the only sprig in it. Washington watched him with remote tolerance. The boy was already better behaved than he had been on that distant December morning.

Beyond young Lee was Caesar, helping French's John sort the dogs and send the select pack with the huntsman. He was good, and Washington knew it—knew with satisfaction that several neighbors envied him his luck in finding the boy. He'd won a footrace at a fair and a small purse with it, and more for his master in wagers than he had cost in Jamaica. But Washington couldn't warm to him, or to the Ashanti airs that the boy seemed to have. Too arrogant by half, and his habit of standing with a hand on his hip like a classical statue irked him, as he must have learned it on the plantation. He never liked to see the scars above the eyes that seemed to deny any possibility of civilization in the boy. Washington winced inwardly at his unfairness, as he had never minded scars on Indians, but then, he was used to seeing Indians in their own deep woods, not on his plantation.

The boy was above himself. It went against the order of things. Why couldn't the boy smile like other blacks when he was addressed? Why did he so seldom laugh?

Mason rode past the estate wall and up the drive, head still bobbing, and as he approached Washington, the latter's worst fears were confirmed. Mason wasn't here to hunt at all. He was ready to travel. Washington was a burgess as much as Mason, but he was holding his return to Williamsburg and the cares of government back a day to enjoy his farms; he knew that Mason would intrude some bill, and despite his warmth for the man, resentment mounted before Mason had closed the distance.

"Scarcely dressed to hunt, Mr. Mason?"

"Colonel, good day. Mr. Lee, Mr. French. Servant, ma'am. Gentlemen, I rode directly to inform you that the government has ordered the closure of the Port of Boston."

Mercer, dismounted near the house and struggling with a new and complex cavalry-style girth, missed the gist and almost lost his saddle trying to get it from Mrs. French. The others murmured, but Washington struck his saddle viciously with his whip, enough to make Nelson, usually the calmest of horses, start. Washington soothed him, annoyed at his own burst of temper, but such news put the whole party out of sorts. It had been hard enough to gather them, and the closure of the Port of Boston was a direct attack on the liberties of every man in the colonies. He said as much.

"I had hoped you would all feel that way. I should like to have the House debate something on the subject—perhaps a censure."

Half of the huntsmen were burgesses. They looked about them, each considering bills up for consideration that would vanish if the governor prorogued them after they attempted to censure the Parliament in London. Washington thought of lingering details of the Great Dismal and the settlement for his officers on the Ohio frontier and cursed, but the matter could not be allowed to drop.

"Mr. Mason, it is no pleasure to hear such tidings, but I thank you for the warning. It remains my intention, however, despite this difficult news, to hunt. What says the company?"

Perhaps, if Washington's views had not been so plain, some would have abandoned the hunt and started back for the capital immediately. Such had been Mason's plan, no doubt. But so committed was Washington to his hunt, and so formidable did he appear astride his charger, that no one said a word. Mason went inside for refreshment, and the hunt went out.

But Washington's mood was foul.

☆　☆　☆

They raised a scent soon enough, and the fox took them up Dogue Run beyond the new mill, up into the marshy country near the eastern bounds of Rose Hill and into relatively unfamiliar country before they lost the quarry in a quagmire. The dogs got muddy to no purpose and both handlers were filthy by the time they had the dogs in order and off on a second scent. It all smacked of incompetence to Washington. He had not been riding right forward with the hounds where he liked to be, and he felt the burden of the lost fox on his shoulders and was sure the field blamed him for the loss. Mrs. French, a very Artemis-like woman but a witch for gossip, was regaling Mercer with some unnecessary tale, doubtless exploring the debt problems of the Posey family, or some such. But he heard her say "Muse" in a suggestive way, and he heard Hugh Mercer laugh a certain laugh, and his resentment at the day reached a new height. What were they saying about Muse, that coward? Muse had not even responded to his letter. Was he up to some new calumny? Washington fumed while the dogs searched for a new scent, casting wider and wider back toward the Rose Hill barns. The country above the marsh was relatively unknown to Washington; he had been over it often enough, but never at speed. And when the pack began to move, he was not really minding the ground or his mount.

Nelson shied at something. Washington felt the shift of weight for the jump and raised himself for it, but as the back legs pressed him forward, he rolled his barrel to avoid the snake, and Washington, angry and bemused, felt the unthinkable—the gradual change of weight that told him he was going to lose his seat. He wasn't thrown quickly—that would have been a mercy. He fell with great slowness, and indeed for a few seconds he was sure he was going to save the jump and regain his seat. He lost a stirrup at the first, and the uneven landing cost him the second, but he had a toe back in his left stirrup when Nelson gave a little twist and he slumped past the regained stirrup. He couldn't quite get a leg down to dismount, and his hunting sword caught on a buckle of the girth and turned him around so that he fell only the last few feet. Nelson was barely moving at the time, which made it worse; it looked like Virginia's best horseman had just fallen off a standing horse.

He had to roll off his sword, which had punched him in the side on landing. The ivory of the hilt was cracked, the copper-green dye showing white. Mrs. French was laughing in the distance; closer up, young Lee was hiding his guffaw in his sleeve and trying to look anywhere else. And Caesar, the dogs boy, was grinning broadly as he held out a hand to help his master up.

Washington ignored the suggestion that he needed help to rise and got to his feet only to find his swordbelt had come down around his knees, and he stumbled badly before he caught himself. The movement was so comical that it finished both Lee and Caesar, who lost themselves in laughter. Washington fumbled with the lion's-head buckle for a moment before settling the ruined sword back on his hip. Dogs were barking, pandemonium reigned, and Nelson was sidling away uncaught. He had torn his scarlet coat in the fall—the thrust of his shoulders had been enough to tear the seam under the arm.

He had not been a laughingstock since before he went away to the war, and it didn't suit him, but he strove to cover his feelings. He couldn't blame Nelson, the most reliable of mounts.

"Master yourself, Mr. Lee," he said in a tone so dark that Lee went pale.

Caesar continued to laugh while he ran ahead of Nelson, brought him to a stand by a fence, offered him a carrot, and caught him. He couldn't stop laughing. Old John, Mr. French's John, thought of stepping in, but he could tell that the boy was doomed; no fake attack by another black man could save him, and besides, he preferred Queeny a little freer with her favors. He stood and watched, and Caesar laughed, and the world changed.

Chapter Five

Great Dismal Swamp, September 1774

The trees were larger than anything he had seen since he had left Africa, and the swamp smelled a little like the land by the great river where he had been born. But any notion of home, any similarity that might have recalled a better time and made the place bearable, was instantly erased by the crushing weight of the work.

He was back in the barracoon, locked down at night with chains, sweating to move great clods of mud all day. No woman lay beside him; he did not have a natty jacket and fine leather boots to show his calves. He was naked but for a loose cotton shirt that was gray with dirt and sweat and some Russian linen trousers that had been old before he had arrived. The last man had died in them.

They rose before dawn, cooking tin kettles of cornmeal in the early gray light, forced to endure the first torture of the day as the smell of the overseers' bacon wafted down the slight breeze. Caesar had not eaten meat since he arrived. He ate his cornmeal in silence, as did the other men. Every one of them was a "cull," a slave who was so troublesome, or lazy, that his master would give him to the reclamation project for the swamp rather than have him at home. Few of them talked; most looked deeply stupid. Caesar couldn't help but notice that he was the only Ashanti and that most of the rest were Ebo. It seemed his lot in life to fall among Ebo and still be considered less than they.

What little coolness the night generated was gone long before he took his shovel and mattock and followed the file of slaves down the trails into the swamp. They were cutting the drainage ditches envisioned by Washington, a few feet at a time. The overseer was stupid, and often drunk, and the neat trenches that Washington designed were executed in a very haphazard manner, never deep enough and often running in curves. The easy days they simply cut trails, or attempted to till the fetid ooze they brought up in digging and piled behind them in neat fields. They might someday be neat fields, but so far looked like small lakes of mud.

When he first arrived, Caesar was almost overwhelmed by the futility of it and the almost-certain knowledge that he would die here, cutting into a swamp. But as time went by, he saw tiny changes despite the corrosive atmosphere, the incompetence of the overseer, and the complete obstructionism of the slaves. Bit by bit, they were claiming land from the swamp. Some of what they drained actually stayed dry. It almost seemed a further offense, that his labor would, in fact, build more fields for his master to till. But another part of him rejoiced that the work was not utterly wasted.

No one spoke. The men with him sang sometimes, but their songs were badly sung and he didn't know the words, which were a mixture of African and local patois. They needed a caller, but any slave talented enough to control the pace of the work as a caller in the fields would never end up here. He would be leading the workers in some happier place.

The daze lasted Caesar for some time—time he was never able to reclaim in his mind, until in later years he wondered if he had had a sickness or a fever that kept him from thinking clearly. He remembered leaving Queeny, and her pressing his store of coins into his hands as he left; he remembered Washington dismissing him with the wave of his hand, as finished business, his thoughts elsewhere; he remembered arriving, and some hazes of work and sleep and the smell of the cornmeal in the morning. He remembered thinking that before this he had never fully realized what being a slave was. But then he awoke, so to speak. He never forgot that waking because he was swinging the great ill-balanced pick, the only one they had that wasn't broken, and another man was trying to pull the stump before he had even cut the roots with the pick, just the sort of inefficient work that typified the whole. And then a new man began to sing a song he knew a little of, a hymn he had heard in the carriage barn. He knew the song and he began to sing with it, swinging the pick over his head and down into the morass and the roots, gradually breaking them to the point that his partner for the day could wrestle the whole mass out with a snap and a sucking noise. Water pooled into the hole left by the stump, and with that water Caesar's will returned, all in a rush. The man who told himself that today he was a slave returned and the mindless automaton who had swung the pick recoiled forever.

He couldn't really remember the time that had passed, except to know that he had lost his place on the plantation for laughing at the master, a knowledge that finally and fully exposed to him his foolishness and filled him with rage that he had fallen so easily into the snares of the fine clothes and Queeny's embrace. The swamp was different only in details. He was a slave, and the property of another man.

✷　✷　✷

He sang and sang that whole day, and in the evening he met the new man, a Bakongo man who had served the Lees. He was called Virgil, a tall, strong man with large eyes that seemed always asleep.

Caesar had all but lost the habit of speech, though he still sought to enunciate. Habits die hard. "You look too good to be here, Virgil."

"I ain't, though. I ain't. I lucky be alive."

"What'd you do, man? Kill someone?"

"Tried. Tried with a pitchfork." When Virgil said it, it sounded like "pithfoak." He had missing teeth on top of his thick patois.

Virgil shrugged. "He took my woman once too often. Let him stay with his own white gals, that's all I says."

"And did you hurt him?"

"I nevuh even ma'ked him, the white bastu'd. He had a little sword, cut me up."

Other men, the less stupid-looking ones, nodded, though none of them was talking. It was as if Caesar and Virgil were alone with a group of ghosts who murmured and ate, but never spoke.

Virgil leaned over to Caesar and whispered. "You have plans to run? You seem the smaht one, heh?"

Caesar was at once chagrined that he did not have plans to run and instantly focused on them. Yes, he would run. There would be no more money and no chance of working his way free from here. He realized in an instant that he had seen things, even in the daze.

"We are locked down each night, Virgil."

"Yeah. Barracoon. I see it. And day?"

"Overseer has two guns, fowler and a pistol. Both loaded. Means business. Shot a boy before I come. He has another man and another party off north, not far. There be more of 'em than we can see, too."

"So we needs to go at night, get a start. You go with me?"

Caesar thought a moment—thought that Virgil might be a plant to lure him—but he couldn't imagine any punishment worse than where he was. And it was time to change, time to strike out. "No, Virgil. Not how I see it. We got to take the man and kill him, get his guns. Then we run."

"Whoa, boy. We do that, we dead if they take us. No whipping. My back plenny hahd, you see? But no hahd 'nough for no musket ball."

"You look and see. We have lots o' time, man. Lots o' time."

★　★　★

It was several days before the overseer shot a man, the first time it had happened since Caesar came to the swamp. Caesar never knew why—whether the man tried to run or whether he was shot for poor work, or on a whim. They heard the sharp, high-pitched sound of a pistol. Later another slave, Old Ben, said he'd seen the body. Caesar worked with Virgil now. He looked at Virgil while Ben told the story, and when the other man was gone, Virgil looked determined.

"You got it right, Mr. Caesar. Boy gotta die."

"How?"

"I don't know. We think, then we get him. But he gotta die 'fo' he kill us all."

Philadelphia, October 1774

Washington's parlor was not all he could have asked, and the size and bustle of Philadelphia so greatly outran that of his native Williamsburg or Alexandria that he had had trouble sleeping his first few nights with the constant rumble of carts and the calling of wares. In time, the habits of his military youth won out, and he slept better.

The business of the Continental Congress crept along, each faction hesitant of the others, each region jealous of its own case and its own traditions, but a few men, like Franklin, kept the business of the continent moving, and with that, Washington had to be content. He did his bit to keep the factions happy, but he could not speak in public. He sometimes felt that it was a mistake for the Virginians to have sent him, the more so as Virginia was now fighting the Indians in the very territory that he had just ridden over. In his absence he had missed the opportunity to command the last major expedition of his time. He regretted the talk of massacres—indeed, the Philadelphia Quakers made it sound as if Governor Dunmore had provoked the war himself to suit his own ends—but the campaign might have suited him.

It didn't matter now. But the short campaign had revealed any number of predictable defects in the Virginia Militia. Washington had before him on the table a letter from some of the officers of Fairfax County, asking him to procure muskets, drums, and a pair of colors for their companies, which he had every intention of doing for them. He would want the militia of his county to appear to advantage, just as his parish church should, if compared to others.

The phrase that caught his eye, had made him rise and pace the room, was one of the last. "We leave it to you, sir, to determine whether it may be proper or necessary to vary from the usual colors that are carried by the regulars or militia."

Colors were the life's blood of a military unit, the flags around which they rallied, the sacred symbols of their country's trust. Roman legions had built temples to honor their eagles; the regulars of Great Britain were not so much different, lodging and bringing out their colors with elaborate ceremony. And in Virginia, the better militia did the same, learning from local regulars or veterans like Washington.

He looked out on the bustle of his continent's largest city and pondered on varying the colors of the Virginia Militia from those carried by the regulars. It was a most sobering thought—it gave him more hesitation than all the empty talk of the Congress, all the moving speeches by Patrick Henry or young Jefferson—the thought of troops, troops he might yet command in Virginia, serving under colors other than the king's.

Men in the Congress talked of war with England. It was that open now. Most of the men who talked and talked had never seen a day's service and had no idea what such a war would entail. Every member was convinced that as native sons, their own valor and honor would stand any affront. Washington thought of the regulars he had seen, of the Fairfax Militia's lack of coats or muskets, and the desire to know what pattern the flags should be. It was a question vexing much of the continent, and until war struck them, Washington preferred to endure the Congress. He feared the talk of war from men who hadn't seen one and wouldn't have to pay the price.

Charles Lee, who had been a guest of the Lees in Virginia but was no relation, had already offered to raise a battalion for the defense of the Congress. His offers hadn't been accepted; neither had he been sent away.

Men asked Washington questions, ignorant questions for the most part, about war. He resented them; he resented how little they knew about the supply of a battalion, or its feeding. He bought several books to help him answer the questions and to drive home his points, that war would be expensive, that the continent lacked some of war's most basic necessities. Men listened to him, or didn't, as their inclinations went; and he sat in his window and tried to imagine a body of Virginia men without a king's color, and for the first time since the whole sad business began, he hesitated. But around him, the pulse of the city beat faster, and increasingly, it beat a martial air.

II

Taking
Off Terror

*Negro servants returning hence [from England], with new
and enlarged notions, take off that terror, and shew them all
the weaknesses of whites . . .*

—MORNING CHRONICLE AND LONDON
ADVERTISER, MAY 21, 1772

Chapter Six

Even as their tools ate at the swamp, the swamp ate away at the men. As the weeks blurred into months, the toll mounted, until Caesar's hands were numb most of the night. He couldn't always grip the tools he had to use during the day, and sometimes they would slip. One day, with his hands wet from the blood of cracked calluses, he had swung his sharp mattock into the roots of an old stump. He'd missed, hit the top of the stump a glancing blow, and the tool turned on him like a live thing. The blade had gouged his leg deep, right into the muscle, and he had dropped like a cleared tree onto the wet ground and watched the blood flow. The wound didn't hurt like a cut, at least at first, but ached like an enormous bruise.

It bled fitfully for days and then began to ooze a noxious pus. He couldn't stop working, although he was certain he had some kind of fever from it. The blood drew flies, and the flies were like one of the plagues of Egypt that the preacher at Mount Vernon had spoken of. He seldom thought of Mount Vernon anymore. It seemed almost like a paradise compared to this hell—a hell of flies and eternal work, of slaves who had recently become too afraid even to break their tools or protest the abuse.

Other men died. Not every day, by any means, but the fever took some, and the pistol took others. A broken bone was as likely a death warrant as a bullet to the head; neither Gordon nor the other whites seemed particular about nursing the injured. Caesar worked on with the hole in his leg, and limped, and knew that he would never be as fast as he had been, even if he lived, but the wound never got the smell of death to it, though it oozed an oily white pus for weeks and in time it left a deep dent and a scar and an ache every time the sky threatened rain, which was most mornings in the winter.

The wound changed him—as a man, and as a slave. At first, he was so certain he was going to die that he began to work less and to devise ways of cheating the overseer that would have seemed petty to him once. He rested longer, took slower swings, made simple mistakes. He never broke a tool—that was worth a beating—but he stopped leading the others in his party. He let them return to drifting and asking Gordon for every bit of direction. That was his greatest protest, although he didn't know it at first.

Caesar hadn't appreciated that he had become the leader in his work party until he stopped. It had seemed natural to him to console, prod, and help his mates, no matter how dull they were. But he lost interest in them when he hurt himself, and his crew returned, almost without thought, to being a band of lost individuals. None of the other men was interested in leading the work party. Most had been broken before they came; the rest were certainly broken now. If Gordon noticed, he didn't say anything; perhaps he preferred their puzzled docility to unified work. Perhaps he was himself too stupid even to see the change; Caesar had known his type before, in Africa and Jamaica, and doubted there was much behind those close-set eyes but hatred.

Caesar had expected a pack of rebels, but almost all the men were broken, except those who had been sent there for being too stupid to work on the big farms of their owners. The smart ones had already run, sometime in the misty past before the overseers were given guns. Mr. Gordon, their overseer, was a brutal man with a terrible fund of energy. Even in the worst of the heat, he continued to hate every black man and woman ever born and muttered endlessly under his breath. Each time he walked up to a group of men, he made a show of checking the prime in the pistol at his belt. He carried a fancy little flask and reprimed with it often. Caesar noticed these details because he still thought of killing Gordon, but the chance never came.

Twice they received drafts of new slaves from other plantations, but none came from Mount Vernon or any of the other Washington farms, and Caesar had no news. He rarely even saw Virgil, though he had taken to the man immediately. Virgil had been moved to another crew after a week, and Caesar suspected that Gordon had seen them talking and was wary of allowing them to be partners.

Sometimes his rebellion hurt him. When he stared down Old Ben because the man wanted his help; when the boy who came and cooked their corn hurt his hand and Caesar simply let him run off injured; a thousand other cuts, tiny abandonings of responsibility. But they were men, and they were not his men; they were slaves. He thought about these things in a distant, unconnected way, as if they were events going on in a fireside story. He couldn't concentrate on himself.

After weeks of petty rebellion and hoarded rest, Caesar finally reemerged from the hell of flies and pain and expected death. As it closed, he began to believe that this wound, at least, would not be his death; and he began to fear from his own action, his carefully developed habit of flinching at the sound of Gordon's voice, that he had allowed himself to break inside.

Long afterward, he thought that the wound must have fevered him, because one afternoon he found himself leaning on his mattock, ankle-deep in ooze but well apart from the others, and he was listening to a voice trailing away:

"... you jes' slow down, boy," he heard. It was his own voice. He had been engaged in a spirited argument with himself, although the sides and the arguments were slipping away like a dream to a man awakening. But the other voice had sounded more like the preacher's, he was sure, and it scared him to the bone that he was possessed, or that the whites had broken him at last.

He shook his head, to clear it, and looked back to where he could see other men working in a line stretching for a hundred yards, with the ancient trees hanging over them and birds in the high canopy. The men seemed to have as much consequence as the birds, and again he thought of the preacher and that he had said that the Lord saw even the fall of a sparrow. *Why a sparrow?* he thought. *Why that bird in particular? Those tiny hummingbirds, now, they was small. Smaller than a sparrow.*

And again he realized that he had been speaking the words aloud, and again he was afraid, both that he was broken like the other broken men and that he would stand and talk to himself about sparrows until Gordon put a pistol ball in his head.

Later he caught himself weeping, and he didn't know why, but if that was a fever, it broke then, because he didn't talk to himself again.

Virginia Convention, Richmond, Virginia, March 23, 1775

"The establishment of such a militia, composed of gentlemen and yeomen, is at this time particularly necessary, by the state of our laws for the protection and defense of the country, some of which have expired, and others shortly will do so; and that known remissness of government, in calling us together in a legislative capacity, renders it too insecure, in this time of danger and distress, to reply that opportunity will be given of renewing them in General Assembly—"

"Make your point, Mr. Henry."

"I will, sir."

"Rather, Mr. Henry, you have done. You want us to vote an extraordinary militia act because it is unlikely that Lord Dunmore will call the burgesses?"

"Yes, sir. May I continue?"

"If you must."

"Sir, I must." Patrick Henry, the prime orator of the House of Burgesses, raised his papers for a moment, recalling his place, and his voice continued in a deliberately humdrum manner.

"Ahem…General Assembly, or making any other provision to secure our inestimable rights and liberties from those farther violations…" The rumble from the convention seat was not all royalist; and Henry's tempo began to change as he added emotion to his voice. "*Violations* with which they are *threatened*. RESOLVED, therefore…"

Washington's neighbor leaned over to him. "This isn't about defending ourselves from the Delaware, is it?"

Washington smiled carefully, hiding the remnants of his teeth.

"I think not." He thought back to his review of the Dumfries Independent Company a few days before. They had their new colors, a company standard with a motto, and a dark blue color with the union in the canton. It was a gesture toward the king's men in the county, but a far cry from the king's color that had traditionally graced every regiment of militia, a union flag two fathoms across. They were uniformed in blue and buff, his favorite colors and the traditional colors of the liberal Whig party in England.

Washington's other neighbor leaned across him to George Mason, two down on his right. "It's rhetoric like this that costs us support in England. Let this man go on and we'll lose every friend we made with the Congress."

Down on the floor, Patrick Henry raised his face to the men in the benches and drew himself to his full height. He looked around him like a man entering a ball and searching for friends. "We must fight." Uttered with regret, but uttered.

A silence fell over the hall; the royalists sat thunderstruck. It had been whispered. Now it had been said. A murmur from the back benches.

"You do not care for the sentiment? But it is being forced upon us by unprecedented tyranny. It is not our property that is threatened, but our liberties, not the pennies of taxation, but the pounds of chains that this government would load upon us. Did I say we must fight? Perhaps what I should have said is, we *must* fight. *We must fight!* There, 'tis said."

Mason and Andrew Stephen were talking so fast that Washington had to crane forward past them to hear Henry on the floor; indeed, the only thing he heard clearly was the reiteration that he must fight. He nodded. It was obvious that it was now to come to blows; every thinking Whig saw it. Many men looked shocked, or angry, even at this late date; Washington could see Benjamin Harrison, red in the face; and Pendleton, Bland, and Nicholas looked as if close friends had been murdered before their eyes. Behind them, one of Washington's grooms gestured to him from the doorway; forbidden in the church, he could only try to catch his master's attention, but it was now riveted to the floor before him.

"...and so retain our liberty, regardless of the cost. Is life so dear, or peace so sweet, as to be purchased at the price of chains and slavery? Forbid it, almighty God! I know not what course others may take, but as for me, give me liberty or give me death!"

The groom's head rose with every word, but no one paid him any mind.

It was a brilliant piece of rhetoric; it stifled opposition, though the royalists tried valiantly to change the course of debate and delay the call to arms. None could match the heights of eloquence that Henry had reached; none could banish the fear of "chains and slavery." And so, with many a beating heart, the Virginia Convention voted to put the colony of Virginia into a "posture of defense" and named a committee of twelve men to be responsible to the colony for embodying, arming, and disciplining such a number of men as might be sufficient for the purpose. Patrick Henry was the first man named to the committee. The second was George Washington.

Great Dismal Swamp, March 26, 1775

"They arming the militia. All ovah the country they be gettin' guns and men togethuh. I seed 'em down by our place, men marchin' and trainin'." The new man was from the Lee plantation on the Chesapeake, and he was a fund of information. He was not a broken spirit, either, but had been sent to the Dismal for insubordination.

"I jus' don' think the time to run is when ever' white boy in Virginny has got his gun to hand." Virgil had come in with his crew the night before. The rising sun barely slanted through the canopy yet, and they were all enjoying the only cool breeze they would have for the day while a young boy with a torn foot stirred a battered copper pot of cornmeal. It contained several frogs; both Caesar and the new man, Lark, had developed some skill in catching frogs, and they were plentiful. Virgil had set himself to learn the art.

"Maybe the governor will arm the slaves."

"That's foolishness, Lark." Caesar was surprised to hear his own voice. "Who's gon' arm slaves?"

"I heard it happen' befo'. Not just one time, neithuh."

Old Ben spoke from the gloom of his blanket. "They done it before this, boys. They armed us in Carolina once. We was to fight Cherokees."

The little group fell silent. Caesar gave the boy by the fire a little slap and pointed him off to another fire. The boy looked at him, pleased somehow, even at being sent away, and Caesar wondered what he had been like these last weeks.

"You run 'long." He tried to sound kindly. Perhaps he smiled. It didn't come easily. The boy showed his teeth and hobbled off. He waited till the boy was out of earshot. "We have to kill Gordon."

Only Virgil met his eye and nodded, but the others made noises, softly.

"Any o' us could die, any day," Caesar continued. "He don't give a damn whether he shoot us or we die o' fever."

" 'Bout time you come back to yo' senses, boy!" Old Ben spoke out of the darkness and then leaned into the firelight.

"Where do we go?" asked Virgil.

Old Ben threw off the blanket. "Run to John Canno!"

"John Canno's a myth, old man." Caesar had heard of John Canno from Queeny, from old Ben. He sounded too good to be true, a black bandit in the deep woods to the south. No one ever seemed to be able to say just where he was from, though.

"If he be, then where all the slaves that run? Who steal the cattle? Who take the folk to Florida?"

Caesar looked at them with a little impatience. "It ain't time for talk. You run to Florida if you wan'. I say we kill the overseer and go into the swamp. We steal what we need. Wi' his pistol and another gun, we can hunt, if we have powder. I was a warrior, and I could be again, and I'll start here. I'd rathuh die killing this Gordon man than live fat, whether here or at Mount Vernon. I'm tired of being a slave. And if I stay here and talk, I'll be a dead slave. Better die free."

"You have a plan?"

"Yeah, Virgil, and it ain't fancy. When he come to the barracoon, he take us to the tools, every morning, wait while we hoist what we need. Yeah?"

"Yeah." They all nodded.

"So when I get my pick, I raise it and throw it, grab the nearest tool, and charge him. I'll go first, but every man of you better be behind me. He get one shot. He hit me, I die. You kill him, you run. Or he won' hit me. Then we fin' the other man, the one we never see. We kill him, too. After that, we have some o' their food, make a plan."

"That's it?"

"That's all I have, man."

Virgil smiled. "I got one thing bettuh, then. Listen. I carry the corn-meal with me. When he stand to watch us get the tools I throw it at him. It burning hot, wet his gun, too, I hope."

Caesar nodded. "Wet gun might not fire."

Lark smiled at both of them. "When do we go, boys?"

Caesar looked at both of them, and past them. "We'll go when I give the word. First morning everything is right."

"I wan' do it now," said Virgil. Lark gave him an odd look; Caesar saw it but couldn't interpret it.

"Wait, Virgil. Jes' a little while."

Virginia Convention, Richmond, Virginia, March 27, 1775

"It all comes down to logistics, gentlemen. We lack arms, we lack wool, we lack powder and lead to make ball; we have precious few cannon, and those of smallest caliber; and we have no magazines to assemble these items even if they were to fall on us from the heavens."

Patrick Henry looked at Washington, usually silent and taciturn, as if he had been struck by a thunderbolt. "Surely every gentleman in Virginia has private arms. Many have fine fowlers, even rifles."

Washington smiled, although the smile didn't touch the skin on his cheeks. He waved a hand to a slave by the tavern's counter and pointed to top his tankard. "I'm not sure how many gentlemen want their fine Durs Egg fowlers being handed out to the yeomanry to repel invaders, at ten pounds and more each."

"If their liberty requires it!"

"Mr. Henry, you are a warm friend to liberty, but not, I think, a soldier. Those fine fowlers have fine parts; the cocks and hammers are slim as a pistol. You'll have noticed this, I think?"

"I have, sir. I have handled arms and need no lesson."

"I mean no insult, sir, but you *do*. Those fine, slim cocks will break when a scared boy pulls them back too hard; the springs will burst when overused, or let to wet and rust. A Queen Anne musket like this here is a heavy thing and built to be used by scared boys. The springs are such that it takes a heavy pull to cock, but see how much metal there is throughout? You can drop it and it won't break. And your fowler has a smaller bore—perhaps sixty or sixty-five caliber, some as small as twenty or twenty-five balls to the pound. A military musket is bigger in the bore, faster to load, and uses a heavier ball that carries farther in the flat or in the brush."

Henry nodded. He had not become a great debater by failing to note when other men knew more than he. And Washington knew the tools of his former trade like no one else on the committee.

Washington rose to his feet. "Your rifles can be pitiful things, sir, because the balls they fire are even slighter, but mostly because they are fragile, and take a man trained in their use, of which we will have too few. Neither they nor the fowlers will take a bayonet, either. A soldier needs a bayonet, either to try conclusions with an enemy at close quarters or to keep the enemy's horse at bay. Without bayonets, you'll never get a man to stand when he is charged. We need muskets, and proper ones—made careful and with bayonets to fit—and cartridge boxes, slings, and bayonet carriages. And we'll need our powder and ball rolled up in cartridges—faster to load, as the men have only to bite off the ball and pour the powder down the barrel. Loading from the horn is too slow."

His old allies from the militia acts of 1757 knew all this; they'd heard it all too often before. But it was news to the new firebrands, and if it didn't cool their ardor, it certainly caused them to start counting their shillings. But Henry never relished defeat in any debate; he deemed his opponent knew the subject better than he, but couldn't let the opportunity to speechify pass.

"You seem to have little confidence in the yeomanry of Virginia. Scared boys and men who won't stand, to hear you."

"Well, sir, I've seen 'em run a few times. Never been a man born not scared when the first balls fly. No gentleman asks too much of his soldiers. General Braddock said that. He may have lost Monongahela, but he was no fool."

"Our men will have the courage of true patriots!"

Washington shook his head. To him, the issue of true patriotism was not germane; no one could recruit or feed an army on it. "Virginia will need three thousand stand of arms for the foot alone. And where the furniture for the mounted companies will come from is beyond me. Muskets will be hard enough, but musketoons and carbines and sabers..."

"New York has been making muskets." Mr. Lewis had sat quiet until now.

"We don't need New York goods to fight Virginia's wars." Patrick Henry seemed divided as to whether the colonies would rise together or as discrete entities.

Washington was not slow to respond. "Oh, but we do, and we will, sir, if we propose to fight the mother country. To raise an army and face British regulars, we will need an army of the whole continent, trained and mustered. And we will need the support and equipment of every colony to face them."

Henry turned to Peyton Randolph, who had entered a moment before and sat quietly against the wall. "Colonel Washington becomes the orator at last."

Randolph, who had a longer experience of Washington, smiled grimly. "Washington only speaks when he knows his subject and his passions are moved. When you speak of war, you meet both those conditions."

Randolph stood when Washington ceased. "Gentlemen, I have to ask your committee to rejoin us in the church, as we are to vote on the members for the Continental Congress."

As the chairs scraped back and the men began to move, Henry leaned past him. He was a man who always separated the battle of wills in debate from the true demands of politics. "Make sure we take the soldier," he muttered, and cast a significant glance at Washington. "I think we shall need him."

Great Dismal Swamp, April 1775

The next two days, they were sent to plant tobacco instead of going into the swamp. It rested them all and gave them a chance to exchange news with the slaves from the other gangs. They got a little more to eat each night, too. Caesar assumed it had to do with newly delivered supplies that had come with Lark, another slave who never spoke named Tom, and several new white men.

Days passed, and still the circumstances they needed for the plan didn't arise.

The third and fourth mornings, Gordon sent one of the new whites, a boy named Keller, to unlock the barracoon while he himself stood well back with a long fowler across his arm; the next morning, he did not appear at all. Keller was unarmed, except for a large knife. He was surly, and Caesar could feel his fear of the blacks, which put him on his guard. The other men ignored his curses, took their tools, and went to work, tensions easing only when they were at the heads of their trenches into the swamp, hacking their ditches a little deeper. But something was different; Gordon hadn't watched them go out, and on a spur of impulse, Caesar stayed with Virgil's party rather than going out with his own. The sullen boy said nothing; he didn't even know the slaves apart yet.

Caesar cut at the roots of a large tree for almost an hour, working his hands into steadiness, cracking the knuckles where he had to force them to respond. The knuckles were getting more swollen every day; they had never looked like this before, even early in his service in the Indies. The black blood around the edges of his calluses made him queasy. He was not a weak man, but his hands looked as if they would never again be adept at anything. Even swinging the pick had become a matter of fine judgment. He tried not to look, then looked again, with the vanity of a handsome man who sees his body being ruined.

He wondered if the plan to kill the overseer had been betrayed. He was sure of Virgil, less sure of Lark. Lark was new. Old Ben would never; he was too old to care one way or the other. The cook boy, perhaps. He stayed all day at the barracoon, cleaning and cooking; perhaps his loyalty was with the whites. But if Gordon knew the plan, *what was he waiting for?*

Caesar decided it was time to act. The decision came suddenly; it didn't seem to result from conscious thought. It was there. *Time to go.* He had assumed that the attack should come in the morning or perhaps in the evening, because they were all together; but what entered his mind now was the idea that there was little to be gained from involving the other slaves.

He sank the head of the pick into a root on purpose, tested it to be sure that it wouldn't come out easily, and crept off into the swamp. If discovered, he could say he was looking for another man with an ax or mattock to help him cut the pick free. He climbed a short ridge to his left and followed a game trail along it, then moved as quietly as he could through the undergrowth, parallel to the line of workers. He had to know where Gordon was. He was not going to lie sleepless another night and be disappointed. Freedom was no longer something he wanted in the future; his hands and his maimed leg demanded it immediately.

He came abreast of Virgil, who was working silently. All the singing had stopped; they had figured that it could be used to track the location of their work and that if it stopped on the day they went for the overseers, it might warn them. No one questioned the end of the songs. Very few of the men knew why they stopped. Virgil hefted his ax and slipped a fascine knife from behind a tuft of brush. He handed it to Caesar.

"Now?"

"I'm goin' to fin' him. *Find* him."

"And?"

"And then we take him, you an' me."

"What about Lark?"

"Just you and me, Virgil."

"I'm with you." Virgil didn't sound calm, but he was clearly resolved. It lifted Caesar's spirits.

If Virgil wanted to question why Lark had ceased to enjoy Caesar's confidence, he didn't. Caesar slipped back into the brush, the heavy fascine knife held in his left hand. It had a vicious hook and an ax blade on the back, meant for cutting brush. This one was painted bright red, to make it easier to find when a careless man left it on the ground.

Caesar's heart began to beat faster. He moved easily now, the sun having warmed his aching bones but not yet sapped his strength. Virgil made considerably more noise. Caesar stopped and pointed. They were past their own gang, back toward the barracoon, the cabins, and the tilled fields. Keller was relieving himself into their ditch. He had the large knife at his belt and no other weapon. Caesar looked at Virgil, whose lips were a little pale, and he nodded. Caesar moved warily into the open to a patch of cattails, making the dry winter grass rustle, but Keller didn't move, still splashing the ditch with his urine and grunting a little, as if pleased with himself. Caesar made it to the reeds. He stood very still, hidden only by the man's position and the merest fringe of green, and breathed slowly through his mouth, spreading his hands wide for balance. He had practiced with his brothers, but his one experience of combat had not prepared him for this. His hands ached as if maimed. He took one long delicate step into the reeds that stood between him and his prey, placing his weight gradually down on a rotting stump that supported the little patch of dry ground. Keller began to button the flap of his breeches, his little grunts odd and faintly disgusting.

Caesar could smell his urine and his fetid breath. He waited until he heard the boy exhale, then he leaned out carefully and pounced, his hand gripping Keller's throat like a band of iron. The boy's eyes were huge. Only now did Caesar really see how young he was, but he ripped the big knife free and stabbed, upward as he had been taught, through the vitals and into the heart, pressing the boy back against his own chest and twisting the knife while his other hand kept the wind from the boy's lungs. Virgil appeared in front of him and his ax shattered the boy's skull.

There was no end to the blood from the head and from the heart. It stained all the water in the ditch in a moment. The boy was dead; he hadn't made a noise, and already the flies were coming. Caesar took a deep breath and stripped the boy's shirt, slave cotton, as poorly made as his own, over the corpse's head. It was soaked with blood, but he used the back to mop his hands and face. He threw it to Virgil, who was still standing, shocked, by the corpse, staring at the ruin he had made of the boy's head. Caesar ripped some ferns from the ground and used them to wipe the blade of the knife. It was a better knife than he had expected, a heavy blade with fine decoration on the backbone and a riveted wood grip. It reminded him of trade knives in Africa, a little heavier, but much the same.

"Come on, Virgil."

Virgil just stood. He wasn't whimpering, but his breath was loud and the sharp edges of his face were pale.

"Come on, if you're comin'." Caesar grabbed his arm. At first the ax came up, but the mad gleam in Virgil's eyes faded in a heartbeat and the big man nodded dully and followed him.

They headed back toward the cabins. It was almost a mile to the clearing, and they moved along steadily, Virgil starting at every forest noise. Caesar had started to breathe freely. The killing had shocked him. He regretted the age of the boy, but he was old enough to be a warrior anywhere Caesar had been, and he carried a weapon. Virgil had it worse. Somehow Virgil's continued reaction helped to steady Caesar. He put his hand on the older man's shoulder.

"Halfway home."

"Never killed nobody."

"Just stay with me."

There was a horse in the paddock with the saddle still on, and a man in a greatcoat talking to Gordon in the yard of the cabin. Chickens clucked around their feet. The man in the greatcoat wasn't large, but he looked fit, and his complexion was burned red even this early in the year. He and Gordon seemed to be arguing, though they were sharing a jug of corn liquor. His greatcoat had a velvet collar and silver buttons, and his fine hat and top boots, even covered in spring swamp mud, made Gordon's work smock look drab and poor.

A few drops of rain began to fall, although the sun still cast a pale light over the dooryard. Caesar slipped closer to the cabin, aiming to use it as cover. He could hear their voices but not what they were saying. Virgil was still behind him. Caesar sank to his knees at the edge of the clearing

and waited, as rain could only help them. It came, harder and harder, and
Caesar waited patiently.

"What you doin'? I can' jes' wait here!" Virgil was quiet, but urgent. He
had the need for action on him, something that Caesar had seen before in
men, a reaction to danger.

"We just wait awhile, Virgil. Be still."

Before long the April rain fell in sheets, the watery sun was gone, and
so, too, were the men's voices. The horse walked about the paddock,
dejected and puzzled that her saddle was still on. The men were in the
one-room cabin. Caesar could hear them through the thin walls of the
mud-and-stick chimney. He had helped lay the chimney; he knew how
flimsy it was.

"We nevah take that cabin with they inside," Virgil said, his voice
rising.

"Don't you move, Virgil. You stay right heah. *Here.*" He slipped out of
the mire, up the bank to the high ground, and along the rail fence of the
paddock to the horse. The cabin had no windows. Unless one of the men
put an eye to one of the many chinks, he was safe. He put a hand in front
of the horse's nose and breathed on it. The horse made a soft noise. He
ran his other hand back along the neck to the top of the saddle and felt in
one of the holsters. A pistol. Rather than drag it into the rain he felt
for the buckle to the holsters and found it, unbuckled the pair of pistols,
and moved back to the edge of the swamp.

"Ever shoot a gun before, Virgil?"

"Nevah."

"This ain't your day to learn, then." The pistols weren't fine, like some
he had seen; these were local made and had heavy locks. The priming
was sound in one, damp in the other. He recharged it from the flask in the
holster. Something didn't look right, but his experience with firearms was
entirely through observing other men with them. He knew he would have
to pull the cock back to full before he pulled the trigger, and he carefully
did so now. The cock came back and there was a soft *click,* almost pleasant. It made the piece look more dangerous. He examined it for a moment, then opened the pan and let out the priming and held the cock as
he pulled the trigger. It forced forward a little against his thumb, and he
lowered it into the pan and then pulled it back one click, then the other.
Half cock, full cock. He had heard both terms. Now he knew the feel. He
did it over and over again until he was sure of the feeling, and then he

replaced the priming and put both pistols on half cock. An unlucky drip from the trees hit the lock of the second before he had it stowed away in its fur-covered horse-holster, and he had to open the pan, clear it of the black mud that had formed there, and refill the pan with powder. He didn't trust the piece, though; he had heard masters say that once a gun was wet, it stayed wet.

Virgil was silent through the whole performance, and he looked miserable.

"Soon, man, soon," Caesar reassured him quietly, but the words seemed to go right past him.

Caesar felt more alive than he had in months, indeed, since Mount Vernon. He felt sure of himself; he was balanced pleasurably on the edge of danger. He smiled at Virgil, a smile that shocked him because of its sheer happiness, and moved across the edge of the paddock to the back of the cabin, his steps covered by the sound of rain. Virgil set his jaw and followed, clearly terrified but determined. His face was a mask of tension, and Caesar became apprehensive that Virgil would do something rash.

Caesar stood under the eaves of the cabin and put the fascine knife under the rope that held his trousers at the back. He drew the wet pistol with his left hand and the dry one with his right. The men inside were making a bargain; Caesar could hear them huckstering. It struck Caesar that Gordon was selling some of the slaves, perhaps in preference to killing them, although he didn't care. He moved to the long porch, where the roof protruded forward beyond the front of the cabin, and made it there with both pistols dry, cocking them with his thumbs as he crossed the step. The door was open a crack.

"Who's there?" Gordon's voice. Caesar didn't hesitate, although he'd hoped to wait and ambush them when they emerged. He shouldered the door, which swung inward. The stranger in the greatcoat rose and turned and Caesar raised his left hand and pulled the trigger. The cock fell and there wasn't even a spark. Caesar pointed the second pistol and it fired into the man's face. The man catapulted back across the crude table, dead.

Gordon pulled a pistol from his belt and snapped it in one motion, but his prime was wet from the rain as well. He flung the big gun at Virgil and stunned him, then dove off his seat for the fowler in a corner. The cabin was full of smoke from the bad fire and the one shot, but Caesar stayed on the man, hurdling the table without thought, drawing the big fascine knife so fast that it cut his back. Gordon raised the fowler, his thumb on the cock, and Caesar cut his right hand off at the wrist with one hate-filled blow. The blood from the arm sprayed him, and the painted handle slipped in his hand and dropped to the floor. He pushed Gordon with his numb hand, as hard as he could, and the wounded man fell back across the fireplace, his back bursting through the mud and sticks even as his legs began to burn. He screamed, clearly past fighting, and Virgil's ax finished him.

Caesar wanted to rest, even to sleep; but the shot had been loud, even in the cabin.

"Not done yet," he said. He was almost unhurt and had killed three men. They had killed Gordon.

He smiled, and though his hands shook, he set about loading the pistol that had fired. Virgil was sick.

"You done?" he asked, when the noises stopped.

Virgil muttered something. Caesar found a leather pail of water and drank half of it, surprised that his mouth was so dry. He passed the rest to Virgil, who finished it.

"They other white boys be coming," Virgil said, looking over the rim of the bucket.

"If they heard the shots, I expec' they would."

"We gon' kill them, too?"

Caesar recognized that Virgil was done. It was something he knew instinctively, that the man could not handle further violence just then. Caesar considered their position. He moved through the cabin, collecting a side of bacon and a bag of meal, a hunting pouch with a horn for the fowler, the blankets. He searched both the dead men's bodies. The wealthy one had a fancy clasp knife, a watch, and two English guineas; Caesar kept them all, and a little pocket glass that the man had. Gordon had less, some shillings, another clasp knife, and a pocket tinder kit. Virgil leaned in the doorframe, watching the yard. He was still trembling at the knees.

"Search the horse, Virgil. We need any food she got, and the man's blanket."

Virgil nodded and stumbled out. As soon as he was gone, Caesar began to strip the dead men. It was miserable, gruesome work: the bodies were clumsy and flaccid; Gordon had soiled himself as he died. For that reason, Caesar left him his breeches. But he needed their shoes. The slender man's boots fit him near enough, and he took the man's stockings as well. He had no illusions about walking barefoot any great distance in the Great Dismal.

When he was done, he took the piles of useful goods out to the yard and added them to the spoils from the horse. He expected it to be late afternoon in the yard, somehow; he walked out into morning and realized that little time had passed since the rain.

"Go get the others."

Virgil looked at him. "What if they don' wan' come?"

"Then they can stay and get hung."

Virgil frowned. "I don' like this. Too many killing. It won' lead to no good."

Caesar smiled, a hard smile with no humor in it that hid his teeth— Washington's smile. "I doubt this will be the last of the killing, my friend. But let's run. We'll have a long start."

★   ★   ★

It took an hour—an hour that frayed Caesar's nerves and made him lash out several times at the other men. He had to explain what had happened over and over; many did not like the sharing of equipment; and some simply stood slack and looked at the blood in the cabin. If the white men had returned, they could have taken the lot, Caesar suspected, but they didn't. Caesar didn't know how distant they were or what they were doing, but if they heard the shots, they either hid in fear or fled. At the end of the hour, Caesar's party was finally ready to move: Caesar at the head, followed by Old Ben; three men he barely knew, carrying an iron pot and most of the food; the cook boy; Tom and Virgil closing the file. Lark was nowhere to be seen. The other slaves were huddled in groups, some eating their share of the cabin's provisions, others already drunk on the corn liquor. Caesar had tried talk and he balked at force, but it angered him to leave them to face the wrath of the whites. He looked around the clearing; then, moved by an impulse, he walked back into the cabin, drew the little tinderbox, got a spark on charred linen, and blew it to light on some tow. He lit a tallow candle and some fatwood with the tow, and made it a bundle. Then he kicked a hole in the wattle and mud chimney and set the sticks of it on fire with his fatwood. He threw another stick into the marsh straw of the roof for good measure, and in a moment it went up with a rush. He took the bundle of tallow and wood out and threw it on the straw in the barracoon. Then he took the long sharp knife he had gained from the first boy and killed the horse. The others watched him, stunned, as he moved purposefully through the clearing, destroying the corn crib and every other structure.

"Stay if you want, you Ebo fools." The cabin was starting to burn in earnest. "Stay and be slaves, or hang!"

They watched him; a few actually ran from him. He thought a few might follow his group when they went. He was too inexperienced to realize that, just then, most of them were more scared of him than of the hazy and uncertain future.

"You gonna die!" shouted one man, backlit by the fires.

Caesar shrugged wearily, too tired to argue, and he led his group into the swamp. Behind him, the cabin roof and the barracoon both caught, and a pillar of smoke rose slowly into the sky. But he thought, as they left the line of drains and plunged into the real wilderness, that today, at last, he was not a slave.

Chapter Seven

Mount Vernon, Virginia, May 3, 1775

It was a curious gathering, and Washington thought that the men who graced his house on the eve of his departure for the second Continental Congress could not have been more unalike. What brought them together was a desire to profit by his patronage; they were friends, most of them, but every one of them wanted something. It was a role to which he was used in a small way, but it was heady, nonetheless.

Major Gates, a half-pay retired officer who had served with Washington under Braddock and had a depth of military experience unrivaled in the colonies except for Washington's own, desired a command if the Continental Congress should see fit to raise an army. Washington smiled; he knew Gates, and knew the man felt himself Washington's superior in the art of war. Washington had never precisely warmed to him and had always feared his ambition; and he had odd, overly ingratiating manners, the product of too many years as an inferior officer in an inferior independent company. But he would need every skilled soldier he could find if Virginia went to war.

Richard Henry Lee wanted a commission in the militia; he had proposed to raise another independent company of horse for his son Henry. He was traveling with his brother Thomas, who wanted nothing but news. Charles Carter wanted the Continental Congress to enact land legislation that Parliament in London had refused, and young Henry Lee seemed pleased to sit with the gentlemen after dinner and sip from his share of one of Washington's famous pipes of Madeira.

"Will Dunmore fight?" asked Carter.

Washington shook his head. "He took the powder from Williamsburg to rob us of the means to violence, not to provoke it. He is a careful, thoughtful man, perhaps even a devious one."

"Thomas Gage never had the repute of a hothead, sir, and I believe he has led the way to a greater act of violence than any seen in these colonies." Gates looked particularly satisfied that Gage had blundered. There was some history there—had Gage refused Gates a commission when he raised his Light Armed Regiment for frontier service? Washington couldn't remember whether that was a fact or a rumor.

"The attack was utterly unprovoked. 'Tis in the express. They marched out of Boston to take powder and stores in Concord, and the Massachusetts men gave them a drubbing."

"While we let Dunmore take our powder and then sit on our hands and take no action!" cried Henry Lee. "All the horsed militia are formed and ready at Fredericksburg."

"And they refused to say the words 'God save the King!' and insisted on 'God save the liberties of America,'" interjected Richard Lee. "Exciting times, Colonel. Is this the time for Virginia's foremost military son to travel to Philadelphia?"

"Dunmore has nothing but a half-company of marines and some sailors. We could take the palace tomorrow and hold him until they bring the powder off the ships." Henry Lee was excited at the prospect.

"On what grounds, gentlemen?" Thomas leaned forward in the big library chair. "I misdoubt this talk of open rebellion. If we must show our mettle to preserve our freedoms, then let's to it and no more debate. But attack the king's appointed governor in his palace, with the only cause that he seized powder that's legally his? I stand with Peyton Randolph and other moderate men on this; he'll give it up without violence. Ben, I know you admire the spirit of those Massachusetts men, but they have taken a step that may lead us, God forbid, to civil war. And war's an ugly thing."

Washington nodded. His thoughts were far away; Virginia had not seen fit to offer him the command of her militia, and he had responded by moving his duties to the Continental Congress to the forefront of his mind. "It is in my mind, gentlemen, that we have left my lady alone far too long. As she has no other ladies to support her, I think it only courteous that we restore the conversation to her."

"Hear, hear," said Thomas, who had not relished the conversation. It was becoming harder to be a moderate.

"I should never have thought to be so inconsiderate," said Gates, as if searching Washington's words for a hidden insult.

* * *

But when they were all abed, Martha smiled at him and chided him firmly. "That's a lonely way to spend my last evening with you."

"I'll be back soon, like as not."

"You won't, though. They'll give you the command."

He looked at her, surprised to have his innermost secret thought divined. "I had not thought..." The words came perilously close to a lie, and he bit his lip and looked at her.

"I have waited for you to open your mind to me, husband. It is plain as the eyes on my face that the Virginia Convention is sending you to the Philadelphia Congress as a soldier. Why else do you not have the command of the militia?"

"It would be unmannerly of me to expect such a command, and villainous to hope for such a thing that could portend such dire consequences."

She turned her head on the pillow and looked him in the eye, hers glinting with humor. "But you do. Is it hard, husband, for one vessel to hold so much honor and so much ambition?"

"You still possess the power to mortify me, madam."

"None of your other friends dare. Your careful silence does not fool me, sir. I know you."

"True enough. What can I fetch you from Philadelphia?"

"You can arrange that the clever fellow who manages all my estates and has so suddenly become a man of the first consequence be returned to me with all his limbs."

"You honor me with your commands."

"Do you remember promising me to leave the army, sir?"

"I remember that the subject came up when we discussed marriage."

"I haven't changed, sir. I dread every time my son leaves this house. Do you think I shall not dread ten times as much for you to face the cannon?"

"Hush, madam. It will not come to that."

"It will, George Washington." *For if they give you this command, nothing will stop you, if you have to force them to war yourself.* But she had made her point, and had no intention of spending their last night in further contention. Rather she smiled at him in a certain way, and changed the subject.

Great Dismal Swamp, late May 1775

"They at war!"

The boy was their most reliable contact with the world. Invisible in his poverty and his lameness, he could enter the settlements and buy goods, or tell them where to steal. That they were not the only band of runaway slaves in the swamp was for certain, as every community on the edge seemed to have a militia ready to turn out against them, but Caesar's careful scouting and the boy's tireless spying kept them safe.

They had covered dozens of miles in their original flight, and more since, slogging through the water or forcing a path through the deep tangles of the high ground. The column had to move at the speed of the slowest, which was not Old Ben or Long Tom, but a beaten-looking man called Fetch who seldom spoke or even looked at others. Caesar didn't know why he had followed them, but he had, and he moved more slowly every day. Twice Caesar looked at his body, but it had no unusual marks or wounds, nothing more than the casual cruelty and hard work of a life of servitude.

"He gon' die," Old Ben said, watching Caesar run his hand down the man's leg.

"Why? He ain't snakebit, and I can't find anything else. He got a fe-vuh? *Fever?*"

"No. He jus' don' wan' live. Simple as that."

So Caesar, to cheat death, let them build a camp on a hummock in the northwest of the swamp. Virgil showed them how to lay up wigwams of reeds and poles, the way an Englishman had shown him. They built four. And Caesar went off every day to scout the area around them, and when he found the settlement to the north a day's walk, he sent one of the men to find the boy.

"That boy need a name." Old Ben seldom prefaced his remarks.

"Why?"

"He gon' die young. Shouldn' die called 'boy.' "

"You name him, then."

"I ain't the big man." Old Ben never seemed to miss a chance to re-mind him of his responsibility.

"You got a name, boy?" Caesar sat on a pile of brush bound up with roots. It made a passable seat.

"Not as I remember, suh."

"Well, then." He thought over all the names he knew. Others of his lit-tle band gathered around, or lay on pallets.

"Do you all know who James Somerset is?" he asked. He saw the flash of recognition from Virgil and Old Ben, but none of the rest seemed to stir.

"He was a man, a black man in England. He went to court to prove himself free. He won. He's free, and there ain't no slaves in England be-cause he won."

"What kind of court would let a black man speak?"

"Courts in England, I guess. He had a white man lawyer called Sharp, way I heard it."

"Where'd you hear this?"

"I heard it from a free black sailor named King who been to England himself."

They nodded, satisfied.

"So that's what we call you now, boy. James Somerset, or James. Mostly Jim, I suspect. But you remember where that name is from, a brave man who made other men free."

The boy—Jim—smiled so widely it looked as if his teeth might burst out of his mouth.

And Caesar sent him on his first mission to spy out the little town.

"Who they fightin'? War with who?" The men clustered around the boy, eager for the cornmeal he had but more eager for news.

"British soldiers fought some men in 'Choosets. They marched down a road and the militia killed 'em all dead. They killed some militia, and now it be war against the British."

Caesar had heard talk of war with England for months, back before he was sent away from Mount Vernon. It was a persistent rumor, but this seemed to say there had been an actual battle. He had never felt much pity for the Virginians, when they talked of it, but perhaps that was just because they were the masters and he the slave. Perhaps they themselves were mistreated by the English, although he never saw any sign and the Englishmen who came to Mount Vernon had seemed little different from any other white men.

When the excitement of the news had died down, Jim told him the bad news in private, which was smart of him. Other overseers had reported the bloody escape and militia were seeking them in the swamp. Jim hadn't heard much, just a hint from a little black girl that there was a hunt in the swamp and a garbled version of the killing, which had clearly magnified in the telling.

"You only killed they three men, I know. I saw them. I counted. Stories say you killed ten or mo'."

"Didn't bother you none, Jim?"

"Oh no, suh."

"Get something to eat, Jim." Caesar looked at the comfortable camp, with two brush huts and a covered fire pit. They'd been there for several days and his hands were less numb. None of the men would want to leave.

But they were hunted, and it was time to move.

Schuylkill Tavern, Pennsylvania, June 16, 1775

Peyton Randolph, acting as speaker for the Continental Congress, was seated in the center of the head table. He rose carefully to his feet and demanded silence of the hubbub around him. The tavern's common room was filled with members of the Continental Congress and well-wishers, some of whom had already adopted military dress, so that the dinner had something of the appearance of a council of war.

"Any man who studies the classics will tell you that the ancients knew that most good generals were good farmers," he began, and Washington winced. Most of the great generals had never farmed in their lives; Caesar and Alexander leapt to mind.

"If that be true, then we have among us a man uniquely fit to command, a veteran of our wars with the French and a farmer whose success is a byword in Virginia. If the cause of liberty must resort to arms, therefore, I think we can ask no better than that those arms be borne and led by my friend." And here he indicated Washington with a gesture.

"I give you the commander in chief of the American armies."

Every man in the room rose to his feet. Men who had never worn swords in their lives but to funerals were wearing them now, even in the cramped quarters; and among the coats of hunting plush and dark velvet, Washington saw more than a few worn laced coats from the last war with France. Every glass rose as if in salute, and he stood, utterly at a loss for words, though the appointment had been his for a day and the dinner was in his honor. He had not expected to be so moved, and he looked at them—solemn and armed—with his heart full of fear.

"Gentlemen . . . I am not . . . I am most sensible . . . that is . . ." He stopped and tried to raise his eyes from the table in front of him, abashed for the first time in many years, and wished that he could have a tenth of his neighbor Mr. Henry's eloquence. But his courage stood by him; he was not nervous, only moved that they should stand so.

"Gentlemen. I am honored beyond words that you . . . that you have chosen me to lead this enterprise. I fear the result more than I wish, and I hope . . . I hope that no man present enters lightly into the notion of war. I fear my merits will fall short of the magnitude of the task. I should thank the gentlemen of the United Colonies . . . I should thank . . . them, for so much confidence in my abilities; but I dread to fail, and ruin my country and my reputation in such a task."

He looked up then, aware that he had spoken mostly to the table, mortified that his speech must sound so craven, but every eye was on him, and no one seemed to censure it. Their glasses were still raised.

"I will bring to this contest a firm belief in the justice of our cause, close attention to the prosecution of it, and the strictest integrity. If these are sufficient to the task . . . If it must be war, so be it. I will lead as best I may, and may God be with us."

Someone at the first table said "Amen" very loudly, and there was a rustle as men drank off the toast, but those sounds served only to accentuate the silence of the crowd, and they stayed standing for some time, thinking of the war to come.

✵ ✵ ✵

Billy hadn't stood at his elbow in the tavern as he might ordinarily have done; northerners seldom thought to provide space for a gentleman's slave as would have happened in Virginia. So Billy had to wait until Washington returned to his lodgings to hear of the evening, and Washington was in a far more solemn mood than Billy had expected.

Billy had his boots off without complaint and had laid out his waistcoat for a brushing before Washington spoke, his shirt open and his stock hanging from his hand.

"I don't think they know what war is," he said suddenly.

Billy took the stock and nodded. It wasn't really his role to speak.

"They think making me their general shows that they are in earnest, and perhaps it does. But none of them has seen a real war. Indeed, I think that veterans of Frederick would laugh at my pretensions to knowing war. Do they expect me to keep them safe?"

Billy took the silver buckle off the sweat-stained stock and threw the stock on a pile of laundry.

Washington drank off a glass of wine from the stand next to the bed and pulled his nightshirt over his shirt, as he often did. Billy grimaced inwardly. Wearing shirts at night meant more work for the laundresses.

"We have no army to speak of, no artillery, no ships, no fortresses, no magazines full of arms." Washington snapped around and looked at Billy. "And when we are beaten, they will blame *me*."

Billy thought that Washington had invited the appointment, but kept quiet. He had Washington's coat over his arm and Washington gestured at it.

"You can press that and send it home," he said.

Billy looked at the coat, perfectly good broadcloth in dark blue. "Sir?"

"I'll be in uniform tomorrow. And until this contest is done."

Great Dismal Swamp, June 28, 1775

Long Tom and Virgil had the pistols, though neither had fired them often; he had the fowler. Each had powder for a few shots, and no more; every man had a knife and an ax. The militia all around them had good muskets and hatchets; some had swords. What they lacked were dogs, because the dogs had balked at the deep swamp and the pepper Long Tom had used.

They were all lying in a deer hollow. The militia were close enough that every movement could be heard, every complaint about the heat. One man was sure he had seen a footprint; the others were less sure.

"Ain't no bunch of 'em," said one man. "Just the one print."

"That ain't no print, you fool."

"Deer might make that mark, if'n he slipped on the bank."

"Deer don't slip."

"Do, too."

"Shut up. Crafter, go back and look at the last crossing again. We all have shoes, so you look for barefoot marks. Dixon...*Dixon*."

Caesar looked and looked for the speaker, who seemed to be right in front of him but had to be on the other side of a finger of open water. *If he could shoot the officer...*

...Then all the other men would rush in and massacre them. He might try to kill the officer to redress the balance, but they were nearly doomed. Caesar wondered what Dixon had done and if he was as dull as Long Tom. He continued to make useless plans as fast as his mind could work, all the while wishing for some luck.

Fetch saved them. Perhaps his nerve broke, or perhaps he chose to sacrifice himself; later most of the men chose to believe the latter. But he moved away as silently as he had lived with them and suddenly rose to his feet and began to run. It drew the attention of the militia gradually; he wasn't loud, and he didn't shout. But in a few moments all the militia were after him, too experienced to risk shooting in the dense cover of the high ground in the swamp but excited enough to crash through the brush after him.

Caesar waited only a few moments; he couldn't afford to hesitate.

"Move! March! This way!" He plunged off to the south, away from Fetch's flight. The running militia didn't hear them, and their luck held.

Fetch's did not. A few minutes later there was a shot and a scream, then a fusillade of shots and some shouting. Caesar thought he heard them laugh.

✫   ✫   ✫

They camped without a fire, hot and miserable in the flies and mosquitoes, with little food. Someone had dropped the black iron kettle in their flight, the cornmeal bag was long empty, and Caesar didn't dare risk a shot to bring down an animal, even if he could find one. The water was brown and warm and tasted of mud. The dead man's boots were beginning to separate where the sole met the upper, and his stockings had rotted away inside the boots.

The boy was already asleep, utterly exhausted. Old Ben wasn't much better.

"We can't live like this," said Virgil, giving voice to what every one of them felt. But to Caesar, it sounded like an accusation. He was too young to feel it otherwise. He flared.

"I'm doin' the bes' I can! *The best!* Would you rathuh be slaves? Be workin' till you bleed?"

"Hey, Caesuh. Don't fret so. We got nowheahs else to go. But we can' live like this long. Boy and Ben'll go next, when the food stay sparse." He smiled a little. "And they ain't no women." That raised a murmur of a chuckle.

Frustration and anger and fatigue warred in Caesar. He wanted to walk off and leave them. He wanted to tell them how inadequate he was to the task of keeping them alive. He had never expected the militia so deep in the swamp. He had made so many mistakes about camps and food, and he felt that they all knew his every error.

"I don't think I can get us free," he admitted. "I ain' made a good decision in days."

"Don' fret yo'sef, boy." Old Ben sounded sleepy. "Tiuhd men don' think straight. We all 'live 'cept Fetch, and that was his own choice."

Virgil leaned forward so his face almost touched Caesar's, and he whispered, "I ain' sayin' you done nothin' wrong. I'm sayin' we ain' gon' make it like this, and we need a new plan. I says we leave the swamp."

"An' go where?"

"South, to Florida. Spanish let you live free, I hear."

"That famous man, John Canno, lives in Florida," said Caesar. He still didn't believe in John Canno. He knew how fast his own single victory had been embellished. "Let's stay here a little longah. *Longer.* The militia may leave. We ought to get free o' them tomorra anyway. We'll go south an' west."

"Gon' need food."

"An' powder an' shot."

"Wheah we gon' get all that?"

"I don' know, Mastuh Virgil. But we need a li'l...a *little* luck. Say a prayer."

Cambridge, Massachusetts, July 3, 1775

The day had turned warm, but Washington didn't show it. His stock was buckled, his smallclothes spotless; he looked very much a commander, and much more so than most of the Massachusetts officers who had gathered for general orders.

"I should like an immediate return, by battalion, of the troops and their equipage."

"Who would take that? I suppose one of us can ride the rounds."

"I would expect that every battalion has an adjutant?"

Many of the officers looked at each other. General Ward, still irked at being superseded in a New England army by a Virginian, felt the criticism was personal.

"Many do, right enough, General. Not all."

"And I expect they are formed in brigades, each of which has a brigade major?"

"I expect so, General." Ward sounded dangerously close to anger.

"Gentlemen. I mean no censure, here, but these are not trivialities that I have cooked up with my staff. We need to know the state of the army's powder and ball. We need to know what we have and what we lack. And to be frank, we need to know these things every day, and we will. Please see to it. I do not expect to see my officers riding the common from camp to camp to gather the numbers. Rather I expect to see every battalion adjutant report to his brigade major, and that major to his brigadier, and hence to my chief of staff, General Gates. In his absence, to General Lee. Am I clear? Excellent." He looked around at them. Any hesitation he had felt as recently as the night before was gone; this morning he had seen the sentries of the Fourth, or King's Own Regiment, on Boston Neck. He was in the face of the enemy, and operations were under way.

"Gentlemen, you have done well, and the entire continent applauds you. But whether we end this year at peace with the mother country, or whether we are doomed to civil war, we must not lose here. We cannot afford that the king's troops mount a successful coup de main against our works.

"We do not need to win any great battles, and I wish to reassure you that I have not come before you seeking useless laurels. But neither will I squander the reputation you have garnered. Our defenses are, to be blunt, pitiful. Over the next few days I will ride over them with you, gentlemen, and our staff. But you have only to look at the two great redoubts the enemy has constructed and filled with guns on Boston Neck to see how this matter should have been carried forward. The defenses immediately below this town are insufficient, and as this is our headquarters, I have little reason to believe that matters will be better elsewhere."

None of the New Englanders could be expected to listen to this thinly veiled criticism with pleasure, and Washington had been warned that Ward, at least, thought that the religious superiority of the Massachusetts men was a stronger armor than any regular entrenchment. He was certainly red in the face.

"God has granted us great victories, at Concord and Monroe Tavern and Breed's Hill, General Washington, and no one can doubt that His cloak lieth over this army and His shield stands before it."

"I am sorry, General Ward. Does that mean you do not feel we should improve our entrenchments?" Washington spoke coldly, his courtesy strained. He did not intend to give an inch on his first day in command, lest his authority be eroded.

"I mean, General, that the hand of the Lord is more to us than all the science of the Romans."

"General Ward, God's cloak and shield would be greatly strengthened by a proper redoubt with ravelins below this town and some strong entrenchments on Dorchester Neck, if I am not very mistaken. I would add, for your private ear, that God may not forever tolerate behavior in a camp like I saw last night—with both alcohol and lewd women—and that as long as this army behaves in such a manner, it would be hubris, sir, to expect special consideration. If those observations are not sufficient, please remain behind when this meeting is dismissed and we can discuss the matter."

Ward seemed likely to explode, but several of the other officers were smiling. A colonel standing behind General Ward raised his hand as if to be recognized. Washington looked past him, but the man began to speak anyway.

"We can best get men to dig—"

Washington stopped him in his tracks. "This is not a council of war, sir. When I want your opinion, I shall ask it." Washington realized how that sounded as soon as the words crossed his lips, and he forced a small smile. "Gentlemen. Only one man can command. I do not wish to be here as a foreigner, taking command after your notable victories, but here I am at the behest of the continent." He looked around the room, ignoring Lee's open amusement and Gates's solid presence, looking for reaction from the New Englanders. They looked back, sullen and closed. He sighed. He knew himself to lack the temperament to court men to his way. "General Ward, if any of my remarks could be interpreted as illiberal, please forgive me. I am moved only by my zeal for our duty and mean no disrespect to the efforts of this army."

Ward bowed in return, but his face remained red.

Wherever the conversation might have gone, it was interrupted by cries of "Alarm" in the camp on the common. Washington looked at Ward; the man had handed over the command, but Washington didn't even know the names of all the brigadiers. He should let Ward respond to the alarm. Ward glared at him, and Washington stamped on his impulse.

"Get me a report of the alarm."

A young man in a good brown cloth coat and a round hat, wearing a fine silver smallsword and sea boots, was introduced to the room in minutes.

"Captain Poole of Marblehead," said one of his aides from the doorway.

"We can see the British moving on the Neck, sir."

"In what strength?"

"Five or six regiments and a battalion of light infantry."

"Do they have packs?"

The man looked crestfallen. "I don't know."

"How long until they are ready?"

"They are just forming, sir. An hour."

Washington dreaded an assault on the nonexistent fortifications opposite the Neck. He looked at the door. "Get me General Lee."

Charles Lee was an enigma to Washington, more like a British officer than an American, with a vicious turn of phrase, a certain contempt for other men, and little habits of dress that made him stand out. Today he wore blue and buff, as prescribed by Washington, but gave it a fashionable air utterly at variance with Washington's severity. His lapels were unbuttoned, which gave the coat a look of informality; his beautiful smallsword was thrust through a pocket; he wore a small tricorn unlike any other in Massachusetts; and his watch fob dangled below a double-breasted waistcoat that in no way matched Washington's views on the dress of his officers. Yet alone of all the men on his staff, Lee entered and presented a perfectly correct salute, bowing and putting off his hat without flourish or awkwardness, every inch the soldier.

"Ward is a hypocritical fool. I don't know how you stand him, sir."

"I don't wish to discuss General Ward."

"All the better. I await your orders."

"Are the men standing to arms?"

"I think they fancy they are. No full battalion is under arms, much less a brigade."

"Ride through the camp and send every battalion to the head of the camp. Tell them to line the road and prepare to march off to the right by companies."

"Very well, sir. I took the liberty of sending your slave for your horse." Lee saluted with his hat and withdrew, his spurs making a martial noise on the red pine floor.

Great Dismal Swamp, July 3, 1775

Virgil and the boy Jim slipped into the brush behind the log barn and crouched, safe in the green and screened by high grass. There were voices in the barn, all African. Jim started to move, but Virgil waved his hand.

"No rush, boy." He listened, and in a moment heard the white woman's voice from the cabin. Two whites, two slaves. And two extra horses. The extra horses grazing at the short grass beside the house's chimney made him cautious, the more so as one had a long gun of some sort tied to the saddle.

"I got cornmeal heah befo'," said Jim, just audible. "Black folks is ol'. Whites is po'."

He watched the clearing. Far across it, against the other edge, the white man and the male slave were girdling a tree in a field where crops and stumps seemed evenly intermingled. Men laughed inside the cabin.

"They is too many men heah, Jim." He turned his head as slowly as he could, but Jim was already gone.

He missed the boy's ghostly advance through the grass but saw him just as he reached the edge of the barn, and then there was no sign of him for a while, except that he noticed that the black female voices in the barn disappeared in a moment. Virgil checked his priming.

The woman who appeared around the log barn with Jim was the first that he had seen in some time, and that may have added to her appeal. She wasn't wearing a jacket; most girls didn't, in the little farms around the swamp. She had the sun full behind her and he could see the shape of her legs and most of her top through her shift, and her breasts, outlined in sweat, made him smile. She had a tiny, pointed face, too small for the body, but nice.

Jim had a small sack of meal; far more precious, he had a brass kettle like the ones the whites gave to Indians to store dried goods in. He was almost bouncing as he crossed the grass, and the woman stood with her hands on her hips and watched the boy go.

"Ol' Nellie say those men be aftuh us!" said Jim, ducking into the brush. Virgil watched the girl, who walked along behind the barn with deliberate coquetry.

"You nevuh said they was a gal," Virgil hissed.

"They wasn't, las' time. Maybe they bought her?"

"Ol' lady say they slave-takuhs?"

"That what she say."

"They got dogs?"

Jim looked guilty. "I didn' ax."

"Don' fret. You done good on that kettle. If'n they had dogs, I reckon we'd know by now. We gon' have to do some walkin' round befo' we goes to camp. Jus' in case they follow us." He smiled back at Jim and rose for a last look at that handsome girl, but she was gone.

"Let's git."

Cambridge, Massachusetts, July 3, 1775

He sat on Nelson and watched his army, a chaotic mob, as they attempted to form themselves in battalions. Men ran from company to company, yelling for their own officers; in fact, several approached him directly. Some had the sense to look for their militia banners displayed in the center of their regiments, but the lack of uniforms and the total want of standard places for assembly told against them. It was over an hour before he had six regiments formed and marching on the roads; he had failed to find any of the ranger companies that he knew abounded to scout the way, and the Massachusetts general officers were conspicuous by their glacial inefficiency or by their absence. It seemed possible that General Ward resented him more than he hated the British; it seemed that Israel Putnam was nowhere to be found. Washington sent his own aides as scouts to keep watch on the enemy, but eager as they were, they were untrained and talkative, and he waited in the summer sun, baking in his uniform and watching his motley army of militia while imagining his outworks stormed, his camp taken, and his reputation ruined before he had learned the names of his own staff.

His six battalions marched slowly, the sixty different companies all marching with different steps when they marched at all. Gaps opened and closed all down the line, making any thought of complex maneuver impossible, and Washington began to wonder if he could actually form a line and fight if he had to. He could only hope that a show of force would be sufficient.

He rode up to Dorchester Neck at the head of his staff, the six battalions fifteen minutes behind him and strung out for a mile and a half. If the British were assaulting the Neck, he had fifteen eager gentlemen to stop them, all mounted. He was half tempted to try and avoid the consequences of disastrous defeat; indeed, he had thought of ordering the troops back to Cambridge rather than face the British with them. The truth of the battle at Breed's Hill was obvious. Unless these untrained men were sent into entrenchments, they would never stand in the field, or even form; they lacked the ability to march up in column, form line under fire, and give their volleys.

But no thick red column ascending the Neck met his eyes. The Neck was empty. Away toward the British lines and their south battery, two companies of light infantry were drilling, their files extended wide. Washington was comforted to see that they did not appear overly proficient.

"Where is this column?" Washington looked over the Neck, relieved that he would not have to fight today with such a clumsy instrument. No one answered. A single understrength company of Marbleheaders stood farther down, where a rough tangle of felled trees had been thrown across the Neck to slow an enemy approach.

"Captain Poole's company?" Washington asked, sitting his horse easily. The man smiled and nodded.

"Where are the British?" Washington waved his crop down the Neck toward Boston.

Another man came up, smoking a pipe. "Oh, they formed up, right 'nough. Jus' a field day, I'd say. A walk in the pahk."

"Where is your captain?"

"He went to find the Virginny general."

Washington shook his head, and the smoking man wandered off. He rode back to Lee. "Turn them around and march them home. Tell the general officers I want a complete muster and a complete return of military stores tomorrow."

"What do you want me to tell the churchwarden, General?"

"I fail to take your meaning."

"General Ward, then."

"Tell him the same as the others."

"He should have turned to with the rest. Sir."

"That will be enough, General Lee. I mean to have absolute command, but I will not stoop to personal remarks about my officers."

Lee, unfazed, looked back where the first four companies, hundreds of yards ahead of the rest of the column, were wandering toward them, each company a small crowd of men without formation.

"I imagine the only way to use them would be to ride up and down, showing each man his place and how to load his musket." Lee laughed at his own sarcasm.

"On your way, sir." Washington tried to sound cool; Lee both amused and irritated him. Lee swept him a bow from horseback and was gone.

It was a byword among farmers that often you had to make a tool before you could even start a job. He would train the army and officers and bring the Massachusetts men to heel. They would obey and respect, and men would not smoke pipes while talking to generals. It would all be a great deal of work, and it wouldn't succeed if the British attacked him before any part of it was done. He headed back to Cambridge, already composing his notes on the drill of the army, but as he began to pass through the chaos of the leading battalion, a thought occurred to him and he pulled up.

"You there," he shouted at a man in a good coarse smock and proper military equipment. The man looked something like a soldier.

"Sir?" The fellow at least had the sense to come to the recover, still the manner of a soldier.

"How many cartridges do you have, soldier?"

"Ten rolled, sir! Powder for six more."

Sixteen rounds. Washington saluted and rode on, checking soldiers as he went. By the time he reached the end of the column, he knew his Massachusetts men a little better, and he knew they averaged only nine rounds a man.

Sometimes, before a farmer built a tool, he had to get the materials for it. Washington started a new set of notes. He was still dictating to his secretary when he climbed the stairs to his rooms and flung himself in a wingback chair.

"What can I get you, sir?" asked Billy.

"An army, Billy. Saving that, a staff of professional officers, sixty thousand rounds of ball cartridge, and ten thousand muskets."

"I'll just get goin', then, sir."

"I'll settle for brandy and water."

"They have ice from an icehouse, sir. It's prime."

"Better and better. Iced brandy, then."

Washington turned to his secretary. "I've led you a damned chase today, sir, and you've held up well. Put down the notes about sashes as badges of rank and then get yourself a glass downstairs. I won't trouble you again today."

The young man bowed and retired. In a moment Billy returned, with a glass and some Naples biscuits. Washington devoured the biscuits and drank off half the glass. "They have no concept of discipline," he said.

Billy polished a silver salver quietly.

"They do not seem to believe in subordination. Every man must have his say, no matter how half-witted."

Billy nodded to him.

"I do not intend to discuss every notion of fortification with some Yankee captain who has read a book on the subject. Braddock may not have been the greatest general of the age, but his staff was a tool in his hand, an extension of him. He thought out the plans and gave orders. When will I reach a state where these men will obey me? I doubt that General Gage shares these troubles in Boston."

"You want to get those boots off, sir?" asked Billy, unmoved by his master's tirade.

"I thought that commanding this army would be like running a plantation, Billy. I would plan, dictate my orders, and the army would execute
my designs. I'm not sure these men even know how to obey!"

Billy looked up from the boots and smiled. But he didn't speak his
mind, and Washington didn't note it.

Chapter Eight

Caesar peered through the fringe of magnolia at the arm of open water stretching north from their new camp. "Where's Virgil?"

"Don' know." Old Ben looked shifty when he said it, and he probably did know. Something was going on; all the men smiled when they looked at Virgil or tried to cover his absences. Caesar shook his head and rose carefully to his feet, the fowler crooked in his arm.

"What *are* you all smiling at?" he said to the other men. "Come on. I'm gon' teach you to use this gun."

It was by no means the first attempt, and Virgil and Old Ben had at least passed the stage where the guns scared them, but Caesar was determined that they would all learn to use the fowler well, even the boy. In a corner of his mind, he had considered trying to hit the militia for more muskets; if he had one for every man, and they could shoot, he would have a force to be reckoned with in the swamp. The militia was wary, and hadn't come as deep in after the first foray, as if by the killing of one slave they had justified themselves and could go home.

He led them, single file, well away from their camp to a sun-drenched clearing in the high tree cover. Some time back, a storm had knocked two big trees down, and their huge, dirt-clogged roots made pyramids at either end of a clearing long enough to run a horse.

Two men lit pipes and sat down, and the rest stood in a loose knot. Caesar wondered idly where the tobacco came from; he suspected it was of a piece with Virgil's forays, but only today did it strike him that the tobacco smelled fresh. He also wondered if he should have a man out watching the trail from the settlements. That would have been Virgil's job.

"Everyone look at this gun," he began. "This is the butt, where you place her against yo' shoulder. *Not* yo' chest. *Not* yo' arm. Like this." He suited word to deed and tucked the fowler into his shoulder. He was quite familiar with it now, having fired it more times than he could count and killed any number of birds and several deer. He still preferred to get right up close to them, though.

"This is the *lock*. She make the gun fire, and she mus' be dry an' clean all the time. This part, with the flint, be called the cock."

He looked up. Several men were smiling. Long Tom had taken out his folding razor and begun whittling at an old stick.

"Bigger 'an yours is, Lolly," Long Tom said.

Caesar rolled his eyes with the earnestness of the young and plowed on.

"The cock holds the flint. She strikes against the hammer, like this." He pulled the trigger so that the flint in the jaws of the cock struck the hardened face of the hammer and made sparks. "Them sparks fall in the pan, heah . . . *here*, and touch off that powder."

He took the small horn out of the pouch that had come with the gun, a tiny thing that barely filled his hand. He twisted the stopper out with his teeth and tapped the lip of the small horn against the pan of the lock until he had filled it with powder. Then he shut the hammer so that its L shape covered the pan, drew back the cock past half cock to full cock, and pulled the trigger. The cock flashed forward, struck the hammer, and snapped it back from the pan while making a shower of sparks that fell into the exposed pan. The priming powder went up with a small *whoosh* and a finger of smoke that trailed away over Caesar's shoulder.

He held the priming horn and the fowler out to Jim, the youngest. "You try, Jim."

Jim set his face in a look of concentration made a little comical by the fact that throughout the operation his mouth opened and shut slowly like a fish underwater. He balanced the long weapon in his hand and found it lighter than he had expected. Then he pulled back the cock as Caesar had told them and took the stopper out of the little horn and tapped powder. It took him a long time to get the right amount of powder, much longer than it had taken Caesar, and his careful attention was almost spoiled when he saw the mermaid carved generously into the little horn. Then he shut the hammer on the pan, raised the fowler to his shoulder, and tugged at the trigger, turning his face away from the expected flash of the priming. Nothing happened.

Caesar hit him lightly on the shoulder.

"Nevah turn yo' face away." He scowled for a moment. "Never turn your face away."

Jim forced his head down over the fowler's barrel and pulled at the trigger again. The whole barrel moved, but nothing happened.

"You're still on half cock," said Caesar, indicating the lock.

"He still only got a half cock!" called Lolly, laughing.

Caesar glared at the man, and the laughter died slowly.

He knew he wasn't old enough to give them orders, but none of them seemed to want to be in charge; they all simply wanted to make his life hard for trying to give orders. Joking when he was talking was common; if he fought it all the time, it just made things worse. Usually he laughed with them. Today he wanted them to learn.

Jim pulled at the cock, and it came back far more easily than he had expected, clicking home into the full cock position with a small and sinister noise. Jim was afraid of the gun, and more afraid now that it was full of potential to fire; the cock looked ready to leap at the hammer with the smallest provocation. He was very hesitant when he pointed the piece; he jerked the barrel several inches when he pulled the trigger. But the pan flashed, and it didn't burn him, and he felt a glow of satisfaction.

"You has to keep the barrel pointed at yo' target. No pulling it. Like this." Caesar aimed over the barrel and pulled the trigger, and the barrel stayed steady. Jim watched.

"When you can flash the pan without twitchin', I expec' I'll give you powder an' shot." He smiled at Jim, then at the rest of the men.

"Jim can do it, I expec' the res' of you have no trouble at all." Caesar held the fowler out like a dare. "Who wants to try next? No one wan' to step forwar'?" He looked at them all. They weren't scared; it was just that years of slavery had eliminated any tendency to volunteer. He looked at Lolly, the joker, sitting on a downed giant and puffing at the blackened stump of a clay pipe.

"Lolly. You try. Here." He handed Lolly the fowler, and Lolly shrank away until he felt its sleek wood and the lightness of the thing, and then he held it with an almost proprietary air. Jim handed him the little priming horn, and Lolly smiled at him.

"There's somethin' I haven' seen none of in a whiles!" Lolly laughed, looking at the horn and the mermaid's breasts.

"I tink Virgil be lookin' at dat now," murmured Tom, normally a silent man.

Lolly was determined to excel, and he thumbed back the cock, pulled the stopper off the horn with his teeth, and primed the piece in seconds, then shut the hammer on the pan and pushed the stopper back into the horn and tossed it to Jim. Then he raised the fowler to his shoulder, seating it firmly where the muscles of the arm and shoulder knit together. The fowler looked tiny in his hands.

He pointed the fowler squarely at Caesar and pulled the trigger. The pan flashed, but no one laughed with him.

Caesar didn't glare. He took the gun away from Lolly and looked away for a moment.

"Don' never do that. Not even in fun. Man don' know whether it be loaded or not. If'n the pan flash, man might turn some pair of breeches brown." He said it all with such solemnity that it took them a moment to realize that he had made a joke of it.

While they laughed, Lolly leaned over to him and hit him on the arm. "Didn' mean nothin, Cese." He looked sheepish, as he always did when a joke went wrong or no one laughed with him.

"No harm done, Lolly." Any rancor Caesar might have felt was expelled by the man's obvious competence. Joking or not, he had watched and learned.

Next it was Old Ben's turn; although he had fired the gun before, he wanted the practice. Caesar gave him a ball and enough powder to drive it; Ben had earned a real shot. He put powder in the pan, spun the musket in his hands, and put powder in the barrel and pushed a ball down atop it, seated on a little patch of oiled muskrat hide. He had to push hard on the ramrod to seat the ball, and he looked carefully at Caesar's mark on the ramrod to make sure the ball was fully seated. Then he took careful aim at the billet of wood across the clearing and fired. He didn't hit the wood, but sandy soil flew in the sun close to his point of aim, if a little short. The others cheered his shooting.

Caesar swayed a little as he recovered the musket. He coached Tom through the motions of loading, but he looked green and seemed to be struggling with his body to stay upright.

"You sick, Caesar?" Ben asked directly.

"Somethin' I ate. I feel like somebody kicked me."

"You get out o' the sun, then, an' don' be foolish." Ben took control of the gun and its associated pouch and began to move the whole party back toward their camp. By the time they reached it, Tom and Lolly had to carry Caesar.

★　★　★

She never closed her eyes, not when he was in her, not when he stroked her, not even when she crooned to him at the end of her passion. But those odd golden eyes looked at him with some intent, and he could lose himself in their light. When they were in the half-dark barn, those eyes seemed to have a slight glow, like the last of a sunset, and the first time he had loved her, he had put a hand in front of her eyes to see if they really cast some light. It was like that for him; she scared him a little.

At first Virgil had thought that tremor of fear came from his long abstinence. It had been a year or more since he had been in a woman—any woman at all—and his wife, a fine woman, had never had the fire this one had, or the shape. But as he came back for her again and again, against his own judgment, he began to be afraid that she had taken something of his soul, or had bound him. He even wondered if it was all the power of her eyes.

The men at the camp knew he was with a woman. Jim had been quick to tell them about the first encounter and had probably watched the second. Caesar didn't know; he lay on a pile of brush under a bower in the camp, and they had to carry him back and forth to empty himself. Virgil tried not to think that Caesar was probably dying. He lost himself in her eyes again and reached beneath her to slip his hands under her and raise her body into his strokes. She liked to be touched constantly when he was in her and pouted if he paid her too little mind, but she never talked. In fact, he didn't know anything about her, except that the slave-takers owned her.

But just as he lost himself in the act again, that last thought burned through him, so that his whole body stiffened a little and she made a little grunting noise like a question. She was very good at reading him.

She belonged to the two slave-takers. He knew their names now:

Bludner and Weymes. And he wondered why two white men owned the most beautiful black woman near the swamp and didn't use her.

It was his third time with her, and only now, at the brink of his own vast satisfaction, did he really wonder why she lay with him. It might have unmanned him completely—the icy hand of betrayal on his prick—but she opened her eyes wide, and her cunny gave a little pulse, as if grabbing him to her, and he was past his fear, and she seemed the only thing in the world. He pinched her nipples, hard, and held her face in his big hands, and they both spasmed together, beyond ecstasy for a moment. Then he didn't know where she went; he went straight back to the fear of betrayal.

He rolled off her, stroking her with his left hand to keep her passive while he looked out of the long crack between the barn's boards. He could see down into the yard. The old slave couple were willing conspirators, warning them when anyone approached the barn, but Virgil had known from the first that the old woman didn't fancy young Sally one bit. Perhaps her man wanted Sally, old as he was. That would be no odd thing. Or perhaps Sally didn't talk to the old couple any more than she talked to him. She was odd, a sort of magical creature, too handsome for the dirt and tangle of real life. Even now, as he watched for the two white men with the long guns and assumed that she had betrayed him, he wanted her.

"Them slave-takers comin' fo' me?" he asked suddenly.

She turned her face a little away.

"Sally," he started, and then couldn't think of what to say. A profession of love didn't seem appropriate; he lacked the will to threaten her. He turned her head to face him and stared into those deep golden eyes that seemed guileless. "Sally, I need to know. Wheah ah they?"

"Don' know."

"Is they comin' fo' me?"

"They don' wan' you." She turned on her side so that her heavy breasts rolled onto the straw, a movement that always caught his eye. She smiled when she saw how he watched her, even now.

"They know I'm heah?"

"They don' wan' you. They wan' the otha man, the one killed all the white folk."

"They know wheah he is?"

"They follow you, big man. An' they wan' follow you today, to be sho'."

He stopped stroking her. Somehow, she had said too much—enough to let him know how well she knew the slave-takers, how much of their plans she understood, how little she cared about him. He didn't really expect her to resist them; it was too hard for a slave woman to resist a man, and he knew it too well. But there were other ways to rebel, and she wasn't following them. He thought now that he could guess why the old woman disliked her. He pulled his breeches on and his shirt; he had laid the shirt under them to keep her off the scratchy old straw, and it smelled of her. She just watched him, naked. The first woman he had ever known for whom nakedness seemed to mean nothing, as if she preferred it to clothes. His wife had been much shyer.

"I won' be back. You need to get clear of they two slave-takers, girl."

"I may. Fat lot you know about me." She wasn't sullen, just direct, and again he wondered at how little he knew her. He still had one of their two pistols, and he checked the prime, stuck it in the back of his waistband. Then he jumped, caught a beam, and swung to the hard-packed floor of the barn, avoiding the creak of the roped wooden ladder that let on to the little loft. He didn't know where they were or how they were watching him; for all he knew, she was signaling them even now. That didn't seem so bad, if he could get one of them before they got him, but he suspected they knew he was armed. He suspected they knew all about him. The barn had only one door, and he slipped through it and into the tall weeds in seconds, expecting a rifle ball in the back as he moved, but there was no shot, no movement, no call for a chase. He began to breathe a little easier, and then he realized that there was no sound of voices anywhere, that the farmer and his old male slave were still in the field, but no one else seemed to be around. He had expected to find the boy, Jim, who waited for him every time. He wanted, suddenly, to *know,* and he looked for Jim in the brush at the edge of the clearing. Failing that, he moved as cautiously as he could into the brush pile behind the little windowless cabin where the two old slaves lived. He slipped up on the little cabin from the big cabin's blind spot and scratched the door with a stick.

"Who theah?" called the old woman.

"Virgil," he answered softly, going through the door.

"You best be off, boy." She was cooking on her little mud hearth, making johnnycakes on a flat rock with some meat fat. They smelled delicious.

"You seen my Jim?"

"I seen more than Jim. Damn, all you young men is fools. They two men is followin' yo' Jim, and they'll take him, an' you, too. All because you have to wet yo' prick."

Virgil felt his face get hot; it was like being admonished by his mother or aunt. But he could think quickly when it mattered, and he knew that the camp was in danger if Jim was running for it with the two whites on his trail.

"How long back did they start?"

"Half an hour. They took guns, boy. You bettah run."

"I got a gun of my own, Momma. You take care."

"It's that Sally, ain't it, boy? She sets you up and they takes you?"

"She jus' does what she has to, Momma." He couldn't raise an anger for Sally, and the old woman really reminded him of his mother. Virgil found himself thinking about things he hadn't troubled himself about since he came to the swamp. He shook his head as if to clear it of thoughts. He slipped out the door and back into the weeds, found Jim's trail, and started to notice what he hadn't seen before—clear signs of two big men in boots following the boy. He checked his prime again and set off at a run.

Up in the barn, Sally wiped herself with a bit of tow she kept to hand and then wiped her body with straw before she pulled her shift on, and then pulled her petticoats over her head and then over her breasts. She never liked taking a man in her clothes; it was so much nicer being naked. She wriggled a bit to settle the petticoat and then pulled her strings taut and tied them off, and began to look for her pockets and her apron. The men who owned her didn't care if she did a lick of work beyond what they kept her for, but she didn't like to be called useless by a wise old woman like Old Sukey. She went down to the garden where Virgil had found her and got her hoe, humming a little in her throat.

☆　☆　☆

Virgil ran and ran, slowing from time to time to listen to the swamp, or just to get his breath. After the third stop his breath was ragged and uneven, and he felt winded. He was in good shape, but the uneven diet told, and running in the swamp was as fatiguing to the mind—which had to make judgments every second—as it was to the body. He checked his priming again, tapped the powder back to the bottom of the pan, and moved off no faster than a quick walk. It was the best he could do.

☆　☆　☆

Caesar squatted over his log, emptying himself into the pool of filth he had created over the last few days. It stank so badly that the other men went somewhere else. They were afraid of him now—afraid of his fever and the death they all thought they saw on him. Sometimes, in the evening like this, he was pretty lucid; he could look around and see that he was not being chased through endless swamp by some nameless horror that had pursued him for days since the fever hit him. In the evening the horror abated and he knew himself and the camp, although he was so weak he couldn't raise his hands for water. And he seemed to want water all the time.

But the dream was still apparently with him tonight because he could hear Jim shouting something from the trail at the edge of the camp and then there was a shot. It wasn't their fowler; it was a sharper bang, almost like a crack of lightning, and adrenaline put a little energy in his body, although it had taken the whole force of his will to drag his near-naked body from his pallet to this log.

Someone was screaming, and there was a second shot that cut off the scream like a knife cutting off the last squeals of a hog. Caesar threw himself forward and pulled his breeches up, trying in vain to button them and feeling filthy for not having wiped himself, but the unmistakable sound of a third shot, this one from the fowler, drove him on. He tried to crawl forward, but the effort was too much for him, at least for a moment, and he lay, still and defeated, and listened to the renewed screams from the camp.

He wasn't sure if it was the dream or not, but for a moment a tall, ferret-faced white man was towering over him, pointing a little pistol at his belly, and he felt very alone. Then the man spoke, and it was all very clear and slow but not, terrifyingly, a dream.

"He's skinny as a polecat, Mr. Bludner. Thin. Got the swamp fevuh. He's dead already."

"Leave him. We'll get him when we round up the othuhs." And the narrow face was gone.

Slave-takers. If he wasn't in the dream, he needed to get away. If they knew he had killed Gordon, he couldn't allow himself to be taken. He began to crawl toward the water, only a few feet beyond the trail. It was deep here—full of things, but deep. He pulled himself along and kicked with his legs, sweating away every bit of water his bowels had left him, and he heard the sharp crack of the rifles again, not far away in the bush, and then he was sliding into the water.

He had some distant notion of hiding. Indeed, he had little expectation of anything after he reached the water. But it was so cold that it seemed to wake him up and charge him with energy, and he swam out into the deepest part, where they bathed, and then across toward the green scum where the big fish and the biggest frogs lived on the far side.

☆　☆　☆

Virgil heard the shots and knew he was too late, but he didn't slow himself, bursting into the edge of the camp only a few moments after the first flurry of fire. He couldn't tell, as Caesar could, the different pieces by their different sounds, but he was unsurprised to find Lolly lying dead in a vast pool of blood, his gut shot and a small hole in the middle of his face, right at the top of his nose. The back of his head was all over the inside of their little wigwam. His eyes were wide open. It might have made Virgil sick, but he was too angry, and he blamed himself. He ran on.

Old Ben lay in the clearing, the old fowler fallen beside him. He was mewling like a kitten, making pitiful noises every time he exhaled. Both hands clutched at his belly, which was caked in mud and blood and something worse, something gray that was leaking out of him. He didn't scream. He just lay and made that dreadful noise. Virgil paused and looked at him, and then reached down and stripped the little pouch and horn for the fowler over the old man's head. Old Ben didn't resist, but he didn't seem to know what was happening, either, and he let out a mournful sound when Virgil rolled him back on his side. Virgil tried to be gentle, but he knew he was hurting the old man by the time he got the powder horn. It had to be done.

He picked up the fowler and moved along the trail where, apparently, Ben had fallen while the others ran. The whites must be right on them, although the forest was somehow quieter. He moved to the edge of the camp and took shelter in the shadow of a giant tree, then elected to wait. He had learned this while hunting with Caesar: when you don't know exactly what your quarry is doing, be silent and wait.

Something moved in the deepest part of the river, but he didn't pay it much mind. Twice he heard voices, soft, but the day was fading fast and nothing seemed to get any closer to him, and then, suddenly, they were both in the clearing, and Virgil realized that it was much darker than he had thought.

"That thin boy crawled away."

"No mattuh, Weymes. We kilt the old man with the gun. We'll claim his bounty an' the younguh one, too. We got the one I caught." He laughed. "If'n they was all this easy, this would be a good an' godly way to live, Weymes. Wheah'd you leave the one you tied?"

"Up the trail. Come on, Mr. Bludner. If you don' min' the swamp in the dark, I do."

"I don' think of you as a delicate flowuh, Brother Weymes." The taller of the two men bent over Old Ben and cut his throat, then cut the whole top of the skin of his head away. The shorter man did the same to Lolly. Ben's little moans had stopped some time since, and Virgil told himself that the poor man had been dead before his throat was cut, but the image of the act stayed with Virgil for the rest of his life.

Virgil thought of shooting at them, there and then, but they had the boy, Jim, and only they knew where he was. Virgil waited some more and followed the two white men when they started back. It was several miles, and they set a fast pace, clearly unconcerned with pursuit. Their contempt for any opposition from the black men burned Virgil like fire. He knew he was responsible for Ben's death and Lolly's, and he flamed with desire for revenge, expiation, and freedom from the knowledge that he had killed his friends—perhaps killed them all.

He padded down the trail and thought about death.

He might have run right on them and died, he was so lost inside his own guilt. Then the sounds of the swamp changed, a subtle change, more of a *lack* than a presence, but Virgil felt it and he stopped, disoriented, and listened to the silence. A crow cawed away in front of him. Something had spooked the crow and everything else.

Ahead of him, Jim began to cry out in pain. Virgil was determined not to lose the boy, and he pressed on, no slower but with his attention focused on the task at hand. He saw a flicker of white among the trees, and then another. One of the men was in a shirt and the pale linen gave him away. They were stopped by a tree on the trail.

They were cutting the boy down from the tree.

He was almost on them; the boy was there, and his heart rose.

Virgil didn't hesitate, or plan. He ran down the trail—better trampled today than ever before—until he came to the little space where it crossed two tiny streams in a dozen feet. The two whites and the boy were just beyond the streams, where the boy had been tied tightly to a swamp oak. His returning circulation caused him to flop on the ground with more force than he could have used in full control of his limbs, and for a moment he was free of his captors, though too far gone to help himself. He rolled and spasmed, the agony of the returning blood more powerful than any desire to run.

When Virgil was just a few feet from the taller man, whom Virgil had marked as the more dangerous, the man looked up and bellowed a warning. He tried to lever himself up from the crouch he was in and move back off the trail, but fell backward, helpless and off balance. Virgil snapped his pistol in the big man's face, and the prime flashed, but the barrel didn't fire. Virgil kicked the man as hard as he could and whirled, dropping the pistol and looking for the little man, who was pointing a rifle at him a few feet away in the soft moonlight and smiling. The smile died as the man realized that his rifle was uncocked—that he had made a fool's mistake and not reloaded after the last shot. Virgil's fowler was loaded with shot, and the shot flew a little high in his inexperienced hands, ripping into the man's face and hands. He screamed, but he was not new to pain, and even as he fell he reached in his hunting pouch for a pistol. Virgil, his mind suddenly clear of doubt and his actions written out for him like morning orders, held the fowler, picked up the pistol he had dropped, plucked the crippled boy off the trail, and ran into the dark. A shot barked at them, and then another, but Virgil clutched his precious burdens and ran.

Boston, October 1775

Washington sat atop his charger, his heavy greatcoat bundled about his ears, and regarded Boston through Charles Lee's new Dollond telescope. It was a beautiful thing: wooden barrel twenty inches long and a fast resolution in the hand. Washington hadn't owned a glass in the Pennsylvania wars. Truth to tell, there had seldom been a vista long enough to use one, through all the trees. This was a different type of warfare, a slow siege where logistics would matter more than tactics. Washington had the patience for a siege, and he wanted the time to train his army.

Incongruous thoughts of the season wouldn't leave his head this morning. He wondered if either of his farms had managed a winter crop of wheat; he longed for a report from his manager. He thought of his farms every day and wrote advice to his overseers whenever he could.

Below him, spread like a printer's study of an untidy siege, were the British lines; closer in, his own lines, stronger than they had been. The sentries, long-suffering militia or temporary "regulars," had blankets, and one lucky fellow a watch coat. Watch coats were the proper military garments for winter sentries; they were coming, slowly, from Philadelphia. Washington centered his telescope on the three figures. One man was quite old; the other two were prime. They all had cartridge boxes. Washington smiled grimly. He would be lucky if they had ten rounds a man. Powder was still the critical element.

As he watched, a British fieldpiece fired—a tiny white blossom of smoke against the bleak gray landscape and the darker lines of their revetments. None of the sentries moved. The ball fell just short, splattering them with mud, hopped a little on a short graze, and rolled over the harder ground by the parapet. One of the sentries leapt after it, placing rocks in its path to slow it. It was a small ball—perhaps a four-pounder, or a six. At this distance, Washington couldn't tell, but he hoped the sentry wouldn't be fool enough to try to stop it before it had lost more energy. Men had lost feet by such antics.

It stopped on its own, and the man flourished it triumphantly at his mates and carried it back to his post, where he put it on a small pile of shot. All three men appeared animated.

Washington folded the telescope and handed it to its owner. "War does not seem to have a terrifying aspect today."

Lee brought it to his eye in a practiced movement. He swept it over the harbor, then over the town, then slowly along the lines.

"That's the King's Own in the lines today," he said. "Blue facings, and those well-cocked hats."

Washington smiled. A sharp regiment. Both had noticed over the months the careful attention the Fourth gave to their uniforms and drill.

A wheelbarrow pushed by two men came down the road past Washington's staff. Neither man saluted, particularly, although both inclined their heads in a civil enough way. They pushed their barrow down the long slope to the advanced post where the sentries were once again huddled against their flèche.

"If we allow these enlistments to run out, every watch coat and blanket we issue will be lost. It is not so much that we lose the army"—Lee was never at his best when talking about the Massachusetts men—"as the difficulty we endure in losing the arms and accoutrements."

"Nevertheless, General, I wish to procure more blankets, and see them issued immediately."

"Of course, sir."

"How many requests have we written for blankets?" Washington turned and held out his hand for the glass again, and one of his staff dismounted and opened a saddlebag to retrieve a volume of the army correspondence. They had such volumes now, and daily returns for equipment and ammunition. The Virginia farmer knew how many bayonets were available in every regiment (too few) and who had muskets with slings. That much he had accomplished, and just the lists had taken him a month. Equipping them might take years, and the pressure from Congress was mounting. He had to evict the British from Boston before they were relieved by a huge fleet and thousands of men who might break his lines and boil out into the countryside, or so the Congress feared.

Lee handed the glass over again.

"A very fine instrument, General."

"Thank you, sir. I had it last week from London."

Most of the staff were dismounted now, pulling at flasks or lighting pipes while they all ran through whatever documentation was handy. Washington insisted that when he was away from headquarters, business must continue on horseback. He smiled ruefully at the provenance of the telescope; his sword was from London, and his pistols, and much of his war matériel. So far, the war had served better than all George Mason's sermons to impress on him how essential were the ties of trade between the American colonies and their mother country.

The wheelbarrow had arrived at the sentry post. The three sentries were helping the two other men load their collection of British cannonballs into the barrow. There were several calibers, four-pounders and six, and one larger ball that might have come from a ship in the harbor with her big twelve-pounders. One of the men with the wheelbarrow paid the sentries. Washington could see the paper scrip changing hands. He shook his head. The wheelbarrow began creeping crabwise across the hill, toward the small battery that the Massachusetts gunners had sited and built so laboriously in late August.

"General Washington?" An apple-cheeked staff officer with the diction particular to the graduates of the Yale divinity school. Washington nodded courteously and looked down.

"We have written for blankets eight times, and watch coats twice, sir."

The man smiled, proud of the speed with which this gem of knowledge had been discovered and polished.

"Pray mention it in the draft for a ninth letter."

Lee chuckled mirthlessly. "In time, there won't be a farmer in this colony we haven't provided for."

"General Lee, I do not always find these remarks helpful."

Lee turned his head, respect warring with an almost overwhelming desire to answer sharply and the struggle plain on his face. Washington put the glass back to his eye. He meant the rebuke, but hoped that Lee would accept it and not reply. General Lee was a first-rate soldier, and Washington could not imagine what the summer would have been like without him. Certainly General Arnold's expedition would not have been sent to Quebec even as late as it had been. If Washington now commanded the army, Lee commanded the staff.

The wheelbarrow had finally reached the distant artillery. Washington was warm from the waist down, where the heat of his horse bathed his legs and coat. Above the waist, the wind pushed through his coat and the salt sea air kept him damp and cold. His fingers were becoming painful in the mornings. He kept the glass to his eye, shutting out Lee's possible insubordination. The Yale man was still by his stirrup. *I should have held my tongue until we were alone. That was ill done.*

The artillerists were loading their six-pounder. Washington knew it was the six-pounder because it was bronze, a captured French piece from the last war and one of the truest in the service, and the polished barrel glinted in the gray light. He could see the gun captain whirling his flaming linstock in the air over his head, a very martial sight that stirred Washington faintly.

The linstock came down across the breech of the gun, and it responded instantly with a fine mushroom of smoke. The sharp *bang* of a good shot and dry powder followed a moment later. The depression of the shot was too low for anyone to follow its fall or its line, but within a few seconds there was a commotion at the British advance post. Washington looked at it through the glass. Three of the smart King's Own men were gathered around a fourth, prone. Washington could see from the numbers that they had been changing the guard. The downed man was spasming hard, probably screaming, but his voice was lost in the wind and the distance.

"Hit with their own ball," said Lee in an odd, strained voice. He had friends in the British army, but then, they all did.

Washington watched the British pickets making shift to move their wounded man. Every man of them had a watch coat, a musket, and a bayonet, made by the same mills that made most of his army's equipment. There was blood visible on the mud, even at this distance, and Washington knew from experience that the human body held a prodigious amount of blood. The shot must have taken off a leg.

Washington handed Lee his glass and turned his horse away as the British artillery fired again.

Great Dismal Swamp, October 1775

It took Caesar another week to break the fever, and he was thin and listless, gradually moving from total apathy about food to a raging hunger that he lacked the energy to satisfy. In his fever, he couldn't imagine what had happened; during his daily moments of lucidity, he still couldn't understand where the others had gone or where he was himself. Unbeknownst to his rational mind, he crawled every day in his fever, dragging his hot and exhausted body through the tangle of undergrowth in a circle, so that he never awoke in the same place.

When he finally came up from real sleep, listless but in possession of his faculties for the first time in days, he was unable to guess his location. He had nothing to hunt with and he couldn't see open water where he might catch a frog. He tried eating the bases of cattails, but the bitter flavor made them hard to eat despite his hunger. They gave him a little energy, though, and he began to move north, as best he could, hoping to see something he would recognize. He had no reason to think he had drifted south from the camp, but he had to choose a direction, and north was the choice.

He was almost naked: his shirt gone, his breeches a ruin that barely covered his legs, no boots, no jacket, and caked in mud and the fine vegetable matter that lay over every inch of the swamp's floor. He was growing desperate for water. He began to suspect he was going to die after all, having survived the fever. When he tried to think back, he couldn't decide whether the slave-takers' attack had been real or part of his fever, although logic suggested that it had to be real or he wouldn't be alone in the swamp. That depressed him further, as it meant that he alone had survived.

The utter defeat and extinction of his little band made him a failure as a leader, and he tried to think what he might have done better. He mourned the men, even those he hadn't liked so well. He felt tremendous guilt. Eventually he stopped walking, although a fitter man would have heard from the bird cries that he was near open water. Caesar slumped down at the base of a giant ancient swamp willow. He didn't so much sleep as surrender. His eyes, puffy and dry, were open but unfocused. He began to lean a little sideways, gradually slipping down the trunk, curling a little to ease the griping in his gut, sweat dripping off his nose.

He considered the possibility of standing up. It seemed reasonable. He was at the end, and death was near, and he decided that he would push himself up the trunk until he could stand if for no other reason than to spite the pain in his gut. And it occurred to him, as if from a distance, that despite his many failures and the ruin of his body, he was going to die free. That was worth something. He began to rise, slowly, almost glacially, and then with a misstep and a stumble back against the trunk, he was erect.

The movement saved him. Jim saw it away across an arm of the open water, like a deer moving, and he ran around the water and found Caesar standing on trembling legs, rocking back and forth. Jim didn't have the training to recognize that Caesar had a ghost spear and a ghost shield and was holding them ready. Jim couldn't see that, but he could just see that it was Caesar—his hero, almost his god—and in minutes Caesar was gulping water from a stolen leather fire bucket in a new camp. He was alive.

☆   ☆   ☆

It took him another week to recover, with food brought to his side every day. Virgil tried to keep the story of the slave-takers from him, but day by day he learned the whole of it, from the apparent treachery of the woman to the last shots in the woods.

"How bad was they hurt?"

"Little one huht bad, Caesar. I shot he face off!" Virgil was anxious to expiate the sin he had committed. The lives of Old Ben and Lolly were heavy on him, and he had buried them in the old camp with good crosses over them, although Lolly had not been a Christian man at all.

"What about the woman?"

"I won' be goin' to her again, Caesar."

Tom was sitting on a stump, whittling with his long razor knife. He looked up and laughed bitterly. "She'll be long gone wi' them slavers, you ninny. How'd a boy like you grow up so simple, Virgil? She was jus' honey to catch flies."

"How bad was the othuh, the *other*, one hurt, Virgil?"

"Jus' roughed up, I think. I kicked him pretty hahd in the weddin' tackle."

"So they won' be back after us right away?"

"No. No, Caesar. We safe fo' a whiles."

"Time to move again, though. We should go north. We haven't been north in a long time. If they send militia, they look fo' us down here, I think. An' we need to hit a farm."

Long Tom looked at the pistol in his lap. He hadn't fired a shot at the slave-takers, and he was in a mood.

"We should hit that farm that this fool an' the boy keep goin' to." He waved his hand. "They gave them slave-takers a home. Let's burn 'em out and take what we want."

Virgil stirred. "They got black folks, and them slaves has helped us and helped us. We burn that farm an' who's gonna pay for it? Them black folks. I say no. I say we steal something, or just ax for it from the ol' woman. But burn 'em out ain't fair."

"He got happy memories o' that place." Tom sneered. The others murmured assent. They wanted blood.

Caesar rolled off his fern pallet and looked around, his eyes still bloodshot.

"We will go to the farm. We will not burn it!" He looked around at the survivors. "If we burn it and kill the farmers, we will jus' draw the militia after us. Let's jus' take what we need an' git. We might make it free that way. Tom, you shut it. You jus' jealous that he got somethin' you didn'. Now everyone jus' go sleep. We'll do it tomorrow."

The survivors of the band grumbled, but they went. And Caesar, still miserable over the losses, puzzled to figure out why he was still in charge.

★　★　★

They moved well, the remaining men almost silent on the trail and then moving up to the back of the pole barn. There were no horses in the little paddock, and the only smoke came from the slave cabin. The white man wasn't pulling stumps, either.

Jim led the way to the back of the barn and then darted across the yard to the slaves' cabin, where he knocked quietly. Then he disappeared inside. He was gone long enough for Tom and Virgil to check their priming, for Caesar to start to sweat from the exertion. He was out of condition and needed to eat better. He was still thin. The size of his forearms startled and disgusted him every time he looked down—like sticks. The weight of the fowler on his arms was enough to make him want to lie down.

The door opened and an old black man emerged, clearly Bakongo, with Jim following behind and hopping along with excitement. The old man came up the edge of the barn and stopped, peering into the bush.

"No one heah but us, boys," he called, and Caesar moved carefully into the open, well covered, he hoped, by the two pistols.

"You do look a sight, mistuh," said the old man when he saw Caesar's scarecrow figure draped in rags. "You boys been livin' hahd!"

"That we have, old man." He *was* old, too, with most of his head white; yet he still glowed with vitality like a village elder. Caesar was respectful of his age and knew that Tom and Virgil would be the same.

"Since the man and missus ran off, we got bacon." The old man smiled. "Come in an' have some."

A regiment of slave-takers couldn't have stopped the rush for the cabin.

☆ ☆ ☆

"That scatterbrained gal left with those men," the old woman said while she laid another few slices of bacon on her griddle. Then she busied herself pouring the fat into a little betty lamp on the hearth.

"Ain't had this much fat since I can' remember when." She sounded almost smug.

"What abou' Sally, ma'am?"

"Don' you ma'am me, you cock turkey! She gone off with they louts wha' own her, and good riddance, though I mus' say she did work she didn' have to. They kep' her for her coney an' nothin' else, an' that's hard on any gal, so I shouldn' talk mean. But I ain't sorry to see her gone." She looked daggers at her man. He laughed as if it were a compliment and went back to entertaining young Jim. Long Tom was fast asleep, full of cornmeal cakes and bacon, and Caesar had a hard time staying awake himself, although it was clear that Virgil still wanted to know where his Sally had gone.

"Why'd the white folks here run off?"

"Afeared! An' of you, I reckon. You hurt that mean little fella bad. He los' an eye an' I'm not too sure but he'll die. That othuh one, that big fella . . . He was beat! Lef' heah like a whipped cur. Said there was twenny of yous, an' you was right behin' him. The man, he jus packed his mule and tol' us to stay put an' lef'. But we heard othuh tales from Sally, too."

The old woman's head shot around. "What othuh tales, missuh? What you heah fro' that gal that I don' heah?"

"You don' know everythin', now, do you, Sukey?"

"I don' take gals fo' no rides in the hay, now, do I? An' that gal young enough to be my granddaughter? I imagine she said things under her shift that she don' say to no ol' woman with a hoe."

The old man just shook his head and chuckled.

"I think you tryin' to flatter me, woman." He looked at Caesar. "Sally says that they's rumors that the governor in Virginny is gon' free the slaves to fight for him agin' the farmers. You know 'bout that?"

"We heard something like that back some months."

"Yeah, well, now seems to be fo' sho'. Sally said they was gon' have a proclamation in Williamsburg. I ask her how she know and she jus' rolls that bottom and smiles."

"They slave-takers came heah fro' Richmond. They knew a few things, too."

"They said they came to take the bounty 'cause all the militia is gettin' ready to go aftuh the governor."

Caesar tried to assimilate all this. He tried to sound the old man out on the sides forming up in this war, but to the old man it was just the governor and his soldiers against the back-country farmers.

"Same thin' happen a few years back," he said, leaning forward over the hearth to light a pipe. The night was dark and the cabin completely without light except the little betty lamp burning a scrap of rag in the fat above the fire's last coals. It was deadly hot in the cabin, but no one seemed to want to leave it for the cooler outdoors, at least not while there was well water, tobacco, and bacon to be had.

"Farmers down south decided not to pay the Carolina Assembly taxes. They got an army together. Then Tryon, he the governor, he gets an army loyal to the assembly an' kicks they tails right back into the mountains. He threatened to arm the slaves, too. But he didn'."

"Will Dunmore do it? Will he free an' arm the slaves?"

"I don' know him that well, boy!"

Tom laughed in the half darkness on the other side of the hearth.

"Virgil? Tom? What do you say?"

"Say to what?"

"That we get us going up to Williamsburg an' see if we can join Governor Dunmore?"

Tom laughed his cynical laugh. "Then we can be the militia an' hunt white boys in the swamp! We'd be good at it, too."

Virgil was less assured. "Long way to Williamsburg. Lot o' bad men between heah and theah."

The old man's face showed for a moment in the dark as he sucked on his pipe and the coal glowed.

"You jus' go quiet, you be all right, I reckon. If all the white folks is as scared as these"—he waved his pipe toward the larger cabin—"an' you take care, you ought to get theah."

"Don' have to decide tonight," Caesar said, walking to the door in search of a breeze. But he had already made up his mind.

✫ ✫ ✫

"You jus' wan' go an' follow that gal!" Long Tom's head hurt and he was not happy that they were heading straight off in the morning, away from what he saw as free food and an easy life.

Virgil so obviously wanted to follow the girl that it was pointless to argue. Caesar left them to it and went to the white cabin, where he lifted the latch and went in. There wasn't much left but the furniture and some food, although he got enough powder in a keg to fill his horn and the little mermaid horn, as well. And he took the man's clothes. They didn't fit him well, and the breeches were almost like trousers, the man had been so tall. He hadn't left any shoes, and he'd taken his greatcoat. There was a small woman's cloak, and Caesar took it. Virgil hoisted out a side of bacon and cut it in half with a sharp little ax he found, and gave the half of it to the old black couple.

"Tell 'em we held you at gunpoint." Tom laughed. "Stand and deliver the bacon!"

Young Jim picked up a shovel and an old pack, which they filled with cornmeal and made him carry. With the cornmeal and the bacon, they were good for five days, more if they skimped, though Caesar doubted that they would. He had them on the road before the sun was very high, walking quickly as the shadows shortened and the bugs came out.

Somehow the stinging ones seemed thicker on the little one-hump trail than in their own heart of the swamp. Jim, used to moving unencumbered along the trails of the swamp, thought he was going to drop under the burden of the pack and the torment of the bugs.

Every time they heard a sound they melted into the woods, turning ankles on roots in their hurry to clear the road, but they never saw another soul, and by the end of the long day they were too tired and footsore to care. None of them had even a scrap of shoe left, but the swamp had not hardened their feet even enough to deal with the soft mud that made the road for most of its length, as it still had rocks and pebbles and gravel where farmers had filled the wettest spots.

They passed six farms, most of them new. All were abandoned. One farmer had left his slaves, but they were as scared of Caesar's runaways as they were of whites and wouldn't unbar their doors. At the last empty farm, they tried the door but found the bar across, and slept well in the barn. An early winter rain on the shingles woke them, but they were dry. Jim built a little fire that barely smoked the rafters and made bacon, and they wasted the day. Caesar encouraged it; they were as safe as they ever might be again, and dry and well fed, and he needed the rest. They had come a long way the first day. They had a very long way to go.

The third morning they moved on again. Their track was punctuated with crossroads and bypaths that confused them more and more. When the road forked or offered a branch, Tom or Virgil would run off down it a bit and come back and describe what he had seen. Then they would all decide, although Caesar's vote began to hold more and more weight as he was proven correct. He wasn't infallible, and one of his choices came to a dead end in a clearing with a tiny plot of vegetables and the start of a cabin. It had been abandoned, and wasted them a mile of walking, but it was well off the road and safe, and he decided that they would make camp there. They built a big fire and piled brush over the cabin's base to make a hut. Caesar got two rabbits with as many shots—a poor use of powder, but he had enough for the moment and refused to worry overmuch. The shots were loud in the wild silence and somehow made him tense, but he was tired of the bacon and wanted to make it last. They were wandering lost at the edge of the Great Dismal Swamp, and until they got clear, he would be worried about the food and the threat of pursuit.

It wasn't a good night, but it wasn't impossible to sleep, although

Caesar's new breeches had chafed him unmercifully and he couldn't find a way to lie easy. They didn't fit at the crotch at all. None of them had a needle and thread, either; that was all gone with Old Ben. They talked about him and Lolly, and even Fetch—all their dead. Caesar worried a little about Jim; he was seeing too much death for his age. He wouldn't be right later. But the boy seemed cheerful enough, delighted with the notion that he was going to be a soldier. It was a cold night, and they had no blankets. They all huddled in a ball together and slept by turns, those on the outside too cold to sleep, those on the inside warm but crushed.

In the cold and wet of early morning, it was hard to get them to move. The walking kept taking its toll, and the tedium of constant anxiety was sapping their desire to go to Williamsburg at all. They were all tired from bad sleep, and a little hungry all the time. The wet was new. Their camps in the swamp had been snug. The rain was hard on their brush shelter and beginning to drip through, the drops cold on Caesar's skin as he considered the others, mumbling to each other as they tried to crawl deeper into the shelter for warmth. He let them lie awhile, and the rain brought warmer air. Caesar stayed awake. Four days of walking and good food were building him up. He felt better than he had since the fever hit. After a bit he threw the woman's cloak over Jim and got up into the light rain and cleaned their pot with ash from the fire, a very rudimentary job. Then he wiped down his fowler, checked his pouch, gathered their few belongings, and woke them all up. In a few minutes they were shambling off back up the track to the road, although Virgil had slowed them while he fetched a coal from the old fire and tried to get his pipe lit. As soon as they reached the road, they were faced with choices of direction.

Caesar looked at the three paths heading off into the endless trees. "They all go north now."

"Right enough." Tom had a strong sense of direction.

"Williamsburg is north and then some."

"And across the bay, too. How we gon' cross the bay?"

"Deal with that when we get to it. I reckon we can get a boat, or steal it."

Caesar looked at the three trails and reached out for Virgil's pipe, which was lit and making the round. He didn't usually smoke, but it helped his energy, and it kept the flies at bay. "I figure it's time to go east a bit. So we take the right."

No one argued, and off they went.

By the end of that day, Caesar was tempted to head across country even if it meant facing the wet edge of the swamp. The trails and roads at the edge of the cultivated parts of Virginia were so unmarked, so empty, and so winding that he feared they might be going in circles. The added fear of discovery settled the issue. After a warm camp and no rain, they set off across country the next day, leaving the rough roads. The shortage of food that now worried Caesar was a cause for Jim's secret rejoicing; the wallet of cornmeal was three-quarters empty and no longer hurt him to carry. Virgil's quarter of bacon was well down, too, although it still drew a cloud of flies every time they stopped.

Perhaps because of the lightened loads, or perhaps because they really were out of the swamp, they moved north quickly, and nightfall found them on the edge of a big plantation, the first they had seen. Caesar gave the word, and after a hasty meal in the woods they moved in the dark across the fields. No dogs barked, although the houses they saw now were lit. They clutched their guns and moved as quietly as they could, every one of them conscious that capture with a gun in hand would mean certain death. When they were too tired to go farther, Caesar kept them at it past several lesser farms until they reached a wooded break extending off into the dark on both sides. The trees were large, and Caesar thought the area had been left for the master to hunt. All the better. He led them in on a deer path, and in an hour the rising sun found them buried in fresh fall leaves, warm and asleep.

He wouldn't risk the smoke from a fire when they awoke. They grumbled, but thirst drove them out of the woods before the sun was fully set, and they slipped down to the stream at the base of a long shallow ridge. The water was brackish and muddy from recent rain, and Caesar didn't want to drink it, but he did. They all did. The sun went down in a blaze of color, somehow startling after the swamp. Sunsets happened in the swamp, but far away above the ever-present trees. The open country stretched away, beautiful and alien after the limited horizons they had lived with for months. They all stopped together in silent wonder. They sat on rocks under the bank of the little stream and watched the sun until the western sky showed only a faint trace of pumpkin afterglow and stars, and then Caesar led them away.

They moved in better moonlight that night, as the half moon was tending toward full. Caesar couldn't remember the moon waning, and he could only figure that he had lost some time in his fever. Superstition and the sunset tried to tell him that time might pass differently out of the swamp, where things were open and it was harder to hide.

He didn't want to try the loyalties of other slaves as they passed plantations and farms. He was afraid of betrayal and afraid that any slave who helped him would be dead if his own little band was caught and questioned. But as they headed a little east and stayed parallel to the road he knew they needed a fire and food. They had about one good meal left.

★ ★ ★

He led them east for half a day and got into some trees along another little muddy creek. It was miles from the nearest house and the country seemed wild. The last plantation was two days behind and they had seen only scattered cabins. Caesar judged it safe to build a small fire and cook the rest of the bacon. He risked a shot at a goose on the water, which Jim swam out and retrieved. They didn't do a thorough job of cooking the goose, but it was fatty and it fed them, with the bacon as a breakfast, and corncakes to fill in the nooks and crannies. Grumbling decreased immediately, although Caesar knew they were at the end of the food.

He had a hazy idea that Williamsburg was on the other side of the bay; that much he remembered from the day when he had sailed into the Chesapeake as a new slave. He had no idea how they were going to cross that huge body of water, and he knew that it was miles around and with many inlets, bays, and rivers, all populated by slave owners. This was Tidewater, the heart of plantation country. By comparison, the Great Dismal Swamp was a haven. They were going to need food before crossing the bay. Caesar felt that the obvious solution would be to kill and butcher a big animal like a deer, if any could be found, and he was out early looking at the ground. What he found was both good and bad.

They were all awake when he returned, a tiny fire burning among the roots of an old oak. The smoke ran right up the tree and got lost among the branches, a good trick they had learned in the swamp. It didn't cover everything, though.

"Smelt that fire a mile away," he commented acidly as he entered their little camp.

"We kept you some tea, an' it's hot," said Jim. He didn't seem apologetic for the fire. They didn't really believe that anyone would be looking for them, thought Caesar. Every one of them had been pursued, or had fought the slave-takers, and yet they didn't really believe.

"There's tracks down by the creek," he said. "Man tracks, in boots."

"Dogs?" asked Virgil. He was suddenly more alert.

"No dogs. But three men, moving fast. They went off north and east, the way we have to go."

"Boots means white men," said Tom.

"That it do. I saw deer tracks, too, over the hill."

"Can't shoot no deer while there's men out there."

"I'm goin' to see if I can do jus' that, friends."

"We should all go."

"Nope. I'll take Jim. He's the quietest. Virgil, you an' Tom stay here, don' make much fire, and keep your ears open. We need a place to go if we get spotted. Build us a frame to hang a deer and sharpen the knives. We need the meat an' I'm goin'."

It was a long speech, for Caesar. He sounded firm and decided, and none of them saw much point in arguing. It was the way he had—sure of himself, and sure of others. Jim followed him with the eagerness of a young dog, and Virgil rubbed out the little fire. Tom pulled out his razor knife and picked up a branch.

Tidewater, Virginia, October 1775

George Lawrence was a picture of martial ardor. He wore a fine blue coat with scarlet facings, like the Virginia Provincials had worn under Washington in the war against the French except cut in the latest style, with narrow lapels and less cloth everywhere. Followers of the military arts knew that this style reflected the growing military passion in Europe for all things Prussian; Frederick the Great had decreed that there would be less material in coats.

Lawrence had never paid much attention to his Latin or Greek, and his knowledge of mathematics was not on the firmest ground, but he had devoured all the military science that the booksellers of Williamsburg and London had to offer, against the day when he would don a uniform. And now he commanded a company in the Virginia Militia. It was a start on his path to better things. In Boston, George Washington, another Virginian, was the commander in chief of a real Continental Army, the regular army of the colonies. Lawrence aspired to command a company in that army. To win the trust of Virginia would require success in Virginia and money. That started right here, at the recruiting table, where he was completing his company with any decent body he could get to sign the bill and take his bounty. Not every company offered a bounty, but he had the money, and it allowed him to pick and choose a little more.

His recruiting table sat in the yard of the King's Arms Tavern, the best tavern in the town. No one else had yet seen the humor in the conflict between the name and his purpose, but he smiled every time he looked at the sign. Englishmen—that is to say, bankers and brokers—had driven his father to bankruptcy, broken them as a family, and taken their plantation. Patient work and a great deal of luck had restored the family fortunes through trade, but George never forgot the attitude of his father's London brokers. They were greedier than Indians, and more rapacious. That is how Lawrence saw Parliament in London: as a group of brokers and bankers seeking to do unto America as Bailey and Callis, Brokers, of Bristol, had done to his family. He would raise men at the King's Arms, but the arms they would bear would be against the king.

On his table lay broadsheets advertising the rates of pay and a rather hopeful view of the possibility of land grants at the end of the war, as well as the bounty and the country's need. His best sergeant, Rob McCoy, sat behind the table in the same blue coat with red facings, a powerful image of martial splendor. Behind him stood Lawrence's drummer, a young black, in reversed colors, a red coat with blue facings. Few of the militia companies had drummers, and even fewer had the money to ape European professionals and provide their musicians with reversed-color clothing, but Lawrence was a stickler for such things. Besides, the boy was free and quite a talented drummer; with the coat, he got as many admiring stares as the sergeant.

Captain Lawrence nodded at the drummer, young Noah. "Point of war."

That was the black boy's great talent; he had actually spent so much time around the military camps that he knew most of the military beatings. He could beat for firewood details and signal officers' call. He lengthened his captain's reach beyond the sound of Lawrence's already powerful voice. Lawrence spoiled him, because next to his veteran sergeant, the boy was the most valuable member of his company.

The boy smiled and the drumsticks flashed as he raised them beside his head, held them rock steady for a moment, and then brought them down like thunder on the taut skin of the drumhead. He rattled through the point of war like a regular army drummer, and every head on the street turned to watch.

"Serve your country and earn the bounty!" called McCoy. A piece of silver flashed in his hands.

"Five shillings hard specie! Drink to Virginia on the colony's money! Preserve your rights against the grasping king! Drive Dunmore into the sea!"

It was as much excitement as the market town had seen in a long time. Rural Virginia didn't see a great many fine laced coats, or drummer boys, or martial sergeants. Men began to come around, reading the proclamations and broadsheets on the table from a safe distance.

The first recruit they attracted here was typical: George Lake, an apprentice. He was healthy and fit, not indentured, and had enough teeth to bite a cartridge. He didn't own his own weapon, which cost him part of his bounty, but he still got two shillings and a place to sleep. He looked intelligent and delighted to be part of the army. Once Lawrence had his name on the books and had given him his bounty in cash, he asked the young man if he would stay with the company if it were taken into the Continental service. The boy replied that he was sure he would.

"I do long to see the world."

"Can you read, George?"

"I can read some, sir."

Lawrence let him go, wishing he could have a dozen such. The boy left, glowing, to find more friends to join.

After the first man tested the waters, there was a rush—a mix of patriotism and economic necessity, as the poorer classes who had been hardest hit by the troubles with England rushed to the bounty and the hope of regular pay. There were other recruits, too: several decent yeomen's sons, and one young man who himself owned property, a small farm in the local red soil. Lawrence took him aside and ascertained that he came from the Carters, a distant relation, and that his people were prominent in this part of the county. Lawrence was holding his lieutenant's commission vacant for a friend, but he was allowed two ensigns. He had heard that some of the militia companies were electing officers and sergeants, but he had no intention of letting such rot spread in his own company. He wanted them to be like regulars, and hoped that he would be able to place the whole company on the Virginia establishment or, better, the Continental establishment, when he had filled his roster. So it was natural enough that, although this young farmer was willing to join in the ranks, Lawrence took him aside and offered him a commission, which the man instantly accepted.

He filled a platoon in the morning, although a few of those who took the bounty were sorry men who would make dismal soldiers. Most, however, were strong men, farm labor, with some experience of arms, or eager boys like George Lake. Lawrence liked Lake. Good material.

The afternoon was slower, as he expected it would be. Most who would join did so in the first rush; those who went home to have a think seldom came back. The original militia raised by the counties had all the best local men already; it was the additional companies that had to be completed in this difficult and expensive way. Lawrence was already doubting what he had heard, that the Continentals were going to have to recruit from scratch as well, and not out of the militia. Farms still had to be farmed, and magistrates could not all go off to be officers.

He sat well back from the table and drank sherry as the afternoon wore away, unaffected by a pint or so, and tolerably happy with the success he had. At two by his big silver watch he went in and dined, and sent good meals out to the sergeant and the drummer. By three they were all tempted to doze off, and Lawrence kept the drummer at it to keep them awake.

"Find us a fifer, lad!" he kept saying. "There must be a blackie here who can play the fife!"

And the boy would smile, a little shy, and look away.

Sergeant McCoy thought that they should take their recruits and march away. "Rendezvous at the camp is in two days' time."

"We can get there in a day, Rob, and every man we have at muster is going to be gold when we have to fight. This town's been good to us; give it the afternoon. And don't be in such a rush to leave the comfort of a bed. Especially when it comes with something in it, eh?"

McCoy laughed mechanically. The captain may have had something bouncy in his bed; all McCoy had for companionship were little biting bugs.

"Let's see if we can't complete the company. We'll march in the morning."

Just after three, two men rode up to the tavern on spent horses. They looked badly used: One had his face swathed in dirty bandages, and the other rode with his knees up so high that he looked like an old sack on a tall horse. The two men had a look of meanness that might have deterred normal approaches, but it was like an invitation to the recruiting sergeant.

"Do you gentlemen fancy five free shillings hard currency?" Sergeant McCoy held up his big fist with the money.

The taller man smiled a little. "Milishee?"

"That's right."

McCoy could see that there was old dried blood on the filthy bandage that the smaller man had on his face.

"Could have used you boys in the swamp. Had a set-to with some runaways."

"We aren't being raised for slave-taking, friend. We're raised to fight the governor, drive the British out of Virginia."

The taller man nodded. "Regular pay, though?"

"Regular as clockwork, friend, and paid every week. Victuals at the colony's expense and the best of living for every soldier."

"Save it, Sergeant. I've served with the milishee before, an' so has Mr. Weymes here. No one ever offered us no bounty, though. I think we'll sign."

"You both have your own weapons?"

"Yep."

"And horses?"

"You ain't blind, is you? Them's our horses, then."

The other man opened his mouth and then shut it, like a fish. No noise came out for a moment, and then he opened it again. "Our black girl runned off."

"Pay him no mind."

"They the milishee, Bludner. You tell 'em about our black girl, Sally."

"We're joining the militia, Weymes, and we'll find her in our own spare time."

"Make your mark, here, and here. And I'll sign for your horses and arms."

"I don' have to make no mark, boyo. I can sign my name."

Lawrence had never liked back-country ruffians, and he stood up smoothly and walked forward. "If you want to serve in my company, keep a civil tongue in your head."

Bludner looked at him, meeting his eye unblinking. They stared at each other for just a moment—too long, in Lawrence's book, but not long enough to count as open defiance. Then Bludner bowed his head, a quick, jerky motion—a man who retreated before superior social position but reserved judgment.

"I'll ax your pardon, then, sir. Didn' mean no harm. Just plain talk. I ain't ignorant."

On the whole, Lawrence liked him now that he had retreated. And men who could read and write were too rare. Perhaps Bludner would make a corporal; he had the skills. The little man looked like death, though, and Lawrence didn't think he'd last long.

Virginia, October 1775

They didn't really follow the deer tracks, as Caesar had a strong idea that the deer were headed across the little creek and up the flat ground toward the next little wooded ridge. He could neither see nor smell a cabin, and yet the fields looked like they had been tilled at one time. They might have been overused; Caesar knew tobacco could play the soil out. But it seemed odd that Washington and others were trying to drain the Great Swamp while there was good ground like this right near the coast. It didn't stand to reason. The red earth showed through the early fall stubble of browned grass, and weeds shot through with the still-vibrant green of autumn thistle. He followed the deer by watching the ground, sometimes confirmed by bent grass and the occasional deep mark in the soft soil.

The deer had stopped suddenly; that much was plain. Caesar thought he knew why and in a moment the smell of blood and ordure made it obvious. Someone else had killed the deer, right here. Caesar suddenly felt hunted himself, down in the low ground between two ridges, and he was stooped to the ground in the dry grass before he had given it any thought.

Jim flattened out beside him. "I smell smoke."

Caesar had scented something several times, well away to the north, carried on the wind. He wouldn't call it smoke just yet. "I smell something, right enough."

"Someone else killed our deer."

"Like the man who owns the ground. Shush now."

He lay still for a while as the morning passed away toward noon, and nothing seemed to move. He felt hunted, and he couldn't lose the feeling. He had checked his priming too many times. He had to move, although his instincts were to lie low.

Or were they telling him that the threat was to the camp? He was suddenly haunted by the image of the slave-takers appearing during his fever. He couldn't let that happen again. He raised his head, and a little eddy of breeze brought him another smell of fire.

"Somethin' burnin'." He nodded over the ridge. "We got to know. Stay quiet."

He moved as quickly as he could over the rest of the autumn grass to the base of the ridge and started up it, his heart easier with cover over his head and his back. It was pure panic that led him to worry about Tom and Virgil; no one could have got round him and Jim, leastwise not with enough men to take his friends. He climbed up the ridge, his legs pumping him over fallen timber, his footsteps light on the leaves and broken branches. Jim was just as quiet. When they crested the hill, they saw a line of fires off west, less than a mile away and mostly showing as smoke in the afternoon light. Beyond the line of fires was a low ridge with cabins, tents, and brush huts, and another line of fires. As far as they could see at the distance, there were no patrols.

"Is that the governor's army?" asked Jim. He sounded eager.

"I don't think so. I don't see no red coats." It struck Caesar then that if the governor had enough redcoats, he wasn't going to need black soldiers. "We need to get closer."

The ridge gave an excellent vantage point of the ground to the north, and Caesar saw another, several miles away and even higher. He crept back away from the opening he had used to look north and across the summit to the south side, where he could clearly see the little creek and the small ridge where Tom and Virgil were. Then he looked out to the east, where the ground was broken by patches of cultivated land and woods. He slipped back into the cover on the north slope and lay there for almost half an hour, watching the sun angle change and the movement in the distant camp. Men came on horseback, and tiny figures moved about, although no one seemed particularly on guard.

At his feet, a tiny watercourse ran into some low ground to the northwest. Beyond that, across a few hundred yards of muddy fields, was a patch of woods, the woodlot of a small cabin well off to the west.

"Jim, you go on back to the boys and tell them to be ready to move. We'll be going hard tonight and there won't be no food unless they gets it themselves."

Jim nodded soberly.

"I think that's the militia, a whole army of slave-takers." Caesar nodded his head. "Gon' make sure, and meet you back to camp."

"I could come with you."

Caesar smiled. He suspected that Jim could do this better than he could himself, but he couldn't order a boy to do something like that, because Jim would do it in a flash, with no thought to the consequences.

"You could," said Caesar, and smiled broadly, to show that he understood the boy's point. "But you ain't."

☆　☆　☆

He moved briskly enough down the face of the ridge and into the muddy rill of water. The brush along its bank was still green and gave good cover, but the muddy water was colder than he had expected. The bottom was mud and gravel, and as he approached the low marshy ground he found the creek bottom turned to pure mud. He sank in a hole so deep that it took him several moments and a great deal of thrashing to free himself. He crawled out into the night air, and the breeze cooled him more, so that his teeth chattered. Then he moved, crouched right down, around the marsh; he couldn't stand to be any wetter, even if he risked detection. He crossed the open ground at a run and entered the trees with relief. Had he been more experienced in the ways of armies, he would have expected the militia to have a post in the wood to cover the rear of their camp, but his luck was in and his inexperience was shared by the summer soldiers. There was no post.

Nonetheless, men were moving on the other side of the wood. Caesar lay silent for minutes, his body heat seeping away into the damp ground, before he crawled forward a little and realized that all the movement was that of men going to and from the downed trees along the northern edge of the wood that they used as latrines. That made him smile; men are seldom at their most alert when dealing with such fundamental issues.

He crept closer. There were no sentries, but the conversation of two men using a latrine told Caesar that this was the encampment of Virginia Militia. He gathered from their conversation that they had been digging trenches and that both wanted to be home getting their crops in. Mostly it was griping, little different from the daily staple of Virgil or Tom. But a third man, noisily settling himself on another downed tree, brought the real news; he had been with a patrol and seen the enemy camp—the governor's camp—which he indicated was not too far to the north.

Caesar had a long way to go to get back to his friends. He ran across the open field, slipping twice in the mud, running as much for the warmth as for the speed. He leapt the creek and headed straight up the ridge, pulling himself up the steep slope by grabbing the smooth trunks of smaller trees in the failing light. He paused at the top, half afraid, perhaps expecting Jim with bad news or an ambush on his back trail. He was conscious that he was going back exactly the way he had set out, a serious mistake, but he didn't know another way and didn't want to waste the time finding one in the gathering gloom.

Once down the other side, though, he felt free, and he was almost unwary as he began to cross the open ground to the south. The smell warned him just in time—the fresh smell of a dead animal. That deer carcass wasn't too far away. Then he heard the movement and he froze, his fowler coming up to a line with his eye and pointed at the sound. He moved to his left, cautious now, his heart thumping away like horses' hooves in his chest.

Wolves or coyotes. Maybe dogs. They were all bad, if they caught you alone. And his one shot might not slow them, might just bring something worse, like militia. He kept walking off to his left, the fowler tracking the tearing, rending noises. It sounded like fiends from hell ripping bodies asunder—too many for one poor deer carcass. Caesar shivered again and moved a little quicker, back to the small creek and then up the side of the ridge he'd made camp on last night. He smelled fire and thought he smelled roasting meat, which made him suspicious. He was so worried that he crawled right up on them and listened for a minute to make sure that slave-takers hadn't left an ambush for him, but it was just Virgil griping nervously to Jim about how late he was.

He wanted to say something about the fire, but he was so cold that he needed it, and he was so relieved to see them that he wanted to hug them all. There, at the base of the last hill, with the wolves close, he had thought it might be some dreadful devil's trick to let him hear how close they were to the governor's army and then take his hope away. With warm tea in him and a blanket on his shoulders, he almost had to cry, but he covered it.

"Governor's army isn't far, friends." He looked around at them in the flickering light of the tiny fire. "We gon' make it tonight, or we won' make it at all."

They nodded. They could all see that wherever he had been, it had been a hard place—not just in the cold, but something in his face.

"I got a rabbit," said Jim.

"How'd you do that?" asked Caesar. "I didn't hear a shot."

"Damn thing walked into here bold as brass, just as the light started to go. Jim gets up nice and slow, then *fzzt!* And he's off after the thing."

"Caught it, too," said Virgil. "Never seen nobody catch a rabbit with their bare hands."

Jim drank in the teasing praise. "You said we needed food, an' we'd have to catch it ourselves, so I did."

Caesar sucked the marrow out of a bone and shook his head.

"Never seen *nobody* catch a rabbit with their bare hands," Virgil said again.

☆ ☆ ☆

The moon was just rising when he started them north, even farther east than the night before. He aimed for the little ridge he had seen, but he wanted to make a big circle around the militia camp, going well east, and come back on his ridge. He had done such navigations in the swamp with mixed success, but the moonlight helped, as did the rabbit. By the time he had been moving for an hour, he was warm again. They were in the low ground where he had seen patches of cultivated land. He thought from the furrows that it was slave-cultivated, not tobacco but food. The slave cabins must be close but he hadn't seen them and he guessed they must be farther east, nestled up against an invisible plantation house. He kept moving, his little band right on his heels in Indian file.

The rabbit was just a memory by dawn. The men had been on their feet for nine hours, and they had started short on sleep. They were done. The rising sun was at their backs, as Caesar had hoped, as they moved west, aiming for the slope of what he still thought was the ridge he had spied while he watched the militia camp. He led them quickly despite their fatigue; more and more he used speed to cross open spaces instead of stealth. When they were in among the trees on the ridge's wooded slopes, he felt as safe as he permitted himself to feel.

"We'll get up to the top and take a break," he said, glancing north through a break in the foliage.

"Thought we was gon' get to the governor tonight," Tom said.

Caesar nodded. "We didn't. I hoped we'd find him out to the east, but he's still north. I think I smell some smoke out there." He waved his arm. "I'll go see. You stay here and rest."

Caesar had some energy left, from some reserve he always seemed to cache away, and he left them in a hollow on the wooded ridge. He thought he could see the Chesapeake in the distance.

He was light-headed, and for a bit he just stopped and breathed, afraid that he might have the fever again. But his breathing steadied and his mind was clear, and he kept on across two fields that had been in wheat and one with corn stubble all the way across. He had to burrow through the hedges where they had been allowed to grow, and suddenly he was at the edge of a road and men were talking on the other side of the trees—white men. There were more fires, the fires he had smelled from the ridge. The hedges covered their smoke.

He slipped into the trees and crawled forward until the men were clear, backlit against their fires. He paused for a moment to think how foolish they were to put the fires behind them in the dark; but they clearly had sentries, and the fires helped him see that the sentries were soldiers in coats, and the coats were red. The local civil war was anything but straightforward, but Caesar was sure enough that men in king's coats had to be the governor's men. Their fires and their sentries faced the militia, a few miles away. He moved forward to the edge of the trees and watched awhile as the regulars changed their pickets and shivered in the fall air. One smoked and another cautioned him about it. The sun rose higher, and as it did, Caesar saw that the relief party coming down the track behind the sentries was composed entirely of black men in sashes, all armed with muskets. Their officer was white. He relieved the regulars and his own men settled in their places. They tended to talk more, and they all smoked. The officer sat down a little to one side, almost at the edge of the track, and opened a book. Caesar began to crawl that way, moving carefully but with joy rising inside him. Those men—black men, with muskets—weren't runaways, but black soldiers. *It was all true.*

He made it to the very edge of the trees, only fifty feet or so from the officer. Caesar didn't know why it was so important to get to the officer without being caught, but he moved as slowly as he ever had in the swamp, out from the protection of the trees and on to the field of high grass, golden in the autumn sun beyond. He stopped frequently to listen; he could no longer see the other sentries without raising his head. After a long time, he thought he had gone far enough, and he lay still a moment, gathering his strength and his courage, and then he rolled to his feet. One of the sentries saw him instantly, but the officer was a little slower, or just lost in his book, and when he glanced up, he saw Caesar's wide smile very close to him. The man showed no fear, only lowered his book.

"Good day to you, sir," said Caesar, bowing, speaking carefully in a way he hadn't in months.

The man laughed. "Damn, that's civil. You a runaway?"

"Yes, sir."

"Speak well, I'll give you that. That your gun? You alone?" He seemed to be speaking for the benefit of someone else.

Caesar felt the sentry glide up behind him, but he held his ground and his smile. "I heard that any slave that joined this army was free."

"True enough." The man looked Caesar up and down. "I'm Lieutenant Edgerton. What's your business?"

"I want to join. There's others with me."

The man behind him put a hand on his shoulder.

"I know this boy," he said.

"Very well, Sergeant King," said Edgerton, his eyes going back to his book. "Enter him and see to his friends."

"Yes, sir." King smiled at Caesar and took his gun for a moment, looking at the priming and the state of the piece. Caesar stared in wonder. He hadn't expected to see King ever again.

King was all business. "How many with you?"

"Two men and a boy."

"Good as you?"

"They can all shoot. Even the boy."

"We get some every day. But not many as bring their own guns, nor can shoot."

"We've been in the Great Dismal."

"I'm sure you have tales to tell. Let's get your friends. Where ah they?"

"Over the ridge. Almost a mile."

"You came *through* the milishee?"

"Yes, sir."

"I'm *Sergeant* King. You say *Yes, Sergeant.*"

"Yes, Sergeant."

"Good boy." He turned back to the officer. "Permission to take a party of men and retrieve the rest of the recruits, Mr. Edgerton?"

"Carry on, King." King doffed his hat, a rakish round hat with several plumes, and then turned to Caesar. "Stay right here."

Caesar watched as he went past the picket and came back with a group of black soldiers. Some looked clumsy with their arms; a few looked dangerous.

"Fall in the marker. You, Jonas. Right. Fall *in*!" The men moved quickly into a fairly crisp imitation of the two precise ranks the regulars had used to march. King stood facing them, a big Queen Anne musket over his left arm like a sportsman.

"We ain't tryin' to impress the king here, boys. We're goin' to get a few o' this boy's friends, waitin' over the hill near the milishee. So we best go fast an' quiet, in a single file. If it comes to shootin', you jus' form a line an' follow me. Got it?" Everyone nodded, although several of the clumsy men looked so nervous as to be comical.

"I forgot your name, boy."

Caesar thought for a moment. "Julius Caesar."

"Very well then, Caesar. You're the scout. Take us to them."

Caesar's energy was renewed, at least for the moment; he could still feel the fatigue, but it was far down and he kept it there. He loped off, moving quickly through the woods and over the fields, trying to guide the little file of soldiers through the hedges as best he could. By the time he got to the hollow at the top of the wooded ridge, it was full day. All three of his men were lying at the bottom of the hollow, unmoving, and for a moment of heartbreak he thought they were dead, but then Jim's head came up and Tom pointed his pistol. And they saw the black men with muskets, and Tom smiled, and so did Virgil, and even Jim.

Sergeant King was looking out of the little wood down the ridge toward the militia camp. "You're no fool, Caesar. This is as good a watch post as I've seen."

Caesar thought that King had learned this new clipped way of talking from the white officer.

He told off all three of the dangerous-looking men and two of the clumsy ones, and told them to observe the militia until he sent a relief. "If you ain't heard nothin' when the sun is at noon, you jus' come back. If'n they attack you, jus' come back. Otherwise, stay here and learn what you can."

The dangerous men all nodded. Caesar went over to the largest; closer up, it was obvious he had been a sailor like King. He had tattoos all over his arms.

"There's a trail comes up from that creek. See it?"

The man squinted, then nodded.

"They didn't have no sentries out las' night, neither."

The sailor nodded at Caesar and smiled. "Thank ye."

And then they were going back down, past the hedgerows and the fields, through the wood, past the other sentries, and farther back, through another line of guards to a field covered in gray linen canvas tents. King took them all to an officer who asked them some questions, and when they left his big white tent each of them had a shilling and a paper chit.

People stopped and watched them because they looked so savage. Eventually this made it through their fatigue, and they began to be embarrassed. There were women in the camp, and quite a few were black, and several were bold enough to comment on Tom's breeches, or Caesar's.

"What's the paper say?" asked Tom. He liked the shilling.

"It says you are a soldier in the Loyal Ethiopian Regiment," said King, and he stopped at a firepit where a big group of black men and women were cooking. "This is your company. Listen up! These men run a long way to join, so treat 'em right. Your corporal is Mr. Peters, right here. Mr. Peters, this is Julius Caesar."

Caesar looked through his fatigue and saw a much older man, who nodded gravely.

"You lads hungry?"

They all responded.

"Well, that's about the only good thing 'bout being in the army." He had a curious accent, like a very educated white man. He was only the second African Caesar had ever heard speak so well. But Caesar was beyond curiosity just then, and when a mess kitty full of salt pork and thick pea soup was placed in his hands, he didn't stop eating until it was empty. When he raised his head, most of the men were gone, and his own three were asleep on the ground. Corporal Peters was watching him with a benign air.

"How long have you been on the run?"

"Near on six months, I think."

"You speak well. What were you, a house slave?"

"No, sir. I was a dogs boy."

"Those dogs must have spoke to you uncommon civil, then." The older man smiled at his own humor. "Get some sleep, lad."

Caesar was boiling with questions, but he was safe and well fed. He let his head slide down onto a forage bag full of straw. He fell asleep there, but his right hand was still wrapped around the wrist of his fowler, and the corporal smiled at him, shook his head, and lit his pipe.

Cambridge, Massachusetts, November 8, 1775

"It is curious that you and I share a name, is it not, William?" Charles Lee was leaning against the doorjamb, his coat fashionable, his hat in hand, watching Washington's black manservant powder his hair. Billy Lee had the mask over his master's face to keep the powder off and was dusting away industriously. He never could tell whether General Lee was joking or being serious, and he didn't like the game.

"Yes, suh. Very curious."

"Perhaps we have a parent in common, or are cousins."

"William does not appreciate this sort of humor, General, and neither do I." Washington spoke from under the mask. "It scarce does you credit, abusing a man who can't answer back."

Lee laughed his cynical laugh, two quick barks. "I think I'm perfectly civil. Inviting the fellow to be a relative ought to be taken as a compliment, I think. I certainly meant it so, Mr. Lee."

"Thank'a, suh."

"Think nothing of it. General, we have dispatches from General Arnold."

Washington's head came up eagerly, but he restrained himself as William Lee was just starting to club his hair. "You have the advantage of me."

"General Arnold is in good spirits and his advance guard is past the second portage to the Dead River. He's through the worst of the high ground and well on his way to Quebec."

Washington's breath escaped audibly. "We'll take Quebec yet."

"Please stay still, suh," said Billy quietly.

"Sorry, Billy."

Billy brought a freshly pressed black silk ribbon, three full inches broad, from the side table and brought it up under Washington's heavy club of hair. He began to tie it. Washington held his head perfectly still.

Lee spoke again. "General Arnold dated this the thirteenth of October. Did I say he's in good spirits, as are his men?"

"Does he give a return of supplies?"

"He notes near the bottom that he has provisions for twenty-five days."

"That's news worth hearing."

"I took the liberty of giving the messenger a few dollars. Added to General Montgomery's dispatches of yesterday..."

"We begin to show signs of having a winter campaign. It's far too early to be sure, but if we can take Canada..."

"...the war is won. No Canada, no bases, no place for their navy to anchor. Yes, sir. Of course, there is Governor Dunmore in Virginia."

"Nothing that need worry us. What do we have in the notes for today?"

"I'll send you Captain Hamilton, sir."

Washington's head emerged from the mask. His hair had just one curl to each side but was crisply clubbed at the back. The coat of silver-gray powder was exact and even and not a speck of it was on his dressing gown. William Lee helped him into his heavy blue and buff uniform. After he had his sword belt seated properly, Lee began buttoning on his heavy epaulets. Washington and Charles Lee wore virtually the same uniform, but each adorned it differently. Lee gave it an air of carefully planned unconscious elegance, while Washington lent it a spartan dignity. As Washington finished his toilette, they glanced over each other as if duelists measuring an opponent's prowess.

"Had any thoughts on provisions?" asked Washington.

"Only that it's time to make demands of the other colonies."

"And enlistments?"

"I expect we'll enjoy recruiting another army when this one marches away with all our equipment, but I'll be damned if I can think of a way to avoid it."

Washington looked pained when Charles Lee swore, but let it pass.

"I think the Connecticut regiments will stay."

"Perhaps, sir. Are you ready for correspondence? I have to be in the saddle. The 'line' regiments won't send in returns unless I bully their adjutants."

"I would like to deal with my household first. Ask Hamilton to wait and send me Mr. Austen."

If Charles Lee resented acting in lieu of a butler, he stifled it, smiled a very small smile, and bowed. "Your servant, sir."

William Lee waited until the room was clear, then started in on his master's neck stocks. He could trust the girls with the shirts, but stocks took a different touch.

Williamsburg, Virginia, November 8, 1775

"Make ready!"

Every man in the company held his musket barrel up by his left cheek and cocked it.

"Present!"

Every man brought his musket sharply down and aimed it across the field.

"Fire!"

Forty flints struck forty hammers and turned them over with a soft *click* and a shower of sparks. Most of the men immediately rotated on their heels until they were half turned to the right, and their right hands reached for their cartridge boxes. The white sergeant in the red coat walked along to one man who hesitated.

"Are ye ready to load then, lad?"

The young man instantly rotated on his heels and reached back. Other men who were slow at the drill did the same. Sergeant King stood behind the company, speaking quietly to the newest recruits in the center of the back rank, which included Tom, Caesar, and Virgil. Jim was so small he had to be in the front rank, but he was a fast study and it had been days since he had been reprimanded at drill.

"Prepare to prime and load. Handle your cartridge!" Forty hands reached in and removed a paper tube full of powder from the wooden blocks in their cartridge boxes. Less than half of them had boxes; the rest had various contraptions they had made themselves or that had been made for them by Williamsburg contractors. Then they bit off the top of the cartridge between their teeth and brought the now-open paper tube to the height of the pan on the musket's lock.

"Prime your pan." Every man poured enough powder to ignite the priming into the pan and raised his fingers to the back of the hammer, or frizzen.

"Shut your pan." Every man closed the L-shaped cock over the priming pan, and...

"Cast about."...rotated the musket smartly at a pivot formed by the swell forward of the lock, so that it was held, lock down and barrel up, in the left hand. The right still held the paper tube with the remainder of the powder.

"Charge with cartridge." The three ranks tipped the contents of the tube and the tube itself down the barrel.

"Draw your rammers." Every hand grasped the rammer at its iron tip and pulled as far as the arm could reach, then those same right hands moved quickly back down to the newly exposed base of the rammer and caught it there, "shortening" the rammer.

"Ram down cartridge." The shortened rammers were drawn fully from the pipes, rotated through a half-circle so that the iron tip was in the top of the barrel, and thrust strongly home.

"Withdraw your rammers!"

"Return your rammers!"

Now every man stood with a loaded musket held tight into his left shoulder. No ball, of course. The king was sparing of his lead.

"Make ready!" Sergeant King was pushing the new recruits at the rear.

"Lock up. Lock up there, Tom."

The white sergeant paced to the center of the line.

"Every man in the second rank should have stepped over. Every man in the first rank should be kneeling with his leg well back. Every man in the third rank should have stepped a little forward to lock up. You should be one machine, capable of delivering one fire. In battle, if the king should ever be so unlucky as to send you there, we will not be loading a step at a time. We'll only tell you to 'prime and load.' But this, the 'make ready,' is the most important step if this long fellow here is not to shoot off the ear of this little fellow in the front rank. Are they ready, King?"

"Yes, sir."

"Very well. Remember what I told you. Every musket comes down together. You all seem to have muscles. Use them. *Present!*"

Thirty or so muskets came down together. Most of the back rank was too slow.

"Not good enough. Back to the make ready!...*Present!*"

This time, the motion was, if anything, weaker than the last. The sergeant seized a musket from one of the front-rank men. "Look, you cretins. First, I'm at the make ready. Yes? Present! One swift motion. The left arm is actually pulling the musket down. If you execute the make-ready motion correctly, you will not hit your mates in front. Right. And again. Back to the make ready...*Present!*"

It was a passable effort and would not have disgraced most companies of volunteers in England. The sergeant let it go with a head motion that showed his gentle contempt for their best effort. *"Fire!"*

The volley, fired with blank squibs, was quite crisp. He did not praise it.

"Prime and load! Quickly! Faster, you idiot! You, the long one, step over, damn you. Cover your file leader! Faster. Six, five, four, three, two... Make ready!"

Most of them got it right. The white sergeant noticed that all the new recruits in the back were on the right foot, had their bodies in the right position. Perhaps King was coaching them, but what of it?

"Present! Do you want to shoot your mate in the back, coneyhead? Yes, you, you great gowk! Lock up! *Fire!*"

He walked back to King, who was standing behind Caesar in the rear rank. "Pretty sorry, King. But given a few years, we'll make soldiers of the survivors."

"Yes, sir."

"That very tall fellow needs some, shall we say, strong measures? He's going to be an embarrassment in the field. He's afraid of his musket."

"Yes, sir."

"Very well, then, King. Bring them along. We're parading with the battalion in a few minutes."

King paced out to the head of the company. "Company will form column by wheeling to the right by subdivisions!"

A murmur in the ranks as the men who knew what this meant communicated it to the ignorant. King was wise enough to wait it out. "By the right wheel! *March!*"

With surprising precision, the company split in two, and each small block wheeled through a quarter-circle to stand in a column. They shuffled uncertainly to a halt. King shook his head, chagrined. He should have told them to continue marching once the wheels were performed, but he couldn't admit it in front of the sergeant from the Fourteenth Regiment.

"At the quickstep! March!" The little column started forward.

In the rear rank of the second subdivision, Private Julius Caesar of the Loyal Ethiopian Regiment set his face and marched. His body was beginning to respond correctly to the commands, and he felt the first gleams of hope since the endless drill had started. Days of clumsy fumbling had reduced him to a deep frustration and anger, the more so as the white sergeant seemed to have no method of teaching but impatient repetition. He never called them *niggers*, but his contempt for them was not very well buried. He seemed to resent even having to drill them. Caesar felt it, and he knew that King and many of the others felt it, too. The drill was difficult enough without the added sting of the contempt that made every evolution seem like a test.

But as he began to master the drill, he began to understand better why it mattered. He could see how the big volleys of fire would replace the inability of most of the men to aim well, and he could feel how terrifying the volleys would be even aside from the execution they would reap. He began to enjoy drill. He also savored the changes in himself, wrought by daily exercise that included rest, good sleep, and regular food. The mattock wound in his leg was finally just a memory, and he thought he might get his speed back in time. His arms were filling out. He stood straighter than he had since the swamp. Girls looked at him when he strode by. And he wasn't alone. Virgil seemed stronger, and Jim had gained an inch and was filling out like an animal being fattened for market. Most of them had hats now, and their clothes were better.

Williamsburg residents still treated them like a raree show, coming to their doors or windows every time the battalion paraded there. The catcalls were mostly gone, although many of the residents made sure that every black soldier knew that they resented the arming and freeing of so many slaves. It was getting harder to find a slave in Williamsburg, and few of the middle-class families had avoided the consequence. Most of them had lost quite a bit of "valuable property."

Caesar's corporal, the well-spoken man, had been butler and majordomo to Peyton Randolph. Other men in the ranks with Caesar had been field hands or blacksmiths or house slaves belonging to Loyalists. None had been reluctant to join the British army to leave slavery. Governor Dunmore had hoped to raise a regiment of whites and a regiment of blacks, and the black regiment was growing faster, though it did alienate some of the white Loyalists. The whites were not coming so quickly, and the governor's detachment of regulars and marines was stretched thin trying to cover all the possible lines and train the new recruits.

Caesar glanced under his hat and saw that they were well up the green by the governor's palace and that two other companies of blacks were already drawn up there, as well as a detachment from the Fourteenth Regiment. Sergeant King halted them when they were aligned with the front marker of the second company.

"Company will form line from column by wheeling to the left by subdivisions." Caesar was prepared for this, could already see the result in his mind. These maneuvers were becoming clear to him, and their purposes, though many of them seemed slower than simply telling the men where to go. It was all about harnessing and controlling the firepower of all the muskets. Caesar understood that to the marrow. He still wondered about the power of individual men aiming carefully, but so few of the blacks were trained in the use of arms that they were unlikely to make good marksmen, and observation of the white militia had suggested that they weren't much better.

They were halted in line with the other companies. A white officer, not one he recognized, in an elegant brown velvet coat and a bright green silk sash, walked smartly to the front of the parade. He began to read from a proclamation and general order from the governor about martial law. Caesar understood it, but it didn't seem to have much to do with him. He spent a few moments thinking about "clubbing," or reversing the company, and why that was such a bad thing. His attention snapped back to the white officer when he coughed and his tone of voice changed.

"*I do require every person capable of bearing arms, to resort to his Majesty's standard, or be looked on as traitors to his Majesty's crown and government, and thereby become liable to the penalty that the law inflicts upon such offences, such as forfeiture of life, confiscation of lands, and etc. And I do hereby further declare all indented servants, Negroes, or others that are able and willing to bear arms, they joining his Majesty's troops, as soon as may be, for the more speedy reducing this colony to a proper sense of their duty, to his Majesty's Crown and dignity.*

"*Three cheers for his Britannic Majesty George the Third and an end to tyranny!*"

"HUZZAH!

"HUZZAH!

"HUZZAH!"

Caesar looked at Tom, who was beaming, and at Virgil, who looked very serious indeed. Jim was too far away, in the front rank, to be reached with a glance, but Caesar could see a little of his smile tightening the skin at his temples. They were free men—and soldiers.

Chapter Nine

Caesar had an eye for ground and a head for tactics, and he never doubted that they would be beaten. He could see that most of the white troops, the soldiers of the Fourteenth Foot, felt the same. They were quiet, looking at the enemy entrenchments across the bridge. No one seemed to doubt that they would be ordered to storm those lines, or that even the ragged militia would be able to kill them in the long narrow defile of the bridge. Caesar couldn't understand why they had to try, but he waited with the others in the cold morning light, where the dew was so heavy it seemed like rain. Everything was wet. He wiped his lock again, directed his file mates to do the same. Caesar was now a file leader in Corporal Peters's section; everyone said he would be a corporal soon enough. He liked that, and he tried to look out for his own. His file consisted of Tom and Virgil; Jim was next to him at the flank of the company, a place he held by both his small size and his competence.

The handsome officer in the brown velvet coat who had read the proclamation was from the third company. Peters called him "Mr. Robinson," and the two seemed to know each other. Caesar hadn't thought to ask, but the man seemed a good officer and his company was the best appointed and the best drilled. Their own officer, Mr. Edgerton, was not as wealthy, and seemed more interested in books than in war. He was still in

Williamsburg, down with the fever. That left King to command the company, a situation fraught with complication, as he was not invited to the meetings the white gentlemen held.

Mr. Robinson could be seen arguing vociferously with the two white officers of the regulars, a very young man and an older one. Both of them kept their voices down. King watched impassively.

"They gon' send us ovuh the bridge fuhst!" someone commented from the rear rank.

King glared back. "So what?"

"It's madness," Caesar murmured from the front rank.

"Their powder might be damp. They might be so scaret they can't shoot. Anything might happen. I done seen it at sea, boys. You don' know what the fight will be till you in it, and then it's too late to change you mind!"

He looked over at Caesar and nodded. "Course, it does help to have a better plan. But we ain't doomed."

Both men watched the movement of the militia over on the far bank. They didn't look scared.

Mr. Robinson came up to them and ordered the sergeants to wheel the Ethiopians onto the road, so that all his men were facing him. There were only about a hundred, less than a third of the regiment. The rest had been left in Williamsburg, for reasons not stated.

"Boys, we are going to follow the Fourteenth Foot across the bridge. They are regulars and better used to standing the fire, but I expect you to follow them with a will and fire as soon as you form line on the far side. I will lead you off myself. If I fall, you must look to Mr. Cowan and your sergeants. The Fourteenth officer is Mr. Crowse. Follow him as you would me. Remember that you fight for your king, and consider that your honor is the honor of your race. Please form the battalion in a column of half-platoons formed from the right, and remind the men of how to form to the left. Carry on!"

The noncommissioned officers moved through the ranks, reminding the men of what the maneuver would be if they crossed the bridge: each half-platoon marching up to the left to form on the one beside it. It was one of dozens of maneuvers they had practiced, and Caesar thought that if he had been in command he would have made the men practice it again. Although the verbal reminder helped all but the dullest, Caesar knew that most of the men in his platoon had only the shadiest notions of marching to an incline. He shook his head. It was interesting that the regulars were going first.

It was, to some extent, his second battle, and he was much better prepared than he had been for his first, far away at home against a sudden attack of slavers. He looked to the right and left at the men in his section and platoon and smiled a little, because he was young and such things touch the heart. He had been a leader since the swamp, and that meant that he had to wonder how many of them would die.

The regulars formed on the road ahead of them, and did it in a way they had not been taught; Caesar watched it curiously. They marched off by files from the center so that they were only two men across. Caesar couldn't see how they would re-form in a hurry, but they certainly looked crisp. Most of the men had reversed their hats and let down the back cock, so that they had a shade for their eyes; it made them look more like scarlet farmers than the usual crisp soldiers. They also talked more at the moment of battle than they did on parade. One fellow near the back turned and waved at Caesar and his men.

"See that you follow us, blackie! No shirkin'!"

Caesar remained silent as befitted a good soldier, a little ashamed that the white regular should have broken discipline, but Virgil leaned forward and shouted: "Leave some for us, lobsterback!" For some reason, the insult caused a number of the other white soldiers to turn and wave. It was an odd moment of camaraderie. Caesar wondered distantly where the white Loyalist militia was. Clearly they were less expendable than either the regulars or the blacks.

"We all gonna die," said one man from Robinson's company. "But I like that them white boys is gonna die first."

And then the regular officer raised his hand, and the column began to cross the bridge.

★　★　★

It was far worse than Caesar had imagined, because they didn't even get across the bridge the first time. They made it a little over halfway, and the wall of fire stopped the regulars. They took hits and slowed to a crawl, then stopped and began to fire back sporadically. No one ran, but no one seemed to be getting any farther. Caesar didn't even have his foot on the bridge yet. His impatience soared, sure, in his strength, that he could make a difference. After a few minutes of ineffective return fire, the regulars retreated in good order. They had lost men, and several were wounded. They were angry.

The Ethiopians were placed in front, but Robinson's company was first, and though they did a little better, moving faster across the bridge, they, too, were stopped by the volume of fire from the far side. Men were killed, or maimed, and they screamed. Caesar made it onto the bridge this time and began to hear the bullets making their whirring noise as they passed close enough to cause other men to duck. He couldn't fire, while other men in the column seemed to be shooting at the water, or nothing at all. The smoke actually gave them a little cover.

And then they retreated again, called back by their own officers when it was clear that they weren't going any farther. Both regiments had brought back their casualties, who were now lying in rows on the dry ground well to the rear, their calls for water and the mercy of God clearly audible above the fifes of the Fourteenth Foot and the popping of musketry from the far bank. The officers had a conference and the older regular officer, his arm in a sling, led his company to the front of the column. The men stripped off their packs, loaded their muskets, and looked grim.

King pointed to a young officer and an ensign with a handful of men from the Fourteenth. "Know what they call that, Caesar?"

"No, sir."

"That's a forlorn hope. Them boys is gon' run across as fas' as they can an' draw fire so that the rest of that company can get across."

Caesar watched them with wonder. The men were pulling off their coats and putting their waistbelts over their shoulders, giving all of them a faintly piratical look. The officer, barely old enough to be called a man, was whistling tunelessly and stabbing at things with his smallsword. He didn't seem afraid, and Caesar loved him for it, because he was certainly going to die. He seemed almost happy. He was fencing with a patch of ferns, showing off his skill, and he lunged, just decapitating the nearest of the plants, then turned and caught Caesar's eye. Caesar smiled uncertainly, and the boy smiled back, then turned and trotted to the head of his men.

There was no longer any joking among the men, and the redcoats were as silent as they had been in Williamsburg on parade. When the order was given, the young officer dashed across with his little party of men on his heels, and then the rest of the Fourteenth followed at the double. Caesar couldn't see what happened because he was in the column, but although the volume of enemy fire increased, the column didn't slow, and suddenly he could see figures in red on the ground in front of the entrenchments. He moved onto the bridge himself and then continued to jog forward. There was a sudden crash and it sounded like one of their volleys; he thought that perhaps the Fourteenth was across and firing. He was half-way, and the bridge was slick with blood from the men who had fallen in the first and second attempts. And the whole column slowed, but they seemed barely under fire. The enemy had a real foe to face now, he thought, and no time to waste on the bridge. The amount of blood on the bridge was a surprise. A man held about as much as a deer, it seemed.

The Fourteenth fired again, precise as on parade and fast, and then the column leapt forward for a moment and stopped, with Caesar and the front of his platoon right at the edge of the land. And just under him, his fine boots caught in the bridge, was the boy-officer, dead. His sword was gone, and one hand seemed to clutch the bank of the swampy ground.

The Fourteenth had formed well, and they were firing steadily, but both they and the entrenchments were so shrouded in smoke that neither seemed to offer any targets. The Ethiopians, whether from indiscipline or native spirit, had formed a loose line instead of the tight line of platoons they had been taught; and they were all intermixed, their ranks and files lost as the men had tried to push forward through smoke to fire their rounds. Caesar didn't hesitate, but led his own men to the left so that the line would continue to form. Mr. Robinson was simply encouraging men to load and fire, and not trying to form them up, so Caesar ran to his flank, stopped near a man from Robinson's company, and began to fire into the smoke.

The triumph of the rush across the bridge was short-lived. Inaccurate as the militia fire was, their superiority in numbers and the advantage of their entrenchments quickly began to tell. Caesar saw men fall around him, some hit badly enough to go down without a groan, a few unlucky ones screaming in anguish, and others, perhaps wiser, taking minor wounds and moving off quietly to the rear. The fire of the enemy never slackened, and Caesar began to doubt that they were hitting any of the rebels. He looked through the smoke and saw a regular officer go down, then stand again clutching his shoulder. He and Robinson stood together for a moment. Then Caesar's attention was brought back to his own narrow frontage, where it was obvious that too many men were down.

They were going to break and run.

A few, mostly younger men, began to edge back, some of them lightly wounded. When they reached the water's edge, they began to move more quickly to the bridge. Sergeant King stopped them.

"Stand still, you bastards. If'n you run, slavers will take you. Stay and fight!"

Caesar hadn't left his spot, determined to die. He cast his musket about crisply and rammed another round down the barrel. The younger men forced themselves forward, although most seemed to lie down or kneel, and few of them were firing. The fire of the Fourteenth Foot had slackened, too, and then it stopped.

"Regulars is retreating!" shouted one of the young men, hysteria plain in his voice. Caesar kicked him, hard, so that the man doubled over.

"Ethiopians!" a voice bellowed out of the smoke. "Two more rounds and we will retire. Make your shots count!" It was Mr. Robinson. He sounded old.

King was trying to form his own company. Caesar had no idea why, but the familiar voice in the smoke was giving orders that he could obey. Tom and Virgil were still with him, and he found young Jim and then Peters and then there were more men. Other men were firing sporadically.

"Everybody loaded?" A ragged volley of assent.

"Make ready!" Caesar knelt and his back foot kicked Virgil, who hadn't moved fast enough. All around Caesar, men were moving slowly.

"Present!" Caesar tried to snap his musket down, but he could see that some of the front rank were out of place, and other muskets late.

"FIRE!"

It was not a crisp volley, but it had a sound that seemed to lift some of the soldiers out of their fear. It was easier to be shoulder to shoulder in the smoke than strung out in a skirmish line, intentional or not. Closer, they seemed invulnerable, and they could hear the voices of their leaders.

"Prime and load!" Caesar rotated sharply and reached for a cartridge, his eyes trying to pierce the gloom in front of him. He dreaded a charge by the militia, now that the regulars were gone. He sensed that the men from the other companies were slipping away as well. He could see King, standing just beyond Jim in the smoke. Then he had cast his musket about and was ramming the cartridge down the barrel. The barrel was red hot and it burned his hands, and the smoke burned his throat. He had bitten the cartridge badly and had the foul stuff on his tongue. He raised his musket to the position that showed he was loaded. As he was one of the fastest to load, he had a moment to look around him. The smoke had cleared, just a little, in a flaw of the breeze, and they were alone, the redcoats drawn up in good order on the far side and a good deal of Robinson's company spread across the bridge in retreat.

"Make ready!" King's voice sounded louder in the sudden sunlight. The company functioned more smoothly, the men kneeling together in the front.

"Present!" Every musket seemed to come down together. It was an amazing feeling, like being part of a great beast of war. Smoke appeared from the enemy entrenchments, and men fell. King went down with a small shriek. He lay silent, but his arms were moving. The seconds stretched on unbearably, and Caesar breathed deeply and yelled, "Fire!"

They fired very much as one, a crisp volley that roared their defiance.

"Mr. Peters! Sergeant is down!" Caesar yelled. He slung his musket and, with Tom and Virgil, moved to King. The man was clearly alive, although a rifle ball had gone through his cheek and there was blood everywhere.

Peters began to order the men to reload, but Mr. Robinson, hatless, appeared beside him. "Back across the bridge, boys!"

The company melted away from the center in seconds as men fled at the best speed their legs could make. They had permission. It didn't seem necessary to wait for orders.

The little group carrying King were almost the last, although a few men stayed to cover them with sporadic fire, and one of them died. Mr. Robinson ran ahead, and then returned to urge them on. The bridge seemed shorter going back, even with the bulk of King, and soon enough they were placing him in the line of bodies that stretched away along the dry ground above the bridge.

And then they went back to where the remnants of the company waited and simply lay down. Later that day they marched away with their wounded and left the bridge to the victorious militia. They didn't talk much.

Cambridge, Massachusetts, December 11, 1775

"I think we'll keep most of those who are left," said Lee, adjusting his sword belt and watching General Gates with a lifted eyebrow. "Does that man consciously seek to imitate a clown?"

Gates was struggling with the collar of his greatcoat, and one of its capes continued to fly up in the wind and disarrange his hat. No such thing had ever been seen to happen to General Lee. He looked up, took note of Lee's regard, and flushed. There was little love lost between them.

Washington ignored Lee's pettiness about Gates. "I understand that the Connecticut men are ill-received on the road."

"I imagine their own sweethearts may spurn their charms when they arrive," Lee said with a certain sparkle in his eye.

Washington caught the look, considered carefully if he wanted to know the means by which the Connecticut regiments had suddenly become so unpopular, and decided that he did not need to know after all. Gates had his coat under control and was striving to sit his horse in the wind like a portly hero. Most of the officers of the staff were in their finest, although much labor on powder and hair was coming to naught in the wet wind.

The Connecticut men had signed on to serve the army and the siege of Boston until December. Washington had held them a few extra days until the Massachusetts and New Hampshire militias had come in to fill his lines, but for a moment, the entire structure of the army had tottered. Now he had "long-faced" militia in the lines; but instead of leading a mutiny against the new Continental Army, the Connecticut troops were being treated like lepers by all New England. It was a satisfying reversal of fortune. Washington looked at Lee again, a man of elegant dignity, yet some subterfuge against the men of Connecticut left him with an ugly look of smug satisfaction, like a cat that has played with a mouse until it died.

"They were actually hissed when they passed Bridge's regiment. That's a good man, Ebenezer Bridge."

Washington hated that look, and he spoke up. "General Lee, I would point out that these men served loyally and that it is the British, not the men of Connecticut, who constitute the enemy."

Lee bowed his head, as he always did on being rebuked. Washington disliked the habit, and would have preferred if the man held his eye. He sometimes suspected Lee did it to hide anger.

"With all respect, sir, I will maintain that two days ago you offered to hang the lot of them as mutineers."

Washington sat straighter in his saddle, unused to such direct rebuke, but it was, alas, true. He had been away from other men too long, was too used to the ultimate authority on his own farms. Here in the world, even as the military "master," his staff felt free to question him. He stifled the start of anger and barked a laugh.

"So I did, Charles Lee." He held Lee's eye, and Lee smiled, his whole face illuminated for a moment. When the man smiled, it was like a clear day—enough to make anyone like him. But he rarely smiled.

The perfect distraction was just turning from the Mansfield road. It was a coach pulled by six matched horses and surrounded by a company of gentlemen led by the staff's own Colonel Baylor. They all looked splendid as the coach and escort dashed up the last of the green and rolled to a stop opposite the gathered staff.

Washington smiled thinly, then made a comment to Lee over the confusion. "If Knox's guns were to arrive, I think my day would be perfect."

Mrs. Horatio Gates and a seemingly endless stream of Virginia travelers emerged from the coach. Lee bowed in the saddle to each lady as she emerged. None of them was likely to be Mrs. Lee, and Washington thought inconsequentially how difficult it would be if Mrs. Lee were to arrive, as her place was so clearly occupied by a local woman General Lee took no care to hide. But then Martha was there, and he dismounted to smile down at her and bow. She curtsied as if to open a dance, the essence of good breeding, and her eyes sparkled.

"Did I just hear myself compared to Colonel Knox's guns?"

Washington always forgot what she was like, and he bowed again to hide his usual confusion.

"I am *so happy* to hear myself ranked with an event that must be important to our whole continent." But she smiled and began to introduce him to the other ladies, and in moments they had the making of the first celebration most of them had known since they joined the army.

On board HMS Amazon, Chesapeake Bay,
December 21, 1775

"I nevuh thought we'd get beat so bad."

"I never thought."

"I never thought. Right enough. I'd wager we didn't kill a one."

"Nor did we. Slave came in last night, into Edgerton's company. Said the same."

Caesar looked at the older man, his hands still moving through the process of reassembling his lock. It was perfectly clean, and he had stripped it twice. It was as if the action of seeing to his musket had acquired a religious purpose to Caesar.

Peters looked out over the flat water that stank with the filth of three hundred seamen and two hundred soldiers. The cold winter weather was probably all that kept them alive, cramped as they were. The ship remained at her moorings just off the land, and every item that went over the side stayed there, a trash heap and a dunghill combined into a great wet midden just at the surface of the water, getting fouler every day they spent on board. Ten days had passed since the "battle."

"We lost a mort of men."

"Yes. So did the Fourteenth. More than we."

"For *nothing!*"

"Caesar, nothing is for *nothing.*"

The younger man glared out, thinking of Sergeant King falling wounded, of the twenty men left dead or carried away only to die later.

"Watch yer 'ead, mate." A sailor swung by on the ratlines, walking the top of the taffrail above them rather than along the crowded deck. He was blacking the rigging as he went, touching up spots where birds and salt had ruined the perfect black of the tarred lines. Caesar nodded, always pleased when offered courtesy, but the man was gone to his next spot of gull white. The *Amazon* was not a hard ship, but she was smart, and her captain didn't leave a lot of leeway because his decks were full of soldiers. The sailors' relative cleanliness and security was contrasted all too often with the soldiers' filth.

Caesar dreaded asking the question, but Peters was likely to move off now. He often did when Caesar complained about the battle or about the conditions; he didn't care to listen to matters he could not change. Caesar had his measure, and it was high. He was not the natural leader that King had been, but his education and the power of his words, his air of manners and quiet confidence, were more than enough to fill the sergeant's shoes. Other companies had done worse, losing leaders and having no one to fill their gaps. Caesar knew he had been suggested for sergeant's rank in Mr. Robinson's company. He knew that Peters had turned it down.

"Why'd you tell them I wasn' ready to be sergeant?"

"You are not." Peters smiled. "No more am I, Caesar. But you cannot read or write, and the duties do require that you keep accounts, figure, and write returns."

Writing. It hadn't occurred to him; he had built an ugly structure of his own failings, but never thought it might be something as simple.

"Can you teach me to write, sir?"

"I'm quite certain I can, if you place the same emphasis on't that you do on that musket. Would you care to begin this evening?"

"Yes, sir!"

"Excellent. Do you know the Bible at all, Caesar?"

"I can't say that I do, sir. I've heard it read, oft enough. It be a fine book an' all. But I don' know it like some."

"Pity, as knowing it by heart can speed a man's learning. Still, I reckon you've heard enough for it, once you start. Know your letters?"

"No."

Peters nodded. "Well, you are in for a long and difficult experience, my friend. Well worth the effort."

"When I can read, will you recommend me for sergeant?"

"When you can read, you'll be a better soldier than I. Which is to say, yes."

Peters moved away, off to his other corporal to see how he fared.

Virgil sat on the hatch cover sewing himself a jacket. None of them had uniforms, but Tom and Jim had returned to the ship after foraging ashore with the regulars with a good piece of brown woolen cloth. Virgil considered himself a fair hand with a needle, as he had tailored a little on his plantation. Winter was cold on men in shirts and linen jackets made from sails past their prime; Caesar longed for a woolen jacket. He nodded at Virgil to get his attention, then at his own equipment in a neat pile under the bulwark by a gun. Virgil nodded. There were light-fingered men aboard; it didn't do to leave your belongings alone.

Caesar went up toward the bow where the white soldiers were. They had better equipment and more of everything, so that he always looked at them jealously, but they were either amused or tolerant of a black soldier who sought to emulate their standards. Most were friendly; a few were bad. Tommy Steele, a big redheaded man, called the bad ones "awkward sods" in a voice that Caesar couldn't emulate. Steele was friendly. Caesar sought him out, waited patiently at his elbow while the man finished talking to another. Caesar couldn't bring himself to interrupt a white man's conversation—a slave habit that he recognized but had yet to overcome.

"Good day, there."

"Mr. Steele, sir. May I use your black ball?"

"Och, Caesar, don't you call me Mr. Steele or ma mates'll think I'm comin' it a bit high. Of course you can use ma black ball. Why don't I jus' get you one? Have a penny?"

Caesar thought about it for a moment and produced a penny. He wasn't sure of the man, and a penny was a penny, but it seemed worth the risk.

"Back in a flash, mate." The soldier slipped off down a companionway into the bowels of the ship. He was gone so long that Caesar, who didn't want to doubt him, began to, and figured his penny lost and his fledgling friendship as well. He had seen worse on board. Some men couldn't stand the black soldiers and made that all too clear. But then Steele appeared at his elbow.

"Done me a favor, really. Here you go. Mind the wax. No, really, I paid the sergeant a penny for it an' told him I lost mine. Now I'm the diligent soldier of the world, he says, paying good drink money for a new black ball."

Caesar took the hard wax ball gingerly. If the stuff came off on your hands, it was like to spoil white leather or good linen. He already had an embarrassing tar stain on his jacket.

"Thank you, Mr. Steele."

"Think nothin' of it, mate. Now, seeing as how you've done me a good turn here, I have a little tobacco I might share with a needy man."

Caesar looked at him, trying not to appear suspicious.

"Go on, then. I don't want nothin' for it. Do you have a tin?"

Caesar shook his head, but he reached into his hat and took out the stub of a clay pipe, broken so often that the bowl had less than an inch of stem. Steele pulled some tobacco off a hank, rubbed it between his hands, and pushed it into Caesar's pipe.

Someone behind him among the men of the Fourteenth made a comment about black balls and black boys. It was the sort of thing that Caesar had expected for some time. He hunched his shoulders and ignored it. Steele looked up, made a face over Caesar's shoulder, and finished packing the pipe.

"Must be hard as sin being a blackamoor," he said quietly. "I'm a Borderer in an English regiment, an' that's nae walk in a country lane."

Caesar was embarrassed by such talk. He didn't know what a Borderer was, didn't want to be a *blackamoor*. But he decided to push a little. The pipe was packed, and he could escape quickly enough if he had to. "What's a Borderer, then?"

"A Borderer is a natural thief, a lazy man who lies in wait to steal and kill and never does an honest day's work as long as he lives." The man who spoke had an educated voice, like Peters, but he was white, and an officer in the blue coat of the navy.

Steele's face was expressionless. It was unusual for an officer to intrude on any conversation of the men; usually the officers seemed as if they were on a different vessel. Steele was standing straighter, almost at attention. The officer looked at both of them and the look on his face was at odds with the harshness of his opinion.

"What's your name, soldier?"

"Steele, sir."

The man nodded. "I'm a Nixon," he said as he turned and climbed the ladder to the quarterdeck. Caesar watched him go uneasily, aware that Steele had thought himself in very great danger for a moment and now was fairly sighing with relief.

"What's a Nixon, then?"

"He's from the Borders himself, the gentleman. Not that my da' would have been strong on Nixons, mind. But here they seem like brothers."

Caesar gathered, then, that Borderers were a tribe of the British, which pleased him, as it made them all seem a little more familiar. He nodded and waved his pipe. "My thanks, Mr. Steele."

"Just Tom. I forget yours... Pompey?"

"Caesar." Mortified.

"Sorry. Your lot sound like a play—Virgil this and Caesar that. Along wi' ya, then, an' have your wee smoke."

"Thanks, Tom."

He walked back down the deck to his spot, still empty through the power of Virgil's glare, and settled his back against Tom's.

"I've a full pipe," he said.

Heads turned all around. Since they had been on the ships, tobacco had become a rarity among the men, especially the blacks. Caesar scarcely missed it, but Tom did, and some of the other men in his section. Mr. Edgerton's man Tonny was one, a regular smoker. They gathered round, and Tom took out his tinder kit and, crouching by a gun, got a spark into his char and lit the pipe. The sweet smoke fought the stench over the side, and even the cold, for a few minutes.

"Next time pack it in my pipe."

"I didn't have it handy." Caesar, getting better at these exchanges, smiled broadly. "If'n you don' like it, don' be smokin' it!"

Virgil's coat was beginning to take shape; he pulled it on over his shirt, the left sleeve on and the right at his feet. It fit snugly. He hopped down off his grating and reached out for the pipe and took a long drag, rolling the smoke slowly out of his nostrils. Several of the sailors admired the jacket, but they kept their distance. Virgil nodded at them; one smiled and one frowned.

It was that sort of ship.

Caesar leaned his head against the gun behind him and began to black the cover of his cartridge box, thinking of the future.

Cambridge, Massachusetts, January 6, 1776

"I protest, sir! That was my plan, a plan that required subtlety and decision, two properties you will not find in General Sullivan."

"General Lee!"

"Sir, I appeal to your sense of fairness. Was that not to have been my command? Was it not my plan? Is there to be no glory in this war for me at all?"

"General Lee, this war is not about personal glory. This is a war fought against our mother country to free ourselves from the chains of tyranny. Every man can only contribute—"

"Spare me, sir. You are the commander in chief. You may direct or subordinate every action. I am on your staff; I have no regiment of my own and command precious little respect outside this headquarters that I have not slaved like an African to get, riding the lines and browbeating adjutants. I have spent weeks in Rhode Island trying to clear the ground of Loyalists and sympathizers so that we don't find ourselves outflanked by a fleet in Newport, and I return to find that the one command I might have expected on the actual field of battle has been given to an incompetent bungler who traipsed across the ice in full view of their sentries. I have no right to make this complaint and that I will allow. I admit freely that the good of the service should come first, but a man is allowed a little vain-glory, I think, and—"

"Calm yourself, General." Washington took a deep breath, distressed at a decision that he had suspected was poor from the start, and doubly distressed that this clash was taking place in front of the staff. He couldn't apologize. To do so would injure the integrity of the office he held. But he must make amends; he had been wrong, and Sullivan had botched the attempt. "I expect more of you than this shouting. Our people are about."

Lee glared, a cat with his back up. He had done yeoman work in Rhode Island—nasty work at the ugly junction where intelligence and politics met—a job no one else had wanted. Washington was again conscious that he had wronged the man, and wounded that he seemed so often to wrong him. There was something about Lee that lent itself to wrong, or a certain injured dignity that seemed the only dignity the man could muster.

Which didn't change the fact that he was a good soldier and that he and Gates were the only two men approaching professionals in his army. They were not easy men. Washington suspected that each felt he might have had the command. They were not easy men again because they had difficult ways; all three of them were accustomed more to being obeyed than to obeying. That had been Martha's phrase. Perhaps Gates resented it as much as Lee; the thought made Washington wince. He wanted a band of brothers like Henry V. He seemed to be leading a band of squab-blers, and there was a fair share of blame with his own name on it.

"General Lee, I will see to it that you have the next important active command. There is some talk of a southern command in our recent letters with Congress. I will see that you have it, if Congress will agree. Or the command at New York." This last in an undertone.

He heard the intake of breath. They all wanted independent commands. He wanted a united army that would serve more than six weeks.

"General Greene?"

"I have a new set of returns with new numbers on the regiments, sir. They are lower, as we feared."

"Whose returns?"

"General Sullivan's. He is not here to defend himself."

Lee shook his head, rubbed his face with his hands, and looked up. "How low?"

"Possibly below ten thousand, although word of the king's proclamation has brought a fair number of recruits."

Lee shook his head again, weary disdain mixed with none-too-secret elation on his narrow features. "The rumor in Rhode Island among the Loyalists is that the British will stab at New York."

Washington looked keenly at the maps in front of him. It was reflex, really; he had looked over the terrain a hundred times. An attack on New York was the only logical step: It was full of men loyal to the Crown; it lay virtually undefended; it had a marvelous anchorage for the Royal Navy.

"They are certainly preparing to leave Boston. I think we can consider the siege victorious."

Washington glowered at Greene, his eyebrows lowering a fraction. "No talk of victory until we have triumphed, gentlemen. I, too, have heard that they are readying a fleet and boats. We must pray it is not for a repeat of Breed's Hill. We don't have the lines to stop them tomorrow if they come."

"I don't think they want to." Lee was more relaxed. "I think my friend Burgoyne has written off Massachusetts Colony. It may be punished later; it may see raids. But the Boston garrison knows they have only foes here. They will go and find greener pastures, like Rhode Island or New York."

"And you think the most likely thrust is New York."

"Yes, sir, I do."

Washington looked around the table at his staff. Gates, unruffled by the tempers shown, looked as if his thoughts were elsewhere; he often did, but they never were. The others were still a little distanced by Lee's outburst, but every face was attentive. They were not scribbling figures to balance the latest returns, which was too often the case. "New York must be defended. I would like a letter drafted to Congress asking for permission to raise troops and appoint martial authority for that defense."

"Sir." Lee was deferential, but firm. His use of *sir* had acquired a new proportion, as if it were a substitute for *my lord*. "You do not need the authority of Congress to place New York under defense. Congress made you commander in chief of the entire continent."

Washington smiled a little, a smile that didn't show his teeth. *How much he would like to believe that he could exercise such powers!* He was satisfied, if somewhat distantly, that every face around the table seemed to reflect approbation for Lee's words. They were loyal to him, even if fractious among themselves. He no sooner felt the thought than he banished it. If he would not allow Lee his vainglory, no less could he allow himself a hope of dominion.

"I am not sure of that. Congress is our master, Charles; we must be wise in choosing our displays of authority." It was said softly; every man in the room could hear it, but said so, Lee would take it as a personal aside.

"I honor that, sir. I honor it deeply. But I have the greatest reason to believe, from the most authentic intelligence, that the best members of Congress expect that you would take much upon yourself, as referring everything to them is, in fact, defeating the project."

Tempted as he was to ask after the "best members of Congress," Washington was pleased, but he controlled it as efficiently as he controlled his anger on other occasions. "Draft the letter regardless, and show it to me later. General Lee, draw up a plan for the defense of New York. If Congress accepts, it shall be your command."

Perhaps Gates flinched; perhaps Greene was jealous. Sullivan was absent. But soon enough he was going to have to send them, every one, away to lead armies. The war would only broaden. Perhaps Canada would fall; perhaps Great Britain would see sense. Neither seemed likely. He had begun to think it would be a long war, and even as he reached to grasp his first victory, he had begun to feel his own monumental confidence slipping.

Along the Chesapeake, Virginia, January 28, 1776

As soon as the governor decided that the peninsula might be suitable for a winter camp, he ordered it scouted. Although the marines were excellent soldiers, they knew nothing of the terrain, and the word came down to the Loyalists, black and white, that scouts were wanted to learn the ground. Many of the Ethiopians volunteered, but Caesar and Jim were taken. They were issued two pistols apiece and sharp knives, a tarpaulin of oiled canvas, and a haversack of naval rations.

The next morning the two of them were taken ashore with a midshipman from one of the Royal Navy ships that accompanied the governor. Mr. Harding was nominally in charge and had the knack of making maps, but his small size and urchin's face did nothing to inspire Caesar's confidence. But he proved reasonable enough once they were ashore.

"Captain said I should listen to you, sir," he said with a civil nod to Caesar. In the boat, the boy hadn't even looked at him. Caesar felt as if he had become a different person on the beach. Behind Caesar, the sailors splashed in the cold water as the bow oars pushed the keel of the big boat free of the sand. Their mates pulled them aboard, their bare legs flashing in the weak sun, and then the oars were out. With surprising speed, the boat began to grow smaller.

"Best be getting inland, sir," said Caesar. He ended the sentence more kindly than he had started it; the enormity of being alone on an enemy beach was just coming to the midshipman. He looked a little gray.

Jim bounded ahead. He was gone into the woodline at the edge of the beach in a second, and Caesar wondered if he was going to have to call Jim back like a runaway puppy. The thought of two days ashore with two boys struck him as less like scouting than minding children. He took a moment at the edge of the beach to gather a pile of driftwood for a fire. Then he pulled a big sheet of old bark over his pile. He thought it looked like rain, and he meant to camp near the beach.

Jim found a big meadow with a stream just to the east of their landing spot. Caesar thought it would make a good camp, screened by trees from the bay and by deep woods from the land. There was a small cabin site, as if the ground had been cleared for a farm that had never succeeded.

They made their way across the small peninsula in less than three hours by the mid's watch. They crossed one track, a pair of paths with a low hump of grass between. Mr. Harding walked along it and came back.

"No horse on this path for some time," he said cautiously.

"We can come back to it, if'n you like," said Caesar.

"Aye, that would be best." He made a mark on his paper and they carried on, walking easily between the big trees on either side. Caesar listened to the white boy counting his paces.

Jim went ahead, mostly. He very quickly caught the habit and the intention of counting his paces, and he would come back with a bound, reporting the distance he had traveled. He kept going down to the shore. Caesar, watching Mr. Harding, noted that the mid already had the whole coast of the peninsula drawn in great detail and that every time Jim came loping back, he'd question him until he could determine where on the coast Jim had emerged. Caesar watched little lines drawn across the paper, began to see in his head how the lines corresponded to places they had been. The only maps he'd seen were decorations on walls in rich houses. He understood how a map could show all of Jamaica, or all of

Virginia. This was the first time that he or Jim had seen a map made small enough to show something on a more human scale. He liked it, but his enthusiasm was nothing next to Jim's.

"That's the trick!" Jim said on one of his returns. He was perspiring, despite the cool air, but he leaned down close to the white boy, watching the pencil move along a straightedge. The white boy was clearly proud of his accomplishment, and he explained to Jim as he went how he measured degrees with his pocket theodolite, how even Jim's forays to the beach were along measured lines, and the paces made for distances, so that they slowly covered the ground.

"Like a net," said Jim. "It's like laying a net of us over the ground. We the cords o' the net."

Mr. Harding considered this for a moment. It didn't sound mathematical enough to suit him. His mathematical knowledge was hard won, and he didn't wish to belittle its power.

"It's like it, I suppose." The white boy couldn't remain indifferent, however. Jim's enthusiasm was infectious, and both boys began to work well together.

Caesar understood well enough, and he relegated himself to guard and make a little coffee when they stopped in the afternoon. The boys drank the coffee, but they were burning to return to the track in the woods and follow it. They saw the whole expedition as adventure. Caesar was oppressed by the emptiness of the peninsula and the constant fear of capture, with the added responsibility of the two boys.

After coffee, he buried his fire and they walked back to the track. Jim loped off, following the track toward the sea. Caesar took out his pipe and filled it. He had little tobacco left and few pennies with which to buy more. He'd saved a coal from his coffee fire and used it to light the pipe. Harding looked over at him and Caesar held out the pipe.

The boy shook his head. "Mids aren't allowed to smoke."

Caesar thought about that, about all the rules they lived with. Harding could give him orders, but he couldn't smoke. That had some humor to it. Caesar looked at the locks of his pistols and changed the prime out of the little horn from his bag. He looked at the sky.

"I think we're going to have rain," he said.

The white boy nodded.

Jim came running back, his energy still a tangible thing. "Four hundred fifty-five each way. Curves to the north. Nice even curve, I think."

Harding took a note. Then he drew on his sketch. "Like that?"

"Yessuh."

Caesar didn't like the track. "I think it's a plantation track to the beach for loading."

"Let's go find the plantation, then," Harding said cheerfully, and they were off.

An hour later their packs were feeling heavy and the rain was imminent. Indeed, the first cold drops had already fallen around them in spurts, as if the sky were indecisive. The track had crossed two fence lines, and they could see fields in the middle distance. Darkness was not far away.

"We need a camp." Harding said it flatly.

"We're a long way from the beach," said Caesar. "I had thought to camp on the beach, where the boat could see a signal."

The two boys looked at him.

"It's a long way back," said Jim.

"An hour."

"We'll be wet through by then." Harding was less cocksure now. He was tired. "And I want to see the plantation, get a sketch of the house. The governor will want to know. We're here."

"If we camp here, we're a damn sight surer of gettin' caught, suh. *Sir.*" Caesar tried to look for alternatives. Getting the boys back to the beach, building them a shelter, then coming back here? It seemed possible.

"We'll make camp here."

"No fire, then," said Caesar. Jim nodded. Harding seemed surprised when Jim joined Caesar and looked at him reproachfully. Caesar took both of them by the sleeve and pulled them off the little track and into the shadow of some trees.

"We ah' standin' in the open. We *are standing* in the open."

Jim looked at Harding apologetically. "We been hunted in ground like this. Smell of a fire carries a long way. Suh."

Harding looked like he was going to be angry, then thought better of it. "You're the scouts. I want to see that plantation. What do we do?"

"We go to the plantation, quick as we can. Then we go back to the beach to camp. That's what's safe." Caesar was already looking at the ground between his stand of trees and the fields. "Don't want none of the slaves there to see us."

"Won't they protect you?"

"Maybe. Maybe not, too. An' if'n they see you, might be different."

"I'm willing to take the risk, Mr. Caesar."

Caesar stopped watching the fields and turned back to face Harding. The boy looked earnest. "Mr. Harding, if'n you get took here, you'll be a prisoner for a few weeks, kept in houses by folk. If'n Jim or me gets took, we'll be hung up dead on the spot, or made slaves. I don' wan' you to think we're afeared, but I wan' you to know what you ah askin' us to risk to take a look at that house."

The rain began in earnest.

"I'll go alone, then," said the white boy. "I'm sorry. I had forgotten."

"That's wrong, too. Jim an' me'll go. You stay here and stay dry an' keep our packs."

"But you said . . ."

Jim sank down on his haunches next to Harding. "We good at this, suh. We'll take a little peek an' be back in no time."

Harding looked miserable. "I'm in command. I should go."

Caesar felt himself admiring the boy a little. "Good for you," he said. "But you got to know we can do this bettuh . . . *better* than you."

He didn't wait to argue. The boy spoke quietly to Jim and handed him something. Jim nodded. He and Jim checked their pistols again and moved off across the ground, now wet. They walked up some dead ground to a creek bed, and then followed the creek bed through a few fields, until Jim, crawling up the bank, could see the chimneys of a big house. Caesar worked his way farther along the bank and then came up himself.

The plantation was a fine one, although small. The main house was solid brick, with five large windows on the top floor front over four windows and an elegant entrance with a fanlight. Brick outbuildings stood to the right and left. Even in the gray of a winter's evening, the building had some warmth to it, and the lighted windows glowed orange as if inviting cold men to come inside and be warmed.

Behind the warm house lay the slave quarters, two rows of dark huts. None of them had an orange glow to them. Without servants to keep fires going all day, the fires went out on cold afternoons, and the huts were always cold.

A proper road ran from the front of the house off to the north. A great stand of trees grew at the northern edge of the fields, which stretched for half a mile. Caesar nodded to himself. The plantation was too far inland to make a good headquarters, but it was too close to ignore. He understood that much. He crawled back to Jim and found him sketching the positions of the buildings. His heavy, clumsy strokes were very different from Harding's, but his eye was sure and the heavy square of the house was proportionate to the two barns and rows of slave cabins.

Caesar pointed at the nearest shed, an openwork log barn with a shingle roof. "Tobacco barn," he whispered.

Jim nodded.

Caesar mimed smoking. "Gonna steal some."

Jim shook his head in exasperation. "Mistuh Hardin' is waiting for us. You jus' tol' him not to take risks."

Caesar crawled over the top of the bank and began to run toward the barn. Jim went back to his drawing, but now he couldn't do it. He was tense. He wanted to follow Caesar, but thought that only increased the risk. He could see slaves working in the fields just beyond the barn, and he could hear a white voice, probably an overseer, shouting in the middle distance.

Then he saw Caesar at the side of the barn, and then slipping into it, a dark shadow against the near dark of the barn. Then Caesar was out again and running toward him, his legs pumping. Jim wondered at how fast he was. He'd never seen anyone run as fast as Caesar. In a moment the man was over the edge of the bank and down beside him. The rain was coming faster. Caesar had two armfuls of tobacco leaf, dry and pungent, and the sweet, dry smell filled the air.

"You done drawing?"

"As good as I can get it."

"I wan' get this under my tarpaulin an' keep it dry." Caesar had a fortune in tobacco, at least by the laws of economy on their ship.

The darkness covered their retreat. It was somehow shorter back to where they had left Harding than it had been sneaking out. Harding looked as if he hadn't moved, and his relief at seeing them was so great that he laughed aloud. Caesar didn't pause to greet him but pulled out his oilcloth and wrapped his precious tobacco in it. Then he slung the whole package over his shoulder and stood up.

Jim was showing his sketch to Harding, but the dark and the rain made it impossible to judge or add Jim's work to the map.

"Must we go back to the beach?"

"If you want a fire." Caesar didn't mention that he had piled firewood that morning, or left it in a dry place.

Harding nodded. His hat was collapsing in the rain, and the dye from his blue uniform jacket had run into his shirt. He was small and wet and cold, but he still had some indefinable air of command. "Let's go, then."

It took them much less time to walk back down the trail, even in the dark and rain, than it had to walk up. Caesar had experienced this before, and knew that careful approaches in unfamiliar ground took much more time than a simple walk down a clear trail. They were all soaked through and shivering.

The tide was up when they came to the beach, and had come up high, so that the shingle was only a few yards wide at the top before the open woods began. Caesar had to hunt for his woodpile for a while, but he found it by stumbling over the slick old bark. Then he used the bark as a shield while he lit the fire under it. First he got a spark from his flint and steel on his charred cloth, all out of his fire kit and the driest thing he had. Then he used dry punkwood from the center of a rotten log to take the spark and make it a coal, and he carefully built a tiny fire of dry twigs on that one coal, building and blowing until he had a flame, and then adding scraps of bone-dry bark and twig and a twist of paper donated by Harding.

Through the whole performance, the two boys sat on the wet ground in the rain, only partially sheltered by the trees overhead. Jim fell asleep, despite the cold. He had been out in worse. The white boy had stood his watches on the deck of his frigate in all weathers, and he rested his back against Jim's and tried to sleep as well.

If the transition from spark to coal to flame had taken a long time, the leap from flame to roaring fire was swift. Caesar fed his dry wood until he had a blaze, and then he put wetter wood on and it burned regardless. He looked over at Harding, who seemed fascinated.

"On a dry day you can build a tiny fire. On a wet day you need mo' fire jus' to burn the damp wood."

"We don't burn much wood on board ship," said Harding.

Caesar smiled and nodded. He took his brass kettle, fetched some water from the stream, then boiled some salt pork and biscuit together and woke the two boys. They ate voraciously, but without really waking up. They made him feel old.

He stretched a tarpaulin across the opening between two trees and lashed it with pine roots. Then he pushed the boys under it, threw a second tarp over them, and prepared himself a pipe of his new tobacco. It tasted wonderful, if a little damp, after a month or more of stale rations and ancient stuff issued by the navy and sold on by the sailors. He drank a little water from his canteen, ate the rest of the salt pork and washed the kettle, and crawled in with the two boys. Mostly, he was content.

The boat came for them the next day, on time and even a little early. Caesar received his share of praise. It appeared that Mr. Harding's map was to everyone's satisfaction, as was the site of the camp and the peninsula as a whole. The governor decreed that they were going ashore.

Harding came back to thank them that same evening. He gave Jim a metal pencil with some leads and a little book of blank sheets, and he gave Caesar a clasp knife.

"I've never had so much praise from my captain all at once."

"What did the governor say?"

"He told Captain Lovell and the marine officer that he wanted to put the force ashore to keep you all from dying of disease. And then he laughed and said that he could at least be thought to be campaigning in Virginia if he was ashore."

Caesar shook his head. "We're better off here."

"Will we make more maps, suh?" asked Jim, and Harding nodded.

"I'll ask for you."

☆   ☆   ☆

The British marines were the best soldiers Caesar had seen. They led the landings from boats provided by the navy, dashing ashore and forming loose lines, every man using the cover along the shingle. There was no opposition; the rebels hadn't smoked the landing and were forty miles away or more.

Command had responsibilities that Caesar hadn't anticipated. As a corporal, he knew more than the other men about these landings. He knew that they were not intended as a step in a campaign to reclaim Virginia from the rebels; the sergeants and officers had made it clear that Governor Dunmore had abandoned any real hope of retaking Virginia for the king by force of arms. But taken together, the need of the men for exercise and the threat of disease on the ships mandated a landing. Five weeks' waste lay in the bilges and around them in the slack water of the Chesapeake. The governor intended to take this little peninsula, hold it, and make it an exercise ground for his army.

✮ ✮ ✮

The wind was bitter coming over the open bay. Caesar's men all had brown wool jackets, but some of the newer recruits had only shirts and navy slop trousers or petticoat breeches. They were nearly blue with cold. They gripped their muskets with white-knuckled hands, and Caesar knew that they would be useless in a fight.

The whaleboat holding his men landed on the sand with a hiss.

"Up oars," called the midshipman, a stranger. He turned to Caesar. "This is as far as we go, Corporal."

"Yes, sir." The midshipman was so young his voice was still high, and he had no real authority. That came from the coxswain, a burly man behind him, who simply smiled and jerked his thumb over his shoulder in the universal sign for "get out." Caesar grasped the gunwale and leapt over the side into less than a foot of water, and then Virgil followed over the other side, just as they had practiced. The rest of the men walked up the thwarts between the rowers, and the sailors handed them their muskets, which had been stored along the bottom boards. It went very smoothly, and Caesar was pleased to see Lope, his newest man, standing on the beach with his musket, bayonet, and cartridge box, as it meant that his was the first boat unloaded. Caesar enjoyed the little courtesies of command; he touched his hat to the midshipman.

"Thank you, sir."

The boy returned the gesture. "First on the beach, after the marines." The coxswain, a decent sort who smoked constantly, waved his pipe at Caesar. He had offered a good price for any tobacco they could "liberate" in the course of their jaunt ashore; had purchased half of what Caesar had brought from the mapping party. The coxswain was sure that the expedition was doomed and even claimed to know where they were bound next.

"Marker! Second Section marker!" Caesar called the ritual words, even though his marker man, Virgil, was ten feet away. Virgil pulled himself erect and put his musket on his shoulder with a negligent air, but the completion of the movement left him in the position of a soldier, the very personification of his section.

"Second Section! Fall in!" The rest of the men, even the recruits, ran to their places in the line, forming two ranks with the tallest in the center and the shortest on the flanks. Caesar's section was almost a platoon since the latest draft of runaway slaves. He had twenty men.

The other boats were hanging back in the current. Caesar didn't know enough about the water to understand what was delaying the second wave of boats. His were the only Loyal Ethiopians on the beach.

In the manual of arms he had learned, he could remember no order that would enable him to disperse his men in the rocks as the marines had done. He turned to Virgil. "Spread them out along the scree, Virgil. I'm going to find an officer."

Caesar grasped his musket across the body and ran to where he could see an officer of the Fourteenth, a naval officer, and a man in a blue velvet coat, whom he thought to be Captain Honey of the marines. He stopped a few feet away, uncertain, and then stood at attention with his musket at the recover. It was a position designed to attract the attention of a higher officer; it meant that a soldier was requesting permission to speak.

The officer of the Fourteenth was the eldest, but apparently not the senior man in the group. However, he was the one man Caesar knew; he had led a company at the disaster at Great Bridge. When he caught Caesar's eye, Caesar stepped forward. "Sir!"

The man in the blue velvet coat turned and looked at him with distaste. "Is this an example of our slave militia, Lieutenant Crowse?"

Caesar felt the blood run to his face and sweat break out all over his body, as if he were about to fight.

"Yes, sir."

The man looked at Caesar, barely touching him with his eyes as if the sight were too painful. "What do you want, darky?"

"Where would you like my section, sir? My officer has not yet landed."

"Get those men's guns away from them before they shoot someone and have them start hauling boxes up the beach." He wasn't addressing Caesar, but Crowse. He took a little silver whistle from his waistcoat pocket and blew it twice. The marines rose to their feet and began to move forward. On the far right, Virgil got the Ethiopians to their feet and moved off on the flank of the marines.

Blue Coat whirled around and stabbed a finger at Crowse. "If I wanted those blackamoors stumbling through my skirmish line, I'd ask for them. Now get them hauling boxes."

Caesar was still standing at attention. Crowse, a man he barely knew, looked at him with a spark of pity, but that was all.

"Have your men stack their arms," he said. "And then get them moving with the stores."

"As you say, sir."

Crowse looked unhappy.

★ ★ ★

Over the next six weeks, Sergeant Peters had them up early to drill with their muskets. It was the only time they handled them; otherwise, the guns were locked away in the magazine by the blockhouse that the Ethiopians had built in the first week of labor. They spent every waking hour building: first sheds for the men to sleep in, then the blockhouse and its chimneys, then a set of entrenchments along the front of the camp. None of their officers could change the situation, and the white troops, many of whom had started to fraternize with them, began to grow used to the idea that they could order a black soldier to do all the dirty work. Some of the blacks accepted this; others, especially the veterans of Great Bridge, resented it. The resentment lowered morale, and the men became listless. In fact, to Caesar's attentive eye, they began to show signs of act-ing like slaves. They moved more slowly and the joking disappeared, at least when any white soldier was about. The men became furtive.

Visits from the sailors provided their only relief. The sailors seemed im-mune to any notion of color, perhaps because so many of their own were Africans or lascars from East India Company ships in the Far East. The ratings of the Royal Navy came in every color of the rainbow. The cox-swain of the *Amazon* continued to pay well for tobacco and to talk to Peters and Caesar as if they were members of the same mess, as they had been aboard ship.

The sick were brought ashore to recover from the fever that had them in its grip on the crowded ships. Once ashore, smallpox began to ravage the men who had survived the fevers onboard ship. The white Loyalists seemed to die faster than the blacks, but Jim caught it and had the fever for almost two weeks. He lost all the weight he had gained since they had joined the army and then even more, until he looked like a tight leather bag stretched over sticks. The others from their mess group, even the men like Tonny who hadn't been in the swamp with Jim, took turns bathing him and cleaning him. As he lay there, his bright, intelligent eyes burned with greater intensity, as though he could cling to life by will alone.

Twice he had loud, angry dreams. Once, when Caesar was minding him, he was somewhere in his own distant past, forced to watch another man being beaten. If the sounds he made in the dream were reliable, the beating had gone on for a long time. The second dream came when Tom was tending him—a reliving of the battle of Great Bridge. Long Tom said it was eerie, hearing Jim say the words again, like being there, except they were lying on the ground in a dark hut.

The white soldiers continued to get Jesuit's bark for their fevers, but the supply ran short and the black men no longer saw any of it. There was no medicine for smallpox, and the men died, black and white together, and as often as not the Ethiopians were ordered to bury them. The dead men seldom got anything like a funeral, just a deep hole and a few muttered words from an officer with a scarf over his mouth.

The surgeon hurried to explain to Sergeant Peters that his people were tougher and less affected anyway. It might have been true, as far as any of them knew; certainly, more blacks survived the fever than whites, but it didn't help the black soldiers with the notion that they didn't rate quite the same treatment as the whites.

The winter winds bit through the tents and hasty cabins that had covered the meadow with a patchwork of rude shelters, military tents, and mud. The constant movement of hundreds of men had worn through the grass. The incessant rain turned the ground to thick mud, and they never had the straw or forage to keep it from their tents. Some of the men went and slept in the woods. As the labor of camp building declined, there was more time for the men to brood on the unfairness of the white soldiers. Caesar began to encounter resentment when taking the men out for early drill. Men who had been eager to learn grew hesitant; men who had had little interest in the work to start with became rebellious. Caesar sensed that even the survivors of the swamp were losing interest.

Two mornings after Jim raved about the battle, Long Tom went down with the smallpox. Spirits were low as Caesar marched the men early to the magazine and stood them in front of the arms racks. Sergeant Peters was laying out a new storehouse, and Caesar was to command the morning drill for the first time. He was trying to pay close attention to what went on, but his thoughts were with Jim and now Long Tom.

"Take up your arms," he said as if by rote.

"Ain't no need, Corporal-man," said Willy, a man from Peters's old squad of inspection. "We ain't soldiers. We slaves."

"I am *not* a slave," Caesar answered hotly. "Now get in line and pick up that musket."

"Nope. Not taking no orders from no black mastuh, neithuh."

Caesar had no experience with mutiny. His men mostly followed his lead because he had led some of them out of the swamp and the rest because of the trust of the first. Some of the new men were not so loyal.

Caesar snapped out of his reverie. He could see that Willy was keyed up and that he was looking at his mates, Romeo and Paget, flicking them expectant glances. He knew that this confrontation had been building since they landed. Caesar was astute enough to recognize that he and his authority might never have been challenged if not for the hostile attitude of the marine officer. As it was, he became the focus for his company's discontent because he was both the newest noncommissioned officer and in some ways the most demanding.

Caesar took a step toward Willy but transferred his attention to Paget. Keeping his eye on the other man, Caesar spoke low. "Get on the line and take your musket from the rack. Do it!"

Virgil recognized from Caesar's tone that something serious was taking place. Tonny shifted his weight a little, as he was the file leader of the next file over from Willy. The others looked vacant. They might know that something was up, but they had chosen not to take part.

"Wha' don' we jus sit somewheah fo' a bit?" Willy asked in a slow, almost affected way. It was blatant disrespect. It was also no different from the way half the men behaved every day. Caesar was tempted to ignore it, or to jolly the man along. He expected he could do that; it worked well enough on slaves.

But these men were soldiers.

Caesar moved like a cat springing on its prey, his left foot stomping directly on to Willy's instep and the butt of his musket smashing into the man's midriff, doubling him in pain and surprise. He collapsed and Caesar stepped past him, thrusting the muzzle of his empty musket deep into the pit of Paget's stomach and then kneeing him in the face as he bent over with the blow. Paget fell atop Willy.

"We are soldiers, not slaves. We got some troubles here, but we'll get through 'em by working harder. On your feet, you two. You ain't dead, but if I hear a peep about drill again, you'll wish you were. Move."

Willy got up slowly, but Paget just lay and moaned. Caesar knelt by him, his musket cradled across his thighs. "You think it ain't fair I hit you so much harder than him? He isn't smart enough to buck me without you helped him. You think I don' know? I know. An' I know how hard I hit you, so get up before I make that show real."

"You broke my nose, you bastard!"

Caesar grabbed the man's head and lifted it off the dirt floor of the magazine. He lifted until he could look into the man's eyes. It was quite a display of strength and it must have hurt the man a great deal.

"You get up now," Caesar said gently, "or I'll kill you."

The whole magazine was silent. Then Paget got a leg under himself and raised himself to his feet. He moaned, but he stood. Caesar ran his eyes over the whole platoon, hurt to see that even Virgil and Tonny seemed to flinch away from him a little. But he had chosen a hard way, and he couldn't falter now.

"Count off from the right," he said. And they did.

★ ★ ★

After an hour's ferocious drill, he took himself to Sergeant Peters and reported the incident, angry that he had lost control, angry at the marine officer and the army. It was the kind of helpless anger he had felt working in the Great Dismal—the first time he had felt that way since his group had found the army.

Peters had a good tent, courtesy of Mr. Robinson, and he sat on a tiny stool that had probably started life next to a fireplace or a kitchen hearth. He was so much too big for the stool that it vanished under him. Next to him was a small straw pallet in a forage bag. His pack was open at the far end of the pallet.

"Ah, Caesar. I would like to offer you a place to sit, but..."

"Sergeant Peters, I have to report that I struck two of my men in suppressing a mutiny."

Peters looked up his long nose at Caesar thoughtfully and fumbled in his waistcoat pocket for his eyeglasses. "The ground is hard even with the straw, and the nights are cold. The rest of you can curl around each other for warmth, but I have the solitary splendor and the lack of warmth it brings, and I'm stiff in the morning."

His fingers couldn't work the catch on the eyeglass case, and he had to concentrate for a moment and press it repeatedly till he opened it. Then he brought the glasses out slowly, as if treasuring them, and slowly unfolded the lappets before he pulled them over his ears and tied the ribbon. They transformed his face from that of a tired man to that of a scholar.

"Tell me about this mutiny, Caesar."

"Willy, Romeo, an' Paget—"

"Willy, Romeo, *and* Paget."

"Willy, Romeo, and Paget refused to take up their muskets for drill."

"Perfectly understandable."

Caesar, bent over in the entrance to the tent and looking down at his sergeant, almost vibrated with shock. "Sergeant?"

"I'm sure it has come to your attention that we are being used as a labor force and not as soldiers?"

"Yes, Sergeant."

"So the mutiny is quite understandable."

Caesar shook his head, almost imperceptibly.

"Caesar, when men are treated badly, they behave badly. Willy and Paget have always been slaves, correct?"

"Yes, Sergeant."

"As such, they know only one code: When mistreated, slow down. You are lucky they didn't spoil their muskets. Breaking tools is an honored practice, as I'm sure you know."

"I've done it myself, Sergeant."

"Good. Now you see their point of view. I'm glad I've shocked you, Caesar; you need to understand how other men think and feel if you plan to lead them. You expect too much from men; you expect them all to behave as you do. How did you handle them?"

"I beat them."

Peters looked at him, his head tilted a little, and he reminded Caesar for a moment of Colonel Washington speaking to a particularly intelligent puppy. He had tilted his head in just such a way. "And did they drill?"

"They did."

"It sorrows me to say it, but that is definitely one way of dealing with a mutiny. The best way, I think."

"Thank you, Sergeant."

"No, Caesar, you mistake me. It is the best way of dealing with a mutiny once it has become open. But I want you to consider how it became open and how that might have been avoided. I have feared this for some days. I believe I mentioned it to you. In future I hope you will keep such instances from eventuating by giving the handling of the men your very best attention."

"Yes, Sergeant."

"Do you have your roll? Give it here. That is still the most oddly formed *R* in Christendom, Caesar. Look at the letters I wrote out for you. Tonny deserves a surname; only slaves have just one. See to it."

"Yes, Sergeant."

"Same for Long Tom."

"Yes, Sergeant."

"Lessons tonight, after dinner is cooked. And our women are being landed tomorrow. Take your squad of inspection down to the beach and see to it that we get the same women we had before. No harlots, if you please."

Something in his tone gave Caesar the hope that he would be forgiven. The shock of censure had not been so deep. He recognized, even as Peters was speaking, the essential truth of his words, and realized that he had felt guilty about the incident and his use of force even as it happened. Yet he did resent that it had happened at all, and he was torn by conflicting feelings of anger and guilt. If Captain Honey were a decent man to the black soldiers, none of this need have happened.

Peters watched him with concern. He wanted to reach out and touch his shoulder or offer some gesture that would ease the sting of rebuke, but he had dealt with young men all his adult life, and he knew the lesson would have more effect if he carried his coldness through to the end. Tomorrow would be soon enough to relax his appearance of ill will. Poor Caesar. Being a leader was difficult enough. Training one half his age was almost too much, and though Peters loved his newfound freedom, sometimes the former butler missed his warm bed under the eaves.

★   ★   ★

Caesar made his way down the tent row that housed his platoon, listening to the men as they patched garments or smoked, idle or busy according to their own inclination.

One of the greatest complaints that the black troops had was that they were not allowed to patrol; the patrols inevitably returned with useful items, from barn boards to chickens. Kept in the camp as a labor force, the Ethiopians were missing out on what little there was to have. What they did have was tobacco. The plantation north of where they had landed was planted in tobacco, poor-quality stuff that had stripped the soil, they all agreed, but worth something anyway. Virgil had led the other men in building a small drying shed and putting up some of the tobacco. Most of it was saved from the plantation's own drying barn, but a little was from a field left unharvested in the autumn of war. It wasn't much, but the sailors seemed to like it and it gave the Ethiopians something to trade. It also gave them a larger building in which to stay dry.

When Caesar didn't hear the voices he expected in the streets of the camp, he followed the stockade until he came to the little drying shed. Inside, he was surprised to see Mr. Edgerton. He was stooped over under the low roof, his hat in his hand and his greatcoat wet. He seemed quite at ease.

"Caesar. Just the man I was looking for. Could we step outside?" Edgerton sounded polite, distant, and Caesar feared that the mutiny was still with him.

"Good day to ya, suh," called several voices from inside the shack. The sweet smell of dry tobacco filled the air. Outside, it had started to rain again, a cold rain that felt greasy where it touched the skin. Caesar expected that they would stop out of earshot of the shed, but Edgerton kept walking.

Caesar elected to strike first.

"Sorry about the . . . trouble, sir." He turned his head and met Edgerton's eyes directly. Some white men didn't like that, but Edgerton didn't seem to mind.

"Quite the little incident. Yes. I thought you handled it well, Caesar. But keep in mind that it had roots. . . ." Edgerton looked away for a moment and then back at Caesar. His look had been in the direction of the marine camp, and it was as eloquent as it needed to be. "It had roots elsewhere. Is my meaning plain?"

"Yes, sir."

"Good, but that's not why I left a warm fire and a book just to find you. I didn't want to alarm the other men in your platoon, but one of our men has just died."

"Little Jim?" Caesar tried to hide the hurt in his voice. Jim had survived so much to fall to a fever in the relative comfort of the army.

"No, Caesar. Jim's no better, but he isn't dead yet. It's Long Tom."

"He's only just been sick!"

"He's gone. Come along."

Caesar walked through the rain, tears flowing unnoticed down his cheeks, head up, almost blind to the camp around him. Long Tom had been with them from the first—after Virgil, his most trusted man. Caesar could see him standing a watch in the camp in Great Dismal, or whistling tunelessly as he whittled a stick down to slivers with his long razor in the woods of southern Virginia. He thought about how far they had come from the swamp and wondered if they would keep it. Even the attitude of the white soldiers was a far cry from life as a slave or a hunted runaway. Tom had died free. But he had died, and in the dismal light of the hospital, Caesar wondered how many of them would live to the end of the war, or whether they would even win through and keep their freedom. Sometimes it seemed like a hard life to live just to lose it all again.

The hospital was worse in the light of day than it ever was lit by fire in the night; the men looked paler, their filth was more evident, and the hopelessness stood out on every face. Tom lay just under the shed outside the door, his dirty white blanket thrown loosely over him. Caesar stripped off Tom's brown wool coatee—they had so few he couldn't bear to waste one—and then he rolled his friend gently onto the straw, laid out his blanket, and rolled him up in it. He did these things almost automatically; it wasn't really Tom, and he thought obscurely that he needed to get back to work. He didn't worry especially about the smallpox; he thought he'd had it already. Mr. Edgerton stood under the shed, water trickling down his greatcoat, his once-fine tricorn now just a shapeless mass.

"Sergeant Peters told me to make sure Tom had a surname on the next muster." Caesar was breathing hard as he tried to lever the body over without seeming disrespectful.

"I beg your pardon?" Edgerton sounded distant.

"Apologies, sir. I was just...just saying that Tom, he had no family name."

"I suppose not. Many slaves don't. Pity, that. The army should issue them along with freedom. Perhaps he could be called 'Hanover,' after the king." Mr. Edgerton kept his head turned away from the corpse.

Mr. Robinson stepped under the roof of the shed. "He's welcome to mine, Caesar." His greatcoat was soaked through, and he had the silver crescent of a gorget around his throat. He was the officer of the day. He hadn't shaved and looked rough.

"Thank you, sir."

"No thanks needed. I remember Tom at Great Bridge. He stood until the end, and the Robinsons can always use a few brave men." Mr. Robinson looked at Mr. Edgerton for a moment as if willing him to say something, but Mr. Edgerton took a snuffbox out of his deep pockets and took snuff, then blew his nose into a handkerchief from another pocket.

"I'd like him to have a military funeral." Caesar stood up from the body to make this announcement.

Edgerton just shook his head in the negative, still playing with his handkerchief.

Robinson leaned against one of the pilings supporting the shed and put his chin in his hand. He looked at Edgerton and raised one eyebrow. "Mr. Edgerton, I daresay we could give him a military burial. The Fourteenth do it every day."

"Captain Honey would never allow it. He barely tolerates us as it is."

"Captain Honey already uses our troops as a labor force, Mr. Edgerton. He should be the soul of tolerance."

"This is not the place for this discussion, Mr. Robinson. But if you insist, on your head be it."

"Truer words were never spoke, Mr. Edgerton. Corporal Caesar, please see to arrangements for a military burial party. Three files with muskets and full equipment, the rest of the platoon in work shirts, turned out in thirty minutes in the company street."

"Yes, sir. Military burial party. Three files armed, rest of Mr. Edgerton's platoon in the street with work shirts and no arms."

"Carry on."

Caesar saluted smartly and marched off, leaving Tom lying between the two officers with his old white blanket around him as a shroud. As he headed off toward the streets of the camp, he heard the two men continue to argue.

✫ ✫ ✫

The only difficulty turned out to be from the soldier on duty at the magazine, who had no orders to allow any troops access to the arms stored there. He was a soldier of the Fourteenth, and he stuck by his orders until Sergeant Peters stepped forward and ended the contest of wills between the sentry and Caesar.

"Private, we have orders from our officer to conduct a burial party. We need six muskets for the firing party. We'll be back with them double-quick. Didn't the Fourteenth have a burial party yesterday morning?"

"We did, at that." The man was hesitant, knowing that a positive answer would weaken his case. He was divided, as the white soldiers often were with the Ethiopian noncommissioned officers—training versus prejudice. He shrugged, as if dismissing responsibility.

"You are ordering me to give you the arms?"

Sensing victory, Peters smiled mirthlessly and nodded.

"Right, then, Sergeant. Here are the keys. Please sign the book."

In a moment, the three files in coatees had their arms and accoutrements, consisting of a cartridge box, bayonet carriage, and bayonet. They fell in at the head of the parade, bayonets fixed. Peters, Caesar, and the other corporal, Fowver, took their arms as well. The officers joined them with their swords belted on and their greatcoats slung like capes. The last two files carried picks and shovels. The whole platoon marched briskly outside the palisade and over the field that had been cut to give the defenders a clear line of sight, to the little cemetery at the edge of the apple orchard.

"Halt!" Mr. Robinson held his hand in the air. The rain fell harder. "Work detail, dig the grave. The rest of you, under the trees and see to your arms."

The burial detail was commanded by Virgil, who had volunteered, and otherwise consisted of the morning's mutineers, looking a little the worse for wear.

Virgil and Paget dug the outlines of the grave with the spades they had carried, cutting deeply into the sod and lifting squares clear until they had a hole six feet long and three wide. Then Romeo and Willy began to break the ground with their picks. Romeo cut away with a will, clearly anxious to please; Willy looked as if every cut hurt him. The platoon watched them work in total silence. Mr. Edgerton took snuff; Mr. Robinson removed a tiny tinderbox from his pocket and got a pipe lit, quickly and easily. Several of the men watched enviously; none of their tinderboxes was waterproof enough to keep their tinder dry in the rain.

Mr. Robinson was an astute man, and he caught the looks soon enough. "Got a pipe packed? Bring it here." He took Tonny's pipe and lit it from his own and passed it back. The spark was passed to other pipes, and gradually all the men who smoked either had a pipe or shared with another. The grave went down, and the platoon sat under the apple trees, cold and wet.

When the men with picks had broken the ground, the men with spades would come in and throw the earth up out of the grave. By his third round of breaking ground, Willy looked used up. Caesar took off his brown cloth coatee and laid it on the ground, then went and took the pick out of the other man's hands.

"You go rest awhile." Caesar jerked his head sharply toward the trees, where the others were resting. Then he began to break the ground. When he was done with his half, he found that two more men had stepped forward to take the places of Virgil and Paget. Tonny took the pick from him, and two by two the whole platoon dug down through the red clay and the sand until the grave was deep and wide.

⋆ ⋆ ⋆

Another month of waiting and working. The camp was more orderly now, laid out in streets, long rows of hordled tents with planks gray in the sun, stretching out like small houses facing one another across an empty street of mud. There weren't enough tents for all the troops, and many of the Loyalists, black and white, had built huts of brush in the shape of tents. Boards from the plantation's barns had been used to hordle some of the tents, and many of these were now thatched in straw. Every day the camp looked more permanent.

Caesar was out alone, standing in the rain under the same apple trees and watching Captain Honey drill his men. He had them strung out across the whole field, each file of two men separated by some yards, and every man seemed to be loading and firing his musket on his own time. There was so much to it that was different from the soldiering Caesar knew that at first he couldn't see that the men were under command at all; it looked as if each man were making his own decisions. But after an hour of drill, Caesar could see that they expanded and contracted on the captain's little silver whistle. They could also halt or advance on the whistle, and when they fired, Caesar gradually sorted that each man in a file was aiming while his partner was loading, so that half the line was loaded at any given time. It looked like a very sensible way to fight in close country, but it asked more from the soldiers because they lost the comfort of the solid wall of their fellows.

He heard Captain Honey give an order, although it was indistinct, and there was a groan from the ranks, a sense of levity that Caesar hadn't seen from regular soldiers, but he knew that Honey was well liked by his men. Then both ranks threw themselves down on the wet ground and seemed to roll on their backs and then on their stomachs like acrobats. Caesar stepped out from among the apple trees to see better, his movements not quite conscious, until he was halfway toward them in the dying light.

They were practicing loading and firing while lying flat on the ground, firing prone. Caesar had never seen the Fourteenth do it, and he resolved to ask Steele whether he knew the trick of it. He could tell that it was not simple; the movement of the ramrod in the barrel while lying on your back clearly took tremendous coordination, and the men were all now soaking wet. But it was the last drill of the evening, and as the rain began to lash down, Honey had the sergeants form them up again and march them back to their cantonment. Caesar followed at a fair distance. It wasn't that any of the marines had shown the hostility that Honey had to the black men, but that Caesar didn't feel he wanted to give them an opportunity to show it. He was becoming careful.

Instead, he crossed through the lines to where Steele and his mess group had a hordled tent on the right of the Fourteenth. Three men of Steele's six were sick, making the tent seem empty. Caesar knocked on the pole, taking extra care not to give rise to any resentment. White soldiers in groups were not always friendly.

"Who's that, then?"

"Julius Caesar."

"You know, mate, from anyone else, that name would be a joke. Come in out of the wet, then, and don't bring it with you."

Caesar unhooked the tent flap and slipped in. There was a dense fug of pipe smoke and unwashed soldier inside, but it was warm and snug, like the tobacco-drying shed. The men of the Fourteenth were veterans, and they knew how to live in the field. Even their mess fires were covered in brush wigwams that occasionally caught fire but kept the men warm and dry while they cooked, a habit they had "learned in Germany." Germany was just a name to Caesar, although it occurred nightly in his readings with Sergeant Peters. Germany was a place the real Caesar had fought in, where the barbarians were hard men and cruel. Caesar liked to think that the Fourteenth had served there.

Caesar sat on another man's pack when an outstretched palm indicated that he was welcome to it. He reached into his haversack and pulled out his tobacco box, offered it around. One soldier filled his pipe and the others simply nodded, as if accepting that he hadn't come empty-handed. No one spoke for a moment and pipes were lit. The period before the drummers beat last call was too precious to be wasted in idle chat.

"I have questions about the drill, Tom."

"God in heaven, look at this one, mates. He's still on about the drill. What is it, then?" Steele turned a tolerant eye on Caesar, whose passion to learn the military arts brought a patronizing amusement in most of the regular establishment noncommissioned officers.

"Do you know how to fire lying down, Tom?"

"You've been watching the Jollies, you have," said another man, Herbert Atkins by name. "They have a different manual from us, any road. No knowing what them buggers will do. All that 'expanding' and 'contracting.' Poor bastards won't know how to form a company front, soon enough."

"Looks useful, though," said Caesar. "Think of Great Bridge, when the rebels were in entrenchments."

"Think how long it would take you to get to your feet and get your kit stowed if you had to move fast," said Steele, but kindly. "I was in the Light Company, back in '74. I probably will be again. We did some of those antics—and not another word from you, Bert Atkins. Sure, I can show you some of it. But it's gey hard, I'll tell you."

"I'd esteem it a favor, Tom. And another thing. What's an adjutant?"

Steele just shook his head. "Adjutant is an officer doing the job of a sergeant, to my way of thinkin'. He takes the rolls an' musters, and keeps the men at their drill, but in the old days when the army was in Europe, the sergeants and the sergeant major did all that."

"We don' have either one." Caesar hated going to the officers of other regiments with his accounts and muster rolls.

"You don't have ten companies, mate," said Bert Atkins. "Stands to reason that you don't get all the extrees until you've met the establishment of a regiment."

Steele looked embarrassed. "Every company has a barrack-room lawyer, Caesar. Bert's ours."

Caesar nodded at Bert, encouraging him to go on.

"Aye, well, you lot are lucky to have the likes of me to keep you from abuse, is all I can say. Caesar, when you have filled ten companies with recruits, and when the King has granted commissions to all your officers, so that every company has sixty men, and a captain an' his lieutenant and perhaps an ensign, why, then they call your battalion 'complete.' An' from that date, they muster you and give you a number, an' you are regulars, or they muster you only for local service an' call you provincials."

"We don't have ten companies," said Caesar.

"That's why you don't have a sergeant major or an adjutant, then. Every complete battalion has ten companies of sixty men and three officers, and one of those companies are grenadiers in their high fur hats and fancy clothes, an' the other is the poor light bobs in regiments that have them, always running about or being on patrol like huntsmen on a hunt day. They wear short coats and little leather helmets."

"The Fourteenth don't have a light company just now, Caesar. If they did, Bert would be in less of a hurry to speak ill of them."

"Why not?" asked Caesar, regretting the question immediately from the gleam in Bert's eye.

"Because light bobs cost money, don't they? And the colonel runs his regiment like a business, don't he? An' is the purpose of his business to win wars? No, boys, it is not. Is the purpose that Bert an' Tom and their mates be comfortable and warm in the field? No, mates, it is not. Is the purpose that the colonel makes a tidy profit on every cheap coat he sells us?"

Caesar interrupted the indignant flow. "Sells you?"

"Oh, aye!" called another from the back of the tent, and Steele turned a tolerant eye on Caesar.

"We buy all our gear, don't we? Every copper is charged against our pay. But is it ours? No, lad, it ain't. Can a lad sell his musket for a few tots? Not unless he wants a bloody back."

"Some regiments is run different," said Bert. "I've seen some as the colonel don't care to make a copper on his lads, an' they have all the best. Good coats, rain shirts, fancy packs that keep the wet out."

"Like the marines?" asked Caesar, and they all looked at him as if he'd grown an extra head.

"Marines ain't in the army, lad," said Steele, shaking his head at Caesar's ignorance. "They're in the navy."

"Paid more an' us, too," said another voice.

"Better an' more o' everything."

"So they're in the navy. And you don't have a light company?"

"Even though we are required to by the warrants," Bert said triumphantly.

"But until we have one, we won't get our own adjutant?" asked Caesar. Steele nodded.

Caesar nodded back at him, with much to ponder, and silence fell again, until Bert poked forward a little from his place in the back, hesitant.

"Saw you bury your man today."

The other three white soldiers nodded solemnly.

"Very proper, your lot looked. Sorry you lost another—we've been hit hard our own selves."

Caesar nodded, surprised to be so affected by their comment. "Thankee, gentlemen. I'll pass your kindness to my company." He rose as the drummer at the head of camp began tapping his drum and pulling the head taut, no easy feat in the rain, but a fair warning that the camp was about to close up. "Good night."

"Good night, Julius Caesar!" they called from the warmth of the tent, and men in the next tent laughed.

Chapter Ten

Head of Elk, Pennsylvania, April 6, 1776

Of all the drummers in the regiment, theirs beat the best assembly. He was the best at all the calls, which didn't keep Bludner from hating him. He was standing in front of them now, beating the call to arms like an important man, and Bludner couldn't abide it. The drummer was the captain's pet. He turned his flare of temper on his men.

"You bastards going to take all day?" Sergeant Bludner watched the men fall in with something like contempt. "This ain't the milishee anymore, *boys.* This is the Continental Army. An' we don' jus' fall in whenever we feel the urge." He had the iron ramrod from his Brown Bess musket in his hand, and he used it viciously, cutting at the last man into the line. The man fell down.

"Jesus Gawd!" the man gasped.

"Get up! Get up before I hit you again." The man climbed slowly to his feet and Bludner regarded them all with amusement.

"I'll say this one more time, *boys.* We ain't in the milishee no more. And when Captain Lawrence tells you to fall in, you fall in. You don' dawdle around looking for food, or whatever you last few was doin'. Listen for the drum. That drum will tell you everything you need to know to keep me on your good side. You hear assembly, you jus' drop what you're doin' an' get here with your kit on an' your musket clean."

He looked over the company, mostly raised from men like himself and Weymes—back-country men, hard men. But a few were farmers' sons from the Tidewater, and they resented his bullying. He didn't care; they were fit, but they were soft, and he had to lick them into shape.

Bludner had served in Dunmore's campaign against the Indians in '74. He had a low opinion of militia at the best of times, and the politically charged militia that had come out to fight the British were the worst of the lot. Most of the men who had stayed to enlist in the Virginia Regiment and join the Continental Army were men to whom a steady job of soldiering came as financial advancement. The promise of land grants was too good to be missed. Everyone in Virginia knew someone who had been enriched by the land grants to the veterans of the last war. So most of the big talkers were gone, but a few lingered, and Bludner was watching them.

"Sergeant Bludner?"

"Sergeant McCoy. Your company, sir!"

McCoy nodded and Bludner walked back to his position on the left as the company's junior sergeant. McCoy stood in front of them for a moment as if considering them. "On the drum. Poise your firelocks!"

Beat.

It burned Bludner that they had to go through the motions to the nigger's drum. He didn't resent McCoy, who was a soldier, but he hated the appearance that the darky was giving orders.

They weren't ragged. Every musket came up, and every eye was looking through his trigger guard at some invisible point in the distance.

"Rest your firelocks!"

Beat.

Almost crisp, the muskets sank to a position over the right knee, firmly grasped in both hands.

"Order your firelocks!"

Beat.

Every musket was brought down to the ground next to the owner's right foot, held upright by his right hand. Sergeant McCoy had served in various armies since he was a very small boy; he had seen both better and worse. They were lucky to have such a fine drummer. It gave the men an advantage that they already knew how to follow the drum, because in battle the drum would still sound when all the voices were shouted out. He needed powder and ball to get much further. That, and time to drill with the rest of the battalion. McCoy executed a sharp about-face, glanced up and down to see if the other senior sergeants were in line, and took off his hat to indicate that his company was ready. Throughout the battalion, the same orders were repeated. Some sergeants walked along the ranks inspecting the men, while others simply talked to their men, made jokes, or stood silent. No two companies were commanded the same way.

When they were all ready, the adjutant, a small man with livid smallpox scars, called the regiment to attention. "Fall in the officers!"

A long line of the regiment's officers marched on to the parade. Captain Lawrence marched stiffly up to Sergeant McCoy, now posted on the right of the company. Lawrence seemed inconvenienced by the spontoon he now carried at the commander's insistence, a weapon like a spear with a six-foot haft and a short spear blade and crossbar. McCoy fell back a step and Lawrence stepped into his place. Off to the center of the regiment, the adjutant passed command over to the colonel, who saluted him with his sword.

At the other end of the company, Sergeant Bludner was allowing his body to run like an automaton; his mind was elsewhere. While the colonel addressed them on the seeds of tyranny and love of liberty, Sergeant Bludner was examining the captain's drummer and seriously considering how to seize him before they marched into Philadelphia.

Because on the docks in Philadelphia, he'd fetch them a pretty penny.

Near Philadelphia, Pennsylvania, May 5, 1776

George Lake wanted to whistle along with the fifers, his heart was so high as they marched through Philadelphia. The regiment looked splendid, in good brown coats and new breeches, all of Russian linen that wore like iron. Their hats were already showing the signs of shoddy workmanship and poor edging. George had made his share of hats as an apprentice, and his own was stiff with shellac and as fine as any regular's, as well as possessing the fine quality of shedding water. And George had a white mohair knot on his shoulder, indicating that he was a corporal in the Virginia Regiment, and hence in the Continental Army. He'd obtained the knot only because he could read and write, but he'd held it fair and square, though there were other men with more experience.

His company looked well, and they marched well, too, thanks to the drummer. Although more than half the men were back-country hicks who were fighting only for the pay, the other half were men of conviction, who had read all the letters from the Continental Congress and felt honored to be allowed to stand up for their colony and their conscience. George was honest enough to admit that the back-country men were harder, tougher on the long marches coming north, and stronger in the daily camp fights, but the younger men were coming along, and George thought they'd have the edge when it came to battle.

He'd heard a great deal about battle from the older men. Some had fought Indians in the West, although that seemed neither here nor there. McCoy had fought in Europe and been in a real battle. Simmons, another older man, had been all the way to Fort Pitt in the last war, and though he'd never come to grips with the French, he knew his way around the camp like the other veterans. But all the veterans agreed that it was no easy thing to stand and receive the enemy's fire, the great crashing volleys that sent thousands of musket balls whirling about your ears. And it was there, where it came to standing your ground, that George felt the younger men had an advantage. They believed. They wanted their liberty with a passion, and that liberty had some very concrete meaning. Other men might fight for rations, comrades, or a land grant in the Ohio country. They might stand the enemy's fire, or they might not. But the true believers would be there until the end; of that George was sure.

George could see the second platoon sergeant, Bludner, slightly out of place as he always was on the march. Sergeants had their spot in the line, marching even with the front rank and just to the right of the rightmost man, and Bludner was never quite there, as if he wouldn't quite admit he belonged to the regiment despite his rank. He tended to carry his weapon, one of the company's few rifles, in the crook of his arm instead of at his shoulder or at the advance like the other sergeants in the regiment. But Captain Lawrence seemed to tolerate him, despite the fact that even now he *wasn't in step*. George had heard him tell his men that "marching in step is taking orders from the Negro." It made George wild. He'd never seen much of black men, working in a trade as an apprentice until his master went broke and headed west, but Noah was the company's pride, the best drummer in the regiment, and he made them look better in the drill.

Bludner enforced discipline with a cheerful violence that Lake hated. He didn't want the Continental Army run by bullies like the despotic

British, but an army of men of conviction who didn't need petty tyrants to beat them into line. Lake was determined to outshine Bludner. He wanted Bludner's type out of the army, and he wasn't alone. As the true believers hardened their muscles, they also became firmer in their convictions: The old ways had to go; there could be no compromise with the king; America must be free and independent. He had heard the rumors that the Congress intended such a declaration, and it raised his heart to think that soon they would not just be defending their liberties but taking the cause of liberty to the enemy.

He looked across the front of his rank. Tanner was inching up and just out of rhythm, although not quite out of step. He prodded the man with his eyes until Tanner caught the signal and adjusted himself, and then they were entering the main concourse of the city of Philadelphia, and the cheering began. Lake knew from the meetings in camp that many of the inhabitants were Tories or worse, or Quakers who wouldn't fight for the cause. But he saw many a pretty face under black bonnets in the crowd, and many in caps as smart as anything he had seen in Williamsburg. Philadelphia was the largest city he had ever been to, and he was finally seeing the world.

He tried not to turn his head to watch the crowd, but he did from time to time and what he saw always pleased him: men cheering lustily, and women waving and yelling with shrill, clear voices. They halted several times, not from purpose but because the long column of companies regularly jammed when an inept officer timed his wheeling motion badly, or just because of the different marching rates of all the battalions. When they halted, men and women would come out and offer the troops bread or beer.

Near the City Tavern, in the prosperous heart of the city, they halted in the sun for so long that men were calling out to Captain Lawrence, asking if they could fall out. Tanner took his tinderbox from his coat and lit a pipe, which the men passed around while Lake glowered.

A very young girl, barely old enough to be thought a "young lady," came out to them from a fine brick house with a stone pitcher of milk. Another older woman in an apron followed with another pitcher, and they began to serve it to the men. One of Bludner's men laughed.

"I thought all you Phillydelps was Tories or Quakers."

The older woman stopped and glared at him. "I think it no shame to say that I remain loyal to the king. He has some poor ministers, that I'll allow, and no man serving this province should stand in the sun in front of my house without a drink. But if you want to argue politics, lad, then you can just hand me back my pitcher."

The man looked shamefaced, then he laughed along when he was jeered by the others.

George smiled at the pretty girl. "That your ma?" he asked.

"Yes," she said, her eyes cast down. Close up, she was a little older than he had thought, perhaps fourteen or fifteen. She wore a printed cotton gown from England that would have cost him a year's wage and he grew shy.

"She put him in his place," George said, at a loss for anything better. She looked up from under her cap, and he saw her eyes were dark blue, with a sparkle he'd not seen before. She smiled impishly.

Tanner jogged his elbow. "Don't keep her for yourself, George," he said.

Ahead of them, the column was moving again, and George regretted it, although this little sprig of a girl was three years his junior and several classes above him.

"Betsy, is your jug empty?" asked the older woman, coming up George's file. George handed the jug back to Betsy, aware suddenly that he must be wearing milk on his mouth like a fool. She smiled as he wiped it off, and gave him a little wave when they marched. And then they were gone.

Sally's Neck, Virginia, May 18, 1776

Jim was gaining weight, and the Ethiopians had their women back. Caesar thought that the two might be connected. Virgil took sick soon after he saw Sally coming up from the boat—went down, lay sick, and then began to mend on his own. He was the last man in the company to go down.

It seemed odd now, because after Long Tom's death they had all taken for granted that Jim would die, too, but he didn't. For a month, he just lay there, neither alive nor dead. Jim just lay sick, a sickness that seemed endless, and there were men in the ranks who knew their drill and had never known him except as a sick man. Caesar knew that Sally had nursed him, brought him treats and both food and wine from the officers'

table. Caesar knew that she lived with Captain Edgerton and made no secret of it. Her nursing, first of Virgil and then of Jim, won her some grudging praise within the ranks, but she wasn't liked by the men, especially
those with wives of their own. She was the only unmarried black woman
and she was loose. Many thought it brought them all down.

Caesar went every evening to see his sergeant and get a lesson. Back in
the winter he had helped the other men build a cabin for Peters and his
wife, and later they had built cabins for every mess, until their billets were
better provided than the marines or the Fourteenth. Peters kept him at
reading and writing, and started him on basic mathematics. None of it
was pleasant for Caesar, to whom learning came late and seldom without
pain. But he wouldn't let it go.

Mrs. Peters, once installed, was an education in herself. Alone of the
married women, she spoke well of Sally and had her in the cabin sometimes, sewing or speaking softly in the fire corner while Caesar and
Sergeant Peters sat at the desk by the door. When Sally was not about,
and her name came up for censure, Mrs. Peters would simply look over
her sewing and say that some people had to find their own way, or that
uncommon looks weren't always a blessing. It was always said in a tone
that reduced a corporal's or private's wife to silence.

As the weeks of inaction stretched to months, Caesar's grasp of reading went from ignorance, through frustration, to accomplishment. And
once accomplished, he wanted to use it as a key to unlock all the things
he didn't understand. But the foremost thing that interested him was the
origin of his name, and on that head Sergeant Peters could give him immediate satisfaction. They began to read together through Colonel
Bladen's G. *Julius Caesar's Commentaries of His Wars in Gaul*, which Peters
had, bound in vellum. It was difficult going, both in style and content,
and Caesar began to see patterns in Peters's speech that were affected
from this very book, which interested him. He also learned that the original Julius Caesar had another name—Gaius. And that Caesar understood something about war, and spoke of it with a detachment that he
had never experienced in a warrior.

And that Caesar sold slaves by the thousand.

No night with the Peterses passed without discussion, or even argument, because the matter buried in G. *Julius Caesar's Commentaries of His
Wars in Gaul* was too important not to be argued. And sometimes Sally, or
another woman, would be there, or Virgil, when he started to mend, lying

on their good bed and listening. Virgil was too quiet a man to contribute when he had so little to say, but the quality of his silence always suggested that he took a great deal away with him.

It was after one of these evenings that Caesar emerged to the first rattlings of the night drum, paid his respects from the doorway, and started back down the line to his own hordled tent, only to hear an argument in progress in the next street—Mr. Robinson's company. Caesar crossed his street of tents and then walked between two of them into the Robinson company street, where he found that Mr. Robinson himself and Captain Honey were the combatants. Caesar stopped dead. They were both obviously the worse for liquor and cared nothing that their voices could be heard throughout the street.

"If we use your black savages to fight this war, we will be dishonored! This is a white man's war, a war of ideas. These primitives have no place in it." Honey was drunkenly adamant, almost pleading for Robinson to understand.

"There's no moral difference between using them to dig your ditches and using them to fight, Captain. But I'll leave that argument aside, because I can see that moral philosophy holds no interest for you."

"What do you mean by that, then? I can take moral philosophy as well as the next man, I think."

"You cannot, Captain Honey. You are a slaver and your family is all Bristol blackbirders, and you stand condemned as such. You cannot bear the weight of reasoned morality."

"You sneer at the trade? When it is the lifeblood of England's riches? When six in ten of our ships carry goods for the trade? When seven in ten of every yard of cloth we produce goes to Africa? Where will we replace that? In the *palm oil* trade? Who will work the plantations in the Indies? No white man would stoop so low, and even if he would, his body wouldn't last the labor."

"I find your 'trade' so iniquitous that, rather than suffer it, I sold my plantation. Rather than suffer it, I lost my fortune. And now, moved by the hypocrisy of those who live off that trade ranting about 'freedom from tyranny,' I find myself at war with all my former acquaintance." Robinson didn't slur a word, but his face was bright red, even in the light of the lantern he carried, and his tone carried a vehemence that belied his usual manner.

Heads were coming out of tents and cabins. Honey was not on friendly ground. He was in the Loyal Ethiopian lines, and the next street held the Fourteenth, where he was scarcely more popular. Caesar knew that the two men were far enough gone that they were heading to violence, and he feared the effect on discipline that this argument would have. But he was also fascinated because the arguments about slavery and trade were among those that came up in Peters's cabin.

"And you prove your love of these animals by living with them and fucking one!" Honey's anger swelled by this thought, he stepped forward and raised his lantern. Robinson stood his ground so that they were standing nose to nose.

Robinson could hardly argue that it was not he but Mr. Edgerton who lived with a black woman, or that such cohabitation was common as common on the plantations. But he did resent Honey's tone and his advance.

"Lower your lantern, sir."

"I'm looking to see if your skin is really white."

Caesar caught Robinson's arm as he reached for his sword. Later he wondered why Robinson had to react to the last as a mortal offense; he seemed to accept blacks totally, but then couldn't accept being identified with them.

"Gentlemen. Your pardon, but the drummer has beat the night call and I must inspect the street, gentlemen." Caesar kept his voice low and calm, willing them to move on to their separate quarters, to get his message and act on it.

Robinson started like a man coming awake and stepped back.

"Saved by your slaves, you cowardly bumpkin!" Honey, sure he had the situation in hand, glared.

"I cannot challenge you as you are my commanding officer," Robinson said calmly. "But the moment you lose your authority over me, I'll show you who is a coward, Captain. Good night."

Robinson walked up the street to his own hut, quite steady. Honey stood for a moment, glaring, and then subsided, perhaps even embarrassed by his last outburst. He glared at Caesar, then began to stumble toward his lines. It occurred to Caesar to help him. Part of Caesar still admired the man for his skills as a soldier, but he couldn't bring himself to help the man back to his quarters, and he turned back to his own.

★ ★ ★

It had been a wonder to all of them that they had made it through the winter without contact with the rebels. The word in camp was that the rebel army had melted away after the battle at Great Bridge. It was an army composed entirely of militia, and they were farmers and shopkeepers and needed to be home. Nor did they have the discipline or the equipment to live out in the fields. And the winter had given Caesar a taste of the cost of such camps, the rations that had to be rowed ashore every day by the navy, the two little brigs kept moving constantly to bring supplies to them from somewhere far to the north. But as the spring began to turn the gray landscape back to green, the rebel army was recalled to its duty. The farmers were grudging, because it was time to plant. But they came.

A marine patrol encountered rebels beyond the creek, ending their isolation. Without any fighting, their outposts were called in. A large force of rebel militia began to dig trenches across the top of the peninsula. Two days later, the governor decided to withdraw his troops back to the boats.

Embarkation was orderly, and the navy did its usual workmanlike job of transporting several hundred soldiers and their wives and matériel from the small cantonment out to the waiting ships. The guns came off first, and the marines last.

The Loyal Ethiopians worked from dawn until dark, packing their equipment and then dismantling the lines they had dug with so much labor, hauling the cannon that had been landed from the ships, and loading the longboats. There was no time to drill, or talk, or learn to read. For two days, they labored every hour of daylight.

Virgil, back on his feet and almost healthy, managed to secrete several barrels of their tobacco among the military stores, ensuring a continued supply of cash. They were supposed to be paid as soldiers, but they hadn't received pay since Williamsburg. The lack of hard coin was hardly limited to the black troops. Most men of the Fourteenth hadn't seen their pay since the start of the campaign.

On Tuesday, the guns went into the boats, a piece of engineering that delighted Caesar as he watched the sailors set up a spiderweb of ropes and hoist the guns off their cradles and crane them into the ships' boats, one tube at a time. On Wednesday, they loaded the Fourteenth's baggage and women, and on Thursday, they loaded their own. The marines had no followers or women, and they loaded their own kits.

Friday morning dawned bright and calm, the sun already giving the promise of great heat in the first moments of dawn while the drummer beat. Caesar got his section up and in their jackets, and then marched them to the parade, where they met the other sections and formed their company. Gradually, all three of the companies formed up in the new light, and then Mr. Robinson led them down to the magazine, the last structure left in the cantonment, to take their arms and accoutrements. Two sentries from the marines were waiting for them, and they looked unhappy.

Their confrontation with Mr. Robinson was far to the front of their column, but the rumor filtered back to Caesar fast enough. *No arms. They won't give us our arms.* Caesar heard Mr. Robinson quite clearly when he lost his temper.

"These are not slaves! These men are soldiers!"

And the sentry replied, "We have our orders."

They stood for a while in the rising sun, and then Robinson marched them back to their own parade. It had a forlorn look, no longer surrounded by huts and tents. The tentage had been folded and packed out to the boats, and the huts knocked down, and their parade was just an open space in the middle of the wreckage of their camp. They all felt naked, standing here without muskets—here, where every morning of the winter had seen them parade under arms and drill, even if the drill was followed by a day of labor. Robinson paced up and down in front of the three companies; Mr. Edgerton had already found a stool, sat upon it, and opened a book. Finally, Robinson called for the officers and sergeants. As Caesar was acting in lieu of a sergeant in Mr. Edgerton's company, he moved forward hesitantly, but no one seemed to resent his presence.

Robinson spoke angrily. "I'm going to the governor. Mr. Edgerton, please do not take the men to the ships until this matter is resolved. Remember, there are other companies in our battalion, at other posts. We owe it to them to resolve this. I don't need to tell you, gentlemen, that it will be very difficult to keep the men to their duty if we lose our arms. Frankly, it will be difficult to keep me to my duty. That is all. Have the men rest on the spot. I'd like them ready to move at a moment's notice."

And then he was gone.

An hour later, Caesar was sitting on a broken twelve-pounder ammunition crate, sharing a smoke with Virgil. Caesar's pipe was foul, and he thought he might start a small fire to rebake the pipe and burn it clean. He mentioned this to Virgil, who agreed enthusiastically.

"Won't get another chance when we're on board ship," he said. "I heard we goin' out for months."

"I heard they're sending us to Jamaica," said Caesar. He shrugged. "I don't want to go back to Jamaica, even less if I don't have arms."

"We wouldn't stay free a minute," agreed Virgil, already digging in his pack for his tinderbox. Caesar laid up a fire from the abundant scrap, and in a moment they had a small blaze. As soon as they had coals, other men came and placed their pipes in them. A few minutes in the coals would burn a clay pipe back to the chalky whiteness that meant it was clean and restore the taste. So absorbed had most of Edgerton's company become in this ritual that they missed the first navy midshipman altogether. He came and demanded that the Loyal Ethiopians board their transports. Edgerton refused, pleading orders.

They all heard the second messenger. By this time, the only troops ashore were the Ethiopians and some marine pickets out beyond the former earthworks. There were rebels in the area, although they seemed as anxious to let the British and Loyalists leave as the former were to be gone. The second messenger was an older midshipman, blond and heavyset and glowing red in the heat. He towered over Edgerton, who would never have been called large.

"Sir, we must get your men aboard."

"Sir, please inform your officer that I have orders from my superior that these men are not to march without their arms."

"Your arms have already been moved from the magazine. It is not a navy matter. My captain assures you that once we are aboard ship the matter will be looked into."

Edgerton held firm. Caesar was surprised. Edgerton had never seemed as firm in their cause, or in any cause for that matter, and that he now stood up to a growing queue of naval dignitaries raised the man in his estimation. But they all began to wonder at the absence of Mr. Robinson.

As the morning wore into afternoon and Caesar's fire died and the pipes became cool enough to be enjoyed, the rank of the navy officers reached a new height when the captain of their vessel himself came ashore. He didn't appear angry, though. He walked purposefully up to Edgerton and took him off to the side. Every man in the Ethiopians watched the exchange, although none could hear it. The captain spoke for a while, and Edgerton suddenly straightened as if struck or shot, then slumped. The impression of injury was so strong that several of the Ethiopians started forward but halted when they saw him shake his head and address the captain briefly. Then he bowed, wiped his eyes, and moved slowly back to the men where they waited, defeat written on his features, and ordered the sergeants to have them fall in. The navy captain stood nearby, clearly unhappy. When the men were standing in their ranks, Edgerton looked them over, and when he spoke, his voice had aged.

"You are to march aboard the boats immediately. The navy doesn't wish you to know, but to hell with that. Captain Honey has shot Mr. Robinson. They say it was a duel. Any rate, we are to go to a different ship lest there be a 'difference of opinion.' "

Sergeant Peters spoke up strongly from his place at the right of his company. "How is Mr. Robinson? Sir?"

Edgerton looked at him, his eyes red from tears held back. He looked older, a broken man in middle age. "He's dead. Now get them moving."

Philadelphia, late May 1776

Weymes held back, the lantern under his watch coat, an enveloping garment provided by the grateful ladies of Williamsburg. Bludner stood in his sergeant's uniform at the edge of the parade, his arms crossed, the picture of impatience. The camp was dark; the last drum call had sounded. Weymes had to strain to see Bludner, but eventually the man nodded to him, and Weymes began to pick his way through the camp, counting tents and brush huts until he came to the one where their fifers and drummers lay. It was a cunning work of layered brush and added thatch, both warm and dry but a refuge for every mosquito in the camp, even on a night as chill as this. He tugged at the wool blanket that hung across the entrance.

"Noah?" He mimicked McCoy's Irish accent. "Yer wanted on the parade, my lad." He kept his voice low, to make the disguise work the better, and as soon as he heard a response and movement from the hut, he pulled the watch coat around him and, lantern visible, began to walk back to the parade. Decoying blacks had long been part of his trade; he was almost pleased to be doing something more useful than shouldering a musket.

He looked back once, to see that Noah was close behind. It wouldn't really matter now if the boy identified him; it was important that the other musicians remember McCoy coming to the tent, not him or Bludner.

Weymes didn't understand the plan, but it didn't trouble him. Bludner tended to make large plans and Weymes knew he need only play his parts to get his share of the reward.

As he passed out of the streets of tents and wigwams and on to the parade, the boy caught up with him.

"Wait, suh! I need ma' drum!"

"Not where you're going, my lad!" said Bludner, and clamped a huge hand over his mouth. The boy tried to fight, squirming and scratching until Bludner pulled him close and hit him almost gently, just behind the ear.

Weymes held the sack while Bludner dropped him in. They hoisted it and were out of the camp in a minute. The night was hardly even old before they passed the lines of sentries, and the buyer was waiting in the old apple orchard by the river, just as he had said. He opened the sack and ran his hands over the boy, inside his mouth and over his teeth and gums, then over all his limbs—nothing sensual, just the rough touch of the horse trader.

The buyer looked happy. "Just as you said, gentlemen. Did he put up much of a fight?"

"He took it 'ard. They always do, the poor beggars. But he'll be happier when he's back to real work. They're bred to slavery. Freedom don' suit them."

"Right, then. Here's the price as agreed."

Bludner counted the money. Spanish dollars and some English silver, well over ten pounds English, and hard currency.

"You're a real gen'leman, sir. A fine price. I think I must add that it wouldn' be fair for you to sport this lad around 'ere for a while. The company would know 'im if they saw 'im."

The other man laughed, a hard laugh that might have touched Weymes if he'd been alone. "He'll be in the Indies in five weeks, given a fair wind. Good night, then." He hoisted the bag and headed off toward the city. They split the money there, and Bludner repeated their story until Weymes had it right. They knew the game.

In an hour, they were asleep in their straw.

☆　☆　☆

George Lake never really believed that McCoy had anything to do with the disappearance of Noah, but most of the men did, although the true believers muttered that Bludner had been a slave-taker and that once a man had fallen so low he was there forever. George never quite figured what Captain Lawrence thought; he never mixed with the men, and after Noah vanished he seemed harder than ever. The other drummers insisted that McCoy had called Noah to the parade at night, which he sometimes did when he wanted to practice an alarm. McCoy repeated to anyone who would listen that he had never called the black boy, that he was innocent, that the whole company was hurt by the loss.

It was the wonder of a few days, and much discussed. Bludner beat a man very badly for suggesting that he had been involved, but didn't bother to hide his satisfaction that the boy was gone.

"He made us look low" was Bludner's response to any suggestion that the boy had been valuable.

The other drummer was passable, although he did tend to mix his signals when he got flustered. His sticking was good enough, and he started training a young soldier from Lake's own section. For two weeks, their marching suffered, as the new drummer beat his drum a little too slow or a little too fast, throwing the men off in one evolution or another and forcing an angry Captain Lawrence to demand that the drummer stay silent so that the men could perform their maneuvers.

The aftermath of the boy's loss split the company even more deeply. Bludner blamed the new drummer for being "unfit, like all these soft boys," and the true believers rallied behind their own and suspected that Bludner had shown his colors and taken the boy. Fights got worse, and McCoy had suddenly lost the authority to deal with them. Too many still suspected him, and someone had whispered that he blamed Bludner to cover his own guilt. It was an ugly time.

But rumors that the British were moving on New York City began to drown the concerns of their company, and by early June, when they were issued with ball ammunition and three days' rations for a march, it became clear that they were going north. No one knew where the British would land, or whether there would be a fight, but at last they were leaving Philadelphia. They didn't march so well, and Captain Lawrence never seemed to be pleased, but they were done with the camp and going to the war.

III

War

Do you not know that life is a soldier's service? One man must keep guard, another go out to reconnoiter, another take the field. It is not possible for all to stay where they are, nor is it better so. But you neglect to fulfill the orders of the general and complain, when some severe order is laid upon you; you do not understand to what a pitiful state you are bringing the army so far as in you lies; you do not see that if all follow your example there will be no one to dig a trench, or raise a palisade, no one to keep night watch or fight in the field, but every one will seem an unserviceable soldier.

. . . So too it is in the world; each man's life is a campaign, and a long and varied one. It is for you to play the soldier's part—do everything at the General's bidding, divining his wishes, if it be possible.

—EPICTETUS

Chapter Eleven

Sergeant King returned to them briefly. He had recovered from his wound but was almost unable to speak from the damage to his mouth, and eating was a labor. He went back to the navy immediately, stopping only to shake hands with the men who had been in his platoon. He convinced a few to join the Royal Navy.

"No bastard will treat you like they treated ye," he said, his voice full of gravel. "Navy needs men, an' don' ask too close about their past or their color."

That much was true. Both of the frigates that had waited out the winter with them in the Chesapeake were clearly short of men. The war had caught them unprepared, with peacetime crews meant for chasing foes no more dangerous than the occasional smuggler. The heavy crews that were needed to fight the great guns and sail the ship were kept only in wartime. Sailors were better paid than soldiers, and such crews were too much for the navy to maintain when there was no one to fight. The war with the colonists changed that, and the ships on the American station were taking any men they could get.

The rumors that they were bound for New York as a labor force grew to the point where Sergeant Peters, now a sick man, confessed to Caesar that if he didn't have his wife to care for, he'd consider enlisting as a sailor himself. Mr. Edgerton took no action to stop the navy from taking his men. Indeed, he was barely visible for most of the spring, and then one day they heard he had been posted to the board of ordnance, leaving them without an officer, which seemed a dangerous development.

Caesar didn't trust the navy. And he had had a taste of the army, and wanted to try it again. He had exercised command, and liked it. But it was more complicated than that, in his mind, and he sought to understand it all. Perhaps it was the acceptance from the Fourteenth Foot when they were about to go on to the fight at Great Bridge, just the acceptance of other men. Perhaps it was the thrill of the fight. Caesar knew he had been bred to love that in Africa. He fancied the army, and he meant to make his way in it.

The Fourteenth changed transports and went off to the Indies with the navy, bound for a different campaign. Caesar had no warning and no chance to say good-bye, but understood from the sailors that France, another great power over the water, was threatening war, and the ships and men were going south to the tropics to defend the sugar islands against them. Caesar smiled a little to himself. He didn't think his heart would have been in any defense of the sugar islands, even if the devils of hell had been the enemy.

☆   ☆   ☆

They were moved to the *Penelope*, a transport that now held most of the remaining Ethiopians and their women, and the frigates left them, taking away the chance of freedom within the harsh discipline of the navy and the chance of riches in prize money.

Jim, once he recovered, grew at an astounding rate. Sally had brought him food every day, whether he ate it or not, and once he was well enough to eat, the richer food seemed to extend his bones a little every day.

Willy and Paget began to creep into their circle as the rumors flew and the treatment on board ship grew more like the treatment they had endured on land at the end. At first, Caesar kept them at arm's length, as troublemakers, but Tonny and Virgil pleaded their case, and, in time, they were allowed to sit and smoke in the section of cable tier that the group had marked down as their own. Lope stayed with them as well. He wasn't bright, but he worked hard, and he could sew a bit.

The *Penelope*, of Liverpool, was well found and relatively new, but she sagged to leeward, couldn't sail anything like a bowline, and her captain spent much of his time drunk. The weeks wore into months and the ships remained anchored in little pools of their own filth, and *Penelope*'s little flaws of sailing became more obvious every time she moved to leave her waste behind her. The sailors had no animosity for the blacks, but what fellow feeling they might have shared was tempered with a lively inclination for the women the black soldiers brought with them, and only constant attention and some rumors of disease kept the situation from becoming deadly.

A bad storm would move them all out to sea to ride it out in safety, but a return to gentle weather meant back to the heat and the stench. The smell was all too familiar to the black passengers. The *Penelope* was coming to smell like a blackbirder, a slave ship.

Peters and Caesar maintained their authority. The mere fact that Caesar's circle stayed together gave them an edge; they were the largest group aboard, and the toughest, and they were willing to use force to keep order. Other ships might have become floating brothels or worse, but not the *Penelope*. The brief southern spring gave way to summer, and the heat and stench drove past unbearable and into hellish. And still Caesar walked the decks, talking to this one and that one, keeping their spirits up, holding them to the standards they had learned from the Fourteenth, both to drill and appearance. He paraded the women every so often, looking for bruises and split lips, for pregnancy, for all the things that the British soldiers looked for when they paraded their women. The women supported him, too. Black Lese, a big woman who had been a slave in New York and spoke Dutch, became their spokesman. She was not a "good" woman like Sergeant Peters's wife, and she cared nothing for the Bible, but she had become the mouthpiece of the women on the *Penelope*.

They no longer had arms, or if they did, the arms were stored in another ship, and no one troubled to tell them. So Caesar and Peters drilled the men with brooms or bits of spar that the sailors could spare, and drilled them every day, even as the heat became infernal. All the men grumbled. Most of those on board were Loyal Ethiopians, but not all; some were members of other units, or just blacks swept up in the last withdrawal from the peninsula. Peters decided early that they would all drill, and Caesar enforced this order.

Behind Peters's easy authority and educated air, there was another, distant mentor for Caesar in his Roman namesake, whose cunning and ruthlessness began to seem natural to Caesar in the hot air of the ship, whose lessons about war were there every night when he went to read with Sergeant Peters.

Caesar was learning to quell mutiny before it came to violence, but twice he missed his moment, or someone mistook his sincerity for weakness. Both times he crushed his opponent in the darkness of the lower deck, first winning and then punishing until his point was clear. That weakness was no kindness was a lesson he learned, and perhaps over-learned, from the crushing of the Gauls. The Gauls, whom the Roman Caesar made slaves.

Caesar's authority grew with practice until it was natural. And as it grew, he noticed that Tonny and Jim and Virgil seemed a little distant. It troubled him. The Roman Caesar never mentioned having a friend while he destroyed Gaul.

★　★　★

Rumor was part of daily life, but toward June the rumors flew thicker and faster. Every department seemed to have its own source of rumor and its own light to shine on possible futures. The sailors said they were going north, the soldiers maintained that they were going south, and the board of ordnance and the governor's staff suggested that they were going to Long Island, off the port of New York. Caesar knew enough former Ethiopians who were now servants aboard the governor's flagship to trust the latter, and began to pin his hopes on passage north to Long Island, and a summer campaign. The British army had been defeated in Boston as in Virginia, and by the middle of June hopes among the white Loyalists as to the outcome of the war seemed to be at an all-time low. But as the Royal Navy vessels set off one by one for the south—indicating that, as far as their own service was concerned, the sailors' scuttlebutt was as accurate as the servants' gossip—and the little fleet broke up, Caesar watched the trash around the ship with new hope.

They finally sailed away from the Chesapeake one day in late June, al-most the last ship to depart. The governor had left days before, and it had begun to seem to the blacks as if they were unwanted when the ship sud-denly trembled with new life. A few more passengers came aboard, the last white Loyalists to leave Virginia, and then, at the change of the tide, the sailors moved briskly for the first time in months, sails were hoisted, and they were away. The moment they dropped sight of land the breeze cooled, and although squalls had them all in the scuppers, sick and feeble for days, the cool and the rain were a welcome relief from the endless heat and the stench of the long delay. They were away north, and were leaving behind those unspoken fears that had plagued Caesar since the wait began: that they might be abandoned or sacrificed, or simply turned ashore.

After the first few days they were all well enough, and most of the hale men joined in the working of the ship as well as they were able. There was never a shortage of hands to pull on a rope or sweep the ship, flogging the last of the slave-ship stench out of her. There was no answer for the thick weed that now clung to her below the waterline, taking whatever fine points of sailing she might have had clean away, but what human hands could do aboard they all did. The captain sobered up to do his navigation, and the ship was happy enough.

Four days off the Chesapeake they saw a strange sail at twilight and the captain doubled back, sailing along his own wake half the night and then setting a new course. The Yankees were known to have privateers out in every water and every weather, and every black man and woman aboard feared them and the necessary return to slavery that would follow capture at sea. But the captain's simple ruse worked well enough, or perhaps there had been no threat to begin with. Either way, the morning found the horizon clear again, and so they sailed for days and days, the women sewing and singing, the men still busy at their drill or helping with the work of the ship.

On a Sunday early in July, they sailed into the great anchorage at Sandy Hook off Long Island, coasting into the midst of the greatest fleet any of them had ever seen, even the sailors aboard who had served in the last war. Through repeated hails they found the governor's ship, and came alongside long enough to report their presence. None of the blacks ever found the reason why their own *Penelope* had lingered so long, if there was a reason at all. But the great fleet brought hope to every Loyalist, black and white, that the king would not be defeated, that they would be upheld. For the whites, it suggested the possibility of the return of their property, and for the blacks, the hope of liberty.

On the third of July, the fleet landed troops on Staten Island, and Caesar and the remnants of the Ethiopians received their first taste of their new role in the army; they were dispatched ashore to dig entrenchments. It was easy work; there was no opposition, and the ground was soft after it had been broken up by picks. Despite the separation of the work from the drill under arms that constituted the "art of war," Caesar and all the Ethiopians set to it with a will. It offered a change from the cramped quarters of the ships, and they received their first pay since the last parade in Williamsburg, many months before. They were not paid to date; few soldiers were, but the existence of any pay at all at least confirmed that they were not slaves.

They dug under the supervision of officers from the engineers, a different breed from the other British officers they had met. Engineers were men who went to a difficult school in England. They did not purchase their commissions like other officers, but won them after long study in mathematics and gunnery. Peters and Caesar both came to the commanding engineer's notice quickly, because they could read and write, and Peters could do mathematics. Jim had stuck to his drawing, at least as long as they had been on board Mr. Harding's ship; he was also learning geometry from Peters. Murray, the senior engineer, had them copy his notes every day and read them back, as well as use their skills to get more out of the men. He complimented them absently (as if unaware that men needed such praise to get on with work) but mentioned the unit in his daily reports to the commander, Lord Howe.

The rebel army made no attempt to contest Staten Island, and soon afterward, Lord Howe's brother, the admiral, arrived at Sandy Hook with more ships and more men. There were so many vessels that Sandy Hook appeared a bare pine wood floating on the sea, with branches and trees as far as the eye could see. The Ethiopians went back to their ship, their ranks enlarged by some few Staten Island blacks they had liberated from farms there. A few spoke only Dutch, and Black Lese had to translate for them. Their odd words and overdone facial expressions gave them a comic air, but they dug as well as other men, and Peters placed them under Virgil to learn the basic drill, although few of the former Ethiopians really expected to see arms again. It was rapidly becoming a rite of passage that all the men knew how to perform the manual.

The armed sloop *Tryal*, anchored next to them, began to invite visitors to their drill, and it became part of the spectacle of the fleet. Sometimes officers would come and watch, as amused by the sight of black men at drill as they would have been by a bear dancing or other frolics that seemed to go against the natural order. But they drilled anyway, and gambled, and dreamed of ways to spend their pay.

After a few days, the *Tryal* and some larger frigates dropped down the river past the rebel posts there, and there was firing for several hours. Royal Navy ships around them beat to quarters, but they never knew what the purpose of the maneuver was, unless simply to strike confusion and terror in the king's enemies.

It was the middle of August before they showed any signs of disembarking again; most of the army lived in camps on Staten Island, but the Ethiopians were kept aboard their ship. It was cleaner, in the cooler air of Sandy Hook, the breezes were more frequent, and the spirits of the men and women aboard were higher than they had been in the Chesapeake. They waited. They watched the preparations, witnessed the arrival of Sir Henry Clinton's force that had failed to take Charleston in the south, watched the seaborne skirmishes up the river and the attack by the rebels with fire ships on HMS *Rose* and the *Tryal*. No one seemed to know why they were waiting or for what.

On the twenty-first of August, everything began to move. Peters received orders through the former governor of Virginia that the "black pioneers" would be wanted with the advance column, and they were issued tools and forage bags—but no arms. They disembarked among strangers who paid them no regard. No one exchanged remarks with them, or treated them as comrades. They were placed in the middle of the grenadier column, with the baggage.

It was not an auspicious start to his second campaign, but Caesar watched it all with anticipation. The grenadiers were magnificent in their fine uniforms, taller than the average soldier, and older, deadly. They performed the motions of the manual with an air of efficiency that was different from the mere expertise he had become used to with the Fourteenth. The grenadiers appeared to him to be hard men, practiced at war. He longed to be one of them. They ignored him. The army prepared to march to war on Long Island.

And the Loyal Ethiopians, those who were left, were carrying only picks and shovels.

New York City, July 9, 1776

The enemy had come.

At first, when he had sat in New York, listening to the news of disaster from Canada, Washington had begun to fear that he had guessed incorrectly and that Lord Howe had taken the British regiments out of Boston and used them to defeat Arnold and Montgomery at Quebec. Then it became possible that they had gone to Halifax, and from there would move to Rhode Island, or the Carolinas, or even into the Chesapeake. They controlled the sea, and they could go anywhere, and he sat in New York with all the army he could muster save those regiments he sent to repair the disaster in the north, watching and waiting, hoping that the enemy chose New York and not some other, defenseless morsel of the great coast he had sworn to defend.

He sent his best generals away, to support the other theaters of war, just as he had expected in January. Charles Lee was off to the south, to defend Charleston and direct the southern war. Horatio Gates and John Sullivan were both off to the north to take commands against Guy Carleton, who had already eaten several generals, capturing some and breaking others. Carleton had held Quebec all winter. He was cutting through the Continental forces like hot iron through snow, driving the remnants of the northern army all the way from Quebec to Sorel.

And all Washington could do was sit near New York, building and training his army as he had in the siege of Boston. It was ironic that he had opened the war with the siege of the British army and now bid fair to stand a siege himself.

He worked, and worried, changed his staff, appointed new officers, wrote regulations, and worried more. He and Charles Lee had guessed that the enemy *had* to take New York. In the moments after victory at Boston, it had seemed obvious, but now, in light of the other news, it appeared an irresponsible guess. He had built an army. He had raised a corps of officers in his own image, who believed in discipline. He had given them a body of regulations and a manual of arms, and he had created a staff and a series of systems to govern the army, feed it, provide recruits for its continuance.

And then the first sails were sighted, and soon hundreds of masts appeared off Sandy Hook. He had caught a tiger. And now his army would fight.

He read through the day's reports, noted with moderate surprise that the enemy was digging in on Staten Island, and called for the day's general orders, written out fair by Colonel Reed, the adjutant general. Only one thing was wanting for the army, besides wagonloads of new equipment, and that was a spirit different from mere rebellion, which Washington privately abhorred. Rebellion would lead individual men to rebel, which was not his purpose.

Colonel Reed had written the orders well. Desertion would now be punished with thirty-nine lashes on the bare back, a sufficient punishment to deter the casual deserter; there were new regulations on obtaining passes for soldiers wishing to travel or visit nearby towns, and an order to provide chaplains for the regiments that did not possess them. Then he came to the meat of the day's orders, whose meaning would change the army and the whole nature of the war. Washington had a draft of the original document by his elbow, and he had read it with growing delight, the magical words expressing precisely the steps that had led *him* to war. Once it was read to the troops, they would know exactly what the stakes were in this war, and it would no longer be a mere matter of rebellion.

> The Continental Congress, impelled by the dictates of duty, policy and necessity, having been pleased to dissolve the Connection which subsisted between this Country, and Great Britain, and to declare the United Colonies of North America, free and independent States: the several brigades are to be drawn up this evening on their respective Parades, at Six O'clock, when the declaration of Congress, showing the grounds and reasons of this measure, is to be read with an audible voice.

Washington cleaned the nib of his quill on a rag, dipped it, and wrote carefully at the bottom of Reed's copperplate.

> The General hopes this important event will serve as a fresh incentive to every officer and every soldier, to act with Fidelity and Courage, as knowing that the peace and safety of his Country depends (under God) solely on the success of our arms: and that he is now in the service of a State, possessed of sufficient power to reward his merit, and advance him to the highest honors of a free country.

✯ ✯ ✯

George Lake mustered his men quickly enough and fell in on the parade. Neither of the drummers who had replaced Noah had the spirit or the strength of wrist to beat any call as loud as Noah had, and the muster now involved the corporals racing about the camp, yelling for their men, and the sergeants going to their place on parade and yelling for the company to be brought to them. George missed Noah. He had made them a better company. In his absence, they had lost some hard-won skills, like the ability to load and fire volleys to the drum. Noah had had some peculiar mixture of skill and intelligence that allowed him to listen to the sergeants and officers and beat the order just fast enough to allow the best fire.

Lake thought of Noah often, because he now had to contend with Bludner every day. Bludner was very much in command of the company. Mr. Lawrence mustered them, and stood at the front during inspections and reviews, but it was Bludner who set the tone. Lake missed the skill that McCoy had exercised, and the attention to detail, but most of all, he missed the distance McCoy had placed between himself and the other men. And he knew that Bludner had driven McCoy out as surely as he knew that McCoy had nothing to do with the loss of Noah. Bludner was friendly with the other back-country men, and no friend at all to the other apprentices.

Despite which, Lake continued to serve as a corporal and knew he was being considered for sergeant. He was smart, smarter than Bludner, and he only needed experience. He read everything he could find, borrowed manuals from officers in other companies, used his pay in Philadelphia to buy books. His section looked smart and drilled well, and they were often the first on parade. This evening, for instance, he'd taken the precaution when morning orders were read to tell them off and ask them to "lie handy" for a six o'clock formation, and they had.

Walters and Miller still had a lot of baby fat in their faces, and Miller still used a fowler from home that couldn't carry a bayonet, but every one of his men had a cartridge box and a bayonet strap, even if Miller and Neldt lacked bayonets. Their hats were cocked just so, and they looked like soldiers. That could not be said for every man in the company.

The company fell in gradually, a section at a time, a few men running up late, and they were no longer the sharpest company in their battalion, as they had been before Philadelphia. Other officers worked their men harder, or perhaps had better drummers and sergeants. Either way, the battalion formed with the brigade, and Captain Lawrence, who was serving his turn as brigade major, stepped to the center of the parade with grave steps.

"Shoulder your *firelocks!*" he called, and they did, in passable unison, twelve hundred muskets going to twelve hundred left shoulders.

"Attention. General Washington has directed that the following be read at the head of every brigade." He looked around, cleared his throat, and held a piece of paper before him.

"When in the course of human events..."

It took several minutes to read, and muskets quickly get heavy, but no one noticed, so solemn was the moment. No one grumbled in the ranks, or demanded to be allowed to go back to the order. No one made jokes. They stood together at attention as the powerful words flowed over them, until the very end.

Captain Lawrence rolled the papers crisply and looked from left to right along the front of the brigade. "Three cheers for the Continental Congress and the Independence of the United Colonies! And let them hear you in Philadelphia!"

He raised the hand with the papers, and the first cheer rang out over the parade.

"*HUZZAH!*

"*HUZZAH!*

"*HUZZAH!*"

Long Island, August 29, 1776

John Julius Stewart was a short man, and no one who had not seen him in action would call him graceful or even handsome. His red hair was thick, but it wouldn't stay in a queue, and his features were snubbed, as though someone had pushed his face against something hard before they were set. His wide-set green eyes were too large for fashion, and gave him a faintly comical air. His limbs were too long for his trunk, and he never seemed to have gotten around to learning the use of them: long legs that he stuck out at odd angles, long arms that his tailor couldn't really conceal.

But it was the hair that his vanity hated most, and it was his hair that generally got the most attention from various dressers, though to little effect until he met Jeremy.

Jeremy had received every boon of nature denied to his master. He was as handsome as a Roman statue, proportioned aptly, so that, though he stood an inch less in height than his master, people who had met them in London or on a hunt remembered the man as towering over the master. Jeremy had brown eyes and carefully straightened dark hair that always sat perfectly on his head. In fact, it was the experience of dressing his own hair and his family's that prepared him for the struggle of his new master.

John Julius had no more been born to the aristocracy than Jeremy had been born to service. John Julius Stewart was the son of a prosperous Edinburgh merchant, and had been to Smyrna and Alexandria before he was fifteen. His father had packed him off to the army lest he run away to sea. Being an officer made him a gentleman, though his mercantile connections ensured a certain number of sneers.

Jeremy's father ran a prosperous and fashionable grocers in London. As a boy he had gone away to serve the earl of Linsford's lovely, silly wife. She had a passion to have a black boy, and treated Jeremy more as a pet than a servant. He first loved, then resented it, but he received the best education possible, as well as an accent and a set of manners that couldn't be learned in any other school. In fact, he had more breeding than his master, which John Julius readily owned. Of course, when the pretty plump black boy became a young man, the lady was done with him. Black men were not the beau ideal of society; besides, his apparent age served all too well as a reminder of her own.

Jeremy went home for a while, but home was a difficult, cramped place after an estate and a series of grand London houses. His mother and father seemed a little vulgar, his peers simple or just *low*. He had no way to make a living, nor any particular interest in learning one, and black men who could fence and write verse were not as much in demand as he had hoped. Despite his father's desire that he follow in the shop, he had chosen service as the best of a bad set of options, and had looked for a military man. His former mistress's husband had been a colonel of militia; the pageant had fascinated him, and so had the toys.

The two men shared a passion for popular novels, a knowledge of the military sports, and a hope for adventure. Jeremy looked around the tiny bedroom of their marquee with satisfaction, enjoying the rustic comforts of the folding beds, the padded close stool, and the campaign desk. A curtain of linen canvas separated the bedroom from the tent's sitting room, where his master might have his brother officers for a glass of brandy or a cup of chocolate or coffee. Jeremy had a proprietary air toward the marquee, which he had earned by supervising its manufacture according to a

French book on castramentation that he had found in a London book-seller's when they were making up their equipment. It was the best furnished in their regiment, which gave them both a great deal of quiet satisfaction.

When the regiment left England to take the field in earnest, several of the more aristocratic officers who had given Stewart to understand that his position as a Scot and a merchant's son was very low indeed had quit the regiment, exchanging with officers who sought active service. Those who stayed were either more tolerant or simply quiet.

The Edinburgh merchant's son had one thing most of them lacked—ready money. He used it carefully, and without too much display, and bought a vacant captaincy in the light company, the regiment's scouts and skirmishers, and good horses and weapons. Jeremy saw to their comforts; he ordered the tent and the desk and the beds. The four good chairs in the sitting room had been "acquired" by a patrol of the light company, and had probably adorned a local house.

"I left *Evelina* on your bed, Jems." The touch of the Scot was still there, although London had removed a great deal of it.

"Sorry, sir?"

"*Evelina!* The book we heard so much of on the ship. Don't be woolly-headed, Jems, there's a good fellow. Remember Lieutenant Burney?"

"I do, sir. A naval gentleman. He was out with Cook."

"Just so."

"And knew the Tahitian, Odiah."

"More to the point, Jems, he has a sister."

"Who writes. Yes, sir. My pardon, I don't know where my head was at. Miss Burney, who writes."

"Just so. Her first is on the bed, called *Evelina*. A novel of very deep sensibility."

"Are you finished, then?"

"Oh, yes. I had it off Waters. He recommended it, and I daresay I devoured it."

Jeremy found the little brown volume, still only paper-bound, with the covers curled and many pages bent. He sniffed at it—horse sweat. Most things smelled of horse lately. Horses had a handsome aroma anyway.

"Did you get us any mail while I was off, Jems?"

"Yes, sir. Two from Miss McLean."

"Give, you criminal!"

Jeremy walked to the little door between the tent's two rooms and poked his head around. "They're on your hat."

The hat, a small and fashionable bicorn trimmed in the regimental manner and boasting a spray of cock's feathers, was the sole ornament of the tent's central piece of furniture, a camp table. Tucked upright in the stiff Nirvenois back of the hat were two letters in travel-smeared outer envelopes.

"Ahh!"

Jeremy smiled and muttered "Just so" as he went back to tidying the bedroom.

"I'd like to get a piece of Turkey carpet to put in here, sir." Requests put during one of Miss McLean's letters were apt to be granted.

"Jeremy, when this army moves, we have to move all this, you know."

"We have bhat horses and baggage allotment."

"Jeremy, trust a man who's at least chased the odd smuggler in Ireland. When we move, half this stuff will vanish, never to be seen again, and by the time we see action we'll be sleeping in greatcoats and drinking soldiers' tea."

"I can get one for a shilling or two, sir." Patiently, because John Julius did not always know what was in his own best interest.

Jeremy had not expected to like his employer. He would have left a man he detested or who misused him. When he applied to be valet to a merchant's son with manners to match, he had not expected humor, or tolerance, or a master willing to be a student in the arcane arts of the culture of the upper class. If John Julius Stewart had any flaws, they were the flaws of idleness. He seemed to have no temper at all, he didn't fight duels, and his taste in women seemed entirely limited to just one, Miss McLean, a daughter of property and gentility in the wilds of Scotland. And Stewart had much to teach: He was a superb horseman, a crack shot, and had other skills that seemed, like the blades of a folding knife, to appear when wanted and then vanish, never to be hinted at. On board the naval ship that had carried them to America, he had endeared himself to the officers by knowing the names of every line and spar, a rare feat for a passenger and rarer for a redcoat.

When the regiment was ordered for American service and he had secured command of the light company, they had located cloth and tailors, and had every man in a dark blue watch cloak before the ship sailed, a little miracle wrought by hard guineas and Stewart's merchant knowledge. These were the things at which Mr. Stewart excelled.

"Don't start the book until my hair's done, Jems."

"Sorry, sir." He had been looking out of the little window formed by dropping the wall of the tent a fraction, watching the dragoons at drill on the hillside above the camp. He picked up the leather sack that held his hair tools and pushed through the canvas drapes to the other room.

John Julius was sitting in the tent's most comfortable chair, reading from a leather-bound book. His unruly red hair was unbound and unbrushed, all over his face and somewhere down his back. It gave him the comic air of a threepenny-opera pirate. His *robe de chambre* was pulled over his regimentals; he had risen early to ride the rounds, as he had been duty officer the night before.

Jeremy rubbed his hands together hard; they were cold, although it was just July. America was cold. He brushed the hair with quick, practiced flicks of his wrist, working the eternally tangled ends apart. "You were riding in the wind without even tying it back."

"Don't be a shrew," said Stewart with a little show of temper.

"Just reach the ribbon round and tie it back! It can't be that hard."

"It was dark." It was a terrible excuse, and they both knew it. A tiny skirmish in a long war that had started with his sisters and mother and would, Jeremy thought, eventually be continued by Miss McLean.

When the strands were well separated, he began to pull the brush through to stretch the hair. Every so often, he would use hot tongs to straighten it, although that was a major labor.

"I have to take the company out past the lines today. Bit of a probe this afternoon. I'll expect you along."

"Most pleased, sir."

"We didn't beat them as badly as I thought the other day. Their marksmen are quite active."

"Yes?"

"Phillips, from the Forty-third? You remember him?"

"I don't believe I've had the honor of his acquaintance, sir."

"Horseman. Tall fellow . . . never mind. But he caught a ball. They hold a little wood in front of their lines, and post their infernal marksmen there. I'm going to wait for the afternoon sun and drive them out."

"I look forward to it. Honored, most pleased."

"Yes, I expect you are. Horse, pistols with new flints."

"Yes, sir."

"I say, no powder, I think."

Jeremy nodded, which was Jeremy's way of conveying that he had never, at any time, considered using hair powder on a day of active duty. Then his lips curled a little, a very slight smile. A servant's smile. "Right, sir. New flints and no powder in the pistols."

"Damn you, sir, you know what I mean."

"Please don't move, sir. It makes all this even harder."

Jeremy whipped most of his master's hair together in a queue and tied it off with a strip of leather. "Which hat, sir?"

"Hmmm. The good hat, I think." John Julius Stewart wanted to fight in his best, a habit shared by most of his compatriots.

Jeremy reached into the brazier and tried the heat of his crimping irons. Then he rolled a side curl with a practiced finger, placing it low enough that John could wear his hat in comfort, and set it, the smell of burning hair filling the tent. He set the other to match and dodged around to the front to check that they were even. When he was satisfied, one of the curls had slipped a touch and had to be redone, but its position was established and the rest was easy enough. Then he went back to the queue, releasing it from its little leather tie and brushing it out again, the tie held in his mouth. When it satisfied him that it looked something like fashionable hair, he spat out the tie, wrapped it as tight as he could and tied it off, then covered the leather with good black silk, bound the queue all the way down as the regiment required, and tied it off. The result was very good indeed, although it took quite a while. John Julius simply continued to read, with the obligatory grunts and cries of pain whenever his hair was pulled.

Jeremy picked up the hand mirror and held it so that his master could see most of the result.

"Splendid! Doesn't look like my hair at all."

"Sir."

"Right. I'm off to see the adjutant about next year's coat issue. I left you some money in the drawer; see that the bhat-man has new forage for the horses and so on, and meet me in the horse lines at one." He pulled out his silver watch, glanced at it, and looked up. "Pass me the time?"

Jeremy pulled his watch out by the fob, opened the case and listened, then took a silver key and wound it several turns. "I have a quarter past eight."

"And I the same. Thank you, Jeremy."

He took his best hat off the table, waved farewell, and pushed through the front flap.

Jeremy went back to his bed, picked up his master's greatcoat, and returned to the sitting room in time to hand it over as John shoved back through the flap.

"Horse lines at one, sir."

"Just so."

Brooklyn Heights, New York, August 28, 1776

"Dig, you bastards!" Captain Lawrence stood in the open and bellowed at his men.

George Lake was too tired to resent the insult. The shovel twisted in his grasp, his hands were so numb they could barely close on the wooden grip, and the cold rain kept on falling. Out in the long green fields below them, the British skirmishers could just be seen, moving casually as if they expected no resistance.

No resistance was about what they had received, at least from George's standpoint. His company had been hurried across the river to Long Island when it became clear that a major action was brewing. But they hadn't seen any action; they had simply marched back and forth for two days and then become part of the broken army streaming back into the trench lines on the Brooklyn Heights. Perhaps General Washington knew why they had lost the battle without any of them ever firing a shot, but it was a mystery to Lake.

Someone had been shooting, though. They had seen the casualties when they came across the river, piled in boats. Some men had turned white; some had feigned nonchalance. George had just been sorry—sorry that so many had been lost, and later, sorry that they had been lost for so little. There was a rumor that Washington had had to sacrifice his best regiment, Smallwood's Marylanders, and that they had all been killed. Other men said that the German mercenaries killed every man they caught, and took no prisoners. Rumor was rife, and their company was digging alongside men from New England and Pennsylvania who had lost their regiments, lost their way, and been rallied by whatever officer caught them first.

George plunged the shovel into the mud again and scooped it full, then threw his cast onto the low rampart that was being formed by the upcast of the ditch. The ditch was spotty, shallow, and wouldn't hide a man, and the upcast didn't help much. George knew men were slipping away whenever Lawrence wasn't looking. Most of those leaving were from other regiments, but a handful were their own comrades from Virginia, and their treason made George's heart burn.

Bludner dug next to George. He was better at it, and tougher; George had to admit that. Weymes, his partner, wielded a pick, breaking the ground so that Bludner's shovel could bite deeper. George watched them for a moment, watched their detachment and their competence. He hated Bludner, was sure the man had sold the drummer as a slave or killed him; he despised Bludner's backwoods arrogance. But there was a great deal about the man to admire. He tended to get the job done.

"Here, then, Mr. Lake," said Bludner, swinging another scoop of mud over his shoulder. "Get a mate to break the ground for you, like Weymes." He didn't sound exhausted, just conversational, as if digging in the rain were an everyday part of life.

Lake turned to one of his men. "Get a pick. In fact, get five picks. Form teams. Watch Bludner and Weymes."

"Where the hell have they been, they don't know how to dig?" Weymes asked contemptuously.

"Town boys, Weymes. They never had to dig no cellars. Don't mind them, Weymes. They want to learn, mostly." Bludner spat, wiped his hands to get a better grip, and dug again. His hands were hard as rock, even in a downpour; Lake, that leader of the "town boys," would probably be bleeding in a few hours. That didn't bother Bludner especially, although now that it looked to come to a fight, he worried that he would have to depend on the likes of Lake to cover his flank.

"Will you look at that?" asked Weymes, and pointed away over the fields to the south.

The British skirmishers were firing into a wood to the left of their front. The wood seemed to be held by their own Continentals; a sharp fire came back. But it wasn't the deadly little skirmish that occupied Weymes; it was the column of black men moving up the track, well to the rear of the British skirmishers. Even in the rain, Weymes could spot a black man at a great distance.

The black men walked up to a spot where several enemy officers were standing. They wore various coats, one red, one blue, another green, and Bludner had no idea what that meant, but soon enough, the black men spread out and started digging.

"Sergeant Bludner, shall I send you down a hammock?" Lawrence's voice carried very well.

"Sir, there's movement on our front, I think. See that clump o' officers? An' then the blackies? That's new."

There was a stir behind Lawrence, and then a whole party of mounted men came over the ridge and right among them, all in a rush. Some of the digging men were alarmed, thinking for a moment they were under attack. Lake couldn't see for a moment and a sense of panic was communicated to him by the men around him, but when he wiped his eyes he could see that it was a group of officers. The leader had to be General Washington: He was tall, and his horse was white.

Captain Lawrence didn't lose a minute in communicating his own name, or that his men were the general's fellow Virginians.

Washington looked at them digging in the rain, which was slacking off. "Were you in action yesterday, Captain?"

"No, General."

Washington didn't dismount; he just sat on his horse and watched the British for a few moments. "Just as I thought. Colonel Reed, send to General Mercer and the Flying Column at once."

"Sir?"

"I believe that the British intend to take our defenses on Brooklyn Heights by regular approaches, by digging. Look at the arrogance of that work! It's being constructed in our faces."

Another officer shrugged. "They know we have just lost our guns, General."

Sergeant Bludner tugged at Lawrence's sleeve. "I'd wager we could bust up their digging some, if you gave me a free hand."

Lawrence nodded at him and then stepped in closer to stand at the general's stirrup. "They just started work, sir. We still have men in that wood to the left. I don't know whose they are."

"Riflemen, from Pennsylvania," said the tall man who looked like Washington except his horsemanship was not of the same order. "I'm Joseph Reed, the general's adjutant."

"John Lawrence, of the Virginia Regiment."

Washington didn't appear to be paying them any attention. He had a telescope out now and was watching the black men dig. They were digging fast. They were digging a great deal faster than these Virginians, and that annoyed him.

Lawrence pressed on with Reed, since Washington didn't seem interested.

"That party of officers came an hour back and ran ropes. Just before you came, the blacks showed up with tools and the officer in the red coat."

"He's an engineer." Reed spoke softly.

Lawrence stopped and looked. "How can you tell?"

"Black facings, but not from the Sixty-fourth Regiment. You'll know them all soon enough. He came up with the tools. *Ipso facto*, an engineer."

"And the other men, sir? The officers in the colored coats?"

Washington looked down at Lawrence and smiled. "I'll wager the man in the blue coat is General Howe. He's dressed for hunting. Odd time of year for a hunt, but I honor his spirit." The telescope went back to the black men, swept back and forth while he measured the pace of their digging, and then froze for a moment. His face darkened with an angry flush. Colonel Reed, aware that something was wrong, turned from Lawrence and rode up to him.

"General?"

"I must be mistaken." The general wiped the lens of his telescope carefully with a cloth and then closed it sharply. When Reed leaned forward again, he just shook his head.

Lawrence waved his hand at the woods. "We could send a patrol to rough up their diggers, sir. Down the ridge and through the woods."

"I will inform your brigadier, then. Do it as soon as seems best, Captain. Bring me some prisoners. I want to know why those blacks are digging. Are they slaves?"

"They sure dig fast, for slaves."

"You are Virginian, Captain?"

"Yes, General."

"Where are you from, Captain?"

"Norfolk, sir."

"Lawrence, you say?"

"My father ships tobacco in a small way, sir."

"Of course. Carry on, then, Captain." He raised his voice. "I look for strong action from my Virginians."

Lake had considered falling the men in, but the digging seemed more important. He watched Washington every moment he could, though. If the cause was in tatters, no one had told General Washington; he was neat and shaved, his hair tight, his clothes clean. He looked confident, and as he gathered his staff, his eye seemed to catch every man in their company for a moment.

George hoped he would say something, but he simply rode by them, watching them. And then he smiled a little, his lips thin, wheeled his horse, and rode away.

"Well, boys, looks like we ain't done yet." George watched the general ride off with satisfaction.

Lawrence and Bludner asked for volunteers, and the whole company clamored to come, so when their ditch was just tenable, he let them have an hour to rest and clear their muskets, and then they started down the slope in Indian file, one man at a time with a few feet between men. They angled well over to get in behind the wood from which fire continued to come in spurts. The British hadn't tried to take it and gave it a wide berth, suggesting that Colonel Reed had been right; the men within did have rifles, which could kill at a much longer range than the typical smoothbore musket.

They made it to the base of the slope without attracting undue notice, and moved quietly to the rear of the woods. Captain Lawrence, at the front of the column, exchanged some sign with the men in the woods and then they moved on among the trees. It was a woodlot like those any farmer might have kept at home, big old trees and some new growth. Lake halted with his section at the base of a large tree that grew like a tower in the middle of the wood.

He could smell the powder that the riflemen were firing from just a few yards away, and hear the distant replies of a few British skirmishers. A tall thin man in a linen hunting shirt and a small gorget stepped forward and took Lawrence's hand.

"We've pushed them back almost half a mile. Of course, they can push us out anytime they like if they are willing to pay the price."

"General Washington asked us to disperse the men digging, there."

Down the rank from Lake, Weymes looked slyly around him. The movement caught Lake's eye, and he listened as Weymes muttered to the man next to him, another back-country man.

"Gon' take some of they *diggers* for oursel's," he wheezed, and laughed. The other man laughed as well. Lake thought it typical of men like Weymes that they saw the war in terms of their own profit.

Bludner slipped out from under Lawrence's eye and moved along the ranks to Lake. He paused a moment, looking at Lake as if judging him, and smiled a little. It was a threat, and Lake hardened himself to keep his head up and look directly at the man. Bludner moved past him, down the line of men to Weymes.

"Take a dozen men—not Lake's. Go along the draw an' get in behind that little fort. When they *diggers* make to run, you take 'em and drive 'em back to me."

"M'pleasure," rasped Weymes.

Up at the head of the column, the rifle officer leaned back and laughed at something Lawrence had said.

"What, them blackamoors? Have at 'em. We'll cover you. I don't think the British have much else here right now. I take it they are digging a fort?"

"That's what the general thought."

"So it will only get harder to get at 'em." The rifle officer took out a little antler whistle and blew it, then waved his men to the left of the wood, away from where the Virginians were going out. The rain had nearly stopped.

Lake heard a wet *pop* next to his head and Ben Miller, the man next to him, sighed and seemed to burst, red spray everywhere. It was so fast that George wasn't able to sort out the order of events. He didn't hear the shot, either. George had never seen a man shot, and neither had most of the other men in the company. Ben Miller was one of his own men, someone he had cooked with and yelled at for losing the mess pot.

"Damn, you Virginnies is plain unlucky. We haven't lost a man all day." One of the riflemen was slumped under another tree, smoking. He didn't seem very concerned. He inhaled deeply, looked at one of his mates, a short man in a dirty linen shirt. "Plain unlucky."

The Pennsylvania voice and the flat pronouncement stayed with Lake.

Bludner appeared, his face red with exertion. "Face front. He's dead, and nothing we do is going to help him. We'll get his equipment on the way back."

The rifle officer nodded. "Come on, boys, let's help these Virginny boys get the blackamoors."

"You boys sure you're tough enough to take some unarmed black folk?" asked another of the riflemen. He didn't sound mean, just spoke flat, but Bludner bristled. Lawrence pushed Bludner forward, past the riflemen.

"Check your prime," called Lawrence. He gave them a minute to check it and replace it if the last of the rain had turned it to sludge. "Form front when we pass the edge of the wood. Eyes front . . . march!"

Brooklyn Heights, New York, August 28, 1776

Jim saw them first, as the rain slackened off, coming from the little patch of woodland that they knew was full of rebels with rifle guns. They all looked off that way from time to time, because there had been shooting in the morning. They were covered in sweat, despite the rain and the cool breeze, but they had a good trench and the upcast was getting to be three feet high. Already a man swinging a pick in the trench had nothing to fear from a rifleman, no matter how proficient. The knowledge of the rifle guns had helped them dig. So had the quick praise of the engineer, Mr. Murray.

"Rebel soldiers comin'. They fo'min reg'lar like, an' I think they comin' fo' us."

Caesar could see that Jim's words were lost on the engineer, and he swung out of the ditch where he was working, took in the approaching soldiers for himself, and turned to where Sergeant Peters was writing for the officer.

"Enemy coming, sir. A full company, if I may." He was quite proud of both the tone and the sentence. Calm and soldierly.

The officer stood up from his stool, handed Peters his lap desk, and ran forward to where he could see over the scarp and down the hill.

"We're buggered," he said. "Where the hell are the dragoons we were promised?"

His lone soldier, a corporal of the Sixty-fourth light company, spoke up hesitantly.

"My company is the other side of the woods, sir," he reminded the engineer.

"Not the same as dragoons, lad, but fetch them. Leave that musket. You won't need it, and we may."

The soldier shucked his cartridge box, bayonet belt, and musket. The engineer scribbled him a note and he ran off. He was fast, Caesar noted. Not as fast as Caesar himself, but Caesar had other plans. He walked over to the engineer and grasped the musket.

"I'm a fair shot, Mr. Murray."

"Who are you, then?"

"I'm called Caesar. I fought in Virginny, for the king."

Murray smiled, given the situation, at the tall black man's earnestness. "I'm sure you did him credit, too. Now show me. Show me, and be quick about it."

Caesar put on the cartridge box and reached back, taking a paper cartridge in his fingers and biting off the base, priming the pan and then ramming the whole cartridge, ball, paper, and all, down the clean gun. You couldn't load that way with a dirty or foul gun. Murray could see immediately that he knew his business. Sergeant Peters folded the camp desk closed and began to run to the edge of the trench. He was smiling at Caesar.

Caesar stepped down into the trench and placed the musket to his shoulder. He raised his head above the upcast, found the target, and fired. The flint snapped down hard and the trigger pull and the flat bark of the big musket were simultaneous. Caesar had never fired at soldiers formed in a line before, and it was easy. There was a body lying on the ground and a little disturbance. He smiled.

Rifle fire sounded from the woods below him, and one shot actually creased his scalp. It made him leap and sit suddenly in the ditch. Tonny laughed. None of them noticed that one of the rifle balls had gone through Sergeant Peters's chest.

Caesar looked right and left.

"Keep your tools to hand and don't stand up till I tell you," he said, and started to load again.

☆   ☆   ☆

Mr. Murray was right down in the trench with them, his coat off to keep it out of the mud. He cursed the mischance that had caused him to wear his only good coat today. He had expected the visit from Lord Howe. Now he was crouched in a muddy trench on a wet day in his best smallclothes and he was damned if he was getting mud on his only proper coat. He rolled it tight and put it inside a linen forage sack that one of the black men handed him silently. The tall fellow fired the musket again. Murray knew his type—a killer, if ever he'd seen one.

Murray was puzzled that all these men were staying. He'd watched work parties run off at the first sign of enemy activity throughout his career, in Holland and Germany and Spain, and he'd never seen a parcel of native diggers grab their tools as if they meant business. His professional honor and maybe his advancement were at stake. They had nothing to gain or lose.

Another patter of rifle balls against the lip of the upcast earth. The tall black man was lying behind it now, covered in mud that made him even more difficult for the enemy to distinguish. He fired again, and some of the black men raised a small cheer. Murray saw that his assistant, the black man who did his writing, was down. That was a waste. Peters had been as educated a man as Murray had seen in the army.

The black man next to him was pointing down the field.

"They gon' be some mad now!" said the smallest black, a mere boy. He laughed.

☆ ☆ ☆

The advance across the low autumn grass was exciting at first. The silent parapet of the distant earthwork seemed like the pretend enemy in one of Captain Lawrence's exercises. They formed their front rapidly, although slow for the lack of the drum, and then they moved forward. Their line was steady enough, bowing slightly and recovering as the men tried to overcome their nerves and remember the lessons of the drill fields.

The first shot was a shock, as the little earthwork had seemed undefended. A man went down off to Lake's left. He couldn't see who it was, but the man screamed and flopped on the ground. George snapped his head back to the front, tearing his attention away from the downed man, but others didn't, and the line bowed badly.

The second shot missed. It passed close enough to George that he could hear the distinctive sound that the passage of the bullet made. He looked around and met the eyes of his friend Isaac. Isaac had heard the sound, too. His eyes had a hurt quality that they hadn't had before, almost like the shot hadn't missed. George knew that the bullet had passed between them. His heart beat even faster.

The third shot took Captain Lawrence just in the middle of the chest. It hit both his gorget and his silver belt plate, and the combination saved his life, but he had no way of knowing that at the time. He went down hard, and there was blood and pain. He screamed. Men ran to him, and several competed to lift him up. Bludner shouted at them and finally dismissed two men to carry the captain back.

"He's one man, ya' bastards! The niggers won' fight. Now *come on!*"

Bludner seemed enraged by their hesitation after the captain went down. Lake settled his pack on his shoulders and pushed forward. They weren't so much a line anymore, even after just a few shots, but most of the men were going forward, a little quicker than the parade ground had taught them. The enemy musket fired again and George tried to imagine what whole volleys of musketry might do to a line like this.

✷ ✷ ✷

"...niggers won' fight. Now *come on!*"

The words sounded distinct over the few yards that now separated them. Virgil and Jim knew the voice instantly. They both started shouting at Caesar. He was loading again, eyeing the range. Murray grabbed the shoulder of the black man crouching next to him.

"Are you lads going to fight?" Murray had to know.

"Oh, yas, suh!" said Tonny. His eyes were almost glazed. He didn't turn his head. He was looking just over the top of the upcast.

Caesar was listening to Jim now. He brought the musket up to his shoulder and fired again, but missed. He thought he had time for one more.

"Those men is slave-takers, boys!" he shouted. A low, dangerous noise came from the black men.

"Are ye slaves now? Or *Ethiopians!*" Caesar's voice carried over the field. Even the blacks who were really only day labor lifted their voices and roared.

Murray was too stunned by the events to consider giving orders. This black man, the tall one, was giving the orders. Murray was used to letting the infantry do the killing while he built the forts and the machines, and he let nature take its course. He knew he was seeing something, though. He drew his sword, a short saber of no particular quality.

Caesar slammed the bayonet onto the end of the musket. It was empty, and the enemy was close. He didn't think it would suit the men with him to wait in the trench, now that their blood was up, and he stood, tall among the others huddled under the upcast for cover, and bellowed. "At them, Ethiopians!"

They swarmed up the short pile of earth and right into the enemy line. There was no time for thought, or flinching.

✷ ✷ ✷

The black faces appeared out of the earth at his feet and Lake swung his musket hard, punching one of them straight off his feet. Next to him, Isaac took another down and then shot him on the ground and George remembered that his own musket was loaded. He saw the flash of red and white among the workers and he aimed at it and fired, hitting the officer. Isaac was clubbed from his feet and another man from the rear rank stepped into his place.

"Stand your ground!" he cried, and he felt men rally to him, press alongside him in the chaos. This was not how he had imagined it, but *they were going to hold.*

★ ★ ★

Caesar leapt into the midst of the enemy, his musket and bayonet low in his right hand and a shovel in his left. He blocked a feeble blow with the shovel and pounded the bayonet home in the man's chest as he had been taught since childhood, ripped it clear and stepped on his victim to close with the next, who was paper white in the sun. Caesar killed him, too. He was bellowing, his heart was charging within him and yet the world came to him with perfect clarity, and he realized that if he broke through the rear of the enemy line the rifles would shoot at him from the wood. He whirled on another man, pushing him off his feet with the shovel and then pinning him to the earth with the bayonet. The man squirmed, and the smell of his guts filled Caesar's nostrils, but he stepped on the man's chest and pulled his bayonet clear just as something sliced along his ribs and he stumbled back.

A big man, as big as he, thrust at him again with a bayonet. Caesar swung the shovel up to block and lunged with his own musket and bayonet, but the man rotated on his front foot and brought the butt of his musket up into Caesar's shoulder and he dropped the shovel as the wave of pain hit. Desperate, he jumped back, his bayonet licking out to cover his retreat and going deep into his adversary's right arm.

Caesar caught the other man's eye for a moment as he drew back the musket for another stab, but a body cannoned into him from behind and almost knocked him down. The other man took a pistol from his belt and snapped it at him, but the priming was gone and the frizzen open, and it wouldn't fire. His adversary threw the pistol at his head and he ducked, and the big man slipped away into the maelstrom behind him. Caesar glanced around and just avoided being spitted by the man who had struck him in the side. He twisted and parried with his own musket. His new opponent was young, gritted his teeth like a fighter, and struck rapid blows in an attempt to overwhelm Caesar's defense.

☆　☆　☆

George Lake had thrown himself into the big black to buy Bludner a moment to finish him, but Bludner was gone, and even one-handed the man seemed to shrug off his best effort. He parried once, then again, and realized that the tide had shifted and he was now the prey. He backed, stumbled, and went down, tangled with another man. Even as he began to lose his balance, he tried to keep his musket up, but he was too slow, and he watched the man slide the bayonet down his gun barrel and smash his hand. He was suddenly looking into the other man's eyes, curled on his side and unarmed, and the other man towered over him. Then he seemed to nod; at least, that's how Lake told the story later. He nodded, smiled a little, and backed away, leaving Lake hurt but alive.

☆　☆　☆

Caesar was content to let the young one live. He had eyes full of courage, even when his last defense was taken from him, and he was injured—he would not fight again today. Caesar backed up three steps, free of the fighting for the first time in what seemed like hours.

There were men coming up from behind them, more men in rebel coats.

☆　☆　☆

"Sergeant McDonald!"

"Sir!"

"Take the two left files off to the flank and try to locate the source of that firing."

"Sir."

"If you please, sir, I'd be most happy to go myself." Jeremy was a little surprised at himself. He usually remained silent during any military activity, as it was not his business and he feared that he would be excluded if he spoke out of turn. But he had a good set of eyes and the fastest horse.

Captain Stewart listened as the sound of another single distant shot echoed back to them. He considered Jeremy, his quality as a rider, the speed and wind of his mount, his steadiness.

Stewart rode up close. "Give me a picture. Who's shooting, what the target is. Quick as you can, and Godspeed."

Jeremy gave a sketchy wave with his riding whip, as close to a salute as he dared, and his horse sprang away. Behind him, Stewart turned the head of his company to the left and ordered them to extend into line.

Jeremy cantered easily over the wet leaves under the trees. So far, all America looked like woods and farms, with nothing as extensive as an English market town anywhere, with the possible exception of the town of New York, still just a smudge of woodsmoke on the horizon ahead. He came over a little ridge and saw the enemy works on the opposite height, and then the sound of a shot drew his eye closer, to the little redoubt where a single red waistcoat showed in the trench among a small band of black laborers. One of them was lying out over the parapet and firing a musket at a full company of rebel infantry advancing resolutely from the woods at the base of the ridge. He saw it at a glance, even recognized Mr. Murray of the engineers kneeling, coatless, in the trench of the redoubt. He whirled his horse just in time to see a section of rebel infantry break from the taller trees to his back and start toward him.

Jeremy's horse was already in motion and he smiled, a feral grin of elation and fear together. He fumbled with drawing his smallsword, as the scabbard hung from chains and wasn't intended for a clean draw on horseback. It took time, and his horse's hooves took him closer to the rebels with every second. One of them was bringing his musket to his shoulder, but the others were either looking openmouthed or smiling.

★ ★ ★

"Get the darky on the horse," Weymes called to the lead file. "Get the horse! An' don' hurt him none, or I'll have your hide!"

Gorton had his musket up to fire and he brought it down even as he caught the gleam of a sword being drawn.

"Nigger's going to ride us down!" he yelled, and leaned forward, musket to his shoulder, and fired.

★ ★ ★

The shot went somewhere. Jeremy was past caring. He had his sword out, his seat was solid, and he took a pistol from the holster on his saddle, leaned forward as he had been taught since infancy, and shot the first man he passed in the chest. Another man grabbed for his reins and he ran the man through, his sword point catching in bone for a moment and almost pulling out of his hand. He felt the horse gather itself for a jump and he dropped his heels, sat square and gave the animal his weight where she would want it, and they were up and over some obstruction he never glimpsed and in among the trees.

Jeremy cantered under the branches until he saw the welcome line of red moving toward him. He arrived in front of Stewart in a spray of leaves, his sword still clutched in his hand. It was red halfway down its length, with a curious blue-red shimmer that looked like an armorer's finish. The tip was broken clean off, about two inches up the blade.

"Trouble, Jeremy?"

"Company of infantry going for our post. Mr. Murray in command of a group of laborers. They seem to be resisting. Shots are one of the laborers firing. I ran into a spot of trouble, a section going for the rear of the post." Jeremy's words came in bursts, and he was trying to find all the breath he had possessed only a few minutes ago. His chest was tight, his throat nearly closed, and his voice was coming out in short, high pulses.

"How far, then?"

"A quarter mile. Less. Two minutes at a canter."

"Right, then. McDonald! Forward. Have the men trail their firelocks and move at the double. Enemy will be front, in . . . in what, Jeremy?"

"Blue coats, Sergeant."

"Blue coats and at the double it is, sir." McDonald began to bellow orders.

✮   ✮   ✮

Caesar saw the blue coats coming from behind them with something akin to rage, because he thought they might have driven the first party off but sensed that the addition of this further handful from behind would finish them. He wiped his head with his arm and his shirt came away covered in blood, and everywhere he looked there were men down, men he knew. He flung himself at a man fighting Mr. Murray, determined to die well. He might have been encouraged by the sound of the bugle to his right, but he didn't know that only the British light infantry used the instrument. If he thought about the sound at all, he thought it was more rebels.

Jim was down right at his feet, his head and shoulder all blood from a musket butt. Virgil and Tonny were back-to-back with shovels, and the results of their determination were laid about them. Some of the laborers had already run, and several had been taken. Mr. Murray fought on, his cheap saber well handled. The rebels seemed to have lost the stomach for the fight and had mostly drawn off a few yards, or run up to the top of the new earth wall. Caesar ran Murray's opponent through, and the man groaned and fell like a puppet with its strings cut.

The big rebel who had wounded Caesar raised a pistol and shot one of the laborers. "Down yer weapons, you Nigras, or by God we'll shoot you like dogs." He seemed to see Virgil for the first time and he raised his empty pistol.

Virgil was clearly hurt, but he began to hobble toward the big man. Caesar knew they had to charge the rebels now, before they were shot down, helpless to resist. He never thought of dropping his weapon, but others did, more than a few.

The new group he had seen coming were yelling from fifty yards away, but Caesar was beyond caring. He gripped his musket close in his right hand and flung himself at the big man.

The big man saw him and took a musket from one of his men, who was standing openmouthed as the two black men staggered toward them.

★ ★ ★

The red skirmish line moved through the woods swiftly, like a disciplined herd of deer. Jeremy could hear the Scots and English voices calling to each other to *Keep up, Jock,* or *Get that line straight.* Discipline was different when battle was imminent.

He was alive, and had fought, and now he was going to do it again.

"There's the open ground," he said to Captain Stewart at his elbow.

"And there are the rebels. *Sound skirmish!*" The last to his bugler, running at his heels like a good dog. As the notes sounded, the whole line stopped and muskets came down to aim, the file leader in every file pair picking a target and firing in their own time. The range was long, there was brush, and only two of the bluecoats fell, but it was enough to disperse the party that had tried to take Jeremy.

"*At them!*" cried Stewart, the first order he had given directly, and he was off through the trees. Jeremy crouched down, clutched his broken sword, and followed him, spurring his horse to catch up.

★ ★ ★

Weymes didn't see the redcoats until two of his men fell. Their red coats were the same color as the autumn leaves, and his whole focus had been on the resistance of the blacks. Before he could say a word, the rest of his party took to their heels, running back to the cover of the woods nearly a quarter of a mile away. He paused a moment and fired his musket at a horseman, but he was alone, and he ran.

Bludner heard the shooting and instantly guessed the cause. It had all gone on too long and the redcoats were on them. He pointed the musket at the man who had shot Weymes back in Virginny and pulled the trigger, but the pan was full of water and there wasn't even a spark. He threw it at the black man shuffling toward him.

"Form your front! Fall in and *rally,*" he yelled. He wished he had a drummer. One boy was down, probably dead, and the other was too scared to beat, his sticks clenched uselessly in his fists, his eyes glazed.

✳ ✳ ✳

Rebels ran right past them to get back to the safety of their own ranks, and most just kept going. Caesar and Virgil were so spent that they weren't able to pursue, although there was one more sharp fight as a small band of rebels tried to take them. Caesar felt a jolt as someone bumped him from behind and he saw a patch of muddy scarlet in his peripheral vision. Murray was behind him.

Jeremy saw the group of rebels run for the woods off in the valley and determined that he would cut them off. He rode the last one down and saw it was the little man who had shouted orders. The man turned, but too late, and Jeremy hammered the broken tip of his sword into the man's back and through the lung, and he fell, his weight dragging straight off the point. Little puffs of smoke came from the distant woods and something hit his horse a hammer blow, and she stumbled and reared. A bubbling red spot had appeared on her withers. She was difficult to control for a moment and then she settled, and he pulled her around and spurred her back up the hill.

At the base of the half-constructed redoubt, he saw a big black man fighting. He was head and shoulders taller than his adversaries and the other two men fighting beside him, and every blow seemed to fell an enemy, and it struck Jeremy that he was watching something from *The Iliad.* Even as he watched, the man felled his last opponent with a vicious upthrust of a bayoneted musket held short, like a spear, and he turned his head, catching Jeremy's eyes across the field.

The rebel line was only half formed. Some had fled directly, running past their comrades to the apparent safety of the woods, while others either stood dumbly or fumbled to reload their muskets. Stewart's company ghosted up to the edge of the redoubt even as Jeremy cantered in behind them.

"Rifles in the wood," he called to his master.

Stewart looked at him and smiled a welcoming, friendly smile that Jeremy treasured.

"Best keep your head down, then," Stewart said. He was always good-humored in moments of danger. The rebels were melting away at the sight of his whole company moving up on their front. The knot of resistance by the black laborers almost at his feet blocked the fire of his left platoon. Several rebels fired and one of his men fell.

"Right platoon! Make ready! Present! *Fire!*"

The volley sounded like a single shot. There was smoke on the breeze for a moment, a deep smell of sulfur, and then screams from freshly wounded men, and the enemy were gone.

"At them, lights! At them. Sergeant McDonald, don't let them rally! Stay on them into the woods. I want those woods cleared!"

"Sir!" McDonald sprang off after his men, who were already pouring down the hill. Stewart waited a moment, looking to the left and right, checking his flanks. His glance passed over the blacks, many of whom were busy taking up muskets dropped by the rebels. He walked his horse over to Murray, the engineer officer. Murray looked stunned.

"Thought I might have lost you there, Lieutenant Murray."

"Aye. Thought the same myself."

Stewart waved his riding whip at Murray and started down the hill. He saw one of his men spin and fall, hit by rifle fire from the deadly wood, and he leaned low over the neck of his horse, spurring it on down the hill. He quickly overtook the line of his men and plunged in among the fleeing rebels. Suddenly the air was full of the buzz of bullets, and he was hit, but he carried on. His men followed him, and now they were over the open ground and pressing into the brushy edge of the wood, screaming and shouting as they came. Most huzza'd; a few yelled older, darker things from the Borders or the clans of the north, and his junior lieutenant, Crawford, kept baying "George and England" over and over.

"This way, sir!" Jeremy had stayed close by Stewart's side down the hill, his horse still bleeding and moving erratically. He thought she was hit again. As they reached the base of the hill he had seen a small trail leading into the wood, a path well worn by generations of woodcutters.

Stewart was on the trail in a breath. His sword flashed once as he found a target in the woods, and then Jeremy and his own men were all about him, and the woods were theirs. The rebel rifles could be seen in the distance, flying over the ridge, the last of them vanishing just as Jeremy jumped the last stumps into the open ground. They were too canny to be caught in the woods where the bayonets of the regulars were more dangerous to them than their rifles were to the enemy. The rebel infantry company was rallying on the Brooklyn Heights, their numbers sadly depleted, and many of the men had thrown away their muskets.

Crawford came up with McDonald, flushed with triumph. McDonald was all business. A little spat like this was nothing to Sergeant McDonald.

"The price, McDonald?"

"Nixon lost the number of his mess on the hill, sir. Lyle and Somers wounded. I wouldn't give much for Somers's chances. Lyle looks all right. And Guibert burst his musket, the useless gowk. He overcharged it."

"We'll hold this wood until I can get us some relief."

"Aye, sir. Ye should see to yoursel' sir. You're hit."

"Crawford, see to it that Sergeant McDonald instructs you on how to post men in a wood. You are in command. Don't interfere with McDonald."

Crawford looked up at him with something bordering on adoration.

Stewart picked his way out of the wood and cantered up the hill, a little light-headed. To every section of his own men that he passed he called out some praise, or a joke. Keeping his seat seemed to be harder, and he wondered absently where Jeremy had got to. He looked down and saw blood flowing easily over his right boot, and as his eyes traveled up his body he saw that the river of blood went down his thigh and over his knee. His white breeches were redder than his scarlet coat. He swayed a little.

The blacks had formed into a very passable line at the top of the hill in front of the redoubt. Most of them had muskets. As he rode up, the tall one ordered them to present arms, a surprising compliment given the situation, and he took off his cap.

"Well fought, lads. Well fought." His voice was weak. He shook his head to clear it and wondered where Murray was.

"Who's in charge here?" he asked, his voice barely a whisper, and started to slump from his saddle. Suddenly there were strong hands on him, and Jeremy's voice in his ear. He was down in the mud, lying on his back, and someone was pulling a bandage tight on his thigh. He hadn't lost consciousness. The big black man was leaning over him.

"You'll be fine, sir. Ball passed right through and into your saddle."

"And you are?"

"Julius Caesar, sir."

Stewart leaned back in Jeremy's arms and smiled up at the familiar face as if at a joke.

"Of course you are," he said, and went away for a while.

⋆　⋆　⋆

Caesar watched the black man on the horse with undisguised admiration as he rode off, following the handcart pulled by four of Caesar's laborers. Impossible as it seemed, his first thought had been that the mounted black man was an officer, although his dark blue coat and feathered turban looked different from every other uniform he had seen.

His muscles seemed to have seized up, as if he had worked too hard all day without rest. The fight had been short, but he had spent energy recklessly. Virgil looked old, his face pinched, and his shoulders stooped. Caesar hadn't seen him so done in since the swamp. Jim looked as bad, although Tonny, who had fought like a tiger from the start, looked fresh as a new calf. Their men were spread out over the hillside, looking for any wounded and plundering the dead without a shadow of remorse.

"Sergeant Peters be dead," Virgil said, thrusting his chin toward the little redoubt they had all fought to save.

"I'll jus' see to him, then. Go get us some good equipment."

Virgil nodded and moved away slowly, like an old man.

Jim followed Caesar with a mattock and a shovel. They didn't say much for a while. Caesar picked the older man's corpse up easily and carried him back to the edge of the broken ground, far from the redoubt and the little patch of woods where the rebels had hidden themselves. He thought that maybe the war would linger here, as it had at Great Bridge, and he didn't want Peters to be dug up when some other unit put in trenches. Once he had a spot, he looked over his shoulder at the view, and it was a good one, right over the little redoubt and then over the valley to the Brooklyn Heights. He broke the ground, his muscles protesting every stroke. He let the pick do most of the work. Then Jim stepped in with a shovel and started to dig. It was the shovel that Caesar had used in the fighting, but the blood on the blade was quickly scoured away by the damp earth. His wound hurt him. He wanted to smoke.

One by one other men came and dug, or used the pick. It reminded him of Tom's grave in Virginia, and his eyes filled with tears unexpectedly.

He walked a little apart so that the men wouldn't see him, and almost ran over Tonny.

"Virgil says you have to see this an' come quick!" said Tonny. Caesar followed him down the hill, toward the wood where the regulars were. They were smoking. He could smell the smoke. Virgil was well down, on a little flat.

" 'Memba this man?" Virgil asked. A small white man, his face a mask of old scars, lay broken like an abandoned doll on a trash heap. Caesar shook his head.

"One of they slave-takuhs came fo' us when you was sick. I shot him back in the swamp, an' now he daid." Virgil laughed aloud. "He came all this way and he daid!"

Caesar looked at the little knot of wool on the man's shoulder marking him as a corporal. He knelt and cut it free with his clasp knife. "Now you're the corporal, Virgil."

He looked down on the body and spat. So did Virgil, and then Tonny.

"Reckon they was chasin' us?" asked Virgil. "The other one was there. The big one. I saw him."

Caesar nodded. "They was after us fo' slaves, Virgil. Nothin' mo'. *Nothing more.*"

Virgil frowned, and he and Tonny had a brief struggle to get the knot of white wool onto Virgil's jacket.

"Any orders?"

"When the hole is dug, we form them up and fire the volleys, just like we used to." Caesar was eyeing the bodies around them for equipment.

"Reckon we can keep our arms?"

Caesar knelt by a young man whose life was gurgling out of a hole in his chest the size of a dollar. He was squirming in pain, moaning, his eyes rolled back in his head. Caesar watched the boy writhe for a moment and then knelt, drew his clasp knife and used it under the boy's ribs, and the boy died, quietly, without even a kick. Then he took the boy's accoutrements, including a nice bayonet and a leather hunting pouch with a priming horn. The priming horn was engraved with *Isaac Stark, his horn.* His musket was a fine one, too, and the pouch had a pipe and tobacco.

Caesar nodded at the body, a little queasy from the killing. The boy had been in pain, gut shot. He hoped he'd done right. "Bury him, too," he said, and Virgil agreed.

Mr. Murray hobbled up to the ring of blacks, where they were watching the last scoops of earth removed from the graves. He watched as Virgil formed them into a line at the graveside. The old Ethiopians formed easily, almost like regulars. Other men had never held a musket before, and Virgil put them in the back rank.

Caesar was smoking, his pipe upside down in the rain. Isaac Stark had made good char and kept his tinder dry, and Caesar thought he must have been a good soldier for all his youth. He was conscious that Virgil had the men in hand. He knocked his pipe out on the sole of his boot, careful not to snap the stem, and then walked to the front of the company. Murray stood off to the side with his sword drawn.

"I take it you're the sergeant now," Murray said.

"Yes, sir."

"Then get on with it, Sergeant."

One by one, the shots for the dead rang out over the hillside, and the smoke of their volleys hung in the damp air for a moment, covering the little mounds of wet earth until the wind came and blew the smoke away.

Chapter Twelve

The rain fell in broad sheets that soaked a man through his coat before he could walk half a mile. Washington sat on his horse and watched his men plod down the last turn in the road and onto the ferry dock where boats were waiting for them. The movement of thousands of men and their weapons and supplies across the narrows to New York was the product of careful planning and meticulous staff work, and his army was already saved. Only the sentries were left.

He had held a council of war to discuss the abandonment of Long Island. Before this war, he had thought such councils to be the sign of a weak commander. He didn't like to have to share momentous decisions with other men. And yet, in the new army, autocracy had no place except in direst need and immediate crisis, and the withdrawal from Long Island had been neither. The British had maneuvered them smartly from each strong position, enjoying all the advantages, from the superior training of their soldiers to the complete mobility of their enormous fleet. The council had helped to share the responsibility and helped him master the rapid blows to his reputation.

Only the commander of the local militia had argued against the abandonment, fearful of retribution against his men who had already pillaged their Tory neighbors and could expect the same in return. Leaving Long

Island had all the power of sense behind it, and now that his generals had faced the British in the field, they had a much healthier respect for the foe. Sullivan and Stirling were gone, taken as prisoners in the loss of Brooklyn Heights. Reports that the Royal Navy had penetrated into the waters east of Governor's Island served to reinforce his point that their flanks were open to British troops landing from the sea at any moment. The agreement of the council was, in the end, unanimous.

And now he sat in the rain and watched his men march onto their boats, pausing from time to time to note a company that had served well, or badly, and occasionally to praise one of his subordinates for the efforts he had made to find the boats and rescue the army. He was conscious that they would live to fight another day and that it would be easier to hold New York from the other shore. But his mind kept slipping away to the inevitable fact of defeat. He had lost his first field action, and lost it decisively, beaten twice in battles and then ejected from his positions by the maneuvers of the enemy navy. He worried that he had lost the confidence of his army, and he worried about the future.

He had taken Boston. Now he looked likely to lose New York. And the army he had preserved by retreat had already begun to desert.

New York, September 6, 1776

Even inside the house, the sound of picks and shovels raising fortifications on the flats below competed with the movement of horses and carts. Most of the wealthy citizens of New York had already left, and now every citizen who had cause to distrust the return of royal government was moving off Manhattan Island. The pro-Congress faction of New York seemed to have little confidence that the city could be held. Their contempt for their own army was returned with interest.

"Burn the city!" The voice belonged to Nathanael Greene, still in pain from the wounds he had received at the Battle of Brooklyn, but every face at the table reflected his sentiments. "Two thirds of the property here belongs to Tories anyway. This town is a nest of traitors. Burn it."

"We have already spent so much in treasure and sweat to build these fortifications, General Washington. We must fight to hold them. If we abandon them so easily, the enemy will think we are beaten." The speaker was General Heath, of the New York militia. He did not take kindly to his city being described as a nest of traitors, but he made allowances for Greene, who was in pain, and whose bravery was highly regarded all around the table. Already, some of the best young officers were called "Washington's sons." Nathanael Greene was one of them.

Rufus Putnam, acting as the army's chief engineer, shook his head and spread one of his hands meaningfully over the map on the table before them. "There are simply too many routes onto the island. They control the river. They can reduce any one of our forts, given time and inclination. They can land almost anywhere, and worst of all, they can bypass us and trap our men on this island."

Washington pushed his chair back with his long legs and stood carefully to avoid entangling his sword with the table. He still smarted from defeat on Long Island, and he already sensed that New York was lost. "We have lost the best part of three thousand men in the last week. We will lose more. Till of late I had no doubt in my mind of defending this place, nor should I have yet, if the men would do their duty." He looked them over, and most of the brigadiers couldn't meet his eye. The men were melting away, and the militia coming to fill their places were very poor soldiers, anxious already, made fearful by the rumor of a defeat they hadn't suffered.

Greene, the firebrand, met his eye but shook his head. "This is not the place, General. And this is not the army."

"I agree. I despair of these men doing their duty. If I were called upon to declare on oath whether the militia had been most serviceable or hurtful upon the whole, I should subscribe to the latter. The army we had at Boston was better. We had a winter to train it, and now it has gone home and we must start anew." He walked up and down the room, pausing twice to look out of the window at Virginia troops, most newly arrived. They looked healthy and willing, and their drill was good, but the Long Island veterans were shy, and had shown it. He could barely hold his temper.

"Send a letter to the Congress and inform them that I must consider the destruction of this city to deny it as a base of operations and winter quarters to the enemy."

His military secretary began writing immediately.

✮ ✮ ✮

Within two days, he had his answer.

"Resolved, that General Washington be acquainted, that the Congress would have especial care taken, in case he should find it necessary to quit New York, that no damage be done to said city by his troops, on their leaving it: The Congress having no doubt of being able to recover the same, though the enemy should, for a time, obtain possession of it."

"They have lost command of their senses."

"Congress is driven by money, and that the New Yorkers have in plenty."

"Not ours to speculate, gentlemen." Just two days later, and Washington was looking down the same table. His defenses were no better, and indeed might be thought worse. There were Royal Navy frigates on the rivers, and his desertions had just reached a new high. "I suspect that the gentlemen of Congress have made a serious error here, but it is they that command us."

"If Charles Lee were here, I daresay he'd have something to say," commented one of the aides. He meant to be heard, but kept his voice low. Lee was not known for his patience with their political masters.

Washington had accepted Lee's jibes, even approved of them. Congress knew nothing of the conduct of war and insisted on tying his hands and appointing generals of little use and withholding rank from the best men. Congress had lost Canada and was now making a fair bid for losing New York. He wondered at himself, because just a year ago he would have bridled at allowing any man authority over his own decisions, but with every day he thought that such authoritarian ways led to the abuses of Great Britain, and he tried to submit meekly to his Congress because they represented a greater will than his own, even when they were wrong. And now they were ordering him to hold miles of coastline with untrained militia and a handful of regulars, against the finest navy in the world and their equally fine army. He could only make his dispositions and bow his head.

"Send to Congress again," he said. He began to describe the defenses of the city, and the limited troops he had to defend it.

"How the event will be, God only knows," he closed. His secretary dipped his quill one more time and it began to scratch again. "Circumstanced as I am, be assured that nothing in my power will be wanting to effect a favorable and happy issue."

No one at the table met his eye, not even General Greene.

New York City, September 13, 1776

The Virginia Continentals were drawn up under Captain Lawrence to greet Colonel Weedon and his men as they marched into the flying camp. Lawrence was still parchment white, and he moved very carefully, but it seemed he would survive his wound. George Lake was now a sergeant. He and Bludner were the only noncommissioned officers to survive the fight at the little redoubt. During the Battle of Brooklyn, they had been thrown in twice with the Marylanders and again on the darkened road back to the ferry they had tried to keep the British light infantry off the army's heels, while their mocking horns sounded foxhunting calls all through the long retreat.

View Halloo.

His friend Isaac was dead, left behind in the mud at the little redoubt on Long Island. So many other men were gone, dead, deserted, or sick, that there were no longer any lines between the "true believers" and the "backwoodsmen." The new line was between the men who had survived Long Island and the new drafts up from Philadelphia. They were still fired with enthusiasm. They also believed everything they had read in the papers there, and insisted that they knew more about Long Island than George did.

George Lake still held Bludner responsible for the wreck of the company in its first fight, but he kept a tight rein on his resentment. Bludner was an arrogant clod, but he was also a good sergeant with an eye for detail. He had led the survivors out of three traps and an ambush in that wet retreat.

Colonel Weedon made a joke to Captain Lawrence out on the parade and his horse fidgeted a little. George kept his hands clasped on his musket and stared straight ahead. Parades no longer interested him much. Colonel Weedon had missed Long Island. He was a tavernkeeper from Fredericksburg, a known social climber and an acquaintance of General Washington. That last stood in his favor with some.

The Third Virginia had also missed Long Island. They were the regiment to which Captain Lawrence's company would now be attached. They would have a great deal to learn.

Down the Hudson River, the British battery on Montresor's Island opened fire again.

Montresor's Island, September 14, 1776

The artillerymen worked like no team Caesar had ever seen. There were dozens of them on each gun, yet every man had an exact place to stand, a path to follow as he performed his tasks. And every man's task was different. Some fed the brass guns, taking paper cartridges of powder from stores well to the rear of the gun line and carrying them forward. Others loaded the powder charge down the barrel, or brought the iron balls from another store, or moved the gun to aim it. Each gun fired in its own time, and yet the impression Caesar received was rather like that of watching a perfectly tuned flintlock, or the innards of a watch at work.

He and most of the other Ethiopians were leaning on their tools well back from the guns. Caesar never tired of watching them fire, but the other men smoked or played cards. Their work had been finished when the gun platform had been dug, leveled, and completed, but the engineers had expected the enemy to dig a counterbattery and return the fire, and had wanted them handy to repair any damage.

Instead, they had had three days of inaction due to what Mr. Murray described as "Mr. Washington's incompetence." Caesar kept them at their drill, and Mr. Murray, the engineer, had become their honorary officer. He had drilled them several times, marching in front and using his sword to indicate wheels and turns. He knew the drill much better than either Mr. Edgerton or Mr. Robinson had, although as an engineer he had never commanded troops. Caesar was learning about how the army worked. The red-coated officers were often well trained, but some were not. The engineers and artillerymen were all professionals, middle-class men who attended schools and knew the business. Caesar thought they were lucky to have Murray's interest.

Virgil was back to scrounging wool and sewing jackets. No one had come to take their arms, and so, unlike all the other work parties digging around New York, Caesar's men had good muskets and all the accoutrements that went with them.

Bang.

The sound of the gunfire no longer made any of them jump. Virgil was making a jacket for a new boy called Isaac Vernon, a very thin runaway from the Jerseys, just across the water. He had swum to them during the night and said that there was a rumor among the blacks over the water that the British army was offering freedom. Willy and Romeo and Paget were dealing cards. Tonny and Fowver were working on a captured musket with a lock that wouldn't make a spark.

Murray came over to Caesar, who stood up and removed his hat smartly, and bowed his head.

"Carry on, Caesar."

Caesar relaxed a little.

"We'll be taking New York in a few days."

"So I figure, sir."

"Captain Stewart wants to put your company on the provincial rolls, Caesar. That will get you paid, and some money for equipment."

Caesar just smiled, suffused with happiness. To be regular soldiers, with pay and standing, would be a fine thing.

"When the army takes a city, things happen. There is usually some looting. Some men get rich. Others get hanged. Do you take my meaning, Caesar?"

"No, sir. I can't say that I do."

"You're going to want cloth for uniforms, and more muskets. You'll want barracks space. There are a host of things you'll want. I guarantee that whatever officer you get will be poor. I'm poor myself, so I know. So there's a chance to pick up some cash, or maybe a few bolts of cloth."

Caesar nodded along before Murray was finished. "Now I understand you, sir."

Bang.

"Church is being rigged in the rear of the battery, if any of you are of a mind to attend," said Murray. "I don't wish to be indelicate, Sergeant Caesar, but as the minister is both Anglican and a gentleman of color, I thought your men might feel comfortable in attending."

Caesar was still lost in thought about brown wool and the possibility of better equipment. He knew that in the long run his company had to find a way to be mustered and placed on a regular status, but he hadn't expected the path to be made smooth so suddenly. He walked back to the lounging work party and squatted down next to Virgil, who took a draw on his pipe and passed it to Caesar.

"He wan' us to drill, Caesar?"

"Mr. Murray says we might get on the rolls as a company."

"That'd be fi-ine." Virgil nodded, a slow smile spreading. "And paid?"

"If they're goin' to make us soldiers, I guess they'd have to pay us."

Caesar watched the battery moving a gun, always interested. They used levers to move the wheels on the biggest guns. It was an education just watching them, but that wasn't where his thoughts were.

"Ever think where we come from, Virgil?"

Virgil laughed. "Every day. Every single day. Every time I swing that pick, I think, *It's still bettuh than bein' a slave.* Every time I drill, I watch them runaways from Jersey look at me like I'm some big man. I know I ain't, but I won't nevuh forget what I was."

"Long way from the swamp." Caesar was still watching the guns. He couldn't quite meet Virgil's eye, because he still felt the losses of the swamp. And Peters's death at Long Island. "An' we didn't all make it."

Virgil sat up, dusted his jacket. The new Virgil, the soldier, was a fastidious man. "I don' wan' to hear none of that talk from you, Caesar. You got us here. Some died. They died free. What I wan' you to look on is whether we stay free."

Caesar turned sharply to look at him. "What are you saying?"

"I'm saying that there's plenty of Loyal folk that own slaves. I'm saying that if we win, there'll be plenty looking to take our guns away, an' if we lose..."

Caesar stood up. "I don't want to hear any of that talk from you, Virgil. Come on. Mr. Murray wanted us for a church parade."

"I could use some church," said Virgil, and started calling for his section to fall in.

Caesar fell the men in and led them to the river, where they washed some of the sweat off. They had a number of recruits, men who had swum the river to freedom, wearing nothing but shirts and trousers, and he arranged them in the rear ranks so that, at least from a certain angle, the company looked like soldiers with muskets and brown jackets. Then he marched them to the base of the battery, Corporal Fowver berating the new men in his singsong Yoruba accent to keep the step.

The minister was a tall man, his altar a table and a drum with a Union Jack spread over it, and he stood quietly as Caesar marched the men up and halted them in front of the table. He tried to remember what they had done in Williamsburg when they had church parades, and the only thing he could remember was to open the ranks, as if God were going to inspect them. When he was done, he thought of saluting the minister, but that seemed wrong, so he took his place on the right of the company and waited.

The minister was thin and elegant in his black suit. Closer up, Caesar could see that he had dirt under his nails and some mud on his breeches and stockings, probably from assembling the little table and putting up the little tent, but he still carried an air of dignity. Caesar still felt he should say something, and so he stood straight and reported.

"Company of Loyal Ethiopians assembled for church parade, sir!"

He was aware of movement to his right and turned his head, expecting Mr. Murray, but what he saw was a girl, very young, just backing out of the little canvas tent and then rising with considerable grace from the straw-covered ground. She caught his glance and looked down in amiable confusion, and her pale darkness flushed. Caesar tried to snap his attention back to the minister, but there was something in her glance that kept him pinned a moment longer, and so he saw her look at him again from under lowered lids.

If the minister gave any sign, he did not show it, but walked along the ranks like a general, greeting every man and complimenting them on the turnout of the company.

"You are the first armed blacks I've seen. It is a pleasure to meet all of you, and a sign of great things. A pleasure, sir." This to Jim, who was shy, as usual. On and on, through forty men, greeting each individually. He came to Caesar last, as if he had planned it so.

"An admirer of yours said that I should come here and meet you. I am Marcus White, a minister of the gospel."

Remembering Sergeant Peters, Caesar gave a civil bow, his musket inclined away from his body.

"Your servant, sir. I am Julius Caesar, and temporarily in command of the Company of Ethiopians." Caesar was still trying to trace the idea of an "admirer." He must mean Lieutenant Murray.

"Several officers have spoken to me of this body of men, sir. Perhaps I should say that I was trained by the Society for the Propagation of the Gospel?" Seeing Caesar's confusion, he said, "It would not be correct of me to explain myself more fully this moment, except to say that we men of color do have friends in England, Christian men who abhor slavery, and they have some influence in this army. I hope we will soon speak more fully." They both bowed.

"I look forward to it, sir," he said.

Marcus White beamed at him and moved with imperial dignity to the head of the company, where he turned and put a hand on the Bible that was the sole ornament of the table. Raising his right hand, he began the service of morning prayer.

"*When the wicked man turneth away from his wickedness that he hath committed, and doeth that which is lawful and right, he shall save his soul alive,*" he said.

New York City, September 15, 1776

The cannonade was short, and by the time he was ahorse and riding to the sound of the fire, the battle was lost.

Washington began to pass running men well before he came to the flats, and nowhere could he find an officer or even a company making a stand. New York and Connecticut militia flew past him, some disoriented. One man even threatened him with his musket when Washington tried to slow his flight. General Parsons rode up and joined him as he and his staff tried to make them stand. Again and again the knot of officers found themselves alone against an onrushing tide of red and Hessian blue sweeping over the autumn fields, their bayonets gleaming like the white tops on the ocean on a clear day, and always moving closer. Again and again Washington rode to the rear, found a good stone wall or a copse of trees, and tried to rally men there. They merely waited until he rode off for more men before they, too, melted away. Washington began to hate them.

Whole brigades broke as soon as they were formed. Washington watched with horror as Fellows's brigade failed to fire even once, but simply dropped their packs and their muskets and ran from the Hessian troops in front of them. A few were foolish enough to run *at* the Hessians, who promptly shot them down. The British didn't misunderstand so easily, and began to reap a rich harvest of prisoners.

Again he tried to rally them at the edge of a cemetery, where the walls would have held the Germans for an hour. And his men melted away. Again, in a churchyard, where men he sent into the little stone church simply broke a window, jumped free, and ran. On and on, a nightmare of failure and cowardice that stunned him, sapped his resolve, and made him question the worth of his cause, that so many young men would refuse their duty.

At King's Bridge Road his staff ran into a column in full flight. A captain, his uniform torn and muddy, was beating men into ranks when Washington rode up. One of the men the captain had just prodded into line waited until the captain had passed him and then swung his musket into the officer's side, knocking him down. The rest fled.

The captain climbed to his feet right in front of Washington.

"It's like herding cats," he said, more in wonder than in anger, and ran off down the road after his men.

Washington watched the wreck of his army huddling on the road, and saw muskets lying everywhere in the muddy fields, with packs and blankets spread among the stubble. The wealth of his new nation had been spent to provide these men with arms, and they were throwing it away.

Just then a company of British light infantry appeared to his front, moving quickly toward him. He and his staff were badly outnumbered, and virtually unarmed except for the pistols in their saddle holsters. To his right, another group of men appeared from the trees, and Washington saw that they were black. For a moment, he hoped that they were some of his own Rhode Island troops, but they had black cockades and white rags on their arms. They began to fire at the wreck of the Tenth Continental Regiment behind him on the road, which flinched and broke again, their colonel racing to the rear on his horse. The British had only two companies here, and a *Continental brigade* was fleeing from them. It sickened him.

Washington wheeled his horse and cantered back to the routed column. He was humiliated, his whole being suffused with rage at having to run in front of the British.

One of the blacks started to run with him. He was well away to the north, but he was moving quickly, and the other black men started to follow the man. He was *fast*. His gait was familiar, somehow.

He was going to try to cut Washington and his staff off from the column all by himself.

The man leapt a stone wall and Washington, fifty paces away, leapt it on horseback in the same moment. His staff was just behind him, riding hard and making their jumps as best they could.

The black man stopped, raised his musket, and fired, not at Washington but at someone behind him. There was a shout and they rode on, and the black man was not quite fast enough to catch the mounted party. Washington jumped another fence, his greatcoat flying off behind him, low on his horse's neck as if he were hunting. He hadn't buttoned his greatcoat, only wearing it loose on his shoulders. Now it was gone.

He galloped, his face red with anger, his back already cold in the bracing, damp air. To *fly* from the enemy like this, in the face of his own men, was not to be endured. He rode right through the column and turned his horse to look back. His staff was clear, but someone had been taken; a big horse was wandering and a group of the black men were surrounding a man in a blue coat on the ground. The tall black man waved his greatcoat and laughed.

It became the focus of all the day's humiliations.

★ ★ ★

John Julius Stewart slumped a little in his saddle, the cool air biting through his clothes, now damp with sweat. He still wasn't himself. He had lost a *great* deal of blood before the surgeon had closed the wound in his leg, and two weeks hadn't healed everything. He saw spots when he rode too hard.

Jeremy reined in behind him. "There he is!" he called, pointing at Caesar, the black sergeant.

Stewart walked his horse over, too tired to trot.

Caesar was wiping the lock of his musket. His men had a prisoner, a wounded officer. None of Washington's army had regular uniforms, and rank was often difficult to ascertain, but this one looked senior.

"Was that your Mr. Washington, Caesar?"

"Yes, it was, Captain Stewart."

"We almost had him."

Caesar finished wiping his lock, stuffed the linen rag into a leather hunting pouch, and stood up. He turned his back and pointed at something rolled tight across his pack. "That's his cloak."

"Who's your prisoner?"

"Some officer from his staff. He's not hurt bad, if you want to take him." Caesar looked up at Stewart and saluted, raising his musket across his body and then up by his face, erect in the air in the correct position for an enlisted man to greet an officer. Stewart wondered wryly why he bothered at all. Caesar met his eye. He was clearly happy, his whole face suffused with warmth. Stewart could see that he had a hunting sword on his hip, a lovely sword not much bigger than a knife with silver fittings and a green-dyed ivory grip.

He pointed at the sword. "Was that his?"

Caesar laughed. "Well, sir, he didn't seem to need it."

"Rest easy, Sergeant."

"Thank you, sir."

Stewart thought that Caesar was like some of the great craftsmen he had known. Men whose brilliance was wholly in the art of what they made, except that Caesar's art was war. He was slow to salute because cleaning the lock of his musket was so much more important.

☆ ☆ ☆

Stewart's company came up quickly, their bayonets gleaming. The shattered rebel column was near, well within musket shot. Stewart raised his hand and closed his fist, and in response his bugler sounded a call.

Skirmish! Skirmish! Skirmish!

Caesar looked down the road and then back up at Stewart, still smiling like a man who has found paradise. "We're gon' to be in a *whole* lot of trouble when they fin' we only have a few men."

Stewart nodded. "The harder we press them, the less likely that will be, Sergeant. If you will be kind enough to keep your lads nipping at their flank, and we stay on the rear of the column, we should move them along briskly enough."

Beside him, Sergeant McDonald blew his whistle, and the first shots began to be fired by his company. They were tired, but happy. All day they had driven the rebels like cattle, without the loss of a man. File leaders aimed and took their shots, and across the field, a man in a brown woolen shirt fell, coughing out his life as his lungs filled with blood, the shock of the big bullet already taking him away. His mates broke again, pushing to the rear, crying out that there were cavalrymen behind them.

Caesar took his men and ran off to the left. He didn't have a whistle or a bugle, and he wanted both. He wanted the quick communication with his men that Stewart had. Stewart was better than Mr. Robinson, better even than Captain Honey. Caesar wanted to know everything that Stewart knew.

He ran, his nostrils flared, breathing easy, his shot pouch riding high on his hip, his boots comfortable and easy. He looked back over his shoulder and slowed his pace to stay with his men, none of whom was as fast or as easy in their gait as he. Virgil was laboring, and Jim looked done in, and there were other faces already gone. Not lost, or shot, just fallen by the wayside because the pace was too fast. But the best were still with him, about a platoon, all armed, and he circled a little woodlot with a stone wall, coming back to the wall when it ran out parallel to the road, and throwing his band behind it. Most of them lay down, panting, even though there was a whole army of rebel stragglers just a pistol shot away.

For all the training the Ethiopians had done, it wasn't for this kind of fight, and he had to run along, crouched behind the wall, and tell every man what he wanted. It took time, and energy, and he couldn't just raise his fist and start them firing. In a few minutes, though, the first shots rapped out, and the column began to flinch away from the wall.

Virgil was breathing like a bellows, and he took so long aiming his shot that Caesar thought he was hurt. Finally he fired, and Caesar pushed his own musket across the wall. He took careful aim and pulled the trigger. In the press of enemies, he couldn't tell if his shot hit or not.

"I'm dry, Caesar," said Virgil. "You have any mo' powduh?"

Caesar nodded and reached into his pouch. He ran his hand across the bottom and realized that he was out as well, although he continued to feel around for a moment. He didn't carry a proper cartridge box, with the paper cartridges lined up in a wooden block. There was always the possibility of one more, but not this time.

Farther along the wall, Jim stared down his musket with feral concentration and it barked. Once Jim would have flinched his head just a moment before the snap of the lock, but that habit had gone. Caesar saw his hand go back to the box on his hip and come back empty.

Men who had missed fire, or simply loaded more slowly, fired a few more rounds, but then they were out, and the column was moving by them, either unaware of their presence or uncaring. Many of the fleeing men were unarmed.

Caesar saw Jeremy riding up behind the little woodlot and waved both arms. Jeremy rode up to him directly.

"Can you ride back and tell Mr. Stewart we're out of cartridges?"

Jeremy stood in his stirrups to look at the road and then back down at Caesar. "I'll tell him, Julius, but I think you'd be as well to gather your boys up and bring them back. I think we're about dry on powder ourselves."

Caesar wasn't clear on Jeremy's role. Sometimes he seemed more like an officer, at others like Stewart's slave. It was too complicated to discuss right there, but the advice sounded good.

"Where is Mr. Stewart, then?"

"Just the other side of this wood, pressing their rearguard. But as I say, they won't be pressing very hard." Jeremy smiled. "I must say, Julius Caesar, I am jealous of that exploit with Mr. Washington. Please do send me a card the next time you plan something like that." He tipped his hat.

Jeremy always called Caesar "Julius" and he liked it. He slapped the rump of Jeremy's horse. "I'll be most pleased to invite you, suh. *Sir.*"

Jeremy leaned down and spoke quietly. "Get back with us soon. I think we're going into the city. We might be the *first.*"

Caesar nodded, ran back from the wall, and yelled. "Fall in!"

☆ ☆ ☆

The army ran to McGowan's Pass. Harlem Heights was barely held, the best position on the island. They didn't stand on the road and they wouldn't hold the line of trenches north of the road. He would have cried, if he dared.

New York was lost. His army had run without firing a shot. For a moment, when the black tried to run him down, he had thought the same dark thoughts that he had had all those years ago in the Pennsylvania country, when Braddock had lost an army, and he had lost his first military career. He was beaten. His army would not stand again for months after a panic like this, and he could not find anyone to blame except himself.

But this was a different war. He was no longer a young colonel with a life before him. In a way, he was now Braddock, and he owed it to his men, and to his nation, such as it was, to try to keep the army together. He would not cry, nor shout, nor vent his rage on the fools who had run. He would have to wait, retreat, and rebuild, and he watched the faces of the men around him on his staff to see if they still trusted him. As for himself, he no longer trusted his army. He rode back to the rear, sullen, angry, and outwardly his usual icy calm.

Despite his worst fears from midday, the camp had not been lost, nor the magazines. There were solid battalions in front of the camp, formed and ready to meet an enemy. He rode along their ranks, the wind cutting through his coat. He missed his greatcoat.

No one cheered, but no one jeered him, either. He ordered his staff to rally any troops who came near the camp and went to his marquee, set on a rise with a view of the parade and the fields over which the enemy would come if this was the end. He didn't think so. He didn't think that the British were ready for the magnitude of today's victory, and would settle for the occupation of New York. He had several thoughts for limited counterattacks, more to hold the army together and raise its prestige than for any strategic reason. Manhattan Island, and with it, New York, was lost.

"You want something warm, sir?" asked Billy.

Washington realized that he was standing in front of the map on his camp desk, unmoving, his limbs chilled to the bone.

Billy held out a mug, steam whirling up from the top. "I have some hot flip, sir."

The mug was porcelain, from his traveling service, hot to the touch, and Washington cradled it like the touch of life, warming his hands for the first time since before dawn. He thought, *I am not a young man.*

"We lost today. Badly." Washington sat, still pressing the mug to his breast, inhaling the steam. Billy nodded, more like an accepting parent than a slave. Washington sighed and went on. "I have lost New York. I could blame others, but what use? I am in command, and I have failed. Should I resign?"

Billy busied himself at the back of the tent, putting wood on the fire in the small earthen fireplace that had replaced the tent's back door.

"They wouldn't stand, Billy. These men are fighting for their homes and property, their own liberty—and they ran. No one stood his ground. Are we a nation of cowards? Billy, men ran without a shot fired at them. It is one thing when a company breaks because they have seen too many of their comrades shot away. It's another when they run before they see the enemy."

He took a deep drink. "Perhaps they don't trust me. Don't trust the army. Or the Congress, God save us." He gazed into the distance, while Billy looked for another chore to keep him close to his master. He missed a comment about the loss of the city while he seized on Washington's hat and began to brush it. Then he stopped.

"Where's your greatcoat, sir?"

"I lost it in the field." Washington reflected for a moment, and thought, *I ran, too.* He smiled grimly. "One more defeat like this and we might lose the ability to fight. Men will simply walk home and there will be no army." He shook his head. "I wonder if this job is beyond me. I think I expected it to be more like farming: a set of tasks to perform, men to obey me, and a drive to complete the work. A steady pull in harness. Now I wonder if Charles Lee could do better."

Billy looked up from brushing the hat. "I doubt it, sir," he said firmly, and Washington looked at him, startled. Billy flushed and put his head down, but Washington laughed, a laugh of pure mirth, his first in twelve hours. "You, too? I thought everyone loved him but me."

"Not for me to say," said Billy, trying to hide his own laugh.

Washington slapped him on the shoulder. "Lend me your greatcoat, Billy. I'm going to check the posts."

Harlem Heights, September 16, 1776

Once New York fell, Caesar realized that he had expected the war to end in the aftermath. The truth was harsher. His men had been among the first into the city, and as Murray had predicted, there had been benefits. But within hours the city was under British martial law, and within days his men were marching north again, following the wreckage of Washington's army. The generals seemed hesitant to finish Mr. Washington, or so it seemed to Caesar from his very recent knowledge of war. So where the Continentals ran, they marched slowly behind, feeling their way cautiously as if they feared a sudden reversal of fortune. And Caesar knew that the war was not over.

The blacks were not yet an official military organization. They had remained with Mr. Murray through the taking of New York, and then, as the army began to move up Manhattan Island, they attached themselves to Captain Stewart's company, because they were familiar and welcoming.

Caesar was tired all the time. He felt grimy, and his eyes felt like they were full of sand. His mouth was so dry he might have spent the night drinking. He had been in the field too long.

He moved cautiously through the low brush at the base of a tall ridge. Captain Stewart and all the men in the Second Battalion of light infantry were extending their lines to the right, hoping to move their posts forward as inconspicuously as possible and "render Mr. Washington's posts even more untenable," as Mr. Stewart had said. Jim had already been around the hill, alone, making a map on the back of an old tax record. He couldn't read, and his markings on paper were like no map any white officer had ever seen, but Jim had gained a little fame in the last three days for the accuracy of his scouting. Mr. Washington's army was here, in the flat ground on the other side of the ridge. Mr. Washington's army had post on the ridge, and they were finally going to contest them.

He looked back at Jim, just behind him. The rest of his company was moving in two long files, one to each flank. The brush was too dense to move in line. He raised his foot to place it on an old stone wall, long abandoned in this tangle of undergrowth, and he wondered who would go to the trouble of clearing a field and moving the stones only to abandon it. Something caught his attention and he froze.

There was a man right in front of him, just a long throw away through the brush. He was wearing a smock or a shirt. There was another one, next to him.

Caesar raised his musket to his shoulder in one smooth motion and fired. All along the brush line to his front, smoke blossomed in return. He threw himself down behind the jumble of rocks that had been a wall and started to load, already looking for possibilities. There were a great many men out there. He could hear them shouting orders.

Caesar thought that if he wasn't lucky, he might die right here. It didn't bother him much.

"Get to the wall!" Caesar yelled. "Get behind the wall and skirmish!"

He grabbed Jim by the rough material of his trousers and pulled him down.

"Go tell Captain Stewart it's a whole parcel of men. More'n I can count. Maybe a hundred."

Jim nodded.

"I'll jus' leave you ma' piece," he said, and handed Caesar his musket. Then he pushed himself up and ran. There were shots, and he stumbled, but he didn't fall, and then Caesar had other concerns.

✯ ✯ ✯

Washington watched the messenger run the last fifty yards. He could hear the firing, and he ached with the effort not to knee his horse down the hill to meet the panting man halfway.

"Knowlton's..." He panted as he closed. "Colonel Knowlton's rangers. In that wood, right there, fighting redcoats. Their light infantry, I think." Washington thought the man might fall at his feet like the runner from Marathon, but instead, the man bent over and then straightened, color flooding his face.

"Colonel asks for support, and says there is three hundred all told, an' with help he can take the lot. Nothin' on their right."

Suddenly they heard bugles from the woods, the contemptuous call of the kill, as if the redcoats were hunters who had taken their fox. Joseph Reed, the adjutant general, rode up, furious.

"Damn it, we had them." He seemed to feel personally disgraced by the calls. "Damn it!"

Knowlton's men could be seen running from the wood now, a few red-coats at their heels.

Washington looked around, suddenly decisive. "We may yet. Get me..." He looked back to the troops who had formed in front of their tents at the first shots and saw Weedon's Virginians. "General Reed, if you will have the kindness to take Colonel Weedon's companies that are already formed? Right up Vanderwater Heights, and into their flank. Take this man as a guide." Washington rode over to the Virginians, who cheered him. There was a different feeling in the air, even if the redcoats were still sounding their calls. He rode directly to Colonel Weedon.

"I need your best, sir. Your very best effort."

George Lake was less than a musket's length away. Washington was right in front of him, his face severe but unworried, his seat on the horse a picture of control. Washington whipped his hat off and pointed it down the hill toward another ridge and said something further as Major Lietch and Captain Lawrence came up to join the little knot. Lake cheered. Washington turned his horse away and it curveted a little and he rose, his hat still off, and looked back along their line. His eyes seemed to rest di-rectly on George Lake for an instant. That frozen image of the general with his hat off, his horse's front hooves raised like an equestrian statue in Williamsburg, would stay with George Lake forever.

George cheered—they all did, it was everywhere, a wall of sound—and Major Lietch was shouting for them to go forward, and the general was gone.

☆　　☆　　☆

Caesar fired again, ran his hand along the bottom of his pouch, and realized that he was again out of cartridges. His mouth burned from all the powder he had eaten biting the bottoms off his cartridges, and no wa-ter for hours. Jim was back, long since, lying in a little hollow to his right and firing slowly. The brush and the smoke made choosing a target almost impossible, but every time he reached back for his canteen, the rebels tried another rush.

Suddenly there was a horse above him, and Jeremy looking down, and legs with wool breeches and sharp black gaiters like little boots moving past him in the brush. The rebels fired, and a man went down right in front of him, and then there was a roar from the redcoats all around him like a savage beast let loose, and the bugles called a "view," as if a fox were in sight. He was fluent in this hunting language, and though the soldiers weren't from Stewart's company, Jeremy's presence told him they weren't far, and he rose to his feet.

"Ethiopians! Forward!" And then Caesar was pressing into the smoke, tripping over the heavy brush, and a twig of thorns tore at his leg, another lashing his hand, and then he was through the smoke and a musket fired just over his head as he fell over another wall. He rolled, his equipment tangling for a moment on his back, and rose as smoothly as he could, the butt of his musket catching a man cleanly in the side of the head and knocking him down and out, his body falling with the boneless limp-ness that Caesar now knew to indicate total unconsciousness, or instant death. Fowver fired at something farther on and then stopped to fit his bayonet. He was yipping like a mad dog, a sound that some of the other Yoruba men made when at war.

All the redcoats were intermingled now, and then there was firing again, coming from their left. Caesar couldn't see anything, and he looked around for Jeremy, who was gone.

"Ethiopians!" he called. "On me! Fall in!"

Men began to appear out of the smoke. He continued to shout, his dry mouth forgotten. Men would be spread all over the wood by now, and his shouting seemed to rally only a dozen or so. Other voices shouted for the light companies of the Forty-second and the Sixty-fourth, and bugles sounded, confusingly, all through the undergrowth, and then the firing was almost in front of them, and a Virginian voice was ordering his men to "get in any covuh an' shoot!"

One of them showed himself clear, an officer or a sergeant, and Caesar raised his musket and pulled the trigger before realizing that the gun was empty and he had no more ammunition.

✯　✯　✯

Ten yards away in the smoke, George Lake never knew how close his death had been, and shouted for his men to keep in line and look for tar-gets when they fired. He shouted again. An arm's length away, Bludner was pushing some new recruits with his musket, shoving them to the exact position where he wanted them. He never turned his head to look at the enemy. He heard the enemy trying to rally and knew they had the redcoats at a disadvantage. His glance caught George Lake's and they both smiled in the same instant, as if sharing the secret. They were winning.

☆ ☆ ☆

"Crawl!" Caesar suited actions to words and began to burrow back toward the stone wall where he had started the action. A volley crashed out behind them, and he hoped all his men had been down on the ground, although a few low balls flung wood splinters and gravel around them. He moved as quickly as he could, and there it was, the little wall, and he was over it and on the trail. He wasn't lost; his head cleared, and he felt as if he could see the whole action in his mind like the chase of a fox or a deer at Mount Vernon. The rebels were all along their left, but not strong on their front.

He looked down the ruined wall and saw that some of the men had never gotten up to join the first rush. He had seen enough action to know that not every man was brave every day, and he waved to them.

"Time to go, Ethiopians!" he yelled, and started down the trail at a crouching run. He stopped twice to look back and see that they were with him, and they were. Another volley crashed out behind him, too far to hurt them. He had "gone away" like a smart fox on a spring day, whipping the prize out from under the nose of the hunter. He couldn't see Stewart or Jeremy at the wood edge, and he knew that their horses would make them prime targets in the woods, but they weren't his concern. He waited as men he knew tumbled out of the wood on his heels, the stream becoming a trickle after about twenty-five. There were several men from the Fortieth and two from the Sixty-fourth. They looked a little bemused to find themselves with a body of black men, but they stayed silent.

"Anyone has more than one cartridge, give it to your mate. Load! Now!"

They were shuffling around, unformed and worried. They thought the enemy was right behind them. Caesar could see it all so clearly in his mind and he forgot that others could not.

"Ain't no one behind you right now. Them Virginny boys is shootin' at trees. You stay with me, lads. I'll see you right." Excitement robbed him of his hard-won accent, but he could feel the fight shaping in the wood as the British swung more men to their flank and steadied their line in the center of the wood. It was all in the balance, and he could see it, he could save it if only these men would load their muskets and follow him.

Muskets were coming up as men got their bullets rammed down onto the powder and replaced their rammers. The regulars looked like they were on parade, already making a line, while many of the blacks who had never served in the Ethiopians in Virginia loaded casually, their musket butts on the ground. Virgil slapped a cartridge into his hand and he primed his pan and cast about, careful of the eighteen-inch bayonet. He was the last man to load, and by the time he returned his ramrod he had his plan.

"We're going left 'round this wood. As soon as we see rebels, we form a front and give fire. If we have the number, we're goin' right at them."

Some of the men looked uneasy at that. By no means did all the blacks have bayonets.

"You men follow me. We'll have 'em," Caesar said, looking hard at one of the regulars who seemed like he might protest. The man just shook his head. Caesar began to jog off to the left. He could see a column coming up from the south, grenadiers with two artillery pieces, but they would be too late for the wood whatever happened. He looked back and saw that his men were coming well, a long single file with the redcoats in the middle. He turned the corner of the wood and could see all the way down the ridge and up the other side, where a column of rebels was shaping up, and he spotted an officer in blue and buff sitting just at the base of the wood, less than a quarter mile away, and he *knew* he was right. The whole rebel line was just in those woods and he was now on *their* flank. The fox had turned and bitten the hunter, and now the hunter was ready to bite back.

"Form front!" he called, and they did, but his voice alerted someone in the wood, and there was a scramble in among the trees as someone flinched away. In a moment the edge of the wood was full of men, right in their front.

Caesar watched it as if in slow motion. He had time. He was calm, even happy, his plan proven correct.

"Make ready!" he called. The regulars didn't really know where to stand in the Ethiopian line, but the order stiffened them and they obeyed automatically. The rebels were close, emerging from the trees and scrambling in the thick brush at the wood's edge.

"Present!" he bellowed, and the rebels began to flinch away, the race lost. They weren't the Virginians, as he had hoped, but other troops in neat blue coats. He owned them. They were caught in the brush, clear of the cover afforded by the wood's edge. Behind them, other units were suddenly at the edge of the wood, too, and halfway down the hill he could see the Virginians and that same tall ugly man he had wanted to kill at Brooklyn when they fought in the little redoubt, but there had been no time.

"Fire!" he said with finality. For just a moment he saw the rebels to his front frozen, their faces slack, as if life had already left them, and then the volley slammed into them like the collapse of a burning barn.

Off to his right, a horse burst from the wood and Captain Stewart, hatless and bleeding, rode up beside him.

"Bloody marvelous!" he shouted, and thumped Caesar on the back, before starting to call for his men to form their front.

★ ★ ★

George Lake pulled himself free of the raspberry tangle at the edge of the wood and held his musket in the air yelling for his men to rally. They were different today. They ran back, yes, but they leapt into the ranks. No one ran past. They had *licked* the redcoats in the wood, got on their flanks and clawed them hard, and the woods were full of redcoat bodies. George Lake knew they were fighting light infantry, the very best the redcoats had to offer.

Certainly they had taken a whack in their turn, but they had seen the backs of the regulars for the first time. They were learning.

He got his men formed and found that his company was the foremost in the field. The Marylanders who had been on his right in the wood had vanished and suddenly he saw why, with two companies formed on his flank. He and Bludner didn't try to form to meet the new threat. They were veterans now.

"Back!" they yelled, and the men ran again. And again, when they yelled for the company to rally, it did, facing the right way, a good space of a musket shot between them and the redcoats. George thought that he might have seen the blacks again before he had to pull back, but he wasn't sure. He waited with his company, and other companies from the Third Virginia came and formed on them. The British formed, but no one came on. Their ranks looked thin. George looked at his own and knew he had lost men, too. Men around him called taunts at the British, and he let them.

They were learning.

Morris House, New York, October 1776

General Charles Lee had not changed. He had won a famous victory, repulsing Clinton's ships at Charleston, South Carolina, and he had dazzled Congress on his road north, stopping in Philadelphia to proclaim his own success and to convince the doubting that there was no other path for General Washington than the one on which he had embarked.

He was still well groomed, wore his coat with most of the facings unbuttoned, like the younger British officers, and his little Nirvenois tricorn was worn rakishly aslant on his head. He tossed his reins to an aide and embraced Washington, to everyone's surprise. It smacked of theater, but then so did a great deal about Charles Lee.

Washington, a man whose bad teeth dictated that he should smile as little as possible, smiled for Charles Lee. Lee smiled back, and gave a bow.

"Welcome back, General. We ought to have a bower decorated in laurel for you."

"Nonsense, sir. A small matter of logistics. A few well-sited forts and many brave young men."

"Perhaps the laurels should be for your dealings with our masters in Congress."

The assembled staffs laughed together. Lee raised his hand for quiet, another theatrical gesture. Washington could tolerate his posturing, indeed, would tolerate almost *anything* to have Lee back.

"General Washington," he said, making sure he would be heard by the whole assembly, "I have nothing but contempt for the Congress. I do not mean one or two of the cattle"—he paused for emphasis—"but the whole stable."

There was a shocked silence. Washington hid his darkest feelings about the Congress from his staff, and they in turn rarely shared their frustrations with the line officers and soldiers who made up the army. Here was Charles Lee, the hero of the hour, speaking to their private, outraged thoughts. Congress, who refused to burn New York City, refused to raise the regular regiments to prosecute the war, tied their hands, held back money, appointed incompetent commanders, pandered to privilege and money. *The whole stable.*

But Washington smiled and gave Lee his hand again, leading him toward Morris House, in which he lodged. "Charles, I had forgotten what it was like to have you about."

And in that moment, the shocked silence turned again to laughter.

They rode along the new lines while Washington described the campaign to date, its many reverses and his plans for the next action. Lee listened in silence, his concentration bent on Washington's report.

"Are we losing the war, General?" he asked, turning to Washington suddenly. They had pulled ahead of their staffs and had what counted as privacy among the great.

Washington shook his head. "I couldn't say. This isn't the war I expected. It is less about battles than about desire. The war of words is as vital as the war in the field. Losses shake men's faith in the cause, and gains strengthen that faith. It is there that the war is being fought."

Lee nodded. "It is a new kind of war. But our enemies adapt as quickly as we do. In the south, they have offered to free slaves who come to the army. They deride our notions of liberty."

"That will lose them any friends they had among men of property."

"Perhaps, General. But what of Parliament? What will our supporters there say when someone of the stature of Burke or Wilberforce denounces slavery instead of praising our resolution for liberty?"

Washington looked over his horse's head for a few strides and nodded. "Slavery is an issue of property, not liberty. But I see how it could be used in other ways." He pointed at a set of ridges in the distance. "That's where I intend my magazines and winter quarters, beyond those hills. May I take it you wish a command?"

"You know me, General. I do."

"Welcome back, Charles."

Jackson House near New York City, October 18, 1776

Captain Stewart had met Sir William Howe on several occasions, but the Howes represented the very top of the Whig aristocracy and John Julius

Stewart was the son of a Scots merchant. He did have the advantage that both he and his wealthy father were Whigs, that is, men who felt the good of the realm lay in liberal government and the House of Hanover, not conservative government and the House of Stewart. In Scotland, this last was often the more important argument, as blood had been shed there in living memory. But in the south, in England, the issue between Whig and Tory was about liberty, the protection of property, and the rights of men.

Sir William and his brother Richard were joint commanders of the entire war effort. Sir William had the army, and Richard had the fleet. They were famous men from a famous family, and many Americans remembered the family name with fondness. Their brother, George Augustus Howe, had died at Ticonderoga in 1758 fighting alongside many Americans. The Howes had not been sent to win a war this time, but to find an end to it as quickly as possible, and they were both capable men who understood politics and war and the dangerous middle ground between the two.

Sir William was dressed for the cold, in a dark blue velveteen hunting coat trimmed in red. He wore heavy riding boots and was leaning back in a deep settle in front of the house's main fireplace when one of his aides stepped in and said softly, "Captain Stewart of the Second Battalion light infantry, Sir William."

Sir William rose and bowed slightly. "The hero of the hour."

"You are too kind, Sir William."

"Nonsense, Captain. By all accounts, your quick action and that of this company of black men prevented a very ugly situation."

"Thank you, Sir William. The men did the fighting. The black men—"

"Yes, I've read your report and that of your brigade major. I needn't tell you, Captain, that a less impetuous advance might have prevented the whole situation. The damned rebels say they've seen our backs now. And where'd I have been left if I had lost both of my light infantry battalions?"

Stewart thought that he had come to be praised, but Sir William's tone was now very uncomfortable for him, and he stood straight, as if ready for a blow. Sir William changed tack suddenly, his voice changing, his chest relaxing. In the next room, a woman was humming and then singing a tune.

"I'm of a mind to grant your request to have this group of Africans embodied formally. I note that your petition to that effect is signed by General Clinton, by your own major, your regiment's colonel, as well as

John Simcoe from the regulars and Beverly Robinson from our Loyalist volunteers." *Whigs to a man,* thought Stewart, *and with votes in Parliament.*

The woman's singing, clear and light, floated out from the closed door.

> An old man came courting me, Hey, ding derry now,
> An old man came courting me, me being young!
> An old man came courting me, fain would he marry me,
> Maids when you're young, never wed an old man.

They both listened until she finished, a lovely clear young voice. Sir William smiled wryly.

"I assure you she is not referring to me," he said.

Stewart merely bowed, hiding his smile.

Sir William waved at a pile of documents on his fireside table. "I cannot simply embody your blacks without consultation, much as I would like. I am aware that there is a body of opinion in this army that we should make ourselves the army of Zion, rescuing this lost tribe from the slavery of the rebels. I also have a clan of Tory officers who believe that blacks are savages, and their employment will bring down on us the condemnation of all Europe."

Again Stewart bowed. When in the presence of the great, a modest man should only marshal his arguments when asked.

There was movement outside the door. It opened, and a cornet of the Sixteenth Light Dragoons leaned in, the silver buttons gleaming richly on his dark blue facings, followed by a severe-looking man in a red coat, with a recent wound, and a pleasant-faced Loyalist in green. A little after came a self-important–looking fellow in a civilian coat of pale blue.

"Captain Simcoe. Major Robinson. Mr. Loring."

Stewart had never met John Graves Simcoe, although his reputation as a soldier was already formidable and he was known to have political connections at home. Major Beverly Robinson was an American who led Loyalist soldiers and was known, despite his Virginian antecedents, to have misgivings about slavery. Mr. Loring was someone important in the emerging British commissary. John Stewart shook hands with Simcoe and Robinson. Both complimented him on the action the day before, compliments from men who had led such actions themselves. Loring merely touched his hand absently with two fingers, a habit so contemptuous that Stewart stiffened.

"Gentlemen, I have asked you here for your views on arming and embodying black soldiers." Sir William smiled at all of them. He had risen politely to greet them as if they were guests, but having done so he was slumped down in his chair with his feet up. Stewart had heard that he suffered from gout.

"My brother and I have to move carefully in these colonies. It is no secret in the army that crushing the rebels in the field will not settle the issue, nor will it heal any wounds. Government at home requires a negotiated settlement, and at the moment, the rebels will not negotiate. Thus the issue about black soldiers is not one of humanity or military expediency, gentlemen. It is one of politics and, oddly, of avoiding conflict with our own adversaries. *Anything* that prolongs this war or provides our rebels with political ammunition to continue the struggle must be examined very carefully. Am I clear?"

Mr. Loring stepped forward a little. "That is quite a relief to me, Sir William. I had understood from the tone of your note that you were leaning the other way, toward employing these savages."

Sir William smiled at him and nodded a little, as if urging him to continue, and the small man bowed his head as if in agreement.

"Employing blacks as anything but labor will harm our cause in several ways. First, it undermines that knowledge of inferiority which is essential to the maintenance of the bonds of slavery. Many of our Loyalists here in New York and across the river in New Jersey own slaves, Sir William, and it is essential that they rest easy knowing that their property is not threatened by the very authority that has been sent by the government to protect it."

Sir William nodded, as if accepting his point.

"Second, blacks are savages. If released upon the rebels, they will commit atrocities that will reflect badly on the honor of His Majesty. Ignorant of the uses of civilization, and totally unable to understand the courtesies of our forms of warfare, they will reduce us to the level of Africans. We will be lampooned in the press."

Again Sir William nodded. One of the doors flanking the fireplace opened and a very handsome young black woman with an abundant bosom only partially concealed by her gown came in softly, carrying a tray. Stewart suspected that she had heard the whole of Mr. Loring's infamous speech, as her face was showing a deep red under the dark skin. Loring paid her no heed. Stewart wondered if she had been the singer.

"Finally, Sir William, despite the arguments these men might urge on you, please remember that England requires the slave trade for her commerce. It is our cloth, our mills, our gunsmiths, and our ships that drive the trade, and without it, what would we have? Any step you take here will be questioned in Parliament, where they will wonder what notions you have learned in America that you seek to smash the trade."

This last was so clearly above the level of converse that was acceptable to Sir William that he turned and stared at Mr. Loring, but Loring had now noticed the girl and seemed immune to his patron's anger.

Sir William waved at the girl. "Polly, pour for the gentlemen. Captain Simcoe, I know you disagree, sir. Please state your views."

Simcoe was a wealthy man from an old naval family. Although he was vastly junior to Sir William in rank, every man in the room knew that the Simcoes grew up to be the Sir Williams. Stewart would never be a general, and Robinson and Loring were Americans. But John Graves Simcoe would rise far, everyone said. He had the connections and the looks, the charisma.

"Sir William, it would be foolish of me to hide from you that I support the universal abolition of slavery. It will happen. The ownership of one man by another is pernicious not just to our morals but to our trade, which is why such ownership is already illegal in England."

Sir William didn't move his head.

"Sir William, I know that you have to concern yourself with the whole of the theater of war and all the politics, so I will refute Mr. Loring's points in reverse, on that basis. First, as to Parliament, Mr. Loring knows nothing of your support there, as he is himself a Tory, and we are Whigs. The Whig interest is inclined to the end of slavery, Sir William. More important than that, though, is in the refutation of the very liberal principles on which our adversaries base their pamphlets and their struggle. Every Yankee Doodle wears a cap with the word *Liberty* embroidered by his sweetheart, and he wears that cap while he beats his slave. When we protect the blacks, we refute the most fundamental of their assertions: that their cause represents that of liberty. It is *our* army that fights for liberty."

His face was flushed. The serving maid clapped her hands and beamed at him for a moment before she saw what she had done and put her head down again to pour more tea.

Loring didn't even glance at him. "A pretty speech."

"Pray, Mr. Loring, be silent. I was silent for you," said Simcoe. He didn't turn his head, and his tone suggested the absent reprimand of a man to his servant.

Loring flushed and ran a finger around the inside of his neckcloth as if it were too tight.

"Second, blacks are not savages, however much Mr. Loring's inflamed imagination may carry him to such thoughts. Here in our lines we already have a black congregation of Anglicans with its own ordained minister, as well as a black man of law. And your brother has, I believe, a black officer on board HMS *Rose*, does he not? Blacks are men, like us, both good and bad. And they will be soldiers like us, if we train them."

Sir William looked at him absently, now searching the table in front of him for something. "Captain Simcoe, you offered to raise a company of blacks in Boston, did you not?" The serving maid reached up above the mantel, rising on her toes so gracefully that Stewart had to look away. She came back to Sir William with a long-stemmed pipe, which he seized eagerly.

"I did, Sir William."

He nodded.

"Finally, Sir William, Mr. Loring says that to provide freedom for the slaves would undermine our role as the authority of government in protecting property. Much as I should like to argue with Mr. Loring that a man should never be considered property, I will rest my case more exactly on the reality of the situation here. That is to say, we control a very small part of the slave-owning population and our enemies control the greater. Any effort on our side to provide safe haven for escaped slaves will harm the economy of those provinces most loyal to Congress *far* more than such a move would harm our own Loyalists, who might even be indemnified, as Governor Dunmore did in Virginia."

Sir William had his pipe packed, and the serving maid, as if completing some household ballet, now leaned over the fire, her back perfectly straight and her legs bent as if in a curtsy, her elbows well out and her head leaned to one side like one of Monsieur Boucher's paintings of a nymph. She lit the taper and turned back to Sir William, offering it to him for his pipe. Stewart, whose thoughts on women were almost entirely confined to his sweetheart in Edinburgh, was moved in a way he had seldom experienced. He smiled at himself, as he was often quick to advise others that the Scots did not feel the effects of Cupid.

"Major Robinson?" asked Sir William, as he puffed the pipe to life.

"Sir William, I can scarce add to the eloquence of my friend except to agree on all his points and bring my own small experience to bear. The loss of their slaves would cripple the southern landowners like Mr. Washington, at least until they understood that hired labor is always more willing than slaves. I might also say, with a certain reservation, that the use of blacks will create a horror among those who own them, and a fear that might well work to our advantage. I do *not* mean to imply that they will behave badly, but only that those who own them fear their rising to such a degree that it might paralyze their councils."

Sir William turned back to Stewart, who was now looking openly at Polly. She curtsied slightly to him, which confused him for a moment. Sir William caught the direction of his glance and laughed aloud, one short bark like a dog.

"Polly, get you gone. You'll have the whole of my army sniffing after you in a moment."

She inclined her head and moved away, stopping in the doorway to curtsy to all of them before retreating through it, all the motions of a lady, not a serving girl. A suspicion flared in Stewart's mind that this was stage-managed, that Sir William was trying to send a message. That young black woman didn't work in this house. If she did, he'd have heard from his friends on the staff.

"Sir William, the body of soldiers who have placed themselves under my protection were raised in Virginia by the royal governor there. They desire to serve as soldiers and not be reduced to the status of laborers, and they have already served you and His Majesty well. I cannot add to the eloquence of the arguments here. I am only a plain soldier. But I can say that these men are fine soldiers, fast and able, and that I would be honored to continue to command them.

"If I place them on the rolls of the provincial corps, they will eventually require an officer of their own. Indeed, I have so many Loyalists clamoring for commands every day that I doubt I could hide them for long. But having heard you, gentlemen"—and he glanced briefly at the closed door through which Polly had passed—"I think I will allow this body of men into the service. Perhaps there will be others, and perhaps not. In the meantime, though, I will permit any runaway to pass our lines."

Mr. Loring shrugged. Stewart had expected him to remonstrate, and was surprised at his easy acceptance of defeat.

The rest was mere formality. Sir William signed several documents that gave the Ethiopians status as a provincial corps called the "Company of Black Guides," as that was how Stewart intended to use them. Ethiopians was thought to be too colorful a term. Having signed, Sir William proceeded to compliment Stewart again on his action.

"And what do you plan after the war, Captain Stewart?"

"I'll continue in the army, Sir William."

"I shall keep my eye on you, then, Captain."

"I thank you, Sir William, and I'll take my leave with my grateful thanks for the compliments and for your services."

"That's fine, Captain."

And with that, Stewart was out in the main room of the house, with men like himself, free of the presence of the great and near great. Simcoe was waiting for him by the smaller fireplace, smoking a small cigar of the type the Havana traders carried. Major Robinson, the Loyalist officer, was lighting his pipe.

"Better than I had expected," he said as he came up. Jeremy was somewhere about, because his cloak was hanging on a peg, neatly, not the way he had left it. The whole room was smoky. The front door was always open as men came in and out, and it ruined the draw of the fireplace. *There* was Jeremy, away through the smoke, at the entrance to a corridor. He was talking to the girl, Polly, who had on a charming mantle and a very proper black silk bonnet. She was clearly going out.

"I knew he was with us the moment I saw the girl," said Simcoe, turning an appreciative eye over Polly.

Robinson laughed. "She can never work here."

"No, it would be chaos. I know her. Her father is the black Anglican minister I mentioned. He brought her to show us which way the tide was running, and to give Loring and the Tories a place to hang their hats."

Stewart looked at him blankly.

"Sorry, Stewart, but you are such a Scot. Loring will assume that Polly is Sir William's latest fascination, shall we say? And so, rather than labeling him a hopeless liberal to the other Tories, they'll just assume he's been led by his cock."

Stewart wondered if the smoke was getting to his head.

Simcoe held out a little leather case. "Cigar? If you have to breathe smoke, you might as well enjoy it."

Stewart took one and lit it. The draw was much easier than a pipe. He coughed a little, rolled a little more smoke around in his mouth.

Jeremy came up next to him. "This young lady requires an escort back to her father in the camp, sir. Might we provide it?"

Stewart looked at her gravely. His immediate impulse was over, but she was still bewitching.

"I suspect she is in more danger from some of us than she knows," he said. Had he said that? He rarely assayed at gallantry. She smiled, without flirtation but with considerable calm.

Major Robinson choked on his smoke. "You Scots are like the rest of us. You simply hide it better."

"I'm sure I would be in no danger with you, sir," said Polly, in a modest way that acted as a reproach to Major Robinson and a compliment to Captain Stewart at the same time.

Simcoe tossed his cigar in the fireplace with a laugh.

"My best compliments to your father, Polly." He straightened his coat and a soldier came and hung his greatcoat on him as Jeremy did the same for Stewart. "Stewart, come and dine with me. I have hopes of getting a good provincial command, and I understand you to be the master of getting cooperation from regimental agents."

"I know the trade, yes," Stewart said carefully. Admitting to knowledge of a trade was often the fastest way to end a relationship with the well-born.

Simcoe just nodded. "You're the man for me, then. Have your man and mine set a day, eh? Major? If I can ever be of service?"

"Your servant, gentlemen. Miss Polly," said Robinson with a bow.

Stewart followed him to the door as Jeremy went for the horses.

"Just so, Captain Simcoe."

Chapter Thirteen

Dobb's Ferry, October 27, 1776

Jeremy rode easily through the quiet evening, enjoying the crisp air and the feel of the horse moving well beneath him. The small force of light infantry had landed that afternoon at the ferry and easily driven off the small picket left there by the rebels, who seemed to be in retreat everywhere north of New York.

Most of the sentries knew him by now, and he moved from one company to the next, trying to locate Caesar's little company, which had come across last and without official sanction. Major Stilson and Captain Stewart had already come to expect that the Ethiopians would be attached to them. Light battalions were always informal composites, and the addition of local or native troops to a light battalion was not a matter of great moment.

Jeremy found Caesar lying on his pack in the yard of the ferry house, his coat off and his neckerchief hanging loose. Caesar was reading. Jeremy already knew that Caesar *could* read, but in his experience the ability to read and its direct expression could be very different things. Jeremy seldom read farther afield than the *Gentleman's Magazine* and the occasional novel.

Around the yard, black men were cleaning their muskets with tow and charcoal, or gambling. The other big man, whom Jeremy knew as Virgil, was leading a sewing circle where new recruits sat on the ground with their legs folded. Each had a little pile of sundries. That pile represented the makings of as much uniform as the Ethiopians possessed, a brown short jacket and coarse sailors' trousers.

It was the largest group of black soldiers that Jeremy had ever seen. He had never aspired to be a soldier himself; to be an officer was so far above his station as to be beyond his ability to ascend, whereas to be a common soldier was in almost every way beneath him. Despite that, he was already enjoying the campaign, and he was obscurely pleased that Caesar had created a body of men that Captain Stewart so patently admired, as such an achievement was clearly respectable.

Caesar himself, reading in the cool autumn sun, seemed almost respectable. He looked his age, in repose. His youth was more obvious when he was still than in action, where he seemed ageless, a trait he shared with Stewart, except where Stewart lost years, Caesar gained them.

Jeremy was amused that his arrival on horseback was greeted from many quarters in the yard but that Caesar didn't so much as raise his head. Jeremy thought he might be shamming until he came up close and heard Caesar mouthing the words softly, his finger tracing along the page of a well-worn and heavy book.

> Caesar, who had immediate notice from his scouts, apprehending some stratagem, because he as yet knew nothing of the Reason for their Departure, would not stir out of his trenches. But early in the morning, upon more certain intelligence of their retreat, he detached all the cavalry, under Q. Pedius and L. Arunculeius Cotta, his lieutenants, to harass and retard them in their march. T. Labienus had orders to follow with three legions. These falling upon their rear, and pursuing them many miles, made a dreadful slaughter of the flying Troops.

Caesar could easily visualize the scene, as his namesake's men fell upon the rear of the Belgians, who looked in his mind's eye like the unvaliant remnants of the Tenth Continental Regiment that had broken at the first shots from his little group of Ethiopians. His pack had "X Con'l" painted on it, as did most of the packs carried by the other black soldiers. He could see the Belgians flinching away, the front ranks striving to hold their ground while the rear ranks began to run. He was reliving it, seeing

Washington fleeing him and smiling with the memory when he realized that a horse was taking grass at his back and there were polished riding boots at the edge of his vision.

"Beg your pardon, Mr. Green."

"At your service, Sergeant Caesar."

Caesar scrambled to his feet and brushed wood chips out of his trousers.

"What are you reading, Sergeant?"

"The *Gallic Wars* of Julius Caesar," he said, holding up the thick volume. It reminded him of Sergeant Peters, and how easily he had adapted to being the sergeant.

Jeremy smiled. "I doubt there's another sergeant in this army who would willingly carry that volume in the field, Julius."

"I think you do them wrong, sir. Caesar's commentaries have lessons that apply to every aspect of our war here, from entrenching a camp to setting a picket. Indeed"—he opened the book and began to flip pages—"see here in the plate, where it shows how to fortify a bridge."

Jeremy shook his head. "A sad state we'd be in, if the works of a general dead these two thousand years were better than our modern manuals. My master has in his tent all the latest works, whether the siege books of *Monseer* Vauban or the very latest from Mr. Muller. Indeed, I bought the most of them for him myself."

Caesar looked at him with round eyes, and Jeremy was struck again with his youth, and the difference between the man in action and the man at rest. Like those round young eyes and the scars above them.

"You mean to say there are modern manuals ... but of course there are." He looked at Jeremy with a certain wonder. "I don't suppose ..."

"I'm almost certain the captain would lend them, or let you read one near the tent, if you had a mind. Indeed, I've been sent to find you with the purpose of inviting you, if you were at liberty, to join the captain."

"I'll come directly."

"Julius Caesar, it really is time someone polished you. Your language is better than the common run, but 'I'll come directly' is too plain. You should send me with your *best compliments* and say that you will *attend* Captain Stewart directly. That's the pretty way to say it. *Attend* is genteel."

Caesar looked at Jeremy for a moment, and Jeremy thought that he could see the other, dangerous Caesar for a flash of an eye, but then it was gone and the eyes were serene. "Mr. Green, pray send the captain my *best compliments,* and tell him that I will *attend* him directly."

"Splendid. I recommend a clean shirt, if you have one."

"In fact, the rebels have provided us with all the shirts we could wish, many beautifully sewn, left on the ground for the first comer. We thought it *uncommon generous.* We attempted to *attend* them directly, to pay them our *best compliments* for the shirts, but they all had prior engagements."

His last was greeted with little grunts of laughter from the men in the ferry yard. Jeremy just smiled back.

"We shall expect you, then." He turned back. "Do you fence, by any chance?"

"Fence? I don't understand you."

"I see you wear a sword. Do you know how to use it?"

"Not any better than I could use it to cut cane, but so far I haven't needed it. Why?"

"I have some skill in the art. Perhaps we'll find a time, young Caesar."

"I would be delighted to attend you."

Jeremy just laughed.

Captain Stewart's marquee was rather grand, but when the army was moving, he had only one packhorse and lived with Jeremy in a simple private's tent. Of course, when the army was moving, the privates left their tents behind altogether.

Jeremy and the company quartermaster had between them arranged for the captain to take over the barn, yard, and shop of a blacksmith. The smith and his family were attempting to continue with their lives while soldiers were living all around their home. Neither Caesar nor Jeremy had any idea if the smith had children, which suggested to both of them that what he had was *daughters.*

The tent was set up in the barn, but used as a screen to make a private room on the threshing floor. It was cold but spacious. Caesar could see from the sentry post that Captain Stewart was sitting with another man dressed in an old hunting coat over very fine smallclothes.

Caesar stopped to return the sentry's salute at the entrance to the barn. Stewart saw him and waved him on. The sentry saluted smartly, jerked his head toward the two officers, and gave a quick, almost invisible smile.

"Good news for yor'n, Sergeant," he whispered.

Caesar walked back and saluted the two officers.

The stranger rose in his seat and returned the salute gravely, while Stewart simply fluttered his hand and told him to "carry on, carry on." Jeremy appeared with a light chair, probably obtained from one of the nearby houses. He took Caesar's musket and carried it off beyond the screen of canvas.

"Have a seat, Sergeant. This is Captain Simcoe of the second grenadier battalion. He commands the grenadiers of the Fortieth Foot."

"An honor, sir," said Caesar, sitting and then standing again, embarrassed at having accepted the invitation to sit before he had been introduced. He hovered uncertainly by his chair.

Simcoe smiled warmly. "Your servant, Sergeant. I had the pleasure to observe your pursuit of Mr. Washington's staff during the affair at Kip's Bay."

Caesar beamed at the praise.

"I tried to bring my company up into action, but mine cannot run quite so fast or far as either your blacks or Captain Stewart's Scots, and so we had to be content to watch the closing acts."

Caesar stood silent. He knew that the grenadiers were saved for the really difficult fighting in major engagements, and he had never before considered how frustrating it might be to watch the lights fight every day in the war of outposts and never participate themselves. For himself, he had seen so much fighting in the last month that he felt rattled, but this didn't seem the time to say so.

"Nonetheless, Sergeant, we haven't brought you here to listen to our war stories. You must know that Captain Stewart has petitioned Sir William Howe to have your company placed on the provincial establishment as a body of regular Loyalist soldiers."

Caesar leaned forward eagerly. "Yes, sir."

Stewart interjected. "Julius Caesar, sit *down*. Jeremy, pour him a glass of rum. Carry on, Captain Simcoe."

Caesar sat stiffly, his pack catching the rungs of the chair back. The rules of this conversation made him uncomfortable, the two white officers apparently pretending that he was their peer. But he was not, and his experience of white gentry suggested that they would be quick to anger if he put a foot wrong. He saw himself laughing at Washington on the hunt so long ago. He'd been sent to the swamp for that.

Jeremy came and stood beside him. Jeremy's presence was reassuring. He could ask Jeremy what to do, if they had a moment alone. Jeremy handed him a small horn cup, and the sweet scent of the rum made his empty stomach flip over.

Simcoe waited until Caesar had sipped his rum and then produced a heavy folded parchment from the saddlebag under his chair. "This document is what is known as a 'beating order.' It entitles Captain Stewart to raise a company of soldiers to be known as the Black Guides to serve for the duration of the conflict. We would like the Black Guides to be based on your men, Sergeant. Can you read?"

Jeremy leaned forward. "He's reading Caesar's *Gallic Wars*. He has it in his pack, sir. Ask him."

Simcoe looked interested. "Are you, by God. Do you have it with you? May I see it?"

Caesar stripped off his pack with Jeremy's help and produced it. Simcoe leafed through it, paused at some illustrations, and smiled. "I read it in Latin for school, and again at Merton College. It seems so modern in English, as if the war were happening now."

Caesar was trying to read the beating order, whose language was almost as arcane as Latin.

"I do not wish to offer anything to you gentlemen but praise," he said carefully. "But can we not continue to be the Loyal Ethiopian Regiment?"

Both white men shook their heads. Simcoe took the lead. "The governor had the authority to raise that regiment only within his own province, Caesar. How far are you in *Gallic Wars*?"

"I'm well along in book three, sir."

"So you understand how his authority worked? How he could command legions only in Gaul, and not throughout the empire?"

"I do, sir."

"And so it is with us, Caesar. Governor Dunmore's right to raise troops doesn't extend outside of Virginia. Commissions he has written have the force of his intent, of course, but they won't get very far. And all the officers of the Ethiopians have moved to other commands."

Or died, thought Caesar, remembering Mr. Robinson. He wondered idly if Major Robinson was a relation. They were of a type.

"So we should join Captain Stewart's corps of Black Guides." Caesar spoke slowly again, because, much as he wanted to like the new officer, and much as he respected Captain Stewart, he felt that somehow *something* was being taken from him.

Stewart stood up and walked back and forth a moment. "I told you he would take it this way, Simcoe. Look here, Caesar. It's me who's joining you, not the other way around. I'll be your officer for a while, and then another will be appointed, perhaps a whole slate of three. We'll recruit you up to a double company, which is what Sir William has authorized. Perhaps eighty men. A powerful force that can operate on its own or provide guides for the light infantry. We should have foreseen that you'd have a pride in your corps. We do, and Sergeant McDonald wouldn't lightly tear off his buttons and join the Fortieth."

Simcoe said carefully, "Did you think you'd be the officer, Caesar?"

Caesar laughed. It wasn't an easy laugh, because since Kip's Bay, he'd met British officers who didn't deserve their rank, and he'd even been ordered about by a few. He knew he could run a company, but the world was as it was, something Jeremy often said. "No, sir. I'm just not easy about leaving the Ethiopians."

"If I said that the Ethiopians would *become* the Black Guides?" Stewart looked at Simcoe for assistance. "Would that help?"

Jeremy pressed his back.

"*Do it, Caesar.* Trust me," Jeremy whispered hoarsely, not really covered by the noise of the soldiers in the barn.

"And we'll be paid regular, and uniformed?"

"Absolutely."

Caesar nodded. He was happy that they would become regular soldiers, and he feared to offend the two officers by not falling in with their plans, but he still felt that something was lacking. He trusted Jeremy, though. Indeed, for the most part, he trusted Stewart, who was the bravest man he had seen in action, and that was worth something.

"I'm very pleased, then," he said. If you have to accept another's wishes, do it with a good grace. So his mother had always said. He smiled. Jeremy squeezed his shoulder. The two white officers shook his hand.

"We'll muster the men you have tonight, so that you can be paid immediately. Do you have women?"

"A dozen or so back on Staten Island. One or two that the new boys have collected here."

Simcoe counted quickly. "You can have only sixteen on the rolls, Sergeant, so best choose the ones who will work and push the slatterns off on another corps."

"Yes, sir."

"You choose them and get me the names when you can," Stewart said hurriedly.

Caesar knew it was a matter of great importance. Women on the rolls of a regiment were members of the army. They got preference for barracks space, they drew rations, and they had a place. Other women, the camp followers and slatterns, could expect to be drummed out of the tents on a cold morning, or worse. He thought of Sally, and Big Annie, and the local girls who had black skin but spoke Dutch. Sixteen women would be hard. Of course, none of them had anything at all now, and none of the boys was really married except Angus to Big Annie.

Whatever he decided, there would be fighting. He was far away when he felt Jeremy jostle his shoulder.

"The problems of command, eh, Caesar?" asked Stewart. "And I see you came off New York Island with a bolt of brown cloth. Shall we continue in brown jackets?"

"I'd rather, sir. They are serviceable enough."

"Round hats. I notice most of your men have no hats, or old rebel hats."

"I like the round hats well enough, sir, but most of our equipment has been donated by the rebels, and we haven't come across a company wearing just the hats we desire."

Simcoe laughed and Stewart smiled.

"Jeremy, give Caesar part of our cold chicken. We're off to walk the posts for a bit. When you've had a bite, Caesar, meet us at your company so we can muster."

Caesar stood up. "Yes, sir."

"Just so, Caesar. Carry on."

✯　✯　✯

The men mustered eagerly enough. Few of them cared if they were Ethiopians or Guides, and the prospect of regular pay, allowances for quarters, proper uniforms, and status was so alluring that even Caesar's band of veterans seemed to think he had accomplished a miracle.

"Bettuh than I evah expec'," said Virgil. "An' Captain Stewart, he's good. Been good to us, too."

Virgil was holding a crown, a large silver coin worth five English shillings. Stewart had given one to every man as "bounty," he said. Caesar thought of the last time he had received a crown from a white man, when Washington told him not to be *familiar*.

"You look like someone walkin' on yo' grave, Caesar," said Tonny.

Caesar tried to shake off his unease. He thought it might be that from

Peters's death until today he had been in sole command, and now others would be above him. Perhaps his freedom had been unbounded, at least within the war, and now it was bounded.

Caesar could see that some of the men of Stewart's company were coming in, despite the late hour, and shaking hands with the Black Guides. Pipes were lit, and rum began to make the rounds. Some men were dancing, and suddenly there were women.

He put his hands on the shoulders of the two men.

"And now you'll both be corporals," he said.

"Gon' hav' to learn to cipher from Cese's big book," said Tonny, poking around in Caesar's pack.

Jim came up from the dark, with a girl by the hand. He didn't introduce her, and she kept her face half turned away, perhaps embarrassed to be in a camp full of men. Caesar nodded to him, and Jim smiled back, a huge gleam of delight.

"Nevah thought it would be so good, when we was in the swamp," he said.

Caesar felt his elation begin to conquer his misgivings, and he nodded. He thought of Virgil calling him Cese just now, a name he hadn't heard in months, and it brought it all back to him. Then he frowned. "You be careful with that girl. She from here?"

"Belongs to the big house."

"What's your name, girl?"

"I'm Morag, if you please," she said shyly, with a little curtsy. Then, "I never see so many black folk before."

Africans were thin on the ground in New York, Caesar knew. Many of the men in camp were recent recruits, escaped slaves from New York or New Jersey, and they were capering with excitement. One, Silas, kept telling all the men around him that he "ain' never going to be slave, not no more" in a strong Dutch accent. Caesar listened with amusement.

"Listen up, here," he called, in his parade ground voice, and the little yard grew still.

"We are a company in the army now, and under discipline. Drink the rum and enjoy your money, boys, but don't you do nothing to bring us infamy. Do you hear me? What we do here will decide what a lot of folk think of black soldiers."

He looked around the yard slowly, trying to catch every eye. "Some of us started this war in Virginia. Some of us just joined today. That's fine.

But all of you remember that just getting to here, where we are free men, and soldiers, has cost us. Remember that better men than us died just to get us here. Remember that we are free and there are a lot of folk that ain't. And remember that the army is marching early tomorrow and we'll be right at the front, so no hard heads and no missing kits."

He looked at them all with something close to love, and it was too much for him, and he turned away from the fire in the yard and walked off a little, and he heard Virgil lead them in a cheer that mixed the company with the white soldiers around them and the shriller voices of women, so that by the third cheer the *HUZZAH* almost lifted the night away.

He saw two officers standing in greatcoats at the edge of the big fire. Simcoe and Stewart were there. He thought they might have drifted off after the parade, but they hadn't.

"Forty-one men, Sergeant. We'll want to recruit up to strength as soon as may be."

"Yes, sir. With respect, sir, there are so many runaway blacks around these parts, we shouldn't have any difficulty." Caesar watched his men around the fires, and he was glad. "Where do we march, sir?" he asked.

Stewart looked out into the night for a moment. "It won't last, but until someone comes and takes the company away, we'll just add it in with the Second light infantry. Do you have tools?"

"Yes, sir."

"Make sure you have picks and shovels when we step off tomorrow. I don't know the plan as well as I'd like, but I'll opinion now that we're to have a go at turning Mr. Washington off the heights at White Plains, and that may mean some digging."

"Yes, sir. But we'd rather fight."

Stewart nodded. "Need money, Sergeant?"

Caesar looked puzzled. "I have a little, sir. What would I need it for?"

Stewart nodded as if he had discovered something he suspected. "Here's five guineas. You talk to Sergeant McDonald and Jeremy about what it's for. Keep an account, mind. It's my own money. But everything in this country costs, and I suspect that won't be different for black men."

Caesar had never held so much money in his life as the five heavy gold coins, together worth one hundred and five shillings, or half the price of a young, fit slave in Virginia. He put the coins carefully inside his hunting pouch, as neither his waistcoat nor trousers had any pockets.

"Thank you, sir. I'll keep a good account."

"Get some sleep, Sergeant. We'll be at it before dawn."

Simcoe pulled his greatcoat tighter around him in the chill air and reached out to get Caesar's attention. "Sergeant, is it true you were a slave in Virginia?"

Caesar stiffened, but nodded.

"Nothing to be ashamed of, Sergeant. Pirates took your namesake, Julius Caesar, and held him as a slave, you know. It was quite common in the ancient world."

Caesar was impressed at Simcoe's knowledge, interested in spite of himself. His inclination was to join the party, despite the prospect of action in the morning. Talking to Simcoe worried him. But the idea that the great Julius Caesar had been a slave held his attention. Why had Sergeant Peters never told him that the mighty Caesar had been a slave, taken by pirates?

"How'd he escape?"

"Oh, his family paid a ransom. And then he hunted the pirates down and crucified them."

"What's that, sir?"

"He nailed them to crosses, just as Pontius Pilate did to Jesus."

Caesar was a little stunned, but then he smiled wolfishly. "I like that, sir."

Simcoe nodded seriously. "I thought you might. And is it true you were a slave of Mr. Washington's?"

Caesar nodded again. He was still thinking about Julius Caesar coming back with fire and sword on the men who had enslaved him.

"Can you tell me anything about him? Was he cruel?"

Caesar thought for a moment. It was difficult sometimes for him to remember his life before the swamp. "He sent me to the swamp for laughing at him. That's cruel, I think. But in the main, he was fair."

Simcoe nodded, clearly dissatisfied. "Can you say anything else, Caesar?"

Caesar smiled. "He's the best horseman I've ever seen. He hates being crossed, but most people do, I've found. He don't like arguments, especially from the young. I'm sorry, sir. I was a slave, an' I kept his dogs. I don't know him like a house slave might."

Simcoe nodded distantly, and Caesar sensed that he might be nearing the line of too *familiar*.

"Do you hate him?"

Caesar shook his head. "No, sir, I do not," he said. He couldn't see himself crucifying Mr. Washington. The men who had hunted him in the swamp, now, or the men who had made him a slave . . . That was worth some thought.

Simcoe nodded. "I'll give you good night, then, Sergeant."

"Thank you, sir." Caesar watched him go. No one had ever asked him about Washington before, but Caesar sensed that Simcoe had an intensity that carried him past other men, made him capable of asking harder questions. He walked back to a large fire that his men were feeding from a rail fence. The ferry master would not be pleased.

Virgil and Tonny were waiting for him, and he was pleased to see them sober. Paget and Romeo, once malefactors, were now pushing the new men into their blankets.

"An' now we really are soldiers," said Tonny. His eyes were shining.

Virgil bit his crown again and smiled. "We gon' have some fun."

"Tomorrow we may be fighting," said Caesar. "Mr. Stewart says we may fight at some place called White Plains. Get the boys to ask around about the lay of the land, see if there are any black folks off that way we can meet in the morning. Start with that girl of Jim's."

They were already practiced at using local slaves for information. Local slaves had helped them all the way up the island.

"Better catch 'em quick, then, befo' the interruptin' is too messy." Virgil laughed. Caesar thought that Virgil had laughed more in the last few days than he had ever laughed in the swamp.

"White Plains?" asked Tonny.

Caesar nodded. "If we're going to be Guides, better get ready to guide."

☆   ☆   ☆

"May I trouble you for your glass?" asked General Lee, reaching for an aide's telescope.

It was the dawn of a beautiful autumn day, and the two senior generals and their staffs had ridden forth early to go over all the ground south and west of the heights in hopes of finding a position where they could make a stand. Lee was already laying out lines in his mind. He looked at the bulk of Chatterton's Hill rising in front of them and turned to Washington.

"Let us have a look from the height," he said, and they rode on up the slope, the two staffs chatting amicably. The shadow of the defeats on

Long Island and Manhattan was still there, but the air was different. Lee had beaten the British in the south, and Harlem Heights had given them all a ray of hope.

Washington listened to the accents and he smiled to hear the Virginians and the New Yorkers gossiping and showing away, each eager to impress the others. They were young, and most of them were personable. He walked Nelson over by General Lee, who was looking through his aide's glass at the works in progress behind them.

"Do you ever consider the wonder of it, that these young men go along so easily together?" Washington said quietly. "But for the war, they would not even know each other. They would be New Yorkers, or Yankees from Massachusetts, or Marylanders."

Lee nodded, still looking at the ground, his face largely hidden by the heavy wooden telescope. "If I may, sir, it is your achievement. Most of the rest of us *are* yet Virginians and New Yorkers." He snapped it closed and gave Washington one of his rare looks of total loyalty—tenderness, almost. Then he pointed back down the slope, to the ground well to the north, beyond their camp.

"This hill stands alone. It dominates the plain, but it is too easily flanked and too hard to hold. Yonder," said Lee, "is the ground we ought to occupy."

"Then let us go and view it," said Washington. He took in the broad sweep of the heights at a glance, and led his men back down off Chatterton's Hill just as the sun began to clear the heights.

They were well on their way, past the camp and riding hard, when a trooper of the Light Horse came up the road after them, his horse lathered with sweat. He rode straight up to Washington and touched the back of his hand to his iron-rimmed helmet.

"The British are on us," he said. Washington took in the man's evident panic and whirled his horse. He showed no sign of fatigue.

"Gentlemen," he shouted, "we now have other business besides reconnoitering."

They flew down the road with the wind of their passage ripping at their cloaks and greatcoats and streaming them well out behind them, the iron-shod hooves of the horses striking sparks from the stones in the road. They stayed at that breakneck pace until Washington drew rein in front of his headquarters, where Adjutant General Reed was just mounting his horse. His relief at the presence of the army's senior command was palpable. Washington caught a look between him and General Lee that puzzled him.

Washington curveted his horse in a circle and addressed all the officers in the yard. "Gentlemen, you will repair to your respective posts and do the best you can."

And to Charles Lee, he added, "Put more men up Chatterton's Hill."

★   ★   ★

Chatterton's Hill was the piece of ground that dominated all the ground south of the Heights. That's what the girl in Dobb's Ferry said, and that's what was reported by every farmhand they approached as the column moved through the dark. Caesar passed the information back to Captain Stewart, and he, in turn, passed it through Major Stilson and right up to Sir William Howe.

Their knowledge of the country was sketchy nonetheless. A farm slave from just north of the ferry had been east of his farm only twice, and he was as confused in the dark as any of the Guides. Caesar felt a kind of fear he never felt on the battlefield, the fear that he would fail the trust placed in him, and twice he halted the whole column behind him while Tonny and Virgil took tried men out in little sweeps north and south of the road, probing for enemies and for a better clue to the lay of the land. It was a new art for Caesar, and it seemed almost as new to Captain Stewart, who came right up to the head of the column at the first delay and stayed by Caesar as he directed the scouts moving forward. He stayed there, but he offered no word of criticism. Caesar valued him for that.

Twice they moved forward in the dark, only to strike another small fork in the road. By day, these forks might have been clearly marked as side tracks or farm lanes, but in the darkness it was impossible to tell without sending a man or a file down the lane for information. They crawled forward, trying to find the base of Chatterton's Hill and looking to link up with the main column under Sir William.

Jeremy was everywhere, using his horse to become Caesar's messenger and an additional voice of command as well. It was the first time he had worked so close to Caesar, as he usually stayed with his master, but some unspoken cue had passed between him and Captain Stewart. He rode hard, his horse steaming with sweat every time he returned to the little clump of men at the head of the column.

After three hours, the sky grew paler. Caesar had begun to get the hang of feeling his way across unfamiliar terrain, although he was certain that he had much to learn.

"I should have had a party out here last night, sir," he said to Stewart.

"Sir William wouldn't have wanted that, Sergeant. A contact last night might have alerted their sentries to the surprise."

"It's not going to be much of a surprise if we can't find them before noon," Caesar muttered, and Stewart smiled while affecting not to hear. They moved forward.

Light changed everything. The looming bulk of Chatterton's Hill was suddenly clear and close, blocking out the emerging morning sky in the east. They were almost at its base, their farthest party under Romeo just starting up the hill and unaware that it was their goal.

Suddenly Romeo was running back toward them. He was sweating hard even in the chill air.

"There's troops cooking up the crest o' the hill, suh." He panted. He pointed up to where the command group could just see new smoke rising at the crest, half a mile away.

"Is your horse sound?" Stewart asked Jeremy, who was rubbing her down. He nodded, alert, and leapt into the saddle, apparently fresh after four hours' hard riding.

"Go back to Major Stilson and tell him we have rebel outposts at the crest of the hill and we're not detected yet. Then straight on to Sir William and tell him the same, unless the major gives you some other message. Off you go, then, and Godspeed, Jeremy."

He turned to Caesar. "Get your men into the shelter of those trees, quick as you can."

Caesar wanted to speak, but Stewart was motioning for Lieutenant Crawford and Sergeant McDonald. He waved to Tonny and Virgil. "Get the men into those trees and lie quiet. No smoking, no fires. Go on, now."

They nodded and moved off. Caesar turned back to Stewart, who was edging his horse into the shadow of the hill while talking to his subordinates, pushing them into the same wood edge that now held the Black Guides. McDonald gave Caesar a quick smile and ran off, and Crawford just looked up the long hill.

Caesar held his musket correctly at the carry, just as Sergeant McDonald had, and waited for Stewart to notice him, but Stewart was looking up the hill and shaking his head.

"I bought a Dollond glass, a really good one, just before we came over.

Jeremy tried ten glasses and said this was the best. It brings things right in close, you understand. And here I am trying to see the top of this damned hill and I have the perfect tool. And where is it?"

Caesar shook his head, not even sure that he was being addressed.

"It's in Jeremy's saddlebag, of course. I'd lose my head, if it weren't attached. You have the air of a man with something on his mind, young Caesar."

"I do, sir. I'd like to send men up the flank of the hill now, to get the lay of the land. Once it's lighter we'll be seen."

Stewart peered into the gloom as if he would really learn something from the darkness.

"Don't get caught is all I'll ask." His own company began to file past, no longer marching but moving quickly into the trees. Stewart motioned to Crawford. "Get a picket line out. I don't want to get bit while we wait here."

"Certainly, sir. I'll see to it immediately."

In an hour, the road to the south was thick with redcoats and any real hope of surprise had been lost. Caesar was content that his men had not lost it. They had scoured the hill, climbing almost as far as the top without being detected before coming back with their reports that there were two battalions of militia and two of Continentals in strong positions along the stone walls at the top. The group of officers at the base of the hill had swelled to uncomfortable proportions, as the mounted officers of half the army rode to the head of the column to view the ground. Caesar thought that if ever the famous Pennsylvania riflemen caught on to the huntlike gatherings at the head of British columns, they would reap a terrible harvest of officers. But he kept his views to himself and kept his men scouring the hill. By midmorning their legs were burning from the ceaseless climbing.

When they were ready, though, they were quick. Suddenly the light infantry and several companies of grenadiers deployed into line across the base, and a second line of more lights formed behind them, and they started up the hill at a gentle marching pace. Some of these troops remembered Breed's Hill at Boston, and they were not contemptuous of the militia. They left their packs behind.

Caesar led his men well off to the left of the main line, in a loose screen covering the flank of the line, with Captain Stewart's company formed in two ranks, but well spaced out, at the very left end of the front line.

Thanks to the Guides, the British knew every fold in the ground and every gully before they started, and Caesar was stunned to see how cunningly the front line used the contours to stay hidden from the crest. He had never seen the British line except in a big field where they stood out like scarecrows, but here, on an autumn day, they moved like red ghosts in the clear air, their bayonets already fixed and shining before them with a thousand pinpricks of brilliant light.

The Guides encountered the first opposition, a lazy morning patrol taking their ease in a gully. Tonny was on them before either side knew the other was there, but he had the quicker wits, and in a moment he had ten prisoners and an officer, dangerously belligerent with shame at his failure. Caesar sent them back under a strong guard and moved on, his company weaker without a shot having been fired.

Stewart was right. They needed more men. He felt naked on this giant hill with so few men covering the flank of the advance. He sent Jim running to Captain Stewart to tell him of the prisoners and his concern, and then he waved his hand, and the Guides, now a little behind the line, moved on.

Too fast, he thought, and there was a shot.

Romeo went down and rolled over, clutching his guts and screaming. Paget ran to him, and Virgil, but Caesar grabbed Virgil's jacket and waved him down. Romeo screamed again and the new men looked gray with worry.

"Watch your front," called Caesar, and he spotted the smoke coming from a clump of trees surrounded by stumps to his left, a little blind that flanked the advance. Romeo was flopping now, his heels drumming the soft autumn earth in convulsions. Paget looked back at the company.

"Help him!" he cried.

"Stay with me!" Caesar shouted, and he knelt. "Those that has bayonets, get them on. We'll be charging that little wood there when I give the word. Go as fast as you can an' kill what you find there, and *then* we'll see if we can help Romeo."

Jim ran up, returning from his errand to Captain Stewart. Caesar watched the men fixing their bayonets and he sketched the situation for Jim. Romeo began to moan. His smell drifted back to them. Caesar thought that the rifleman, if he was one, had reloaded by now. He didn't want Jim going next.

"Don't you head off to Captain Stewart until we charge," he said.

"Ready?"

A nervous chorus. Virgil looked scared, and many of the others were shaking. Caesar was calm, although he greatly feared that the little wood was full of men. Not the moment to worry.

"Charge!"

They were off like racers. Caesar had time to note that every man left the cover together, and no one shirked; scared or not, they were good men.

Crack.

Someone grunted and there was a clatter, but it wasn't him and he ran on, now well in front because he was the fastest. Then there was another shot, flatter, like a fowler, and then several muskets, but none of them hit him, and he paused for just a second to look back, and there was Virgil close behind, eyes mad with fear and perhaps passion, and the rest of them coming along as best they could.

He waved them on, knowing that he was only a few paces from the nearest enemy and that if anyone had a shot in reserve he was a dead man. Then just as Virgil caught up to him, he turned back to the enemy and charged at them. A young man, perhaps a boy, appeared to his left and Caesar killed him, the whole weight of his charge plunging the bayonet into him so that the muzzle was buried in his breast. When Caesar ripped it free the bayonet bent and then came off the barrel, ruined. He pushed through the undergrowth to where two men had a shallow pit covered in branches, a good blind that they were in the process of abandoning. Virgil clubbed one of them to the ground with his musket butt and Caesar hit the other with his shovel twice, the first blow landing flat and the second almost severing his head. Suddenly there were Guides all around him, screaming with the suppressed fear of that rush over open ground. Paget went by him, his face a mask of rage over scared eyes, his bayonet bloody and the blood running down the barrel and over his hands.

And then it was over.

✶ ✶ ✶

It was the first time George Lake had watched a battle, rather than participated. He stood on the road below Chatterton's Hill and listened to the Royal Artillery pound the militia positions on the ridge above him. The Royal Artillery were on the other side of the ridge, well over a mile away, but he could hear every round fired, count the batteries now with the experience of the veteran as each fired its salvo.

Bang bang, bang, bang, bang bang. Six guns, each a four-pounder from the noise. They'd fire again before he breathed ten times. They were that good.

Their fire was pounding Brook's militia. George had watched them go up the hill with weary cynicism, knowing that they were hopeless just by listening to their chatter. And so it proved. Before long, the first of them came running down the long slope. His officers made no attempt to stop this flight, because they were so inexperienced they didn't know that when one fled, the others were close behind. He watched it like some distant show, the way he used to watch a service in church, with detachment. The big guns kept firing, and in a few more salvos the whole of Brook's was coming down the hill.

George kept looking back to his left, where Wadsworth's brigade stood casually. They could see the British columns beginning to form front to attack Wadsworth's positions, but as they lacked the artillery that the British had, they couldn't interfere with their deployment. Then he turned his attention back up the flank of Chatterton's Hill. He could now see Smallwood's Delaware regiment redeploying. It seemed like a terrible waste to countermarch in the very face of enemy fire, and yet it was admirable to watch American troops march so coolly while the shot fell thick on them. The Delaware troops had the reputation as the best in the army, and George Lake wanted to cheer them.

Bludner came back down the line to him.

"We're beat," he said quietly, pointing up the hill to where the remaining militia were already showing signs of flight. "Goddam but them milishee is *wuthless.*"

"We was all milishee once," George said.

"We oughta shoot them milishee," said Bludner. "Teach 'em it's more dangerous to run than stan' their ground."

Bludner's attention strayed to the regiment halted beside them, a New York regiment in gray coats. They looked smart, and they marched well. George could see that Bludner's attention was on some black soldiers in the front platoon.

"There's meat on the hoof," said Bludner, with a smile that froze George's heart. He hadn't thought of their drummer in weeks, but in that moment he was again sure that Bludner had sold the boy.

Bludner looked at him. "You squeamish? They ain't soldiers. They don' know a thing about your *liberty*. They just serve because someone's filling their bellies. I know. I know their kind."

One of the black soldiers looked over and saw Bludner staring at him. He laughed and turned to his file partner and they both laughed. Bludner turned red.

"No nigger's gone make game of me," he said, but George grabbed his arm.

"We're moving," he said. Captain Lawrence was shouting about handling arms.

✷ ✷ ✷

Caesar pulled his men together after the skirmish and counted heads. The little outpost had held less than a dozen men and they were all dead, a shocking result of such a small affair. Romeo was their only casualty. Paget was gone again, back beside the now-cooling corpse of his friend. Caesar watched as Stewart's company halted a musket shot away and began to fire at some opponent he couldn't see. He told Virgil to form the company and walked back to Paget.

"Come along, Paget. We'll all come back and bury him."

Paget looked up at him, his hands sticky with blood.

"Wipe your hands, Paget, an' come along." He kept his voice low and soothing, as if talking to an unhappy child.

Paget wiped his hands on the grass and stood up. His eyes were unfocused.

"We know each othuh all ouw *lives*, Caesa'," he said, his voice trembling like his hands.

"Remember what I said last night?" Paget just looked at him. "Never mind. We'll come back an' bury him, Paget. Now get back in your place," he said kindly, and walked back to the head of the company.

As best he could see, they were now on the flank of the enemy, or could be if they moved to the crest of the hill. He couldn't see what was happening through the brambles and hedgerow at the edge of the field. Somewhere in the next field, Captain Stewart was, or wasn't, fighting the same war. He looked for Jim and realized the boy hadn't come back, and he worried for a moment, but there was no time.

"Follow me," he said, and started climbing over the low stone wall toward the crest.

✷ ✷ ✷

The Highlanders and Hessians to his front maneuvered slowly and precisely from column into line behind a deep screen of brush in the next field, but they made no move to attack. George Lake watched them with the intensity of a predator watching distant prey, but he could not conjure them to attack, and his views on the subject were deeply divided. Despite the victory, or at least the absence of disaster, at Harlem Heights, he still feared them, especially the Germans. Before he could really work through his worry, they were moving again, leaving other troops to face the Hessians and Highlanders.

Bludner continued to watch the heights they were now climbing, leaving the staring contest with the Highlanders to the plain below. The firing from the crest rose to a crescendo, and George was proud of the Maryland and Delaware regiments. Their volleys were breaking down into little barks of fire from the platoons, but the volume of fire said they were holding their ground, and that made him proud.

He couldn't see anything beyond the next stone wall for the smoke. There was little breeze, and every round fired on the crest renewed the cloud. The acid sulfur smell, like hot rotten eggs, drifted over him and roused him to a new pitch of attention. He turned in place, still marching, but now facing his platoon.

"Pick up the step there, Jenkins. Watch your interval." Jenkins, while bright, didn't seem to understand that if they didn't keep their dress and their intervals, they'd never make the wheel that would carry them back into line. George had learned that all these minute defects had to be cured before they were under fire, because once the balls started flying by, no one thought enough about anything. Most of the men would start to huddle together, loading and firing like automatons, or lying down and refusing to rise. It wasn't cowardice, he now understood, but he didn't know what it was, except that in every battle he had to fight it himself, the urge to get behind someone or something.

The Delawares looked magnificent. He watched as one of their companies loaded, the rammers going up and down so near together that they sounded like they were demonstrating the firings for inspection.

Lawrence held his hand in the air, made a fist, and jerked it down.

Halt. They had started to make signals for these things, because they had learned that no voice could carry the orders over the sounds of battle.

He began to hear that low murmur that wouldn't leave his ears for days, the mumble of screams and curses from the wounded that lay as an undercurrent beneath the main flow of the battle. If he listened, he would hear them more clearly, and he hadn't the time or the inclination. He was afraid that they would tell him something about the battle, that it was his turn to feel the ball in his guts, or the destruction of a leg. He didn't fear to die, or not more than any other young man, but the maiming he had seen and the results scared him. He'd seen men thin as rails with huge scared eyes, wasting away from fever and despair with a leg gone, or a foot, and he swore he wouldn't be one. He had a little pistol, something for a lady's muff or a gent's pocket that he had picked up after Harlem Heights. He thought he might be able to use it, if ever he was hit and became part of that horrible murmur below the battle.

There was a giant volley, a great crash of fire like the long roll of a massive drum, and then the field seemed to be silent. The murmur grew louder, and the insects, undisturbed by all the violence, droned on.

The Delawares had held. They were cheering.

★　★　★

Caesar heard the cheering and looked to his right, trying to see through the scrubby trees and the smoke, but he couldn't. Jim was still missing and he sent Tonny off to the right to find Captain Stewart and get a report. Caesar was at the crest or even over it, in some wasteland that had never been enclosed with a stone wall. He placed his men in the cover of some larger, older trees and crept forward on the same path that Tonny had taken. He went a certain distance and froze, undecided. He wanted to go forward and talk to the captain, but he hadn't left Virgil with any clear orders and Virgil needed to know what was expected of him. He stood there in the smoke for a moment and then went back, running, suddenly panicked by a vision of disaster, but there was nothing under the shelter of the big trees but his men, many of them lying down to rest.

"Virgil!" he yelled, and Virgil came toward him, a small pipe clenched between his teeth.

"I'm going to find Captain Stewart. You hold here with the Guides and don't fall back unless you is hard-pressed, do you hear me?"

"I hear you, Caesar. Don' worry none about us." Virgil waved his hand, almost a salute, and went back to the rock where he had been sitting as another great cloud of smoke drifted over them. Caesar started back into it and there was Tonny, his eyes staring wide.

"Tonny!" he yelled. He was tempted to slap the man, he looked so pan-icked, but Tonny straightened up immediately.

"Ah thought I'd lost you for sure, Sergeant," he said. He was covered in sweat. "I got turned round in that smoke. Lord, be kind."

"Did you find Captain Stewart?"

"Ah nevuh saw him, Sergeant. He ain't ovuh theah. That's rebels be-hind a wall, and they look like they just won the battle."

"Won the battle?"

"Ah saw the redcoats pulling back. They was beat. An' the rebels ovuh theah is cheering like they jus' won money."

Caesar pointed him over the stones and brush to the woods. "You go talk to Virgil. Tell him I said stay there anyway, but put some pickets out in case we really have lost and they try to surround us. I'm going to find the captain."

Tonny nodded. "Pickets out, stay where we is. Yes, Sergeant."

"Good," said Caesar, and he ran off to the right, now aiming down the hill. He ran well, fast when he had a clear path, and just loping when he didn't trust the footing or the smoke obscured his vision. He had already gone farther than he wanted and he began to worry about the company when the sound of firing was renewed, the steady British volleys easy to follow and just to his left. Any farther forward and he'd have been in front of them when the shooting started.

He passed the flank of the Sixty-fourth lights and ran along behind them, past the Fortieth lights. And there he was. It took Caesar a mo-ment to realize that Stewart must be commanding the whole battalion, or that the ranks were thinner than he remembered. He ran to Stewart's stirrup and saluted, waiting for a chance to speak. Stewart was busy, sur-rounded by officers.

"We're going back up. We're going to fire six more volleys by alternate fire and then we're going up the hill in one rush, do you all understand? No stopping to fire, no pause, no conversations in Greek. Just fire, listen for the whistle, and go. Any questions?"

If there were any, his manner defeated them, and they bowed, many doff-ing their hats. Caesar loved that they kept their courtesies even in battle, be-cause it reminded him of his own father, who was renowned for such little acts of bravery. His father would certainly have doffed his hat and bowed, even under fire. Caesar hadn't thought of his father in weeks, and the little memory in the midst of the smoke and fire seemed to him a good omen.

"Sir?" he asked, trying to get Stewart's attention. Stewart was standing in his stirrups, trying vainly to see through the smoke. Bullets from the enemy buzzed past them every few seconds, sounding slow and harmless, like big bees on a summer day.

"Sergeant Julius Caesar, as I live and breathe. A pleasure to see you. I take it you are somewhere to my left in the smoke?"

"Yes and no, sir. We're at the crest, in a little wood."

Stewart whirled, his whole attention suddenly fixed on Caesar. "At the crest? On your honor, now."

"We're on the crest. We had a little fight with an outpost and swept them, and then we were at the crest. We're all alone."

Stewart was already riding toward his own company, where McDonald was handing out paper cartridges to men nearly black with smoke and powder from their muskets.

"Crawford?" he called, but McDonald shook his head.

"Down, sir."

"McDonald, Sergeant Caesar here says his lads are *on the crest* off to our left. Take our lot and follow him. The two of you try to get into their flank. Do it *now*. I'm taking the lights up this bloody hill in three minutes."

McDonald yelled "On your feet!" at his men. They were up like hounds on a hunt day, despite their losses or perhaps because of them.

"Advance by files from the center! Follow me!" said McDonald, and he was off into the smoke following Caesar. He was older than Caesar, but powerful, and he kept up easily.

"They'll fall behind, Caesar. They're good lads, but the wee ones haven't the legs for this kind of run."

Caesar slowed his pace a fraction. He was trying to see the next step.

"If you will..." he said carefully. McDonald always seemed a good man, but he was senior. Yet Caesar *knew* what to do. He could see it.

McDonald nodded. "Unless it's daft, I'll follow your lead."

Caesar smiled. They ran on.

Crash.

A great volley rang out beside them. McDonald's men were opening out, the better-conditioned men forging on and the others falling back. Still running.

Crash, bang.

The second volley, and some answering fire from ahead. Caesar could see his trees. The pause in firing had thinned the smoke. He fell back a pace and loped along beside McDonald, who was equally effortless in his running. His words came out in bunches to the rhythm of the run.

"If you...form front there...and start forward...I'll bring mine...in above."

McDonald simply nodded and put his whistle in his lips. He didn't blow it, but began to look around him. Caesar increased his pace and left the regulars behind. He bounded over the low rocks until he was in among the trees. He felt as if he could fly, he was running so fast.

Crash!

Threeet! From McDonald's whistle.

"Guides! Form on me! Guides! Form front on me!"

They were all around him in a moment, Virgil stepping into the space behind them as easily as if on parade. Many of them were smiling. They didn't look like the British soldiers, because they still weren't really in *uniforms* and because McDonald would never have allowed Tonny to finish his smoke in the ranks. Even Virgil was smacking the remnants of his clay against his boot heel to clear the coal. They all seemed unconcerned.

"Tonny, I want you to take us into the flank of that regiment along the wall. Do you know the way?"

Crash!

"I'm a Guide, Sergeant!" Tonny said, as if this explained everything. He loped off into the brush.

"Skirmish line on the move, then. Spread well out and keep going forward. See Stewart's company there? Virgil, you link up on their flank. Now go, go, go!" Caesar ran ahead and turned back to watch them come up onto line and dress themselves. The new men could never be trusted to keep the dress, and would sag the line or bell it out, making it hard to maneuver. But there was Virgil, and Paget, and Jim, thank the Lord, back from wherever he had gone and pushing some new boy back to his place, and they were rolling forward almost at a run.

Crash! Louder now, and closer, the great volley was like a hammer blow on a great anvil.

The Guides were level with McDonald's men now, and they formed a line together, the redcoats to the right of the brown coats, all the men dark in the smoke. Caesar paused just for a moment to watch them, a single mighty machine like two great horses yoked to the same plow. He had never been so happy, though so much of war was so grim. Here, in the heart of the battle, he was the master. He knew it. He could feel the mastery, the knowledge of time and space. They would strike the flank of the rebels just *there*, and at just the moment when they were preparing the volley that would crush Captain Stewart's attack. It was like powerful magic running through him, the mastery, and it was powered by these men who went like horses on the same team, pulling him to victory. He no longer saw them as Yoruba and Ashanti and Bakongo, but just as soldiers. He had never felt it quite this way before, but it was the most powerful thing he had ever known, and he wanted to stop them and tell them how brave they were, and how he honored them, every one.

But war never stops, and he reached for his bayonet and remembered throwing the bent thing away just a few minutes ago. He ran until he was in his place at the right of the company.

Crash. That was the last. Stewart would be ordering the bayonets fixed, and then he'd order them to march. Caesar went over the corner of a stone wall without a pause and turned to make sure the line was kept as the men negotiated the change in terrain. The other side of the wall was a field, open and flat, running along the crest, and there were rebels in crisp blue coats, a long line of them running off to the left. They were behind them a little and their appearance was greeted with consternation. Caesar ran down the ranks.

"Dress up! Look to your right and dress the line!" McDonald was just clearing the low wall with his men. If they were attacked now, they'd be destroyed, divided and spread too thin. There was no cover in this field and no way to stand in the scrub of the last field and be cohesive. Caesar could see that they had to strike a strong blow here, not a little raid, or Stewart would still walk into the guns.

McDonald was on line. He nodded to Caesar and Caesar yelled the orders.

"Make ready!"

Even in open order, all the muskets went up crisply as every man cocked his firelock smoothly.

"Present!" The end of the rebel flank was flinching away, retreating already. Caesar didn't blame them.

"Fire!" The volley swept the corner right off the rebel battalion, like a tool loosening a rock from the earth.

"Fire!" McDonald's volley was a sharper sound. The rebels fell like wheat beneath a scythe, and they began to run. They didn't run happily, like militia, but slowly, bitterly, like men who were close to a great victory and were suddenly deprived.

★ ★ ★

Stewart's men came up the hill in lines. They weren't very deep, and the last part of the hill sloped very steeply, but they felt, or heard, the support at the top and suddenly they came on strongly, covering the last few paces in a rush. Stewart jumped his horse up the last incline, the big mare gathering her haunches and then leaping, scrambling for purchase, and then Stewart was at the top, among his own company. The Sixty-fourth lights and the Fortieth came up all together, suddenly too many to throw back, and the crest was theirs. Jeremy came up then, riding his smaller mare easily through the brush and into the field. Stewart waved at Jeremy, and the two met in front of Caesar. Jeremy had a smoking pistol in each hand, a look of triumph on his face and blood all over his front.

"That was splendid!" said Jeremy. He had a deep cut on his face, and the turban on his hat was shredded where a ball had cut it, but he was unaware of it. Jeremy waved at the second line, now coming up the hill.

"I've never seen anything to beat it," said Jeremy.

"Shall we do it again?" said Stewart. He laughed, all tension draining from him. He was watching the rebels pull back behind their rearguard lower on the slope.

"They won't come back at us," he said, answering his own question. He clapped Caesar on the shoulder wordlessly, then rode over to McDonald and said something that made that hard man smile broadly.

Somewhere, lower on the hill, a rebel fife was playing "Roslin Castle" like a lament, and Caesar sobered from the high spirits of survival and victory, and went to count the cost.

★ ★ ★

They didn't run back down Chatterton's Hill. They marched. The rearguard was strong, and the effort of taking the crest so costly for the redcoats that there was no pursuit.

It didn't matter. George Lake watched the line ripple and fold, struck in the front and the flank, and knew that again the British had beaten them, and again they would be driven from the field, from a fortified position. He wanted to understand why the British were such good soldiers. He wanted to be that good himself. He wanted revenge on the

Highlanders and Hessians who had chased him around Long Island and Manhattan and were now combining to chase him from here.

He hadn't lost a man today, because they had never made it into the action. That had its advantages, including that a great many new recruits had seen a battle without fleeing, and would, he thought, be less likely to flee the next one.

If they stayed. George Lake would stay until victory, or until Washington gave up. He was here for the cause. But other men were asking hard questions again, and tonight he knew all the militia would go home again.

☆　☆　☆

Washington rode slowly over the plain behind Chatterton's Hill, still angry at the precipitous flight of the militia. This defeat was his own fault, for again trusting militia in his forward posts, for accepting battle in a position that could be turned. Howe was teaching him a great deal about warfare, and he wondered how his opponent would do with an army composed of militia, second-rate regulars, and men who only served for a year. He shook his head, angry at himself for the weakness of his argument. Sir William's soldiers were better, but he had had to train them himself, too, after Boston.

The loss of White Plains meant he would lose his depot of matériel. He couldn't rebuild his lines in the ridges behind the town now, as Lee had planned. In fact, he'd be lucky to keep New Jersey. He was running out of terrain in which to fight, and Howe would soon start pressing him toward Philadelphia.

Washington had always contended to others that the task was hard, but he admitted to himself that he had said this at least in part from a sense of modesty. Now, watching his army retreat from the field at White Plains, he began to think that this task was beyond him. Again the militia would defect. Again he would have to train new men, find them muskets and uniforms, and keep them together through the winter.

Behind him, there were bodies on the ground, men he had ordered into action and who had died—some of them because he had made mistakes in his deployment. He stopped his horse, to the consternation of his staff, and looked back over the field. In some way, the desertion of the militia was a direct judgment on him. He was killing his men while he learned to be a general.

Last winter he had barely kept an army together while beating the British at Boston. If winter was difficult for a victorious army, what would it bring for one that had suffered defeat after defeat?

★　★　★

A few paces away, Lee surveyed the British army advancing carefully, not really bothering to maintain contact with his rearguard, treating them with contempt. Most of the regiments had fought well, and the men, and the cause, had deserved better. He realized that the adjutant general, Reed, had ridden up beside him, and they sat together in bitter silence.

"I could have won this battle, had I been allowed," Lee said, wishing the words unsaid as soon as they left his lips.

"I think he must go," said Reed. And both of them looked away, stricken that their doubts had finally been voiced.

★　★　★

The Black Guides stood in two neat ranks at the top of Chatterton's Hill. They were standing at their ease, and their muskets were grounded. Men smoked, or talked in low tones, and each, even the newest men, took his turn to bury the four dead men they had lost in their fights on the hill. Caesar dug first, and then waited for Virgil to finish before the two of them shared a pipe.

"Evah think this war gon' kill us all befo' we win her?" asked Virgil. Caesar took out his tinder and struggled with relighting the pipe, which he had let go out. Paget had just finished his turn at Romeo's grave and was walking stiffly toward the treeline. The weather was beautiful, the sky a deep blue with the setting sun red and pure in the western sky.

Caesar puffed hard, still trying to get the pipe to light.

"An' is it jus' me, or ah them Doodles gettin' better ever' time we meet them?" Virgil hunched his shoulders. "You plannin' to marry that pipe, or you wan' give it here so I can fix yo' foolishness?"

Jim, no longer Little Jim, had an arm around Paget. Some other men were near them, and then others stood in different groups. Every death affected someone in the company directly and then spread in little ripples to the rest. Caesar thought himself hard to the deaths, like he had been in the swamp, but Romeo was different, somehow. A foolish man, and sometimes a brutal one, but Romeo's trust in Caesar had been absolute since the day Caesar beat him. And that trust had killed him.

Virgil snapped his tinder kit shut with a little crack and lit the pipe in three deft motions. He inhaled deeply and passed it to Caesar. "You in charge, Caesar. People gon' die. It ain't you' fault unless you want it to be."

They smoked, and the sun sank, and then they marched away and left a row of graves, like the rows they had left the other times.

Chapter Fourteen

New York City, November 28, 1776

Taverns in the city of New York were, by and large, cramped affairs, with a snug and a few small tables close around a central fireplace, and perhaps a private room. They didn't have dance floors, and rarely had music beyond that offered by a vagabond fiddler.

The Moor's Head across from the barracks at 10 Broadway was a different animal altogether. Perhaps because the building had started life as a warehouse with a comfortable front shop for clients, it had the space for dancing that the other taverns lacked. The tavern was larger, better furnished, and better served than any of the sailors' dives or public houses along the waterfront on Burnett's Key or Water Street, and infinitely better in air and spaciousness than the narrow drinking shops between Stone Street and Marketfield where the soldiers tended to congregate. Perhaps it was better because the consortium of owners were black men, to whom a tavern license had been forbidden for all the years until the conquest of the city by the British army.

The Black House, as it came to be known, was the regular off-duty home for the Company of Black Guides, who had their winter quarters across the street. Many of their women worked in the kitchen or did the house's laundry, augmenting their army rations with the hard currency paid by the house's many well-born white patrons. Almost as soon as its blue door opened, a peculiar military demimonde sprang into being at its tables. The male patrons were often members of the best families, and if the same could not be said for the majority of the female patrons, it was not that their manners, or indeed their costume, seemed in the least beneath the quality of their "friends."

The central fireplace, a behemoth of brick and mortar that cast its heat well back into the cavernous common room, saw gatherings of red-coated officers and their Loyalist compatriots as soon as the weather stalled their advance through New Jersey. Before November was very old, a map of the northern colonies taken from the *Gentleman's Magazine* was framed and mounted in the good light by the fire, where campaigns could be the more easily planned by ambitious subalterns and armchair brigadiers. The claret was passable and cheap, the landlord had a number of cubbyholes to hide the shy, and Mother Abbott's, the most genteel brothel in the city, was an easy walk away.

If any of the regular patrons were surprised by the familiarity of the black patrons, they were never allowed to forget that this was a black tavern, the first such to be licensed in the city, and that it owed its existence to its black clientele. The white officers came for the space, and after a time for the fashion of the place, but for the blacks it was the only tavern where they were welcome.

✷   ✷   ✷

The black woman pulled at the heavy petticoats around her hips and drew them up above her ankles, showing the dark slimness of her legs under white silk stockings. She had her tongue clenched in her teeth in a most engaging manner, and James Julius Stewart thought her the handsomest woman in the room, and possibly in New York.

She moved her legs again.

"*Pas de bourrée*," she said, concentrating on her feet. She seemed to curtsy, then rise and float. Stewart and the three other officers—and a crowd of delighted onlookers—watched her slippered feet as she rose onto the points of her toes to walk straight-legged for three steps before gliding back down into the curtsy, or *plié*.

Monsieur, the French-Canadian dancing *maître* who had attached himself to the Moor's Head, was giving another officer a private lesson, and he came back across the room to the thick crowd around Mother Abbott's girls where they were attempting to repeat the steps he had just demonstrated.

He glanced at Stewart with mock venom. "If *Monsieur le Capitain* wishes to learn to dance, he would do better learning from me"—and he rolled his eyes at the women—"even if I lack some of their obvious attractions."

Jeremy, silent until now but admiring the women from a safe distance, prodded Stewart gently with one finger.

"Do it," he said in a whisper.

While Stewart stood, indecisive, Monsieur stood in front of the women and paused, beautifully at rest in his *plié* position.

"*Pas coupé,*" he said, and performed one. None of the women was as good as he, but the black woman with the magnificent legs was graceful even in her hesitant approach to his steps, and he fixed on her.

Mother Abbott shook her head from a settee near the fire and called out. "Sally, you behave yourself, child. This is not our house."

The men laughed, but she continued to keep her eyes down and her tongue clenched between her teeth.

Jeremy led his master to one side. They made a handsome pair, Jeremy resplendent in gold-buttoned scarlet and his master in a plain frock coat of plaid.

"You've always wanted to dance, sir. And I'll say respectfully, there is no better place. Consider, if you will, returning to London as an able, or even accomplished, dancer. Consider how it marks you in any society, that you lack this accomplishment, so necessary among the gentry. No one here can tell tales about you. It is not at all the same as going to some public dancing master in London who may ridicule your efforts and your age. And if I may speak from some experience, this man knows his art."

The bitter truth was that without dancing, Stewart was marked even in America as a man whose origins could not be the best. The ability to dance a minuet, or even open a ball with a small ballet, denoted a childhood of affluence with dancing masters and tutors.

"I'm sure Miss Mary would prefer you to return to Edinburgh with this accomplishment."

He regretted the statement as soon as he made it. Miss Mary, the object of years of Captain Stewart's devotion, was not a subject that he could find suitable in a tavern. He looked dourly at Jeremy, who stared woodenly back, hoping he had not spoiled his entire attack. Jeremy was an able dancer himself and had looked forward to spending afternoons here, watching the lessons and impressing the ladies with his own accomplishments.

A group of women, accompanied by two officers of newly raised Loyalist corps, came in a rush, interrupting them and filling the space with a fine sparkle of femininity.

"The flowers of the field," commented Stewart a little wryly.

Miss Poppy, who was well known to all the gentlemen present, was a blonde, and wore her golden-yellow gown with more humor than dignity. She smiled on all, as if she expected life to be a constant delight, and a circle of admirers surrounded her. The girls from Mother Abbott's shrank instantly against the wall, eclipsed by "proper" women from the city's better families.

Behind Miss Poppy was her older sister, Miss Hammond, who managed in a single glance at the huddle near the far wall to convey that there would be no conflict.

"I told you that this was the sort of place a woman could go," she said graciously, as if recognizing one of the sisters from Mother Abbott's as an acquaintance. Her escort, a thin, elegant man of middle height in a fine green coat, raised his glass a moment and turned a trifle pale.

"Surely, miss, you don't mean that..."

"I think, sir, that you should consider your ground a little, before you tell me what I should mean." The archness of her reply was ameliorated a little by her touching his sleeve with her fan. The other women with her laughed and hid their faces, and one giggled noticeably. The other man turned from a side conversation to reveal himself as John Graves Simcoe in a fine velvet coat. Stewart had seldom seen him out of regimentals, and he hurried forward to make his bow.

"Captain Simcoe," he said, smiling broadly.

"Captain Stewart," returned Simcoe. "May I present Ensign Martin of the Loyal Militia, and Mr. Chew, currently without a regiment but desirous of serving His Majesty?"

Stewart bowed to each in turn. They were young men, both clearly in awe of Simcoe, and now of Stewart.

Miss Hammond paused by Simcoe, and he presented her as well.

"Captain Stewart, Miss Hammond, a local family, and her sister, Miss Poppy." They curtsied. "And Ensign Martin's sister, Miss Martin, and her friends, Miss Amanda Chew and Miss Jennifer. Mrs. Innes, whose husband is in the commissary line. And Miss Hight."

Miss Poppy was clearly the prize, with a freckled English face and golden hair, but neither Miss Chew nor the Martin woman was anything but pretty, and Miss Hammond had more presence than all the other women together. She wore a fine modern traveling gown that showed off her waist. Stewart thought privately that the tall black girl, Sally, was her equal for dignity of carriage, but it was an odd comparison to make, and he didn't pursue it. The two younger women, almost girls, wore dresses a year out of fashion and in materials not calculated to endear them to Englishmen, but Stewart gave them his best smile. They were all children to him. Mrs. Innes was handsome in spite of her giggle, and Miss Hight so became her name that Stewart thought she looked more like an officer of grenadiers than Simcoe.

"Captain Simcoe, I understand that there is to be dancing here, with a dancing master," said Miss Hammond, more in an answer than a question. Simcoe nodded gravely to her.

"Stewart as much as lives here, Miss Hammond. I think you would better address him."

She looked at him gravely. "Is there to be dancing, Captain Stewart?"

Stewart looked toward Monsieur for help.

"I give lessons here for a fee, to any who wish them," Monsieur said. "I also put on the occasional ballet. It remains to be seen if I will ever have the quality of student to perform a proper dance here."

"There isn't anyone in the *town* who wouldn't benefit from a lesson, sir. Excepting Miss Hight, who is the best of us. But I had hoped we might have dancing, perhaps by subscription. The Moor's Head is the only common room of a size."

Sally, the tall black woman, came cautiously closer. Stewart identified immediately both that she had something to say and her clear desire to avoid giving offense, as she had no business mixing with proper women. He looked at Jeremy, who read his glance and intercepted Sally, a prospect that he clearly enjoyed. They murmured together for a moment.

Jeremy moved back to Stewart and whispered in his ear.

"I think the tavern would be delighted to host a weekly subscription if it were to be by daylight, so no accusation of lewdness could be made," said Stewart. Jeremy nodded imperceptibly, and Stewart wondered how he, a Scots Protestant who could not dance, had become the intermediary for the principals. He felt like the second in a duel.

Miss Poppy laughed. "Faith, sister, it's only by daylight we'd be allowed near this place." She gestured at Sally. "You dance, I'll warrant."

Sally nodded and dropped a very nice curtsy.

Ensign Martin stepped forward. "I don't think your mother would approve of any direct contact..."

Miss Poppy looked at him, the vacant happy eyes suddenly sharp.

He desisted immediately. He looked at Miss Hammond as if for support, got the same visual slap, and retired in some confusion.

"Perhaps we could clear the floor and just...try it!" she said. "It wouldn't really be right to go to the trouble of a subscription without having tried the floor. And"—she glared at the men—"I wish to *dance*."

Every male in the crowd immediately began to move the tables and chairs against the wall, while Miss Hammond extended her hand to Captain Stewart.

"I expect Captain Simcoe will wish to dance with my sister," she said, apparently ignoring Ensign Martin. Stewart knew the meaning all too well, but he affected not to understand, and bowed, withdrawing a pace, flushing a little from an old wound to his *amour-propre*. Miss Hammond glared at him a moment and then turned on her heel, only to find herself looking into the yellow eyes of Jeremy.

"I'm sorry, miss, but the captain does not dance, and it mortifies him to be reminded."

Miss Hammond seemed to grow, and her smile returned.

"Ah," she said. "I thought..."

"Yes." Jeremy bowed and made as if to step away, but she kept him with a glance.

"These women are...I...I would rather these were honest women."

Jeremy smiled a little cynically. "They are as attached to the army as I am, miss."

He left her coughing in her attempt not to give an unladylike snort of laughter.

★ ★ ★

Jeremy saw a familiar cap and a pair of well-set shoulders in the gloom near the door to the private room and he made his way there, pushing past Caesar and Virgil as they watched the dancing.

"Miss Polly," he said gravely. She looked up, her arms full of a large and unhappy cat.

"Sir!" She curtsied. "I lost my cat. Had I known you would be here, I would not have asked my father to escort me."

Jeremy had to look up to meet her father's eye. He was one of the tallest men Jeremy had ever seen, and he wore his quiet black minister's coat.

Polly kept her eyes down and said, "Father, this is Mr. Jeremy Green, of London, who serves Captain Stewart over there. Mr. Green, may I introduce my father, the Reverend Marcus White, a minister of the gospel."

Each bowed to the other. The Reverend White had a magnificent smile that tended to overwhelm all comers. Jeremy had seen its child on Polly and had already been overwhelmed.

"Your servant, sir."

"You serve Captain Stewart? I long to meet him. He commands the Black Guides, does he not?" Mr. White had a very slight Dutch accent.

"Indeed, sir, and I'm sure that he would be honored to make your acquaintance." Jeremy considered him for a moment. "Please accept my apologies if I seem impertinent, but do you have a parish?"

Mr. White boomed out a laugh that carried clear across the room to the people forming for the dance. Heads turned. "I currently serve the Society for the Propagation of the Gospel in America, those gentlemen who were kind enough to arrange my freedom and ordination. My parish is become New York, and there are thousands of black souls here. I try to care for them. I have the honor of the ear of Sir William on some matters."

Jeremy bowed again, impressed. So many blacks in America had angered him with their ignorance, and here was one in whom learning spoke with every word. Jeremy wondered if the Guides would warrant a chaplain.

Three black men dressed in military smallclothes with colorful sashes pinned around them came in by the back with instruments. They arranged chairs for themselves and other men, and two maids came bearing music stands and instruments. Jeremy saw Caesar approach them and a spirited conversation occur.

Suddenly Miss Poppy was with them. She exclaimed, "A kitten!" and reached out, gracefully and softly, to run her hand over the cat's head. He didn't appear to resent the familiarity. Miss Poppy looked into Polly's eyes and smiled. "I cannot resist a kitten."

"He's hardly a kitten, miss. He's just a grumpy old cat."

"I've never met one I didn't like," she said. "Most like me, too. May I introduce myself, as this seems an informal kind of place? I'm Morag Hammond. Most people call me Poppy."

"Your servant, miss. I am Polly White." Miss Poppy merely inclined her head instead of the full curtsy that Polly gave her, but her smile went beyond civility.

Ensign Martin appeared at her shoulder. Jeremy noted his clothes with approval. Martin was the best-dressed Loyalist officer he had seen.

"Is that the famous Sergeant Caesar?" Martin asked, looking at the group around the musicians.

"It is, sir," said Jeremy. He beckoned to Caesar and enjoyed the wariness of his approach. He was introduced. Jeremy was so busy watching the admiration shown by Ensign Martin that he did not spare a glance for the contact between Polly and Caesar. It might have caused him to dismiss his own prospects with Miss White, had he seen the almost palpable spark that flew between them.

"Surely I have seen you before, Sergeant Caesar." She sounded cool.

Caesar nodded mutely. Polly White was beyond his experience of black women, and the added burdens of the admiring Ensign Martin, the beautiful Miss Poppy, and the approach of Captain Simcoe combined to render him mute. Virgil, ever the bolder when it came to the fair sex, at least so long as Sally wasn't involved, came up to his elbow.

"You was at the battery when your daddy gave us church," he said.

She nodded, her slim back straight, and turned to face the music.

The musicians, including a fifer Caesar had just engaged for the company—playing, however, an old fiddle—began to play. They played some piece of formal music through, and Caesar enjoyed it, but not as thoroughly as Miss Poppy and her sister, who were clearly enraptured.

"What did we do for musicians before all the blacks came?" they asked each other, while Monsieur arranged the couples for country dancing.

They danced a set and declared that another would be required before they could certify the floor. Then the tall, thin woman, Miss Hight, came and partnered the dancing master in a complicated ballet that had them all rapt, though it was short. There was a great deal of laughter. Simcoe danced and teased Stewart about his ignorance. The black men and women, away from the fire but tacitly included in the coaching of the dancing master, danced separately. Caesar danced, his own steps hesitant but capable as Sally led him along through the country dance. He didn't trust her, knew that Virgil still longed for her, but she was somehow part of the company now, even as a prostitute. Her courage and bearing reminded him strongly of Queeny, and he realized with a guilty shrug that he hadn't given that woman a thought in months. He danced with Sally and smiled, and she smiled back, a tiny hint of artifice visible in her face. She had a little velvet patch on the top of one breast that he wanted to admire, and she *would* raise her skirts to show her ankles. The music stopped as she pulled him through a last round.

"Thank you for the dance," she said. He bowed to her. There was always a hint of restraint between them, but he saw her eyes were elsewhere and he let her go.

He found that she had left him standing with Polly White, and they both studied the floor in sudden confusion. Caesar had no memory of asking her to dance, nor she of accepting, but in a moment they were attempting a much more difficult dance that the white dancers were doing with vigor. She was the soul of grace and her very pretty dancing raised him above himself, so that Jeremy, resentful that both of his beauties were otherwise occupied, couldn't help but applaud them. Indeed, when they ended, she rising prettily on her toes and then sinking in a curtsy, and he simply happy to have the right foot on the ground at the end, they had a little round of applause that included the white dancers. Caesar flushed and looked at Polly. She met his eye, hers half lidded with exertion and perhaps something else, and she flushed, but she didn't turn away. Her smile was enigmatic. He bowed to her and then reached for her hand, but she slipped away through a doorway and vanished.

☆   ☆   ☆

Stewart was not precisely disconsolate, but he stood near the mantel of the fire, smoking and thinking some bitter thoughts. He found a glass of wine being put in his hand and looked around to find the tall, handsome black woman looking him in the eye.

"I could teach you to dance," Sally said. It wasn't done broadly, just a hint that there was more to it.

"I imagine you could at that," he said. He drank the wine.

☆   ☆   ☆

He had never lain with a woman who was naked, and he rested on an elbow, just admiring her, running his hand over her breasts and her waist down to the swell of her hips. She was black, and that was different, although he had known women in Smyrna and Algiers who were darker. The gleam of her skin was magnificent, rich like the best old furniture, a simile that made him smile because he didn't think she'd be flattered. Then he thought of Mary, and frowned a little, because she wouldn't approve and he was Protestant enough to regret the lapse, but Sally was too much in the bed to ignore or feel guilty about just then.

"I could teach you to dance, Captain darlin'," she said. He placed his hands around her waist and drew her to him, but she held him off easily and pouted.

"I mean what I say. I saw how you looked there. Let me teach you some steps, and perhaps you'll be less afraid." Her manner was such that he couldn't resent the word *afraid*. He moved his hand all the way down her back. The hand trembled a little.

"Why do you take off all your clothes to do it?" he asked her. She shook her head.

"I want to know!" he said, a little too loud, his hand still on her back. She shook her head again. She was looking somewhere else, but he wanted the woman back that had been there before, asking him to take the lessons. Sally had been there, not just the shell of her, and he kissed her neck, smelling the warm grass smell she carried with her. She shrugged him off, impatient now.

"I like to dance. I thought..." She sounded curiously defeated, as if the prospect of dancing was the only thing that had held her interest, and in an unaccustomed moment of insight he saw that it probably was. The act itself was of little consequence to her, even naked and lewd. He stretched, his frizzed red hair around his head in the candlelight like a halo, or horns.

"You can really teach me the steps?"

She bounced back to him, her face alive again. "Only the simple ones. I *shan't* lie. But then we can have *Monsieur* to teach us privately." Her manner of speech was odd, and a little stilted. He thought perhaps Mother Abbott had been teaching her to speak.

"You expect that I have money, Sally."

She nodded, still smiling. "Jeremy says you are a rich man. Surely you can afford a few lessons?"

He pulled her on top of him, noting the gooseflesh all along her arms and hips. It was cold in the room, now that he was cooling. November had more bite to it in the colonies.

"Just so," he murmured.

★　★　★

Caesar kissed her again, holding her around the waist with one hand, the other roving her well-protected body. She was wearing layers of petticoats and a full set of stays with a jacket over all, a set of clothes more impenetrable than armor. He ran his hand under her skirts and up her bare leg, the feel of it overwhelming him as they kissed on and on, his hand higher, on her bare hip, and then she bit his tongue and her hand slapped his ear and he stepped back. She sighed and shrugged, moving her stays and smoothing her skirts. They were in the little hallway that led from the kitchen to the woodshed. Caesar looked at her.

She shook her head as if to clear it, and fled, and he stood there, alone and disconsolate, his lust still cresting but more concerned that its object was offended or worse. He called after her, walked through the whole of the tavern, and went back to his barracks, wanting to weep, or talk to someone. She was nowhere to be found, and the common room was empty of any acquaintance except Sergeant McDonald of Captain Stewart's company. Caesar moved past him warily, not sure that their professional lives would stretch to the tavern. White men had proved uncommonly touchy about these things, and Caesar, possessed of a temper himself, tried to avoid placing himself in a position to give or receive offense. But McDonald hailed him as soon as he looked up from his tankard.

"Julius Caesar, as I live and breathe. Come and have a glass, Caesar."

Caesar joined him, oddly grateful for the company.

"You look hipped, lad," said McDonald.

"Nothing to it, sir." Caesar looked around. "You came on your own, then?"

"Nah, lad. I came with some others, but they had to be chasing the ladies and now there'll be no finding them before morning parade."

Caesar motioned to a barman for wine, and McDonald called for cards and pipes.

"Do you play, Caesar?"

"I have played, sir."

McDonald lit a pipe and fanned the cards. "Gambling is a sin, clear as the devil. So's killing, though, so I reckon I'm done on those lines. Care for a hand?" He was examining the cards, which seemed to depict the battles of the Duke of Marlborough, except for a few, which must have come from a different deck. They depicted engagements of a very different sort.

Caesar played with him in a desultory manner for a few hands until two more men appeared, both soldiers from the Forty-second who seemed to recognize McDonald immediately. Then they wished to change the game to whist, which Caesar didn't know.

"It's easy," they all chorused.

Virgil was snoring when Caesar got to his bunk in the barracks. He hadn't taken so much wine in his life, but he knew how to play whist, and just then that seemed a fine accomplishment.

★　★　★

Jeremy drank steadily, knowing that his master had taken one of the women he fancied and that Caesar, as close to a friend as he had ever known, was well on his way to taking the other. He drank, but he was a man of the world, and he did not end the night alone, nor did he and his partner ever snore.

Brunswick, New Jersey, November 30, 1776

The outpost that spotted the two wagons couldn't believe their luck. Their glee was passed back along the chain of command until George Lake wrapped a sergeant's sash over his blanket coat, took his musket from the hastily built rack lashed between two saplings, and ran off into the hard bite of the early morning air. He was the senior man when he came up, and he was immediately relieved to discover that they weren't under attack. He sent many of the alarmed men back to the camp, a good two hundred paces distant, and only then turned his attention to the cartmen.

"Who are you?"

"Free men, Sergeant. This is my uncle and my boy Sam."

"Where are you from?"

The black man, hunched against the cold, glanced back at the river behind him. "Over Jersey way."

"Where'd you get the straw?"

"We bought it, mister. It be ours. We bought it to sell to Mr. Washington's army."

One of the other blacks with the wagon nodded. "We reckon you be needing straw. We know where to get it cheap, an' we jus' walk it across the Jerseys an' bring it to you."

George looked at them. They were strong men, neither well dressed nor ill, wearing strong shoes and heavy coats of the shaggy material known as "bear fur." They seemed a little nervous, but George put that down to the effect of approaching white men with guns.

"How much?" he asked, poking at the straw. It was good and clean, and he needed it for thatching the little wigwam huts his men were building, and for bedding. There was no straw within a day's march of the army.

"Six shillings the load. We got two loads." The older man smiled a little.

The price was certainly fair.

"They're spies," said Bludner, from behind him. The black men froze. The boy, Sam, raised his head.

"This ain't your post, Sergeant Bludner." George had suddenly reached a point where he wasn't going to deal with Bludner by avoiding him. The change was sudden.

"Take the straw if you want," said Bludner, paying him no mind. He motioned to a file of his own men he had brought. "Take them Nigras."

The older black met George's eyes and shook his head. "We don' want no trouble," he said slowly. But he was reaching for something.

When the shooting was over, George Lake was still standing there. He had never moved, not shocked but deeply sorry. Three of the blacks were dead and the older one was weeping quietly, gut-shot. Bludner walked over and kicked him, and he screamed. Then Bludner reloaded, slowly, savoring the old man's fear, and George stood by, wrapped in conflicting hatreds until it was too late and Bludner suddenly reached out and shot the man dead. Only the youngest was left, cowering on top of the highest hay wagon. He was pale under the dark skin, gray with shock.

Bludner pulled him down easily and showed him to Lake.

"He's the only one that 'ud fetch a price, anyroad," he said.

The black boy suddenly hit Bludner in the ear and Bludner dropped him, and then hit the boy as hard as he could, a great crashing blow with his fist. The boy went down as if hit by an ax.

Then the man closest to Bludner fell, and the snow under him was suddenly a vivid red. Somewhere far distant, a shot rang out.

Bludner reached for the boy, who was struggling to his feet; George pushed Bludner down flat in the road and crouched behind one of the carts. He looked at his priming. Something whispered through the straw of the cart and he heard another crack.

Bludner was flat on his back where George had pushed him down. The black boy was weaving and sobbing, but heading away, for the most part.

"Hessians," George hissed. "Jaegers." The short, heavy rifles that the Jaegers carried could kill at three hundred yards, and the best of the men who carried them were professional huntsmen at home. They could shoot.

The shots had drawn the attention of an enemy post. Or perhaps the little party of blacks and their straw had been a ruse to draw them out. The Germans were already famous for it, attacking foragers, using deserters as spies. They had a cunning that the British seemed to lack. Most men feared them, but George Lake's mother was a Palatine, and he thought he knew them better.

They simply had different notions of war. Given his mother's stories, perhaps it was because all they did was fight.

Bludner lay still, but he spoke quite clearly. "I want that boy."

"Go get him, then."

"See them Hessians ain't shootin' of that boy? They was spies. I know that kind."

"I see that they are shooting the men with guns, Bludner. Lie still." He marveled that he had been afraid of Bludner so long. The man had no thought beyond making money and causing evil.

The exchange of shots was drawing attention from the camp, and more men came out. There were more shots from the distance, and another man went down. The Jaegers hit about one man every four shots, which George thought was very good practice for the range.

"Bludner, we've lost four men now," he said. "All a'cause of your greed."

"You're a dead man, Lake."

"I jus' saved your life, Sergeant Bludner. Most o' the company watched me." He leaned out and fired at the distant stand of trees where puffs of smoke located the enemy. He didn't have a prayer of hitting, but he thought that someone should fire back. "You come for me, I'll be ready. I could kill you now, for that matter, but I ain't like you, Bludner." He felt that he had just drawn an important line.

"I'll have you for—"

"You ain't worth a turd, Bludner. You jus' shot an ol' man for fun, you ignorant bastard. Now lie still or I'll laugh when the Jaegers kill you. Maybe I'll kick you when you're gut-shot."

"You're a dead man."

George shook his head, a calm in him that he thought might never go away.

"No, but you talk big if it suits." He had another round loaded, and he fired into the trees.

Another man went down, somewhere on the road behind him. George lacked the interest and the will to lead a charge across the open snow-clogged fields to clear the Jaegers. They'd lose more men that way. He wished they had some of the rifles on their side; there were some riflemen with several regiments, but none of them close by. He wished that Bludner had not killed the blacks. It all made him tired, and it made him wonder if he would ever go back to a shop and polish boots or make hats. It didn't seem likely.

But the black boy, probably crippled, wandered across the field toward the distant wood and eventually disappeared.

★ ★ ★

Despite desertions and expiring enlistments, the want of provisions, the litany of defeat, Washington could listen to the young men of his staff exchange their jibes and mannerly quips with something like real pleasure. He missed his best counselor, Adjutant General Reed, who could be counted on to hear a quip or an aside and keep it to himself. Washington had just thought of the very line he wanted to describe what he saw happening on his staff, and in the best remaining regiments of his army.

"A crucible," he said to himself. "A crucible for forming Americans from the disparate colonies." That was what he had wanted to express to Lee as they descended from Chatterton's Hill. Lee was not American born, but surely he felt the change?

Washington looked down the main table in his lodging with something like benevolence, and sent his cup back for another fill of the landlord's coffee. Outside he heard the stamp of feet that indicated a sentry saluting, and he raised his eyes from the report from an outpost of the Third Virginia about an encounter with German Jaegers to see a messenger in a greatcoat.

"I have an express for Colonel Reed?" asked the man, holding up a twist of paper as if to prove his errand. One of Washington's young men took it from him, sat him at the table, and gave him his own cup. They were a well-bred set of men, and Washington was proud of them.

"You are from General Lee, I gather?" said Washington, looking at the express. The man nodded, his mouth full of bread. The letter was sealed and addressed to Colonel Reed, but as it was official from General Lee, Washington broke the seal and read it without any hesitation. He always read Reed's official correspondence when the man was absent.

Camp, Nov'r the 24th, 1776
My Dear Reed,
    I received your most obliging, flattering letter—lament with you that fatal indecision of mind which in war is a much greater disqualification than stupidity or even want of personal courage. Accident may put a decisive blunderer in the right, but eternal defeat and miscarriage must attend the man of the best parts if cursed with indecision . . .
    . . . I only wait for this business of Rogers and Co. being over—shall

then fly to you—for to confess a truth I really think my Chief will do better with me than without me.

It was signed by General Charles Lee, with a flourish.

Washington sat quietly, the buzz of the table lost to him, his morning contentment smashed and replaced by an awful hollow of personal betrayal and a darker fear that it was true. He sank and sank, whirling into alien depths of self-examination and despair. Only the total silence of the room brought him to his senses, or at least back close to the surface. Every officer in the room was looking at him, and he realized that he had crushed the note in his great hand and he thought he might have cried aloud. Their looks of shock were too eloquent.

He made his way to the door and out. His man, Billy Lee—*curse the name*—brought him his greatcoat and he shrugged it on and went for his horse, blind to salutes and courtesies on all sides. He was so seldom angry that the soldiers didn't know what to make of this mood. They watched him go in wonder.

He rode off, alone as he was never alone, blind to direction and purpose, anxious to get away from those eager young men and their accusing faces. Was he indecisive? He held councils of war and asked advice. Was that not the way of liberty that he had learned since Boston? Was he to rule alone over the army?

Washington had never much fancied any role but that of command, and whether on his estates or in the Virginia Regiment, he had always given the orders or avoided situations where other men could order him. He had served under Braddock willingly enough, but so great was Braddock's authority that serving him rendered the server all the greater. The hard lesson Washington had learned in this war was that the inclination of liberty demanded constant subordination and that he, the commander, was little more than the servant of the men who fought for their liberty. It was that acceptance that moved him to accept counsel, that and some modest hesitancy on his own part to exercise sole authority even when offered it.

... that fatal indecision of mind which in war is a much greater disqualification than stupidity or even want of personal courage. ...

Or perhaps he was an indecisive blunderer who could not win a battle, and was best out of the way. Unaccustomed to self-examination, he rode and thought, compared his accusers and his own inner voice as if he were casting the accounts of his plantation, and calmed himself. His horse, wiser than he in some things, brought him back to the inn before the cold and wind made his internal debate moot, and he dismounted, already weary. There, in the babble of his officers in the yard, he discovered that the routine crises of the day, the movements of Howe and Cornwallis and the defection of his militia, could sweep his personal discontent aside.

Later, when the routine was dealt with and the staff had gone to their beds, he climbed the stairs to his room on the second floor and stopped in front of the door. It all came back like a kick from a horse, and he turned and slammed his fist into the wall. The house shook.

Billy flung open the door to his room, clearly startled. "I'm sorry, sir. Did you need me?"

"No, Billy." It was said with desperation, a hint of emotion in the throat that Billy sensed immediately. He looked closer and saw tears flowing down his master's face and he flinched, afraid of something nameless, the end of the world, perhaps.

"I'm losing the war, Billy. And I'm losing the goodwill of my generals."

Billy let a breath escape him in a rush, and he realized he hadn't breathed since he saw the tears. He almost laughed for relief. Something understandable. He pulled Washington into the room and closed the door. Then he took Washington's greatcoat and sat him on a chair. He pulled off his boots.

Washington recovered his composure under the constant attentions.

Billy took the silk ribbon out of Washington's hair and laid it aside to be pressed. At Mount Vernon, he'd have cut a fresh one for tomorrow, but silk wasn't so available here.

"I am indecisive, it appears," Washington said, gone from tears to anger.

"If you are going to move about, I'll brush you' hair later," said Billy.

"Damn it! First they think I'm a tyrant! And then, when I open my counsels and my heart to 'em, they think me indecisive!"

Billy poured out a glass of Madeira and handed it to Washington. He picked up the brush from the camp table and walked around behind him, where he was invisible. He looked out of the window for a moment and gathered his courage, and when he spoke, his voice was very quiet.

"I don't think you can ever do harm, opening your heart to men worth your trust. General Lee ain't worth it. Never was, though he claims the same name as me."

Billy was a little shocked that he'd spoken aloud, but Washington nodded.

"It shook me." The admission was flat, spoken without timbre. Washington might have been commenting on the weather.

Billy just nodded.

☆   ☆   ☆

Washington returned to the yoke.

It became obvious that he must retreat again and that General Charles Lee would be late in meeting him with the part of the army that Washington had assigned him. In a day's work, he dealt with the wholesale defection of the militia in the flying camp and the instant need for hard money to pay bounties and keep the regulars who were willing. When he returned from hours ahorse, visiting his colonels and trying to keep a tired and dispirited army together, he finally sat back at the head of his table. He actually had the strength to laugh, because his "young men" of the staff looked gray with fatigue, and he was not yet tired. And when he had laughed, he took a fresh-cut pen and paper and wrote to Colonel Reed. Whatever Reed's failings or feelings, he was invaluable as the adjutant general.

> *Dear Sir,*
>
> *The enclosed was put into my hands by an express from the White Plains. Having no idea of its being a private letter, much less suspecting the tendency of the correspondence, I opened it, as I have done all other letters to you, from the same place and Peekskill, upon the business of your office, as I conceived them and found them to be.*
>
> *This, as it is the truth, must be my excuse for seeing the contents of a letter, which neither inclination nor intention would have prompted me to.*

Personal issues decided, he then changed to a separate sheet and addressed General Lee. He didn't mince words, as he had on three prior occasions. Washington directly ordered Lee to bring his part of the army to him, by forced marches if necessary. He made the order as plain as day, lest Lee think he could flout it.

Washington had the glimmer of a plan whose execution would require every man in the failing army. A plan that was bold to the extreme, and would not, he thought, leave him open to any accusation of indecisiveness ever again. And it would require him to trust his subordinates to execute independently.

He was learning.

Chapter Fifteen

Caesar saluted and sank quickly into his *en garde*, his legs bent and his feet making a perfect L as Jeremy had instructed him over and over for months. He bent his elbow slightly, stiffened his wrist until his point was up, and advanced on his toes. Jeremy met him halfway and they both circled, first one way and then another, until Jeremy chanced a thrust, which Caesar parried. They then exchanged simple thrusts for a minute, back and forth as if they were doing line drills. It was a game. London's finest *maître*, Monsieur D'Angelo, had taught Jeremy. D'Angelo did not teach secret thrusts and twirling parries like some of the fashion fencers and mountebanks, and he insisted that a perfect thrust, well delivered and fast as lightning, could defeat any guard. Indeed, Jeremy did hit Caesar several stunning blows, especially when he varied his tempo or stamped his foot for a distraction. Caesar, in turn, pleased himself immeasurably by planting his foil's rawhide-bound point high on Jeremy's breast in a simple attack that was so well executed that Jeremy had to stop to congratulate him on it. So Jeremy and Caesar thrust and parried like mad, until both of them were lightly covered in sweat and they began to make use of some of the feints and *caveats* that were more the norm in the swordplay of the day. Caesar's *caveat* was still too wide, too slow for Jeremy, and he backed up a step and held up his hand.

"That *caveat* is near to being vulgar, Julius."

"Vulgar?"

"Can you think of a better word? It is too big and too slow for fashion. I'd call it showy if it had any right to be shown."

Caesar all but hung his head. He whirled his blade through a smaller *caveat*.

"Use your fingers, not your wrist! That's it. Just a tap on my blade and then around. Like this and look! I have hit you again. Tap and hit. And again. I really must teach you the parry to that—this is not the place for a display of temper." They exchanged parries, and then Jeremy stepped inside his guard, grabbed his wrist, swung his own sword around behind his back, and pricked him in the side.

"Oh, well struck," Caesar said, surprised. Jeremy looked pleased with himself.

When they were finished, they were replaced by Sergeant McDonald of Stewart's company and an officer of the Highlanders, who looked at them with considerable respect.

"Ah won't be givin *you* any trouble, then," said McDonald to Jeremy as he passed.

Jeremy laughed and pointed at the wooden baton in McDonald's hands. "I'd rather not face a broadsword with a smallsword, though."

"Oh, aye! A duel of broadswords wi' a fencing master like yourself!" Both the Scots laughed. McDonald waved to Caesar, who nodded back. They had been closer since he learned whist.

"Come on, Caesar. I have to be back before Captain Stewart needs me."

"You wait on him all the time as it is!"

"Yes, well, he rather needs me all the time."

"You like him, don't you?"

"I do, then." They were putting on dry shirts and waistcoats in an outer dressing room. The *salle*, an open floor in a former warehouse, was another location in the city that was colorblind. Indeed, Jeremy was quite popular. Caesar had heard men—white men—suggest he was the best swordsman in the city. Caesar thought of Washington. He had almost liked Washington, of all the masters he had had. But Washington had *owned him*. Perhaps it was different if you were a servant, but free.

★　★　★

When they walked back into the Moor's Head, a group of soldiers was singing.

> How stands the glass around?
> For shame, ye take no care, my boys
> How stands the glass around?
> Let mirth and wine abound.
>
> The trumpets sound
> The colors they are flying, boys
> To fight, kill or wound,
> May we still be found
> Content with our hard fare, my boys
> On the cold, cold ground.
>
> Oh why, soldiers, why
> Should we be melancholy, boys?
> Oh why, soldiers, why?
> Whose business 'tis to die.
>
> What, sighing, fie!
> Damn care, drink on, be jolly, boys.
> 'Tis he, you or I,
> Cold, hot, wet or dry,
> We're always bound to follow, boys,
> And scorn to fly.
>
> 'Tis but in vain
> (I mean not to upbraid you, boys)
> 'Tis but in vain
> For soldiers to complain
>
> Should next campaign
> Take us to Him who made us, boys
> We're free from pain,
> But should we remain,
> A bottle and kind landlady,
> Cures all again.

Simcoe and Stewart were installed in chairs under the map of the northern colonies. Simcoe was in uniform, his gorget hanging loose at his throat, while Stewart wore a neat plaid coat and heavy breeches suited to riding in the weather. They had pipes and cards on the little table between them, but those diversions had been pushed aside.

"He's done," said Simcoe. "Look at this bend in the river. Washington has to defend the whole navigable stretch, all the way along the front of Philadelphia. There are four ferries and his front must cover all of twenty-five miles. Grant says that Washington has less than four thousand men. All we require is a cold snap to freeze the river and we're across. Then Philadelphia falls and we all go home."

The two men contemplated the extremely serious position in which the American commander had placed himself.

"I had rather counted on a longer war," said Stewart.

Simcoe cleaned a long clay with his penknife, scraping the inside of the bowl. Then he ground some tobacco between his hands until he liked the texture of it and filled the bowl carefully, pressing the tobacco with his thumb.

"I have always liked these long pipes," he said. "They give a cool smoke, and you can light them from a fire without singeing your eyebrows." He suited his action to his words. While he was stooped over the fire, Stewart waved for another pint of Madeira. When Simcoe returned to his seat, he nodded, as if the conversation had never been interrupted.

"I, too, had hoped for a longer campaign. The action at White Plains was as close as I've been to glory, and neither of us managed to get mentioned at all." It was a sore topic, as Stewart had actually commanded his battalion in action and not been recognized for it despite being the first to take the crown of the hill. Simcoe, with the grenadiers, had been similarly ignored.

"I had expected you to be appointed to your provincial corps ere now." Stewart toyed idly with a lock of his rebellious hair, which, having escaped from its ribbon, was now living a life independent of its fellows.

Simcoe inhaled his pipe. "As did I." He looked into the fire. "I had imagined that after Major Rogers proved unsuitable, I would have been chosen, but I gather that there is a list. Perhaps I am third or fourth."

Stewart brightened. He thought a moment. "Remember the officer who beat Rogers's camp?"

"Certainly. General Charles Lee, formerly a captain in our service, I believe."

"Just so. General Charles Lee has been taken prisoner."

Simcoe shook his head ruefully. "A pretty stroke. Who got him?"

"A party of dragoons. Lee left his camp behind by some miles to stay at a tavern, and a young officer who got word of it rode twenty miles to surround and take him."

"He was their best man, I think. Mr. Washington seems a master at retreat, but he has yet to face us in the field and win. Lee was the more dangerous man."

Stewart was silent, as he often chose to be when he disagreed with his friends. Simcoe looked at him carefully, registered his disagreement, and changed the subject.

"I know why I want a longer war, John Julius. But you? You are a prosperous man, I think. What do you want from the army?"

Jeremy came up behind Stewart and replaced the bottle of Madeira with another. He bowed slightly to both men and noticed the sprig of red hair that had escaped from Stewart's careful sidecurls. With a smile, he slipped away. They heard him calling for Polly before he was out of the common room. Stewart was staring off into the gloom at the back of the room. Simcoe began to think he would not speak.

"Love, I suppose."

Simcoe straightened his shoulders a little, as if the word made him uncomfortable. "Oh, my apologies."

"No, no. It is not anything shameful, merely too common. I pledged my troth to Miss Mary McLean, daughter of a man who fancies himself a great aristocrat in Scotland. My people are in trade; indeed, I was myself until I met Miss McLean. Her father informed me that I might only have her if I did something honorable and covered myself in glory."

"That seems a trifle old-fashioned, surely?"

Stewart nodded sharply, clearly unhappy.

"How long have you waited?"

"Six years."

Simcoe whistled softly, and Jeremy reappeared as if by instinct, with Polly close behind and Caesar at a distance. Only a blind person would have failed to note that wherever Polly went, Caesar was seldom far behind. Polly sometimes affected to dislike his suit, but no one believed her. Even her father, whose reputation for rectitude was a byword in the city, seemed to favor Caesar.

"Your pardon, sir," Jeremy said with his usual half-smile. Polly busied herself at the fire. Caesar went and fetched logs at her request.

Simcoe watched her for a moment.

"Polly, do you enjoy the conquest of the best soldier in New York?"

She hung her head a little, but Simcoe thought he heard a giggle.

Stewart turned in his chair. "What are you about, Jeremy?"

"Sir, you are not leaving this house with a devil's horn planted on your brow. Sit still, sir." He whipped the offending curl open, then combed it and the stray wisp of hair ruthlessly together. Polly handed him a pair of tongs, ready heated, and the smell of burned hair suddenly filled the room. He held the curl for a moment and then withdrew the tongs.

"Thank you for your kindness, Miss White."

She curtsied. "Your servant, gentlemen."

Simcoe stopped Caesar, who dropped a load of logs in the bin. "Will your Mr. Washington surrender, Sergeant Caesar?"

Caesar looked at Jeremy a moment, trying to imbibe some of his poise. The question might have been serious. It was always hard to tell with Simcoe whether he wanted a short answer or a long one.

"He won't surrender, sir. He may be beat, but he will not give up."

Simcoe inclined his head politely. "Even if we take his capital?"

Caesar caught Polly's eye and felt that he was on parade. "Sir, my knowledge of war is confined to the management of a company. But it seems to me that Mr. Washington and his army have shown an inclination to survive and retreat after the loss of the continent's greatest city, and perhaps the loss of Philadelphia will affect them no more. At the very least I will say this, though I only knew him as a slave: Mr. Washington will not surrender while he has the tools to fight. And he's a man whose quality is only seen when he's pressed, sir. That much I saw even on the hunt."

And Stewart thought, *They have that in common, then.*

Polly smiled one of her rare, quick smiles that showed she was pleased with him. Simcoe and Stewart both nodded to him. Had Captain Simcoe really told Polly he was the best soldier in New York? He bowed and followed Polly to the door, catching sight of the tavern's proprietor and the Reverend White sitting together in a booth. They both bowed slightly to him. White motioned him over.

"You do us credit, sir, both in the manner of your speaking and your message. I have seldom heard a man declare himself a former slave with so much dignity."

"The ancient Julius Caesar was a slave, if only for a little while," Caesar replied. "But I thank you for your compliments."

The Reverend White accepted this assay into education with a smile. "Epictetus was also a slave, and that for his whole life, Caesar. And while I honor your choice of books as pertinent to your chosen path, I might have wished you'd chosen a man who led a better life. Caesar made fifty thousand Gauls into slaves and conquered whole nations. Epictetus founded a philosophy that is with us yet, strong under our Christian ways. Yet he lived and died a slave."

"I would be happy to attempt Epictetus, if you would lend him to me," said Caesar.

The innkeep, a portly man with a broad face that totally belied his open and intelligent nature, laughed aloud. "It is a pleasure to hear the two of you. Julius Caesar! Epictetus! An' this from two men as black as me! It's a new world, is what it is."

Caesar slipped away. Military praise he took as his due with the arrogance of the young, but the praise of Marcus White was another thing entirely, both for itself and for the light it cast on his suit with Polly. Sometimes she seemed taken with him, and other times not interested at all. And Marcus puzzled him on a different plane. Marcus White seemed to know some very powerful men and to be welcome everywhere. He traveled through the lines with ease and spoke freely of visits to men in the Continental camp, or in Philadelphia. And he seemed to spend considerable time and energy on Sally. Caesar had thought that the reason might not go beyond the obvious, because he felt that few men would be resistant to Sally's charms. But Marcus White made no secret of attending her, and even allowed Polly to take messages for her and do her fine sewing, a most remarkable circumstance in a decent girl's life and one that could reflect on her reputation. It puzzled him.

He found that he had stopped in the hallway to the kitchen by the private room. He had lost Polly while talking to her father, and now he cast about the kitchen, expecting to find her at her sewing, but all he found was Jeremy, drinking small ale with Sally. Virgil sat on the other side, silent. Virgil was almost always silent these days, as it became apparent to him that winning Sally was beyond his means. She wouldn't be won. Caesar thought to speak to him several times, but Polly, or the equipping of the company, always seemed to be first. So he sat, silent. Caesar sat next to him and grabbed his arm for a moment, and Virgil turned his head and smiled a little sadly.

"That was well said in there." From Jeremy, who put a hand on his shoulder, so that they were all linked for a moment. "I wish they would consult me on tactics and politics. I'm jealous, Julius Caesar. But well said."

"I try to speak the way you do, Jeremy."

"That's just it, Julius. You do."

Jim, almost a foot taller than when they met him, hurtled through the big kitchen, chasing a maid, who shrieked, and then they were gone into the snow out the back. Sally smiled into her beer, and Virgil looked at her. She met his eyes kindly, at least for her.

"No, Virgil. It won't do."

Caesar wondered what he had missed, but the silence told him it wasn't good.

Virgil rubbed his nose for a moment, as if someone had punched it. He rose from his bench and started for the door. Then he looked back at Caesar, happy for a moment because he'd thought of something to break the tension. "I foun' us a drummah, Caesar."

Caesar nodded. "I can put him in a coat tomorrow. Where'd you fin' him?"

"Queen's Rangers brought him in. Got him off some Germans."

"He big enough to take the shilling?"

Virgil smiled a thin, strained smile not at all like his usual easy grin. "He hates the rebels worse 'an us, Cese. They killed his family."

Sally winced. Caesar just nodded. He pulled open his daybook. "Got a name?"

"Sam. Sam Carter, I think."

Caesar wrote the name in his book. "Get him a coat. An' give him a shilling."

McRonkey's Ferry, December 26, 1776

"What are we doing now?" asked one of the new men.

George Lake made no reply. The remnants of the Third Virginia had been awake the whole night, moving to the ferry and then filing onto narrow, evil-looking boats that were slowly picking their way across to the Jersey bank of the Delaware. The trip looked dangerous, and the men were already cold. They all feared that they would be soaked to the skin by the time they reached the far bank. George walked along the ranks and made sure that men tied their hats to their heads, and those with tinder kits or tobacco put those items in their hats first. He looked at their cartridge boxes and made sure that their muskets were empty. A wet gun could be dried, but a gun with a soaked load of wet black powder in the barrel would take an hour to clear and dry.

Bludner stood apart, speaking quietly to Captain Lawrence. George knew that he and Bludner were in a state of quiet hostility and that Bludner would attack him to Lawrence at any chance. George wasn't used to this kind of warfare, and he felt that he was slipping behind. Captain Lawrence no longer sought his opinion on anything, no longer sent for him to lead special patrols. In fact, Bludner had been sent across the river last night and had already seen the town they were supposed to attack. He had apparently done well. George tried not to resent Bludner's success.

They had the company up to thirty men, and they had a drummer again. George Lake had been to Philadelphia twice, looking for their recruits from Virginia and quietly soliciting local men where they could be got. Other regiments had begun to recruit free blacks. George didn't think that he was ready to put Bludner in the way of that kind of temptation.

He decided to light his pipe, and he pulled up the collar of his greatcoat. His eye caught Bludner and Lawrence, who were both watching him. His stomach flipped a little, and then he turned his back and started trying to get a patch of char to catch a spark. In a moment he had a little coal going, to the envy of his company, and after a deep inhalation, he handed the pipe to Corporal Bent, who took it gratefully.

"Sergeant, where are we going?" asked another recruit. "Is the war lost, Sergeant?"

"Silence, Rogers," George said, his voice low. Most of the men thought they might be going to surrender. It was a sad comment on the army. George had figured out where they were going by inference, but he wasn't saying until they were across the river. Once across, no one would desert.

☆　☆　☆

In the handsome stone house by the ferry, George Washington sat at a plain cherry table and took the messages that members of the Philadelphia Light Horse brought without enthusiasm, hiding his feelings.

Colonel Reed sent that Israel Putnam could not be moved to commit his command across the river to support any sort of attack. Horatio Gates had left the army to go to Congress. It seemed possible that he had left to avoid being present when the army was destroyed. He had Mercer and Lord Stirling, of the older men who had been his best resources since he took command at Boston. Putnam, the hero of Bunker Hill and the commander of the Philadelphia district, would not commit to the plan, and Washington would not order him to. Charles Lee had gotten himself captured, a sharp blow even if Lee was waging a subtle campaign against Washington himself. Washington smiled bitterly at that recollection, because this reckless gamble had its roots in that damnable letter and those comments about his indecision. He was not so small-minded as to be driven to excess by the opinions of others, but the sting of those unjust words was still with him. And now, in this one attack, his generals were choosing their paths. Some were staying clear. Others were eager to take part. So be it. The ones that wanted to play a role had been briefed in detail about the attack, in stark contrast to his earlier style.

"Boats are starting to cross, sir," said an aide.

He had a little fewer than twenty-five hundred men to challenge the British army. He couldn't possibly defend twenty-five miles of riverbank if the current cold snap lasted and the river froze to any depth. His men would be spread at the rate of a hundred per mile, and Cornwallis, or Clinton, or Howe, would sweep across, encircle those not immediately destroyed, pin them against the river, and end the war.

He rose to his not inconsiderable height, pulled on his greatcoat and gloves, and settled his hat. Billy had tied his hair very tight against the wind, at his request. It pulled at the corners of his eyes, a comfortable sort of pain. Billy put up with a great deal. George Washington was not a dramatic man. If he had been in his youth, then a middle age of farming and married life had driven such notions from him. But as he walked to the ferry followed by his staff and his horse, he thought about the great Roman, Julius Caesar, leading his army to the bank of the Rubicon River. Perhaps just such a night as this, with snow and wind. Caesar had said something like "The die is cast," meaning that he was taking a great risk. Washington toyed with saying some such as he sat in the boat, looking at the enemy shore and trying to guess whether he should prepare the army to form to the right or the left once they encountered the Germans. He tried to imagine where their posts would be today, or whether they would patrol with Christmas still ringing in their ears. He tried to imagine whether the British dragoons would be out on the roads, ready to report his column as it moved up the road. In the end, he said nothing, except to ask an aide for the map as soon as they got off the water.

By the time they had the army across, they were two hours late. Any chance of a dawn surprise was lost. Washington considered briefly the consequences of loading the men back in the boats and recrossing, and he could not imagine what would happen to the army if the British caught it here against the river, or how demoralized his men would be if the whole of their Christmas had been given up for nothing.

He looked around in the early dawn light, nodding to Greene and Sullivan and Mercer and Stirling. He didn't call a council; every one of them looked at him with a happy resolution that made his heart rise, as if the warm sun had broken through the snow. He didn't think of Caesar and his wars in Gaul and Italy, but of Henry V on the field of Agincourt, and again he was almost moved to say something to his captains about "we happy few," but the drama wasn't in him. Yet they were with him in a way that Putnam and Lee never had been, and he gave them all a rare smile.

"Gentlemen, I think you know the plan." They bowed from the saddle to him, somber yet somehow elated. *They were attacking.* It was a heady thing. He felt that they wanted him to say something to mark the occasion, but he couldn't find the words, and instead he simply pointed east.

"Gentlemen," he said, looking from man to man. "Let's be about it."

✯　✯　✯

The crossing was damp and cold, indeed, but not so bad as he had feared. George Lake got himself free of the boat on the far side and watched the muskets handed up to willing hands. The men scrambled out on the low ferry pier and began to form. The darkness was full of men. He hoped they had sentries out somewhere.

"Sergeant, where are we going?" The same voice, or perhaps a different one. He didn't know all the new men yet.

"You call that a line?" he said, but quietly. They would know soon enough, and in the meantime he wanted them focused on the details of soldiering. "Mr. Clarke, do you have your worm? Get some tow and start wiping the locks and the barrels. Every man is to pick his touch hole and see that Mr. Clarke has his weapon dry."

Men grumbled, because most of the weapons were already dry, but George Lake intended only that they be busy. He knew that the army was late, and he knew the sun was not far off. If they were going to be caught on this open shore by the ever-vigilant British, he thought that his men should be unaware of the possibility until it was upon them.

The snow came in gusts, and the flat countryside of Pennsylvania began to be clearer as the light grew. But soon enough, almost too soon for the busy Private Clarke, the columns began to form and move. Some troops went up the main road to Pennington, and others went with General Sullivan on the more direct route to Assunpink Bridge. Once the column stepped off, they moved briskly, and it warmed their feet and gradually made all their various discomforts into one dull ache. At least they were moving. The snow began to fall a little harder, and George noted that Bludner's hat was developing a little triangle of the stuff, like the top of a grenadier's hat.

They halted for a spell, and the men began to be cold again. Bludner stayed with Captain Lawrence and seemed to have little interest in the company, so George sent out two files to watch the ground beyond the road and tried to cudgel his mind for other ways of keeping the men busy on the march. As he began to consider having them collect wood, the column formed up quickly, and he had to race to recall his pickets before they moved off.

In another mile, they turned a corner. It was almost full light, and they could just see the village of Trenton laid out before them in the middle distance. Then another gust of snow hid the little town of stone houses.

☆　☆　☆

In Washington's experience, war consisted mostly of waiting to see how well other men had understood their orders. The waiting was interspersed with brief flashes of danger and action, usually caused by his attempts to repair his own defects, or those that others had added to his plans through inattention or neglect. He was not confident in this plan, a complex series of three converging columns that depended on luck and timing and the quality of his generals. It was dictated by the shape of the village.

He wanted a complete victory. His idea of victory required that he take or kill the Hessian garrison of Trenton, the dreaded German regulars that his men feared. Their outposts routinely injured his own, and their Jaegers were the scourge of his lines. He was not attempting an easy target, but a very difficult one, and his chosen enemy was not much less in men and guns than his own small army.

Where was Sullivan? He waited as the light grew for discovery, or news. He no longer expected General Ewing's column to show at all. They had been intended for a different ferry, and as he had not directed their operation in person, he had little confidence in them. At this point, in the growing light and the snow, he had little confidence in the whole plan. He began to dread what would lie around each turn of the road. The feeling was unaccustomed. He tried to shrug it off.

His horse was warm, because he kept moving along the column. The men were silent.

A dark, wet man was brought to him near the head of the column, a messenger from Sullivan. He sighed with inward relief. Sullivan was moving well, but concerned about his wet muskets. Washington had watched some Virginians using tow to wipe their muskets dry at the ferry and wondered that the whole army hadn't performed this simple operation.

He nodded his thanks to the messenger and turned to young General Greene, who was waiting on him.

"Let us go as rapidly as we may, General Greene," he said, and pushed his horse ahead. Close by him, a company commander caught the order and raised his voice.

"March-march!" he called. The men began to shuffle along at something like a trot.

★ ★ ★

George Lake's company was in the center of General Greene's column, and it began to move faster and to expand, as columns do when they change speed. As each company and each platoon heard the order to trot, they went off, increasing the distance to the next. George left his place on the front right of his company and began to run down the column, coaching the corporals and sergeants to close up and keep their intervals. The Third Virginia began to form again. He ran back up the column, passing Bludner, who looked at him dully.

"In a hurry to get beat?" Bludner asked as he ran by.

George didn't spare him a reply. He raced for the front of their battalion and passed the word up to the last sergeant in the Fifth Virginia, a man who knew a little, and that man headed off to close his men.

It was the sort of detail that officers generally overlooked, even when they were veterans. The newer ones wouldn't even know how vital a few moments could be in bringing your column up to a line and beginning to fire, had no idea how hard simple maneuvers would be in the blowing snow.

He was sweating now, and his feet were warm. If he had a particular friend left, he would have shared the irony with him, but they were all gone now, and so he kept it to himself, and they trotted on.

There was a flutter of firing ahead.

★   ★   ★

Washington watched the Hessian outpost form rapidly, fire a volley, and vanish in the growing storm of snow. It was well done, as the men fulfilled their duty to provide an alarm and then ran for the town. Washington was quietly impressed by their quality. But his own men moved past the post, a cooper's shop a little outside the town, and began to trot forward again. None of them had been hit.

He trotted his horse along the verge of the road, careful to keep clear of the column. The men seemed afire with enthusiasm suddenly, every one of them racing forward, faster and faster, the column beginning to resemble a giant race, at least in the vanguard. Back in the main body, Washington could see that the companies were moving well, better closed up, which would be vital if the plan was to work. Greene's entire column would have to form line to the right, a complex maneuver. He watched them for a moment and then heard the welcome sound of musketry from the direction of Sullivan's column. The alarm was sounded. Any surprise was over. Now it would be a battle, and in truth, the die was cast.

★   ★   ★

George Lake had plenty of time to watch the last moment of the preparation, as a flaw in the wind cleared the snow for a moment. Off to the south, Sullivan's column was a dark mass on the low road, and his own column lay ahead and behind him. And then, in an instant, all the order was chaos as they reached the outlying buildings. Mercer's men began to hurl themselves at the stone houses, and there were scattered shots. He had no idea who was firing or at what. He could hear the head of the column cheering, cheering like madmen, and his own men began to press forward. He hadn't heard such cheering in all his time in the army. He pressed them back with his musket.

"Keep your intervals!" he bellowed.

A scattering of shots came their way, and he heard one whicker past. It made little impression on him. The head of the column was trying to form in the narrow streets, and Captain Lawrence was shouting for them to "form front by company," but George could see that the guns that the army had moved with so much labor from across the river were trying hard to reach the front.

"Stand fast!" Lake bellowed. He pointed at the guns. Lawrence froze for a moment with a look of pure hatred on his face and then it cleared as he saw the guns moving, and he nodded sharply. The Fifth Virginia detached men to move the guns faster, and suddenly there were heavy bangs and the heady smell of sulfur. The column shuffled forward again. The guns were commanding one street, but it seemed that the Germans were forming on another and suddenly, unexpectedly, George Lake was in the front rank facing them. The rest of the column must have suddenly gone down the other road. An arm's length away, a four-pounder fired, the canister of little metal balls cutting men down in tens. The noise made his ears ring.

Captain Lawrence sprang to the front. "Follow me!" he yelled. Instantly he took a ball and went down. The men, most of whom had taken a step forward, shuffled. It was a moment of hesitation, and Lake wouldn't have it.

"At them, Virginians!" he yelled, and his company followed him forward. Behind the little screen of German infantry were two of their battalion guns, three-pounders that could shred their company in a heartbeat. Screaming their huzzahs, the Virginians raced down the street as the German gunners struggled with the high wind to get the touch holes of their guns primed. George Lake watched it all, his whole being focused on the man placing a quill of powder in the touch hole and then stepping back. The Germans were afraid, caught unprepared in the street, and the man with the linstock that could fire the piece was slow; he fumbled his movement a little and George was there, atop him, sweeping him off his feet. He rolled off the man and hit him in the breast with his musket butt and before he could move to another enemy, the guns were taken.

He picked himself up slowly, covered in the nasty slush and mud of the street, to find that he was standing at the feet of General Washington's horse.

"Well done, Virginians," Washington said, and rode off.

"What's your name, Sergeant?" asked an aide, riding up.

"I'm George Lake, an' it please you, sir." Lake suddenly felt old and tired. The officer looked calm, comfortable, and elegant, all things that were beyond George Lake this morning. The officer saluted him, raising his hat, a gesture that he never expected, and rode off. Lake turned to his men, busy looting every German in sight.

"Form on me!" he yelled.

✩ ✩ ✩

Victory. Not since Boston had he had this feeling, this gentle elation of spirit that held him above the earth as if floating along in a gallop. They had taken nearly the whole garrison of Trenton, three regiments, and more driven off in the snow without their guns. He had a further gamble in mind, a quick lunge against the British concentration at Princeton a few miles away to break up their timing and disrupt their attempts to attack him. It was a technique that every fencing master taught, to attack into your enemy's preparation. He thought now that he had timed it well, that he was across and into the enemy with something like total surprise. He felt his confidence return, and he could see on every face around him that they were confident as well. Indeed, Mercer's men looked like they were drunk, so great was their flow of spirit. But they were under control soon enough, and he would have his attempt on Princeton. More men would come across the ferry today. The word of the victory would spread, and the sunshine soldiers and summer patriots who fought at convenience would suddenly appear to bulk his forces.

There in the snow, surrounded by the adulation of his staff and the cheers of his men, he saw that it would take only a few such victories to put the chance of defeat behind him. The British had to defeat him. He had only to survive.

General Greene, flushed with the success, took his hand in Quaker directness.

"Give you the joy of your glorious victory, General," he said.

Washington smiled broadly, his rare bad-tooth smile that he hid from all but Martha.

"Their enlistments still run out in four days, Nathanael," he said.

Greene shook his head, and Sullivan sneered.

"Let the faint hearts go home. After this, men will flock to us," Sullivan said.

Washington rose in his stirrups, looked at the men about him, and waved to his escort commander to start down the road. "Perhaps, General Sullivan. But in any case, they will need to be trained, and fed, and clothed, and we will spend another winter building the army."

Greene touched his arm, a contact Washington had used to resent. "You sound tired, sir."

"Tired?" Washington held in his horse. The big stallion was unwinded by the morning, restless, his ears pricking for new adventure. "Perhaps I am tired, Nathanael. But I now see why they chose a farmer to lead this army. Farmers are used to having to start anew every spring. And farmers know that before you begin a job of work, you have to build your tools." He looked at his staff, his generals, his army. The tools were there. He had trusted them, and they, him. And they had won.

IV

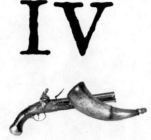

Liberty
or Death

. . . If a clod be washed away by the sea, Europe is the less, as well as if a promontory were, as well as if a manor of thy friend's or of thine own were:

Any man's death diminishes me, because I am involved in mankind, and therefore never send to know for whom the bell tolls; it tolls for thee.

—JOHN DONNE, 1623

Chapter Sixteen

George Lake was on his last days with the company. Spring was bringing changes throughout the army, as had the victories at Trenton and Princeton. Princeton was a confused memory, hazier than the brief fight in the streets of Trenton. It had not felt like a victory until the last moments, when the British line wavered and fell back, leaving the Continentals the field and a clear route back to their own side of the river. But the victories were a tonic, and when the enlistments ran out more men stayed than George had ever hoped. Most of the men who stayed now felt that they would win the war, and the veterans had something that they had lacked before, a steady confidence in their movements and their drill.

One of the changes was that George was being promoted. He was leaving the rank of sergeant and moving up to be an officer in another company, the new light infantry company, supposedly composed of the best men in his regiment. He had watched the men being chosen and was aware that the new company had more than its share of awkward men, new recruits, and lazy men the other companies didn't want, but he also noted that it would have the highest proportion of true believers, young men from trades and farms who had a stake in the new nation, and that meant something.

He had two days left until his promotion became official, and in those days he was the odd man out, with a new tent all to himself and new equipment to find, and he sat on the fresh straw over boards that made the floor of his tent and mended his ragged uniform. In the street outside, Bludner was preaching to his platoon.

Bludner sounded a little too pleased with himself. George Lake told himself not to care—he was on his last days in the company and Bludner's opinion of him no longer mattered. But old habits die hard, they say, and he waited his time as the man went on with his bombast to his cronies, pulling on an old coat that wouldn't mind the April mud. The rain had stopped for the first time in days.

"...found some of my property, gone missing on its legs, as it were. I hope you *gentlemen* take mah meanin'."

George couldn't help but hear him. Now that they had proper tents, everyone could hear everything that was said in their company street. He opened the hooks and eyes on his own and stooped out, passing his sword belt over his shoulder as he did so.

It pained George to see the eagerness with which some of Bludner's men received his words. The divide between the true believers and the backwoodsmen was, if anything, deeper in the new drafts. Too many of the recruits were landless men, or laborers, serving for the land grants promised. Too few were young men from families or from trades. *The war is using up our patriotism*, he thought. *It is going on too long*. He felt it himself. He limped a little as he made his way over to the circle of men around Bludner.

"...nice piece, a *black* piece I mean to recover when this is over. An' she can tell us a thing or two about what them lobsters is up to in New York. She'll be scare't of me from here!" He laughed at the thought, an ugly sound.

George Lake stopped by the edge of the group and stood silent with his hand on his hip.

"Why, lookee here, boys. It's the new *officer* of the light company." Bludner's sneer was all too obvious. George thought the man looked a little drunk.

"Sergeant Bludner?" George spoke quietly. His voice was steady.

"Frien' o' mine jus' got free from New York. He saw one o' mah slaves there. An' he says that the Jerseys is full o' free blacks jus' waitin' for us to take them. Now, that don' interest Mr. Lake here. He wants to protect them niggers, don' you, *Mister* Lake?"

Bludner was looking for a fight, spoiling for it as he had been since the news of George's promotion came down from the regiment. George was ready to give it to him, but wanted the man to make the fight himself. George could watch Bludner looking for a means to be offensive.

"Did you ever own a slave, Sergeant Bludner?" George knew that Bludner always claimed he had, but as he had never owned any land, George couldn't see why.

"I owned a couple, yes. More 'an you, *boy*."

George stepped toward him. "How did you come to own slaves when you didn't own any land?" He was getting angry. He wasn't even sure why he was angry, but the anger was growing in him. Perhaps it was the term *boy*. Perhaps it was just two years of steady abuse. "Was you a pimp, Bludner?" he asked, stepping in close.

Sometimes a chance remark touches a nerve. Perhaps someone else had once made the comparison, some time in the past, but Bludner was all rage, a blur of fists coming at George. Except that George had been ready since he left his tent.

He took the first blows on his arms and retaliated, hitting Bludner twice in the face, snapping his head back. Bludner was relentless, pounding away at his arms, slipping blows through into his chest and belly through perseverance and rage, but George hung on, punishing his man with punches to the head. Bludner tried to close and George leapt back, bent low, and lunged like a fencer, smashing his left fist into Bludner's throat and putting him down. As Bludner started to rise, George smashed him in the crotch with a kick, and then another to his head. He was breathing as if he had run a race. Bludner lay in the mud, spasming like a slaughtered lamb, his eyes open and blind.

George stumbled back and looked at the ring of men, some frightened and some deeply inimical. He stood straight, covering his panting, trying to be like the gentlemen officers he had seen. His voice was remarkably like Washington's when he spoke, steady, commanding. "Clean him up and see he's on parade," he said, and walked through the circle. He felt cleaner.

George needed to get clear of the camp, clear of Bludner and the divided loyalties of the men. He decided to take his few shillings and his loot from Trenton into the city of Philadelphia and get himself some new shirts and a decent set of clothes, so that he could start life as an officer looking like one. He had no horse and no friend who owned one, so he walked out through the camp, got the password for the day at the adjutant's tent, and made his way past the quarterguard and up to the head of the camp and the sentry line, where he showed his pass and started for Philadelphia, three miles away.

It was fast becoming a beautiful spring day, crisp enough to take the sting out of his knuckles and warm enough that he was never uncomfortable, although his right foot was nearly naked in a split shoe. What he wanted more than anything was a good pair of boots. He went over his loot in his mind: two big silver watches, ten silver thalers with Marie-Therese's bust on the front, a silver-mounted pistol, and a telescope. He coveted the telescope, because it was so useful, but he had no place to stow or carry it comfortably, and knew that it would fetch too good a price to allow him to keep it.

Deciding to sell his loot was easier than finding a place to do so. After he had visited several small shops where he was treated as a tramp or possibly a deserter, he found that he was in the middle of town near the City Tavern with no idea where he should go. He looked up the broad street, angry at being made a pariah in the capital he was fighting to protect.

"That's how my cat looks when he's planning to bite me," said a woman.

George turned and found himself looking at the girl who had brought the milk so many months before at this very corner. Her mother was standing beside her, smiling.

"Is that the best General Washington can do to keep you poor boys?" asked the older woman. "You didn't look like such a scarecrow in the summer."

"I'm sorry, ma'am." He *was* sorry. He was standing on a prosperous corner in the center of the city, bringing the army into disrepute by his very presence. He looked too poor to be a private, much less . . .

"You've been promoted!" The girl actually hopped, despite her petticoats and her fur-lined Brunswick. George thought the girl's jacket was worth more than everything he owned. It looked warm. He wanted to hang his head, but he didn't.

"I have, too," he said modestly.

"What brings you here . . . Lieutenant?"

"Yes, ma'am." He indicated his sash. "I am a lieutenant. I'm here to buy some clothes. And to sell a few things, too. But I can't seem to find a place to do that." He smiled at the girl. *Betsy.* Not that he dared use her name.

Her mother smiled. "I don't think we introduced ourselves. I'm Mrs. Lovell. This is our daughter. We live just there, in the house with the roses."

"I am Lieutenant Lake, ma'am." George wondered at the power of his new rank. The word *lieutenant* had visibly changed the woman's demeanor. "Miss," he continued, bobbing his head at Miss Lovell. "Of the light company of the Third Virginia."

"Our pleasure, sir." Mrs. Lovell gave him a level stare. "I won't pretend to hold with Congress or Mr. Washington's war, though such views aren't popular here. My family is Scots. But you seem a decent young man, Lieutenant. It is a sad civil war that would keep us from being civil."

George bowed. In a year, he had learned that answering was not always the thing. Tempted as he was to defend his patriotism, Mrs. Lovell's steady gaze made him feel that this was not a conflict he would win.

"As to selling things, I don't think I've been to such an establishment in some time." She didn't sniff, as George had thought she might. Instead she gave a smile, as if she knew a secret. "But I might go to Dodd's, on the Lancaster Road, if I wanted to sell a few things at a good price. You may say that Esther Ogilvy sent you."

She smiled in secret satisfaction and Miss Lovell looked at him in a way he found very pleasing. He made his bows to both of them and hoped he might renew his acquaintance on a later visit, a turn of phrase he had learned from watching the officers in his regiment. Mrs. Lovell hesitated, and then smiled.

"Of course, Lieutenant," she said, and they parted.

Miss Lovell's face remained before his eyes as he walked the muddy mile of the Lancaster Road to Dodd's. The clerk behind the counter barely spared him a glance.

"I was told to say that Esther Ogilvy sent me," he said, eyeing the beautiful fabrics behind the counter and wondering if his walk had been for nothing.

An older man with lank gray hair pushed past the clerk and came out into the store. "Did she now?" he asked grimly. "What's she called, lad?"

"Mrs. Lovell."

"Well, that's true enough, soldier. An' you've a few things to sell?"

George didn't need a second invitation. He laid the watches, the pistol, and the telescope on the counter. The clerk reached for the telescope and Mr. Dodd (if it was indeed he) rapped the younger man sharply on the knuckles.

"That's a Dollond," Dodd said after he'd tried it. "And it works. May I ask how you came by it?"

"The German officer who owned it gave it to me," George said easily. "I confess that I didn't offer him a great deal of choice, but such affairs are accepted in war."

"Oh, yes. She's a beauty, though. I shouldn't say that, but 'tis true. I'd go to ten guineas real money for the telescope."

George gasped. He'd expected less than that for everything.

"Two guineas for the pistol. It's good work, but guns are easy here. The watches? Well, they're Dutch, not as good as English either way. I'll let you have a guinea apiece."

George nodded. He suspected he should bargain, but it wasn't in him. He'd have boots and good breeches and even a coat. He might visit Mrs. Lovell and her Loyalist house yet.

"I'll keep a watch for myself, then," he said, and picked up the smaller of the two.

Dodd shook his head. "I'd like you to try to bargain, at least, for the form of the thing. Otherwise, I'll know I offered too much and I'll kick myself all day."

George rubbed his chin, eager to get the money. "Throw in a watch fob, then."

Dodd nodded. "That will have to do. Stillwell, count out the money. I take it you want it in hard money? I'd offer more in Continental."

"Thanks," said George with a broad grin. "But we get paid in paper, an' we know just what it's worth."

New York, April 12, 1777

John Julius Stewart had learned to dance. He couldn't dance well, or gracefully, but it scarcely mattered. He could stand up with a woman at a subscription ball or a small set in a private house, and although the act might not give her great pleasure, it was an improvement on a lifetime of mumbled apologies. He danced regularly with Miss Hammond, whom he could now look in the eye, and who tended to tell him the truth of his shortcomings as a dancer; and he could dance with her sister, Miss Poppy, who would prattle about cats and paintings and had he seen the new house being put up on Queen Street? And he could dance with whatever offered on afternoons in the black taverns. He could watch Sally smile with delight every time they completed a set together. It didn't happen often, as there were few places he would go with her, but late at the tavern he would sometimes fight his way through an easy country dance while the musicians played on and on to please her.

And then, as spring came, something happened to change her. She became morose and easily angered, listless in a wooden way, and was drunk nearly every time he came to her. Stewart was sufficiently taken with her to care, but he had never fancied himself her sole supporter.

He found himself making excuses to shun her. He told himself that he shouldn't see her anyway. He spent more time drilling the Black Guides. He was busy enough with shaping the new draft of recruits from England for his own company and seeing that every man in his company had their new equipment and all their clothes that he didn't have time to see her every day. It was the busiest time of year for a company commander. Every spring the army issued new clothes, new equipment, to bring the army back up to the mark. The work took him out to the lines north of the city and kept him from Sally anyway.

But when business sent him back to headquarters for the day, as it did when he had to complain to the regimental agent about the quality of shoes he had received, he still preferred to come to the Moor's Head. Many of the officers in New York did. The music was better, and louder, and the food the best on the island. Jeremy made it plain to him that he preferred to visit the place. It had a rare air to it, with soldiers and sailors and officers, blacks and whites and the occasional Indian, all intermingled in the same rooms.

He often tried to meet Simcoe at the Moor's Head. Simcoe had grown to be his particular friend since the fall. They planned the future of the war together, bemoaned the defeats at Trenton and Princeton together, and wrote letters to each other. Simcoe's company was in the Jerseys, too far for daily conversation, but they corresponded as often as practicable. Soldiers of the Black Guides, who watched over the frequent convoys, often carried their letters.

Stewart was dancing with Mrs. Innes, the handsome sharp-faced woman whose husband was something in the commissary. He was conscious that he had a letter from Miss McLean in his pocket and that his attention was focused on Sally, who was drunk, and Jeremy, who was attempting to restrain her. He could tell that he was not amusing Mrs. Innes, who clearly expected better of him. He was frustrated, and angry, and felt the weight of layers of his own sins in a way that seems to be the exclusive preserve of the Scots. He saw Simcoe in the doorway and sighed with something like relief, a sound that did not escape his partner.

"Somehow, Captain, I don't think I have your full attention." Mrs. Innes giggled and tapped him lightly with her fan. She was unsure herself how much raillery was acceptable with a man so much older.

He bowed to her. "Pray, madam, will you excuse me for a few moments?"

"I cannot promise I will not have gone elsewhere for my dance, Captain," she said. Stewart walked her over to Simcoe, who was just in the process of handing off his dripping cloak to a maid.

"Captain Simcoe?"

"Your servant, Captain Stewart."

"And yours, sir. Have you met the lovely Mrs. Innes?" Stewart said, turning to introduce his partner. Captain Simcoe bowed over her hand. She giggled again, her least engaging habit. Simcoe didn't come in any farther, as he was still wearing boots caked in mud, and spurs.

"I have, too. She giggles. Otherwise, quite engaging. Your servant, ma'am." Simcoe was wearing a green velvet coat and a double-breasted waistcoat, fine clothes for riding or for an evening in town. He got his gloves off and was still fumbling with his heavy riding boots when Jeremy appeared as if by magic with a bowl of water and a small boy who flung himself on the boots with gusto, pulling them off and carrying them away. Simcoe washed his hands.

"That boy is smaller than the boots," said Mrs. Innes.

"Do you have a dry shirt, Captain Stewart?" Simcoe was embarrassed. "I lost my portmanteau somewhere on the road. Never saw it go. The buckle must have slipped."

Jeremy nodded to Stewart. Stewart smiled at his friend. "I do. I have a room upstairs, if you'd like to change."

"Your *humble* servant. Do you ever think, when you are out in the wet on a night like this, how close the comforts of New York are?"

"I do."

"It's a wonder every officer and man doesn't desert the lines and come here, especially with such loveliness as these." Simcoe waved at Mrs. Innes and her friend Miss Amanda Chew. Mrs. Innes giggled. Miss Chew made a face.

Jeremy led Simcoe upstairs. Stewart talked to Miss Chew for a moment, earning a glare from Mrs. Innes for deserting her. He spoke idly, trying to find Sally in the crowd on the other side of the room. It complicated their lives, that he couldn't cross to her side of the room any more than she could seek him on his side. He told himself that he only wanted to know how she was.

Jeremy reappeared with Simcoe, who looked better for Jeremy's attentions. Mrs. Innes made a motion to indicate that another dance was ready to start and she was impatient with her abandonment.

Stewart nodded, his attention on Jeremy, who was trying to communicate something.

"Perhaps Mrs. Innes would be kind enough to accept Captain Simcoe as a replacement while I am gone?" Stewart asked.

"And I suppose you expect me to relinquish this paragon the instant you reappear? Be warned, Captain. I am not an easy man to displace." Simcoe, so often grave, was in high spirits.

Mrs. Innes giggled again, clearly delighted by his attention. Jeremy pulled lightly on Stewart's arm.

"I'll return to see which of us has the better claim, then, ma'am," Stewart said, and followed Jeremy down a passage.

"What's the hurry?"

"Sally is in a heap in your room. I managed to steer Captain Simcoe to another. I think she means herself a mischief." Jeremy stopped and leaned in close to him, a hand up on the wall beside him. They were very much of a size, and their eyes were inches apart.

"You have more power over her than the rest of us, sir. Don't tell me she means nothing to you."

Stewart almost hit his head on the passage wall, he was so taken aback by the look of Jeremy, and his tone. He thought to resent it, but he couldn't. He knew he had some sort of power over her, and he knew she liked him. The letter in his pocket made it all the worse. He suspected himself of the worst of motivations. He wondered if he had taken a black mistress because somehow that wouldn't *count* so much with Mary as a white one. He hung his head a moment.

"She's drunk and angry, sir. None of us knows why she's this way. Caesar says he's never seen her like this, and Caesar's man Virgil is beside himself."

Stewart suspected that his treatment of Sally would reflect in his relations with all of them. He shook his head, feeling as if he had just taken a series of blows. Then he straightened up. "I'll see what can be done, Jeremy. But she's more a force of nature than a woman."

Jeremy nodded. "I apologize for my tone, sir. I wanted you to see the gravity of the situation." Stewart noted that Jeremy didn't look particularly apologetic, and he wondered if his man had a *tendresse* of his own for Sally.

"Never mind, Jeremy. If a man can't bear a reprimand from his manservant, he's pretty far gone, I guess." He walked down the passage to the room that Jeremy indicated, and went in.

It wasn't the scene from hell he had expected. There were no visible signs of carnage, and Polly White was sitting quietly on the bed. She was reading in the firelight.

"I came to see her." Stewart didn't fully open the door.

"I'm glad, sir. If you allow, I'll come for you when she wakes."

"Polly, you're a dear thing. Why is she so bad, of a sudden?"

Polly looked down at her book, as if it could answer his question. She took so long to answer that he thought perhaps she didn't intend to speak.

"I don't think it's so sudden, sir. I think that she's had a hard life, and sometimes it comes home to her. And I think that sometimes she wants a different life, and she can't see how to get to it from where she is. My father says that great beauty in a woman can be a curse. I think it was, for her." She looked at the woman on the bed.

Stewart thought she was going to say more, but she didn't. He looked at the woman lying on the bed, and the woman sitting on the end of it, and shook his head.

"There's truth in what you say, Miss White," he said, somewhat moved. "Please send for me instantly when she wakes."

☆ ☆ ☆

"We'll be off across New Jersey in a few weeks," Simcoe said, rubbing his hands in front of the fire. "I expect the lights will be in the vanguard. We're to clear the ground back down to the Delaware and reclaim some of the support we've lost since Washington's victories in the winter."

"And then on to Philadelphia?"

Simcoe looked around the tavern as if expecting to spot a spy. He lowered his voice. "I wouldn't expect it. There is a great deal going on at headquarters that is not what we might expect, if you take my meaning."

Simcoe so seldom spoke in this manner that Stewart was puzzled to understand him. "I can't say that I do take your meaning, John."

Simcoe actually pulled his chair closer. "There was supposed to be a grand campaign, with Lord Howe marching north from New York and John Burgoyne, or perhaps Guy Carleton, taking an army south from Quebec, with the objective of taking Albany."

"Albany!" Stewart rose to his feet and looked over the map until he found it, up the Hudson. "What the devil do we want with Albany?"

"The plan was that we would meet there, and split the northern colonies from the southern."

Stewart grimaced. "That's an armchair general's plan. Something that *Gentleman's Magazine* might suggest."

"I believe Lord Howe is very much of your mind, John Julius. He has decided to let the northern army take Albany on their own, or perhaps with a little *divertissement* from General Clinton. He himself intends us for Philadelphia."

"Just so."

"By sea."

Stewart sat back in his chair, struck dumb. All the way south to Virginia, into the mouth of the Chesapeake, up the Chesapeake to the Delaware.

"One pounce and we're in his capital," said Simcoe.

"That would be a bold stroke."

"You see why the march through the Jerseys is nothing but a raid in force."

"And I see the necessity. A bold feint that way will pin Washington in place while we go round by sea."

Stewart raised his glass. "A glass of wine with you, then. Here's to a long campaign and many promotions."

Simcoe raised his and drank.

★ ★ ★

"You were supposed to have it for Christmas, but it wasn't ready," Polly said quietly, so as not to awake the sleeper. She handed Caesar a tiny bag of silk, tied off with a fine red ribbon.

"You gave me a silk roller at Christmas," he said.

"I had to give you something, goose!" She rolled her eyes at the eternal blindness of men. He leaned in and kissed her quickly, before she could make an objection, but she didn't resist in the least. They'd had a talk on the subject, and Caesar now knew where the boundaries that might lead to his ears being boxed lay. He did continue to test them, but warily, like a good soldier on patrol. The enemy sentries remained alert, however.

He motioned at Sally. Experience with Polly had taught him that he needed to honor her concern for the woman, although Sally was all one to Caesar—she drank, she made trouble, she was a memento from the swamp and had to be tolerated.

"She's in a bad way, Julius," she said.

"She *will* drink," Caesar said dubiously. Neither Polly nor her father was easily practiced upon, but Caesar rather thought that in this case the soldiers, not the priest, should keep Sally. He had wondered several times why Marcus White continued to help Sally when the relations brought him only gossip and trouble.

"No, it's not just that, Julius. She was happy. I think Captain Stewart keeps her happy, though it's wrong, of course."

Caesar tried to hide a smile. "Does she love Mr. Stewart, do you think?"

"Don't be a goose, Julius Caesar. She don't love nobody. But she likes him. She taught him to dance. And then the other day this man came to her..."

"What man is that, then?" asked Caesar.

"An ill-looking thin white man. You know the sort, that look mean and pinched whether they will or no?"

Caesar nodded, staring at the rich red of the ribbon on his present.

"The man made her afraid. She won't tell me why, but she hasn't been the same since. She was shocking to my father, too."

Caesar thought that Sally might be shocking to Marcus White in many different ways, but he kept his views to himself.

"Jeremy blames Captain Stewart," Caesar said, feeling disloyal to both.

"Sally thought that Captain Stewart would take her in keeping, and not leave her at Mother Abbott's," said Polly, instantly destroying Caesar's cherished notion that Polly didn't really know what Sally did to earn her fine clothes and daily bread, or at least needed to be protected from the details. His surprise showed on his face.

"Oh, Julius Caesar, you can be so blind. Open your present, then."

He pulled the bow apart teasingly, enjoying the feel of the satin ribbon, and then rubbed it against her cheek.

"That's all the present I need," he said.

"If I wanted to listen to Jeremy's compliments, I'd ask for them myself."

He wanted to flare with anger, but the truth was that the line did belong to Jeremy. He looked at her, unsure how to react, but she kissed his hand and then the ribbon.

"Open it, then," she said.

He opened the piece of silk and there was a ball of jeweler's cotton. When he opened it out, there was a gleaming silver whistle on a plaited cord. He gave a startled sound, wordless.

"That's beautiful," he said, wishing to blow it immediately.

"It's the shape of Captain Stewart's, but it has a different note. Sally took his for a few days to get it right. And Virgil plaited the cord."

Polly looked down demurely. Caesar kissed her and she responded vigorously. Her eyes half closed, which moved him. Then she ended the kiss, gently but firmly.

"Listen, will you? I need a favor." She placed the bed and its sleeping occupant between them. Caesar laughed at her and she smiled back.

"What do you want, Polly?" She never asked him for anything, but made him shirts and gave him silver whistles.

"I need to borrow your drummer, Sam. I need him to run some errands for me." Something about the manner of her asking made him a trifle suspicious, but he could hardly refuse. Sam ran everyone's errands. His cherubic looks made him seem even younger than he really was, if you ignored his eyes.

"Thank you, Caesar," she said, coming back around the bed.

Caesar thought that it might be time to test her boundaries again, but Sally picked that awkward moment to wake up, and the chance was gone.

New Jersey, May 19, 1777

A month's military activity made Polly a memory, left in New York when the light troops of the army moved suddenly into the Jerseys. Caesar relished the memory, though, pulling out her whistle and feeling its smoothness with his thumb for a moment, a habit he had developed from the day he got it.

He blew it, and his pickets went loping out to the little hilltop where he had ordered them. Lieutenant Crawford watched him avidly.

Caesar spoke quickly. "Virgil, take the right platoon around through the outbuildings and cover the back. Sergeant Fowver, straight over the hill through the woodlot. Tonny, with me. Leave a file on that little copse by the road to guide the advance guard. If they come before I get back, tell them those woods on the little ridge ain't cleared yet."

This sort of patrol had been their daily bread on the advance through the Jerseys, moving at the front of the army and looking at the ground. They had learned to be well ahead, and to leave men in secure posts to provide some communication with the advance guard. They had learned the fine art of being guides in more than name.

They had another advantage, too.

✭ ✭ ✭

Lieutenant Crawford stood politely in the dooryard of the little farm, resplendent in an old red coat with no lace and decent smallclothes. His fighting clothes were better than any New Jersey farmer had seen in some time, and he overawed the middle-aged man who had presented himself at the door.

"Have you turned out in the militia for the rebels, sir?" asked Crawford. A file of Caesar's men was standing behind him. Not threatening, but very much present.

"I have not, sir."

"Do you own a firearm?"

"I never seen the need, as the Indians are a long ways away." The farmer was anything but friendly. The fear hadn't lasted long, and he was just on the border of respect.

"Are any of your neighbors in the rebel militia?"

"I can't say." His wife was much younger, although already worn. Several children were gathered in the hall, including one young man of sixteen or seventeen.

Crawford tried anyway, his Scots accent minimal. "Sir, you realize we are here as soldiers of the king to protect you and your neighbors from these rebels. We mean you no harm. We are not the army that burns farms, I think."

His words were lost on the farmer, and probably on his brood, as they stood silent in their house. Nearer New York, Crawford had been fed tea or chocolate at the more prosperous houses. Here he wasn't even offered well water.

Caesar came around from the big barn with two muskets and their accoutrements, each with its little tail of straw that told of where they had been hidden. Two young slaves trotted at his heels.

"Bergen County Militia. He's senior sergeant in the second platoon of Captain Meyer's company, and his son is one of his soldiers." The slaves smiled broadly. Caesar made quite a show of handing them the muskets.

"You Christian men? Good, then." He looked them over. "You have names?"

The short one in the little straw hat poked out his chest.

"I'm Moses Shaw and this is my brother Abraham." They both smiled. "We guess we're free." They chuckled with mirth.

"You are free if you swear to uphold King George and serve him in his army." This was now the line that Caesar used every time they met with slaves in the Jerseys, though it was a most liberal interpretation of Lord Howe's orders.

"Raise your right hands and repeat after me. When I say I, you each say your names." Both men raised their hands, smiling less and clutching their new muskets awkwardly. The other Guides, at least those with no immediate duties, formed up in two neat lines in the farmyard, with Sergeant Fowver and Virgil prodding the inept and awkward into the ranks.

"I," said Caesar.

"Moses Shaw," said Moses.

"Abraham," said Abraham.

Do swear that I enter freely and voluntarily into His Majesty's service, and I do enlist myself without the least compulsion or persuasion into the Black Guides commanded by Captain Stewart, and that I will demean myself orderly and faithfully, and will cheerfully obey all such directions as I may receive from my said captain, or the officers or noncommissioned officers under his command, and that I will continue to serve His Majesty in all such services as I may be employed in during the present rebellion in America—

"So help me God."

The farmer tried to protest to Lieutenant Crawford that these were not his muskets and that he couldn't run the farm if his slaves were taken.

Crawford smiled a little wolfishly. "Sergeant—I may call you that, mayn't I? You are hereby a prisoner of war on parole, taken in arms against His Majesty, and it's very lucky for you that I haven't the men or the inclination to take you back to New York."

The man turned pale. Men died in the prison hulks of New York harbor.

"Further, as you are a rebel, your slaves are free men. They have chosen to enlist in His Majesty's army, which shouldn't surprise you. You may, perhaps, feel that they bear you some ill will, and I recommend that you consider well what you are at, sir. I hereby require you to present yourself to the sheriff of this county in the next fortnight to sign an oath of loyalty to His Majesty. If you do not do so, or if anyone reports that you turn out to serve the rebels, we'll return. Do you understand?"

The man was watching his slaves and his muskets filing out onto the road. The loss was enormous, if calculated as property.

"*Do* you understand, sir?"

The man nodded. He clenched his fists by his side and opened them.

Caesar came up to Crawford, saluted, and handed him a military pack.

"In case you had any doubts, sir." In the pack was a set of shirts, a homespun overshirt like those the militia and even some of the rebels wore, and a knitted cap. Caesar pointed to the pack, which was painted with the insignia "III VA." Crawford took out the cap. Embroidered around the base of the cap was the motto "Liberty or Death." He held it up.

"It puzzles me how you Americans can prate about liberty while you own slaves," he said. "I'll keep this. It ought to fetch a good price from the laggards in New York."

Caesar rifled the pack, which had a broken strap, and sniffed it. It smelled of smoke. "This ain't been around here long, sir."

He looked at the farmer. "When did this pack get here? You, there. The tall boy. Step out here."

There looked to be resistance for a moment. In the end, good sense won out and the older boy stepped out. Caesar sent him off to the barn with Virgil.

Crawford nodded. They were learning to question rebel sympathizers separately, so that they couldn't coach each other.

"What are you bastards doing to my boy?" cried the father.

"He'll be questioned. When did the patrol come through your farm?"

"I don't know." He was white and shaking. His wife was clutching him from behind. Crawford hated these scenes, as these people were essentially Englishmen and he despised having to brutalize them. It reminded him of bad times in Scotland. He thought of the slaves outside, the lives they led, and hardened his heart.

"I'd recommend you reconsider. I can take you or your son to New York, and I will if I feel you are placing my men in danger."

"What are you doing to my *son?*" shouted the man. He looked over to where Moses and Abraham were standing with the other Guides on the little road that led past the farmyard. "What did we ever do to you that you would betray us like this?" He raised his fists at them and they both flinched, although they had guns and he had none.

Caesar stepped up to him, very close, where he could smell the man's breath and the fear in his sweat. "It isn't about them, sir. It's about you. You are the traitor. You have been serving the rebels. You get to pay the fiddler now. An' if Mr. Crawford wants to know when the patrol passed, I think you'd do well to tell him. You have a mighty big family to be taking these risks with." He was a foot taller than the man, and he quailed.

"Yesterday, damn you. Rot the lot of you. Yesterday." He spat.

Caesar watched him, unimpressed. "How long were they here?"

"Not long. They told us to hide the muskets..." The man stopped, knowing he had said too much.

"So they knew we was coming? What did they tell you, exactly?"

The man looked at his wife as if he needed support.

"Don't look at her," said Caesar. He had stepped past Crawford now. Crawford couldn't force himself on a man like this. Caesar didn't like it, but he found it was easier with the slave owners. They feared all blacks and responded appropriately. He felt that somehow it made their punishment fit the crime. He thought of the ancient Caesar, crucifying the men who would have made him a slave.

"Don't look at her, little man. Look at me. What did they say?"

"They said..." The man was ready to sob. He looked like a cornered animal. He glanced at his wife and daughters, his younger son, and Caesar, who was doing his best to look like the image of vengeful Africa. "They said a company of blacks might come through, an' we'd best hide our muskets and keep quiet."

Crawford shook his head. "Was that so hard, sir?"

Caesar threw him a glance, asking him to stay quiet. "What else did they say? Tell me, now. They knew we was a company of blacks, you say?"

The man was gray. His wife and family were now crying.

"Want to cough your life out in the hulks?"

"I won't, neither," said the man, clawing for self-respect. The fact that he said he wouldn't, though, served to point out that he had more left to say. Caesar nodded.

"Very brave," he said, and motioned to the file. "Take him."

The man held to his resolve as they tied him and led him into the yard. Caesar went off to the barn, where the boy glowered at Virgil, who sat smoking quietly.

"Any trouble?"

"Boy said he'd kill me if'n I harmed his pa, which is kinda funny considerin' I'm here with him."

Caesar nodded and walked around the barn back to the yard. He had a notion what it was the man wouldn't tell. He knew which unit the Third Virginia was. He remembered them from Long Island. He stood in front of the defiant man for a moment, as if considering. Then he walked slowly around the man until he was behind him.

"Your boy says they came through late last night. He says they meant to lie in ambush for us. That right?"

The man sagged. His whole body seemed to shrink, as if the courage were flowing from him. He tried to turn to face Caesar, but Tonny held him.

"Let him go," said Caesar to Tonny.

The man wouldn't meet his eye.

"Look at me."

The man flinched away.

"Look at me, mister. Tell me what they said."

"Promise you won't hurt my boys."

"I won't if you don't give me cause."

"They were a big company. They said they was goin' to lie for you at Dick's farm, down the pike. Dick's got a parcel more slaves than I do, they figured you'd go there."

Caesar looked at him carefully and nodded, although his blood was up now. "Get his boy and put them all together." He still sounded threatening.

Crawford came up to him. "I hope that was worth it, Sergeant. We just made these people rebels for life."

"I think they were already there, sir."

"I think that war is a lot uglier than I had thought," said Crawford.

★　★　★

"How'd they know we was comin'?" asked Paget. The story was all over the company in a flash, helped by the additional testimony of Moses and Abraham. Virgil heard him and frowned.

"Stow it, Paget. There's hundreds of ways they could know. They have scouts, too." They moved quickly over a hill, well away from the rebel house in the little valley, and then halted.

Caesar ran up and tapped Tonny and Silas Van Sluyt, the fastest runners in the company. "Follow me," he said. They ran to the crest of the hill, where Crawford was waiting with Sergeant Fowver.

"I want to take these two and follow that boy."

Crawford shook his head. "What boy?"

"The one at the house. He'll head off to warn the Virginians as soon as they think they are safe."

Crawford shook his head. "Damn me for a green boy. Of course they will. My apologies, Sergeant Caesar, I should have seen that—"

"Never you mind, sir. I'd like to take these three an' follow on his heels. We'll see how they lie and report back. You can send to Captain Stewart an' bring up the advance guard, if you are of a mind to."

"I do like being managed by a professional, Sergeant Caesar. It is good for my *amour-propre*. Very well, carry on."

"Yes, sir." He winked at Fowver, who gave him a quick smile. Then he ran.

☆ ☆ ☆

They almost missed the boy, because he chose to run right out onto the road, and they had never counted on him being so daring and so blind. Once they had him, however, they paced him easily, running well behind and off to the boy's left. They lost him several times, when they had to go well off the path to detour round woodlots or patches of muck, but his white shirt and old green waistcoat made him an easy mark on the dusty road.

He ran over a mile before he flagged. Caesar wasn't even into his pace yet when the boy stopped, breathing hard. The Guides all lay down. The boy breathed a moment and then left the road, bearing west. Caesar sent his men well to the left and right, so that if the boy tried to mislead them or double back, one was bound to spot him. He didn't do any such thing. Guileless as a lamb, he ran cross-country, as straight as a ball from a rifle-gun, until an outpost challenged him. Again Caesar threw himself flat and then began to crawl up. He could see Tonny off to his right, but he didn't know whether Van Sluyt was still with them. He could hear the boy speaking in a rush, could hear the excitement in his tone but not the words themselves. He moved closer. He motioned to Tonny. Tonny pointed at something off to his own right, and Caesar had to wonder if it was another post. There were a great many rebels out here, if they could space their posts so closely.

Caesar nodded to Tonny and pointed back to where they'd come. He pointed at his chest and made a little gorget with his finger, then patted his shoulder as if he had an epaulet. He saw Tonny brighten as if he understood and begin to move away slowly until he had a few trees between him and the sentries, and then, with a wave, he was gone.

Caesar was alone.

He lay flat and stripped his equipment off until he was wearing only his jacket. He took the hunting sword out of its scabbard carefully and then began to creep forward alone. The post was on a little knoll, shaded by a big chestnut tree and guarded by a loose abatis of fallen branches piled around like an open fence.

There was only one man in the post. The other had gone off with the boy. He hadn't gone far, because his musket was propped against the great chestnut tree that provided the post with its cover of branches. Caesar crept closer, urged to move faster by the knowledge that the boy was getting farther away with every moment, but he relied on caution to take him close, and he crawled.

Time passed. The sun beat down on his back and he sweated rivers through his coat. He was up to the little abatis of downed branches that the pickets had made, and he prepared himself. Far off, carried on the wind, he heard the slight rattle and clank of a well-ordered company on the move, and he knew that the Guides were down on the road and moving fast. They would still be over a mile away. He rolled up and caught his foot in a branch. He saw the sentry flinch in surprise, then reach for his musket, which was a few feet away. He wrenched his foot clear and threw himself forward, but the man bent to his musket, took it, and aimed. The seconds slid by as Caesar ran, already doomed, at the man. He saw the cock fall on the hammer, the sparks, the ignition of the powder in the priming pan, all as if they were separate acts, and he threw himself down.

Damp or ill-maintained, the gun hung its fire for some fraction of time that saved him. He felt the heat from it, and the ball scored his shoulder and down his back. He rose in a leap, the sound of the shot still in his ears. The man had his mouth open to shout when Caesar cut with the sword and hacked him down, but he could already hear shouts of alarm in the distance and he cursed his own eagerness.

The man at his feet gurgled. He was cut badly in the neck and Caesar killed him, squeamish about cutting a man who couldn't fight back but too aware that he was all but dead already and in pain, like an animal. His blood was everywhere and couldn't be hidden.

The shouts of alarm grew and Caesar moved a little forward into the shadow of more of the big trees. He was in an old woodlot, he could now see, and there was the farmhouse below him in a little vale. He could see the coats of the Virginians as they moved about, probably forming up. They looked confused.

One man was running back toward the post that Caesar had just taken. Caesar thought the man was probably the file partner of the dead man. Before he could reach the post a shot rang out and the man went down, hit somewhere low. He gave a sudden sharp scream of pain and then lay still for a moment. Caesar tried to follow the line of the shot and saw Van Sluyt reloading on his back on the next knoll. Caesar broke from cover and ran for his equipment, only forty paces to the rear but now seeming like a mile, and there were shots. None came near him, and he had no way of knowing if the shots were even meant for him. He reached the log where he had left his kit and rolled behind it. His fowler was loaded and ready and he scooped his bag and horn over his shoulder, cleaned the blade of the little sword as well as he could on the grass while lying flat, put it in the scabbard, and then buckled on his pack. The whole process seemed to take forever. He worried about Van Sluyt, left alone on the hilltop. Van Sluyt had seen action, but not like this, not alone, and Caesar feared to have the man's blood on his conscience.

But he was an old soldier, and he hated being far from his equipment. He had feared that if they were driven off he'd never see his carefully gathered kit again. He heard another flurry of shots and rose to his feet, and ran back up the far knoll toward Van Sluyt. He heard Van Sluyt fire, felt relief that the man was still fighting and alive, and then saw the Virginians right in front of him, ten men coming up the knoll.

Caesar fired into them with no apparent effect. The sound of the second shot gave them pause, though. A big man at their head looked to the left and right and Caesar blew his whistle three times, as loud as he could. In the distance, his whistle was answered. He watched the big man as he reloaded, knowing him as the slave-taker who had nearly killed Jim and Virgil in the swamp. He had fought the man on Long Island and he didn't think his presence in an ambush laid for them in New Jersey was happenstance. He watched a man aiming at him and he rolled back behind a tree. His back hurt like hell.

Van Sluyt fired into them and missed. They were spreading out now and moving back toward their main body, which was just visible through the trees in the farmyard. Caesar leaned well out and took his time with his shot. He couldn't get a line on the big man, so he shot another, who went down. He blew his whistle again. The answer was closer.

"Keep them amused," he said to Van Sluyt. It was one of Simcoe's sayings, and he liked it. Silas nodded happily. Caesar ran off down the knoll and back along the path they had run up until he found the Guides moving at the double over the open fields. Lieutenant Crawford was running well, right in the center of the front as if they were running on parade.

"Just over the little ridge, sir. About a company. They've called in their ambush and it looks like they're leaving."

Out of breath, Crawford merely nodded and panted. He turned and trotted back a few paces, looking at the men, and put his whistle in his mouth, then spread his arms wide and blew twice. They began to pound up the hill, the line extending itself as they went, and again Caesar felt that burst of pride in them. Moses and Abraham, green as grass, were following Paget and Virgil. The line extended out and out, seventy strong, and they came to the knoll almost together, as pretty as any company Caesar had ever seen. Van Sluyt was smiling like a loon, nodding his head, and Caesar grabbed him by the shoulder.

"Where are they?"

Van Sluyt pointed past the house to the road beyond it, where they could just see a little rearguard forming on the road.

"Well done, Silas."

Van Sluyt continued to smile.

By the time they swept through the farm, no one was smiling. There was an old black man in the yard, hanging from a tree, and a black woman was dead on the ground, her throat slit. Otherwise, the farm was empty.

They chased hard for over an hour, firing at various ranges and trying to provoke the rebels to stand, but they weren't raw anymore. They ran well, kept together, and both Crawford and Caesar feared they might be led into a second ambush. They had to break the pursuit when the Virginians entered a narrow defile covered in thick woods. None of them wanted to risk that there weren't a hundred enemy sheltered just inside.

The rebels jeered at them when they halted. They halted immediately, over half a mile away, and fired a volley that hurt no one.

Caesar and Van Sluyt together had knocked three of them down, and they had one prisoner, an older man who had not been able to keep up the pace. It wasn't much to show for a day spent running, and they were weary men when they marched back to the farmstead where the Virginians had prepared to ambush them.

☆ ☆ ☆

"We didn't lose a man, though," said Crawford, scraping the pork stew out of his little china bowl. The farmhouse had been deserted, and Crawford had not complained as the Guides pillaged it and the surrounding barns. The owners had decamped, indicating where their allegiance lay.

"Last fall, all these farms declared they was loyal," said Caesar. He looked out over the little hills in the failing spring light. "I remember when we came through here in November."

"Trenton changed that," said Crawford. He looked guilty, as if just saying the words was disloyal.

Caesar nodded and ate.

"We'll win them back when we take Philadelphia and end the war," said Crawford.

Caesar kept eating. He was watching the smooth conduct of his mess groups. Women didn't cook in the British army. The men cooked for themselves, usually in the same groups that shared a tent and fought together. One man carried the tin kettle for cooking, and another carried the shovel or the ax. Mess groups were usually little families within the company, although the newer ones could be more like little wars, as men struggled for dominance or fought to resist tyranny and avoid the worst chores. The new man always cleaned the pot and carried it and most of the rations.

When he looked at them, he saw them as individuals and then as mess groups and platoons. He thought about the surprising calm and courage of Van Sluyt, considered the change in Paget and the steady virtue of Virgil, the quick wit of Tonny, the solidity of Fowver. He watched Moses and Abraham struggle with sand and straw to clean a pot. He watched Jim directing his mess group with unlooked-for authority. Jim was ready to be a corporal.

He thought of how many blacks he'd liberated in the last few days, either into his own ranks or back to New York City, and he wondered a moment why he no longer saw them as Bakongo or Yoruba or Ashanti, but only as black. Perhaps the change had been gradual, but he couldn't remember it. He could remember how important it had seemed on the plantation. The war had changed it all.

"Do you think we'll win the war, Lieutenant Crawford?" he asked.

Crawford looked at him as if he had blasphemed. "Can we fail? We've been beaten a handful of times. We beat them whenever we find them. They'll never build an army that can defeat us."

Caesar ate a little more and watched twilight fall, already concerned for his outposts. Something was nagging at him. "If we don't win, every man in this company is a slave again, sir."

Crawford looked at him with sudden comprehension.

"If you lose, you get to go home to England."

"Scotland, Sergeant."

Caesar was suddenly impatient with Crawford. "Scotland, then. You go home. The white Loyalists will go to Jamaica, or Florida, or Canada. But we'll be slaves. Forever. Or they'll hang us."

Crawford looked at him strangely, like a man who has discovered a friend has a terrible disease.

"We'd better win, then," Crawford whispered.

"Aye. Aye, but it isn't looking that way." Caesar realized he had bottled the thought up since the first defeats at Great Bridge in Virginia. He shook his head. "My apologies, Mr. Crawford."

"None needed. This war...this war is ugly."

Caesar didn't like the look of the future, so he contented himself with the outposts.

"I think we ought to move before we sleep. We made fires here." Caesar pointed at the little smudge of smoke in the sky.

Crawford looked as if he wanted to protest, but the silent Fowver nodded and he was quick enough to nod as well.

"Just so," he said, imitating his hero.

"These people sure hate us," Caesar said, thinking of the family they had questioned and the old man hanged. He stooped to grab a handful of the sandy soil and used it to wipe his little wooden bowl clean. Then he pushed the bowl into his pack and motioned to his mess group to douse the fire and get their packs on. They grumbled, but they moved. He stood up, admiring the quick way that Crawford cleaned his little knife and fork and readied himself without fuss. Crawford was green, but he learned fast, and he never slowed them down.

"What of it? They have betrayed their king, and they will pay the price."

Caesar shrugged, pulling the straps of his pack over his shoulders. He thought he knew a little more about hate than Lieutenant Crawford did, and there was something at the edge of his mind, about hate, and fear, and how it could serve to bring men together the way the Guides were together.

And he wondered how the Virginians had known where to wait for them.

"They do hate us, though," he said, and went to form the company.

Philadelphia, August 1, 1777

Washington squirmed a little in the big chair while Billy dusted his boots. Washington had not grown up rich and had never become accustomed to having other men fuss at him, and he couldn't abide having anyone put on his boots. Lee put the pulls into his hand and he set the right boot on his foot and pulled it smoothly up his calf to the knee before attacking the left, which never seemed to fit quite as well.

"Here's another report that the British fleet has left Sandy Hook, General," said Colonel Hamilton. Hamilton, despite his West Indian origins, was probably the wittiest, most sensible and genteel of the permanent staff. Washington grunted slightly as his left heel finally slid home in his boot and then sat back so that Lee could set about his hair.

"By all accounts they sailed on the twenty-fourth," Washington said quietly.

"Where bound is the question," said his Irish aide, Fitzgerald, with a stretch and a yawn that drew a grave look from the general.

"They can land anywhere they like," said Hamilton. "Up the Hudson, the Jersey shore, or around Cape May and into the Chesapeake."

"It certainly explains the withdrawal of their forces from the Jerseys," said Washington. "I have long feared that Lord Howe, as I believe he is now styled, would decide to use the full mobility that his brother's fleet allows him. I believe that our fears are now upon us. With Ticonderoga fallen to Burgoyne, it must seem to Howe that he needn't cooperate with Burgoyne and can launch some scheme of his own. How I wish for better intelligence."

"How I pray we may yet have it," said Hamilton, arranging the military letters that Washington would have to read for himself.

Lee put a curl on each side of Washington's head with economy and then stood back to measure the effect, smiled, and handed his master a plain buff wool waistcoat. Washington pushed it away.

"Give me a double-breasted one, Billy. I'm always chilled in the morning."

Lee took another from a trunk and brushed it.

"Any other business today, gentlemen?"

"Can you bear another foreign officer, General?" asked Johnson. Fitzgerald made antic motions as if he were an ape. Hamilton rose and took snuff with theatrical gestures that were clearly meant to be French. Even Billy Lee, the slave, felt free to join the laughter.

"What has Mr. Deane sent us this time?" Silas Deane, the Continental Congress's appointed diplomat in Paris, had developed the annoying tendency of granting Continental Army commissions to foreigners on the spot. Some of his appointments outranked existing American veterans, who were angry to find themselves outranked by foreign aristocrats. Most of the aristocrats seemed to feel their time in America could best be spent educating ignorant Americans about their own superior martial virtues. It could be quite wearing; witness Colonel Hamilton's continuing charade.

"A marquis," said Hamilton, desisting from his antics instantly.

"Come," said Johnson. "That's handsome of Deane, I must say. We've had our fill of chevaliers and barons, so a marquis will make a nice change."

An uncomfortable silence fell.

All Washington's aides were young. They had to be, as he led them a rough and hard life, but sometimes the general's rather staid sense of humor oppressed the young men. They knew he was tired of the foreign officers, but each was suddenly aware that they had offended him or, rather, taken their humor beyond some definite line of his approval.

Johnson stood up. "My apologies, sir. I let my tongue get the better of me."

"Not for the first time," Hamilton muttered quietly, and Johnson rounded on him like a cat annoyed by another, but Washington was quicker than either.

"Very well, gentlemen. Let's see this marquis. I do hope we can all master our humor in his presence, as I'm sure that his good opinion of us will carry heavy weight with His Catholic Majesty, the King of France, on whom we are very dependent. Do I make myself clear?" Every Frenchman had claimed that his opinions carried great weight with the king of France, and apparently a few of them were telling the truth.

"Colonel Hamilton, who is the officer of the day?"

Hamilton opened his orderly book and ran through a list of names. "Our officer of the day is Lieutenant Lake of the light company, Third Virginia."

Washington looked at him. "Recall him to me."

"Intelligent, fit, soldierly. Up from the ranks—began the war as an apprentice to a hatmaker, I believe. Led the charge on the Hessian guns at Trenton." Hamilton knew these facts by heart. He had been the one to notice Lake at Trenton. Hamilton liked to see the self-made men rise.

Washington nodded as Billy began to help him into his coat. "Very well, then. Send for him a little after the marquis arrives."

Hamilton nodded and made a note.

✷ ✷ ✷

The man who presented himself in the front parlor was of average height or a little less and well dressed, in a dark blue velvet coat and with a beautiful sword that had already excited the admiration of every soldier who beheld it. It was a hunting sword, short and broad, with a heavy blade and a black horn hilt worked in silver. The coat and the sword went together and spoke of wealth, which made today's Frenchman a distinct entity, in that most of the men Deane had sent were clearly poor, if not destitute.

He was young, too—perhaps only twenty-one or twenty-two—and he stood before them with so much self-possession that his bearing was like a lesson in genteel behavior. Indeed, Hamilton said later that he liked the man before he ever opened his mouth.

He waited until Washington was done speaking. Washington had been addressing the commissariat officer on a scheme to increase their stock of shoes, a subject that could be of interest only to a veteran. The young man stood still, his manner open and yet expectant, a small but wonderfully candid smile upon his face as if to say that, just by being there, he had reached the summit of his ambition. For their part, the staff were content just to regard a man of such wealth and breeding. Washington completed his animated conversation on shoes and Mr. Turnbull, the commissary, bowed and withdrew. Washington turned the full weight of his gaze on the young man and his eyes widened imperceptibly as he, in turn, took in the coat, the sword, and the youth of the man.

"The Marquis de Lafayette," said the captain of the guard.

"Please allow me to introduce my ... self," said the young man, "as our titles are not easy on the ears of a young republic. I am Marie Joseph Paul Yves Roch Gilbert du Motier. In France I am the marquis, it is true, but here, I think not, yes? So I will be just Mr. Gilbert du Motier."

He bowed to them all, managing in a single bow to include every man present but show his deepest respect to Washington.

Washington returned the bow. "How may I serve you, Marquis?"

The young man smiled again, a wonderful smile. "But it is I who seek to serve you!" He drew his sword in a flourish and handed it to Washington hilt first with a bow. He moved with more grace in the instant of that bow than any of them had ever seen, but then, none of Washington's staff had seen a Versailles-trained aristocrat before.

Washington watched him with surprise. Other Frenchmen had been theatrical, but despite the theatrical presentation of the sword, no one present could resent it. Perhaps the other aspirants hadn't smiled quite as well. He touched the beautiful sword hilt and leaned forward.

"Why do you seek to serve with us, Marquis? I understand you have arranged to be appointed a major general. Do you know how rare that rank is here?"

The smile never faltered. "The rank, it is nothing," he said. "Liberty now has a country, and I am here to serve her."

Washington was moved by the young man's frankness, but his experience had made him wary. Washington waved the sword away.

"Then serve her, not me. I am not a king, or emperor, to take your sword." He looked away, trying to hide that he was moved. "Do you have any military experience?" he asked.

"None that would apply in a young republic, Monsieur le general," he said. "I have been an officer, it is true. I commanded a troop in the Mousquetaires Gris de la Maison du Roi until they were, as you say it, taken from the establishment. I was second in command of an *esquadrille* in the regiment of my father-in-law, the Comte de Noailles."

Hamilton nodded to Johnson and bent over him. "A guards unit. Very prestigious." Johnson nodded.

"And then?"

"Nothing, General. I have never seen action, nor commanded more than two hundred men. But I am afire for liberty, and I have brought equipment and money. I will buy you shoes, if that is the only way I can be of service. I am not poor. I require no pay, no special allowance, nothing. I ask only to serve you with my sword and my heart's blood."

The marquis had them all spellbound, and obscurely, Washington wished he had Martha by him to tell him what to think of a man who exuded so much charm, such palpable enthusiasm. Behind the young marquis, he saw his guard captain, Caleb Gibbs, make a motion and the door opened a little.

"Please take a seat, Marquis," he said. All his aides found themselves chairs, and the marquis sank into one with enviable grace. Most of the men felt a little dirty just looking at him in his perfectly tailored clothes, his sparkling white stock and cuffs. Hamilton couldn't resist the urge to look at his own shirt cuffs and, having inspected them, to hide them under his coat.

"Lieutenant Lake of the Third Virginia," said Captain Gibbs.

Lieutenant Lake couldn't have presented a greater contrast to the figure in the chair. His blue coat had faded to a color closer to the color of mud, and his linen was, despite his best efforts, dirty everywhere it showed. A long visible thread at his cuff indicated that the fabric was losing its edging. He wore a captured Hessian sword with the blade cut short, and he carried a plain Charleville musket with the bayonet affixed. He stood straight as an arrow, anything but at his ease, and waited for his doom. It was clear from his demeanor that he expected the worst.

"Lieutenant Lake, I have never had the chance to convey my compliments for the dashing way in which I saw you take the guns in King Street at Trenton." Washington seldom had the time to compliment his officers. In fact, a lifetime of experience warned him against it. Compliments often ruined the young, he thought, but then he had an unaccustomed thought of Braddock, who had been quite free with praise.

George Lake swelled to almost twice his former size. "Thankee, General."

"I understand that you are becoming a fine officer. I thought that as this was your first day as officer of the day for our section of the camp, I would take the opportunity to thank you."

Lake was too moved, and too awestruck, to speak.

The marquis shot from his chair and grabbed him by the hand with both of his.

"This is the genuine hero!" he said, bowing and clasping Lake's hand. Lake seemed to see him for the first time.

"The Marquis de Lafayette," said Hamilton into the silence, trying to introduce the two from a distance of twenty feet.

"A pleasure, Marquis," Lake croaked out. On balance, he thought facing the Hessians again would be easier than this sort of thing.

"Please, monsieur, the pleasure is all mine. You have been a soldier a long time?"

Lake bowed a little, as he had seen the gentry do whenever they spoke civilly to one another, and nodded. "Just two years, sir. Marquis."

The marquis nodded enthusiastically. "It is the same with me, except that I have never taken a Hessian gun. Two years, General, and he is an officer of merit. I will give him my sword"—he suited the action to the word—"and carry a musket for two years until I have performed such a deed."

George Lake found himself holding a sword that must have cost the value of every furnishing in his whole town. The dogs' heads at the ends of the quillons had most amiable expressions.

Washington watched him with astonishment. Hamilton eyed the sword with something like lust.

"Marquis, I think perhaps we can find you a place. May I leave that to you gentlemen?" He turned to Fitzgerald and Johnson. They nodded, bowed deeply to the young man.

George Lake didn't want to keep the sword, worried that he'd do it a mischief. "Please, sir, Marquis. You'll be wanting this."

Lafayette bowed to him. "I give it to you. Perhaps we trade, yes? I have always wanted a Hessian sword like that, and to have it from such a hand as yours makes it beyond price."

"I could never take this," said George Lake.

Hamilton took his arm. "Lieutenant, I think you must." He smiled and tried to wipe the envy from his mind. "See that you take care of it."

"Lord, yes," breathed Lake.

✯ ✯ ✯

"I was struck by his grace," said Washington as he rode down the main street of Philadelphia. Several people called after them, or cheered—a pleasant change from a year before.

"If I may be so bold, sir, I was struck by the handsome way he gave young Lake his sword. Lake's never seen such a thing in his life, and now he owns it."

Washington bowed to acknowledge a group of delegates on a corner and rode on.

"Yes," he said finally, after Hamilton thought the moment had passed. "Yes, he won me there. I wanted to see how he'd play to one of our rankers. And he played up like trumps, I thought."

"Certainly was a lovely sword, General."

Washington was silent again for a while and then he said, "It was the kind of thing our government ought to do. In England they'd give a man a sword with an inscription. Handsomely." He shook his head. "Another thing to organize. Some sort of society for the officers, when the war is won."

Hamilton followed with that last ringing in his ears, because Washington never predicted and seldom bragged. *When the war is won.*

Later, after Billy had taken his coat and pressed a fresh stock and put him in his nightshirt, Washington was reviewing the temerity of his comment when Billy spoke out, a rare event in itself.

"That, there, was a fine young man," he said. He was behind Washington, as he often was when he had something to say.

Washington, still thinking of the sword and the possibility of winning the war, looked around, distracted. "Who, Billy? Lieutenant Lake?"

Billy laughed musically. It was a feminine laugh for so big a man. "He seems fine enough, sir, if a little comic. No, sir, I meant the foreign gentleman."

"Ah, Lafayette?"

"Yes, sir! I liked him directly. An' I thought a funny thing, sir. Which I wanted to say, if allowed."

"Go ahead, Billy. There's never been secrets between us two."

"He's like your son, sir. If'n you had one."

✯ ✯ ✯

As he was on duty for the staff that day, Lake was sporting his best clothes, worn though they were. They had been new when the twelve guineas had been paid over, but constant service had already ruined the two new shirts, and the smallclothes were dull with dirt. The new sword and its beautiful belt of red silk and gold lace looked odd against his stained waistcoat, and he covered the magnificence of the belt with his sash during the rest of his duty.

When he was done, he borrowed a clothes brush from one of the servants at headquarters and gave himself a good brushing, and then took himself to the fine brick house near the City Tavern to pay his respects. He told himself that he owed it to the lady of the house to thank her for her help in selling his plunder.

A pretty Irish girl opened the door and made a curtsy to him, an unaccustomed politeness. He smiled back.

"Lieutenant Lake to see Mrs. Lovell," he said, and she showed him into the hall. She gave a sniff when she got a better look at his clothes, and his spirits plummeted.

She vanished and was replaced a few moments later by a middle-aged man rather run to fat, dressed in resplendent black wool with fancy buckled shoes. George bowed and the man returned it very civilly.

"It is not often that one of Mr. Washington's officers graces me with his attentions."

George was not familiar enough with civil society to know what to make of this apparent raillery, nor to know how to deal with a man to whom he had not been introduced. He bowed again. "I had hoped—"

"To see my wife? She's in the drawing room, where I'll escort you. Damn, don't they feed you in the Continental Army? I'm Silas Lovell, by the way. And I remain loyal to my king."

George was somewhat taken aback by the last declaration and indeed was feeling quashed by the whole experience, so that when he entered the parlor he missed Betsy altogether. He made a small bow to Mrs. Lovell, sitting by the fire in a wingback chair.

"Your servant, ma'am,"

"George Lake. Goodness, sir, have a seat. Mary, put a cloth on that chair. Lieutenant Lake, your breeches are too . . . filthy to be intimate with my furniture."

George sat hesitantly and realized that Betsy was behind her mother, smiling at him where her parents couldn't see her.

"I called to thank you for your kindness in sending me to Dodd's, ma'am."

"I thought he might serve you. But you might have bought some new clothes."

"These are new, ma'am. Or were."

Silas Lovell laughed. "Dear heart, the army of Congress has no money, no clothes, and no food. Mr. Lake is doing the best he can by us, I'm sure. Look at the quality of the sword he's wearing!" He leaned over. "May I see it, sir?"

"With pleasure." George hadn't had it out of the scabbard since he had buckled it on. His reasons were superstitious. He still didn't feel it was really his. He drew it and handed it to Mr. Lovell.

"Superb. French, I think. Yes, a Klingenthal. There is the mark. My goodness, sir, that must be worth a pretty penny. My wife said you were poor?"

"I am, sir." He didn't want to say that it had just been given to him. He'd sound like a beggar or a braggart.

"And you aren't afraid of being marked a Tory by visiting this house?"

"I care little for politics, sir, except that I'm a Patriot and I stand for Congress. But if every man cannot have his say, then there is little point in having liberty."

Mr. Lovell turned slowly, his eyes kindled. "That's a form of sense I haven't heard often in your camp. In this city, we've heard more insistence that every man must love Congress or be a traitor."

George nodded. "I hear plenty of that, too."

Mr. Lovell looked at him. "Come, don't you want to call me a traitor? I'm country born and bred, and loyal to the king."

"Silas! Stop picking a fight. This boy is too well bred to meet you in an argument in your own home."

George wanted to laugh aloud at the notion that he was well bred.

Mr. Lovell waved the sword in his hand. "I'm sorry, sir. I am so used to this ignorant argument: that I'm a traitor because I stay loyal to my king and his government, and that these men who have overthrown all I hold dear are *patriots*."

George rose. Betsy looked unhappy and George knew he would not come off well from any encounter with Mr. Lovell about politics.

"I should take my leave," he said.

Mr. Lovell lowered the sword and smiled warmly. "No, no. I shall apologize for my warmth. Here is your sword. We will sit to supper in a few moments and I hope you will join us. Indeed, I'll support Mr. Washington's army to the cost of a shirt, if my daughter will fetch one from my things. I was not always this gargantuan size, sir."

"I couldn't..."

"I insist. Go change your shirt and join us for dinner."

The dinner was better than anything he had enjoyed in months, and the china dishes and silver were finer than anything he had eaten from in his life, but neither made as great an impression on him as an hour of Betsy's company. Her gaze, under lowered lids, flicked across his with a flirtation he found both frightening and pleasing. She was older than he had thought, perhaps seventeen. She spoke twice, both times at her mother's prompting, and it seemed that she spoke directly to him. When the ladies left the room after dinner, it felt empty. He had a pipe with Mr. Lovell, and then insisted that he had to go or be late passing the lines at camp. Mr. Lovell breathed smoke out through his nose and nodded.

"I'll see that a boy with a lamp escorts you, then. Please forgive me for my illiberal attacks on Congress, Mr. Lake. It isn't often I am allowed to speak freely, and even now I dread that you'll report me to some officer."

"I'm sorry you think I have the look of an informer," said George, rankled. "I care nothing for your politics. I believe every man should speak his mind. But I'll fight for my cause and not apologize for it."

Mr. Lovell had taken a little wine and more sherry. He was not angry at George Lake but he was angry, and the two became mixed. "Fine, then. You've had my hospitality. You've ogled my daughter, who's to be wed in the spring. Now be gone."

Wed in the spring. George bowed and choked out a refusal of the loan of a boy with a lantern. He couldn't be angry at Mr. Lovell, who was clearly a little drunk. And he barely knew the girl. But it stuck with him, and he had a long walk back to camp in the dark.

Chapter Seventeen

The summer seemed to pass away on transports. After their raid into the Jerseys, they were back in New York for a month, and then they marched to Sandy Hook and loaded onto boats to be carried out to the waiting ships. Caesar was struck by how few of the Guides had been in boats. It seemed so little time since they had gone ashore in Virginia, but they had been Ethiopians then and there were only a handful left from last year.

The transports left Sandy Hook and New York and sailed down the coast, then into the Chesapeake Bay. The long, low headlands and the long strips of beach reminded Caesar of his first arrival here. He wondered what might have happened to King, or Queeny, or any of the other blacks he had met in his previous life as a slave. The time before the swamp had a dreamlike quality to it, so that he almost doubted whether it had happened. He stayed on deck for hours, watching the low coast go by. No one joined him but Jim, who kept him silent company. He didn't share his thoughts, but they were gloomy, ruminations on his life as a slave. The longer the war went on, the more he dreaded a return to that condition.

The fleet was the largest company of ships Caesar had ever seen, and they filled the bay from horizon to horizon. On calm days, they were like an extension of the forest from the land, bare poles like dead trees as far as he could see. When the breeze served, though, it was a sight to lift the heart, with shining white sails set in graceful curves all around him. That sight seemed to be the physical expression of the power of the British Empire, her navy and transports of soldiers all laid out for his view. Surrounded by such power, Caesar couldn't believe that his freedom was imperiled. They would win the war and be free. He hid his doubts from his men, all except Virgil, whose doubts were deeper and more like fears.

The voyage seemed to last forever, so that the men grew used to naval rations and endless free time. They sewed and played cards, used up their tobacco and gambled for more from the sailors. Their uniforms improved from the sewing, and Caesar used the time and the cramped space on the brig to best effect, drilling the men in the repetitive line drills that were too often ignored in the hurry of campaign and daily labor. He had to drill them a squad at a time because of the small deck, but this had one bene-fit, that he got to know every man and watch the performance of every corporal. By the time the fleet finally moved all the way up to Head of Elk, the anchorage at the entrance to the Susquehanna River, his men were the best drilled they had ever been. Even the new recruits were passable soldiers.

The landing was difficult. According to the first reports, the enemy had not wholly fallen for the ruse of an attack in the Jerseys and was wait-ing with considerable troops to face the landing in their rear. The Guides were among the first troops to be sent ashore, and Caesar was directed to send two men, Jim Somerset and another of his choice, to scout to the north and east and discover the location of the enemy. Jim took Moses and three days' rations, and moved off too quickly for good-byes.

They moved the camp twice in the next two days, the advance guard feeling its way along small roads, just one cart track wide, that wound be-tween rail fences over the rolling hills. The towns were small but prosper-ous, and the farms were larger than those in New Jersey, with solid stone houses and silent farmers. There were few blacks here and almost no slaves. The Quakers and Mennonites who made up the bulk of the countryside population didn't hold with slavery. They didn't hold much with the British army, either.

The third day, Caesar's men were well out in advance of the army. Shortly after noon, Caesar found himself in the yard of a small farm with less than half of one platoon. The rest were scattered. His company was spread along several miles of roads, providing guides for the light infantry behind them while exploring the country. They had no contact with enemy troops beyond a handful of militia whom they sighted just after first light and chased across a field of tobacco. Caesar broke off the pursuit rather than lose what little organization his company still had.

A party of dragoons came up in late afternoon and told him that Captain Stewart's company was coming along behind them, collecting his guides as they came, and that his post would be relieved shortly. The officer of the dragoons wanted to press forward to look at the road north to Kennett's Square, on the main road to Philadelphia.

"We chased some militia going that way," Caesar said.

The dragoon sergeant looked at his officer. "How many were they?"

"Just half a dozen, but they came from the north, too. I wouldn't want to go past those woods with horse. Not at dusk, when we can't see to support you." Caesar tried to indicate the small size of his force in the yard without appearing to shirk his duties.

The officer sneered. "I can't imagine we'd need your support anyway," he said. He meant it to be an insult. He was the kind of officer Caesar liked least.

"I think we should be looking for a place to camp," said the sergeant. "We just passed an empty farm, sir. We can press on in the morning."

The officer beat his crop impatiently against his boot. He wanted to make trouble. Caesar willed himself to remain still. The officer represented the type of man who reminded Caesar every day that he was a different color and a different kind.

"Without decent infantry, I suppose it would be an error to go forward," he said, the insult plain. His sergeant shook his head, just one little negative nod, as if denying any responsibility for his superior. They turned their horses and left the yard without a good-bye, and Caesar breathed out slowly. It was a beautiful evening, with an autumn sun turning the tobacco red and the wheat gold, but the evening was blighted for Caesar.

Lieutenant Crawford marched his platoon of the lights into the farm an hour before dark. He found Caesar taciturn, but he took no note of it. He was more concerned with getting his men into the dry barn and the carriage house of the farm and hearing Caesar's report. Most of the rest of the Guides were with him. Caesar found Sergeant McDonald, and together they got billets for the other men who would straggle in later. They saw to it that fires were going and food was started, and they set pickets well out in the fields.

Just as dusk was fading into full dark, they heard one of the pickets challenge and the guard stood to arms in an instant. Before Caesar could lead his quarter-guard out, though, Jim and Moses came into the farmyard, both smiling broadly and covered in dust from head to toe.

Caesar smiled in response. Their return lightened a burden he hadn't been aware he was carrying, washed away the stain of the dragoon's insults. Jim saluted smartly, bringing his musket up to the recover and then across his chest. "Sir. Corporal Somerset reporting from a scout."

Crawford motioned for him to take his ease. "What do you have, Corporal?"

"Rebels all over the place on the other side of the Brandywine. Big camp, and a lot of patrols. I can show you better in the light."

"How far off is the Brandywine?"

"Just a few miles. Maybe six. There's a good crossing on this road, called Chad's Ford. That's where their outposts are. There's a crossing every mile up the creek. The stream is too deep for artillery, but we crossed it three or four times in different spots. Gets deeper as you go south. Ain't nothing a few miles north of Chad's Ford."

Caesar, Crawford, McDonald, and a crowd of other noncommissioned officers listened to Somerset's report with growing apprehension.

"They ain't far off," said Virgil. Most of the men felt they could speak freely around Crawford.

"That must have been one of their patrols we brushed today," said Caesar. "I hoped they were just militia going to a muster."

Crawford motioned to Sergeant McDonald. "Better get Corporal Somerset back to headquarters as fast as you can," he said.

"We need to double our pickets and get these fires hidden as quick as we can," said Caesar. As the group broke up, Caesar could see that Jim wanted to say something to him. They walked out of the firelight and around behind the barn. The wind was cold.

"Something else?" Caesar was worried about his pickets.

"I don' know, Caesar. It's for you to say."

"Tell me, then."

"I saw Marcus White on the Lancaster Road."

Caesar tried to digest that. "What did he say?"

"I didn't speak to him. Moses an' me were hid in some trees, watching the road and having a bite. Lancaster Road's north of the rebels, maybe ten miles north o' here."

"Sure it was him, Jim?"

"Sure as death, sir."

"Keep that to yourself."

"Somebody sold us to them rebels in New Jersey. We all knows it."

"Jim, just keep it to yourself." Caesar felt like he had been hit in the head. He sent Jim off to get a hot meal while he tried to understand this bit of news. He couldn't see a way it could be good. When last he had seen Marcus White, the man had been in a church in New York. He had no business, at least no honest business, so close to the rebel lines. But the pickets had to be set, and the army was clearly going to fight in the morning. It would have to wait.

In an hour, Somerset was off to the rear with a pass and Sergeant Shaw of the lights to keep him safe from their own patrols. Caesar made the rounds with Lieutenant Crawford, who was taking more direct interest in the running of the company, and Sergeant McDonald, who was still teaching Caesar the details of a really well-run company. They looked into mess kettles and inspected the fires of every section. Most sections were gorging themselves on three days' rations in a single day. Improvident as this might seem, it gave the advance troops less to carry when they actually made contact with the enemy.

Virgil was taking his ease and smoking while his mess group cooked their second meal. They all showed signs of the consumption of a half-pound each of peas and about the same in salt pork, and none of their overshirts would have borne even the most cursory inspection for cleanliness. They were grumbling happily in the cool evening air despite the lack of tents. The army's baggage was far away, near Head of Elk, and the light troops in the vanguard had had to build hasty shelters from fences and brush. In fact, there was no longer a decent split-rail fence within a mile of the British lines. Everyone used them to construct shelters, and veterans saw them as a ready-made source of dry firewood as well. Fires were springing up across the fields to the south as the army came up behind them. Before the darkness was very old, the wheat and tobacco were trampled for a mile around them.

He sat for a moment on a stump, making entries in his daybook by the light of a lantern. Constant attendance on his reading, first with Sergeant Peters and later with Marcus White, had ensured that he could read quickly and accurately. His writing still lagged a bit behind, and sums were nearly alien.

McDonald came up behind him and read his report over his shoulder. "Very pretty, Julius," he said, kneeling next to Caesar.

"Writing's getting better, anyway." Caesar didn't look up, trying to reckon the value of Private Paget's lost neck stock and trying to remember what last name he had assigned the man. *Edgerton?* That sounded likely. Naming was a dangerous thing, and sometimes men resented the names he gave them. Sometimes it was better coming from the Reverend White, or even from Mr. Crawford or Captain Stewart. Yes, he had it in the book. Paget was Paget Edgerton. It seemed like a good, loyal name.

McDonald took out his daily report and began to run down it, looking at Caesar's as he went.

"Does anyone actually read these?" asked Caesar, trying to work out the "off reckoning" due his soldiers for "lying without fodder" a second night in a row.

"For certain sure, young Caesar. And it should comfort you to know that when your namesake was a pup, centurions were scratching away with their pencils to try to list every item missing and get every man his pay."

"Can I borrow that little book?"

McDonald looked at him with mock indignation. "I presume you mean my little bible on pay and provision?" He took a slim volume from his pocket, worn and stained, entitled *Treatise on Military Finance*, and Caesar skipped directly to the tables at the back of the book and began to reckon the pay due each private. Sometimes he excused men lost gear just to save the trouble of the additional math of deducting lost items from their pay.

"That's a shilling, Julius, not a penny." Jeremy was standing at his shoulder as he added.

"You don't all have to watch me." A little flare of temper, because he thought that they were waiting for him to fail.

Crawford, who had been listening to a tale told by a fire, wandered up and looked over Caesar's shoulder. "Heavens, Sergeant! Time for that after we fight."

"No, sir," said Caesar with a hint of sullenness. "If we lose men dead, then it'll be harder to get their pay for their relatives if I don't do this tonight." He looked at McDonald.

McDonald nodded and turned to Crawford. "Always get the pay straight before an action, that was my first sergeant major's advice, sir, an' I have taught Julius Caesar the same way."

Crawford looked around at them and shrugged. McDonald and Caesar exchanged a glance. He'd learn.

Most of the men went to sleep as soon as their bellies were filled, but, as they all expected a major action the next day, more than a few found themselves unable to sleep and began to talk. Every fire in the army had its share of men, nervous or quiet or shrill, telling tales of battles past. There were veterans in that army who could remember great days in the field, and disasters, at famous places like Minden and Quebec, or smaller actions across Europe, along the shores of the Mediterranean or on the soil of America. Older men, sergeants and officers, could remember battles as far back as the frigid dawn at Culloden, and some camps featured men who had served on both sides of that battle. Wherever men abandoned sleep for talk, the fires coaxed out the stories until the camp was awash in remembered blood and terror and glory.

When his accounts were cast and sealed ready for inspection, Caesar lay down at the fire his own squad had, with Virgil and Paget and their section. The old veterans from Virginia were spread thin now. With Jim's promotion to corporal, all the survivors of the swamp were in positions of leadership.

Virgil was whistling softly, sharpening a knife that didn't need any more sharpening. He had already patched shirts for every man in the squad and resewn several other items. He never slept before an action. Caesar knew that Virgil hated actions as much as he himself enjoyed them, and he wondered why. Virgil was no coward, but there was something to the thought of battle he dreaded, dreaded so much that he never told war stories or relived their battles, although he had fought well in every one since they killed the overseer together. Caesar rubbed the scars over his eyes, remembering. He smiled a little, then went to sleep. Virgil looked at him as he started to snore, kicked him lightly, and went back to his knife.

"Keep us safe, Caesar," Virgil said softly.

Chad's Ford, Pennsylvania, September 11, 1777

For George Lake, it was a frustrating day. The Third Virginia stood in neat ranks or lay in the shade, depending on the emotional state of General Greene's staff. Riders crossed in front of them again and again on their way to General Greene or General Washington. Rumor after rumor came down the ranks to the light company—they were to fight at Chad's Ford; the enemy was marching to flank them up the river; the enemy was concentrating in front of them; they were to attack; they were to patrol across the stream.

The last had proven true, and George had followed Captain Heller across the stream, where they immediately encountered strong enemy patrols supporting the big guns that were exchanging rounds with the Continental artillery posted on the opposite bank. They made it across in relative safety and moved up a small creek, only to find that green-coated Loyalists covered the approach. A skirmish developed that George felt they couldn't win; the enemy fire became brisker as more and more of the green-coated men came up, and their fire slackened as their men sought cover. It was vicious, with men hunting each other from tree to tree and bush to bush all along the little creek, with no quarter asked or given. George had lost sight of his captain in the first moments and now took several chances that would have given his mother great unease as he sought the man along the creekbed, moving from one knot of his men to another. He wanted them to withdraw but lacked the authority to say it.

He lost his helmet to an enemy shot that took it clean off his head and landed it in the middle of the creek. He left it there. While he would expose himself for the cause, he wouldn't do it just to retrieve the damn helmet.

Sergeant Creese was at the outlet of the stream with a party of wounded he was shuttling back to the regiment. He hadn't seen the captain either but concurred that they were outnumbered and in a bad case.

"Shall I go ask Colonel Weedon, sir?" he said, clearly eager to get free of the creek.

"If we wait for you to go to the colonel and get back, we'll all be dead, Sergeant." George raised his head and looked up the creekbed. It was hot, and his coat was soaked with sweat. He was glad his hat was gone, although the flies were dogging him. He wished he didn't have to make this decision. He liked being junior and invisible, and he could see that every man around Creese was now depending on him to do the right thing, to save them all, or whatever they pleased. He wished he knew just what the captain's orders had been. He felt overcome with worry, and then he saw some bluecoats a hundred paces or more away, hauling a four-pounder.

"Sergeant Lilly!" he called, as loud as he could. He heard an answering shout.

"Withdraw! Bring your platoon back through Sergeant Creese's! Second Platoon, stand fast and cover them!"

Lord, his voice was hoarse. When had he done all the shouting? He watched the enemy bullets skip along the water of the creek and thought how nice it might be to just lie down in the cold, clear water. There might be trout in such a cold stream. He'd eaten trout on Long Island and liked them. He thought about Betsy Lovell, and her secret glances at dinner, and he smiled despite his current situation. He had developed the habit of thinking of Betsy when things were low.

He shook his head clear of such notions and splashed some water on his face and then grabbed one of Creese's corporals.

"Get over the Brandywine, find that battery commander right there, and get him to fire grape! Right away. Tell him where we are and that we're hard-pressed by these greencoats. He'll understand."

The man looked intelligent and calm, which was better than he could have expected. He saluted smartly and threw himself across the stream, and Lake watched him until he was up the bank and clear.

The presentiment of disaster had been greater than the reality. Lilly's platoon was pretty healthy as it fell back, and the whole company was still game, although there were men missing in several files. He held them at the edge of the west bank, willing the corporal to get the message across, and his dreams were answered by two loud bangs almost over his head. He heard one of the Tories yelling at his men to lie down, and he waved his men back to the Continental bank of the ford. As soon as they were across, he got them up the bank and fell them in again behind the first good cover so he could count heads. They had lost five men, including the captain and the trumpeter. No one seemed to know where they had gone.

Lake took his men back to the regiment and then left them under Sergeant Lilly while he went to make his report. It was two o'clock.

★　★　★

After a day of slow marches and an age while they waited for other units to cross the Brandywine, and after mistakes of their own as guides that raised tempers all along the column, they were now marching back to the sound of the firing. They had made the long march and they were around the enemy's flank, but the question remained as to whether they would arrive in time to do any good. However, they had begun to move faster and faster, and now Caesar had to keep his men from trotting.

They could hear the guns all day, but they were off to the south and Caesar wasn't sure how they could be part of the same battle. He knew the general plan of movement, because he had been privileged to hear it explained by Colonel Musgrave in the predawn chill by the embers of their last fire. He knew their column was intended to pass the northern posts of the rebel army and swing well into their rear before coming down on them, a crushing blow, as described.

What he did understand was that it was all taking longer than the generals had expected, and that most of the officers and sergeants who had been around him in the dark, listening to the plan, had suspected this very problem. They would be late, and for all they knew, Lord Howe was trying to defend Chad's Ford with a handful of men while they picked their way through the maze of tracks and minor roads north of the rebel positions.

Jeremy and Stewart came up on horseback as they came to a bend in the road. Just beyond, he could see a vista of open ground, farmland, and a plowed hill with some woods in front of it. There were Continental regulars all along the line in front of them.

Stewart watched the line in disgust. Jeremy threw his hat on the ground and then had to dismount to fetch it, which made him angrier.

Caesar grabbed their bridles and pulled them back before Stewart's bright red coat could be seen.

"Go back and tell the column to halt," said Stewart, taking his glass from Jeremy and dismounting. He handed his horse to Caesar, who handed it directly to one of his men and followed him into a stand of trees that shaded the corner of a stone-walled field.

Stewart lay down behind the wall, worked a stone loose, and pushed his glass through. Caesar crouched behind him.

"It appears we are too late," he said. Behind them, Virgil was all but physically restraining a party of red-coated officers who wanted to go ahead into the field. Sergeant McDonald and Lieutenant Crawford came up, and then several other officers from their battalion. The staff officers were kept back.

Caesar could see the Continental troops start to move. Every one of them lying in the corner of the field took a breath together as the long blue and brown lines suddenly began to form columns on their center or rightmost companies and march away. It wasn't well done; every battalion seemed to have its own manner of forming a column, and the enemy brigades were slow to move.

"Appearances can be deceiving," Stewart announced, closing his glass with a snap. "Apparently our country cousins are determined to snatch defeat from the jaws of victory." He ran back to the knot of mounted officers around the bend and reported what he had seen, and the general ordered them forward. It was just past three o'clock by Jeremy's repeater. And the enemy, perfectly positioned to stop their thrust, was marching away.

★ ★ ★

Lafayette reined in his horse by George Lake and looked over George's company. He had an air about him that made other men want to follow him, although he was as young as their youngest man. He *looked* like an officer, and he was well equipped and so well uniformed that he made most of the other officers look shabby. Certainly George Lake, whose only claim to elegance was the superb sword that hung from a double frog at his waist, had no business standing next to the marquis's horse.

"Monsieur," said the young marquis companionably. "Can you direct me to the General Greene?"

"Yes, sir. General Greene is just there at the head of the road. What's happening?" George had seen the fine marquis often enough since their first meeting to qualify as an acquaintance.

Lafayette shook his head. "Our General Sullivan has allowed himself to be flanked again. I gather he does this with some regularity?"

George nodded, remembering Long Island and the painful, rainy retreat. His mouth set bitterly.

"Do not worry, George. General Washington has all General Greene's division in reserve. Sullivan need only hold until we arrive, and we shall win a victory that will end the war." He laughed. Everyone knew that he was ambitious to command a division himself and that he could be a demanding companion. But Lafayette was already well loved, not least because he always referred to the Continental cause as "ours" and "we," where so many of his French and German compatriots referred to it as "yours" and "you."

He reared his horse a little, showing away, and waved his hat.

"Get ready to advance, George!" he called, and galloped off.

Down the ranks in the old company, Bludner said something coarse, and the men around him laughed. But they did it nervously, like schoolboys.

✯ ✯ ✯

The whole battalion of lights raced across the open fields toward the copse at the foot of the little plowed hill in front of them. It was a disciplined run, but they had all dropped their packs at the stone wall and none of them expected to cross so much open ground without a great many casualties. Caesar's men started a little in front, because he had put them there where their brown coats would lie unnoticed in the autumn fields. And they ran a little faster.

They were a quarter of the way there and not a shot had been fired at them. It didn't seem possible, and Caesar had to force himself to look up at the woods rather than down at his feet. If he was about to take a volley, it seemed better that he not know it was coming.

That was not proper thinking for a soldier. He looked up and almost stopped in astonishment. He was watching the better part of a battalion *leaving* the woods and falling back. He couldn't reckon why, and feared a trap, one so cunning that its purpose would be hidden from him or Captain Stewart or even Lord Howe.

More than halfway now. Some of the newer men were panting with exertion. The veterans were running easily. One or two held their weapons high, ready to take a shot the moment a target was offered. Most ran with their muskets across their bodies. Stewart's company was close behind, and the other lights were almost up with them on both sides. Well off to the left, he could see Captain Simcoe and the Fortieth Grenadiers moving along. Simcoe stood out because of his heavy gray horse.

Caesar knew he had slowed unconsciously when he had seen movement in the wood, and the whole company had slowed with him.

Captain Stewart rode up to him. Jeremy was nowhere to be seen.

"I...think...they're...leaving...the wood," Caesar said in time to his pounding feet.

"Get into it and start shooting. Make as much noise as you can. Make them watch us and not what's coming behind us."

Caesar raised his musket in salute and Stewart took off his cap for a moment, and then rode off.

Now he was close enough to start looking for a route in. Usually a wood was densest at the outside edge, where the sun had full play and the brush could grow thickly. Most woodlots had little paths, and this one was no exception. Caesar still expected to be met by a volley any second, and he looked at the company. They were well spaced out in extended order, each file pair two paces separate from the next, across sixty paces, or almost a third of the front of the wood.

He knew they were all loaded. He knew that speed was all that mattered. He blew his whistle twice and yelled, "Charge!" And they gave another spurt of speed, and were into the trees with a crash.

☆　☆　☆

George began to think that they were going to run the whole way to wherever the British might be. The column moved too fast, so that the men got spread out and some had to fall out or fall behind, where the stragglers got mixed into unfamiliar units and wrecked their order of march. Despite all that, they were marching faster than George had ever marched, and they were moving toward the musketry.

Despite their desperate skirmish in the early afternoon, the men were acting as if they had plenty of heart. George had stopped wondering where his captain was. The man was plainly dead, or captured. Now George wondered if he could command the company in action by himself. He was about to find out.

☆　☆　☆

The woods were empty of all but a terrified picket who fired once and fled without causing a casualty. Caesar leapt over some fallen trees and hurried to the side of the wood facing the enemy, who were formed a little over one hundred paces away.

"Keep your order, then!" he yelled. "Come up to me and To Tree!" To Tree was the British army's innovative manner of getting soldiers who were trained to linear warfare to take cover in a wood. The Company of Black Guides had something of the opposite problem, as they generally had a tendency to take cover if cover was offered, whether ordered to or not. They all but vanished into the tree line.

Caesar blew one long note on his whistle. He shouted "Skirmish" at the full reach of his lungs, and all along the line, the file leaders picked targets and began to fire at the Continentals. Stewart's company was already taking the ground to their right, and the light company of the Fortieth had just appeared on their left and was moving into the tree line. Caesar waved at Virgil and Fowver, standing together at the left end of the line. Fowver nodded, saw that Caesar was going for new orders, and moved to take command.

Caesar ran back to the rear of the wood and then along behind it, looking for Captain Stewart or their battalion officer, Major Manley. He saw two horses grazing, but neither was familiar. He ran along the edge of the wood until he reached its southern boundary and there he found all the officers, gathered in a clump and watching the great spectacle of battle laid out by the wood's height.

Caesar was a veteran now, and he had never seen a battle laid out so clearly. The British columns were coming up from the rear and just starting to form their front, first companies forming battalions, and then battalions forming brigades even as he watched.

Across the field and up the low hill, the rebel lines were formed but constantly twitching, or so it appeared at this distance. Caesar knew that the twitches meant they were moving, making little corrections to best occupy their ground. Such maneuvers were common on parade, but most armies in the field depended on the noncommissioned officers knowing the axis of attack and keeping a couple of natural objects, say a flower and a fence post, aligned in front of them to keep the line marching in the right direction. Most commanders left gaps in their lines so that miscalculations in marching by battalions didn't throw off the whole line. The Continental line was clearly in disarray, packed too tight and trying to maneuver in the face of the enemy. And now the Guides and all the other troops in the wood were starting to get hits, causing more confusion.

Far distant, back toward the direction of Chad's Ford, he could see a column of marching men, and in the foreground he saw one Continental brigade intermixed with another and trying to sort itself out. Almost opposite the wood, a battery of Continental guns, masked from the wood by a little hill and sited in a dip, had begun to fire into the forming British line.

Simcoe was closest to him, and he pointed his riding crop along the distant road from which the enemy column was coming.

"That's their reserve, Caesar. We must break General Sullivan in front of us before Mr. Washington can bring all *that*"—he waved his crop at the marching column—"into the fight and stop us."

"Very kind, sir," said Caesar, and he meant it. Officers seldom took the time to explain anything.

Stewart rounded on him. "Seen Jeremy?"

"No, sir."

"Keep shooting. As soon as they start to break, get at them. Wait for Major Manley's call, though. He'll be behind the wood. I'll be there in a moment."

The Continental battery fired, almost together, and an entire company of the Seventeenth Regiment seemed to disappear. Caesar was appalled by the carnage a single battery of guns could wreak. None of the men in that company would ever have had a chance to stop it.

A British battery moved ponderously forward, its hired drivers unwilling to get too close to the action. When at extreme range, the gunners had to drag their guns forward on ropes, and they did it with élan. Caesar didn't have time to watch, and when the Continental battery fired again, he wasn't there to see the execution it wrought.

✫ ✫ ✫

Washington was well ahead of Greene's column now. Too late, he fully understood the confusing welter of messages that had reached him all day. He *should* have attacked across the ford when he felt that Lord Howe lacked the men to stop him. He could have ended the war in an afternoon, and even now he felt that victory was close. If only Sullivan could hold the hill and the wood to their front, Greene's men would arrive and even have time to breathe a few times before Washington sent them into the teeth of the British advance.

He looked at his watch. It was half-past five, and before his unbelieving eyes, the troops in the wood began to leave it and march back. In moments, the whole edge of the wood erupted in a flame as the British, advancing along an axis that allowed them to use the wood to cover their entire force, took the wood and used them.

He rode forward to Sullivan, who was shaking his head in weary disbelief. "I'm sorry, General."

"Nonsense, General Sullivan. You've held together nicely. But tell me why we've just given the British that little wood to your front."

"No help for it, sir. I had to make my line straight or the whole of the British attack would have fallen on the kink and broken me. Marshall and Woodford misunderstood and gave up the wood, and by the time I tried to fix it..." He shook his head wearily. "I've just ordered them to take it back," he said, all too aware of what that meant.

Greene's men were twenty minutes away. Washington watched as the British fire began to decimate the regiments moving over the open ground to the wood that, only a few moments before, they had left.

✯ ✯ ✯

The Continentals came up the hill at them again, firing quickly like regular soldiers and then pushing forward, but this time some hint in their movement, the carriage of their heads or some little flaw in their firing, suggested to Caesar that their hearts weren't in it. Their first counterattack had almost swept the hill, and indeed, over to the right, the Continentals had gotten right in among the trees and only the reserve under Major Manley and a lightning response by McDonald and Crawford had kept them in possession. The second attack had come to a halt just in front of the Guides, so that they had exchanged three volleys with a Pennsylvania regiment at a range so close that men were hit by burning wads of tow or felt the blast of heat from every round. But the Pennsylvanians lost their colonel when he tried to lead them forward for a last charge. The Guides and their friends from the Fortieth kept their heads and kept up a steady fire, although Caesar was already finding a place for his men to run to when they broke—only to find that they were going to hold. He loved them for it, every one. It was the hardest fighting he had ever known, and the bluntest. The two forces simply bludgeoned each other at point-blank range. The Guides had the advantage of a little cover in the wood edge, although it scarcely mattered when the range was so close, and Caesar couldn't imagine how regular soldiers kept their nerve in the open under such an exchange.

The third attack died away before it ever became a serious threat, and all the sergeants in the wood were bellowing for their men to "Cease fire, damn your eyes." It was merciful to the men retreating from their third brave attempt to take the wood, and soldiers like to give each other mercy, when they can, but it wasn't mercy that kept them yelling to "Cease fire, there."

The men in the wood were almost out of ammunition.

✯ ✯ ✯

Washington sat at the top of the little plowed hill and watched Sullivan's wing begin to break up. It went down fighting, outnumbered and outfought, but not by much, and it didn't break like the militia of those early disasters. The enemy was more cautious, and the Continental artillery continued to wreak havoc on the British advance, actually stopping it once when the troops were all broken and swept away. The guns kept firing, and here and there a well-led battalion, or a company that trusted its officers more than it feared the British, held its ground and kept firing. Washington was shaking his head sadly, because Weedon's brigade, his very best troops, were just too far away to save the day. They weren't so far that he would lose his army. Darkness was coming, and darkness combined with Weedon's men would save him from a defeat like some of those around New York, but it was so close to a victory that he could almost say the word aloud in his frustration. Lafayette watched him with something like adoration.

"Let us see if we can rally Sullivan's men," said Washington. If he could buy five minutes, he could save a great deal of honor from the day. He rode down toward the Meeting House with Lafayette and his staff.

☆   ☆   ☆

Caesar watched as the line in front of him came apart, and he listened for Major Manley behind him. Most of the men were drinking water, and a few were lighting pipes. He told them not to.

"We have to be ready to advance," he said. Down the line, Crawford waved to him. He waved back.

Jeremy rode up behind him, somehow silent on a horse.

"Forward!" he yelled, as if he were the officer in command. No one doubted him. They were all used to getting Stewart's orders through Jeremy, and the long skirmish line began to move out of the wood and up the hill at last.

"We have less than three rounds a man. Where's Captain Stewart?" asked Caesar, running to keep up with Jeremy's horse. Jeremy reined in, despite being the only mounted man in the skirmish line and the clear target for any sharpshooter on the hill.

"He's arguing with some well-born fool from the staff. Manley took a ball over at the angle and now they are all uncertain about what to do."

Caesar was struck dumb.

"Captain Stewart couldn't do it, you see?" Jeremy asked. "I had to."

☆   ☆   ☆

The British attack, first sudden, and then cautious, turned sudden again. Just as Washington had a company rallied to send back to the hill-top, he saw red coats and brown appear. The men in brown coats were black, a sight that always moved him strangely. He'd seen the same men before.

The final loss of the hilltop, so suddenly, was decisive. Before he could change the orders of the men he had just rallied, they melted away under his hand. Lafayette was doing no better, and it seemed that his English was deserting him. He had a sword in his hand, and he kept shouting "For liberty!"

★ ★ ★

George Lake was at the head of the column of Weedon's brigade. He could see Washington, Lafayette, and Colonel Fitzgerald on the little road at the foot of the plowed hill. Weedon was riding right next to him, urging him on, but suddenly Lake needed no coaching, and his jitters fell away.

"Form front on me!" he yelled, and the men came panting forward. His company was seventy yards ahead of the column. Washington was alone, except for his staff. Weedon was yelling something about the road, but George didn't care just then, and he yelled "At the double!" and ran the line forward.

★ ★ ★

The lights and the Guides reached the crest of the hill almost together, and saw the whole of Sullivan's broken division laid out before them, with the powerful battery of Continental guns that had been masked by the hill now almost at their feet. And just in front of them, Caesar saw Washington as clear as if they had been hunting together. He waved his hat without thinking.

★ ★ ★

Washington saw a tall man, one of the blacks, wave his hat. The man almost looked familiar, and the insolence of the gesture sparked him to anger, so that he drew his pistol and fired it, barely pausing to aim. Generals do not take direct part in major actions, unless directly threatened. Lafayette was surprised, and he took Washington's arm.

"We'd best be away, General," he said, keeping Washington from drawing his second pistol. Washington nodded, as if recovering from a blow, and turned his horse.

☆ ☆ ☆

Caesar saw the familiar arm come up with a pistol and he dropped to one knee, smoothly aimed his fowler, and fired. The second he fired he wondered a little. Washington was too much to be simply a target on the field. Caesar was confused just thinking about it. But he held his arms out and blew his whistle, running along the company and reforming them in close order.

"Don't fire on the generals. Kill the horses by those guns!" he yelled, pointing down the hill where the teams were waiting to pull the deadly Continental guns clear of the British attack. They had already performed this service several times. They had three rounds. He didn't expect his company to last long. But the guns had to go.

☆ ☆ ☆

Lafayette gave one brief scream of pain as the ball struck his leg and then stiffened in the saddle. He began to slump off, and Fitzgerald and Johnson each got an arm around him to support him. Every one of the staff saw he had just pushed his horse in front of Washington, and every one of them saw him take a ball that might have hit their general. Washington watched it unbelieving and took shelter for a moment behind Lake's company, which was just coming up.

"Fire!" yelled George Lake, and his volley fell on the Guides like a hammer, killing Tonny where he stood on the right of the company and spraying Tonny's blood over Sam the bugler. Tonny had been standing in Caesar's place. Caesar had just stepped out of the ranks to hear Captain Stewart, coming up in the twilight. Moses Shaw, proud as Lucifer of being a front-rank man on so little service, took a ball in his gut and went down with a scream that shook the whole company. A late ball, or a spent round from another volley, caught Caesar just at the edge of the hip and went on to strike his leather hunting bag, spinning him around. For a moment he thought he was gone, the blow was so hard, but then he saw the hole in the bag. He didn't have time to feel relieved. He waved Stewart away and looked at his company.

They held firm despite the casualties. There were men in brown coats on the ground all the way back to the woods, and more here. Caesar rued that he had re-formed them in close order, but only their closed ranks gave them, or any troops, the confidence to stand the weight of fire. Their efforts had already shot down most of the horses on the guns and some of the gunners. He stepped over Tonny and held up his fowler to get their attention.

"Make ready!" he yelled, and he felt them move, the rear rank stepping over to occupy the spaces between the rank in front. Their last bullets. "Present!" And the muskets came down, steady or trembling a little, but every muzzle pointed at the enemy. He had his back to the Continentals, and he could feel that they were halfway through their loading. He was prouder than ever that his men had stood a volley in the open, like regulars, and now they were going to give it back.

"FIRE."

He turned as he gave the order and watched as their fire smashed into the men in the front rank. The uniform was the familiar one of the Virginia Regiment they had faced so often, but their leather caps marked them as light infantry. Probably the best men of their regiment.

The volley snatched four or five men down, and another stayed standing for some reason but screamed, moving along the front of the company and throwing off their carefully trained motions of loading. Just to his right, the grenadiers of the Fortieth Regiment fired into them, and more men fell.

☆   ☆   ☆

George Lake took a musket ball through his biceps and was knocked flat by the impact. The whole hillside was full of enemy and he had no business taking them all on, but Washington was just behind him and he couldn't withdraw. He couldn't lie flat on his back and think it over, either.

"Make ready," he called, trying to use his good arm to rise. He ignored the temptation to stay down. On his feet, he could see that Weedon was forming the Third Virginia to his flank, so that he was the anchor next to the guns, using his company as a shield to get his line formed. The buff facings on the grenadiers just to his front were all too familiar, as he had faced them again and again, and the company of blacks were almost like old friends. He saw the tall man, the one with the scars over his eyes, just to his left despite the gathering murk, and he was tempted to bow. Lafayette had said they did such things in battles in Europe.

"Present," he yelled, wobbling a little on his feet. There was blood everywhere around him on the ground, down his side, all through the right leg of his worst breeches.

"Fire!"

Not everyone was loaded, and the volley was ragged, although game.

✮ ✮ ✮

The second volley was not aimed at them. It struck the grenadiers of the Fortieth just to their flank, and Caesar saw Captain Simcoe fall and he ran to him, forgetting his place in the line for a moment. Then he stopped himself and took a breath and looked over his shoulder for McDonald or Stewart. He saw Crawford running toward him.

"We have to get the guns!" Caesar yelled. Behind him, Fowver was giving the orders. Beyond Fowver, the Fortieth Grenadiers were preparing to avenge Simcoe.

"You get them! Get the guns! We'll cover you!" Crawford pointed at the Continentals in front of them.

Caesar thought of how brave the Guides had been, how well they had stood the fire. They were out of ammunition, tired. Caesar ran to the right of his men.

"One more time! Files from the right!" he bellowed, his ragged voice rising easily above the din of volleys and the great pounding of the big guns. "Follow me!" He saw Jeremy behind him, silhouetted against the darkening sky, and heard Stewart's voice, reassuring in the shadow, getting the regulars up and into the line. And the Guides came.

They raced the Seventeenth Lights into the battery. All the horses were gone, and though the gunners were determined, they hadn't the numbers to stop a determined plunge from the hill on their flank. Caesar fenced for a moment with the officer and then knocked him down with his musket. He yelled for his men to rally. They were on the flank of the company that had clawed them so cruelly just a moment before. He wanted to form, but the men were herding the prisoners from the battery or pursuing those who ran toward the Continental brigade forming to the rear of the position. Some were just stopped in the battery, looking blank. They were done. Taking the battery used the last of their spirit.

The light was fading fast.

✮ ✮ ✮

Washington watched the speed with which the British overran the battery and nodded. The loss of the battery sealed the day. He needed it and Weedon to turn the tide, and he had just lost one while gaining the other. He rode over to Sullivan, Greene, and Weedon, who were waiting behind the force that had become the rearguard of the army.

"In another minute we'd have had them," said Greene.

"Or they, us," said Washington. The muskets were falling silent all along the line, and the light company of the Third Virginia withdrew from the fast-forming British line without taking another volley. Somewhere in the regiment, someone jeered at the retreat, but the cry wasn't taken up.

George Lake was the last man to come from that deadly field, dragging himself by force of will. As soon as they saw how badly he was hit, dozens strove to help him.

The Continental army withdrew into the growing darkness without their guns. They had lost the battle, and with it their capital.

★ ★ ★

In the Corps of Black Guides, Caesar gathered his men and buried the dead at the edge of the woods. They stood in their ranks and took their turns to open the graves in the damp autumn ground. The loss of Tonny hit hard, as the old crew from the first days of the Ethiopians grew smaller. Sam cried, on and on, a lament of sobs that played against the rain and darkness. Tonny had been good to the boy.

Virgil smoked, and dug, and sat with Caesar in the darkness.

"Them Doodles gettin' better ever' time we meet them." He smiled, a barely visible motion around the coal of his pipe. Caesar felt numb over his whole body, from his toes to his brain. He watched Silas Van Sluyt having his turn with the pick, taking slow, measured strokes that broke the earth swiftly.

"You tired of war, Virgil?" Caesar felt light-headed.

"I was tired of war when you killed Mr. Gordon, an' that was a long time ago." He handed Caesar the lit pipe, wiping the stem companionably, and stood up, brushing the wet from his trousers. "We ain't gon' win this thing, Cese."

Caesar was silent.

"I won't be no slave again, Cese. Rather die quick, like Tonny. Most o' the t'othuh boys feel the same."

Caesar nodded. "Amen."

Jeremy rode up on a tired horse and Caesar could feel the heat coming off its flanks. It felt good. He held the horse's head while Jeremy dismounted.

"What'd captain say?" Virgil asked, extending the pipe to Jeremy. "Was he mad?"

"Captain Stewart said I might be a general yet. Some of his comments were more colorful. But taking the hill was right, and we did it right." Jeremy put his hands on his hips and looked at the burial party. He seemed on edge.

"Is that Tonny?" Jeremy handed the pipe back, his hand shaking.

"Yep." Virgil took it. "An' he has plenty o' company."

Caesar put his hand on Jeremy's shoulder. Jeremy was looking at the corpses laid out in rows, and beyond them, where the corpses of the Continental soldiers lay. Other burial parties were at work, from all the regiments engaged. Those not digging were mostly silent, and out beyond the area that had been cleared, men moaned or shrieked hoarsely from wounds that had not yet finished them.

"I killed them," Jeremy said suddenly. His voice ended on a broken note, but he still stood straight. Caesar squeezed his shoulder. He thought of saying *yes*, because that was the truth of command. And he thought of saying *no*, because that was what Jeremy needed. But in the end he simply stood with his arm around Jeremy, thinking that Washington had fired a pistol at him, and he had fired his fusil at Washington, and somehow that made them even.

Virgil smoked until the clay was done and then went back to have another turn at digging. Jeremy stayed a while, and then he stepped away and smiled a hard, forced smile.

"I guess we'll take Philadelphia now," he said.

"No way Washington can hold it." Caesar didn't watch Jeremy wipe away tears. He turned to look at the fires appearing in the dark and winced. Jeremy was on him in a second, pulling at his coat.

"You're hit," he said.

Caesar shook his head. "Nothing. Just my bag ruined," he said, but his hand brushed the tail of his coat and it was dripping wet. Other men were coming up, all around him, and he found it hard to breathe. He reached for Jeremy, and then the ground slipped away.

Schuylkill River, Pennsylvania,

September 12, 1777

The British hadn't mounted a pursuit. Washington's army, tired and beaten, ill-shod and cold, had managed to escape from the field with no further losses. He kept the army moving, as the loss at Chad's Ford meant he had to get well back before the British cut him off from his supply. Philadelphia and his nation's capital were lost.

He rode up and down the column, stopping at the wagons full of wounded to look at the men who would survive. He was hoping for news of Lafayette. The wound appeared to be slight, but until infection had passed or taken hold, any wound could be a killer.

Long after dark, past midnight and straight into the first light of morning, the exhausted army marched, until at last they crossed the ford of the Schuylkill and Washington felt them to be safe. His own light horse had already posted guides and marked the road to a new camp. He let his subordinates take command and rode off to camp.

Billy had his tent up and furnished, despite the immense labor that must have meant. He even had a small fire on a brazier and hot rum punch. Washington gave Billy his greatcoat and slumped into the biggest chair, his muddy boots still on and his spurs leaving a trail of wet leaves.

Billy put the rum in his hand and went out with the greatcoat, and didn't reappear for some time. Washington drank and thought. He savored being alone. All night, he had maintained his facade of stern discipline, a facade not so different from the real man, but in this instance, far from the emotions boiling within him. He wanted Billy to come back so that he could talk to someone.

"You fired your pistol," Billy said from the door. Washington could smell the distinctive odor of black powder being cleaned with hot water. Sulfur and rotten eggs.

"A man fired at me." Washington chose not to say that the man had been black. "He hit the marquis."

"I hope you hit him back, then. The marquis will be all right, sir. It's just a wound in the flesh of the leg, and the surgeon says it's clean."

Washington breathed deeply. "And we lost again. *I* lost again. Damn it, we were this close."

Billy had a wad of tow wound on the end of a double spiral of iron and affixed to a wooden stick: a cleaning rod. He was using this to swab the inside of the pistol. He didn't raise his head. "The army fought well, though, sir?"

"They did, Billy."

"They think they did, too. They don't sound beat."

Washington stretched his legs. "I'm not going to win the war by losing all the battles."

"You told the marquis different."

"What's that, Billy?"

Billy looked up from cleaning the gun. "You tol' the marquis that all we needed to do was keep an army in the field and we'd win the war."

"So I did, Billy." He looked at the black man fondly. "You'll make a general yet."

"No, sir." Billy went back to polishing, but he had a smile on his face. And Washington went to sleep.

★　★　★

Caesar lay on the creaking, jolting cart and watched the cloudy sky. He didn't have the strength to move his head. He wondered how long he had to live. He was alone in the cart. Every time it hit a hole in the road, his hip hurt like fire. The voices around him were strange, not men from any company he knew.

He dreamed of the swamp, where the pain and heat went on for hours and there was nothing a body could do. He woke to find the sun bright above him, his mouth parched and his throat painful. He fought vertigo and pain to raise his head. The man next to the cart had a high brass helmet with something worked on to the front. It was too bright to look at. Hessians.

"Water," Caesar croaked. His lips hurt. Everything hurt.

"*Wasser?*" asked the man. He reached behind him and suddenly was gone. Caesar had to lower his head as the effort became too much, but in a moment the man was on the wagon and was pouring water from an enormous canteen into a cup. Caesar drank it, and another. Then another. He knew he was drinking the poor man's ration, a sorry return on the man's good nature. He drank again. Then he lay back. The man had mustaches, but he smiled through them.

"*Sehr gut,*" he said, and hopped off the cart.

Caesar went back to the swamp, except now he was swimming, and even asleep he realized he had the fever again. Later he thought that the cart stopped for a while, and the Hessian, or another like him, gave him more water. Somebody sang a hymn, except all the words were foreign. And then he was back in the swamp. The flies were terrible, and Virgil was trying to get him to move.

And then it was Virgil, and Polly was with him, and they were both smiling and crying. And Caesar was awake.

Pennsylvania, October 18, 1777

Washington was writing in his study at the back of the stone farmhouse his staff had appropriated for the campaign. The late-afternoon light was fading and Billy was lighting candles and keeping the fire going. Writing to his family and considering the business of his plantations was Washington's greatest relaxation, and Billy defended it zealously. Washington had just finished a letter to his brother John and was considering an addition to a letter to Martha when the house echoed with the clatter of booted feet. Something was happening at the front of the house. Washington reached for his greatcoat, fearing the worst: that in the aftermath of the loss at Germantown, Howe was on him in a surprise attack like the one at Paoli.

He was rising from his chair when Billy came in.

"Messenger from General Clinton, sir."

Washington reached for the dispatch. He threw his greatcoat back on to its peg before Billy opened the door. No need for his staff to see his apprehensions. There they were, though, crowded in the doorway, Lafayette with his leg bandaged, and Hamilton and the others, their faces troubled. They knew the rumors: that General Burgoyne had beaten Gates north of Albany and that Putnam was losing the Hudson forts one and two at a time. General Clinton would have the latest.

Washington opened the dispatch and spread it on the table, but he was smiling before the paper hit the desk.

Gates had forced Burgoyne to surrender. *As well he should,* Washington thought. Gates had some of his best regiments and the whole support of the northern colonies. He had outnumbered Burgoyne five to one. Still. He stood up and faced the staff.

"General Gates has won a signal victory over General Burgoyne. Burgoyne's forces have surrendered."

Hamilton smiled broadly. "Then we're still in the game, General."

Lafayette embraced him with one arm. "France will not be deaf to this."

Washington listened to their celebration and joined in as much as he could. It was the third great victory of the war, after Boston and Trenton. It eliminated one of the three British armies facing them. He cared deeply for the cause, but not so much for the man who had won it.

Later, when they had moved their celebration to the camp and he was alone in his room, Washington allowed his head to sink to his hands for a moment. He rubbed his eyes, added a few words to his brother so that the original letter now forwarded news of General Gates's signal victory, and leaned back.

Billy put his head in the room. "You ready for bed, sir?"

"I suppose."

He stood up and moved to the bed, where he sat. His shoulders, usually square, were slumped. Billy took the ribbon from his hair and began to brush it out.

"You are hurting me," Washington growled.

No more than usual, thought Billy, but he said nothing.

"Damn it," said Washington.

Billy stopped. "Something on your mind, sir?"

"Sometimes the hardest thought to bear is that all the victories in this war will be won by other men." Washington said the words evenly, without a trace of self-pity, but Billy shook his head.

"That sounds more like General Lee than General Washington," Billy said scathingly, and Washington whirled, almost carrying the brush from his hands.

"Damn you!" Washington started to rise, but Billy pointed the brush at him.

"Sit down, sir. Or your hair will be a sight." Billy had been enduring Washington's occasional flashes of temper for too long to be ruffled.

Washington sat a moment. Then he leaned back. "Well struck, Billy."

Billy grunted and brushed harder. After a moment, though, he smiled to himself.

Washington scratched his chin. "In ancient Rome, whenever a great man had won an important victory, he'd get a parade, Billy. It was called a triumph. And in the chariot with him, as he rode through the crowds, there would be a slave. All the slave did was whisper 'You are just a man.' "

"Sounds like a good job for the slave," said Billy.

Washington shook his head. "I'm trying to say—"

"I understand what you are trying to say," said Billy. He went on brushing hair.

☆   ☆   ☆

"You want me to call a doctor?" asked Caleb. He was a Massachusetts man who had been in the war since Concord Bridge, an officer in the Tenth Massachusetts. His left hand had been amputated after a musket ball smashed it. He lay next to George Lake in a tent outside the hospital with a third man, whom they knew to be called William. They were curled together for warmth in straw that was growing damp with blood from William's seeping wound.

Neither one of them knew his surname, because William hadn't been conscious since he was brought in after the fight at Germantown. His uniform put him with one of the Pennsylvania line regiments. His seeping chest wound suggested he would probably be a dead man in hours.

"No one would come, anyways," George said bitterly. His arm was healing, and he had strength in his hand for the first time in weeks. He knew inside that he was better off in the cold tent, where the air was clean, than in the hospital where disease killed more than wounds. But he was angry. The Quaker nurses treated them all like lepers. The doctors were too few, too busy, and too hard. And George wanted to get back to work. He wanted to see if he still had a company, and he was lonely. Caleb Cooke was a good companion, an instant comrade of similar convictions, but Lake wanted one of his men to come by. Some link with the world before his wound. He wanted to write a letter to Betsy Lovell, but no one would give him paper. Philadelphia was lost, anyway. Her father would be happy. And she was marrying someone else. Her mother probably wouldn't even let her read a letter from him.

Someone was riding a horse down the next street of the hospital camp. George could smell the horse and hear the rider . . . *French accent.* Hope leapt in his breast and his heart beat suddenly so that his arm throbbed.

"I am looking for one called George Lake, yes?" said the voice, just a few tents away.

George wanted to leap out of the warmth of his shared blankets, except that to do so would have been to endanger Caleb's precarious recovery.

"Over here, sir." His voice was clear enough. He heard the horse move, splashing through the puddles, and then he could lift the flap of his tent and see the horse itself, and the slim booted form of the rider.

"Captain Lake!" exclaimed the marquis. He was down off the horse in a flash. There were other men behind him.

"You won't want to come in, sir." Lake realized suddenly how he must look, unshaved, with all his clothes on, one shirt over another and his two coats on top, and the third man's blood all over the straw. Lafayette was yelling, summoning, demanding from someone outside his view.

"Want to introduce our guest?" asked Caleb, still curled up tight.

George sat up and pulled his hair behind him, trying to comb it with his fingers. He looked like hell, and the marquis, spotless from head to bandaged leg, was a moving reproof.

"Lieutenant Caleb Cooke of the Massachuesetts Line, this is Major General the Marquis de Lafayette."

Cooke laughed. "Damn, George, I do have the fever."

George shook his head. "I apologize for the conditions, Marquis. Caleb thinks he has fever."

"Pah! It is nothing. George, you need better than this. Myself, I was cosseted by the ladies while you lay here. Jus' today I hear that you are still in hospital, yes? And I come as soon as I may."

"I'll be all right in a day or so," said George. He was elated. Just seeing the marquis made him feel better.

"General Gates has beaten General Burgoyne. Do you know this?" Lafayette was crouching in the entrance to the tent, and the knees of his spotless white broadcloth breeches were slowly soaking up the blood in the straw.

"We heard something." George felt as if Lafayette were bringing him back to life.

"Fetch a litter. I am taking this man with me." Lafayette added something in French to the man behind him.

George shook his head. "I can't leave Caleb," he said. "He's just starting to get better. He's lost a lot of blood, Marquis. He needs warmth."

"Fetch two litters. No, three. Empty this tent."

In a moment, George was being carried by two men of Lafayette's guard. Caleb was laughing. And the third man was in a litter behind them. Gates had beaten Burgoyne. Maybe William would live.

Anything was possible.

✯   ✯   ✯

A heavy rain lay over the city of Philadelphia, from the outposts on the Germantown Road to the comfortable lodgings around the new theater in Southwark. The city's conquest had turned out to be an action of little moment, and although the Continentals fought a second battle for their capital at Germantown, the Congress had to scuttle out the back as quickly as Howe's marching army came in the front.

In the first heady days after the victories at Brandywine and Germantown, Loyalists had rejoiced, sure that the fall of the capital and repeated defeats of the Continental Army spelled the end of the war. But Congress relocated without a sign of surrender, and word of General Burgoyne's "convention" in the distant north suggested that any possibility of victory must now be placed on a far horizon. Burgoyne had surrendered an entire British army, whatever he called the act. Doubts that victory would ever be secured by the king's forces were creeping in. To everyone the occupation of the city seemed temporary.

The British wounded were well housed, even the black ones, but Caesar fretted at his inactivity. The ball that had ruined his pouch had glanced off his hip, plowing a deep furrow in his flesh, but that had healed quickly. Far worse was his rematch with the fever from the swamp. It was weeks before he could hold a conversation with Virgil or ask how Polly came to be in Philadelphia.

He wasn't sure he liked what he heard. Marcus White had come after the army arrived, and seemed to cross the lines without a pass, or so Virgil said. And Polly did the same. Virgil had seen her himself when he was on duty on the Germantown Road, coming into their lines with a basket on her head. It worried Caesar, but he couldn't bring himself to ask her about it when she came to visit, often bringing fresh apples and once an orange from the south. He was weak, so weak that all he could do was eat and watch the world outside the barracks as the fall became winter.

Stewart visited him with the news of Burgoyne's surrender and delivered it in a monotone, so that Caesar knew it was serious.

"Have we lost the war, then?" he asked.

Stewart shook his head. "Not yet. But it's not good. They say the French will enter the war now."

Jeremy leaned past Stewart and fed Caesar an apple slice. "I'm not sure this is calculated to cheer our patient up," he said. Stewart looked shame-faced.

Caesar considered asking Stewart about the ease with which the Reverend White crossed the lines, but he decided it was something he had to look into himself.

Chapter Eighteen

Philadelphia, Pennsylvania, February 14, 1778

The black troops missed their excellent barracks and their taverns in New York. Philadelphia was a very different city, more sober, perhaps more supportive of the king in material ways but more spiritually restrained. It was a city founded by Quakers, and it resented the new theater and the "loose" ways of the British soldiers and their amiable friends. The army retaliated by fetching their baggage and still more of their friends from New York, and the early days of winter saw most of Mother Abbott's and a number of other followers make their way south. Sally arrived in a neat traveling dress and moved into a smart set of rooms over a milliner's. The Guides knew that Captain Stewart, not Mother Abbott, now furnished her lodgings. The Reverend Marcus White and his daughter, Polly, took rooms in a small Southwark church in the late fall, and Polly began to serve the "ladies" of the theater. But the ladies of Philadelphia lacked the happy candor of Miss Poppy and Miss Hammond, and there were no mixed taverns, much less subscription dances. Philadelphia society valued itself far too much for such displays. Indeed, twice in the winter, the Guides were called out with some other black troops to clean the streets of the city or shovel snow, duties they had never been expected to undertake in New York.

Lieutenant George Martin was transferred to them while Caesar was

recovering, and placed on their establishment. He was their first permanent officer, and as such they were prepared to dislike him or find him
wanting. Caesar, in particular, worried that Lieutenant Martin might
somehow change the company in his absence, but no such changes were
manifest when he returned. Lieutenant Martin was conscientious in that
he inspected quarters every few days, he made the rounds with Caesar,
and he stood his posts while they stood theirs. He was still learning the
complexities of the manual, and soon after he returned to duty Caesar
took him out to a big barn south of the city with Virgil and Fowver and a
few steady men to teach him the methods that the company had developed and the drills that were practiced by Captain Stewart's company
and others in the Second light infantry Battalion. Lieutenant Martin
seemed comfortable learning from them, which endeared him as fast as
any amount of his work. And they found that he liked to sleep late and
was pining for Miss Hammond, in far-off New York. They were mostly
pining for New York themselves, and it gave them all sympathy together.

George Martin had larger ambitions. He aspired to be an officer in the
most prestigious of Loyalist corps, the Queen's Rangers, now commanded
by their old friend Captain, now Major, Simcoe. Major Simcoe had recovered from his wounds at Brandywine and had received the Queen's
Rangers as a reward for his participation in the critical closing moments
of the battle. He made some very obliging remarks to the men of the
Black Guides about their help in his reaching this object of his desire, and
they were still drinking his health on a regular basis. Major Simcoe had
told Mr. Martin that there were no positions open in his corps, but had allowed him to know that a year or two of distinguished service in another
provincial corps, especially with the Guides, might win him the honor he
desired. So Martin worked harder than he might have, and made a better
impression.

Christmas had passed with some celebration, and the New Year had
been marked by a party given by the Scots with a barbaric name that
Caesar couldn't pronounce. And then he had entered the round of duties. The winter was hard, and the lines around Philadelphia seemed endless. The rebel army was never far away.

A steady winter of drill had made them a better, sharper company.
They had inherited some worn but serviceable red jackets from the
grenadier company of the Sixty-fourth Regiment, which, with help from
Virgil and a local tailor, allowed them to look considerably more like

British soldiers when they were on duty in the city. For service on the lines, they continued in their warm brown coats and trousers, improved as individuals saw fit with woolen leggings, gaiters, leather breeches and boots, or any other provision against the snow that a man could devise.

The younger generation, in the persons of Jim Somerset, Willy Smith, and Isaac Vernon, were now corporals. Neither Caesar nor Virgil fully credited Willy's conversion from troublemaker to leader, but he seemed to have made it, and his squad was the best turned out in his platoon. He and Jim had developed a near-permanent rivalry between their men that they never seemed to allow to interfere with their own hard-won friendship. Caesar couldn't bring himself to like Willy, but he tried to keep this from his day-to-day management of the company. And Isaac Vernon still seemed like a new boy, despite having served more than a year and fought like a small tiger in four actions. Sam the bugler and sometime drummer was useful, although he shook like a leaf under fire and cried at night. He was often away, running errands for Polly or the Reverend White. He obviously knew the area very well, and Caesar thought the boy might have come from Philadelphia.

The snow was not kind to men on the outer picket line. Caesar and the Guides had done a double share of duty, providing both a woodcutting party yesterday and pickets tonight, and there was some grumbling. Once they had watch fires roaring—the size of them a tribute to yesterday's woodcutting—and food on the boil, resentment settled into a steady undercurrent of conversation.

Caesar was sitting on a clean stump, using a handful of tow in the firelight to clear the snow from his fowler. He never slept in the field until his lock was clean, dry, and bright. The continuing hilarity at the next fire annoyed him, as he could hear Willy bragging about his rush into the Continental battery at Brandywine. He slipped a cover over his lock, pulled General Washington's greatcoat closer around him, and walked along the beaten path to the next fire.

"Willy, you going to take that patrol out to replace Sergeant Fowver, or just shout at the rebels?"

Willy fell silent immediately.

"Sorry, Sergeant," he said without resentment. His men already had their greatcoats on, and packs, as Caesar never let men go out without all their equipment. The fire was throwing a wall of heat, and he basked in it for a moment before he walked over to the knot of men preparing to depart and started looking at their muskets. They were all clean and dry. He gave Willy a smile.

"Tell Sergeant Fowver to come see me if he has any news," he said. Willy saluted.

Caesar walked back to his own fire and burrowed into a little pile of hay with Virgil, who grunted. It was too cold for idle chatter, and anyone who managed to get to sleep resented any interruption.

Nonetheless, it seemed he had only been asleep for a moment when Sergeant Fowver was prodding him awake.

"You wanted my report?"

Caesar did not come fully awake at once. He had been in a pleasant dream that had Polly White and a sort of misty future, and it had seemed both warm and pleasant. Virgil grunted. Caesar sat up, noting how cold his feet were as the big fire burned down.

Caesar grabbed some wood from the pile and threw it on, and then kicked the sentry, who was asleep.

"Laddy, if you can't stop us from being attacked, at least keep the fire going."

The boy, a recent recruit from a farm in Maryland, just nodded. He expected to be beaten. Hocken? Haxen? Caesar couldn't recall his name for a moment, and then it came. *Horton.* Tom Horton.

"Tom, the army is a hard place. You have to pull your weight. Every man here has stayed awake long hours and then stayed awake on guard. In one of those English regiments, they'd have the skin off your back, do you hear? So put yourself on report to your corporal in the morning, and we'll see. Don't fall asleep again."

Horton cringed a little, awake but terrified, and Caesar grunted. He filled a little kettle with snow and put it on the fire.

"What'd you see, Ben?" he said to Fowver.

Fowver looked greedily at the kettle and settled on his haunches. "Never saw a one of their patrols. We went right down to the river and right across toward the Paoli Road and never saw a thing. Found a root cellar with some turnips. I put them on the pile at the head of camp. But the best thing is I found that Marcus White."

"What!" Caesar sat right up.

"Sure as God made us sinful men. I brought him back. He says he has a pass, but he was out beyond our pickets and that ain't right."

Caesar felt like he had seen a ghost, or worse. "Where is he?"

"I have him with my lads at our fire. I didn't want him to talk. He asked to see you."

Caesar nodded grimly. The implications were obvious, because the rebels spent so much effort moving spies and messengers in and out of Philadelphia. He could see that Fowver was as disturbed as he was himself. He had the added complication of being in love with the man's daughter, and he tried to imagine White, either White, spying for the enemy. It made him sick.

"I'll come. Hey, Horton," Caesar called to the sentry. The boy came at the run.

"You boil this water and make tea, and come get me when it's ready, and I might forget I caught you asleep."

"Yes, sir!"

Caesar followed Fowver along the line of fires, thinking dark thoughts.

If he expected the Reverend White to show fear at his approach, he was very mistaken.

"Good evening, Sergeant Caesar," he said gravely.

"Good evening, Reverend." Caesar bowed a little. "You understand that we have to question you, Reverend?"

"I do."

"Can you explain what you were doing in the wastes between the armies?" Caesar began to examine him. Marcus White was not dressed in the threadbare garments of a preacher of the gospel, but in a filthy red waistcoat and leather breeches that had seen a great many farmyards, tucked into heavy boots. It was the costume of a poor laborer. It didn't look like anything that Marcus White should own.

"I cannot, sir, except to say that I have many souls to minister to, and not all of them can be visited in a black coat or by the full light of day."

Caesar bowed again. "Reverend, I understand that, and yet I am charged with taking any man I find between the lines." He turned to Fowver. "Anyone with him or around him? Did he have anything on him?"

Fowver shifted his eyes a little, uncomfortable.

"I didn't search him," he said.

Marcus White stared into his eyes for a moment. It was a look of mingled reproach and question. Caesar succumbed.

"Leave us alone for a moment, Ben," he said, and Fowver moved away.

"Take me direct to Lord Howe," Marcus said. "Don't make a fuss of it, but take me yourself. If a fuss is made, it might ruin everything."

"And you will *not* tell me what it might ruin."

White shook his head. "These are not my secrets, Julius Caesar."

"Now?"

"Better than the whole camp knowing I was here."

Caesar shook his head. "This is not the city, Reverend. I have to take men with me if I go back. I'm not risking capture out here by going alone, and you know what happens to our kind if they are taken. *Do* you still want to go if I take a party?"

"I understand your concern. I'm more worried about too many knowing my secrets than I am about capture."

Caesar nodded. White seemed very cool. He motioned to Fowver, who brought him the steaming kettle of tea.

He drank a cup gratefully, scooped more tea from the mess kettle and handed the little wooden cup to White, who drank greedily in his turn.

"Sergeant Fowver," Caesar said formally, "I am handing the command of the company to you until Mr. Martin rejoins in the morning. I am taking this gentleman back to the city immediately."

Fowver nodded.

"I'll need two files of men, and as yours are still dressed, I'll take them." He motioned to four privates and saw from their weary resignation that they understood. He examined their muskets and then checked their haversacks for food.

"Bad news is, you get to walk all night. Good news is, you get to sleep warm tomorrow."

He sensed he was in for a lot of grumbling, but he wanted to do some of his own.

✱ ✱ ✱

They had to cross seven miles of snowy roads and pass two lines of pickets to get back into the city. It was a dark night, and the going was slow, as every farm corner seemed like a turn in the road, and there were no signs to help them on their way. For a while they followed the tracks of a party of mounted dragoons that had visited them during the day, but then other horses joined and left the track and they could no longer rely on the clear horse trail. The moon came out from behind clouds and the night grew colder, but the men were warm as long as they kept moving. White was silent, and Caesar tried to read his soul and felt bad for it. He wanted White to prove himself good, but he couldn't help but feel that the man had wanted him to take him to Philadelphia alone, or that he was still hoping for a lucky rescue. He couldn't imagine what was behind that stoical face. The Reverend White just kept walking, his head always up, glancing about him with interest even in the dark.

They took a wrong turn at some point and walked a mile before Caesar realized they were going east, straight into the rebel lines, and he turned them around and walked them back until he could see their old tracks and the little drift of new snow that had put them off the main road. They climbed the drift, tired and deeply cold now, and walked north. There was no more grumbling. The four men who had been out all day with Fowver were deeply tired, and Caesar, who had walked posts and watched wood-cutters for two straight days, was catching himself asleep from time to time even as he walked. Marcus White just kept walking, silent, careful, and watching all that they did with what appeared as a happy curiosity.

The challenge of the Fortieth Regiment sentry was a welcome, and they thawed at the fire for a few moments before starting the home stretch into the city. Caesar watched White more attentively, afraid that the man might bolt or attempt an attack, but his demeanor never changed. It didn't change at the second sentry line, where the sergeant of the guard showed some suspicion about the lot of them, or in the streets of the city, just waking as the first carts of the day rolled to the market. Caesar almost led the man home, and his heart was rising in unease as they approached the army headquarters, but he marched his charge to the headquarters guard and passed him into their care. He was not encouraged to wait or give his version of the story, and he explained himself to Lieutenant Crawford at the barracks and went to sleep, exhausted and quite concerned.

☆ ☆ ☆

John Julius Stewart sat in Sally's parlor and read his latest letter from Miss McLean with mingled senses of guilt and unreality. She belonged to another world from this, one where the war did not drag on, where he did not have a black mistress and a group of hard-living libertine friends and a growing mountain of debts to affront his father. It almost didn't seem to matter that she missed him, or rather, he so doubted that he would ever see her again that it seemed unfair to worry about such trivialities. He was introspective enough to dislike these excuses he heard in his mind, and he turned her letter in his hands and tried to see her.

Sally was standing in the doorway of her chamber, a fire filling the grate

of her fireplace and warming her as she combed out her carefully straightened hair. She was modestly dressed in a good print jacket and warm
quilted petticoat, and her face had no hint of the makeup she might have
worn in New York. Philadelphia was a different place, and although the
British officers might play libertines in its Quaker streets, a woman who
didn't want her clothes spoiled or worse took care. Sally took care.

She watched Stewart with tolerance and amusement. He was dressed
to go out, in a long civilian coat of plush and a fancy waistcoat. Jeremy
said he'd be at the theater half the night, which he often was. She wished
she could go, the more so because Polly was sometimes there and other
girls who had followed the army used it as a place to make their little rendezvous. She missed Polly, who came from time to time with a message
from her father. She wanted company, and Stewart seldom offered it.

Jeremy always told her when the letter came, and she didn't feel any
jealousy for an absent rival an ocean away. Stewart wouldn't keep her
forever, but he'd already done fairer by her than any of her previous
boys, and while she missed the company of other girls from Mother
Abbott's, she didn't miss the men or the obligations.

Stewart rose and she helped him put a greatcoat over his elegant coat,
then straightened him and tugged at his ribbons and his watch fob to
make sure he was solidly accoutred. She lacked Jeremy's expertise with
his hair, but she helped him as best she could, patting the stray wisps
down and touching up his curls, knowing it was all a waste as the first
breeze in the street would set it all awry.

"Enjoy yourself, sir," she said demurely. He bowed to her, something
none of her customers had ever done before she met Stewart.

"Your servant, madam. I doubt I'll meet any company tonight that I
will enjoy as much as this."

She shook her head and laughed. "We have a dance lesson tomorrow
with Miss Hallam."

"Just so," he said with a smile, meaning that he would get up for it even
if he had a thick head. She was glad he remembered, as it was her favorite
day of the week. He bowed again and kissed her a little, and then went
down the stairs, cursing as his sword caught in the narrow entranceway.
She heard the bang of the front door and felt the gust of cold air under
her own door, and he was gone.

★　★　★

Jeremy arrived at the milliner's shop later than he intended. He bounded to the door, stopped to check his watch, and saw that a man was just coming down from her rooms. He made a gesture of his mouth in distaste and stood aside, well into the shadows of the little hall where firewood and old furniture was stored at the base of the stairs. The man came down slowly, almost as if he were limping, and as he passed, Jeremy could see that he was a slight man in a bearskin coat, with gray in his hair and a hard face, and white. Not Captain Stewart, at any rate. Silently he made his moue of distaste again and waited for the interloper to close the outer door before he moved up the stairs.

He had to knock several times before she opened, and then it was not any version of the Sally he knew, neither the bold one nor the saucy one, but a woman beside herself with fear and something darker. She was visibly relieved as soon as she recognized him.

"What is it, Sally?" he asked. "You look like you've seen a ghost."

"Nothin'," she said. "Nothin'. I had a fall."

"Nonsense, Sally. Who was that man on the stairs?"

She looked away.

"He hit you, didn't he? Look at me, Sally."

"Won't you jus' give me a minute, honey?" She smiled a little, although her lip trembled. She was making a great effort to master herself. Their evenings together were rare, and she wanted to cry to see it ruined. She liked Jeremy above all men she had ever met, and he was looking at her in a horrible way.

"Sally? Who was he?"

"Does it matter, honey? I ain't your sister." She smiled bravely at him. "One man more or less can't really hurt me."

He glared at her, and then was suddenly calm. "Sure, Sally, and I have no right to take you to task for spreading your favors, except that I don't think the captain would be so understanding." She nodded. "You don't need *money*?" He couldn't believe it. He wrote his master's accounts, and he knew what she received.

She bit her lip and tasted a little blood where the man had hit her. She had forgotten that Jeremy would come. She couldn't think what to tell him. She ached to tell him the truth and see him look at her with something like admiration, but she couldn't.

"Take me out?" she asked, making the smile and the half-lidded eyes that led men along so easily.

Jeremy shrugged. "Just as you like, but we're going where I want to go. Perhaps you'll learn something by it." He waited while she cleaned herself up, helped her into a cloak, and they went out into the snow. They walked quite a distance in silence, and her elegant shoes began to hurt her feet. She had walked the roads of the south for too long barefoot to be able to get her feet into pretty shoes comfortably, and that irked her, but frozen, painful feet irked her more.

"Where are you taking us?"

"A tavern," he said sharply, and kept walking. He took her all the way down to the port, near the river, where merchantmen and a few Royal Navy vessels filled the wharves. The ice on the river was already breaking. They passed several taverns before he led her to one whose appointments suggested that it was for the better class of sailors, with a gilt anchor cut like an officer's button as its sign.

Sally stopped. "I don't like taverns," she said in bitter memory.

"I won't sell you, you foolish girl. Just come inside."

"Black folk ain't welcome in this sort of place."

"I drink here often, Sally." Jeremy looked at her with appraising eyes, and she sensed that he had wanted to bring her here for some time. He led her into the warmth of the place and in a moment she felt her legs flush under her petticoats. She was cold.

The seats by the fire were filled with gentlemen in navy uniforms or in civilian clothes that failed to hide their true profession. A few army officers were there as well, and some merchant sailors. Jeremy was greeted once, by an officer, and he bowed in return and got them to a table near the door to the kitchen. Sally grew warmer by the moment.

"Do you see?" he said eagerly, once they had been served warm wine.

She shook her head. "They treat you nice," she agreed. "You speak like a gent and have nice manners, and they don' know who you might be."

"Not that, Sally. You are a ninny. Look over there."

She looked off into the candlelight beyond the fireplace on the other side of the common room. A black man sitting with a big blond man, or perhaps overgrown boy. They were arguing loudly about something.

"Know him?" Jeremy asked.

"The black one? Is he another servant? He sounds like he's from the Indies."

Jeremy laughed aloud. At the sound of the laughter, the two men turned and looked at him. The blond boy waved at Jeremy, but the other man rose and bowed to Sally before sitting again. Sally looked into her wine for a moment, thinking that men were all exactly the same, but pleased by the bow nonetheless.

"Sally, he's an *officer*. A lieutenant in the Royal Navy."

"A black man?"

"The same. Lieutenant James Crease, born a slave in Santo Domingo."

She drank off her wine. "Still a man like other men."

"Don't be coarse, there's a good girl. Sally, he's an *officer*. Maybe just the first. There's nothing we can't do. That's what I brought you here to see."

Sally leaned back in her seat and put her face very prettily in one hand. "Honey, you was never a slave. I *was*. I was born one."

He nodded.

"It don' jus' pass out of you, honey." She smiled at him, beautiful in the candlelight even with a growing bruise. She thought to say more, but the black man from the table was suddenly standing by Jeremy and bowing.

"Your servant, sir. Crease, of HMS *Apollo*."

Jeremy rose and bowed more deeply. "Jeremy Green, sir, in service to Captain Stewart."

"I hope you won't think me a libertine if I say I stopped here to say that your lady is very beautiful," Crease said with another bow. The big blond fellow called something out and waved again.

Sally smiled at him, and Jeremy bowed. "Thank you, sir."

"My pleasure. Time to shove off, Jack," he called, and went out.

✩   ✩   ✩

"Sergeant!"

Caesar awoke to find that it was midafternoon and one of the men from the Black Pioneers, another black company, was trying to shake him awake.

"Sergeant!"

Leaden with lack of sleep, he opened an eye. The whole of his straw mattress was warm, gathered around him like the thickest comforter in the world.

"An officer for you, Sergeant. And a young lady."

He forced himself up.

In ten minutes he was as clean and neat as his pack could make him. Most of his good shirts were still locked in a trunk at the Moor's Head in

New York, but with what he had to hand and a cup of hot water, he was clean and shaved when he came down the stairs to the guardroom at the front of the barracks house. Lieutenant Crawford was sitting primly with Miss Polly White. They made something of an odd couple, but they fell silent as he entered.

"Sir?"

"I'm to escort you to Colonel Musgrave, Sergeant."

Caesar looked around a little wildly. "Am I under arrest?"

"Not that I know of. Now get a coat and come along."

The walk wasn't far, and Colonel Musgrave was brisk. He had a mountain of correspondence in front of him and was busy signing off items for his regimental agent, all on documents with which Caesar was intimately familiar. Caesar took off his hat and bowed, and Musgrave remained as he was, head down and writing steadily for some time. When he looked up, he seemed surprised to find anyone there. Then he smiled.

"Ah, Sergeant Julius Caesar of the Guides. A pleasure, Sergeant. A word about last night, if I may? Your patrol encountered only a member of this army in distress, and rescued him, then brought him back to headquarters. Nothing more. Am I clear?"

"Yes, sir." Caesar had only addressed Colonel Musgrave once in his military career and was daunted by the second attempt.

"You did very well. Glad you showed some spirit in the thing, and glad no harm was done, eh? Here's a guinea for the men of the patrol, and another for you and the other sergeant. Right? Right, then. Well done. Dismissed."

Caesar bowed and was shepherded out again by Lieutenant Crawford.

"That mean anything to you, Caesar?" asked Crawford.

Caesar nodded, looking at the two guineas in his hand.

"Any idea why I was told to bring Miss White, then?"

She smiled at him and held out a hand.

"I can only hope, sir," he said. Crawford shook his head. When they were outside, she tugged her hand away.

"I have to take you to my father."

"I expect so," he said, still smiling at her. She colored a little and turned away.

"I don't see you as much as I used to," she said.

"This ain't New York, Polly. And you and the reverend aren't always easy to find."

She nodded, looking down. She didn't offer her hand again, but walked by his side until they reached the little carriage house where they lived.

"I wish..." she said.

"What do you wish, then?" he asked, trying to kiss her. She avoided him.

"Never mind, you. Stop that." She pushed him in the door and slammed it.

Marcus White was seated at his own little desk by the window, writing quickly. He took off his spectacles as soon as he saw Caesar and rose. Caesar bowed and White waved him to a chair.

"You got the message, I see."

"I did, sir."

"And you are puzzled?"

"Not in the least, sir. Honored more than ever by your acquaintance, sir, and perhaps not even surprised by your role, now that I have it clear."

The Reverend White nodded slowly. "Do you have any questions, then?"

"Is Polly involved?"

He saw White's hands clasp hard behind his back and had his answer. He had questioned too many guilty soldiers to need any coaching on the subject.

"Never mind, then."

"Do you love my daughter, sir?" The Reverend White was very close to him, and perhaps a little angry.

Suddenly Caesar was on different ground than expected. "Perhaps... yes, I think I do. Which is to say that I haven't given it much thought lately." Caesar raised his chin. "She's a little above me, I think."

"Why? Because she can read? You can read. Because she's modest? You're no libertine."

"You are a man of real education, sir." Marcus shook his head, but Caesar went on. "I decided when we left New York that it wasn't right."

Marcus White nodded. "Yes, yes. You're doing a fine job of speaking all my lines. I agree that you have no skill besides war. It worries me. Julius Caesar, so aptly named! But last night scared me more. I made a mistake and almost paid for it. I think she has a great deal of regard for you. If we all live to get back to New York..."

"New York?" asked Caesar. Fascinated though he was by the subject, he was equally interested by the prospect of a move to New York.

"Haven't you heard? Lord Howe is to go back to England in the spring, and Sir Henry Clinton will take command. He intends to march the army back to New York." This was uttered as if a commonplace.

Caesar just shook his head. "Even barracks rumor has not gone so far."

"It's fact, though, Caesar. The government is going to retreat and try negotiation for a while. Saratoga has scared them deeply. I hope we have not already lost the war."

Caesar shook his head. "You know more than any officer I know, but I suspect I know why, and I won't say. So tell me about New York?"

"Eh?"

"If we all get back there, I think you said?"

"Ahh. Yes. If we do, and if you'd care to court her, and if she's willing, I'd be content."

Caesar saw a marvelous vista opening before him. He smiled from ear to ear.

"Not every day that the woman's father asks you to court her, is it?"

Caesar shook his head again, tongue-tied.

"I told her you'd never ask. She told me you never stopped trying to take liberties." Caesar was suddenly cast down. "I ask that if this comes to nothing, you not bring my daughter down."

Caesar raised his eyes and met the minister's. "Yes. Yes, I promise."

"Good, then. I think we understand each other. Where is my Epictetus?"

"In my pack."

"I have the *Memoirs of Socrates* to trade for it when you bring it. In your pack, you say? Is there anything left of it?"

"I dried it well when it got wet, sir. The pages have warpled a little, but she's fine."

"Perhaps I should save my books as well as my daughter, until New York."

He went out, and she was waiting.

"You have my father's permission." She said it straight, and flat. His heart turned over.

"You don't seem too pleased." Caesar thought that all his suspicions of Marcus White might come back, if it turned out that White was trading his daughter for Caesar's silence about his activities.

"I'd like to hear something from you."

Caesar met her eyes. They stood a long moment, looking at each other. "I want to marry you," he said, straight.

She nodded gravely.

"But I'm a soldier. Polly, I don't know just how to say this to you, 'cept that I ain't so sure we'll win. And then what am I? A black freeman? A slave? Somebody's property? You ain't...you *aren't* like me. I want to marry you, but I want to know that there's something after all this."

Polly smiled for the first time in that conversation. "That's the Caesar I want. The one that thinks. I don't want it all to be snatched kisses and your hand on my thigh, Caesar. I want to be talked to. I learned that equality from my father, and I'll expect it." She started to walk, and made a motion that he should come along. "It's cold. *I'm* cold. As to after the war, what of it? We're black, Caesar. There isn't ever a day we'll rest easy, knowing that the next day will bring us ease. And I don't see you ever being a slave again."

Caesar caught her to him and kissed her, a quick kiss on the lips, and then a longer kiss on her neck. "I'll keep you warm, at least," he said.

She kissed him a moment and pulled free. "New York, then," she said, and turned back to her father's house.

★ ★ ★

The sallow man in the bearskin coat had two more stops to make, but he thought of the black whore for the rest of the evening. She was the favorite of his postboxes, and the only one who didn't make him cringe and feel inferior. Sometimes, when she vexed him, he hit her and liked it. She was terrified of him, and no one had ever been terrified of him before— much the reverse—and he took pleasure in that, too.

He picked up two more packages and then traveled east, carefully avoiding the post at the first line of pickets and meeting a Quaker farmer and his wife exactly on time, just as the sun rose off toward Landsdowne. The little man in the bearskin coat was especially proud when he was just on time for these meetings. He rode up cautiously, because he was always cautious, and stopped a good few paces from the wagon.

"Got any fodder to sell?" he asked. The old Quaker on the wagon frowned.

"Got any *fresh* fodder to sell?" he corrected himself, annoyed that the man needed so much care, but pleased that he could remember the whole phrase. The old man nodded, and indicated the back of the wagon.

The man in the bearskin coat rode back into the city when the transaction was finished, again avoiding the British post on the road, back to his dreary day-to-day life. He liked the nights when he was a courier, a secret messenger for the cause.

The Quaker farmer took his wagon through the lines with a paper signed by several commanders on both sides, selling fodder as he went. Once he was outside the range of all but the most aggressive patrols of the king's army, he turned down a side lane past some fields that had been fallow at least a year and drove his wagon right into a barn. He no sooner pulled in there than armed men surrounded him.

"What you got for me?" asked Sergeant Bludner.

Valley Forge, February 23, 1778

Washington felt the cold right through his spirits. The capital was lost, and his army, a bare three thousand men, were camped in the hardest conditions they had yet endured. He felt that the war might now be lost through sheer neglect and a lack of basic logistics. His men might melt away, starve, or die in the cold.

Washington looked at the man standing before him, able, brave, animated. The very picture of a good officer, and Washington disliked that he had to refuse the man a furlough, but the other generals had been writing passes as if they were free of threat, and with British patrols attacking his outposts every day he could not afford to have his officers absent. He feared desertion. He feared that the army would break up like an ice floe and be gone in a night.

"General, I appeal to you. I've worn out all my smallclothes, and I promised I would wed her by the first of the year. She'll be eating her heart our, sir! Please let me go."

Washington said nothing. The Massachusetts captain was dressed in the remnants of a British coat, and his boots were wrapped in rags. His hat was tied to his head with a piece of old sacking. When he gesticulated, his hand could be seen wrapped in bandages. Yet he stood straight as an arrow in front of his general.

"If I don't go, she'll die."

Washington smiled thinly. "Oh, no sir. Women do not die for such trifles."

"But, General, what shall I do?" The man was not angry at being refused, just plaintive.

"What will you do? Captain, I recommend you do as I do and write to her to add another leaf to the book of women's sufferings." He winced at his own tone, as he could imagine what Martha would say if she were present, but thankfully for his status as the "demigod" of the revolutionary cause, she was not.

When the captain was dismissed, Washington notified Colonel Fitzgerald that he was done with petitions for the day and set himself to correspondence. He read a dispatch from his spymaster stating that an agent in Philadelphia with a code he recognized was confirming the movement of British troops out of the city in the spring. It was not the first report Washington had received on the subject, and he looked out of the window for a moment and considered what it would mean to his army, starving in the snow, to retake their capital, even if it were retaken only because the enemy abandoned it.

A knock at the door interrupted his reflection. Billy leaned in and indicated the marquis a little behind him. Washington beckoned.

"The marquis has a man he wishes to introduce, General," said Billy. "I think you might want to hear him."

Washington nodded. "Some warm punch?" he asked, and Billy vanished.

The marquis bowed elegantly and made way for a far less graceful man behind him.

"My general, may I have the pleasure of introducing Freiherr von Steuben, formerly a general in the service of the King of Prussia? *Monsieur von Steuben, j'ai le plaisir d'introduire le Général des États-Unis, Monsieur George Washington.* General, Freiherr von Steuben has little English."

Rather than Lafayette's courtly bow, von Steuben clicked his heels together and bowed stiffly from the waist. "*Votre serviteur, Monsieur le Général,*" he said.

Washington's French was not good at the best of times. He waved them to chairs. "Please thank the Freiherr for coming. I am flattered to receive an officer from the Prussian king. How may I be of service?"

There was a brief conversation in French, and Lafayette smiled. "The Freiherr wishes that he may serve our army. He makes no demand for rank and says that rather than importune you for some task, it might be best if he simply joined your headquarters and watched to see if he could be of service."

Von Steuben spoke rapidly again. Then he smiled and rose from his chair, bowed from the waist again, and seated himself.

Lafayette nodded and waited until his protégé had finished. "The Freiherr says that he served on the staff of the great King Frederick and also has conducted large-scale..." Lafayette paused. "How do you say it, games, on the *Champs de Mars?*" The two foreigners looked at each other.

Washington smiled benevolently. "Military exercises?"

"*Exactement.* My pardon, General. I speak nothing but English for months and it improves itself, yes? And then I have someone to speak the *langue* of home, and..."

"Please tell Freiherr von Steuben that I would be delighted to make a temporary place on my staff and that he should feel free to ask me anything he likes. I will assign John Laurens to translate for him. Laurens might learn more soldiering, and you, my dear Marquis, are far too busy to be a translator, I think."

If it was a reproof, it was a gentle one. Lafayette's adoration of his general was sometimes a burden, and it imposed on Washington a restraint he had never used with another person, except perhaps Martha, but it was cheering, all the same.

Washington called for John Laurens and Billy served hot punch to all four men. Washington thought of the contrast between the Yankee captain to whom he had been forced to refuse a furlough and the elegant Lafayette in his new uniform and fur-lined waistcoat, and the contrast made him think of Lafayette's unlikely friend.

"How is Captain Lake, Marquis?"

"He does very well. His arm has healed cleanly. The hospital was worse for him than the wound, I think. I will have him out on patrol in a few days."

"What? Doesn't he want a furlough like every other officer?"

"General, George Lake is the true believer, yes? He will not leave this army until the enemy is beaten."

John Laurens bowed from the door and came in, snatching his share of the punch. He was in some middle ground between the ragged soldiers outside and the near perfection of Lafayette, but when the situation had been explained to him, he was able to translate for von Steuben very well indeed. When the three men began to discuss military matters in French, Washington cleared his throat and stood to his dominating height, and the others rose immediately.

"My pardon, General. I meant no rudeness."

Washington smiled, a thin smile that left his teeth hidden, but with some warmth. "I must go back to the army's work, gentlemen. Colonel Laurens, may I leave the Freiherr in your capable hands? Marquis, I thank you for bringing him, although I must say that I would have thought you natural enemies."

"Perhaps in Europe, *mon général*. Here we unite in the cause of liberty." Lafayette bowed deeply and the men withdrew, leaving Washington to plan his campaigns. Somehow, between the Yankee captain, George Lake's recovery, and von Steuben, his mood had changed. He was pleased.

Billy closed the door and smiled.

Philadelphia, April 30, 1778

The army reentered Philadelphia to muted celebrations. The people of the City of Brotherly Love had watched armies come and go for three seasons now, and were inured to the change. The Loyalists missed the British, and indeed, so great a revel had the Mischianza proved that some heads were still recovering from it.

The return of the Continental Congress restored the city to the position of capital, and the government returned with a rush, eager to renew the business of politics and also to seize the property of avowed Loyalists. It was a difficult time, particularly as the enemy was just across the river in New Jersey, busy retreating on New York, and Washington was keen to get across and harry their retreat.

George Lake had marched through the city before, but the last time he had been a corporal. Now he was a captain, and thanks to the generosity of the marquis, he almost looked the part, in a good blue coat with red facings, a smart leather helmet with a visor, and his fine sword hanging by his side. He even wore good top boots in emulation of his idol. Behind him, his company shared in his fortune. Every man had a good wool coat, brought as bounty from France. The coats had been shared through the army by lottery, but most of the light infantry had received theirs first, not least because Lafayette had many friends among the younger officers of that corps. So Lake's company, one of the best in the army, led the parade that was also a pursuit: They were to march through the city and board a ferry the next day.

Reclaiming his company had proved less of a hazard than recruiting it. By the time George was fully recovered, he found his company had shrunk to just twenty-five men under a sergeant he didn't know. In his absence, the other officer hadn't been replaced and no drafts had been procured. George had been forced to tour the other companies and importune Colonel Weedon for more men. In time he'd got them and a new officer, Lieutenant Isaac Ross, a Scotsman from Alexandria with a far better claim to the rank of officer than George Lake. Ross, however, first encountered his new commander having wine with the much-revered Marquis de Lafayette and never thought to question his commander's antecedents.

Ross was better than adequate. He roamed the column and watched the sergeants and made George's life very easy, so that as they neared a certain corner, close by the City Tavern, George was able to turn his attention to a certain house. It was still a block away when George saw men at the windows and someone smashing the front door with an ax. He knew that the Lovells were Loyalists, and he knew the temper of the times.

"Mr. Ross? Indian files from the flanks of sections, if you please. At the double!"

George waited until his men began to file off and then led them up the side of the column, trotting along smartly. The men in the companies ahead were studiously looking the other way, trying to ignore what was happening under their noses.

George's friend Caleb commanded the company just short of the house. "What's your hurry, George?"

George pointed at the Lovells'. "I'm intending to stop the looters."

"Folks inside are Tories."

"Folks looting them are scum, Caleb."

"Aye, then. True enough. I'll back your play."

George turned away and motioned to his men. "Take them. I want them all as prisoners. Smartly now, and no shooting."

He drew his sword and led a few men into the Lovells' central hall. A big man was carrying a sewing table and seemed surprised to see a Continental officer appear.

"This 'ere's my place. Go get your own."

George jabbed him in the face with the hilt of his sword and broke the man's nose. "Take him."

Ready hands grabbed the man and George took the sewing table before it got broken. Around the house, through the great casemented windows, George could see his own men and Caleb's forming a cordon. His sergeant was arresting men in the library.

George called out: "Mrs. Lovell? Mr. Lovell?"

He heard voices from upstairs and ran to the top, where he found a huddle of men, none in uniform. The best dressed stepped in front of George and raised his hand. His voice was shaking, whether with emotion or fear George cared little.

"Halt! Soldier, you are interfering with the orders of the Congress."

"Take him," said George, grabbing the man's outstretched arm and pulling him down the steps.

"Damn you, sir! I am an officer of Congress . . ."

"Are you, now? Where were you at Valley Forge, then? Take him, boys."

The man disappeared into a welter of soldiers. When it had been a matter of helping Tories, the men had been hesitant, but as soon as George made it a matter of taking men who claimed to be patriots but declined to serve in the army, the soldiers were suddenly very active.

The rest of the looters at the head of the stairs stood warily. One man had drawn a pistol.

George pointed. "Is that loaded? Put it down this instant or you're a dead man."

The man hesitated. The barrel swung slowly, as if the man couldn't decide where to direct it.

"Down, I say," George said quietly. Behind him, one of his corporals took careful aim from the steps. The pistol was placed on the floor.

"Take them all outside. *Mrs. Lovell!*"

More cries, this time from farther up in the house, perhaps the servants' quarters. George pushed through the men, sullen now, and snatched up the pistol. Then he turned a corner and went up some narrower steps to a door. The door was shut and there were two men with a crowbar outside.

"Drop the bar and clear the door, lads."

They saw the pistol and cowered away.

"Straight past me and down the hall. Don't make a fuss or you'll be killed. Good lads." They were younger than the rest, perhaps less spoiled, and they did as he said.

"Mrs. Lovell?" he shouted.

"Who's that?"

"George Lake of the Continental Army, ma'am. Your house is clear. You can come out."

He heard a shriek from inside the door. He was thinking of knocking it down himself when it was opened from inside. Mrs. Lovell's face was bright red, and her shawl was wrapped around one hand, which was bleeding. Betsy was behind her.

"Are you all right, ma'am?"

"Mr. Lake? Thanks to God, sir, for your timely arrival. I think they meant more than pillage, and my husband hasn't been home in two days and I fear for him, and one of the dogs was killed by a band, and, sir..."

This was not the Mrs. Lovell who had been so calm in ladling milk to his men. She was badly shaken, like men he'd seen on the battlefield. George moved her downstairs and exchanged a glance with Betsy, who was dressed in mourning and threw her arms around his neck in a manner he found...*very* pleasing. But duty called. He looked deep in her eyes and she gave a nervous smile, as if now embarrassed by her own boldness.

He was afraid to ask her anything, so he left her looking after her mother and went outside. The column was moving on, and his men were hopelessly out of line already, as were Caleb's.

Colonel Weedon rode over, accompanied by the marquis. "Captain Lake? I do hope you have an explanation, sir."

"Colonel, this is a Loyalist house. But the people here have been good to the army, gave us milk the last time we was here, and I'm partial to them. The house was being broken by scum. I took care of it."

Weedon nodded, looking at the group of toughs on the lawn. "They mean to make trouble for you, then."

Lake nodded, and the marquis looked thoughtful. Then he rode over to the group and pointed at them. "I believe every one of these men is a deserter from the Second Pennsylvania Regiment," he said aloud. The soldiers hooted at them. The men looked angry or terrified.

"I ain't no deserter. I ain't stupid enough to be in your army!" shouted the biggest to a chorus of jeers.

The marquis came back. "My friend the Freiherr von Steuben will so enjoy making these men into soldiers. They themselves will someday acknowledge the favor we have done them in allowing them to serve the cause of liberty."

Weedon laughed and slapped his holsters. "Damn me, Marquis. You have a way with you. That's that, then, George. Get your men together and bring your 'deserters' along."

George saluted and went back into the Lovells' house. On the steps he put a hand on Caleb's arm. "Can you do me another favor, Caleb?"

"I suppose." Caleb was laconic at the best of times.

"Have a man you trust wait for the baggage and have William brought here. They're going to leave the wounded in the city anyway, Caleb. William'll be better off with the Lovells, and he'll give them some element of protection as well."

"An' if he ever recovers his wits, he'll be home, like."

"Thankee, Caleb!" George passed back into the parlor, where Mrs. Lovell was sitting in the big chair with her daughter close by. Soldiers were moving furniture back in.

"Mr. Lake; Captain Lake, I think. How can I thank you enough?"

"It was nothing, ma'am. But you could perhaps do me a favor, if you feel I've done you a service. A man I know is badly wounded. Our army hasn't a real hospital . . ."

Mrs. Lovell sprang to her feet. "I'd be happy, Captain. Take me to him."

"I've taken the liberty of sending for him. He's from Pennsylvania, and his name is William. He's been awake a few times in the last month, but he's bad. An' that's all we know. But we shared a tent when I was wounded. . . ."

Betsy looked at him and turned white. She looked down suddenly and sat. Mrs. Lovell nodded. "When were you wounded?"

"I was hit at Brandywine, ma'am. But I was most of the winter recovering. I thought to write, an' then I thought . . ." In fact, he realized that his thoughts were neither here nor there, and that his company was forming outside and Private Locke was hanging on his every word in the doorway. Oh, *lovely* gossip about the captain. He bowed to cover his confusion, but Mrs. Lovell was still too close to her own troubles to notice.

"I have to march, ma'am. May I write for news of my friend?" He looked directly at Betsy when he spoke, greatly daring, hoping she could read his code. She kept her eyes down, but a tiny smile played at her mouth.

"Of course, sir. You are a benefactor of this house, and your letters will always be welcome here." Mrs. Lovell already sounded more herself.

George bowed. "I must go. My apologies for the rush. Mrs. Lovell, your servant, Miss Lovell."

"See the captain to the door, Betsy. Let's look like civil people despite the events of this morning."

Betsy blushed and followed George to the door. He paused, as close to alone with her as he'd ever been and unable to speak a word.

Caleb, out in the street, caught sight of his coat and called out, "Come on, George!"

George looked at Betsy and his feet actually moved, so great was his pull to the street. He shuffled and cursed inwardly.

"My fiancé fell through the ice and drowned," Betsy said, and she kissed him. It was just a touch, but it lit his face like fire.

He caught one of her hands and kissed it, afraid to touch her. "I'll write."

"You had better, Mr. Lake."

"I want..." He was tongue-tied, and he kissed her hand again. She smiled as if she knew and vanished in the door.

Out in the street, his face red as an enemy coat, George trotted to the head of his company.

"Well done, our George!" yelled one of his men. He glared.

"A beauty and no mistake," said his sergeant. Someone gave a cheer.

"March!" growled George.

★　★　★

A few streets away, Washington sat in the City Tavern and looked at the treaty Silas Deane had laid in front of him. It held the seals of Europe's most powerful monarch. Lafayette beamed with pride.

"France has recognized the United States." John Laurens was reading, alternating with Deane. "And will become our ally. They will send us soldiers and matériel."

Washington nodded. They had heard the rumor for weeks, but there was a happy babble of congratulation from those gathered in the great common. Fitzgerald laughed with Hamilton, and Lafayette translated something to von Steuben. Outside, their army, a new army, marched through the streets with a steady pace that von Steuben had spent the spring beating into them. They looked like regulars. Some of them had done before, but now the whole army looked the part.

Washington moved off to one of the windows at the north end of the room and looked out at the city. After a moment, he realized that his inner staff had gathered around him silently while the rest kept up a fine run of comment in the background. Washington nodded to Hamilton.

"I have to thank you, gentlemen."

Hamilton bowed. He couldn't remember being thanked by Washington for anything. Lafayette beamed and Fitzgerald looked puzzled.

"What for, sir? It's Silas Deane as got the treaty."

"You gentlemen taught me to use a staff, and to trust...other men." He paused. "So now you will need to teach me to trust an ally far more powerful than we are. Am I wrong to doubt the purity of France's motives?"

They all looked suddenly grim. And Lafayette nodded. "You are right, General. And yet I think they wish the English defeated."

Washington rubbed the bridge of his nose; he could see a new crowd of congressional dignitaries coming toward the staff. "I would prefer to defeat the British before the French arrive. But for that, we must make Clinton stand and fight."

Hart's Farm, New Jersey, June 24, 1778

"They will stand, and they will fight." Washington was speaking not of the British but of his own men. He could not believe what he was hearing from the men in the room. Charles Lee, exchanged from captivity and now no friend to his commander, was gathering around him a party of discontent. That Washington knew, but until this moment he had no idea of the power their discontent had in his officer corps. The thought struck him that Lee had always been like this, searching for the boundaries of authority. Something crystallized in Washington, even as Lee moved to the map.

Lee pointed. "Clinton is marching back to New York. The British can call it anything they like, sir, but it is a retreat. With all due respect, we gain nothing by attacking him and little by interrupting his retreat. The risk to us is great, however. Right now, every man in New Jersey is ours. Since Saratoga, the tide of Congress is running high. We cannot afford a defeat. If we attack his rearguard, we will be defeated. Our troops cannot stand the fire."

Washington looked around the room. Lee seemed to have polarized the officers of the army, recently so united, and Washington vowed silently that this would *not* happen again. He looked at the marquis.

Lafayette, recovered from his wound and entirely unchanged, uncrossed his legs and popped out of his seat like a marionette.

"I would be delighted to take our advance guard and have a *passage à l'outrance*, General. I do not agree with the General Lee. I believe that my men will stand the fire."

Lee looked at him disgustedly. "When have they yet, sir?"

"You were not at Trenton or Princeton, sir, nor Brandywine."

"I wasn't at Saratoga, either, sir! But by God, even the veterans of those actions admit that they couldn't stop the British when they came on with the bayonet! Right up until he surrendered, Burgoyne was still winning his victories! We cannot afford one of those defeats. We have a good new army and a great deal of public support and a treaty with France. We've won! Let's keep it. Let's shadow Clinton all the way out of New Jersey and claim victory." He turned a look of re-pugnance on Lafayette. "And let's leave him in the nursery where he belongs."

"Contain yourself and apologize!" Washington spoke in a voice of thunder. Lee recoiled. Washington stood to his full height, towering over Lee.

"I beg pardon, sir. The hurry of the moment..."

"*Ce n'est rien*, General Lee." Lafayette was always magnanimous. It was one of the reasons so many of the officers hated him.

"General Lafayette, you may take the advance guard under your command. Give me a plan to attack the rearguard of General Clinton's army and make an attempt on his baggage."

General Lee took a deep breath and swept his head around the room. There were a number that looked to him for leadership. He had gathered a small crowd on his side, distinct from the crowd around Washington. After the victory at Saratoga, there had been a conspiracy to place Gates at the head of the army, but it had failed in part because so few officers knew Gates, or liked him. The same was *not* true of Charles Lee. A great many officers in the army admired him.

"Very well, sir. If you insist on this mission, I will undertake it rather than entrust it to an officer so inexperienced, no matter how good his heart."

Washington looked at Lee with thinly disguised misgiving. "Very well, General Lee."

"But I will not guarantee the outcome." Lee was sarcastic. Washington wondered if he had allowed this behavior before or if captivity had changed Lee.

"I seem to remember you feeling that I lacked decision on a former occasion, General Lee." Lee grew pale. Washington seemed an extra few inches taller. "Don't let me find you the same, General."

Washington held his gaze until Charles Lee turned away.

Near Monmouth Courthouse, June 28, 1778

Marcus and Polly had always been sure they would return to New York, but Caesar had hoped that the war was going better than that. Early spring proved them right. Once the orders to move back to New York came to them, he hoped that they would sail home, as they had come, but they were ordered to march. The women were ordered into boats along with the heavy baggage and most of the stores, but the army stepped off from Philadelphia, leaving it to the rebels, and headed for New York. In the dark of the first morning's march, Caesar felt that the war was lost. They had taken the rebel capital and the victory had not had any real effect. There were rumors that the French would now declare war on England and they would all be on the defensive. Caesar saw his chances of a life of freedom marching away into the dark like Clinton's retreating army.

The march was orderly, but they were attacked every night in New Jersey and many of the days as well. Militia rose up out of the ground to contend the flanks, and every patch of woods had its garrison of local men. They took casualties, enough to make the men angry, and they were in action or worried about it every day.

Soon enough they began to encounter more than just militia. Twice they found ambuscades laid by regular troops, and one whole day they skirmished with mounted dragoons who dogged their patrols just out of musket range, looking for an opening. During those days, Caesar began to rely on the green-coated men of Simcoe's new regiment, the Queen's Rangers. They had their own cavalry and their own riflemen, and twice his patrols were saved by their timely appearance. There were black men in the ranks of the Rangers and in several other units now.

The pressure on the Guides mounted every day. They lost two men in a day, killed by rifles at a distance, and the next day a new boy, Dick Lantern, who had been an ostler in Philadelphia, was captured when he strayed too far out of the pickets in the evening. They all knew he would be sold as a slave. It added to their fatigue and their frustration.

Caesar felt that Washington was following them like the hunter he was. He wondered when Washington would pounce.

The day started hot. The night before had been warm and so damp that Caesar's men lay on their muskets to keep them dry. The rebels had driven some cattle herds right through the outposts, scattering sentries and luring them to fire, which alarmed the camps and kept the men awake.

It was the last alarm, just as the false dawn started in a dark morning already too hot for comfort, when the sentries nearest the light infantry began to fire. Caesar sprang up, more in anger than in fear. He'd suspected for an hour that the soldiers of the regiment on duty were inexperienced ninnies, and this confirmed it. No one around his fires seemed to be asleep anyway, and he roused them and got them into their equipment while he sent Jim Somerset to find an officer. As the first light appeared in the sky, Jim came back with Jeremy, who was wide awake, dressed, and leading a horse.

"I want to take a patrol out and make 'em pay for keeping me awake," said Caesar. "Apparently these heroes"—he pointed to a soldier of a line regiment slouching in a filthy red coat—"don't have the spirit to do the job."

Jeremy nodded and rode off, returning shortly with a German officer and Lieutenant Crawford. Caesar was surprised to find that the German officer spoke perfect English.

"We was troubled all night. We'd be delighted to sweep the ground in front of us, now that there is light to shoot." The German officer waved over the low ground to their front. He looked at Caesar and inclined his head in measured civility.

"Captain George Hangar of the Jaegers."

"Sergeant Julius Caesar of the Black Guides. Your English is very good, sir."

"Damn! I might say the same, sir. But I'm English myself. Just happen to serve in the Jaegers. Love the rifles, you see."

Lieutenant Crawford was looking through his glass at the ground. A ball came past them, announced by a hiss. A second ball struck a stump and sent up splinters. Hangar knelt by the stump eagerly and dug at it with his clasp knife before extracting a ball.

"Rifles, of course. You know how long the barrel is compared to the weight of the ball? All that metal means that they can load more powder, eh? That barrel must weigh a full six pound, and that will allow them to shoot more than half the weight of the ball in powder. Even a small ball like this will carry three hundred yards. And the long barrel means all the powder is burned."

Caesar looked at Jeremy with an eyebrow raised, and Hangar caught it. He smiled and rose to his feet, his command aiguillette bouncing as he dusted his knees.

"Rifles are my passion, Sergeant. I can't help but prose away about them."

Another ball passed between them and made its little musical note.

"That's just seven or eight men firing to amuse us. I'll see to that immediately with my lads. You'll sweep the ground? I think you'll find they have a force in those woods, but I doubt it will prove considerable." Hangar took Crawford's glass, looked for a moment, and handed it back. "A pleasure, gentlemen. Damn me, I hate the heat. Let's get this done."

Lieutenant Martin came up to them and was immediately touched by a ball fired from the gloom to their front. It was a slight wound but he seemed proud of it. Caesar wrapped it with his handkerchief as they scrambled back from their exposed position.

"Good practice," said Crawford. "They can shoot."

"They shoot best when there ain't anybody shooting back," Jeremy quipped.

A moment later they could hear the heavy barks of the Jaegers' rifles returning fire off to their left. Caesar looked at Martin. "It was my intention to take the company out and cover the ground as quickly as possible."

Martin nodded. "I expect you know the business, Sergeant. I just want to see it done." Martin was jealous of Lieutenant Crawford, who was shouting orders rapid-fire at Captain Stewart's company, already formed off to the right. A further company, the Forty-second lights, was moving cautiously down into the low ground off to the right. Captain Stewart could be seen riding that way.

Caesar hated the oppressive heat, which made both uniform and equipment uncomfortable. He used a cloth to wipe his face, shifted his belts to allow a little more of the fetid air to reach his skin, and blew his whistle twice. The company moved forward.

The rifles fired again, off at the wood line in the distance, and their smoke hung in an ugly cloud just over the position of the shooters. Because there was no breeze to move the smoke away, it provided a screen that kept them safe. Caesar could just see the shine of the new sun on a ramrod or a barrel as the man loaded. Caesar raised both his arms and waved them forward and started to trot. Captain Stewart came up behind him on horseback.

"Right to the woods!" Stewart shouted. Caesar just raised a hand in acknowledgment. He could see the riflemen scrambling now, one pausing to take a last shot, another leaping over a log. The last shot vanished into the morning, doing no immediate harm that Caesar could see, and then they were at the wood line. He blew a long blast on his whistle and heard the corporals shouting "Skirmish" just as Stewart's bugles began to send the same signal. He aimed at a retreating figure and fired to no effect. The range was already too long for muskets.

Caesar waved Fowver's platoon forward. Willy Smith passed him, yelling, "Moses, get it loaded, there." From his vantage point commanding the stationary platoon, Caesar watched Fowver's men with pride as they picked their way forward, the files staying together and the men covering both the front and flanks with their eyes. Off to the left, Stewart's company was moving forward more aggressively, and Caesar could hear McDonald pushing them with his voice. Caesar started his own platoon forward.

It seemed only a moment later that Stewart and Jeremy appeared by him at the far edge of the wood.

"No point in it," said Jeremy, looking through his master's glass. Stewart held out his hand for the instrument and shook his head. They had come three-quarters of a mile from their camp and Caesar was soaked in sweat from the little run. Jeremy looked as if he had a private store of ice in his coat, but Captain Stewart's hair was every which way, as if he had come to battle straight from his pillow. Caesar wondered if Sally was with the army baggage back in the center of camp, or whether she had gone to New York by ship, like the Guides' women.

Stewart shook his head, cocked his leg over the cantle of his saddle to steady himself, and looked into the gloom again.

"Damn the heat," he said snappishly.

Jeremy shrugged. "Drink some water, sir."

"I don't want water."

"You should drink some water, sir."

Stewart turned and glared at them both for a moment, and then smiled. "Well, gentlemen, we missed them."

Caesar nodded. Lieutenant Martin approached and Caesar gave him a description of what they had hoped to accomplish. Stewart handed Martin the glass, and he looked into the haze for a moment before giving an exclamation.

"Isn't that the gleam of bayonets?" he said, pushing the glass at Stewart. Stewart finished a long pull at the canteen that Jeremy had held out to him and looked guilty for a moment before seizing the telescope and taking a look.

"Look at that," he said. "Jeremy, get back immediately. Find Colonel Musgrave and tell him that the Continentals are forming to attack our right." He looked for a moment. "Well spotted, young Martin. Look at them all. Tell the colonel that I have no idea of a count in this haze but that they appear to be formidable."

Caesar shook his head. "I don't want to fight in this heat."

"Just so." Stewart motioned at their companies. "I had thought to leave a detachment here, but there is no purpose if they are coming to contest these woods."

"We could give them a little harassing fire as they come up," Martin said eagerly.

Stewart nodded, motioning to his bugler to sound the retreat. "Good thought. Keep the Guides here for a bit. Be ready to move, though—if the army marches, we won't keep this ground."

Martin looked at Caesar. "Did I do right, Sergeant?"

Caesar smiled. "We'll see, sir. But I'd rather be doing the harassing fire than taking it all morning."

★　★　★

George Lake led his company at the head of the column, and he saluted General Lee as he passed him, turning his head to the right and bringing his sword up in a smart salute. Lee waved with his whip.

All the light companies of the army had been concentrated in a single division with several crack regiments. They were all veterans and all tried troops, and George gathered that they were actually going to attack the

British, a thing that hadn't really been done since he was at Trenton. He was excited, but under the excitement he worried about the heat, which was already affecting his older men, and he worried about the dissension. He knew officers who said that General Lee thought this plan to be fatally flawed, and he knew officers who thought that there was no plan. George knew that Lee had not ridden out to view the enemy or the ground in any detail, and this negligence worried him. But Lee was popular, and he looked every inch a soldier, sitting on his horse and watching the columns march forward. Lake could only hope.

✱ ✱ ✱

In three years of fighting, Caesar had never been a spectator in a major action. The Guides occupied the fringe of woods facing west and waited. Twice in the morning they drove off parties of the enemy, but although these actions helped steady the new men, they were minor affairs. The enemy only came in small patrols and were happy to be seen off with a burst of fire. They took one prisoner from the second patrol, an elderly private in the Second Virginia.

To the south, they could just make out the enemy columns forming in the dust and haze. After they repulsed the second patrol, Caesar went to the edge of the woods at Virgil's urging and watched both of the grenadier battalions forming front from columns to attack a steep hill over a mile away.

Caesar nodded. "I wondered last night why we didn't occupy that hill, and today we have to take it back."

Virgil pointed with his chin at the main camp, where the long lines of wagons were moving out to the north.

Caesar nodded again. "I see them."

"So it won't be no big battle. The line regiments is already movin'." Virgil, a great respecter of the British line, thought it unfair that the British generals seemed to fight their battles in America with only their lights and grenadiers. "If'n they never use them boys for ought but re-placements, they'll be sorry soldiers when the day comes."

Caesar looked at Virgil, a little surprised, as it wasn't Virgil's usual line of thought. "What day, Virgil?"

"The day when them Continentals is ready for a proper battle."

✱ ✱ ✱

They marched and countermarched in the heat, and the British artillery played on them like a deadly cloud of insects, the big balls emitting a deadly whine as they flew, or rolling and bouncing ominously over the hard-packed ground. Despite the moisture in the air, the ground seemed as hard as rock, and it reflected the heat like a great brown mirror. George had already lost two men to the cannon, but he had lost five to the heat.

And they hadn't come to grips yet.

He saw the distant columns of red come together and shake out into a line and he watched with professional admiration as the British came on, rounding a little bend in the road with their columns behind. Two of their six-pounders set up at the head of the near column and fired a round of grape into the battalion next to George, and it gave ground. It didn't run, like in the old days, but just fell back a little, giving the British the crest of the hill.

George ran to his commander, Colonel Weedon. "Are there any orders, sir?" he asked, pointing at the British grenadiers.

"None since we marched this morning, Captain." He looked at his watch and then down at the British. "Last I heard, we were attacking."

"Guess no one told them," said George. He turned and found Caleb Cooke at his side.

"I'm holding this position until General Lee should choose to honor me with his commands," said the Yankee captain. His bitterness was obvious.

George ran back to his company in time to see the head of the British column start forward up the hill aimed at the space to his left. He marched his company forward a few paces until they had a clear shot down the hill and ordered his sergeant to open fire. Companies to his right were doing the same. Colonel Weedon was pushing two companies a little down the slope to fire into the flank of the attack when the woods in front of them erupted with more grenadiers. George had never seen an attack like it. The British were in no sort of line, and he watched a group of their officers run into the little patch of swamp at the base of the hill to his right and wade through, a dozen grenadiers pushing along strongly in their wake until the whole group was across. The two companies that had gone forward to flank the first column were now caught in the flank by this second group. Despite outnumbering them heavily, they were so caught by the initial surprise that they ran, with fewer than twenty grenadiers pursuing them to the top of the ridge. In a moment, both his flanks were lost and the hilltop was a sea of red jackets.

He wanted to stand and gape unbelievingly. This wasn't some superior performance by the British, but massive incompetence by his own.

"Get them back!" he yelled to his sergeants, and then pointed at his new bugler, a little black boy of twelve or so that he had found in a cottage. "Sound retreat."

★　★　★

Washington rode forward, listening to the sounds of musketry in the heavy air and concerned at its volume and direction.

"Surely that sounds closer than the last," he said to Lafayette.

He began to gallop and his staff followed him forward. They began to pass panicked men and deserters, and the junior officers of the staff set themselves to round these up. Then they passed a trickle of wounded men moving to the rear.

"Damn the man," Washington said aloud. These were his very best troops, the light companies of the old Continental regiments and the rangers and riflemen, as well as whole battalions of crack veterans. Off to the left he could see a column of Massachusetts men standing to, drooping in the heat. He turned to Fitzgerald.

"Tell whoever commands that column to get those men out of the sun. What is he thinking of?" He rode forward, his horse lathered in sweat but still full of spirit. Washington didn't seem in the least fazed by the oppressive heat. Lafayette was invigorated by his burst of energy, and the little flow of breeze generated by the gallop had helped.

Washington rode into the middle of a rout. The whole of the road was choked with disorganized units trying to force past each other, with officers striving to rally their men and men too panicked to be rallied. A battery of guns had cut their traces and left their pieces sitting on the hard-packed road to get away on the horses. Washington fumed. He rode back and forth, suddenly everywhere, cautioning a colonel, soothing a jittery captain, praising the efforts of the men who suddenly found themselves in the rear guard. All his staff flew about like demons, riding from unit to unit, bringing up clumps of men who seemed willing to return to their duty, in some cases simply giving men heart who had lost it or telling commanders to make their men drink water. It all helped, and little by little they turned the shambles back into the cream of the army.

Through it all, Washington looked for Charles Lee. He found him sitting quietly on his horse amid his small staff, gazing at a distant hilltop where a battalion of British grenadiers were putting themselves in a state of defense.

"What are you about, sir?" asked Washington as soon as he rode up.

Lee looked as if he had been struck. "I told you they wouldn't stand," Lee said bitterly. "Those grenadiers rolled the so-called elite of our army off that hill like so many children. They won't stand."

Washington looked at him with something pretty near loathing. "Sir, they are able, and by God they shall do it! Your retreat is a disgrace. Do me the favor of accepting responsibility for your own errors and not blaming the men who sought to serve you."

Lee rounded on him. "There's irony for you, sir. *You* are going to criticize *my* command?"

"I am. I can see that the scale of this operation was beyond your grasp." Washington turned aside as a trooper of the light horse cantered up and saluted, presenting a message. Washington read it. Lee made no attempt to see it, but sat fuming.

"Was it your intention to attack the enemy rear guard from both flanks?" Washington asked.

"Once I had lured them with a feigned retreat."

Washington looked at the re-forming army.

He turned his horse so that he was nose to tail with the messenger, scanning the distant hill where the grenadiers could be seen. He beckoned to Hamilton and looked at a map for a moment.

"I'm taking command," he said.

Lee was clearly stunned. He rode off a distance and sat quietly. Perhaps he had mistaken his man.

Washington finished his map study, lining up features visible in the endless heat shimmer with marks on the map. He turned back to the messenger.

"Attack!" he said.

★   ★   ★

George Lake's men were not beaten. They made that clear by cheering Washington as he rode up to them in the full heat of the afternoon, despite their parched throats, and the cheer was taken up along the line, even by men who had run from a handful of grenadiers an hour before. They cheered and cheered. Washington smiled a little, hiding his teeth but visibly pleased. Lake stepped out of his spot at the head of his company and caught at Lafayette's bridle. The young general smiled down at him.

"What happened?" Lake pleaded.

"I don't think we will ever know. I am not experienced, eh? But it seems to me that Lee had no plan."

Lake shook his head in angry negation. "We marched out there smartly enough and *then* there were no orders."

"Perhaps he had a plan. And the British attack surprised him. I think perhaps General Lee does not like being surprised."

Lake nodded, agreeing now.

"But war is nothing but a series of surprises and disappointments. That is why this one is so very good." Lafayette pointed at Washington. "He is never ruined by a surprise, eh?"

Lake smiled up at Lafayette. "Now we attack? General?" Lake was never quite sure if Lafayette really was a general as he was twenty years younger than the others.

"It is hot," Lafayette responded warily. "And many of these troops have already fought, whether well or badly. I think that I have learned that most soldiers will only fight once in a day."

The men behind Lake cheered again, as if to prove the young general wrong.

Lake went back to where his company was waiting in the shade and told them to be ready. Then he took out his horn inkwell, suddenly his most precious possession, and started to add to his endless letter to Betsy.

✷ ✷ ✷

Caesar watched the grenadiers attack in the distance and then settled down to a long exchange of fire with some militia to their flank. As the morning wore on, the militia began to come closer and there were some rifle balls among the shots coming at their wood line. Mr. Martin moved up and down the line quite boldly and set a good example, and Caesar developed a new liking for the man. Several of the soldiers of the Guides who had been down on him noted that he did not hesitate to share his canteen with a black soldier—a sin that had been imputed to him at spring drill.

Jeremy visited them from time to time, checking on their position and a similar one occupied by some men from the Queen's Rangers just to the south. In late morning his horse took a ball, and he had to walk back to the light infantry camp. It was quite a feat of bravery, unnoticed on that busy day, but Caesar watched him go the whole distance, under fire much of the way, with deep misgiving, because Jeremy seemed to be above such notions as using the available cover, or running.

He was back on a new horse by early afternoon. He rode up to Mr. Martin, and Caesar trotted over through the heavy air. There were guns firing to the north, or perhaps low summer thunder—it was difficult to be sure. Caesar had soaked his jacket with sweat, and his hatband and even his leather equipment were damp.

"Men are low on powder and we're all out of water," Caesar said without preamble.

"I just said the same," Martin added, a little defensively.

"What's in front of you?" asked Jeremy, scribbling on a little pad.

"Militia and some rifles. Perhaps more rifles now than there were." Caesar looked at Martin, who nodded.

"I think they are just waiting for us to leave so they can get in these woods and start firing on the camp," said Martin.

"Rotate another company out here so we can get powder and water," said Caesar. Martin was proving to have a head on his shoulders. He nodded at Caesar's pronouncement. Jeremy handed them his canteen, which was full, and another.

"All I could bring. Lieutenant Martin, Captain Stewart says that this is not going well and that the column has been very slow to leave camp."

Martin nodded slowly.

"I think the attacks by the grenadiers are an attempt to force the enemy to break contact so that the rest of us can withdraw in something like safety. Captain Stewart thinks the grenadiers have gone too far, and so does Major Simcoe." Jeremy paused as if he feared he was saying too much. "The Jaegers are right there behind you, where we started this morning. If you have to pull back, at least they can fire over you once you are in the low ground."

Martin looked up at him. "I take it that means the light infantry are going forward. To *rescue* the grenadiers?"

"It could mean that, sir. I'm sorry to be obtuse, but it could mean that."

Caesar leaned in. "But Jeremy doesn't feel he can say, because it wasn't in the message he was given, but rather in something he overheard, am I right?"

Jeremy smiled. "Just so, Julius."

Martin shook his head. "We need water and powder." He sounded worried. As Jeremy rode off, Caesar touched his arm and smiled. Martin brightened up immediately.

"You just remind me if I forget, Sergeant," he said in his official voice, immediately cheerful and businesslike.

"You're doing very well, if I may say, sir."

"Why, thankee, Julius Caesar. Thank you for that."

★　★　★

Because they weren't running, they could make their water last, and the shade of the trees was a relief that many soldiers on that field would have killed for, but the heat grew until it seemed the principal enemy. Men stopped firing because they lacked the energy to load, and everyone was wet with sweat. Caesar and Martin moved constantly and were the most tired because of it, but the action was never anything but an exchange of shots at extreme range. Jeremy's first horse was their only casualty except for a graze to Angus's head that ruined his hat and made him proud as Lucifer.

But it went on and on. The smoke simply sat on them and seemed to do nothing to drive off the incessant whine of the mosquitoes. They lay in their sweat and the stink of their powder, coughing at the heavy air and eaten by the bugs, worse than any day Caesar could remember in the swamp.

The firing began to rise again to the south, but the smoke and haze of the day now hid the hill where the grenadiers were all together. Moments later, though, Major Simcoe came riding up on his big gray charger almost white with lather and dust. He had a bugler behind him and two junior officers, all in the dark green jackets and blue facings of the Queen's Rangers.

"Damn, it's hot," he said when he met Martin. He waved to Caesar, and this time Caesar brought Fowver so that they would all have the same story. Simcoe waited until they were near him and then unrolled a little map drawn on the back of a letter.

"I think they are trying to pin the rear guard here"—he pointed at the hill—"and then get around to attack us here and here"—he pointed at the woods they were in and another opposite, where the Highlanders were—"to cut us all off and force our surrender. I think that General Clinton decided this morning to attack here"—he pointed back to the hill that the grenadiers had taken—"to break up the attack and give us time to get free."

Caesar followed it all. It was the most spread-out battle he had been part of, and it seemed to move at a glacial pace, perhaps because of the heat. And even with a map and Simcoe's explanation, it was too confused a battle for him. They seemed to be defending in two directions and attacking in a third.

"It seemed to work, and then something has spurred the rebels to another effort, and I think they are building to an attack right here."

"Where are the light infantry?"

"Gone off to support the grenadiers."

Caesar looked at the camp they had left that morning, now nearly deserted. Simcoe pointed him off to the right, where a column of green-coated men was approaching.

"I want you to launch an attack here and try to get a prisoner. I'll move into these positions behind you. Then you fall back through me, get some water and powder, and join the lights of Colonel Robinson's Loyal Americans as a reserve with the Jaegers and my rifle company." He pointed to the rear, where green-coated men from the Loyalist regiments were moving into the shade.

Martin nodded to Caesar and he had his whistle to his lips in an instant. Fowver ran for the head of his platoon.

It was like a repeat of the early morning. The enemy fired sporadically but wouldn't stand, and the Guides moved forward to a patch of brushy ground by a little stream just a few hundred paces away. The move took them five minutes. Their reward was a trickle of cold water in the stream, and Caesar ignored Simcoe's wave that they should return immediately while he had Willy and Jim filling canteens at a basin in the little stream. The canteens had narrow necks and they didn't fill fast, and their situation in the patch of brush was too precarious to allow them all to fill at the same time, so the corporals moved up and down, risking their lives in the new volume of fire from across the hazy flats. As soon as the last canteen was filled, Caesar gave the signal and they all fired together, not to hit anything but to make a solid screen of smoke that hung, concealing them for a minute or more, and then they ran back as quickly as a day's fierce heat and too little water allowed.

Their wood was full of green-coated men in tall helmets. Caesar knew a few of the men in the Queen's Rangers, and he accepted a little cigar from a corporal who had just taken a long pull at his canteen. Mr. Martin was explaining the frustrating nature of their attack to one of Colonel Robinson's men, a black.

"There's no cover to approach them," he said, and Simcoe just nodded.

"Go on back to camp and rest. I'll send for you if I need you."

They crossed the long field to the camp area, deserted except for the other soldiers in reserve. The Highlanders looked fierce, still capable, but they were so red in the face that Caesar worried for them. The handful of mounted troops were watering their horses all the time, and the Jaegers lay in the sun and burned, their pale complexions betraying them. Caesar kept looking up the ridge to the place where the grenadiers and now the lights had gone. He couldn't remember the last time he'd gone into action without Captain Stewart, and he didn't like the sound of firing to the south.

★　★　★

As soon as they started up the hill, Crawford knew that they were too late. It was obvious that the grenadiers had been clawed cruelly by the artillery fire they had heard during the whole miserable march to the hill. As they started the climb in the full heat of the midafternoon sun, the grenadiers were retiring. They were magnificent soldiers, and not one of them ran, but their companies were the size of platoons and they were withdrawing off the hill steadily. Stewart could see that he had already lost men to the heat and expected that the grenadiers, in action all morning, would be worse.

Crawford couldn't see what pressure they were taking from his spot at the left end of the company. And then he looked to the front in time to see the whole woods fill with Continentals like a bucket filling under a pump. In a moment there were hundreds of them forming just above him on the hill.

"Halt!" cried Captain Stewart, racing down the line. The company next to theirs kept marching and was instantly exposed to a storm of fire. Stewart yelled to McDonald and then rode up to Crawford. McDonald was leading the firing.

"Hold here for as long as you can, but for God's sake give the ground if you must. I'm going to see what the grenadiers intend. I'll be back in a moment."

Crawford saluted and turned to face the front. The rebels, who had been a mob a moment before, were forming like soldiers. Crawford's company fired into them, and they took the volley at close range and continued to form their line. A company off to the left was already firing. Crawford stepped out of the line and walked back to the center, where Captain Stewart usually stood to fight the company. The first platoon was almost loaded. Never taking his eyes from the enemy, he nodded to McDonald, who was preparing to fire. His men were outnumbered badly, and he doubted that these well-drilled enemy troops would fire any worse than they formed. He spared a glance for Captain Stewart riding low in his saddle off to the right and well up the hill, and Jeremy following him, and he saw Stewart's horse go down as if all its legs had been cut at once. Stewart did not rise.

✶　✶　✶

Jeremy leapt his horse over his downed master and fired a pistol at the first rebel to appear in the distance. He looked around desperately, but the grenadiers were just too far off to the right and the rebels were pouring down this part of the hill. He dismounted.

A ball had killed the horse dead. Its whole weight lay on Stewart, and Stewart was barely conscious.

"Get ye gone, Jeremy!" he muttered.

"Nonsense, sir." Jeremy tried to give him a little water but the movement caused Stewart to faint from the pain. Jeremy cushioned his head with his saddlebags and took a moment to do those things he had heard veterans recommend you do when you are about to be captured. He took his watch and put it next to his skin, concealed his ivory-handled dagger in his boot, and put several golden guineas inside his shirt. He saw the rebels forming their company just forty yards away and he worried that they might fire on him, so he tied his white stock to his sword and waved it. The enemy company marched right by him, their officer simply waving at him.

"Come, that's gentlemanly," he said aloud, hoping his words would comfort Stewart, and turned to find another party of rebels with a tall man in an old blue coat at their head. They were moving carefully, formed in open order, and a number of them had weapons pointed at Jeremy. He held out his sword to the leader, who looked faintly familiar.

The leader grinned. "You killed Weymes," he said.

Bludner raised his pistol and shot Jeremy dead.

★ ★ ★

Forty minutes later, Sir Henry Clinton's counterattack with all the grenadiers and lights and all the reserves cleared the hill to the crest, and Caesar ran to the fallen horse. Stewart was gone, but Jeremy lay there, his hands out on the ground and his legs a little apart, lying facedown. He had been plundered thoroughly, his watch and guineas taken and all Stewart's saddle gear ripped clear of his horse. Caesar picked Jeremy up and threw him over his shoulder. Jeremy was still wearing his breeches, covered in blood, and his boots—apparently the tight fit was more than casual plunderers were prepared to face. He carried the body down the hill as the sun pounded on them and the order was given that finally allowed them to start a withdrawal from the field. He carried Jeremy for over an hour, until the first halt, not speaking to the men around him.

When he gathered the men of the Guides and told them to prepare for a burial party, some men from Stewart's company appeared with a cart. The cart had some wounded grenadiers in it, but the grenadiers were quickly convinced that their cart could carry a dead man as well. They stepped off into the heat and marched all night with the cart in their midst, and the moans of the wounded grenadiers were like a lament for Jeremy, and defeat.

★ ★ ★

To the south, George Lake's men stood on the crest of the hill and watched the last of the British light companies march away from them. They were too tired to pursue, and they had taken casualties themselves, although more from the heat than the enemy.

"I think we won," croaked a man in George's company. It was said quietly, as if the saying would break the spell.

George stretched the fingers of his right hand where he had clutched a musket all day. "Well, boys, they were trying to retreat when the day started, and at the end of it, they retreated." He looked at the ranks of his men and smiled. "On the other hand, we're here, and they ain't, which is a sight better than we're used to."

They gave a weak cheer, and another as they saw Washington and his staff ride out of the stuffy gloom again. Lake saw Lafayette peering down the hill at the backs of the last British light troops, and listened to them as they tried to count the casualties, and then, in the boldest moment of his life, George Lake stepped in front of Washington's horse.

"Give you the joy of your victory, sir," he said, amazed at his own voice.

Washington looked up from a map and peered at him for a moment, and then smiled, the thin-lipped smile that never showed his teeth.

"Not much of a victory," he said, but his men began to cheer again, and the cheer spread in waves. And then Washington's grin split his face, and his eyes kindled and the cheers went on. Lafayette shook his hand, and then George's, and then they were all around him, a wave of noise that spread from the center until the British could hear it two miles away.

★　★　★

Caesar was keeping the men together with physical threats by the time they halted, and Mr. Martin was bringing up the rear with the stragglers. But when they had rested for a few minutes and their legs stopped shaking, they took a little water and some hardtack and felt human enough to bury Jeremy.

They took turns digging, as they always did, although he was just one man, and the contributions from Stewart's company made it go fast. Some of Stewart's men had stripped Jeremy's boots and bloody breeches and then put on clean ones from his baggage, and they wrapped him in a clean linen sheet. Virgil carved him a cross from a downed branch as quick as he could, and Mr. Crawford paid the farmer in whose field they were going to plant him to get a stone. They were close to areas that their patrols would operate when they came out from New York, and Caesar thought they might get this way again. He didn't seem able to think of much else, except that Jeremy had become a friend of a sort he had never had before. Jeremy had taught him so much. And that—like Sergeant Peters—he was dead.

McDonald came up to him and just nodded a few times, and then put Jeremy's ivory-handled button dagger in his hand.

"He had it in his boot. We thought you ought to have it." Some other men from Stewart's company nodded behind him.

When Jeremy was in the ground and they had fired a volley over him, some officers came up to protest the firing, but Mr. Martin and Mr. Crawford sent them packing. Virgil, Willy, and McDonald lit pipes, and they passed the tobacco around as they had for their dead since Virginia.

Caesar found that he couldn't get the pipe into his mouth, and it struck him that he was crying, great choking sobs that wracked him until Virgil put his arms around him and hugged him close a moment. He hadn't cried for Tonny, or Tom, or Peters, or any of the others, but he cried for Jeremy, and Virgil sat beside him with his arm around him, as the night suddenly cooled with the passing of that awful heat.

Chapter Nineteen

New Jersey and New York, July 4, 1778

Jeremy was dead.

It hit Stewart at different times, because Jeremy had been there so often and because he was weak and needed the man. Both men, Jeremy the servant and the other Jeremy, who could make a joke about Miss McLean and a suggestion about Sally. Sometimes in one breath.

He would have to do something about Sally. Even in a fever, he could see that.

He lay in a little house somewhere in the Jerseys and watched the sun creep across his white, white quilt. He thought about Jeremy, and Sally, and once he found himself having a conversation with Jeremy, who was not, of course, there. He worried for a little that he was losing his mind, but later he realized that he had a fever.

Men came to see him from time to time, and a girl fed him soup. He didn't really know the men, but he had enough spirit to see that they were Continental officers and that they were kind. He had visited their wounded often enough. It was that sort of war, sometimes.

Then he woke in the night and was well. Weaker, somehow, than when he dreamed and spoke with Jeremy, but better, too. He'd had fevers before, and he knew this one had just broken. He lay awake, thinking about Jeremy in a different way. He smiled a little, and slept.

When he next awoke, one of the men was by his side with a watch, looking at his pulse and counting, while another was standing behind him.

"Quite a credit to the trade, this fellow. Healthy as a horse in no time," the nearer man said, putting his hand down on the coverlet. "You awake, sir?"

"I am."

"It always pleases a doctor when one of his patients does him the courtesy of surviving a treatment."

"Give my man the bill." That little pain. He had no man. "Perhaps not. Give it to me, I suppose."

"I think the Continental Army is footing the bill, sir. But I need to tell you that your leg, while healing, has been shockingly set about, and that I took a pistol ball out of your shoulder, and another out of an older wound low on your back. It was there, and I thought I might as well cut."

Stewart nodded, a little troubled by the number of wounds, and puzzled, as he couldn't remember getting any of them. "Can you tell me what happened?"

"Not I, sir. Perhaps Captain Lake, here. But you are on the mend. I'll look in again later—always a pleasure to see one that heals, eh?"

The doctor indicated some medicines to the lady of the house and bowed his way out. The officer remained, watching him in silence, as the lady moved about the little room, tossing the pillow and sitting him up. His arm was in a very tight bandage that went across his chest, and his leg was in another. He was afraid to look at the base of the bed, so sure was he that one of his legs was gone, but she moved the blankets to air them and roll him over to strip the sheets, and he saw it. It wasn't exactly handsome, and there was some blood and some yellow fluid on the bandage, but the whole leg was there.

The woman prattled as she moved about the room.

"I hope the captain doesn't think we sympathize with the king just because they gave us a king's officer to heal up," she said, smiling at the other man. "But we are all God's creatures, aren't we, sir?"

The Continental officer smiled and bowed his head.

She turned on Captain Stewart. "And you're awake, so we ought to come to be friends, don't you think?"

He wanted to retreat from all that energy. "Your servant, ma'am."

She curtsied. "And yours, sir. I'm Betsy Holding. And you?"

"Captain John Julius Stewart, ma'am." He looked at the other officer. "If you are my guard, sir, I think I can guarantee that I will make no attempt to escape today."

The other man smiled a little nervously and tossed his hat in his hands. He made a sketchy little bow and Stewart thought that he was probably not very well bred, but then wondered what his own bow had looked like before Jeremy got hold of it. Always Jeremy.

"Captain George Lake, sir. I..." Captain Lake clearly had something very difficult to say. He looked out the window, and Betsy, a woman who had several grown children and was widely known for her sense, bustled around the room one more time and withdrew.

"I can see the gentlemen need to talk," she said.

Lake pulled up a chair and sat on it, backward, his chin on the top rung of the ladder back. Stewart noted that he was wearing a very fine hunting sword. French, he thought.

"Can you tell me how I came to be captured?" he asked.

Lake looked at him and there was some sort of hurt in his eyes. Stewart wondered if he had done the man an injury, but it wasn't that sort of hurt.

"Your horse was hit by a ball. I think it was a roundshot from one of our guns, or perhaps a piece of grape. I saw you go down myself, all in a tumble. Nasty fall."

Stewart nodded. "I think I can agree to that."

"I marched right by you. Your men were trying to flank us and the grenadiers were rallying. I didn't think you looked like much of a threat."

Stewart nodded, and Lake looked away.

"Your... your man came and stood over you." Lake leaned forward. His eyes were intense.

Stewart tried to raise a hand. "I know. He was hit. Somehow I remember that part. I felt him fall across me."

"He was shot while he was trying to surrender, sir. I watched it, and I have waited for you to wake up because I wanted to apologize. I can't think why your man was shot. It turned my stomach. And I know the man who did it—Bludner, who was my own sergeant once."

Stewart looked at the other man, who seemed very moved. He was young and gawky, with a colonial drawl, and his uniform was not quite the thing, but he had that air of confidence that Stewart always associated with the better type of officers. Stewart noticed these things because he was quite consciously walling himself off from the knowledge that his

Jeremy had been shot down in cold blood. He admitted to himself that he had been conscious, had suspected this to be true and simply ignored it. He found himself looking into George Lake's clear green eyes. They were wide and deep and didn't seem to hide any secrets at all. He was very young, and for a moment, Stewart felt as old as the hills. *Bludner*, now that struck a chord. It was a name Sally said both awake and asleep. Stewart tried to overcome his fatigue.

"*Bludner?* A slave-taker?"

"I think he did some such, yes. I thought to report him to the army."

Stewart sat back, tired and old.

"Come back another day, sir." He put his head back on the pillow and went instantly to sleep.

★　★　★

They moved back into the barracks easily, as if they had never been away, and all the women came out to greet them. Many of the Guides' women had never gone to Philadelphia because they'd found work in New York or just didn't want to follow the army, and Caesar thought that perhaps none of them had expected them to be in Philadelphia very long.

Big Lese was there, and Mrs. Peters, coughing and weeping a little and happy to see them back. And there was little Nelly Van Sluyt, who looked half her man's size, and others—women and children who seemed to outnumber the soldiers five to one or more. Caesar had seen that the men were paid before they marched to the barracks, and now he watched attentively as money was handed over to wives who hadn't seen much but rations for nearly a year.

He saw Polly standing with Big Lese and talking to her, bobbing her head as she did when addressing someone her elder, the very soul of courtesy. She looked up at him and smiled, a tiny secret smile with a long message attached, and he responded with a great grin that cracked his whole face in two. And then he went back to work, finding barracks space for the new recruits he'd acquired since they marched for the transports a year before and occasionally facing the hard job of throwing an interloper out of a bunk he or she didn't have a right to. Many black refugees came to the barracks first, or last. And there were holes in the ranks, and losses, and women who knew from letters that their man was dead but had come for the parade in hopes there had been a mistake, and other, harder women who came to get their man's last pay, or perhaps a replacement man. It was the same at every barracks in New York, and the men had joked about it the night before. Now it didn't seem so funny, with women and children being turned out because they were no longer attached to the army, and others coming in. They had to find space for new men they had picked up, or move men. Sam the bugler was no longer a child, and needed a bed. Tonny had fallen and a new corporal got his space. On and on. Through it all, Caesar and Fowver worked, each wanting to be else-where or to enjoy some of the happier portions, but they had no time and theirs was the only authority high enough to settle the resentments.

When Lieutenant Martin arrived, Caesar left him with two of the stickiest domestic situations and plunged into the kitchen, where Mrs. Peters and Big Lese were measuring out the allowance of pork. It was a pork day, and there would be some pudding—plum duff, by the smell.

"Where's Polly?" he asked, and they both gave him the knowing look that matrons reserve for the young and besotted.

"She waited," said Lese in her West Indian singsong.

"But she said that as you were so important," said Mrs. Peters, "she'd just go about her business."

They laughed at him when his face fell. "I do like to see you look like a normal young man, an' not just Mars, the God of War," said Mrs. Peters. She had a special privilege: Although her husband was dead and had never technically been a member of the Black Guides, or even the Provincial Corps of the British army, she was mysteriously listed on their rolls and continued there. She and Lese laughed at his confusion and weighed another piece of pork.

"Of course," Mrs. Peters continued, "she did say that if you were decently repentant, she and her father might consider having you to dinner."

"It's not my fault!" he said, looking at the two of them. They, if anyone, should understand. Lese Fowver knew every detail of every scrap of a quarrel in the company, and Mrs. Peters had been dealing with barracks issues for four years, and a house full of slaves for most of her life. They both just smiled again.

"She's in that little church on Queen Street, sewing," Lese said. "Maybe you should find her."

Mrs. Peters stopped him. "Did you leave that nice Mr. Martin to deal with the likes of Hester Black?" Hester was the most married, and most voluble, woman in the company. She rarely lacked an issue for her feeling of grievance.

"I did."

"Shame on you, Julius Caesar. And he wanting to get away and find his Miss Hammond." But Caesar was gone.

★ ★ ★

The next day Stewart was able to sit up and eat unaided, and read the Bible, which seemed to be the house's only book. He thumbed through it idly, looking at stories and thinking about slavery. He could almost feel his bones knitting.

Mrs. Holding sat with him, now that he made decent company. She seemed surprised to find that he didn't have a tail and that the Bible didn't burn his hands. She and her husband were dyed-in-the-wool Whigs, "Patriots," as they called themselves. He tried not to use the word *rebel* in her house. She had two sons, both in the militia, and two daughters, both married to men of property. She reminded him of every good wife in Edinburgh, and yet she was thoroughly American in the same way that the Miss Hammonds were.

"Do you have a slave, ma'am?" he asked suddenly. Her mouth became firm.

"I don't hold with it," she said crossly. "It ain't right for Christian folk." He wondered if she had ever allowed her husband an opinion. He liked her.

"Just so," he said, putting his head back on the pillow.

★ ★ ★

Polly kissed him and held him close, but before they had time to babble ten words, she stopped him and pushed him away. He thought it was because they were in a church.

"Sally's in a state," she said.

He wanted to stay with Polly and she wanted him to stay, but Sally was there between them and he knew he owed it to the woman to find her and talk. He could imagine that Sally was in a state, and he thought he knew why.

He went to find Sally. She wasn't at Mother Abbott's anymore— Captain Stewart had seen to that. She had a set of rooms up two flights of stairs over a hatmaker's on Broadway. It was an expensive set of rooms. He was careful going there. Although it was only a few steps up the street from the Moor's Head, people in New York were touchy about color. He thought of Jeremy, who seemed above such notions and yet completely conversant with them, and he thought of fencing with Jeremy just a few doors along. His eyes filled for a moment and he had to stop. When he was himself again, he went to the narrow door for the upstairs rooms and opened it. A woman in a neat bonnet poked her head out of the door to the shop.

"Are you a friend of our lodger, young man?" she asked.

"I am, ma'am," he said, making a leg as Jeremy had taught him. She nodded as if it were her due.

"Do your friend a service then, young man. Tell her that I will not have a lodger who makes a nuisance! And that goes doubly for a black one. I don't care how solid her money is."

Caesar bowed. He had learned from Jeremy how useful these courtesies were for hiding one's thoughts.

"And no male visitors in the evening, or she is out. I told my husband that it was a mistake to take your kind in here."

He bowed again. He felt Jeremy's voice in his head, and he smiled. "What kind is that, ma'am?"

She looked at him and shook her head as if it were a matter of little importance.

"What visitor did she have?"

"Now, that's a proper question for a brother to ask of his sister, I'm thinking." Caesar wasn't sure what he thought of being Sally's brother, but he let it pass. "A little white man. I didn't like his looks, and I'm certain he hit her. What do you think of that, young man?"

He shook his head.

"Hmmf. As I thought. None of us is any better than God made us, I expect. But I want her quiet or gone, do you hear?" She nodded vigorously and shut the door.

Caesar shook his head at his own thoughts as he went up the stairs and knocked.

Sally answered. She was in a shift, and drunk.

"I heard Jeremy's dead," she said. He smelled the rum on her. She was naked under the shift, and yet he was quite unmoved by it, because she was so clearly distraught.

"He is," Caesar said, coming into her room.

"I loved him." She sat on her bed, a fancy canopy bed from a shop. Her trunks were mostly unpacked on the floor. Her lip was split and she had a bruise on her face and another on her naked shoulder. Caesar nodded easily. He had suspected that Sally was sharing the master and the man, but it hadn't been his place to say, and Jeremy had never even hinted. Jeremy could be very closed about things.

And Caesar wasn't too sure he believed Sally, either. She might just love him now for the drama. She was not a simple woman.

"And Captain Stewart?" Caesar asked. He was surprised at himself, because he didn't *care*. He didn't want to know.

"I think I love him a little," said Sally. "Don' tell me he's dead, too."

"No. He's a prisoner, but Mr. Martin says he's already on the list to be exchanged. Polly said that he needs shirts and the like, and thought you'd help make him up a package to send through the lines. There's a cartel going tonight."

She started at the words *through the lines*.

"What's a car-tel?" she asked a little listlessly.

"A flag of truce," he said. He was suddenly suspicious of her, as he had been of Lark in the swamp and of Marcus White. "Who hit you, Sally?"

She just shook her head. "A man," she answered, as if that were all the answer that was needed.

Caesar shook his head in weary disgust. "You loved them, but you went and found a man? And he hit you? What does Polly see in you, or the Reverend White?"

She was crying again, drunken tears that could have been real or fake.

"I don' know, Julius Caesar."

He looked around the room, at the wreck of her trunks, and smelled the reek of the rum.

"We're going to clean this room. And you. And we're going to find the captain some shirts and suchlike, so that he thinks his mistress likes him enough to bother."

Sally just sat on the bed, shaking with sobs. She was hiding her eyes, and it almost seemed that she was laughing. He shook his head.

"Your landlady wants you gone. How are you going to explain *that* to him? You want to go back to Mother Abbott's? Or just lean your back against a building an' get it done with any sailor trying to make his tide?" He was harsh, and she just sat, her head down, until he finished. Then he went to get Polly. He wanted to slam the door, because it would have made him feel better, but he was afraid the noise would be the last straw for the old woman downstairs.

★　★　★

Stewart got himself up and put on a lovely clean shirt with the embarrassed help of Mrs. Holding. It was one of his own, but someone had rinsed it in lavender and pricked his initials into it since he had sent it north with the shipboard baggage, and he smelled it carefully. It had to be Polly. She could sew, and she took care in matters like this. Sally might dance and talk and drink, but her sewing didn't run to these fine stitches. He smiled, though, because the perfume on the note had been Sally's, although the note was in Caesar's square military hand with another from Simcoe and yet a third from Crawford, all enough to make him dab at his eyes.

And there was a note from Miss McLean. It was a cheerful missive about the turning of summer in the Highlands, the sounds birds made, and her eagerness to be with him. It, too, had a little scent attached. From his bedside, he could read her note and smell her scent, and smell Sally's, and feel little guilt. Just sorrow, really. He had taken a black mistress because it had seemed less a betrayal than taking a white one. But now, at a distance, he found that he liked Sally fine and that Jeremy's death freed him from the guilt of it. It made no sense, but it was fact.

"Your friends, sir?" asked Mrs. Holding. She wanted to get him dressed so that she didn't have to dally with a man in just breeches and a shirt.

"Just so, ma'am. If you could maneuver that waistcoat round my bandage? Well done. And a stock? Yes, I think they included a buckle."

She held up his best paste buckle, a magnificent square of dazzling jewels set in silver. He had bought it behind Jeremy's back. Jeremy thought it vulgar.

"Goodness me, sir. I've never seen such a thing. And this is for a man?" She looked at it with something between admiration and horror. "You'll not see its like in Bergen County!"

"I didn't think I would," he said pleasantly. She got the stock buckled.

"And to think you are going to dine with General Washington," she said reverentially.

"Yes," said Stewart as she tried to fuss with his hair. "Yes, it's quite an honor for him."

She struck him gently on the shoulder. "You are quite a card, I find. Quite the young spark."

He tried not to wince as she tugged at his hair. It made him think of Jeremy, of course, and yet he smiled. Sometimes, thinking of Jeremy made him smile. He opened the letter from Simcoe, and a page from *Rivington's*

Gazette fell out. He shook it open one-handed and read through the items until he saw the notice that he had been wounded and captured, with a little star beside it, and then it struck him that he had been mentioned in dispatches. He smiled. He flipped it over and saw the quote of the dispatch, a very pretty piece of nonsense that mentioned him in a most heroic light.

Poor Jeremy would have loved this moment, he thought. He put it with Simcoe's unread letter as he heard Captain Lake ascending the stairs.

Lake put his head round the door and smiled.

"So you are well enough to come?" He seemed very nervous.

Stewart laughed. "A little banged about, but nothing that should worry Mr. Washington."

"You mustn't call him that, John." Lake shook his head. "It makes him that angry."

Stewart bowed to hide his smile.

"Perhaps you can relieve Mrs. Holding of the odious duties of helping a man to dress by holding that coat, George," he said easily, and Mrs. Holding chuckled at him.

"He's been difficult all afternoon, sir," she said. "I think it the great pity of the world that you have to go and exchange him so that he'll go back to shooting at you directly."

Stewart winced as his hand was thrust into the coat and the abused shoulder took the strain.

"I think it will be some time before I'm shooting at Captain Lake." He smiled at a sudden thought. "Indeed, I wonder if I won't go home to recover." Home to Edinburgh, covered in glory. *Yes.* And then no. He thought of Jeremy, whom he had counted on for humor and for advice in dealing with Miss McLean's father. But life was going to go on. And he would see Jeremy avenged.

George Lake's hands were cold with nerves.

"That's good," he said. He sounded strained. Stewart frowned at him from inches away and Lake closed his coat.

"Are you worrying about a dinner with General Washington and his staff?"

"I don't know how to act like them," he said.

"Fie on you," said Mrs. Holding. "Don't be an ungrateful body, Captain Lake. And poor Captain Stewart, putting himself out all morning to show you how to eat like a gentleman."

Lake hung his head, and Stewart hobbled across the room.

"George Lake, you have, by all accounts, won several actions all by yourself. And now a dinner undoes you, and that with your own general? Look at me, sir. A poor wounded officer surrounded by his enemies, going to eat with the very ogre who looks to overturn the *rightful* government of this country."

"You put me in mind of Mr. Lovell, John. He says such things. But Washington is no ogre."

"That's your sweetheart's da', then?"

George blushed. He had been easy with his confidences, so quickly had he taken a liking to Stewart. And now Stewart was using them to abuse him.

"Oh, fie on it, Captain. She is your sweetheart, will ye, nil ye."

"Oh, shame on you, Captain Stewart," cried Mrs. Holding, laughing despite herself.

George Lake simply shook his head at the two of them. "All very well for you to laugh," he said. "I fairly dread this dinner. And the marquis will be there, too, I have no doubt."

A week on, and Caesar was finally getting to have his dinner with Polly, although it had widened into a dinner with Polly and her father ... and Sally. Caesar hadn't known what to make of Sally since that afternoon. She hadn't been drunk again, and had comported herself soberly, and even sat patiently with Polly, learning to put an initial on Captain Stewart's shirt. Sally did one in the time it took Polly to pick out the letters in five others, but that didn't lessen the accomplishment.

They were to dine at the Moor's Head, and Caesar arranged it, securing a table and ordering the food. The black patrons seldom ran to such an occasion, but it was not so rare for the Reverend White, as he had prosperous friends. And the Black Guides had something of the run of the place. It promised to be a very good dinner, private in the little room off the hall to the kitchen.

Caesar came in his best scarlet coat, wearing a watch he had kept from the days in the swamp and that Jeremy had arranged to repair last year. He had good new boots and fine smallclothes, all of which had been in Jeremy's traveling trunk. It made him feel odd to wear them. Polly had taken them apart and altered them to fit. He was dressed to ask for Polly's hand.

"You look very fine," she said.

She was dressed in a sack-back gown of printed linen that made her look as slim as a young tree, and had a little cap on her head that made her face as beautiful as he had ever seen it.

"You are the most beautiful woman I've ever seen," he said with a bow.

She looked over her shoulder as if looking for someone else in the room and then smacked him on the arm.

Marcus White was dressed in severe but fashionable black, with a new coat and new smallclothes and a white collar that seemed to shine like righteousness. He was leading Sally by the hand, and she was dressed as modestly as she ever had been in Philadelphia. Caesar, who had to judge men every day, knew in his bones that she had dressed to let Polly be the center of attention, and he liked her for it. As they walked through the common room, every eye there was on them. More than one voice suggested that some of the blacks were getting above themselves, but never loudly, and Major Simcoe rose and kissed Polly's hand. He didn't directly address Sally, a complicated piece of social tactics that avoided both offense and impertinence.

"Your servant, miss," he said formally, and Polly showed him just the least flash of her eyes as she curtsied in return, a flash that made him smile unexpectedly.

Then they crossed the rest of the room and left it for their private dinner.

★ ★ ★

Stewart was seated near the middle of the table, with Captain Lake across from him and Alexander Hamilton on his right. Lafayette was close, above Hamilton. Opposite Lafayette sat Colonel Henry Lee, now a famous cavalryman. General Washington filled the end of the table with both size and spirit.

They were all men of culture and civility—except perhaps Lake, and he was learning. They did not discuss any matter that might give pain to a guest who was an enemy, but instead chatted amiably about letters and sport. Hamilton was delighted to find that Stewart was a fellow fisherman, and they discoursed on horsehair lines and the latest fashion in hooks for several moments until they realized that they had spread a sort of wondering silence all down the table.

"A glass of wine with you, Captain?" said Lafayette, leaning forward.

"Your servant, Marquis."

"And perhaps you will then enlighten us all about this multiplying reel?"

Stewart winced in embarrassment.

"I am sorry to be a boor," he said.

"Nothing of the kind, sir, I assure you, and I can guarantee that my friend Hamilton will insist."

"Well, then," said Stewart. "It is a brass winch, for holding line, you see? Except that it has a gear on the shaft so that the user has some mechanical advantage as he winds. Am I plain? So that, instead of just storing your line on a winch, now you could actually use it to land a fish."

"Gimcrack notion," said Fitzgerald. "What if the thing slips and you lose your fish?"

"Does the sear slip on a well-made flintlock?"

"I take your point, sir." Fitzgerald raised his glass, acknowledging it. "But do you really need such an advantage?"

"Oh, as to that..." Stewart shrugged. "I don't use one meself, mind. I was just explaining to Colonel Hamilton here why they are coming into fashion. Friends of mine had them made in Philadelphia."

"Oh, they did?" Hamilton smiled. "Perhaps I can do the same, now that...Oh, I'm sorry."

Stewart smiled at them all. "I'm not so sensitive as that."

Washington, as the senior, could not be asked a direct question; it was not done. But he could listen and by his listening betray an interest. Stewart realized that Washington was listening attentively, and turned to him, inviting a question.

"These are trout you are speaking of?"

"Oh, pah, trout," said Hamilton and Stewart together, which gave rise to a general laugh.

"No, sir," said Stewart. "Although I do enjoy fishing for the trout from time to time, it is the salmon, that prince of fishes, that is the true heart of the sport."

"So I have gathered from Mr. Bowlker and Mr. Fairfax." Washington dropped these names so that they would know that he was not behindhand in matters of sport, although the books were far away with his old life at Mount Vernon.

"Oh, sir, indeed?" Stewart had sat through a great many regimental dinners, and he knew that a great deal of complaisance on these matters was expected of him as a guest. A *decent show of interest*. Greatly daring, Stewart asked him a direct question.

"Do you fish yourself, in Virginia?"

"All too seldom, Captain. We don't have salmon, and the only trouts I have seen are in the mountains. Have you seen our mountains, Captain?"

"Only from a distance, sir. You always seem to be keeping me from them."

This last prompted a burst of nervous laughter. Stewart could tell he was sailing close to the wind, but Washington did not seem an utterly formal man, and was obviously used to men of good breeding and good conversation. Judging by Hamilton and Fitzgerald, better breeding than his own. He smiled for the absent Jeremy, who had trained him so well. He looked at George Lake, who was chewing carefully and trying not to be seen.

"Are you a farmer at home, Captain?" Washington clearly wanted him to say yes, as everyone knew that Washington liked to go on about farming.

Stewart shook his head. "I fear not, sir, although I gather that you are an eminent farmer. My father is a Turkey merchant."

"How many turkeys does he have?" asked George Lake from across the table. It was almost his first comment since they had been seated. The roar of laughter in return was like a volley of musketry, it was so loud and so high. Lake shrank with embarrassment.

"Look how different the language is already," said Stewart into the last of the laughter. "My father owns ships that trade between Edinburgh and Smyrna, in the Empire of the Grand Seigneur."

"Goodness," said Hamilton. "Have you been there yourself?"

"I have, too. A wonderful place, like the Arabian Nights brought to life. I went twice as a lad."

Hamilton nodded along eagerly. Again, Stewart had the ears of the whole table.

"Did you like it much? In Turkey?" asked Fitzgerald. Stewart thought that when alone, he might ask about the women there. Everyone did. Veils made men so curious.

"All but the absolute nature of the place. The slavery had worked its way into the national fabric," he said, and winced. The table fell totally silent.

☆ ☆ ☆

"Polly was never a slave," said her father, looking at her with affection. "She was born one, of course, but her mother and I were free before any man ever told her what a slave might be."

Polly nodded. "I remember England. Most of the ladies were very kind, although I did tire of being a curiosity. Because of my color, I mean, and being from America. Other people were from America, but they didn't have to wear a sign on their skin to say as much."

"And you were a slave for Washington," Marcus said.

"I met Washington once," said Sally. They all looked at her in surprise.

"I was with Bludner. My mother was still alive then, I think. We was taking crabs on his river, an' he came an' near beat Bludner to death. I liked him fine."

"Washington?" Caesar looked surprised. "He beat Bludner? I'd have paid good money to see that."

"Who is Bludner?" asked Polly, quietly.

"He's a slave-taker from Virginia. He almost killed me, and Virgil and Jim when you come to it, back in '75."

"He owned me my whole life," said Sally, her lips trembling, and she spilled a little wine from her glass.

"He doesn't own you now," said Marcus White, but Sally rose and bolted out the door. Marcus made to follow but then came back. Caesar shook his head.

"I don't know what you see in her, Reverend," he said. "She's been trouble since I knew her. And men get ideas, seeing you going around with her."

"Perhaps they should get ideas if I don't go around with her, Caesar. Do you know your Bible?"

"Not as well as you, I daresay. But I've read it, yes."

"Then you know that our Savior spent a great deal of time with prostitutes. And soldiers and tax men, too, I think."

Caesar bowed his head at the answer.

"It's never as easy as you think, Caesar. No matter how hard your life has been, hers was harder. And no matter how brave you are, she has been braver. Think on that before you jibe at her again."

Sally came back with a little powder over the tear tracks she had made, and sat composedly.

★   ★   ★

The silence dragged on. Stewart knew he could end it with an easy apology, but some part of him knew that he had wanted to say those words since he sat down with them and that he wasn't sorry. But he hated to seem a boor, so he attempted to change the subject.

"May I ask what kind of fish they *do* have in Virginia?" he asked. George Lake was white as a sheet.

Lafayette leaned forward, smiling as if he had followed this point for some time. He blinked his eyes, and Stewart suddenly knew he had an ally, someone else who had long wanted to speak out.

"I have always felt that slavery leaves an indelible mark on a country," he said. And the silence deepened.

Hamilton turned to Stewart and shook his head. "This is a most unfortunate subject for this table. Are you a particular enemy to slavery?"

"I didn't think so, before," said Stewart.

"You had a slave of your own, I think?" said Johnson.

"No, sir. A servant. Closer than servant."

Washington spoke up from the end of the table, where he had been silent. "A slave may be close, I think. Both the ancients and the Bible tell us as much." Washington was careful in his speech, and Stewart realized that he was quite angry.

"Oh, aye, they do. But not as close as a true friend, surely?"

Washington considered Billy, and his fury grew. "Surely not only equality can bring true friendship? So that a slave can be as much your friend as a servant?" Washington was just civil. He knew he was berating a guest at his own table, a sin at least as great as the one the guest had committed by starting this fox, this damnable subject, at his table. And yet he realized that his views were not as simple as they had once been.

"And yet, are not these men your friends, though they also serve you?" Stewart thought, *I am contending with a man at his own dinner table. Jeremy would have my head.* And he thought, *This is the archrebel himself. I'll say what I please.* "And how do you know that the friendship of a slave is not compelled or feigned? A servant can leave. Even a staff officer. . . ." He smiled, willing them to laugh.

"And can you speak in comfort of our having slaves when you attempt to impose tyranny over us by violence?" said Henry Lee.

Stewart smiled, relishing his response. He no longer cared to be perfectly civil. "Can you speak in comfort about liberty, sir, when you keep slaves?"

Henry Lee turned a bright crimson. Lafayette leaned forward attentively.

"Yes," he said decisively, as if he had just decided a question. "Yes. Slavery is a blot on the escutcheon of liberty that this country bears."

Stewart feared an explosion from General Washington, but instead he appeared troubled.

"It is not a simple issue." He looked at the table. "I once thought that it was a mere matter of property, but it does have to do with rights. And yet, if a man treats his slaves fairly..."

"They are yet slaves," Stewart said firmly. Washington loved Lafayette like a son, and Hamilton not much behind, and Stewart felt strongly that they were both of his opinion, and it made him bold.

Washington turned on him. "What do you know of how a man treats his slaves, then?"

"I know one of yours, sir."

Stewart suspected that if he had been hale, he'd have been summoned to a duel by half the room, but he was not daunted by their looks, although George Lake was cringing.

"Who?" Like a pistol shot.

"Do you recall Julius Caesar, sir? He is now a sergeant in our army."

Washington sat a moment, as if stunned, and looked at Stewart. He was seeing the black man at Brandywine, and the one who had taken his cloak at Kip's Bay, and the new African boy with the scars over his eyes.

"I remember Caesar," he said softly, as if the man were standing there himself, and Washington had just noticed him for the first time.

☆　☆　☆

"Do you hate Mr. Washington?" Marcus White had asked this before, and it always seemed to fascinate him.

"No. No, I don't hate him. I don't love him much, either." Caesar said, looking through the wine in his glass. "We exchanged shots at the Brandywine. Something like a duel, I think. I've thought that it settled something between us."

"Do you have any happy thoughts from then? When you was a slave?" Polly asked.

"Oh, yes. I was learning a good amount every day. I had a comfortable place to live, and it was so much better than the Indies."

"But what of Washington?"

"He was a distant master. He seldom beat a slave, and he was often fair. He never liked me."

"Why?"

"Oh, Queeny said it was my scars." He rubbed them.

"They do give you a *savage* look," Sally said in a low voice, as if she were wooing him.

"And I had to be free."

Marcus nodded at him, as if they had conspired together. "Yes, it comes to you that way, doesn't it?"

Caesar frowned, remembering.

Sally looked at them both. "How did you 'have to be free'?"

"One day, you know you'd rather die than be a slave," said Caesar. "Some never get it. I grew up with slaves, in Africa. Sometimes one would kill himself, or run. Now I know why."

Marcus looked at him. "Was it injustice that moved you?"

"Perhaps it was. I just remember the little things. I was never beaten while I was at Mount Vernon. It was never a great injustice, and that is why I say that Washington was mostly fair."

Marcus White nodded. "That's the power that slavery has, though. To make a man's likes and dislikes into the power of a god. A man can be the very best of masters, and yet, in a fit of temper, abuse a slave in a way he would never abuse another free man. As if slaves aren't human."

"What else do you remember?" asked Polly.

"He loved to farm and he loved to hunt. He was a master of both. Those skills probably make him a good soldier."

★   ★   ★

"The first time I saw him . . . well, he reminded me of a soldier. He was my dogs boy. He had an eye for ground that . . . well, that has doubtless made him a good one."

Washington took a glass of wine from Billy.

Stewart watched the black man, who pretended a complete lack of interest in the conversation.

Washington spoke carefully, because the subject was so great and so painful that he could not simply dismiss it. Nor was this the first time the subject had surfaced at his table, and he wondered again if he was changing.

"Slavery is an issue that will haunt us for some time, I think."

Hamilton shook his head vehemently. "Can we allow that, sir? When even an advocate like the marquis tells us that it is a blot on our liberty?"

Henry Lee shook his head just as vehemently. "When you speak of the end of slavery, Colonel Hamilton, you speak of depriving us of our property as surely as if you'd come and burned my house."

Stewart was seated at almost the middle of the table, and now he looked back and forth among the young men and realized that it split them all. It was odd, as he had seen so many slaves in the North that he thought the matter was pandemic.

But George Lake, whose accent was as deeply Virginian as Henry Lee's, spoke with quiet confidence. "Can any man, who has fought so hard for his *own* liberty, sit idle while another man loses *his?*"

Every head turned to him, the most junior officer present and welcome mostly as the prisoner's escort and Lafayette's friend.

"What do you say, sir?" asked Henry Lee. In Virginia, he owned property worth thousands of pounds, and George Lake was a tradesman's son and an apprentice, if that.

"I say, with respect, that the men who have fought this war, the handful of us who served from Morristown and will still be here at the end, we know what all these words like *liberty* really mean. And we know when other men who didn't do the fighting . . ." He stopped, as if stricken, and muttered an apology, but Hamilton looked like to applaud.

"The ones who write the speeches and didn't ever serve? Is that what you mean, Captain Lake?" Hamilton asked, rising a little. "I couldn't agree with you more."

Lee looked at Hamilton with scorn. "Free the slaves? Who will indemnify the owners? What will they do with themselves? Will they be citizens?"

"King George might have said the very thing of us, sir!"

"I think that the southern states would go to war rather than lose the full value of the property they have fought to save."

"Perhaps, then, we can see the precious manpower they cannot spare to fight *this* war!" Hamilton was on his feet. "At home, guarding against some fabled revolt of their slaves while *we* face the cannon and the redcoats."

He flamed red in the face. "My apologies, gentlemen. You all know I do not mean Virginia." He turned to Captain Stewart. "And please pardon my fling against redcoats."

"My coat is most certainly red," Stewart said with a smile.

Washington looked down the table sternly and shook his head. "I think this is why we keep politics out of the mess, Captain Stewart."

"I apologize for what I started, sir."

Hamilton turned to him and whispered as a strained conversation covered him from up the table. "You didn't start it, sir. They did. When they bought their human cattle."

* * *

"Can we drink to the happy couple?" Sally asked, and Caesar glared at her.

"I haven't asked yet," he said sheepishly. He was enjoying the mood and the conversation, and he didn't want to come to the point of the evening yet. In a social way, he was afraid of Marcus White, and a little afraid of Polly.

"You're slow, then," Sally quipped.

Caesar looked across the table at Polly, whose eyes were down, and then at Marcus White. He reached into his pocket and pulled forth a plain silver band, hammered by the armorer from a shilling. His hands were trembling.

"Sir, I have not hidden from you my admiration for your daughter, and I would like to take this occasion to ask for the honah, that is, *honor* of her hand," he said. There was a quaver in his voice, but he got it out just as he had practiced it.

Marcus White waved easily at Polly. "You know that you have my consent if you have hers."

Polly smiled. "You have mine."

Caesar went and knelt by her, and placed his ring on her finger. "Then I hope you will be my wife."

"I will, Caesar." She kissed him on the forehead and then looked into his eyes, hers huge and dark. "But my father has to tell you something first, don't you, Father?"

"Tell me?"

Marcus White looked at her, clearly a little frightened in his turn.

Caesar knew what it must be immediately, and went to shush her. "This isn't the place." He looked at Sally, his distrust clear on his face. The scars made him look dangerous at such moments. "Perhaps when we're alone."

"This is just the place," insisted Polly, looking up at him with steady eyes.

Marcus White looked at his daughter for a long moment. "If I must."

He looked around and then stood up to lock the room's only door. Then he busied himself throwing wood on the fire.

"Caesar, you know that I have something to do with gathering intelligence for the army?"

"I do, sir. And you need say no more about it. . . ."

"Caesar, let my father speak." Polly put her hand on his arm and left it there. Marcus White leaned forward over the table.

"My daughter, Polly, often acts as a courier for me." Caesar started, and he raised his hand. "No, please let me go on. I feel that you can know this because you know all the principals, and because it is time we draw this to a close. I do not so much collect intelligence as attempt to prevent the enemy collecting from us, do you understand?"

Caesar narrowed his eyes a little, but nodded. He glanced at Sally, who was looking at her hands.

"Throughout our army, the enemy has his spies. Some of them move around very publicly, because they wear the same uniform as you do but feel that the colonies have been unfairly treated. I can do little about them, and neither can anyone else."

Caesar nodded. Many officers had sympathies with the other camp.

"The enemy also attempts to recruit spies through bribery, coercion, indeed, any method that will result in a flow of intelligence. I fear that this is not grounds for moral outrage, as I am very sure we do the same."

Caesar continued to watch his eyes.

"Some time ago, someone who had been coerced approached me. She wanted to repent her sin. Indeed, she had little notion that I was anything but a minister of the Lord, but all her words fell on fertile ground. I took her under my wing. My daughter became her friend and confidante, because this woman was terrified all the time. I used my daughter to carry messages between us and to follow certain people. This work was dangerous, but not as dangerous as my agent, the convert. Do you understand?"

Caesar looked at Sally. He looked at her too long and wondered what she had passed before she became a convert, but then he smiled.

"I understand," he said, and Polly pressed his hand.

And Sally looked up, and into his eyes. "And I understand what you and Marcus said. One day you jus' can't be a slave no more." She looked down. "I can be a whore. Folks like you think it low, but it ain't like being a slave." She looked up again. "Marcus is the best thing I ever knew, except maybe Jeremy. I couldn't have jumped essept for Jeremy. But now I'm scared all the time."

Marcus said, "We've been feeding her false information for some time, and they are beginning to get on to it."

"So they beat you," Caesar said bitterly. "And I thought you had been with a man."

"Maybe I had," said Sally. "That don't make so much of a mind to me as it does you."

Caesar looked at Polly and at Marcus. "I feared, once, that you were both spies. I even wondered which side you spied for."

Polly kicked her father lightly. "I told you he was quick."

Marcus nodded. "Why?"

"You passed the lines too easily, and Polly seemed to know the headquarters, at least according to Jeremy. And you always seemed to know powerful men. I thought perhaps you were spying."

"Slavery does not beget confidence in one's fellows, does it, Caesar?"

"No, sir. No, it does not."

Polly squeezed his hand again.

"Now you know," she said.

"All's well that ends well," Caesar said, one of Jeremy's favorites.

Sally gave a little sob. "It ain't the end for me until Bludner's dead," she said. And somehow her saying it robbed much of the joy of the day.

V

Care and Labor

*I will plainly set before you things as they really are; and
shew you in what manner the Gods think proper to dispose
of them. Know therefore, young Man!—these wise
Governors of the universe have decreed, that nothing great,
nothing excellent, shall be obtained without Care and
Labour: They give no real Good, no true Happiness on other
terms . . . If to be honoured and respected of the Republic be
your Aim,—shew your Fellow-Citizens how effectually you
can serve them: but if it is your ambition that all Greece shall
esteem you,—let all Greece share the benefits arising from
your labors . . . and if your design is to advance yourself by
Arms;—if you wish the power of defending your friends, and
subduing your enemies; learn the art of war under those who
are well acquainted with it; and when learnt, employ it to the
best advantage.*

—VIRTUE'S ADDRESS TO HERCULES, FROM
XENOPHON'S MEMOIRS OF SOCRATES,
AS TRANSLATED BY SARAH FIELDING, 1762

Chapter Twenty

New Jersey, April 1779

Polly felt as if she had been walking for her whole life. Her legs burned at every step, and only the fact that she was late for her rendezvous and had charge of Sam kept her at it. If she had been alone, she might have looked for a friendly farm and rested.

She had crossed the lines into the rebel-held area outside New York two weeks before. Her first contact had been away, and her second had changed the meeting place twice, scaring her and requiring her to stay close to the rebel camp for too long. The information he provided made the trip worthwhile, but she had walked a hundred miles in a week and she wanted to be home with her father and Caesar. And she wanted to live to be wed.

At first she was cautious, sending Sam ahead to run and play and tell her what the roads were like, but they were both tired and she grew sloppy when she thought they were clear of the last rebel patrol. Besides, there were other people on the road, farm folk, and that made her relax.

She came on the post suddenly at a turn in the road. It was new and unexpected, and Polly wanted to turn and find another way, but her rendezvous was just the other side of the lines here. Her news was too important to delay and she was late. In any case, they had already been seen. Best to brazen it out.

She noted that the men in the post weren't regulars. They were Connecticut militia. That could be good or bad. The militia was notoriously slack, but their men were ill disciplined. She had been groped by militia men enough times to know the difference and prefer the professionals at the Continental Army posts.

She took Sam's hand. Sam was just fourteen, stunted from a life of poor food and small enough to pass as her son or her brother. Polly used him to collect messages and run errands, and on trips like this he had become important for cover. She was afraid she was getting too well known.

There was a wagon and several men on foot ahead of her, and one woman with a basket on her head who immediately tried to sell them eggs. Polly bought one and gave it to Sam, keeping the egg seller in conversation. She hoped to pass the post with the white girl, chatting.

The militia began searching the wagon. Some of them were drunk, and the white girl gave her a worried look.

"I mislike these. They are no true soldiers," she said.

Polly nodded. She took an apple from her apron, hard and wrinkled from a winter in the cellar. As she reached under her petticoat to find her clasp knife she used the movement to check that the ivory-handled dagger was still there. It had been Jeremy's, and Caesar had lent it to her for luck. She touched it. Then she took her clasp knife, cut the apple, and offered a piece to the girl. Sam finished the egg and looked at her with big eyes until she gave him a piece, too. The militia were still rifling the wagon, throwing things around, laughing. The farmer on the box grew angrier.

"You's nothin' but cow boys!" he cried.

All the smiles vanished. The militia began to look ugly, and one of them took an earthenware jug and smashed it on the ground. Cow boys was what the farmers called the Loyalist cavalry who stole their cattle. The name was beginning to spread to all the marauders who worked between the armies.

Polly looked at the white girl, considering. It might be time to cut and run. The militia were dangerous, drunk and angry, and she didn't fancy getting a black eye or worse.

"They ain't gon' to let us cross easy, ma'am," she said hesitantly, playing her part as a poor black from one of the farms.

The girl looked more scared. "My brothers wanted to come, but I said it would be easier for me." She shook her head. "These eggs ain't worth what they has in mind." Two more soldiers came up from behind them.

They looked different. One sat under the tree with his weapon to hand, watching the two girls. The other smiled at Polly. Polly felt a touch of ice against her spine.

Sam was looking at her. He was scared, and Polly was responsible for him. Sam made her trips easier but the responsibility weighed on her. In many ways, it was easier to travel on her own, and she understood Caesar's feelings for his company all the better. There wasn't enough cover by the road to try to run. Even in petticoats, she could outrun most men, especially the lard-assed militia, but in open ground they could shoot her in a moment. And the two were watching her. They looked a little different, harder men altogether, like rangers or riflemen.

The wagon cleared the post, the farmer poorer by some silver coin that had probably robbed him of the whole value of his trip to the Continental camp.

"You pretty things have passes?" The sergeant had lank hair and his bad breath washed over Polly. The two rangers rose carefully and walked toward the sergeant, although both men were suddenly watching the distant woods on the British side of the lines.

"You got a picket out?" asked one, teeth gripping an unlit pipe.

"Jus' my brother up the hill."

"He awake?"

"What business is it o' yourn? This be my post!"

"Not if them Tory horse ride you down. See 'em?" The ranger pointed with his pipe. His motion was very small, careful. "Don't act alarmed or they'll come at us. Maybe they're just lookin'." The ranger looked at the militia with contempt. "What are you boys doin' this far from our lines? Besides stealin' from farmers?'

The other ranger was smiling at the white girl. Finally he came over. Polly tried to listen to both while keeping her eyes down. Demure. Uninvolved. Her heart leapt at the notion that there were Loyalist cavalrymen just a few hundred yards away. They were probably hussars of the Queen's Rangers, all friends of Caesar. They must be her rendezvous.

"I'd fancy one of them eggs, miss," said the second ranger. The white girl smiled nervously and gave him an egg, for which he paid a hard penny. That was a high degree of honor for a sentry post, from Polly's experience.

"Don't you worry, miss. These milishee won't harm you."

The first ranger was still trying to stare down the sergeant. "Well?"

"Captain Bludner ordered us here. We're lookin' for Tory spies."

Polly froze. Just the name Bludner was enough to panic her, but she looked at Sam and thought, *If I lose my head, they'll take Sammy, too.*

The ranger looked at the militia sergeant, hard. "Bludner don't run posts. An' he ain't much better 'an a cow boy. Nor a cap'n, I reckon." He looked at the whole group of men. "What the hell are Connecticut mil-ishee doin' in New Jersey?"

"None o' your business." The lank-haired sergeant spat.

"Bludner has his place up north o' the river. Who sent you here?"

"I'm lookin' for spies."

Polly thought, *Bludner has a post, north of the river.* That was news. She worked to master her fear. The sergeant was focused on the rangers. She thought she might play a part. After a moment, she snapped, "Then go fin' some, an' let po' hones' folk go work!"

The sergeant turned and glared at her, but the rangers smiled. The sec-ond ranger, the tall one with a fancy hunting shirt and a beautiful knife, was telling the egg girl how to find his camp. Polly was scared but she had gotten the line out with real anger and she was waiting for the verdict.

The first ranger looked up the road. "Come on, Elijah. These folk is gon' to get ridden down in a minute, an' I don' wan' to be here."

Elijah held up his hand and bent down to whisper something to the egg girl. He was *good,* thought Polly. The poor girl didn't know what had hit her, she was so taken. She'd probably never been off her farm before.

The rest of the militia were looking all around them, on the edge of panic, but the sergeant wasn't giving in.

"We can hold this post against some Tory horse, I guess. You walk off if you have a mind. I have orders."

Elijah actually kissed the egg girl's hand. Something about it broke Polly's fear, the thought that here on the edge of violence a man was courting, or something like it, and she laughed. She decided to play the saucy maid to the hilt, since she'd started.

"You gon' to defend us, Captain? Or jus' flirt with the lady?"

Elijah laughed. "Always time for flirtin'," he said. His friend had walked a distance off, along the ridge to their right, and now he was suddenly ly-ing flat and readying his rifle.

"They's a-comin'!" he called.

Elijah picked up the butt of his rifle and turned away in one motion, headed for the ridge and his partner. "You'd best clear the road," he called as he ran.

Polly didn't wait for more orders. She grabbed Sam's hand and ran the other way into the field beside the road. The ground was still hard and the footing was good, and she ran easily. The farther she ran, the more scared she was, waiting for a ball in the back.

There were shots behind them. She didn't turn, and so she missed the flurry of fighting as the hussars swept down the road. She dragged Sammy into the cover of a shallow depression. There was still snow here, and it was cold. Her petticoats began to take water from the damp ground. She was breathing like a horse after a run, and all thought seemed to have left her. She rolled onto her stomach and tried to look over the crest of her cover, and the cold April wind took her straw hat, blinding her for a moment. And then she saw the huddle of men on the road and green coats all around them.

"See them, Sam?"

"Yes'm."

"Queen's Rangers."

"Ones on foot be Loyal Americans."

"Let's go an' let them round us up, then."

Philadelphia, June 11, 1779

Riding was still a new adventure for George Lake, and he regarded the journey from the Continental Army camp near Newburgh, New York, to the capital at Philadelphia with some apprehension. He had been sent carrying dispatches, at his own request, as he had his own agenda to follow in Philadelphia. But the journey was a labor.

He had a good horse, thanks to the marquis, who was now absent in France but had left George many of his belongings. He was well turned out, in a new coat and a proper greatcoat, and wore good boots and clean linen. Indeed, throughout his journey, he was accorded a level of respect from innkeepers and fellow travelers that he had not experienced outside his own circle in the army. It pleased him, although he tried not to let it go to his head. At the ferry over the Delaware, the boatman's daughter flirted to the edge of lewdness, which caused him to wriggle. She was pretty enough, but he was too close to Betsy to feel any temptation.

What he noticed most, besides the ache in his thighs and knees, was the change in attitude his uniform provoked. In the Jerseys and Pennsylvania, he was now treated as a figure of authority and respect, whereas just a year or two earlier he wouldn't have been welcome under many roofs. The world was changing. People were finally choosing sides.

He saw other signs that were uglier. Everywhere he rode there were burned-out houses and fields left fallow. Twice he met families on the road, refugees driven out by their neighbors for taking a stand opposed to the majority in their region. The war was hardening attitudes, causing long-standing disagreements to burst forth as violence.

Philadelphia looked prosperous. Even on the outskirts, there were new houses and a new tavern being built, and the river was full of ships. Even a Royal Navy blockade couldn't keep the French out of the Chesapeake or the most ambitious Massachusetts men from trading. The shops were full of goods and the people in the streets were the best dressed in America, but they seemed surly. Perhaps they saw too many uniforms. His treatment was different here, and people all but crossed the street to avoid him.

George took a room at an inn near the Congress and went to deliver his dispatches immediately. He knew the contents intimately: reports on the progress of General Sullivan's expedition against the Iroquois, which George had viewed as a gimcrack strategy; reports on the movement of British ships and men in and out of New York; and a report on the state of the army near New York. Washington was not quite laying siege to the British forces there, but he had them under close observation while he sent many of his troops to face the British attacks on Charleston and other ports in the South.

The entry of France into the war had changed it profoundly and had other effects than just the return of the marquis to his homeland. With France in the war and the loss of Burgoyne's army at Saratoga, the British were forced to place their main effort in the Caribbean to prevent the loss of their valuable spice islands to the French navy. Both sides were now concentrating military efforts in the Carolinas, where a fleet avoiding the hurricane season could relax within easy covering distance of the rich islands farther south. And the British had discovered, perhaps too late, the wealth of Loyalist sentiment that existed in the southern back country.

While armies and fleets skirmished for the possession of anchorages and bases in the South, the war in the North burned on as a series of raids and counterraids. Loyalists and Indians attacked the Mohawk Valley to cut Washington off from his grain supply, and Washington sent Sullivan to drive the Iroquois from their villages in retaliation. Around New York City, spies and partisans fought a skulking war every day. The dispatches covered these new realities in detail and the logistics that supported them.

He handed his dispatches to a member of the Continental Congress, who immediately encouraged him to comment on the papers he bore. George refrained. The army had already survived two periods of intense internal politics, and General Washington had made it clear that he didn't intend to put up with a third. George had little interest in such talk. He requested a signed receipt for the dispatches and found himself in the street, a short walk from his real destination. He was clean and neat, well dressed, and at the end of his duty, and yet he paused, going into a coffee-house.

He hadn't been to the Lovells' since the day of the looters, and despite many letters he feared to put to the test his resolve to ask Mr. Lovell for his daughter's hand. He might no longer be welcome. Sitting alone in the coffeehouse, nursing a cup of bitter coffee, he wondered why the idea of being forbidden a house he had entered only once as a guest made so much difference. He thought it might be that he had spent so long imagining the house and its occupants that he felt a more frequent visitor.

To make matters worse, none of his letters had been answered in two months. It was the lack of letters from Betsy that had spurred him to action. Now that he had arrived, he feared to find out the truth. She had married. She had been forbidden to write. Anything seemed possible.

He stood once again in the street outside the coffeehouse before finally forcing himself to walk the two blocks to the Lovells', whistling the "Rogue's March" as he went like a condemned soldier. He walked up the steps briskly, his boot heels ringing against the brick, and tapped on the door with the force of nerves.

He knocked again a few moments later, louder this time. The door of the next house opened and a maid leaned out. She was pretty, and Irish, like most of the maids in Quaker houses. She ducked back as soon as she saw him. He knocked again.

A small boy was standing at the foot of the steps with a wooden hoop. He had been pushing the hoop with a stick, but now he just watched George.

"Are you a real soldier?" he asked.

"I am, lad."

"May I hold your sword?" he asked, turning his eyes away as he spoke, perhaps ashamed of his own daring.

George laughed and came down the steps. "You can hold the hilt, but I'll just keep a grip on her. There, isn't she fine?"

"Oh, yes, sir."

"So, do you live hereabouts?"

"Oh, yes, sir!"

"What's your name?"

"Alexander Keating, if you please, sir."

"Well, Alexander Keating, do you know the people who live in this house?"

"I used to know them, sir. Mrs. Lovell made the best orange marmalade and Miss Betsy was the prettiest girl on the street, or so my mama said."

"Good for your mama. I can't agree more." George was wrestling with the construction *used to know*. "Where are the Lovells now?"

"They had to clear out. Mama says the Committee of Safety was wrong to make them go, but Papa says I shouldn't talk of such things."

"I imagine he does. Could you take me to meet your mama?"

"Oh, I haven't been rude, have I, sir?"

"Not at all, Alexander. And you handle that hoop very well indeed. Now march me round to your mama. That's the boy."

In minutes he was seated in another Philadelphia parlor, being fed coffee by the matronly Mrs. Keating. She clucked over the Lovells. It was some moments before George reassured her that he was a friend and not a servant of the committee. Wealthy Philadelphia had developed a distrust of uniforms, and George resented it the more for the respect he had felt on his trip south from New York.

"They came several times. I'm not speaking against the government, you understand," she said, almost in a whisper, and with a look over her shoulder that spoke volumes. "I'm not saying that Mr. Lovell wasn't a little too loud in his defense of King George. He was arrested, and he paid a fine. An' most of that fine lined the pockets of the 'officer' who arrested him, I have no doubt. My husband would scold me if he heard me talking this way, to an officer an' all. But a person has to be heard. What's this 'freedom' I hear so much about? The Lovells have none, I believe."

George sat and drank his coffee silently.

"Oh, I've offended you, Captain. I'm so sorry. We're good Americans, really. But the Lovells had always been our friends."

"Ma'am, I'm an officer in the Continental Army." George paused a moment and then spoke his mind. "I'm a plain man, an apprentice when the war began. I've fought since '75 an' I reckon I'll see it through to the end, an' I don't have any time for these Committees of Safety. In New York Colony, we had to use the army to suppress some of them. Mostly they ain't patriots. They are a vehicle for greedy, cruel men to tyrannize their neighbors. If they was anything else, they'd be in the army."

He rose and handed her his coffee dish. "I won't trouble you more, ma'am, with my own seditious talk." He tore out a sheet from his pocket book and wrote on it in pencil. "This is my address in camp. If the Lovells come back, or you get word of them, would you send to me?"

"Of course I will! I'm a goose! You're the officer Betsy was always on about, aren't you?"

George frowned, then smiled. "I reckon I might be, ma'am."

"Oh, goodness. Oh, of course you want to know where they went. Well, I suppose that all the Tories go to England or to New York. I think that Silas had a place in New York. So you and your camp are closer to the Lovells than I am." She laughed a little wildly. She was still very much on edge.

George didn't ask for a second cup because he could tell Mrs. Keating was nervous to have him and unhappy to discuss the Lovells. He went back to his inn, claimed his gear and his horse, and set out on his return trip. He didn't want to spend a night in Philadelphia if he could help it.

Betsy might be in New York, just nine miles from George's camp. *And only the British army between us,* George thought as he started north.

New York City, November 30, 1779

It was St. Andrew's Day.

In the early afternoon the tavern hosted the party for Caesar's wedding. This was not a common event in taverns, and the service itself, performed unflinchingly by the bride's father, was held in an Anglican chapel up King Street a ways, so that the party had to squelch to and fro through the muddy streets. Caesar carried his bride, the length of his former master's great cape wrapped around her so that her French silk gown, imported illegally and with a great deal of anticipation by mercantile connections of Captain Stewart, came through untouched.

Back at the Moor's Head, all the musicians of the Guides, as well as the musicians of several line companies and two very tall pipers come early for the St. Andrew's Day festivities, made themselves into a military band and proceeded to play with loud competence. The rafters echoed with songs both military and profane, but it was the dances that everyone would remember later.

Stewart enjoyed the rare pleasure of partnering Sally in public. He did not disgrace himself and she seemed transformed. He wanted her transformed. She spent too much time considering her shadowed future as it was. She had come in a simple gown, as if to keep her charms from rivaling those of the wedding couple.

Caesar was magnificent in a scarlet coat and half boots. He looked like a martial statue, except few statues laughed as much. The scars on his face were almost invisible when he laughed, and he laughed often. When it was his turn, he raised his glass and spoke of Polly and the Reverend White, and then of Jeremy. Stewart, unprepared, could only weep. But it passed in a moment and he raised his glass, his tartan coat in contrast to the brighter colors all around him.

But it was Polly who took all eyes. The Hammond girls, the elder of them soon to be wed to Mr. Martin, arranged to arrive at a time when they might have been coming early for the St. Andrew's Day party—a thin fiction to fool their parents—but even Poppy's golden hair and fashion couldn't compete with Polly's straight back and the contrast of her complexion and the color of her gown. Polly was the most beautiful woman in the room, and perhaps in New York, and she and Caesar danced to everything, sang every song, toasted their friends, and gave them something good to last the longest winter of the war.

Before darkness had fallen, most of the wedding party was back in the barracks across the street, many barely able to stand. Sergeant McDonald, who had struck up a friendship with the two pipers and felt obliged to stay for the second festivity, pronounced it the best wedding he had ever attended.

★　★　★

The Moor's Head stayed full. There wasn't room for another man or woman to fit under the rafters, and the din roared out into the street and across to the barracks there, and up to Mother Abbott's and down to the docks. Men drank at their cards, a piper played an endless, complex pibroch while a critical crowd watched, and everywhere men sang.

Highlanders and Lowlanders and Scots by courtesy danced and sang, recited poetry, or, if greatly daring, gave voice in Gaelic. Sergeant McDonald and the pair of pipers from Mull had seized the best table early and held it against all comers, proclaiming the superiority of Scotland, Alan McLean, and the Hebrides to all who would listen. The eldest, a white-headed man named Cameron, declaimed from Ossian and challenged any man to tell him the great bard was a counterfeit.

After the wedding, the Scots had begun to arrive in earnest and the character of the place changed. Colonel Robinson was a late addition, along with his guest. Stewart laid himself out to be amiable, aware that he was just a shade short of drunkenness. Jeremy would have been leading him home by now. Sally had given him a meaningful glance when she left, and that had been hours ago. He watched, and sang, and shouted, and drank more.

From time to time the door opened and brought cold and damp and newcomers, often couples coming from other parties. There were several St. Andrew's revels in New York, and it seemed that everyone in the town was Scottish.

Stewart heard the men from Mull singing "Come o'er the Stream, Charlie" and wondered how seditious the evening would become.

Behind him Robinson waved for a waiter. "Some of your countrymen still want the Jacobite pretender, Captain?"

"Not really. Most think he's a useless sod and a drunk. And Roman, to boot. But the resentment is still there. Aye, and some of the songs you'll hear tonight are still illegal at home." Stewart raised his glass. "But we were always Whigs, so I won't drink to the king over the water. I was just born when the prince came over and me da' stayed in his countinghouse like a proper Edinburgh gent."

Robinson laughed. He was Virginia born, well bred, a former friend of George Washington, but he hated slavery and hated the Continental Congress, too. Some said he and Washington had fought over a woman. Whatever the truth, he had married in the North and stayed there, and now he commanded one of the better Loyalist corps. Stewart liked him well enough but he was no substitute for Simcoe, who was away in the South.

"You British make such an issue about countinghouses and the like. No one in America cares. We're all in trade." He waved his wineglass at the room. "Could you have St. Andrew's like this at home? No. Half these men wouldn't be allowed in the same room as the other half."

Stewart nodded his agreement and thought about Caesar's wedding. He might have let the wine lead him astray, because when Stewart looked up he found that they had been joined by a family, a rotund man and his handsome wife and even handsomer daughter. The man bowed to Colonel Robinson, who rose from his chair and bowed in return.

"I took the liberty of inviting Mr. Silas Lovell, formerly of Philadelphia, and his wife to join us. Mr. Lovell is not Scots but something tells me his wife is."

Mrs. Lovell made a face and tapped the colonel lightly with her fan.

Stewart rose to his feet and bowed.

"Mr. Lovell of the commissary, may I introduce Captain Stewart of the army."

"Your servant, sir," said Stewart, racking his brain for why the name of Lovell seemed so familiar.

"And yours, sir."

"You are Scottish, Captain?" asked Mrs. Lovell.

"Born and bred in sight of Holyrood, ma'am."

Mrs. Lovell smiled and nodded. "My family is from Aberdeen."

Mr. Lovell winced at the pibroch, which had reached a level of intensity rivaled only by the complexity of the repetition.

"When did you come to America?" asked Stewart.

"I came as a girl, in one of my father's ships. I'm an Ogilvy."

Stewart bowed again. "I suspect I know your brothers, ma'am. My father is Kenneth Stewart, the Turkey merchant."

In a moment they were off in a rush of reminiscence. Short of meeting a friend from Edinburgh or from his school days, Captain Stewart couldn't have made a happier acquaintance. They spoke for several minutes, animated, exchanging names and laughing, until Mrs. Lovell noticed that her husband had gone off with Colonel Robinson and her daughter was standing by, somewhat listless.

"I don't think my husband introduced my daughter, Betsy."

At the name Betsy, the whole memory crystallized for Stewart and a shadow crossed his face.

Both women noticed the change. For a moment, he was again confronting the loss of Jeremy and the days just after. But he rallied quickly.

"Are you ill, sir?" asked Mrs. Lovell, looking for water.

"No, ma'am. Pardon this question, which might seem a tad brash, but do you know a Captain George Lake of the Continental Army?"

Both of them gasped, although Miss Betsy appeared the more moved.

★ ★ ★

"Captain Lake is getting missives from the enemy," said Caleb Cooke, handing George a thick canvas wrapper. "This came through the lines for you from New York, and the whole staff wants to know why you're so popular."

Lake was sitting in the main room of his host's farmhouse, trying to get his charcloth to cook right by tapping his tinderbox to make it heat more evenly.

"Have a pipe for your messenger boy?" Cooke asked when George continued with his task. George pointed to the mantelpiece, where two long white pipes lay alongside a brass tobacco box. When he had the tinder going the way he wanted it, George took the heavy canvas package and opened it with a clasp knife from his waistcoat pocket.

"Would the gen'lemen like coffee?" asked the farmer's wife.

Caleb smiled broadly. "Damn, you have better quarters than I do. My proprietress speaks only Dutch."

George grunted, still wrestling with the wrapper. When he had it free, he could read the inner envelope. "It's from Captain Stewart!"

"That fellow you had as a prisoner?"

"He's the one. Fine fellow. I liked him. If the British were all like him, I reckon we wouldn't have a war."

He opened the envelope and the size of the parcel was explained. Twenty envelopes fell out, and a small package.

"I guess you two had a lot to talk about," said Caleb, around his pipe.

George gave a shout and bounced out of his chair.

"Bless that man!" he said, pounding his fist in the air. "God bless John Julius Stewart and his family forever."

Caleb watched his usually dour friend in amazement. George had tears in his eyes and he was laughing and then he kissed one of the envelopes. Caleb had to look away, it was so peculiar.

"Don't you get it, Caleb? Stewart's found my Betsy. In New York!"

Caleb sighed and puffed his pipe.

New Jersey, April 15, 1780

Sam had shot up over the winter. He was too big to be Polly's boy anymore and almost too big to use as a child. Food and affection had changed him, too. He had a hard time playing at being a slave, and he resented the slights he met with in the role.

Since she had married Caesar, Polly hadn't wanted to spy much, either. Her own nerves were worn, and now she watched his as she waited to leave. He began to quarrel with her father. He never told her that she had to stop spying, although she sensed he wanted to. Perhaps he knew she had her arguments ready, or perhaps he understood the game and the cost too well.

In April she discovered she was pregnant, but she kept it to herself because she had miscarried in the fall and she didn't want Caesar and her father to treat her as if she were made of porcelain. She took the mission when it came because she thought this baby was going to stick and she might not be able to go again. She wanted to do her duty one more time.

Caesar led the patrol intended to get her through the rebel lines. She had never done this with him before, but this time he insisted and his men treated her like a queen. They landed by boat from Staten Island and made camp. Caesar and his men were going to attack a mill the next day. She would return to New York through the landward side in a week.

They sat around a tiny fire, huddling close and holding hands until long after the other men were snoring. Only the sentry was awake, off in the dark in a hide made of fallen boughs. Their breath steamed in the cold.

"You know I'm going to worry about you every day," said Caesar.

Polly pressed his hand tighter. "Don't talk about it," she said. "I'll be back soon enough. Don't you go and get shot."

He laughed. "Not likely." He pressed her hand back. "Ever wonder what we'll do when this is over?"

She snuggled in closer. "We'll be warmer."

"Sometimes I think that there is a joy in this I might not find in peace."

"Julius Caesar, you talk a lot of nonsense."

★ ★ ★

Polly had no trouble on her rounds. She dropped three documents in three different places, all dead drops so that she wouldn't know the recipient if she were caught. She had to meet one man in person, and he was dismissive of her as a messenger because she was black. He ordered her to send someone of higher rank the next time. She shook her head as she left him. Higher rank? As a spy?

Sam was more of a liability than a help. He made some of her drops and watched for her but twice he got into fights with white boys his own age. He wasn't used to being called names anymore.

Their rendezvous for going back was in New Jersey, which meant she had to cross the Hudson. The ferry proved to be far more dangerous than it had ever been before, with guards who checked papers and were deeply suspicious of her, slave or no. She and Sam made it across, but she feared that the sergeant had sent a description of her ahead. She decided to keep to back roads and stayed with some Dutch Negroes she had met before the war, hiding for a few days and missing her first rendezvous. Caesar would worry, and she wanted to go to him, but that was sloppy thinking, the kind that got spies killed.

She passed the rebel camp on the river, thinking that this was the home of Captain Stewart's friend who was sweet on Betsy Lovell. So easy for her to stop and reassure him. So foolish to think that way. She passed well south of the big rebel post at West Point and cleared a drop there. She had no idea who the post was for, but she thought he must be very important as his was the one post she was to clear regardless of her other circumstances. Her mission complete, she started downriver, looking for roads south and east into New Jersey, and began to use Sam the old way, sending him well ahead on roads she didn't know to look for guard-posts.

They walked for a day and then laid up in a burned-out house, sleeping in the cellar. She was a day early for her second rendezvous and she was a little lost. Her careful walking on back roads had taken an unfamiliar turn and she thought she might be near the old Day House in Bergen County, but the ground was steeper than she imagined. There were patrols out, soldiers moving in the cold before dawn, and she didn't know which side they were on, so she and Sam huddled close. They had no sleep.

Finally they got up and started forward. Polly knew she looked poorly, and that might hurt her if she had to pass a post. She tried to straighten her clothes but her petticoats were soaking wet. She worried that she looked like a runaway. With his wild hair, Sam surely did.

It started to rain. That had benefits, and she determined to go as far as she could while it lasted. They trudged on, heads down, her straw hat pasted to her head. They were both soaked through. Polly's stays began to bite her sides and waist, and she thought she might be bleeding.

The morning passed and still the rain fell. Soon it was all they could do to put one foot in front of another. Sam hadn't talked for hours, and she stopped sending him ahead because she couldn't bear to stop walking. She knew they had to find shelter or they'd die in the open.

Just after noon her heart rose a little when she passed a big red clapboard house she recognized. They were less than a mile short of their rendezvous, and although the road rose steeply, she started to walk faster.

"I don' think mah legs will go any bettah," said Sam.

"*Better*, Sam. Less than a mile to go."

"You jus' sayin' that."

Polly pointed into the wind and panted. "No, I ain't. Over the crest of this hill—"

"What's over the crest of this hill, honey?" asked a voice behind her.

She turned and saw four white men, two on horses, and more men behind them. They had guns, three of them rifles.

"Where you run from, honey?" said the voice. "Take 'em, boys. That's cash on the hoof."

Polly had never met Bludner but she had heard about him often enough from Sally to know the face and the manner. There would be no brazening this out. She picked up her sodden petticoats, summoned her tiny reserve of energy, and ran, long white-stockinged legs flashing in the wet as she dashed up the road. She was past Sam before he had even turned.

"Slave-takers," she said. At least it didn't give away their real errand.

Sam didn't hesitate, either, but he didn't run. As the horseman came up on him, Sam leapt onto the horse's back, tugging at the rider.

Bludner lost a stirrup and got a fist in his mouth before he mastered his opponent with two brutal moves and threw Sam down in the road.

"Take him, you fools. Carter, you're with me." Bludner whipped his horse and it sprang forward.

Polly had no idea what Sam had done, or what the result was. She ran over the crest of the hill and started down the other side, where the road turned steeply. After the first turn there was a boulder, and she left the road and ran into the brambles beyond, tearing her stockings and her bare thighs and carrying on regardless. She heard the horses come over the crest behind her and she broke through the brambles and into some trees.

"Where'd she go?"

"She must be in them woods," said another voice, and she heard horses' hooves on the road. Then she ran again, spurred by pain and fear like a wounded animal, and she ran down the hill, making leaps from wet rocks that would have terrified her on any normal day. She landed badly at the bottom, turned her ankle, and hobbled on, too scared to stop. But surely no man on a horse could come down a hill like that.

She smelled smoke. Not woodsmoke, but smoke from a pipe, and she hoped it might be a party out for her rendezvous. The slave-takers' horses were on the road, coming down the hill the long way, and all she could do now was hobble. She was sweating, warm for the first time in two days. She stopped behind a huge oak and looked for a place to hide.

She saw the Loyalist sentry at the same moment he saw her.

"Rebels on the road. They're after me. They have my brother," she panted. "Where's the officer?"

It wasn't Caesar. She'd asked her father not to let Caesar come out for her because he'd fret too much, but now she wanted him because he'd know how to save Sam. And then something snapped inside her and she sat down on a rock and watched the blood coming down her legs.

The patrol was from the Loyal Americans, with some Jaegers along for the fun, and they were on the road in a flash, but all their priming was wet and Bludner rode away.

Polly sat on her rock and wept.

★　★　★

"We lost that girl," said Carter. "Sergeant at the ferry thought she was a spy."

"She is. Why the British use niggers for spies beats me, but she is. We'll have her the next time she crosses the lines, and then we'll see some fun."

"We got the boy, though."

Bludner laughed and looked at Sam, whom he'd already beaten so badly that the boy's face was lumpy, as if made of clay. Bludner spat. "I don't think he knows much."

"You gon' ta kill him, sir?"

"Kill him?" Bludner laughed. "Kill him? Carter, that's why I'm a captain and you're a corporal. I ain't gon' to kill him."

Bludner looked at Sam and smiled, showing all his stained teeth, and spoke carefully, so Sam would understand. "I'm going to sell him."

Boston, April 28, 1780

The wharves of Boston stretched out into the distance so that the harbor seemed like a winter forest of bare trees. The British blockade was neither close nor thorough and trade was flourishing, although nearby Newburyport had as much or more because there was no British frigate to watch the entrance to the Ipswich River there. Most of the vessels in the harbor were local, although there were Dutch and Spanish ships, and a French warship just arriving, the *Hermione,* toward which George Lake hurried with horses and several soldiers.

George was no sailor, but he watched the great frigate come in with fascination. She had some way on her from a fuller press of sails she had worn in the outer roads, and now she ghosted along under just a headsail through a riot of small boats and other ships. It seemed a miracle that she hit nothing. As he watched, she passed the pier where he stood and turned suddenly up into the wind, so that the last of her way came off her and she stopped, the latest in a long row of merchants and privateers anchored just off the Long Pier. He saw her anchor come down with a splash.

There was quite a crowd gathering as George waited. When a boat pulled away from the *Hermione,* the crowd began to cheer. George cheered with them and then used his men to keep the head of the ladder clear as the Boston crowd pressed closer.

Lafayette came up the ladder with his usual energy and, despite the presence of several dignitaries from the local assembly and the sovereign commonwealth of Massachusetts, caught George in a hug and kissed both cheeks, to George's intense pleasure and embarrassment.

It was hours before they could talk. Lafayette made several fine speeches and visited a number of homes. He gave another officer dispatches from the French court at Versailles for the Continental Congress and he watched the landing of his new camp equipage personally. Finally, at the house of one of his many friends, he slouched down in a chair, watching a servant pull off his boots.

"Tell me everything," he said.

George did his best—from the actions of the Congress to the successes of the British. Lafayette nodded along and drank wine. When George began to slow, Lafayette waved his hand.

"But how is *he*? The generalissimo? How is he?"

George smiled. "He's different, Marquis. Better with the men. He's, well, more open, I think I'd say. And eager to see you, Marquis."

"As I long to see him. I thought of him every day, my friend, while I watched the posturing of the court. Ah, if you could see Monsieur de Maurepas, you would understand the intensity of my frustration. No ships, too few troops, no muskets unless I paid cash. Nonetheless, George, on my ship I have enough uniforms, helmets, and muskets for a division. They are mine, you understand? I purchased them. And I will see to it your company is among the first to be uniformed."

George laughed. "I can't imagine how much money that would cost."

Lafayette made a dismissing motion with his hand. "Nothing. Nothing that I will worry about. I wish to take these muskets and place them before the general. Has he met Rochambeau? But of course he must have done. Is all well between them?"

"I think they got along like good friends, Marquis. And I gather you have a son? May I congratulate you, sir?"

"Ah, you may. Very nicely put, George. Three years as an officer and you sound the gentleman, eh? My little Adrienne has given me a son and I have called him after the general, as George Washington, yes?" Lafayette had a light in his eye and his whole face beamed with pleasure. "And you? You are still a captain? That is because I have not been here to press your claim, my hero. And have you married? What happened to Miss Bessy of Philadelphia?"

"Miss Betsy, Marquis. And now she's 'of New York.' We write, and I daresay we're affianced, except no banns have been called. But I doubt we'll wed before the war is over."

"That is romantic, George. I hope it makes you concentrate on the matter at hand, so you desire victory above all things. But I wrong you. You were always a true believer, and you have already put the cause first."

Lafayette looked at the earnest George, no longer quite so young. He had lines on his face and frost in his hair from five years of constant campaigning, and if he had more of the air of a gentleman than he had the last time Lafayette saw him, he had purchased it in blood. Lafayette thought George might be the archetype of the knight, the warrior who earned his name and escutcheon in the field and founded a great name.

A servant brought the marquis a lit pipe, which he savored. "You know, I have not smoked since I left the field in America. And now I come back to it. Very pleasant." He pulled his feet under him in the wing-back chair and curled sideways so that he faced George, a silk brocade dressing gown pulled loosely around him. No one would have mistaken him for American. He was too small, his features too open and soft. A pretty female servant came in with a pan of warm water, which she placed by the marquis, who watched her with interest. He continued as she built up the fire, and she caught his eye, then lowered hers and smiled. She curtsied and was gone.

Lafayette smiled to himself. Then he looked back at George.

"I have missed this country." He waved his pipe. "And not just the pleasures of it. Do you know if I am to have a command?"

George leaned forward. "I only know the rumor, but it is said you are to have a division of all the light troops in the army."

Lafayette punched the air with his pipe and gave a little shout. "It's true, then. That is what I was promised in France. And, George, I will see to it that I have your company as well. We shall be the elite of the army, and we shall lead the way to victory."

Tatawa, New Jersey, October 13, 1780

George sat in his tent, a fine small marquee he had inherited from Lafayette, and wrote his second letter of the day to Betsy, briefly describing his patrol and then transcribing a poem from a book provided by the marquis. George's preoccupation with writing to Betsy and reading her letters had improved his literacy to the extent that he had been acting as Lafayette's adjutant when Colonel Laurens wasn't available.

His French was also improving. Throughout the summer he had moved between the American camps and the French camps, carrying letters for the marquis and answers from the French staff, all of whom he now knew with some degree of intimacy. He could conduct a conversation with Lafayette's father-in-law the Comte de Noailles, although the content of such conversations usually made him blush. Indeed, Laurens often joked to George that he'd had to learn a whole new vocabulary to deal with the aristocrats. They wanted to fight, and sometimes fought each other, but when no fighting was available their every thought turned to women.

George finished translating the poem, wrote it out fair, and then built up the fire in his brazier, but a soldier called out from the door and asked him to attend the marquis immediately. He picked up the book and walked out of his tent and up the hill to his general. When he saw that Lafayette was entertaining General Washington he turned away, but Lafayette beckoned to him before he could slip off. Washington still had the power of a god for George Lake. He stood at attention until Lafayette invited him to sit. Washington inclined his head in greeting and Lake feared that the great man was angry at his intrusion.

A servant poured George a Madeira in one of the marquis's exquisite glasses, and George touched it to his lips while Lafayette went back to his story about Madame d'Hunolstein. George had suspicions, fostered by the Comte de Noailles, that despite Lafayette's love for his wife, he and Madame d'Hunolstein were more than just friends. Washington apparently thought the same, because he tapped his foot as the story drew toward a difficult conclusion. Lafayette blushed at his hero's discomfort and changed the subject abruptly.

"You know that General Gates has been beaten badly in the South?" Lafayette directed this at George, who shook his head.

"We have lost Charleston and now we look to lose much of the back country. That is not the worst of it, George. I don't want this spread to the camp at large, but you read my correspondence and it is only fitting that you know." He looked at Washington, who turned his head away. It startled George, the raw emotion stark and open on Washington's face: rage and something else. He shrank back into his chair.

"General Arnold has attempted to betray West Point to the enemy. Having failed, he has fled to New York."

"*The wretched traitor,*" Washington said in a whisper.

George gulped. He was adept at handling men under fire, but this was different. He now understood Lafayette's story: He had been attempting to divert Washington from his rage. George searched for something to say.

"That's terrible" was the best he could do.

Washington drank off the rest of his Madeira, his head turned away.

"I am poor company, my friend," he said bitterly, and there was a sharp click. Washington looked at the fine glass he had just broken by the pressure of his hand and shook his head. He tossed the glass through the door of the tent.

"My cloak!"

"But, General. You mustn't think to go yet. Let us entertain you—"

"My thanks, Marquis. Captain Lake. I'll not burden you, gentlemen. Nelson and I will see the evening out."

He shrugged into his cloak and gave a little bow from the door, stooping low to get his head through the tent flap. His leaving was as if a lamp had gone out, so intense was his presence.

"Bah," Lafayette said angrily. "Arnold was never more than the sum of his ambitions. We are better without him."

"He was at Boston with the general. I believe Washington had a feeling for him."

Lafayette smiled at Lake. "You know, you are too good for this world, George Lake. Do you know that many of the generals hate one another and all strive for his approval or that of Congress, or both?"

"Yes," George said simply. "It's all one to me, sir."

Lafayette poured himself more wine. "If he were less a god..."

"How do you mean, sir?"

"Oh, if it were the old Maréchal de Noailles, I would send for one of the ladies of the camp, who would dance and laugh and take him to her bed and that would be the end of his rage. You Americans are not immune to the charms of Venus, but he is. He wants to return to Martha and only Martha. Would that I were so constant."

"You want to return to Adrienne; you speak of her every day."

Lafayette looked at George hard, as if he feared to be made game of. Then he looked away, swirled his wine, and stood up suddenly.

"This has affected me more than I realized. I am a bore. You think only of your Betsy, and perhaps you Americans *are* immune to Mademoiselle Venus after all. You are all great men." The marquis sounded bitter, a side of him George had never witnessed before.

George took a deep breath. "I'm not a perfect man, Marquis. I'm a soldier. I've lain with other women an' thanked 'em for it. But I wouldn't ask one to go to the general. An' he wouldn't want it. An' Betsy seems so far away, for all she's just across the river." He paused in thought for a moment, and then plunged on. "Think we'll ever win this war? When we lost Charleston I thought of quitting. An' you know what held me, Marquis? It wasn't love of my country. It was the knowledge that there's nothing else I'm good for. I've been a soldier so long I can't go back, can I? I can't make hats for the gentry in Williamsburg, although five years ago that was my only ambition."

Lafayette looked at him as if seeing him for the first time.

"I'm not the perfect American, Marquis. Nor is the general." George was no longer seeing Lafayette but the long marches of the last six years. He wondered how he had gone so far afield or spoken so much. He mumbled an apology, suddenly shy.

"I, too, have doubts, George. The general, he has doubts, or Arnold's treason would not have him so angry. You know him as I do. He carries the weight of the cause on him and he can never appear to be weak or all of us will be afraid, yes? He is our Hercules. He carries the labors."

"Yes. Yes, that's just it, Marquis."

"Go to bed, George."

The marquis pulled his dressing gown closer about him. George wondered if he had a girl to warm his camp bed and decided it was better not to know. George had to write out the orders that drove the camp girls from the tents some mornings, and he wanted a clear conscience for his commander.

"Good night, sir."

New York, January 12, 1781

The inn was cold, even though every one of the fireplaces was roaring. New York seemed empty, so many of the officers had gone home on the transports to England for the winter. Only those too poor to make the crossing or with nothing to go home to stayed behind. Even some of the Loyalists had left, looking for employment in the mother country.

John Stewart did not follow them. He had been mentioned in dispatches again for an action in New Jersey, and he expected to be made major in his regiment in the spring. He'd already arranged the purchase. Major Leslie wanted to go home. And Stewart would stay. *Until Jeremy is avenged,* he thought.

Stewart had doubts aplenty. He felt that the war was lost, and his beloved was not growing any younger waiting for him. He had enough military glory to last him a lifetime and enough laurels to win his love and marry her. Each winter Stewart told himself that this was the last, and then he stayed for another. Yet something kept him here.

One reason was Julius Caesar, who was sitting at a table playing whist with three other sergeants. Then there was Sally. He tried not to think of her, although she was often in his thoughts.

Jeremy, and Caesar, and Sally. And the war. He hated it, but not all of it, and when he thought of these things and then of Miss McLean waiting in Scotland, he felt a cold guilt in his stomach.

He shook himself and raised his glass to Mr. Martin. "I thought you planned to move to the Queen's Rangers."

"I did, once. Now I wouldn't leave the Guides for anything. Everything I know I learned here. And besides, the Rangers are in the South."

"Which is damned far from Miss Hammond. I agree. Let's drink her health, you and I."

Caesar had appeared by his elbow. "Captain? Lieutenant? Reverend White begs the indulgence of a word in the private room."

Caesar was tense, his hands clenching and unclenching by his sides. The two officers rose and followed him into the relative warmth of the private room in the back, by the kitchen.

"If I'd known this place was so warm I'd have been back here afore ye," said Captain Stewart, settling in a broad wooden chair by the fire. He started to see Sally sitting in the chimney corner with Polly, dressed modestly. She was mostly modest these days, although every month or so she'd kick the traces, drink hard, and come back to his bed with a bruise on her face. He tried never to ask. He wanted to hit her sometimes, but he had never asked her for faithfulness.

She gave him a nervous smile.

The Reverend White shot Mr. Martin a look and waited for Caesar, who was checking up and down the passage. Stewart had a glimpse of his own Sergeant McDonald outside before Caesar shut the door.

"As snug as you could wish, Reverend. And no one the wiser but them that knows."

The Reverend White nodded sharply.

"Gentlemen," he said to the two white officers. "I beg your pardon for dragooning you like this, but we have a matter of some importance to put to you and we require complete security."

He looked around the room. "We wish to make a plan to kill or capture Mr. Bludner and we need your help."

Stewart nodded. "I would be happy to help. Why now? And what do the ladies have to do with it?"

Sally stood up slowly. Stewart could see she was very nervous.

"Captain Stewart..." she began. Tears rolled down her face, but she smiled and he smiled back. There was no one present who did not know he kept her, except maybe Martin, who would have had to be blind. And Stewart was not one to care particularly. He remembered Jeremy ordering him to see to Sally in the upstairs hall of this very building, and the thought made him smile the more.

"John, surely, Sally."

She bobbed her head. "John. I have wanted to tell you this for a year. I am a spy, honey."

Stewart nodded. It wasn't that he had known, more that he had sensed that something wasn't right, and this fit perfectly. He was even happy, for a moment, because it was so much better than what he had expected her to say.

"For us, I hope," he said, looking around. Of course, the Reverend White was a spymaster. Now he could see the whole thing.

"Not always," growled Caesar.

"Bygones is bygones," said Polly, and then she let her eyes fall.

"What's past is over, and Sally has more than atoned for her sin. She's doubled for me for two years, and she has led us to half the spies in New York. We feed them what we want. They run at our pleasure. And we have Sally to thank for it."

White looked around the room. He had the attention of every man and woman. "Bludner thinks he runs Sally. He sends a man to her every fortnight, who beats her and collects her reports. Now he wants her back in person. We are determined that she won't go. When Sam was taken, we were afraid that Bludner might learn something from him, but Sam must have held his tongue until he was sold south. We honor that memory. When Major André was taken, we held our breath because he knew about Sally, but he has kept her secret so far. I hope he may go free or take it with him to the gallows."

"Amen," said Lieutenant Martin, who knew André.

"But Bludner keeps getting closer, and he's foul. I don't need to tell you, any of you, what we owe to Mr. Bludner. Jeremy. Sam. And he nearly had Polly."

Polly smiled bravely. She feared Bludner now, but not so much that she wouldn't volunteer again. She hadn't been pregnant since her second miscarriage. Caesar blamed Bludner.

"Thanks to something Polly heard a year back, we have one or two clues about where he might have his quarters. What I want to do is beat the bushes until we find him and then use his own messenger to get him into our grasp. Then I want to take him and all his men."

Stewart nodded. "We're capable of that sort of action, Reverend. Do you know where he is?"

"Not yet. We have to do this so that his masters will never know he was betrayed by Sally, or they'll never rest until they get her. We need to take all their men in New York in a single night and parade one as the Judas. Leave me to plan that aspect. I want you gentlemen to plan the military operation and find some way to cover it so that it looks like part of a larger whole."

Stewart looked at Martin, and at Sally. "Just so."

Green Springs, Virginia, July 6, 1781

Captain George Lake watched General Wayne's Pennsylvanians break under the weight of the British fire and retire. Some ran, some walked, and a few units marched back smartly, but there were more than a hundred bodies left behind. The attack had been foolish, and Cornwallis, the British general, had baited the trap and sprung it, just as Lafayette had said.

George waved his arms and blew his whistle, and his company broke into a run. The men at the back of the long files had to sprint to reach the new front, which George formed in the cover offered by a raised road.

"Five-pace intervals!" he yelled.

Men began to space themselves out. In a few moments, his men covered almost two hundred paces of the front, and Caleb's company was doing the same on his right.

Something reached out and plucked away his shiny leather helmet, which hit the ground well behind him. George crouched down. "Rifles! Keep your heads down."

Wayne's Pennsylvanians filtered through his men and started to form behind him, temporarily safe from the fire because of the raised road's embankment. As soon as his front was clear, he turned to his bugler.

"Sound skirmish," he said.

The boy raised the instrument, a fine brass hunting horn bought in France with the marquis's money, and sounded the call. File leaders leaned their heads up over the embankment, picked their targets, and fired. The moment their shots rang out, they rolled on their backs and began to load while their file partners searched the ground ahead for targets. George leaned up against the damp earth and raised his head carefully, one hand over his gorget to hide the flash. He could just see some green-coated men in the field beyond the embankment, lying prone and firing carefully. They, too, had leather helmets with curved half moons as their insignia.

"Queen's Rangers, lads. Always a pleasure to fight the best."

His corporal, Ned Simmons, laughed and then fired, his French-rifled carbine making a crack that contrasted with the softer bangs of the muskets.

George saw cavalry forming beyond the field at the edge of the woods. He looked behind him to see if the Pennsylvania men were rallied solidly. They were not, but behind them he saw General Lafayette and his staff galloping across the tobacco fields and he smiled.

He trotted over to Caleb, keeping his head well below the top of the embankment.

"Cavalry, Caleb," he said by way of greeting as he dropped to the ground beside him.

"Whereabouts, then?"

George pointed to where the cavalry were trying to stay hidden. "Colonel Simcoe hopes to keep us amused with his lights and his rifles until we are well strung out...."

"And then ride us over. Those Pennsylvania boys are done for the day, George. I'd say it's time to get out of here."

"Let's hear what the marquis has to say."

Lafayette dismounted behind them and handed his horse to an aide, who instantly fell wounded. The horse spooked and ran off in a long curve, looking for a place to gallop free. Lafayette shook his head and laughed and started to walk across the plowed ground as if unconcerned by the fire.

"Well done, George," he called. When he was closer he condescended to crouch behind the embankment with the two light officers. "The army will thank you for getting here so quickly. General Wayne is rallying his men, and then we'll be away."

"So we are retreating?"

Lafayette laughed, one short bark. "You wish to attack?"

"Not in the least, sir."

"Excellent. As soon as the Pennsylvanians begin to withdraw, you may move into those woods. You will be the rear guard. There will be dragoons to cover you ... ahh, there they are."

George nodded, trying to time the arrival of the friendly cavalry against the possibility of the enemy horse charging him.

Lafayette slapped his boot. "Come and see me when this is over. I have a job for you, as you Americans say."

He rose and bowed, regardless of the bullets. George couldn't help but return the bow.

★ ★ ★

Simcoe sat on his horse in the shadow of the trees with his black trumpeter, Harris, and his staff and watched the arrival of the rebel horse.

"The enemy have put their house in order, gentlemen," he said, scanning the field under his hand. He made a clucking noise. He had been close to snatching away two of their best companies, but the chance was gone.

One of his riflemen in the tree nearest to him called down. "Colonel? I have a good shot at a general who just stood up. Little fellow. Must be Lafayette!"

Simcoe made his clucking noise again. "Let him go, Dodd." He turned his horse and motioned to his bugler, who immediately started to blow the recall.

★ ★ ★

An hour later George and the marquis watched the end of the British column as they withdrew across the river toward Williamsburg. A shot rang out as one of their rear guard tried the range against Lafayette's dragoons.

"They beat us and then retreat," said George.

"General Cornwallis has limited supplies and quite a few wounded men. He is eager to secure his escape." Lafayette mounted his horse, re-captured by the dragoons, and motioned to an aide.

"What'd you want me for, Marquis?"

"I want you to take my dispatches to General Washington as quickly as you can."

George nodded, already worried about his company in his absence.

"It is essential that General Washington should understand the situation as quickly as possible, George. You know that the Comte de Grasse and his fleet are on their way?"

"I know they are coming this summer, yes."

"They may come here. Perhaps they will go to New York or to Rhode Island, but they may come here. And, George, if they do, you must tell the general that we will have Cornwallis like a rat in the trap."

New Jersey, July 8, 1781

Caesar heard the shots off to his right and stopped in the trail. He had been ordering one of his men to collect all the carts from a farm, but foraging was no longer the primary mission. He turned and ran to his right, gathering men as he went. Across a field, he saw Major Stewart put his horse over a fence and wave his helmet.

Mr. Martin was standing in the farmyard, his whistle to his lips. Caesar waved his musket. "Enemy off to the right, sir."

"I'm with you," said Martin, and they ran through the farmyard and up to a fence where one of the new men, Saul, lay slumped and moaning against the clean split rails. His red jacket glistened with blood from a wound high in his chest. Caesar knelt by him a moment and shrugged to Virgil, who was on the other side of him.

"Rifle," Caesar said. He looked for Saul's file partner, a veteran named Delancy, after his former owner. Delancy was ahead of them in the fenced field, lying under a tree. His musket barked. Caesar tried to follow the line of the shot and saw several men in dirty gray shirts on a low rise to the east. Caesar looked at Martin, who nodded and blew his whistle.

"Form front on the center. Quickly, now. Odd files will cover. Even files advance on the whistle. Listen for it."

Martin was encouraging the men, and then one of them fell and gave a scream. Far off, there was a tiny puff of smoke. Some of the newer men immediately crouched, and one fired his musket. Virgil cuffed him.

"Don' be a fool," he growled.

Faster, Caesar thought. *We have to move faster.*

He blew his whistle. Something hit the barn right next to his head and splinters pricked his face. He shook his head. Fowver was ordering the stationary files to start firing, and they did, slowly and carefully to avoid their own men. They weren't likely to hit much with muskets against rifles at this range, but they had all learned that any enemy shoots worse when he's worried about keeping his own head down. Caesar's men began to trot.

He was reading the ground, looking for cover, when he saw the little fold off to the left. He angled that way and the line followed him. They were well spread out but he began to sprint, the full power of his legs carrying him ahead. There was a fence and he hurdled it, his whole body crossing in one fluid motion, and then he was over and running on the other side.

"Files from the center, follow me!" he bellowed. The men crossing the fence began to run to him. He kept going forward.

Off to his right, he saw Major Stewart moving his men through an orchard. Then he was in the little fold and hidden from the riflemen. He paused a moment to gather his men, few of whom had his turn of speed. There were shots from the farmyard, and then more shots from over his head.

"Ready?" he asked. They all got their breath back, safe in the dead ground and none too eager to leave it.

Martin drew his sword. He looked at it a moment as if it were unfamiliar and then held it up. "Charge!" he yelled, and ran up the fold. Caesar followed him and the moment they came over the little crest they began to cheer.

The rebels didn't wait for them. Surprised by their appearance so close, they bolted. Off to the right, Major Stewart's horse crested the rise and one of the rebels paused and shot him. Stewart's horse crumpled. Caesar bellowed. Virgil stopped for one stride and shot the man down, and Martin gave a cry and ran on, Caesar at his heels.

There was a long hill behind the rise where the riflemen had waited, and they ran up it as best they could, Caesar and Martin now well ahead. The rocks grew bigger until they could no longer see their quarry, and then they came around a great boulder and were on a road. A big man on a horse fired a pistol and the ball went wide. Then he laughed. Another man turned his horse and tried a rifle shot from horseback.

Caesar aimed his fusil and pulled the trigger. Nothing answered him but the clatch of the cock hitting the hammer. The rifle shot ricocheted off the boulder, and Martin took a pistol from his belt, raised it like a duelist, and shot the man's horse. The big man gave one glance at his partner and rode away.

Suddenly Caesar knew the big man was Bludner. He gave a wordless cry somewhere between pain and rage and ran down the road, brandishing his useless fusil like a spear. He ran with the full power of his legs, the iron horseshoe plates on his heels kicking up sparks as he went, leaping the downed horse and on around the bend.

He could see for a hundred yards, and there was Bludner going over the next hill, his horse at a gallop. Caesar put his head down and ran. At the next hill he abandoned his fusil. He ran until he could no longer see Bludner ahead of him. And then he turned and started to trot back.

☆ ☆ ☆

Stewart was lying under a maple tree at the edge of the rise where the riflemen had been. He looked as pale as death. Caesar ran up to him and saw that McDonald was smiling, and he breathed a sigh of relief. He had been convinced that Bludner had killed Stewart.

Stewart had a bandage on his left arm and his shirt, breeches, and waistcoat were as red as his coat. His horse lay dead.

"Sergeant Caesar?"

"My compliments on finding you alive, sir."

"No compliments needed, Caesar. I told Mr. Crawford and Mr. Martin to see to the detail. That shooting will bring the rebels down on us." Stewart tried to move and gave a little grunt. "I think it's time I went home to Scotland, Caesar."

"That was Bludner, sir."

"Really?" Stewart winced and moved, winced again. "And we missed him?"

"We missed him."

Stewart shook his head, but McDonald smiled. "We missed him this time, Julius. But your Mr. Martin took one of his men."

Caesar brightened. "Took him?"

"Shot his horse. Took him prisoner."

"Think he'll talk?"

Sergeant McDonald gave Caesar an ugly smile. "Oh, I'd say."

Stewart wriggled again and closed his eyes. "I'll stay a little longer, then."

Chapter Twenty-one

Dobb's Ferry and New York, July 19 and after, 1781

Washington saw the courier arrive outside his window and signed a general order without flourish, then made a sign to David Humphreys, who was acting as his secretary, to hold his private correspondence. The courier was doubtless about to deprive him of his afternoon.

Fitzgerald leaned in from the common room. "Captain Lake from General Lafayette," he said formally, and withdrew.

Washington remembered Lake well, one of the company-level officers who had been with the army for so long that he seemed to personify it. Lake saluted smartly. Washington bowed a little while remaining seated and held out his hand. Lake gave him a canvas packet.

"I am surprised to see you so far from your company, Captain Lake," he said. The words sounded cold, though he had meant them to be warm. He winced a little. The lack of news about the French fleet had him on edge.

"The marquis wanted his message delivered in person, sir. He says if the Comte de Grasse will come to the Chesapeake, we'll have Cornwallis like a rat in a trap."

Washington smiled. As he repeated those words, George had looked out of the window and his features had undergone a strange transformation, as if he had become Lafayette for a moment.

"We are all waiting on the Comte de Grasse, Captain. If he comes to

Newport, we will act in the North. If he offers the British battle off Sandy Hook, we will attack New York." Washington opened the packet with a knife and began to read the dispatch. "How badly was Wayne handled?"

"More than one hundred men lost, sir."

Washington shook his head. "Impetuous. But Wayne has spirit." He shook himself. What spirit indeed, that he would criticize a general to a captain? Although sometimes he felt that Lake was like his staff, his military family.

He read on. "Ahh," he said, when he read that Cornwallis had retreated on Williamsburg. This was country he knew well, so that he could see the action at Green Springs, taste the air, see the horses trampling the tobacco and smell the result. "So Lord Cornwallis is well down the peninsula?"

"He was when I left the marquis." George continued to stand at attention.

"Captain, please refresh yourself and hold yourself in readiness to deliver my answer. You can join my staff." He gave a hard little smile. "While we wait on the Comte de Grasse."

★   ★   ★

Caesar stood in his room in the barracks and polished the blade of his sword with an oiled cloth and some ash. He moved the blade rhythmically between his fingers while his mind was elsewhere.

The first essential of the plan to take Bludner depended on constant knowledge of his agents in New York. For that reason, someone watched Sally every moment of the day. Major Stewart tended to spend more time with her, and when he was absent from her rooms Sergeant McDonald or one of his friends watched her door. Even so, in late July, Bludner's agent met her, hit her, and terrified her. They couldn't touch him as he left her. It would have ruined the plan. But McDonald told Caesar he had never been so close to killing a man and not done it.

The second essential was to know Bludner's location and to be able to plan to attack it. The prisoner had added to their store of knowledge about Bludner's posts. He knew of three, and the prisoner said that Bludner moved among them often. Only his couriers knew which post he'd be at. But the prisoner knew a good deal about the locations of the posts: one in an old cabin in a wood, one in a big stone barn, and one in an old Dutch farmhouse. They knew a little about each but needed more to strike.

Polly had gone to be with Sally after McDonald's report. She came back toward evening. She had been crying, he could see, and she was subdued. Caesar had been blacking his belts, part of a ritual he did to calm himself. His whole kit was hanging from hooks, the leather gleaming softly, the weapons bright. His offering on a private altar. He wiped the blackball from his hands, reminded by the smell of the regulars of the Fourteenth Foot and his days in the Ethiopians.

When his hands were cleaner, he took Polly's between his. Hers were cold.

"Sally's drunk," she said quietly.

Caesar just sat.

"He beat her, and there was nothing we could do. She's going to break, Caesar. We have to get Bludner before Sally gives up."

Caesar hung his head. "Next time will be the last. I swear."

"Tell Sally that. I'm not afraid, or if I am, it's nothing to her terror."

"We're making a plan. We can't move until we have some cover, or the rebels will know what we were after."

"My father agrees. You know that. And he's trying to sound out . . . other quarters. We followed the messenger last night, through three other stops. We know where to follow him and whom he meets. It will make the big night easier."

Caesar considered Polly. "I worry about you, Polly. I think this is a great deal more dangerous than standing guard with a musket."

She smiled and looked down, and Caesar thought that it was something they shared, the secret love of the excitement. He even wondered if sharing this plan wouldn't bind them in a way that few couples could be bound. He held her close and she kissed him suddenly, her mouth opening under his and her lips melting and unlike anything he had ever known, and her eyes were liquid.

Then she pushed him away.

"I have something else to tell you," she said with her secret smile. Caesar sat on his heels and looked up at her, waiting.

"I think I'm pregnant," she said. "Don't go gettin' any ideas."

Caesar's smile filled his face.

☆ ☆ ☆

"It's a pleasure to have you back with us," said Colonel Robinson, pouring a fresh glass of claret.

They were back under the map at the Moor's Head. Stewart's hair was a mare's nest of red ends, but he was otherwise looking cheerful, if not well. He had a leg up on a chair like a gout sufferer, and one of his arms was strapped to his chest with a black silk sling.

"It's a pleasure to have so much female sympathy and never need to dance," said Stewart, acknowledging a smile from a distant Miss Hammond, who was being instructed on the big floor with Mr. Martin. They were learning a ballet. He inclined his head in return.

Simcoe gave a snort. "I gather that when the use of your limbs returns, we shall find you a very passable dancer, Stewart."

"Lies. All lies."

Robinson looked around the tavern. "I hear that our army in Virginia is in difficulties."

"Lord Cornwallis seems to have been maneuvered into a position where the navy has to retrieve him. My friend Simcoe is not too happy about it."

"Friends of mine outside the line say that General Washington may be preparing to march that way," said Robinson. "And we think it might be worthwhile to have a little raid to keep him pinned to his lines here."

Stewart nodded absently, an idea forming in his head. "How many men would you use?"

"Oh, two hundred at least. We'd beat up one of their outposts and they would assuredly have a covering party behind them, so any trap would need enough muskets to keep the covering party off."

"Quite a big show, then," Stewart said with satisfaction. "Any notion when?"

"We need intelligence. I think they are very careful about their movements."

"But you'd be ready to go soon."

"Oh, yes. Do I sense a spark of professional interest, Major Stewart?"

"I am interested in being active, sir." Stewart smiled dangerously. "And I'm trying to please friends."

☆ ☆ ☆

"We have to be ready to move," Hamilton repeated. The staff was gathered around the table in the main room of the tavern, and to their number had been added a dozen French officers, most very young men in splendid uniforms. The Duc de Lauzon, one of the most powerful young men in the world, lounged on the back of a Windsor chair, his powder blue leg contrasting sharply with the dark wood all around him.

"Move where?" asked a French officer. "We cannot plan a campaign when we don't know the object, surely?"

Washington held out a hand to George Lake, who passed him a large chart.

"We have an opportunity to act in Virginia," he said, showing them a new theater of operations. "Always assuming that the Comte de Grasse will condescend to visit us there. But first I want to secure the ground between the ferry and the river, and perhaps farther down toward their posts. A raid in force, gentlemen, to keep their ears pinned back while we go off after the other fox."

✯ ✯ ✯

Robinson came into the tavern, dejected, and passed Caesar without a word and sat in the fireplace nook. He stripped off his gloves and began to tap them against his boot. Caesar approached him cautiously, unsure of his welcome, but Robinson seemed to notice him for the first time and beckoned to him.

"Sergeant?"

"Sir."

"It's off, Sergeant. Washington has flooded his outposts with men. There must be six thousand militia in the ground along the river. Suicide to try for one of his posts. It's as if he knew what we were up to," he said, and Caesar caught a chill. *Sally might break,* Polly had said.

✯ ✯ ✯

"Can you stir your friends for reports on the rebels?" Stewart asked. Marcus White and Stewart had shared all their information.

"I can't see that it is essential, although I'd be happy to please Colonel Robinson and General Clinton."

Caesar nodded his head. "We have two men from up that way. Van Sluyt comes from one of the plantations on the river. It may be that we could get a report from the blacks up there."

"Is it so important?" asked Marcus White.

Stewart nodded. "They have moved forward in strength. Some of my friends at headquarters think that Washington may be looking at a proper attack on New York. If that's the case, Bludner won't be in our reach. But others aren't so sure. Lord Cornwallis has got himself in some difficulties in Virginia. Washington has been cunning at covering his movements before. He may be moving. If he is, we need to know what those rebels are doing."

White turned to Caesar. "Even if it means sending Polly?"

And Caesar felt a nip of fear.

New Windsor, New York, August 14, 1781

Washington read the message calmly, masking his exultation and the resulting nerves with the ease of long practice. He had his plan in place and he was ready.

"Note to General Knox. Please tell the general to suspend the movement of our siege train north. We will keep it at Philadelphia. Fitzgerald, please fetch me Captain Lake."

"At once, sir."

Washington dictated a series of orders to his secretary. Militia to fill the posts. More militia to be called out from Connecticut. Commands for the Hudson forts. Commands for the reserves. One of his aides handed him a report from a spy, from which he gleaned that the British had no idea what his real target was. He frowned.

"Do I know Captain Bludner?"

"He has his own company in the outposts, sir. Something to do with intelligence."

"Leave him here. General Heath will need all the intelligence he can get if the British choose to strike in my absence."

"Captain Lake, sir."

Lake entered and saluted. Washington took off his hat and bowed. "I'm sending you back to the marquis."

"Sir!"

"Captain, I am bringing the army to Virginia, and the French as well. We are going to have a go at the rat in our marquis's trap. I want you to tell him that I will be on the peninsula, God willing, in three weeks. He must keep Cornwallis occupied for that long."

Lake beamed. All motion in the building had stopped and every man hung on Washington's orders. Word had passed. Virginia. Cornwallis.

"We will march on the nineteenth of August, in four days. And with luck and the benevolence of heaven, gentlemen, we will go to Virginia and win the war."

★　★　★

"The French have moved south and the whole rebel army is in New Jersey," said Robinson, pointing at the map over the fireplace.

Martin took a draw on his pipe. "Mr. Washington can be a deep one, sir."

Stewart favored his arm, now healing well, and reached with his left hand for his wine. "Mr. Washington is marching to Virginia to take Lord Cornwallis," he said carefully, looking into his glass. The other two officers took sharp breaths, and Robinson cursed.

"Gentlemen, there is nothing we can do to stop him. But, Beverly"— this to Colonel Robinson—"in his absence, I think it would be surprising if we didn't snap up some of his posts."

Robinson leaned forward. "Because his army can't be in two places at once?"

"Even Mr. Washington can't do that."

"It will take some time to plan all over again," said Robinson.

"We'll need new intelligence. They've moved all their posts," said Martin.

Stewart raised his glass to a distant corner where Sally sat sewing with Polly. "Here's to Mr. Washington, gentlemen. In his absence, great things may be accomplished."

New York, September 10, 1781

In New York, the weather had turned to rain, a harsh, cold rain that kept everyone indoors. It promised to be a hard fall. Caesar stood in the bow window of the Moor's Head watching a few laborers run through the wet, mud splashing up their thighs. He pitied the soldiers out in the lines.

Major Stewart had a pint of Madeira and a map, and he used them to make his points. "If you really want to leave the impression that the whole thing is an accident, or perhaps that it was about something very different, then I think our best hope is to hide it under Colonel Robinson's expedition. If Robinson attacks the outposts near the Hudson, we can take Bludner in the same sweep with the same men. But we need to know just where the rebel posts are and just where Bludner's men camp. We need the whole layout of the area. When we take Bludner's courier, he may spill all of it or he may try and lead us into a trap. I want to know the ground in advance."

"So we take the courier the night that Colonel Robinson plans to go after the rebel posts?"

"Just so. It came to me when Robinson was telling about his plan. Caesar, do you concur?"

"I do, sir."

"And do you know the area?"

"We were all over that ground last year." Caesar could see it in his mind's eye.

"And Reverend White says that Bludner's covering party is usually by the Van Cortlandt house. Look here. That's less than a mile from the ferry."

"Stands to reason, sir. There are only so many approaches between our lines and theirs, and Bludner's spies need the ferry."

"Just so, Sergeant Caesar, just so. Do you see it, Reverend?"

Marcus White looked at Caesar carefully, as if judging him all over again.

"Doesn't Mr. Van Sluyt have a wife?" White asked.

"He does, but that has never kept him from his duty . . ." Caesar trailed off as he saw that he had missed the mark entirely. Marcus White was looking off into the distance.

"Perhaps his wife would go. Women pass the lines very easily. She could take Polly. . . ."

Caesar shuddered.

"I've done it before, Julius." She fairly bounced with enthusiasm and his heart died within him. He wanted to say, "*But you are pregnant.*" Yet he understood that would be a betrayal.

"But we already know all this," he protested.

"No, Caesar. We *guess* it. And if we're going to commit hundreds of men up the river, we have to *know*."

Marcus looked at Polly and they smiled at each other, a smile of private communication.

Stewart shook his shoulders a little. "I don't like sending them in harm's way. . . ."

"I'd do anything to get Bludner," said Polly.

Mount Vernon, September 9–10, 1781

Truro Church brought a lump to his throat. As he pulled his horse to a stop and looked at the church's pattern of Flemish brick for a little, the church unleashed a flood of memory, of obligations and uncompleted tasks from another life. For the first time in five years he wondered who was a warden and whether the rector's roof had ever been repaired. He could see bricks missing from the churchyard wall.

David Humphreys, the only one of his staff to accompany him on his dash to Mount Vernon, looked ready to fall off his horse. Billy Lee looked better, tired but easy on his tall bay. Washington's decision to go home for one night on the way to his campaign had been the product of a rare whim, and he had ridden sixty miles in a day to get here. Few men had the stamina to stay with him.

Past the churchyard, he was really home. Those were his fields on either side of the road, and the road itself, which needed repair, he was sorry to note, was also his. All the way from Baltimore the roads had been bad, but here in Frederick County they were virtually impassable, just near his home and in the path of his army that needed speed for his troops and more speed for his supplies.

"Good to be home, eh, Billy?" said Washington, turning slightly in his saddle. He was concerned that Humphreys might have a fall, and took the opportunity to give him a glance.

"Yes, sir," said Billy.

The sun was setting as he finally turned his horse through his gates and was greeted by the moving sight of Mount Vernon glowing with the last light, and all the windows lit from inside. A white man he didn't know ran from behind the Greenhouse, calling that there were visitors, and Washington smiled, the spell of his own house strong on him.

"Well ridden, David," he said to his companion. The man bowed in the saddle, stiff with fatigue, and appeared unable to speak. Washington rode past the front of his house toward his stable and dismounted. None of the blacks looked familiar, and he handed his horse to a stranger.

"Do you know that boy, Billy?"

"I don't know any of these folk, sir."

Washington nodded a little sharply, collected his pistols from his saddle holsters, and gave them and his pannier to Billy. Then he walked up the sandy drive to the house, where doors were opened and there was a great deal of movement.

She was standing just inside the door, an enigmatic smile on her face. Older, very much older, but the smile was the same and he laughed to see it.

As he stepped over his own lintel, she came forward. "I thought perhaps you had forgotten the way?" she said, and he lifted her in his arms and kissed her, a rare excess in front of the house staff, but she didn't protest. And he held her, remembered the weight and the smell of her, and he was home.

"You are famous, I find," she said. "Even I have a place in the pantheon."

It was so easy to forget who she was, how the sharp steel of her went along with the flame, and yet when he looked she wasn't wearing her closed face, and he realized she was speaking at random because she was surprised. For five years he had written to her every day, and only now did he think that she might have had the harder life, trapped here by her illnesses and her own will, without him. He took one of her hands and kissed it.

She laughed.

"I have gifts for you from many admirers, my dear," he said. "But I am still the commander of an army, if only a little one, and I must send a letter this instant before I place myself at your service. May I have your pardon?"

"You came home. I can forgive you much for that." She gave him her precious smile of delight and turned into her parlor. "I will await you."

Washington gave Billy a nod. Billy knew which things to unpack and buff up—the miniature from Adrienne de Lafayette, the scent from France—and Washington passed into his study. He couldn't call for David Humphreys, who was barely able to walk, and he was determined to send his letter tonight. He went to the desk, rifled it for paper, and had to cut a quill. All his pens were years dead. Then he had to mix ink from powder, which required the help of an unfamiliar scullery maid. Finally he had his materials to hand and he dashed off a letter to the commander of the Frederick County militia demanding that they turn out the next day to repair the roads.

Then he rose and caught sight of the bust of Frederick the Great on the bookcase by his desk. He looked around at all the busts, Alexander and Caesar and Charles, and he shook his head as a grown man does when confronted with the excesses of youth. The busts put him in mind of something, though, and when he entered his wife's parlor he was holding his own copy of Müller's treatise on artillery and siegecraft.

She was reading a novel by the fire, and he came and settled on an elegant chair that hadn't been in the room when he left for the war.

She put her book aside carefully. "Is the continent safe, then?"

"As safe as my poor powers can make it. I had to order a repair to the roads. Our wagons would mire—"

"It is not just the roads that lack repair, my general."

"Yes," he said, falling in with her conversation. He knew what she was playing at, but he determined to act the part of the man. "Yes, the wall in Truro churchyard also needs repair."

"I heard talk of gifts," she said.

Washington rose and called for Billy, who brought them, gave him an odd look, and left up the stairs. Washington had pounds of presents for her, because no French officer visited him without a gift for "Madame Washington." He presented her with a selection of the best, along with a few that he had chosen himself in Philadelphia and on the ride south. She began to open them, exclaiming softly over the scent and deriding the tastelessness of a gold snuffbox that must have cost as much as a good horse.

"Now everything is from France," she said. "I confess to missing our English trifles."

He brought out a final package from his pocket, and she opened it and looked at him. It was a small etui, a collection of sewing tools in a plain sharkskin scabbard with severe silver mounts. She ran her hand over the shagreen, like polished pebbles set in leather, and clipped it to her housewife.

"We still get some English goods," he said.

"You thought of me," she said. Her eyes were moist, but she turned away. "You..."

"Yes, my dear?" Once the words were out he knew what she wanted. He hadn't told her how long he would be home, and she was too proud to ask.

"I will have tomorrow here alone. The next day my staff and the French staff will arrive, and we will have to entertain. On the twelfth I'll be gone."

"Gone? Where are you going?"

"Down the peninsula, Martha. Cornwallis is near Williamsburg. I hope to catch him with his back to the sea and make him surrender."

"Would that win the war?"

He shook his head. "I no longer know."

She nodded, tears running down her face and neck.

He rose and walked to the window. He saw movement on the lawn and was tempted to give her a moment alone and walk out to see his dogs. The pack would have been broken up, of course, but he thought of the slave, Caesar, and of hunts in the autumn and the feeling of anticipation, so like the feeling he had now. That put him in mind of slaves. He spoke without turning.

"Have we changed a great many slaves?"

"They ran."

"Ran?"

"When Mr. Arnold's army passed this way, and again when General Phillips was across the river. Each time the British came near, they flocked to join them."

Washington looked through the window again. "Can you blame them?"

Martha rose from her chair and looked at him in mock horror. "Whoever you are, leave this house and tell my husband to return!"

He shook his head, laughing with her, and then caught a hand and kissed it. "I'm perfectly serious."

Martha gave him that enigmatic smile and said, "I think it is time for supper. I wouldn't want to keep the generalissimo of the Continental Congress from his bed." She stopped in the door and looked back at him, twenty years younger in the light. "Or mine."

He bowed, happy, and made to follow her, but she stopped him with her fan. "But you have changed."

"I have, too."

New York, October 1, 1781

The Loyal Americans had the outer posts on the White Plains road, and Caesar got to know them as he came out every day to wait for her return. She was supposed to go out with Mrs. Van Sluyt and return the next day.

After the third day of waiting he kept very much to himself. The Guides had recently been ordered to clean streets in New York, a loathsome chore and too much like labor for any of them. They cleaned for a day and grumbled, but Caesar would have none of it. He was quiet, and very dangerous.

On the fourth day he stopped at the Whites' lodging, finding neither father nor daughter. Then he walked out to the first line of posts, saluting officers and accepting the curious salutes of a variety of corps, and showed his pass, and then out alone through the dangerous ground between the first and second line, and so to the Loyal Americans again at sunset. He watched the road that led to Dobb's Ferry and the rebel lines, but it was empty.

The green-coated men were quiet around him. They knew something was up. They knew he had been there when two black girls crossed the lines, and they knew that Sergeant Caesar was a favorite of their own colonel. So they nodded to him, stood stiffly in a post that was probably comfortable in better times, and wished him luck.

He watched until the sun went down, and then he picked his way back in the dark.

☆　☆　☆

On the fifth day, a flag crossed the lines, and Caesar feared it, because if Polly had been taken he fancied that the rebels might announce it, but his real fear was far darker, because he feared Bludner. Sally had turned Bludner into a demon, and Caesar tried not to imagine Polly being made a slave, or raped, or killed for the man's sport. He hated this game, and he wondered if he would forgive Marcus White his willingness to play it with his own daughter.

On the sixth day, the Loyal Americans had been replaced on the post by some of Emmerich's men, a Loyalist regiment that included a fair number of rebel deserters, hard men, and in some cases very bad men. They were not so friendly, and they didn't know him. They had a sergeant who seemed inclined to resent his presence. Caesar was too worried even to react to the slurs they passed casually, until he happened to look at the sergeant in just a certain way, and the sergeant withdrew, muttering. But although two parties of men passed the post, there were no women. It was a week until Sally's messenger would return, and Polly was six days late, and Van Sluyt cried for his wife all day. Caesar knew he would have to resent the day labor soon or do something to show that they were too useful to accept such treatment. But all he could think of was Polly.

On the seventh day, he had no duty. None of the Guides did. They were not in the posts, and the labor order had been withdrawn as mysteriously as it appeared. Caesar took Van Sluyt and walked out through the lines, showing his worn pass to every post and being greeted familiarly as he went. He had done this often now, and he was doing it more from superstition than from belief. He had begun to doubt Marcus White again. He couldn't seem to interest Captain Stewart in the indignity of soldiers being made to labor—Stewart only said that his own men were building a road, and weren't Caesar's men getting extra pay? And Lieutenant Martin said the same. He felt as if he had to carry the concerns of every man and woman in the Guides, and he had to bear them while remaining outwardly unmoved by Polly's absence. Too many people already knew too much. There were so many who could have betrayed her, and he wondered at Marcus White's curious confidence that no black would betray another. He knew blacks in Jamaica who had sold dozens of their brothers into bondage, or back to bondage. He looked at the company at morning muster and wondered if one of them could have sold Polly to the rebels.

When they reached the outer post, they found the Reverend White sitting quietly with a Bible, reading. Caesar sat next to him on a fence rail where he could see the road.

"She'll come today," said White, looking down the dusty pale road at the heat ripples in the distance.

"Where have you been?" said Caesar. "Why didn't you go with her?"

Marcus White looked at him with eyes of sadness and pity.

"Don't you think I wanted to go with her, Julius?" he asked. "They almost know me now, Julius. There are one or two who might take me just for crossing the lines. They seldom molest women, or even question them. Men are different."

Van Sluyt sat quietly, but he was so upset that his hands shook.

"They'll hang my girl," he said. "Or put her back to a slave, an' I'll never see her again."

Marcus White shook his head with a calm like that which Caesar had on the battlefield. "They'll come today."

"Why?" asked Caesar, his tone more accusatory than he had intended.

"I'll tell you when they come."

★　★　★

They hadn't come by midday. The sun beat down, and the Loyal Americans changed their guard, and the surly sergeant was replaced by a courteous one, and there were two black men in the platoon that came on duty. Caesar didn't know them but he went to them somewhat mechanically and introduced himself. It passed the time.

They didn't come in the afternoon, although parties of women passed with eggs and geese, and one pair of very handsome girls leading a pig. None of them was black. None of them had come far, and most were just farm women taking things in for the market.

They didn't come in the evening. The Loyal Americans shared their mess kettle with good heart and Caesar ate well, sharing his tobacco and a little bottle of rum in return. Van Sluyt didn't talk or eat, but simply sat on a rock by the side of the road and polished the lock of his musket over and over again. Marcus White began to walk down the road in little spurts. He walked forward a few paces as if to have a different view, and then farther and farther until he was almost at a musket shot from the post itself. All Caesar's suspicions returned at the gallop and he followed into the gathering gloom, walking fast on the road in such an agitation of spirit that he realized that he had left his fowler propped against the stand of arms in the little post. He was unarmed except for his sword and Jeremy's dagger.

But when he caught up with the Reverend White at a single great oak tree that marked a slight turn in the road, White was making no attempt to escape. He was weeping silently, great tears flooding down his face, a look on him that made Caesar flinch. Marcus White raised his arms and Caesar felt his heart stop, and he looked into the last red shreds of the setting sun.

There were two white caps in the distance, and one had a basket on her head and the other walked in just that way. They were black women, and Caesar's heart beat once, thud, as if all the promises of the world had all come true, and again, thud, and they were closer, the dark coming down like rain between them so that no matter how fast the two women moved they seemed to be getting no closer. He realized that Van Sluyt was still polishing his musket, unknowing that happiness awaited him, and he shouted, and the slighter of the two women looked up and began to run.

He covered her in kisses and her father hugged her and they tried to accomplish all of this as they hurried Mrs. Van Sluyt down the road to her own husband. All the while the two excited women poured forth their story, of lines closed, of messengers missing their appointments, of an endless tangle of mistakes and missing friends. And then Hester Van Sluyt was in her husband's arms, and Caesar had Polly's hand, and they were back within the post.

Without a thought but his own heart, Caesar said, "Promise me you'll never do it again."

Polly glared at him like an angry cat. "Pshaw!" she said. "It suits you! I feel it every time you go out. And worse as I like you more!"

He fell back, astounded for a moment and then chagrined, and caught her hand again and she let him. Marcus regarded them tenderly. To make a change, Caesar turned to him. "How did you know?"

White laughed. It was a shaky laugh at best.

"I didn't know, Caesar, but it was my place to offer comfort if I could. He was afraid for you, my honey," White said to Polly, and she bowed her head.

"That's all?"

"Their passes..."

"He means to say our passes were for a Saturday, and he knew that if I thought we were in danger I'd wait and cross on a Saturday," she said.

Caesar nodded, as if he understood. "You are very brave," he said.

"Pshaw," she said.

Yorktown, Virginia, October 14, 1781

Washington looked out over the lip of the trench into the dark and listened to a dog barking somewhere in the British lines. Lafayette stepped up close to him and cautiously placed a hand on his shoulder. They could see nothing, could hear nothing, but they stood in the cold darkness and waited for the verdict of the battle.

It was less a battle than a siege. Cornwallis, hugely outnumbered, had built a fortress of earthworks around the Tidewater town of Yorktown and had gone to ground like a fox, waiting for the Royal Navy to come and take him off. But the Royal Navy, for the first and only time in the war, had been outguessed and outnumbered, and now it was a French fleet that lay at anchor out in the Chesapeake. Cornwallis had little chance of succor but, being an excellent general and a professional, he was determined to hold his ground as long as he could.

Washington, the farmer, was now the commander of the largest joint Franco-American army of the war. He had dug his approach trenches, planted his guns, and bombarded the star forts and redoubts of the British. He had the advice of the best French engineers and some gifted Americans. He had the support of professional officers from all of Europe. But he was the commander and this was the best chance the fledgling United States would ever have to win the game. He tasted fear tinged with anticipation. They were so close to victory.

Tonight, the picked men of his light infantry and the best of the French grenadiers would assault the most exposed British forts at the point of bayonet, in the best tradition of European arms. It was all managed like a play. In Europe, kings came to sieges to watch the show. In America, there were only the actors. And in a few moments the last act would open and his best men would fling themselves on Cornwallis's veterans, and then...

☆ ☆ ☆

Somewhere in the darkness a dog was barking, but George Lake was elsewhere.

He could read Betsy's last letter in his head, even standing in a dark and muddy trench. She'd said "love," which was a hard thing for a young girl to say to a man she hadn't seen in two years and who served the enemy. She'd said it several times, and constant rereading had imprinted the letter on him to such an extent that he could close his eyes and see the shape of her writing and the color of the paper.

Someone nudged him and he opened his eyes. Even in the dark he could recognize Hamilton, his commander for the night. Hamilton squeezed his arm. "You'll be a major in the morning, George," he whispered, and George just shook his head. He had volunteered to lead the first rush over the top of the trench. It wasn't for the promotion, although it was natural enough for the ambitious Hamilton to think so. It was to get it over with. They were close to the end and George had a chase in view, as the Virginian hunters liked to say. He wanted his Betsy, and a farm somewhere or a shop. It was close. So close that he chose to feel it was just over the top of the rampart of the great British redoubt a few hundred yards distant, if he could only get there.

He shook Hamilton's hand. He pushed through the crowd at the head of the sap and found Caleb Cooke, with whom he had exchanged last letters, just in case. He and Caleb shook hands without words because they had nothing left to say. He passed through men he had known since before Green Springs, since Monmouth or Brandywine, and often they would simply lock eyes, although some shook hands. They were all around him, all the men who had stayed true from the first fights, and those who had come later, until the dark was fuller than it could really be. He had tears in his eyes. He wiped them on his cuff.

He went back to the head of his own men and got his spontoon, the long weapon like a spear. Around him in the dark, other officers and sergeants gave speeches. He didn't have one ready. He put a foot up on a step and looked back over six years, and spoke quietly.

"If I fall, no one stops. Just take the redoubt. That's all that matters."

There was a pause, and even the damn dog stopped barking. And then the first red rocket burned up into the night from the French lines and George was out in the open, running, silent as a shadow.

He could hear the others coming behind him, and he ran through the mud, jumping shell holes where the mortars had dropped their rounds short. Then he was into the ditch at the foot of the big redoubt, and now the British were awake and firing down at them. He heard a scream behind him, and another, and there was a wall of firing over his head and he ran on, his boots throwing mud high in the air, heading for the rear of the redoubt as they had practiced, where the walls were lower. And the firing seemed sporadic and his heart began to rise. He risked a look back and saw that Desmond, the New York boy, had the colors and was close behind him. They were almost at the end of the ditch when Desmond went down and George was tangled in silk. He grabbed the flagstaff and pounded up the steep slope of the rampart, his new breeches black with mud. He slipped and jammed in a heel to keep his spot and lost his spontoon. Above him on the wall, a man lunged at him with a bayonet. George parried with the flagstaff, pushed its point into the man's face, and suddenly he was gone. Finally reaching the top of the earthen wall, George raised the flag.

At the foot of the inner wall a British officer had a platoon formed, and though they were about to be overrun from three sides his men were finishing their loading as calmly as on parade. George admired them even as he collected his own men at the top of the wall and led them down, silence forgotten as they bellowed a cheer, an unstoppable tide of blue coats. Then something punched him in the chest and he felt the British fire and he was down, the cold of the mud catching at his hands and his neck.

New York, October 14, 1781

Jason Knealey liked working in New York better than in Philadelphia, where the people were all suspicious. New York was full of alleys and bolt-holes, and he had no need to do his real work anymore. He was an important man, and spying paid.

He walked up the black whore's steps with a steady pace, trying to draw out the pleasure of the moments before she opened the door. His coat flapped a little behind him. He knocked at the door and heard her familiar movements, the hesitation as she came to the door, and he knocked softly in the code. It was supposed to change every visit, but such things couldn't interest him, and he simply rapped out a little series, four, pause, two, pause, four. She was supposed to answer in code to tell him it was all clear, but he had never even taught her this nuance. She opened the door. She was smiling in a way she had never done for him, and he wasn't sure he liked it, but he pushed into the room boldly.

"I hope you have something worth my ride," he said, and then his riding whip was taken from his hands and he was on his back looking at her pale blue ceiling.

"If ye do everything I say, just the *way* I say, I won't open ye with ma' wee knife and let a dog tear at yer guts," said Sergeant McDonald.

★ ★ ★

Polly kissed him quickly on the lips.

"I'll try to be braver than you were," she said.

"I'll be back in the morning," he said, and then realized that she had said the same. She shook her head, and her father came forward and took his hand.

"I am not supposed to shed blood, and yet I almost envy you this. It's open, compared to the other. Clean."

"Tell Sally I'll kill him."

Marcus White turned his head away for a moment and then back. He was struggling with himself. "I admit that is what I want. I console myself that he is an evil man."

"Reverend, this isn't for you. But I'll kill him." He was calm now. The wonderful clarity that going into action always brought, the way it simplified. He leaned past Marcus White and took Polly in his arms.

"I've been scared enough for both of us," he said. "Now I'll be back."

"See that you are, then," she said, and it was time to march.

★　★　★

The little house on Cherry Street was already familiar to the men of Captain Stewart's company who followed Sergeant McDonald. They'd had it pointed out for two weeks. But it was no part of the sergeant's intention to let his captive know that his information was worthless. McDonald wanted him to betray, and betray again, until his betrayal became automatic and he gave them the thing they most desired, which was the location of the covering party commanded by Bludner. So McDonald walked along Cherry Street until the man blubbered that here was the first house, and that the man inside, Mr. Harris, was his contact. They took Harris in his nightgown, with his wife weeping by the door. He was small fry, and McDonald knew his role. He made sure to let Harris see the unhappy messenger, Jason Knealey. He had his orders, and his orders were that every man they took was to see Knealey. Anyone from the other side who examined the evidence would assume Knealey had betrayed the whole chain of agents. It was a constant danger of the spy trade, and Marcus White planned to exploit it.

★　★　★

Lieutenant Martin had the Guides formed at the top of Broadway, ready to pass the inner post as soon as Sergeant McDonald joined them. There was a large column ahead of them: the whole of the Loyal Americans, as well as a company of Hesse Cassel Jaegers, and some dragoons at the head. It was a small army, and Colonel Robinson was its commander. He rode up and down the column, checking their last details, calling on individual officers and sergeants to describe their targets. The main part of the column was intended to surprise the New York militia post at the ferry, and each company had a particular assignment—this house or this barn or crossroads—that it was to secure. Many of them glanced curiously at the Guides, because they knew, as soldiers know, that the Guides had some other mission, and might join them on their own in some way. There wasn't much talking. The columns were allowed to lie on their arms and men went to sleep on their packs.

Just after the moon set, Major Stewart appeared on horseback.

"They have the spy. He's on his way," Stewart said. He looked very white in the moonlight, and Caesar thought it probably still hurt him to ride.

Stewart had no need to come. He was going home to Scotland, had been mentioned in dispatches again for the action in New Jersey, and was buying his next rank in a regiment still stationed in England. Caesar knew he was there, sitting his horse in some pain, because of Jeremy, and Sally, and he nodded to himself and moved over to his little knot of corporals.

"Get them up," he said. Stewart was already gone, up the column, and men were getting to their feet like ghosts rising in a play or an army summoned from the ground. The Loyal Americans were in a dark green that looked black in the dark, and most of the redcoats in the column had work shirts pulled over their coats to conceal them. His own men formed quietly, each man looking for his file partner and falling in until the whole company was there. Ahead of them, the rest of the column was marching with only a few whistles sounded, leaving the Guides alone on the dark road.

Sergeant McDonald came up out of the dark on a small horse, leading another. McDonald was wearing a greatcoat, and the other regulars with him were wearing their work shirts over their coats, too. They fell in with the Guides and the party moved off, passing the inner post with a whispered password and the outer post in silence. Then they halted for a moment and Caesar looked to Stewart and Martin, caught their eyes, and ordered the men to prime and load.

Martin kept walking up and down, a fund of nervous energy. He had passed his tests of fire, but this was a different kind of war and needed different nerves. Stewart sat in the starlight, a dark figure with an oddly shadowed face. Jason Knealey feared this silent figure even more than he feared McDonald, a deep-in-the-gut fear that made his flesh crawl, and he all but sobbed aloud when he saw the Guides clearly, row on row of black men.

"Bludner talks about them," he said, trying to sound friendly through his terror.

"Which, now?"

"The black men. He talks about them, an' how he'll get them someday."

"Oh, aye. Weel, I dinna think he's going to get this lot, but we'll see." McDonald was chewing tobacco and seemed lost in thought, and Knealey tried the bonds on his wrists. He felt the knife press his guts, just a pressure through his clothes, but firm and very steady, and he moaned.

"You'll live to see the dogs start on ye," said McDonald. Knealey just shook.

The last rammer rammed home the last cartridge while McDonald reviewed their destination with Knealey for the seventh time, and gave his captain the nod.

"Time to march?" asked Lieutenant Martin.

"Time to run," said Sergeant Caesar, and Stewart nodded.

"Just so."

"Van Sluyt, take two files ahead and don't get beyond our sight. Stop and come back if you see *anything*. Virgil, four files to the left of our path. Stay fifty paces from the column and rejoin if you see anything or cannot pass a piece of ground otherwise. Jim, the same on the right. At the double, then. March, march!"

They left the road across the unplowed ground of a fallow field, and in a moment they were lost to the sight of the last outpost.

"Where they goin'?" asked one of the soldiers on duty.

The other shook his head. "Glad they're on our side."

✭   ✭   ✭

They moved for almost an hour without a pause, undiscovered through the night. The scouts reported nothing that could be construed as suspicious, and the column took its first rest halt in a gully at the base of a dark mass of hills. They were making a long arc to their destination to avoid intermixing with Colonel Robinson's party. They had some hope that Bludner was expecting his messenger from the opposite direction.

After five minutes' rest and no pipes, they moved again, now at a quiet march across dark fields. Anything in among the trees was invisible in the black, and the sky was an endless field of stars that covered the heavens and seemed to have a clarity and a depth more suited to a winter night.

They stopped when Virgil called a halt by waving, but he had only flushed a deer, and the astonished column watched as the big doe and her fawn raced down the whole length of their little column. Sergeant Fowver slapped the doe as she ran by and laughed softly.

"Bet she never been slapped befo'," he said quietly, and Caesar glared at him. Then Caesar gave two soft pipes on his whistle, and they were moving again, through an apple orchard full of ripe fruit where Jim Somerset stopped them for reasons he couldn't explain to Captain Stewart in a hurried conference. But Caesar respected Jim's ways, and he sent Virgil forward with three old hands to feel out the last few hundred yards of the approach. Knealey sat and sweated, and the other men made their last checks of their equipment. No one spoke. Men filled their haversacks with apples.

To some it seemed that Virgil returned in a moment, but to Caesar and Stewart he seemed to be gone half the night.

"Sentries out," he said. "An' more under cover, I reckon. Hard to tell in the dark."

"And you have a route?"

"All the way to the last cover."

Stewart called for all the noncommissioned officers down to the lowliest corporal to attend him, and they moved well off from the column to be as quiet as they could. Virgil drew them a hasty sketch in the dirt.

"A big barn heah, an' the house. The yard is open an' they ain't no fence." He was nervous, Caesar could see, almost shaking from what he had just done. Caesar thought of Polly and all the different ways that people were brave.

"Then this is a little patch o' wood, and this is a wall, jus' so high." He indicated his thigh. "They's men behin' that wall."

"Cover for us?" said Stewart.

"These woods is empty, and these other woods, I dunno. We di'n't get to them."

Caesar nodded. "Fowver into the near woods and I go into the far."

Stewart winced as he shifted his arm. He was still sitting on his horse. "One long blast from my whistle and in you go. Remember that we don't want to give the alarm before Robinson. He's only a mile or so away, perhaps two. He ought to open the ball in about an hour."

Martin shook his head. "An hour is a long time lying in the dark."

Stewart nodded. "I agree. Keep them here for half an hour."

★ ★ ★

Caesar moved at the head of his men, cautiously entering the edge of the woods, completely alive and aware of every motion and every sound. The night trees were pitch black, but the gentle hum of insects and the chatter of birds told him the woods were most likely empty. He kept his fowler up and aimed into the darkness as he moved from trunk to trunk, his legs making noise in the underbrush that would easily give him away if there were foes here.

When he was in the middle, the brush was less and he could move better. He changed his posture, rising all the way up on the balls of his feet in silence and then sinking back down to change the weight on his back. He leaned forward, and then back, and felt his spine shift a little, and moved on, placing each foot to make the least noise. He couldn't *see* anything, even the man behind him when he turned, and he had to stop himself from looking up at the sky just to find light for his eyes. In what seemed like an eternity he came to thicker brush, and then light—the far edge of the wood. He peered out softly and couldn't even make out the bulk of the barn, except that there seemed to be a sharp edge on the horizon that must be a roofline. He waited. Virgil came up to him and he patted him off to the right, and then Jim came and was sent to the left. He could hear them make noise, and he expected an alarm at every moment, and he put his own whistle to his lips and held it there like a pipe stem, ready. And still there was no alarm. He realized that it was possible that the farm was empty, and that shook him more than the dread of discovery, but under these worries he was still in the grip of the calm that came in action. He crouched and waited.

The very first lightening of the sky came and with it a gentle rain, almost a mist. It didn't last long but Caesar dumped his prime and reprimed from a little horn. After it stopped, the sky seemed to darken, and then it became difficult to tell the passage of time and Caesar grew concerned that something·had changed, or that the darkness might be a sign of heavy rain.

Off to the north and west, there was a dull thump and the hint of a cry on the breeze, and then another thump as the sky grew brighter. Suddenly Caesar wondered if he had been asleep, because the roofline of the barn and house were each distinct, and the morning seemed farther along out in the open while it was still full night under the trees. A very distant sound, almost at the edge of hearing, so Caesar began to doubt each sound, and they were never repeated, but each was separated from the next by an interminable time. And then, quite close, a whistle blast, and he was on his feet and blew a blast on his own whistle, and the woods erupted, pouring Guides into the open ground.

There was a shot from a window of the house and someone went down.

"Clear the house!" Caesar yelled in a voice of brass. They went forward, right up the front steps and into the first room. There was one man there and someone shot him, and the room filled with smoke. Caesar flung himself at a solid door and fell through it as it came off its hinges. Two shots went over his head, one killing a former slave from Pennsylvania and the other smashing the doorframe and ricocheting to break Virgil's arm. Caesar was up in a second, stunned but game. He tried to get over a table at the closest man, but the man had his hands up. Jim Somerset shot him anyway. The other man fought grimly, pinned against the wall, and managed to knock one of Caesar's men down with his musket butt before he was stuck under the arm with a bayonet. He screamed.

The room was clear. Jim pushed past Caesar into the next room and it was empty, and they entered the kitchen through different doors, together, each of them with his file partner covering. Smoke everywhere. They could hear shooting upstairs and something was on fire, because the reek of the smoke was in their lungs before they could see it. Everywhere, Caesar was looking for Bludner, but he wasn't downstairs in the house.

Van Sluyt appeared at the back of the kitchen. "Just the two upstairs, and they're dead. Roof's on fire a little."

"Let it burn," Caesar said. He knew why they had set it, and it gave him a grim joy that Bludner's men expected help when they set the fire. He looked out the kitchen door toward the yard and a shot whispered past his head.

A new boy, not yet fifteen, came past Van Sluyt.

"Mr. Martin says they have the carriage shed, but Bludner's in the stone barn, an' he would like a word."

"Send Mr. Martin my best compliments and tell him that I will attend him directly," Caesar replied, and fired carefully at the loophole in the barn, just twenty paces away. There was a screech and he gave Van Sluyt and Jim a big smile.

"Jim, just hold the house. I'll be back."

"Yes, Sergeant."

★　★　★

The light was enough that it could almost be called morning. Captain Stewart was annoyed that his whole plan to seize the barn had been frustrated by one man tripping on a root and falling just as the last defender reached the barn, but there was nothing that they could do. The barn had walls several feet thick, and would resist even a small cannon.

Caesar came up behind the low stone carriage house and found the two officers watching warily.

"We have to storm it," Caesar said immediately.

"We'll lose a lot of men," said Stewart, looking at McDonald, who nodded.

"And then we'll get in the doors and kill them all," said Caesar. He looked at them and they at him, and McDonald gave him a little nod. Caesar felt that Stewart was resisting the notion because he couldn't share the danger. Mr. Martin looked like he had his doubts.

Caesar said, "Give me a few minutes, sir. Perhaps we can get fire onto the roof of the barn and smoke them out."

Martin brightened noticeably, and Stewart looked thoughtful. "Let's make sure we have the doors covered, then."

Caesar was back at the kitchen door of the big house. He leaned out so his voice would project.

"Surrender!" he called.

He was answered by an obscenity.

"Come out or you will all be killed. If I have to storm that barn, there won't be any prisoners."

"You better git!" That might be Bludner's voice. "You think we don't have covering troops?"

"That's what I think. All your covering troops is dead or taken, Bludner. That is you, am I right?"

Silence.

"Enough talk," he yelled, motioning to Jim, who was moving very carefully at the corner of the barn where there wasn't a loophole. "You have ten seconds to surrender, or we storm. Are you ready, Guides?"

A roar, and Jim was at the base of the barn. It didn't have an overhang on the top side, and he was safe, right up against the wall. He started to light a hasty torch of linen and tow and fat from a coal.

There were noises from the barn as if in debate, and a single pistol shot.

"No one here is surrenderin'. Come an' take us."

"Try this, then," said Caesar, and nodded to Jim, who leaned back and threw his torch high, high in the dark, where it spun like a child's firework for two revolutions before landing in the thatch of the roof. Jim flattened himself against the building again.

"Don't seem like no storm!" called the defiant voice inside.

Caesar waited. Fire takes time. The morning was very quiet, as if the first burst of musketry had stunned the birds, and they heard a little rattle of shots far off. And then, as if by magic, the thatch caught in one gallant sheet of flame.

Caesar wondered what it would be like to be inside the barn, with the smoke and the knowledge of what waited for them in the yard. He thought of the ancient Caesar and the pirates, and he smiled.

The main door of the barn opened, and a handful of men staggered out with handkerchiefs and neck rollers over their mouths. They threw their muskets out first. No one fired, and they were ordered out to the open ground, where some of Stewart's men took them with ungentle hands. McDonald made sure they saw Knealey, too. Then another group, perhaps five men. Caesar was leaning well forward, looking for Bludner, when he realized with shock that the door closest to the kitchen had opened.

A thick knot of men burst from the door and raced on, scattering as soon as they were clear. One fell over another, and a second stumbled, but the others were running like rabbits from a dog, while the Guides were mostly watching the men at the front surrender.

Jim shot one and immediately began to reload. Van Sluyt shot the one who had stumbled, and Caesar waited too long for Bludner and realized that he had been the first from the door and was already clear of the yard. He shot another man and turned from the door to run through the house. Jim was with him. Virgil fired one-handed from a window and gave him a shout as he whipped through the main room and out the front door. He could see the shapes of four or five men as they ducked into the same woods he and his men had waited in just a few minutes ago, and he reached back for a cartridge as he ran. If Bludner wanted a race, then so be it.

Suddenly Major Stewart was on them, his horse careening into one man and kicking at another, a beautiful capriole. Stewart's saber transcribed a vicious arc, and a third man was down, and then Bludner and another were clear away into the woods, where the horse could not go.

And one of them stopped, because there was movement at the edge of the woods. Stewart whirled his horse and reared it, and the rifle ball caught the horse in the breast, bouncing off the thick bone and leaving a long score and a steady flow of blood. The horse slumped and Stewart fell heavily under it as Caesar went by. He gave Stewart a glance, unable to tell how serious the wound was, and focused on his prey, and Stewart cursed. "Get him!" he shouted.

Caesar bit off the back of a cartridge and stopped for one stride to get priming into the pan, and then dashed on. Behind him, there was another burst of firing by the barn. He thought Jim might still be with him.

"See to the major," he roared. Jim stopped with Stewart, but he looked and saw Virgil, his arm bound against his chest, running along behind. Then he was in among the trees with Bludner and another man.

He could see now. He was surprised at how small the woodlot was in the light. The branches were still moving from their passage, and he followed a little slower, patient. By the time he cleared the wood, he saw them disappearing over a low hill, hundreds of yards ahead. Then he started to run in earnest.

He wanted to catch them before Robinson's men took them. They were headed directly into the Loyal Americans over the ridge, and he didn't want the mess of their being prisoners. He didn't want the chance of escape. He wanted Bludner dead. He ran a little faster, still saving some for the last gasp. He was utterly confident in his running. He could run very fast, and he could run *forever*.

He flew over the ground, and as he crested the next gentle rise he saw them clearly, Bludner ahead and moving well, and the other man slower and laboring. Caesar looked over his shoulder and saw Virgil coming along, his face gray with effort. Caesar stretched into a long sprint, angling a little as he came down the slope. The other man looked back at Caesar and swerved. Then he stopped, clearly done in by the run, and raised his musket. Caesar ran on. If this man was loaded, then Bludner had tried a shot at Stewart and was empty, because neither of them had had time to load. The man aimed carefully and Caesar could see his arms trembling with the effort, and he swerved to make the man reaim. Caesar saw the puff of smoke and heard the report, but not the bullet. The man was too spent to aim well, which was what Caesar had expected. Caesar ran directly at him, bowled him over at full speed, and ran on. The man was thrown aside.

"Finish him, Virgil!" Caesar shouted, and ran on, feeling the fatigue in his thighs. But Bludner was flagging, too, and Caesar got his round loaded and then began to sprint, catching up with every stride. Bludner looked back twice, and then, with a hundred paces between them, he stopped and began to load. Caesar leapt a low stone wall and dashed forward, watching Bludner's loading warily. At fifty paces, Bludner was just putting the ball in the barrel, but he surprised Caesar by rapping the musket on the ground to get the ball down, taking aim, and firing in one motion. Caesar barely had time to swerve, and even then he heard the sound of the bullet close, but the report sounded odd, and Bludner threw the musket down, the side of his face burned and black. Bludner drew a heavy sword, breathing like a bellows. Caesar slowed a little and ran past him, breathing easily. He ran until he was between Bludner and Robinson, still a mile or more to the west, and then he stopped.

"You black bastard," Bludner said, seeing Caesar clearly. "You've vexed me before."

Caesar saw Virgil in the distance, just finishing the man he had knocked down. Although he had the fowler loaded, he placed it carefully on the ground, lock up, and smiled, a thin-lipped grin that showed no teeth. Then he stepped back and drew his hunting sword and began to circle Bludner to the left, drawing Jeremy's little dagger with his left hand and keeping it close to his side. He relished the fear in Bludner's eyes and the way Bludner was edging toward the fowler on the ground. He had seldom felt so alive. He breathed deeply.

Bludner leapt at him with a roar and cut at his head, and Caesar parried easily. He stepped back. Bludner took several deep breaths and cut at him again, an overhand motion that left his side exposed. Caesar noted it and his smile grew. He stepped back again, drew the same attack, met it with the same parry.

"Try harder," he said. Bludner stepped to his right and attacked, one-two, head cuts from opposing sides, and Caesar parried them both. Then his heel caught a branch and there was a rush of action, Bludner trying to bowl him over, his own total contortion as he fought his own body for balance and got a knee under him and his sword up to catch another of Bludner's single-minded blows. Caesar stood up, feigned a little twinge, and made as if to stumble back. Bludner brought his wrist up and cut again, the same side, and Caesar parried, stepped in close, and slammed Jeremy's little ivory-handled dirk right up under Bludner's right armpit.

Bludner stepped back and fell immediately, although he was on his feet in a second. Then he swayed.

"That's for Jeremy," said Caesar, and then, as if to himself, "You are *easy.*"

Bludner waved his blade and said something, and Caesar killed him, a simple feint and a cut to the neck, his whole weight and all his anger, his whole life in one cut, and Bludner fell with a crash, head rolling off in the dirt.

He cleaned his blade, took the man's dispatch case and his rifle, and picked up his own fowler. He looked at Bludner's body and shook his head.

Virgil came up, still in obvious pain from his arm.

"You killed him." He smiled broadly through his own pain. "I knew you would."

"He was easy," Caesar said simply. "I thought he'd be something..."

Virgil just nodded. "Ain't it always like that, though?"

They stood together, savoring the early autumn air and Bludner's shocking corpse, and then they began to run back to the rest of the Guides.

VI

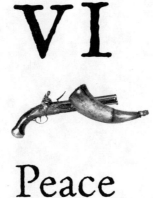

Peace

Peace hath her victories
No less renowned than war.

—MILTON, "TO THE LORD GENERAL CROMWELL"

"Is it your opinion," said Socrates, "that Liberty is a fair and
valuable possession?"
"So valuable," replied Euthydemus, "that I know of
nothing more valuable."

—XENOPHON'S MEMOIRS OF SOCRATES, AS
TRANSLATED BY SARAH FIELDING, 1762

Chapter Twenty-two

Near Dobb's Ferry, May 6, 1783

Guy Carleton was dressed in the full uniform of a British major general, with a scarlet coat whose glare of color was accentuated by the dark blue of his cuffs and collar. The buttons were gold, as was the metallic lace that surrounded each buttonhole. The effect of the whole should have been stunning, but Carleton himself was a cold man at the best of times, and today, quietly enraged, he exuded a chill that could be felt by all the men at the table opposite him. Carleton was almost alone, accompanied only by his military secretary, who wrote quickly whenever either party spoke.

This is almost as pleasurable as Yorktown, thought Washington with an inward smile that never passed out onto his calm face. Years of defeat and deprivation only served to make the years of victory all the sweeter. That Carleton deeply resented Washington's insistence that he should sit here unaccompanied, unescorted, with none of the civilities of war that one general could pay another, was simply the reaping of a harvest of indignity that the British had heaped upon him over the last eight years. Washington was not alone. He was accompanied by his entire staff, and a number of senior officers and representatives of the Continental Congress, who had provided the list of new demands, ancillary to the signed treaty prepared in Paris.

Washington was aware that the forcing of demands after the signature of a treaty was an ungentlemanly business, but he chose, repeatedly and in defiance of the advice of some of his closest officers, to function as the servant of the Congress and not its master. He looked down the list.

"General Carleton, the next two items deal with the repatriation of British prisoners of war taken at Saratoga and Yorktown and other such actions."

Carleton sat unflinching. His face might have been carved from wax. He gave a very slight nod.

Washington read through the first item again, disliking it. Hamilton and Lafayette had both advised him to ignore it, but Washington knew that it was important to the southern colonies and that it was a reprisal for Great Britain's insistence that the Tories, or Loyalists, be reimbursed for property seized or destroyed during the war by servants of the Congress. A functionary from the Congress began to read.

"The Congress of the United States has come to understand that there are at present some thousands of blacks in New York City, who have served the king under arms or in various other capacities. These persons are the legal property of citizens of the United States, and must be returned."

Off to his right, Hamilton was visibly shaking his head. Lafayette had turned his face away, and a member of the Continental Congress from South Carolina was smiling broadly.

Carleton looked stunned, but then he smiled slightly. Washington longed to wipe that cold smile right off his face. The man represented the sort of British officer he had always disliked. His arrogance seemed unbreachable.

"If the blacks are not returned with an accounting of their former stations and owners, a like number of British and German prisoners of war will be kept until such time as this requirement is met."

Carleton shook his head and whispered to his secretary. His secretary laughed aloud.

"How do you answer this requirement?"

Carleton looked at his snowy white shirt cuffs for a moment and then spoke very quietly. "Any arrangement outside of those guaranteed by the Treaty of Paris lies beyond my powers. I must communicate with my government."

"That could take months!" cried the member of Congress.

"I cannot help that," Carleton said coldly. "I am not the one, I think, who seeks to change the treaty."

The rest of the issues drew even less response. Most of them were very minor, and Washington knew that most of them had been arranged as a pretext to force the British commander to come up the river to visit them and to vex him. The slaves were the main issue. He himself no longer took the same view of slavery with which he had started the war, and he saw in Lafayette's indignation a certain reflection of his own feelings in using prisoners of war as negotiating tools for the return of slaves. Lafayette would call it a blot on the escutcheon of liberty, and half the staff would agree.

Washington nodded to himself and paused near the door of the house in which they had met to put on his greatcoat and take up his hat and gloves. Carleton was quite close, only a few feet away, and Washington looked at him curiously.

Carleton had left America in 1776 with his reputation untarnished. He beat every Continental Army to march into Canada, and he routed the army that Washington sent in '76, chasing it all the way back into New York. Now he was back to oversee the turning over of British North America, less Canada, to the fledgling United States.

Carleton had his own greatcoat on and he turned, his eyes suddenly widening a fraction as he took in Washington's proximity.

"I'll endeavor to have my answers for your masters," he said. Washington recoiled. Carleton smiled coldly.

"If you want them, though, don't expect me to go through this process again. You can come and see me," Carleton went on.

"May I remind you, sir, that you are the defeated party? And that I expect to summon you if I require your presence?" Washington didn't believe such things, but he was stung by the taunt of "masters."

"General Washington, you and I recognize that you have no more than three thousand men here. I still have fifteen thousand in New York." The cold voice sank a little further, to a hiss. "Your French friends have all gone home. If you wish to reopen the dance, I will be *most happy* to oblige." He put his hat on with an air, collected his secretary, and was gone, escorted only by some of Washington's light horse.

✯   ✯   ✯

"You intend to stay?" Caesar was incredulous. Jim Somerset was sitting at a table in the Moor's Head with Sally at his side. "You are going to *marry?*"

"With your permission, Sergeant," said Jim, looking mild.

Many comments about their relative ages and Sally's past life came to mind, but Jim had known Sally exactly as long as he had, and there seemed little enough to say. The war had grown Jim up smartly, and he was now almost as tall as Caesar, though still skinny as a rail. And Sally probably only had five or six years on him. It might be enough to harm, or to help, and it wasn't his place to say.

Sally looked at him defiantly. "I have a good sum of money to start us with. We were going to buy a house."

"You'll be taken as slaves!"

Jim shook his head. "I don' think so, Sergeant. Bludner owned Sally, an' we *know* he's dead. Ol' Mr. Gordon owned me hisself, an' I saw you kill him. So I reckon no slave-taker will show up with a claim on us."

Caesar nodded slowly. "I expect you have a point there, although you'll always have to worry."

"That's what it's like to be African in this country, Caesar," said Jim with a smile. "You worry. Lot of folks is stayin', though. We won' be the only folks of color."

Caesar nodded, took a sheet of paper from his map case, and began to write them a certificate showing his approval of their marriage.

"Captain Martin has to sign this," he said.

They both nodded. Sally smiled slowly and looked at him under her lashes.

"I thought you might get him to sign," she said.

"Corporal Somerset, why don't you fetch us some wine?" Jim sprang up to go to the little bar where spirits were served, and Caesar glared at Sally.

"What are you at?"

"I want to stay. They goin' to build a whole new country here. An' I want to stay with folks I don' know so well and start over. You and the Guides might go to Jamaica, or England, or Canada, but I don't want to be with the Guides. They *think* they know me."

"And Virgil?"

"Virgil is a good man, an' he'll find himself a woman that suits him. I don't, an' I ain't." She tossed her head.

Caesar just nodded. He had heard Virgil plan for Sally on many an evening. "He thinks he just has to get it right, you know. Just say the right thing, or know you better."

"He thinks he knows me, but I'll tell you, Jim knows me better than any of you." She was more wistful than defiant.

"And you won't go whoring on Jim?"

"You think whorin' comes natural, Caesar? It don't." She glared at him. "I haven't since the major left, now, have I?"

They both sat in thought for a moment, remembering Major Stewart, now serving in Gibraltar and married to Miss McLean. He had left Sally a wealthy woman. She had benefited from the change, but Caesar was still suspicious of her. And on another level, he knew he'd miss her and Jim. It was all of a piece; the world he had known since he left the swamp was falling apart. Jim came back with wine, and he looked away, his eyes suddenly filling with tears.

"I'll get Captain Martin to sign."

Jim sat and shook his head. "They say at the bar that the Congress is demanding that all the blacks in New York be returned." He shook his head in disgust. "Them rebels really think they won. How come they never won when I was around?"

Caesar spread his hands on the table and shook his head. "They took General Burgoyne, and they took Cornwallis at Yorktown, and the government lost the will to fight. But they won't give us all back."

"They traded the Indians away fast enough."

"Stow that talk, Corporal." Caesar glared at Jim. But a finger of ice touched his spine, and he sat up.

"And what can General Carleton do?" asked Jim. "He's got orders from London not to *make trouble*."

"Government has no money," Caesar said quietly.

"Neither does the rebel Congress, but they jus' print it." Jim propped his chin on a long bony hand. "I read them pamphlets, Sergeant. I do understand."

Caesar changed the subject.

"Polly will miss ya, Sally," said Caesar.

"Oh, we can write. An' I'll miss her, an' your little one. But I want a life, Caesar. An' not as Sally at Mother Abbott's. Sally Somerset has a nice free ring to it."

"You'll tell her?"

" 'Course I will. Not till we know what Carleton's doin', though. If'n you all stay here, I may want to move, or marry someone else." She looked over at Jim, who looked down a little and smiled, then chucked her with his elbow.

✴ ✴ ✴

Caesar looked for Captain Martin at his house. He rarely stirred these days, except to stand his guard and parade the company. Captain Martin was a family man, and his two daughters and his wife took his time, the more so as he had cleared his house and sold most of his belongings. He was about to become a refugee, and he knew it. That didn't make it any easier.

It was a fine house, with plasterwork and fireplaces and delicate tints on the walls, and he wondered when he'd be able to afford the like again. He had thought of staying, and then thought again. No matter how tolerant the new government was, he had commanded the notorious Black Guides, and his wife was a Hammond. He would have to go. There were rumors of land grants in Canada, and that intrigued him. He couldn't farm, but he could survey. He thought that if the Canadian adventure became a reality, he'd probably accept, although many of his fellows were bound for England. He had a map of upper Canada open on the table. He liked the look of the ground around the Bay of Quinte.

He met Caesar in the foyer, answering his own door, because he'd let all the servants go weeks before. Money mattered now. Caesar entered with a lack of self-consciousness that still surprised Captain Martin, coming in the front door as if it were his right—which, of course, it was.

"How can I help you, Sergeant?"

"Need you to sign a wedding certificate, sir."

"With pleasure." Martin sat at his one remaining table and then searched a little lap desk for powdered ink. Caesar was looking at Martin's uniform coat and gorget slung over a chair when Mrs. Martin, the former Miss Hammond, came in carrying a teacup.

"Why, Sergeant Caesar, as I live and breathe!" She put her teacup down and he bowed to her.

"How is Polly? The baby? Splendid. And Virgil? We never see the fellows anymore."

Caesar looked again at the uniform coat, and Martin shook his head ruefully. "I doubt I'll get to wear it again now. They only want to send the regulars into the lines, and it is all I can do to keep our lot from being used to sweep the streets."

Martin was reading the certificate, which Caesar had hoped to avoid, but he signed it without a quibble. Mrs. Martin read over his shoulder and shook her head.

"That Sally . . ." she said, but went no further. A preemptive knock at the door interrupted her.

"I'll see to it," said Martin, and he walked into the front, his footsteps echoing in the empty house.

"He's taking defeat very hard," said Mrs. Martin.

"I think we all are, ma'am," said Caesar.

Martin came back carrying an envelope with a military seal.

"Speak of the devil, and there he is," said Martin. "We have orders, Sergeant. Best uniforms, full dress, polished and ready, at the top of Broadway tomorrow at the break of day."

Caesar felt his heart rising with excitement. "I'll see to the men. Where bound?"

"The messenger couldn't say, or wouldn't."

"They wouldn't send you to fight in the Indies, now, would they?" She sounded concerned. It was the last active theater of war, and indeed, they had seen no action around New York in eight months. The Guides had been in the very last fight, a stiff action fought in boats where Martin and Caesar had both been wounded.

Martin shook his head. "Not with these notes about polished brass and whited belts. I think we are going somewhere to stand guard, but by God I'll enjoy it if it's to be our last parade." He eyed his uniform coat.

Caesar smiled his big grin, the one that hid the scars over his eyes.

✯ ✯ ✯

The gondola carrying General Washington and select members of his staff was crewed by sailors of the Continental Navy. There weren't many of them left, as the end of the fighting and of active privateering launched a race to restore the trade between Great Britain and the Americas, and every sailor wanted a berth when the merchants' bounties were being paid. But there were still enough men to make a creditable crew for a single vessel, and they pulled Washington down the Hudson in style.

At the dock there were two British officers visible from well up the river, holding several horses. Washington expected to be slighted. He knew he had mortified Carleton and that Carleton would take the opportunity to strike back, but he was prepared to bear any reasonable affront with equanimity. The war was over. Whatever Carleton decided, Congress had given Washington the power to agree to. There would be no more attempts to increase the demands on the defeated. Washington had not hesitated to pass Carleton's threat, empty as he thought it to be, and it had worked wonders in bringing Congress to heel.

The dock was closer now, and Washington could see that the British had fortified the old ferry house and dug a small rampart beyond it. In fact, he was pleased to see how well the fortifications of New York stood, as they justified his conduct at the end of the war. New York, as held by Carleton, was impregnable.

"Oars up!" called the coxswain, and every oar was pulled in and set upright. It was as well done as the Royal Navy would do. Washington liked to see his men able to match the British for display.

"That'll show them," he said to Major Lake, standing with Colonel Hamilton at the rail. Colonel Hamilton smiled broadly at him. Today they would reach the end. The real end, the bitter end, the final act that would close out the war. Washington ached to get back to Mount Vernon and his farming. The accomplishment of a life's ambition, to become a great captain and to play a great part on the stage of the world, left him empty. He wanted to go home and farm. He thought that growing things from the ground might heal him.

Hamilton watched the officers on the dock as they drew closer. "Will we all be friends again in my lifetime?" he asked.

Lake touched the hilt of his sword, as if for luck.

"Already the merchants are restoring trade. In ten years, the ties of language..." He was thinking it curious that there were no soldiers waiting for them. He had been requested to come without an escort. Once he would have bridled and made demands, but the time for that sort of thing was past, and he had won. He didn't need another parade to show it.

The gondola brushed down the dock, and a sailor tossed a rope to a man in a gray jacket, who caught it and made it fast. Another sailor stepped nimbly over the rail to the dock and made the stern fast, and a handsome British officer was bowing.

"If you would come this way, General Washington?" said the officer, after he had saluted. "Perhaps you'd care to review your escort?"

That was an unexpected courtesy.

"I would be pleased," Washington replied, and he mounted the horse that was waiting for him. Hamilton came along, as did George Lake and his secretary. The British were not limiting his staff as he had limited Carleton's, and he felt a pinch of remorse.

They rode around the corner and into the little redoubt that had been built to cover the dock, and there was a company drawn up in open ranks, with the sun gleaming on polished muskets and shining brass. They wore red coats.

And every man of them was black. General Washington's horse sensed his hesitation and flicked an ear, hung a moment, and then moved forward smoothly as it felt the power of its rider. He was a well-bred man, and he wouldn't give the British the pleasure of seeing him react if this was intended as an insult. He couldn't decipher for a moment whether it *was* an insult.

He dismounted, tossed the reins to one of the British officers, and walked to the white officer at the head of the company, who saluted smartly.

"Present arms!" the officer called. The stamp and clash of arms was nearly perfect.

"Your servant, General Washington. I am Captain Martin," he said, his hat off and his sword at the salute.

"And yours, Captain." Washington looked back at Hamilton, who returned the captain's salute.

"These must be the famous Black Guides," said Hamilton. Lake was staring at a sergeant at the right rear of the parade. He knew the face, and the scars. The tall black man seemed to know him, too. Unconsciously, both of them touched their sword hilts, and then Caesar snapped his eyes back to the front. Lake turned to follow Washington.

Washington had decided to continue the charade and inspect them. He went to the right of the company. He looked at the first man, a thin corporal, who stood rigidly at attention and looked to his front, and Washington nodded and kept moving. About halfway down the front rank he came to a man and for no particular reason he stopped.

"What's your name, then?" he said.

"Silas Van Sluyt, sir!" the man said, his voice quavering slightly with nerves.

They were clean and neat, the very image of professional soldiers, and he admired the way their blankets were rolled into the folds of their packs, every one the same. He stopped at the left end of the first rank and turned to the captain.

"May I see how those blankets are rolled?" he asked, and the captain stepped past him.

"Corporal Edgerton? Pack off, if you please." Sergeant Fowver, standing three paces behind Edgerton, gazed off into space and hoped, *hoped*, that Paget Edgerton had done his blanket up and not put a piece of cloth in as a fake. Washington watched as the pack came off, obscurely pleased that he had come up with something to look at. In time, the pack was off and open, and he saw the blanket, rolled thin and then folded over along the inside top of the pack. The whole pack was different from those most of his own soldiers used, but it was a useful detail, and the skill with which the man opened and closed his pack spoke more about his life as a soldier than any amount of drill.

Washington walked down the rear rank, taking short steps to avoid overrunning the much shorter captain. He looked at their faces and gazed into their eyes, this company of blacks who had all, most likely, started the war as slaves.

He was all but finished when he saw that, in the British way, the sergeants stood in a line a few paces behind the men on parade. He looked back at the sergeant on the right and came to a stop, one foot poised for another step.

He knew the face so well, and he had thought of it several times since that dinner in New Jersey. He smiled to see the scars over the young man's eyes. It was a hard smile, in that he didn't show his teeth, but he stepped closer to the man. He felt a lump in his throat.

The soldiers *were* the message, of course. He nodded sharply, not to anyone in particular, but to Guy Carleton, who was somewhere else. General Carleton was telling him that the blacks would not be sent back to the Congress, and Washington admired the manner of his reply. He found himself standing in front of the man. *Caesar.* He looked him in the eye. They were of a height, although Washington remembered him as smaller. Caesar carried himself well, and wore a fine uniform and a good sword, and suddenly Washington beamed, one of his rare happy smiles. Hamilton was stunned, and stopped behind him.

"You are the senior sergeant, Caesar?" Washington asked.

"Yes, sir," Caesar answered. He found it difficult to talk, and his voice was subsumed in a whirl of conflicting emotions. He found it difficult not to answer that unexpected smile.

"Very creditable, Sergeant. Very creditable indeed." Washington turned to Captain Martin. "As fine a company as I have seen, Captain." Martin flushed. Sergeant Caesar was smiling fit to split his face.

Washington walked back to his horse and mounted. He bowed from the saddle to Martin.

"A very great pleasure," he said, and Martin bowed.

When Martin completed his bow, he called, "Shoulder your *firelocks!*"

It was well done.

"No need," said Washington, and he turned his horse back to the docks. Martin gazed after him in surprise, and Lake and Caesar locked eyes again, and then Lake smiled and turned away. One of the British officers hastened after Washington, and Martin took George's sleeve.

"You must be Major Lake," he said.

Lake bowed. "You have the better of me, sir."

Martin bowed in return. "My wife has the pleasure of the acquaintance of Miss Lovell."

George flushed and smiled broadly as he wrung Martin's hand.

"We're to be wed as soon as I have a pass for the city," he said. "I hope you'll attend?"

"Alas, I will be going to Canada, Major." Martin gave an ironic smile. "But you have my best wishes, all the same."

✯ ✯ ✯

The British officer had caught up with General Washington.

"General Washington," he called. "General, I hope you did not fancy some slight, sir. None was intended, I assure you." The officer, a major from the staff, was all but pleading for understanding.

"And I took none," said Washington. "But I have received General Carleton's response, and I fully understand it. Please tell him from me that I enjoyed inspecting his troops and that I accept his response in the name of the Congress."

Washington returned to the boat, and he and his staff rowed north. The British staff officers were gone in a moment, and Captain Martin was left looking at the little cloud of dust.

"Who will believe that, do you think?" he said to Caesar as the company re-formed at closed ranks.

"What does it mean?" asked Virgil. He was searching in his haversack for his pipe.

"It means we're free," said Caesar. He threw his arms around Virgil and hugged him. "It means we're free."

Acknowledgments

The research for this book has spanned so many years that I can't guarantee to remember all those who have every right to my thanks. I beg the forgiveness of any who have been forgotten. I have benefited from the research of hundreds of people, from articles on eighteenth-century warfare in West Africa to articles on prostitution in early America. I hope that their hard work is reflected here and can only insist that any historical errors are entirely mine.

From the first, I have had the support of many members of the Revolutionary War reenactment community. Beyond their priceless knowledge of material culture and period life, their ranks contain many professional and amateur historians who have unearthed a great deal of data vital to this book. Jevon Garrett, a close friend from university and a reenactor who portrays a black Loyalist, set me on this road. Todd Braistead (whose article on black Loyalists appears in *Moving On*, noted in the Bibliography) provided signal assistance, as did Jim Corbett, whose detailed knowledge of the staff officers and internal politics of both armies I have only inadequately represented. I would also like to thank the men and women of the British Brigade, the Brigade of the American Revolution, and the Northern Brigade. Dozens of units deserve special praise, but I'll limit mine to several re-created units for their constant enthusiasm and help on details of the period: Gavin and Nancy Watt and the King's Royal Regiment of New York; Fil Walker, Tom Callens, Elizabeth McAnulty, and all the members of Captain Fraser's Company of Select Marksmen, the Sixty-fourth Regiment of foot, and Mike Grenier, their commander; the Fortieth Regiment and Roy Najecki; and Daniel Gariepy and the members of his baroque dance classes. I'll close my praise of reenactors with my thanks to the Queen's Rangers of Canada, both their re-created unit and its commander, Jim Millard, as well as the original and continuing regiment, the Queen's York Rangers of Canada, whose historian, Captain

Bob Kennedy, has opened their armory and regimental museum to me many times.

I'd like to thank many museums and research institutions in the United States, Canada, and Great Britain, most especially the Metro Toronto Reference Library, the National Archives of Canada, The National Army Museum in Great Britain and Brendan Morrissey, the City of London Museum, the Society of the Cincinnati in Washington, D.C., Mount Vernon, and Fort Ticonderoga and Chris Fox, for access to their libraries and their collections over the years.

Bob Sulentic (another old friend from university) and Vivian Stephens provided signal help with research, especially quotes from classical authors in eighteenth-century translations.

Special thanks to the first readers of the manuscript, Nancy and Gavin Watt and Jevon Garrett, all noted above; Allison McRae, who proofread the initial draft (a daunting task), and my incomparable editor in England, Tim Waller. Bill Massey, my American editor, added excellent advice at the last lap, and Fil Walker, Doug Cubbison, Bob Sulentic, and my wife, Sarah, provided a last read for details and accuracy. Sarah also remained cheerful despite many opportunities to be otherwise as I finished this manuscript in the midst of our wedding preparations.

And finally, for my father, Kenneth Cameron, to whom this book is dedicated and without whom it never would have been started, much less finished.

Historical Note

The Corps of Black Guides is a fictional unit, as is Captain Stewart's company of light infantry, who lack a regimental number for the excellent reason that I didn't assign them one. With those exceptions, all the units portrayed in this book are historical. My Corps of Black Guides is founded on a mixture of black units like the Black Pioneers and several others. Captain Stewart himself is loosely based on the character of Captain Stedman, a Scottish officer in Dutch service whose book *Narrative of a Five Years' Expedition to Surinam* is a tale of romance, adventure, and early protest against the slave trade, and on John Peebles, a grenadier officer in the Forty-second Regiment whose journals give a very different view of the American Revolution.

George Lake is an amalgam of dozens of patriotic young men who left us journals to record their feelings and their deeds. If Caesar, Lake, or Stewart seem impossibly heroic, they pale beside the courage of the men, black and white, on both sides whose deeds sometimes exceed the wildest flights of fancy any writer could produce.

I have attempted to portray the language of all parties in a manner that will represent the differences in speech caused by race, tribe, culture, and social status without making the text illegible, troubling to read, or reminiscent of caricature.

The character of Washington is based on his own letters and Douglas Southall Freeman's biography. Many of his speeches (and those of other historical personages in this book) are lifted directly from his recorded comments and letters. While it is possible to find him vain, petty, ambitious, and arrogant (because he was, at times, all those things), it is impossible to think him anything but great. It was a pleasure getting to know him.

★   ★   ★

I have included here a rough chronology of historical events that relate to the book that may not be so well known.

June 22, 1772: The *Somerset* case decides that slavery has no legal status in Great Britain. (This is one of those cases that dealt with a minor issue but were transformed by public interest.) It was widely reported on, and involved the forcible recovery of a "slave" in London. It was discussed in America, and was taken to mean that any slave who reached England was *free*. American and West Indian slave owners took note of this legal development, as did abolitionists. Period pamphleteers saw this as a clear sign that the slave trade would be made illegal, and the idea that England was considering the abolition of slavery was included in colonial grievances.

November 8, 1775: Governor Dunmore of Virginia issues a proclamation freeing any slave whose master is in rebellion against the king, and who joins the Loyalist forces to support "his Majesties Troops, as soon as may be, for the more speedy reducing of this colony to a proper sense of their duty."

Late November, 1775: British regulars of the Fourteenth Regiment and Loyalist black soldiers of the Loyal Ethiopian Regiment attempt to storm the rebel fort at Great Bridge and fail with heavy casualties.

1776: Several corps of black Loyalists are raised to support the British army in North America. One, the Black Pioneers, becomes a "provincial" unit on the establishment (like Butler's Rangers, the King's Royal Regiment of New York, etc.) while others remain in various combatant states without full pay, like Colonel Tye's "Black Brigade," several units of black partisans and horse, the "Black Rangers" raised in South Carolina, and so on. (These informal or partisan units were not regularly paid, but served for rations and, in some cases, plunder, like Brant's Volunteers and scores of white Loyalist militia units.)

1776–82: At least 11,000 blacks served with the British army or served as auxiliaries, boatmen, sailors in the Royal Navy (by far the most egalitarian of the services), or laborers. Another 10,000 to 16,000 blacks followed the army in various capacities, as servants and cartmen, digging entrenchments, as camp followers, and the like.

1783: The Continental Congress is asked as part of its treaty obligations to help restore land and property taken by "Patriots" from "Loyalists." In response, the Congress demands that the British return all the freed slaves in New York, numbering 11,000 to 16,000, because they represent an enormous "property loss" to their owners. Sir Guy Carleton, the British commander, refuses despite heavy pressure and arranges that *every* black in New York gets special manumission papers and passage to Nova Scotia. Despite this, many blacks remain to form the nucleus of the modern black population of New York.

☆ ☆ ☆

Some of the historical players in this unexamined side of the American Revolution include:

John Graves Simcoe: Volunteered to raise a company of black soldiers in Boston in 1775 and was instrumental in the raising and equipping of several black units in New York, often using them as scouts and guides for his raids into the New Jersey countryside. Simcoe (famous in Canada and virtually unknown outside it) was a captain of grenadiers at the outset of the war and went on to command the elite Queen's Rangers, who still exist today as the Queen's York Rangers in the Canadian Army. Simcoe went on to pass the first uniform laws against slavery in the British Empire in Upper Canada (1792).

Colonel Tye: Commanded the "Black Brigade," a unit of as many as 600 to 900 blacks who served as partisans in New Jersey and New York from 1776 to 1782. Tye was viewed as a respectable and honorable adversary by his foes and had several escapes worthy of fiction. He died of a wound in 1782.

Sergeant Thomas Peters: The senior black soldier serving in a regular provincial regiment, Peters ended the war in the Black Pioneers and, with Colonel Tye, is the model for the fictional Caesar. Peters was a slave, escaped to join the British, and served in both the Loyal Ethiopians and in the Black Pioneers. He became the senior black Loyalist in Nova Scotia, and when conditions there became untenable, he led a delegation to London in 1790 that resulted in many Nova Scotia blacks settling in Sierra Leone, where he became one of the colony's leaders.

George Washington: Most of Washington's slaves ran off to the British during the Revolution, although some were recovered. However, at some point between 1772 and 1796, Washington underwent a dramatic reversal in his views on slavery, and despite being a very successful slave farmer, before he died he came to agree with Lafayette that the system was pernicious and a blot on the liberty of America.

Selected Bibliography

The following titles are works that readers may enjoy if they feel that their sense of the history of the period has been challenged or seek to know more about slavery or warfare or the philosophy of the day. It is by no means exhaustive, but represents works that exerted a greater influence on this book.

Anderson, Fred. *Crucible of War: The Seven Years War and the Fate of Empire in British North America, 1754–1766.* New York: Vintage Books, 2001.

Caesar, G. Julius. *Commentaries on the Wars in Gaul* (translated by William Duncan). London, 1779.

Equiano, Olaudah. *The Interesting Narrative of the Life of...* London, 1789.

Fielding, Sarah. *Xenophon's Memoirs of Socrates.* London, 1762.

Freeman, Douglas Southall. *George Washington, Vols. I–V.* New York: Scribners, 1948.

Gerzina, Gretchen Holbrook. *Black London: Life before Emancipation.* New Brunswick, NJ: Rutgers University Press, 1995.

Gronniosaw, James Albert Ukawsaw. *A Narrative of the Most Remarkable Particulars in the Life of...* Bath, England: W. Gye, 1792.

Hodges, Graham Russell, ed. *The Black Loyalist Directory.* London: Garland Publishing, 1996.

Houlding, J. A. *Fit for Service: The Training of the British Army, 1715–1795.* London: Oxford University Press, 1981.

Nash, Gary B. *Red, White, and Black: The Peoples of Early America.* New Brunswick, NJ: Prentice Hall, 1974.

Nosworthy, Brent. *Anatomy of Victory: Battle Tactics 1689–1763.* New York: Hippocrene Books, 1990.

Pulis, John W., ed. *Moving On: Black Loyalists in the Afro-Atlantic World.* London: Garland Publishing, 1999.

Rees, Sian. *The Floating Brothel.* London: Headline Books, 2001.

Stedman, Captain J. G. *Narrative of a Five Years' Expedition* . . . Barre, MA: Imprint Society, 1971.

Stevenson, Captain Roger. *Advice to Officers on the Conduct of Detachments* . . . London, 1769.

Thomas, Hugh. *The Slave Trade.* New York: Simon & Schuster, 1997.

Walker, Ellis. *The Morals of Epictetus Made in English.* London, 1716.

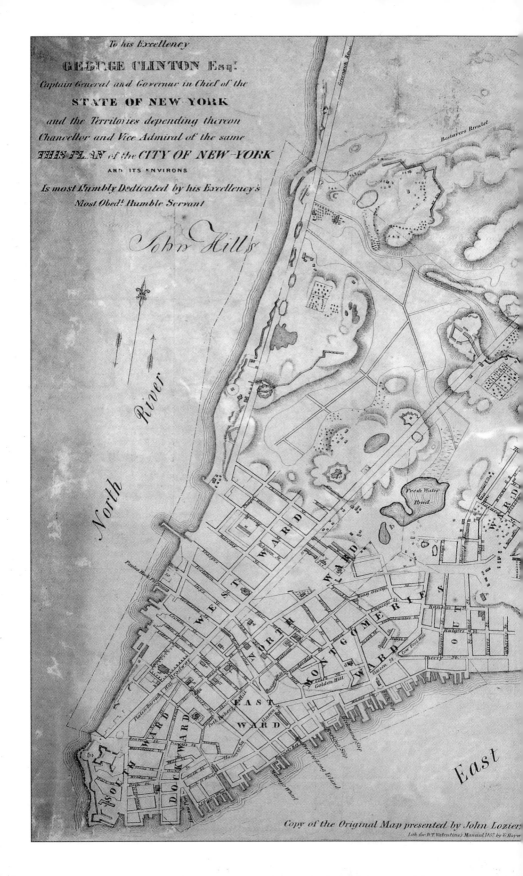

North River

Bestavers Rivulet

Fresh Water Pond

WARD

WEST WARD

NORTH WARD

EAST WARD

MONTGOMERIE WARD

SOUTH WARD

DOCK WARD

Golden Hill

East